THE GREAT
British & Irish
BED & BREAKFAST

Favorite Places to Stay
in Great Britain & Ireland

Interlink Books
An imprint of Interlink Publishing Group, Inc.
New York • Northampton

ACKNOWLEDGEMENTS

We are indebted to the Cumbria Tourist Board (CTB), Derbyshire Dales District Council (DDDC), East of England Tourist Board (EETB), Heart of England Tourist Board (HETB), Irish Tourist Board (ITB), Lincolnshire County Council (LCC), North West Tourist Board (NWTB), Northern Ireland Tourist Board (NITB), Northumbria Tourist Board (NTB), Scottish Tourist Board (SCTB), Shropshire Tourism (ST), South East England Tourist Board (SEETB), South West Tourism (SWT), Southern Tourist Board (STB), Wales Tourist Board (WTB), Worcestershire County Council (WCC), Yorkshire Tourist Board (YTB) for the use of pictures within the text.

First American edition published in 2002 by

INTERLINK BOOKS
An imprint of Interlink Publishing Group, Inc.
99 Seventh Avenue • Brooklyn, New York 11215 and
46 Crosby Street • Northampton, Massachusetts 01060
www.interlinkbooks.com
ISBN 1-56656-454-9

Publisher: Davina Ludlow
Editor: Victoria Rowlands
Assistant Editor: Georgina Ludlow
Administration: Deidri Surtees
Design: Zai Khan
Layout: Oliver Blackwell
Mapping: Philippa Ross
Production: Phil Cory
Research: Victoria Lippiatt

Printed and bound in Spain

The publishers would appreciate any information that will assist them in keeping future editions up-to-date. Although all reasonable care has been taken in the preparation of this book, the publishers cannot accept any liability for any consequences arising from the use of the information contained within this book.

To request our complete full-color catalog, please call
1-800-238-LINK
visit our website at: www.interlinkbooks.com
or write to us at: Interlink Publishing, 46 Crosby Street
Northampton, Massachusetts 01060
e-mail: info@interlinkbooks.com

Introduction

The selection of properties in our book is as diverse as the area it covers. There are thatched cottages, farmhouses, Georgian townhouses, converted stables, manor houses, and former vicarages. Whether you are visiting a historic city, attending a meeting in London, touring the West Country, the Lake District, or a remote part of Scotland or Wales, or vacationing in Ireland, you will find a property offering high quality accommodations at a good price.

The great advantage of staying in an establishment that is proprietor run is the genuine warmth of welcome and the friendly and personal attention that you will receive. With few exceptions, you will be staying in somebody's home and your hosts will be sensitive to your needs and offer hospitality in their own style. In many cases they can provide dinner too, using local or home produced food.

Whether you are a visitor to Britain or Ireland or one of the ever increasing number of people discovering the joys of a "short break," our aim is to give you all the information that you will need to choose the establishment that is right for you. Details of properties have been supplied by the owners themselves and we have now established an annual cycle for visiting each of our homes to ensure that standards are maintained.

For all of those who have bought earlier editions of this book, we hope you will appreciate the many changes we have made to layout and content, and for those who are first time users, enjoy your Bed and Breakfasting with the homes in our book. Very few of the properties listed carry a tourist board or motoring organization rating, our aim is that all of the properties listed are at least the equivalent of five diamonds or five stars, and in many cases higher!

Davina Ludlow
Publisher

Contents

Contents

Ireland Counties Map

UK Counties Map

How to use

Finding the right B & B home

We have divided the publication into England, Scotland, Wales and Ireland. The maps on pages 6-7 detail the Areas/Counties for each Country, and the Contents (pages 4-5) provide a page reference to each Area/County, where you will find a more detailed map showing Map References for each property listed within that Area/County. You should use these Map References to locate properties within the Town or Area that you wish to stay and select your B & B from the description, prices and other information shown within the listings. Also refer to the quick reference indexes at the back which provide page references by Town and, if you are looking for a particular B & B, by property name.

Sequence of Entries

The listings within each Area (i.e North Wales) or within each County (i.e Cumbria) are sequenced by Town name. For multiple listings within the same Town, those in the centre of the Town will appear first in alphabetical property name order, followed by those in suburbs or adjacent villages.

Prices quoted

The prices quoted throughout our book are based on the price per person per night for two sharing a double room, which includes a full British, Irish or continental breakfast, and VAT where applicable. An extra charge is usually made for the use of a double room as a single. Reduced charges may be available for extended stays, you should check when booking. Prices for England, Scotland, Wales and Northern Ireland are shown in British £, and for Ireland in Euros (€). It should be noted that with effect from early 2002 the Euro will become the standard monetary unit in Ireland. (IR£1 = 1.27 Euros).

Meals

Where the B & B offers dinner, the minimum price or 'dinner available' is shown. In many cases dinner is only available by prior arrangement, so check this out when booking. You should also check the description for further information on food, specialities, etc.

How to use

Room descriptions

'Rooms' are described as follows: *Single*: 1 bed, *Double*: 1 large bed, *Twin*: 2 separate beds, *Four poster*: King or Queen size bed with canopy. 'Bathrooms' are described as follows: *Shared*: facilities are shared with some other guests, *Private*: for your own use but in an adjacent room, occasionally abbreviated to 'pb', *En-suite*: private facilities within your own bedroom suite. Again you should check the description for special features of bedrooms.

Smoking

'No smoking' means no smoking anywhere in the house, 'Restricted smoking' means smoking is permitted in certain rooms, or areas of the house and you should check with your host where you may smoke.

Children

We have asked our homes to clarify their policy on this often sensitive subject in one of the following ways: No children, Children welcome or the minimum age at which children are welcome.

Dogs

'Dogs welcome' generally means that you can bring your dog, but you should always check the house rules. Only a few hosts permit dogs in bedrooms or even in the house, but are happy that your dog sleeps in your car or they can provide a kennel.

Symbols

We hate guides that are packed with symbols and have done our best to put everything into simple English. However see 'Payment' below for the abbreviations we have used for credit cards.

Tipping

Few of your hosts would expect you to tip them, but if you have received exceptional kindness you may wish to send a thank you card.

UK Railways Network

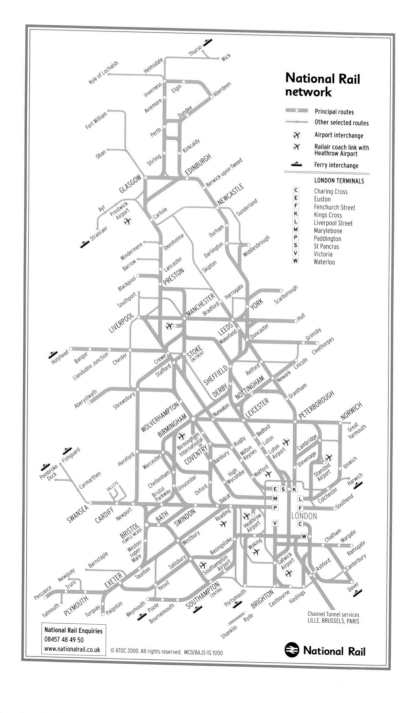

National Rail network

- Principal routes
- Other selected routes
- ✈ Airport interchange
- ✈ Railair coach link with Heathrow Airport
- ⛴ Ferry interchange

LONDON TERMINALS

C	Charing Cross
E	Euston
F	Fenchurch Street
K	Kings Cross
L	Liverpool Street
M	Marylebone
P	Paddington
S	St Pancras
V	Victoria
W	Waterloo

Channel Tunnel services
LILLE, BRUSSELS, PARIS

National Rail Enquiries
08457 48 49 50
www.nationalrail.co.uk

© ATOC 2000. All rights reserved. MCD/BAJS-1S 11/00

National Rail

How to use

Bookings and cancellations

Please refer to page 16 for booking information for London properties. For all other areas, bookings should be made direct with the home by telephone, fax, email or post. A deposit may be required which is often non-refundable if you cancel at short notice and the room cannot be re-let. Your time of arrival and departure is vital information to your hosts who will do their best to meet with your requirements.

Payment

In the UK you can pay by cash or cheques drawn on a British bank with a cheque card, or in some cases by credit card. In Ireland cash (from 2002 in Euros) or credit cards are the normal method of payment. Our listings show whether credit cards are accepted (C-Cards) and which of the following cards are taken (MC Master Card, VS Visa, AE American Express, DC Diners Club). It is generally the case that if the establishment accepts credit cards, switch cards or direct debit cards will also be accepted.

Feedback

Please let us know your opinion of the accommodation that you stayed in. There is a report form at the back of the book and this should also be used to inform us of any delightful homes that you may have come across and you would like to recommend for inclusion in future editions. Feedback is essential for the integrity of our book.

www.stayinstyle.com

All homes listed are featured on our website and those that have their own E-mail addresses or Website addresses can be accessed directly from our website.

We would like to thank those who have allowed us to use their pictures on our front/back cover: Skiary, (Loch Hourn, Highland), The Mill House (Berwick St James, Wiltshire), Firs Cottage (Maenan, Conwy), The Glebe House (North Berwick, East Lothian) and Viewmount House (Longford, Co Longford).

London Underground System

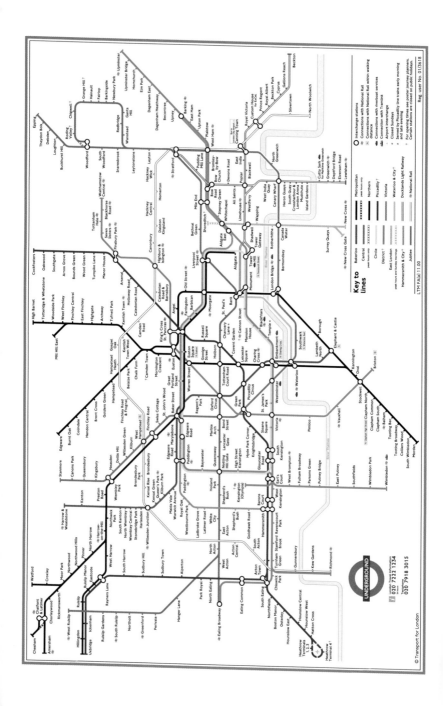

London

Two thousand years of history has seen a Roman settlement by the River Thames develop into a capital city of over seven million people. The strategic position of London was recognised by William the Conqueror who built his White Tower here, the hub of the Tower of London. However, the crowded unhygienic housing was a breeding ground of disease and as a consequence London suffered badly from the Black Death in 1348 and the Plague of 1665. The Great Fire of the following year cleansed the city of the pestilence and in consuming four fifths of the dreadful medieval slums made way for the spacious and considered planning of a new city. This noble city remained largely in this form until the bombing of the Second World War led to another period of rebuilding. For the holiday visitor there is everything here one could wish for and there is no doubt that by far the best way to enjoy the sights of London is from the top of a grand old London double-decker bus.

A large proportion of the city's attractions are to be found in the West End, with Trafalgar Square the undisputed centre. Overlooked by Nelson's Column, the visitor can easily spend the day within a very short distance of this landmark. The National Gallery and the Church of St. Martin-in-the-Fields take up two sides of the Square with the impressive Admiralty Arch taking up the third and leading to The Mall, at the end of which stands Buckingham Palace, the Queen's main residence. On one side of The Mall is the royal St James'

Park, beyond which is Birdcage Walk leading back to the very hub of Westminster, Parliament Square. Here stands the Houses of Parliament with the famous clock tower housing the great bell, Big Ben with each minute hand on the clock faces measuring fourteen feet in length! Across the Square is Westminster Abbey, Britain's most important church, begun by Edward the Confessor in the eleventh century. Almost all monarchs of England have been crowned here since William the Conqueror. The Abbey contains memorials to some of the most famous figures in English history. The City, a square mile of the ancient city of London is the financial centre of the capital and retains much of its medieval street plan. Here stands the other great London church and landmark, St Paul's Cathedral, the baroque masterpiece of Sir Christopher Wren and the burial place of Wren, Lord Nelson and the Duke of Wellington. Nearby is one of the

The Tower of London

capital's most popular tourist attractions; the Tower of London, built by William the Conqueror after 1066, home of the Crown Jewels and regalia, the headsman's axe and the Tower's famous ravens. London is also a city of remarkable pageantry and ceremony where the Changing of the Guard at Buckingham Palace, the Mounting the Guard at Horse Guards in Whitehall and the Ceremony of the Keys at the Tower of London draw a number of visitors everyday. And then of course there are numerous annual and casual events which include the impressive Lord Mayor's Show and the various colourful carnivals. If the history, pageant and tradition of the city becomes too rich a fare then there is the London of world famous shops, Oxford Street and Regent Street cannot fail to fascinate even the window shoppers. For the specialist shoppers there is St James' Street, for the bookworms there is Charing Cross Road, and for the visitor who merely wants a 'bargain' there is a multitude of street markets, Camden Lock, Portobello Road and Brick Lane. There are restaurants, nightclubs and theatres to suit every taste, Soho and Covent Garden constitute the heart of London's nightlife. The National Film Theatre on the South Bank is the leading repertory cinema, and London theatres offer everything from musicals to Shakespeare. However, London also houses some of the world's finest museums and galleries, both traditional and modern, The National Gallery, The National Portrait Gallery, The British Museum, The Victoria and Albert Museum, The Tate Gallery, The Imperial War Museum and The Museum of the Moving Image with its hi-tech displays and hands-on exhibits.

PLACES TO VISIT

This is a small selection of interesting places to visit. Many more are listed in our annual guide to Museums, Galleries, Historic Houses & Sites (see page 448)

Buckingham Palace
London SW1
The State Rooms are open from August to September (by ticket only). The Queen's Gallery reopens in Spring 2002, and the Royal Mews is open all year.

Kew Gardens
Kew, Richmond
The royal Botanic Gardens at Kew cover 300 acres with living collections of over 40,000 varieties of plants. There are also two art galleries.

London Eye
South Bank, London SE1
At 440 feet high, the world's highest observation wheel, providing a 30 minute slow moving hover over London.

Tate Modern
London SE1
The Tate Gallery of modern Art with displays of 20th century art ranging from Andy Warhol paintings to Henry Moore bronzes.

The Tower of London
South Bank, London EC3
Over the past 900 years the Tower has served as a royal fortress, a prison, a place of execution, an armoury, a mint - now and for the past 600 years it houses the Crown Jewels.

London

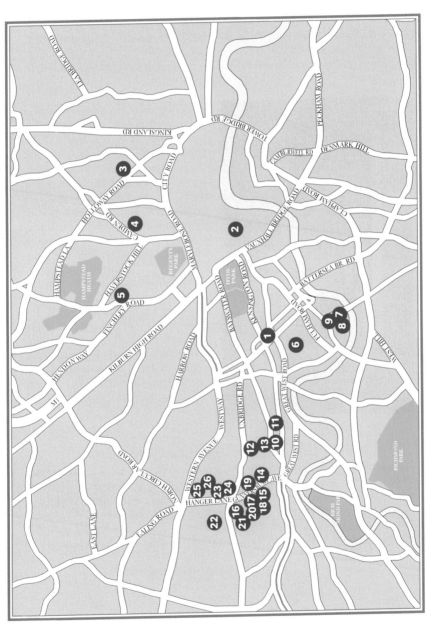

The Blue Map References should be used to locate B & B properties on the pages that follow

Beautiful B&B in London

Anita Harrison and Rosemary Richardson specialise in arranging good quality Bed and Breakfast accommodation in London homes. All have their individual style and charm and offer exceptional value for money - a very affordable alternative to hotels.

Most of the accommodation is located in the leafy west London areas of Chiswick, Hammersmith, Ealing and Parsons Green, convenient to shops and restaurants, and public transport for the central sights. In these areas the average cost for a twin or double sharing bathroom is £26 per person per night: £31 with private bathroom, including breakfast. The listings begin with a small selection of homes in more central areas where prices are higher.

The accommodation has been chosen with great care, with hosts who take pleasure in welcoming guests to their homes. The guest rooms are comfortable and attractively decorated, with the emphasis on cleanliness and warmth. Tea and coffee making facilities are provided and a generous breakfast is included in the tariff. Parking is available at many of the addresses.

HOW TO RESERVE YOUR LONDON B&B

It is recommended that you telephone Anita or Rosemary to discuss your requirements or contact them by e-mail. The minimum booking period is 2 consecutive nights. To secure your reservation, an advance payment of £7 per person per night is required, to be paid by Visa or Mastercard. The balance is settled with your hosts during your stay, but we must point out that hosts are not able to accept credit cards. You will receive an official confirmation of arrangements. Terms and Conditions are shown on page 23.

LONDON HOME-TO-HOME
19 Mount Park Crescent, London W5 2RN
Telephone and Fax: 020 8566 7976
Email: stay@londonhometohome.com
Website: www.londonhometohome.com

Kensington High Street Nanette & Steli
London Home-to-Home
Tel / Fax: 020 8566 7976

A beautifully preserved Victorian town house, which is tastefully decorated and incorporates all modern facilities for guest's comfort, whilst retaining the authentic features of the period. Televisions, hair dryers and hospitality trays are available in all rooms. Vivacious hosts offer high quality accommodation, serving breakfast in the elegant family dining room. A welcoming atmosphere and friendly service is assured. The nearest underground is Earls Court, on the District and Piccadilly lines, ten minutes walk. Buses to sights.

B & B from £52pp, Rooms 4 en-suite double/twin, No smoking

Victoria Area Mrs Margaret L
London Home-to-Home
Tel / Fax: 020 8566 7976

This welcoming London apartment has a theatrical feel and is cluttered with interesting memorabilia. Margaret offers three double/twin rooms with small private bathrooms nearby. Ideally situated, in fashionable apartment block located just five minutes' walk from Victoria station (Circle, District, Victoria lines). Also express trains to Gatwick Airport. Buckingham Palace, Westminster Cathedral and St. James's are within a short walk. Continental breakfasts. Many bus services including Round London Sightseeing tours. No parking.

B & B from £39pp, Rooms 3 double/twin, private bathroom, No smoking, Small dogs welcome

Islington Area Jackie & Oscar
London Home-to-Home
Tel / Fax: 020 8566 7976

Very convenient for the central sights. Hosts offer a pretty, compact double-bedded room with TV and hot drinks facilities. A private bathroom is sometimes available. In the summer breakfast is served in the courtyard garden. Lovely accommodation in a cottage with olde-world feel. Hosts are keen travellers. Single visitors welcome. Handy for Family Records Centre, SoG etc. The nearest underground is Highbury & Islington, on the Victoria line, a six minute walk.

B & B from £33pp, Rooms 1 double, No smoking

Camden Town Area Sue & Roger
London Home-to-Home
Tel / Fax: 020 8566 7976

Guests are made most welcome in the modern home of an architect and his wife. They designed the house themselves in the 1970's, with much use of glass. Two guest rooms available. An unusual double-bedded room where the bed is sunk into a low platform, and a single room. Both rooms share a guest bathroom. Breakfast is served in the open-plan dining area, which overlooks a courtyard garden or in the summer, in the courtyard itself. The family pet is Peckham the macaw. Hosts accept one booking at a time. The nearest underground is Camden Town on the Northern line, 10 minutes walk.

B & B from £41pp, Rooms 1 double, 1 single, private bathroom, No smoking

Swiss Cottage Area Marilyn & Alan
London Home-to-Home
Tel / Fax: 020 8566 7976

Map Ref: 5
Tube: **Swiss Cottage**

Congenial hosts offer four comfortable guest rooms in their modern townhouse. Three of the guest rooms share a bathroom, the triple room is en-suite. Very close to Swiss Cottage tube station, just seven to ten minutes on the Jubilee line to Baker Street (Madame Tussauds) and Bond Street (for the department stores). Finchley Road (Metropolitan & Jubilee lines) eight minutes walk. Many bus services to the sights. Limited parking.

B & B from £33pp, Rooms 1 single, 1 double/triple, 1 twin, 1 triple en-suite, No smoking

Parsons Green Area Jennie & Clive
London Home-to-Home
Tel / Fax: 020 8566 7976

Map Ref: 6
Tube: **Fulham Broadway**

In fashionable Parsons Green, Jennie offers three beautifully decorated guest rooms in her turn-of-the-century townhouse. Breakfast is served in the formal dining room. Nearest underground: Fulham Broadway on District line, is a ten minute walk. Parking is difficult.

B & B from £35pp, Rooms 1 single shared bathroom, 1 double pb, 1 twin pb, Restricted smoking

Parsons Green Area Dolores & Bert
London Home-to-Home
Tel / Fax: 020 8566 7976

Map Ref: 7
Tube: **Parsons Green**

Whether staying for two nights or a week you can be sure of a warm welcome with these cheerful and generous hosts. They offer a double room with queen sized bed, television and hot drinks tray. A futon sofabed available for triple bookings. Shower and wash basin are en-suite. The atmosphere is friendly and informal. A popular choice! Some of London's trendiest restaurants in the area. The nearest underground is Parsons Green, on District line, a ten minute walk. Buses for Chelsea, Knightsbridge and Central sights.

B & B from £32pp, Rooms 1 double/triple en-suite

Parsons Green Area Moira & Frank
London Home-to-Home
Tel / Fax: 020 8566 7976

Map Ref: 8
Tube: **Parsons Green**

Self contained apartment for two to four guests on first floor of a family home. Comprises a twin bedroom with private bathroom, dining/living room with television and comfortable sofa bed, additonal bathroom and fully equipped kitchen. Lounge overlooks a pretty park. Frank and Moira are gracious and welcoming hosts who live on the ground floor. Ideal for longer stays as guests can be totally self catering. A popular area for quality interior design, furniture and antiques. Excellent restaurants. The nearest underground is Parsons Green, on District line, a ten minute walk.

B & B from £30pp, Rooms 1 apartment

Parsons Green Area Dulce & Manuel
London Home-to-Home
Tel / Fax: 020 8566 7976

Map Ref: 9
Tube: Fulham Broadway

A charming Portuguese couple offer a specially warm welcome. In their recently refurbished Victorian home, they provide two delightful double guest rooms, both with en-suite bathrooms. Manuel, who is a chef, serves a Portuguese breakfast or a traditional English one. Many restaurants and shops in the area. One cat. Metered parking. The nearest underground is Fulham Broadway, on the District line, a five minute walk. Buses to Knightsbridge for Harrods and the Museums and central London.

B & B from £35pp, Rooms 2 double en-suite, No smoking

Hammersmith/Chiswick Area Marjory & Christopher
London Home-to-Home
Tel / Fax: 020 8566 7976

Map Ref: 10
Tube: Stamford Brook

Wonderfully close to the tube, this family home offers a very beautiful and spacious twin guest room with wash basin, television and hospitality tray. The room overlooks a tranquil garden. Private bathroom is adjacent. Christopher, a linguist, and Marjory, a teacher, are anxious to make their guests' stay as pleasant as possible. Enjoy an evening stroll along a lovely stretch of the river Thames, passing picturesque pubs and lovely gardens. Good restaurants and shops nearby. The nearest underground is Stamford Brook, on the District line, a one minute walk. Buses to Trafalgar Square and Kew Gardens.

B & B from £33pp, Rooms 1 twin, private bathroom, No smoking

Chiswick Area Peter & Valerie
London Home-to-Home
Tel / Fax: 020 8566 7976

Map Ref: 11
Tube: Turnham Green

Stay in villagey, unspoiled Chiswick, where writers and actors live. On the Bedford Park Garden Conservation Estate, this 1880's Norman Shaw home is just four minutes walk from the tube station, interesting boutiques and eating places. Valerie and Peter offer three guest rooms, a double and twin, either of which can be triples, with guest bathroom, plus a double with queen-size bed. Sitting room for guests. The fine home of a retired architect. Easy access to Heathrow. Buses to Central London.

B & B from £28pp, Rooms 1 double, 1 double/triple, 1 twin/triple

Chiswick/Acton Area Charo & Antonio
London Home-to-Home
Tel / Fax: 020 8566 7976

Map Ref: 12
Tube: Turnham Green

A beautiful loft room is offered in the home of Spanish hosts who have lived in England for many years. Twin beds, television, hot drinks and very pretty and comfortable sitting area. High standard of cleanliness and very warm welcome. Not available in August. The nearest underground is Turnham Green, on the District and Piccadilly line, a ten minute walk.

B & B from £31pp, Rooms 1 twin en-suite, No smoking

Hammersmith Area Catriona & David

London Home-to-Home
Tel / Fax: 020 8566 7976

Map Ref: 13
Tube: Ravenscourt Park

This comfortable Victorian home is situated in the heart of historic Brackenbury Village, Hammersmith. The bedrooms are furnished with flair to the highest standards. Peace and quiet are guaranteed after a long day of sightseeing in London. There is a wide choice of restaurants, pubs and cafes to suit every taste within a short walk. Friends offer similar accommodation in a home nearby. The nearest underground is Ravenscounrt Park (District line) seven minutes walk and Goldhawk Road (Hammersmith & City lines) ten minutes walk. Buses to Notting Hill Gate, Marble Arch and Piccadilly Circus. Parking is metered.

B & B from £27pp, Rooms 2 double, 1 single, shared bathroom

Acton Town Area Janice & Jeremy

London Home-to-Home
Tel / Fax: 020 8566 7976

Map Ref: 14
Tube: Acton Town

Superb accommodation is offered in this home of grace and quality where the hosts delight in providing for guests' every comfort. Beautiful lounge available for guests. The mock-Tudor home has a beautiful garden and is located on a lovely estate with a large park of historic interest close by. Choose between a twin with en-suite bathroom and a spacious and lovely double room with wash basin and private bathroom. Ideal for Heathrow arrivals. Off street parking available. The nearest underground is Acton Town, on District and Piccadilly line, a ten minute walk.

B & B from £31pp, Rooms 1 double/twin, private facilities

Ealing Broadway Area Anita & David

London Home-to-Home
Tel / Fax: 020 8566 7976

Map Ref: 15
Tube: Ealing Broadway

Warm, welcoming hosts offer two attractive guest rooms with twin or king-size beds, each with washbasin and sharing a guest bathroom. Decorated to a high standard. Ealing Broadway, the local centre, is just five minutes' walk for the underground and numerous excellent restaurants, pubs and shops. Non smokers preferred. One dog and one cat. The nearest underground is Ealing Broadway, on Central and District lines, five minutes walk.

B & B from £26pp, Rooms 2 double/twin with shared bathroom, No smoking

Ealing/Acton Area Pauline & Peter

London Home-to-Home
Tel / Fax: 020 8566 7976

Map Ref: 16
Tube: Acton Town

A friendly family offer a delightful twin room with adjacent single room. Guest bathroom with jacuzzi. Peter is a plant specialist. The home overlooks a public park with a museum, boating pond, mini-golf, tennis and bowls. A very welcoming atmosphere. Off street parking. The nearest underground is Acton Town, on District and Piccadilly line, a ten minute walk. Direct line to Heathrow.

B & B from £30pp, Rooms 1 twin, 1 single, shared bathroom with jaccuzzi, No smoking

Ealing Area John & Jane
London Home-to-Home
Tel / Fax: 020 8566 7976

Map Ref: **17**
Tube: **Ealing Broadway**

A lovely family home of great character offering one twin room with private bathroom adjacent, overlooking landscaped patio and gardens. The home, built in the mid 1880's, has been tastefully furnished. Breakfast is served in the family kitchen/breakfast room which leads onto the garden. Hosts take every care to ensure their guests' comfort. Five minutes walk to a modern shopping mall and several first class restaurants. Open parkland nearby. The nearest underground is Ealing Broadway on Central and District lines, seven minutes walk. Ealing Common is eight minutes away.

B & B from £31pp, Rooms 1 twin with private bathroom

Ealing Area Anne & Richard
London Home-to-Home
Tel / Fax: 020 8566 7976

Map Ref: **18**
Tube: **South Ealing**

Cheerful welcoming hostess, an actress, offers a lovely, spacious loft room with king-size bed and en-suite shower bathroom. Lovely outlook. Choice of self-catering or traditional breakfasts. Ideal for two guests, but a single bed can be added to make a twin/triple. The nearest underground is South Ealing, on the Piccadilly line, twelve minutes walk.

B & B from £31pp, Rooms 1 double/triple, en-suite

Ealing Area Muriel & Neville
London Home-to-Home
Tel / Fax: 020 8566 7976

Map Ref: **19**
Tube: **Ealing Common**

This gracious hostess offers three single rooms in a home of beauty and charm, decorated with a traditional English quality. A tranquil setting. Muriel, who is a piano teacher and keen gardener, does not accept smokers. Accommodation is not available in August. At nearby Ealing Common tube station, three minutes walk away, there is a choice District and Piccadilly lines, and a comprehensive range of shops and restaurants. Easy commuting from Heathrow or Central London.

B & B from £36pp, Rooms 3 single, shared bathroom, No smoking

Ealing Area Rosemary & Ian
London Home-to-Home
Tel / Fax: 020 8566 7976

Map Ref: **20**
Tube: **South Ealing**

Bed and breakfast with a difference. Australian hosts offer an airy self-contained studio apartment on the second floor of their beautiful home. Overlooking gardens and pond. Double bed, en-suite shower bathroom, kitchenette with microwave, dining/sitting area with television. Linen provided, also breakfast food. A warm and friendly welcome in a lovely home. Reductions for longer stays. The nearest tube is South Ealing, on the Piccadilly line, ten minutes walk. Buses to Kew and Richmond.

B & B from £31pp, Rooms 1 double, en-suite, No smoking

Ealing Common Area Maria & Damien
London Home-to-Home
Tel / Fax: 020 8566 7976

Map Ref: 21
Tube: Ealing Common

Accommodation designed for a comfortable stay. Warm and friendly hosts offer a large loft room, providing triple accommodation with en-suite shower bathroom and another triple with double and single beds and en-suite shower bathroom. Breakfast served in the conservatory overlooking the garden. Situated in a quiet, tree-lined street, a short stroll from shops and restaurants. The nearest underground is Ealing Common, on the District and Piccadilly lines, seven minutes walk. Very handy for guests arriving from Heathrow. Maria speaks French.

B & B from £31pp, Rooms 2 triple en-suite, No smoking

Ealing Common Area Rita & Geoff
London Home-to-Home
Tel / Fax: 020 8566 7976

Map Ref: 22
Tube: Ealing Common

These welcoming hosts offer a large, self-contained guest room on the top floor of their home. The room is thoughtfully planned, and comprises a sleeping area with double bed, sitting/dining area and fully equipped kitchenette, with private bathroom, and facilities for self-catering. Generous supply of breakfast food provided. Short or longer term rates available. The nearest underground is Ealing Common, on District and Piccadilly lines, five minutes walk.

B & B from £27pp, Rooms 1 double, self catering, private bathroom, Open all year

Ealing Area Diana & Louis
London Home-to-Home
Tel / Fax: 020 8566 7976

Map Ref: 23
Tube: West Acton

Relaxed, friendly hosts offer a loft guest room, comprising a spacious and airy twin/triple room with private shower bathroom en-suite. Television and hospitality trays in room. Modern three storey home, conveniently situated for two underground lines, West Acton on the Central line and North Ealing on the Piccadilly line, both seven minutes walk.

B & B from £31pp, Rooms 1 twin/triple en-suite

South Ealing Area Gill & Mark
London Home-to-Home
Tel / Fax: 020 8566 7976

Map Ref: 24
Tube: South Ealing

Comfortable, spacious twin room accommodation in a family home, located in a quiet residential street, just a couple of minutes' walk from shops, restaurants and the underground. Gill is a gardener. They have a pet labrador and they do not accept smokers. The nearest underground is South Ealing, on Piccadilly line from Heathrow, four minutes walk.

B & B from £26pp, Rooms 1 twin with shared bathroom, No smoking

Ealing Area Sally & Alan
London Home-to-Home
Tel / Fax: 020 8566 7976

Map Ref: 25
Tube: Ealing Broadway

Young professional couple with two young children offer one double room and one twin room with guest shower bathroom. All newly decorated with style. Many good restaurants and shopping mall nearby. Family discounts available. The nearest tube is Ealing Broadway or Ealing Common, on the Central, District or Piccadilly lines, both ten minutes walk.

B & B from £29pp, Rooms 1 double, 1 twin, guest bathroom, No smoking, No dogs

Ealing Area Ursula & Jim
London Home-to-Home
Tel / Fax: 020 8566 7976

Map Ref: 26
Tube: Ealing Common

Attentive hosts offer flexible accommodation in their comfortable home in a quiet and leafy residential street. Two spacious triple rooms, each with a large double bed and single bed and en-suite shower bathroom. Also a twin room and a double/single sharing an impressive Art Deco shower bathroom. Ursula teaches English as a foreign language and speaks fluent German. The nearest underground is Ealing Common, on District and Piccadilly lines, ten minutes walk. Unrestricted parking on street.

B & B from £26pp, Rooms 1 single/double, 1 twin, shared pb, 2 triple, en-suite, No smoking

London Home-to-Home - Terms & Conditions

Cancellation: Should it be necessary to cancel your booking, we will refund your payment, less an administration fee of £40, providing that London Home-to-Home receives at least four weeks' notice. Where a booking is cancelled within the last seven days, London Home-to-Home reserves the right to collect the balance owing on the first two nights, on behalf of the hosts. We recommend that you take out full travel insurance.

PLEASE NOTE that London Home-to-Home acts only as a booking agent between paying guests and hosts. The information provided is based upon the circumstances normally in existence in the homes. London Home-to-Home does not itself actually provide the accommodation nor does it own or control in any way those who do provide the accommodation. Further, your contract for the accommodation is with the hosts. Should there be a dispute regarding accommodation, the matter must be raised in the first instance with the hosts. London Home-to-Home does not accept any responsibility for any matters which arise as a result of events beyond its control. London Home-to-Home reserves the right to transfer the accommodation should it consider this necessary, or offer a full refund of monies paid and will notify guests of any change as soon as possible. Any dispute arising out of the agreement for provision of accommodation shall be governed by and subject to English law and jurisdiction.

Bath, Bristol &
Northeast Somerset

This region offers a holiday venue to suit all tastes. It is an area packed with interest and simply cries out to be revisited over and over again. Such is the appeal of this special locality, that no amount of description can do it justice. It just has to be experienced.

Bristol, in the centre of the region, is the largest town in the south west of England, a major entertainment and also communications centre since medieval times, when it claimed parity with London. Though no longer a commercial port, the docks still dominate the centre of the city, their attraction being the splendid Maritime Heritage Centre and the Bristol Industrial Museum where Brunel's magnificent steamship of 1843, 'The Great Britain', now fully restored can be viewed. Heavy bombing during WW2 destroyed many of the medieval buildings and the city was greatly modernised in the 1950s and 60s. However the Cathedral, once the abbey church, retaining its spectacular Norman Chapter House and fine Lady Chapel, has lost none of its historical charm and is a delight to visit. There are a large number of fine Georgian houses, Queen's Square being the most impressive. Of special interest are the curious bronze pillars known as the Nails outside the exchange, where the merchants paid their accounts, hence the saying 'to pay on the nail'. As befits a city of Bristol's importance, there are theatres, concert halls, cinemas and high quality entertainment of all descriptions, as well as many famous shopping streets and the hectic life of the university.

Of course, if our Georgian heritage is an attraction, nearby Bath offers the finest Georgian architecture in the country. The Romans made Bath their headquarters in AD 44, building baths around the natural hot springs and dedicating a temple to the goddess Sulis Minerva, naming the city Aquae Sulis. To commemorate this unique period is the fascinating Roman Baths Museum. The pride of medieval Bath its handsome monastery, whose early sixteenth century church survives today as Bath Abbey is renowned for its magnificent fan-vaulting and its west front. In the seventeenth century Bath became a fashionable Spa town and the centre of a culture led by Beau Nash, who for 50 years was the Master of Ceremonies here. Many of the great houses, the Circus of 1754, a circle of 30 houses noted for their famous residents of the past, and the Terrace are the work of the architect John Wood. The magnificent Pulteney Bridge was designed by Robert Adam, adding to the impressive architecture of this city

Clifton Suspension Bridge, Bristol (SWT)

The countryside in this region is as glorious a setting as the visitor will find anywhere in England. The National Trust controls Sand Point just north of Weston-super-Mare, a limestone headland which includes Castle Batch, an ancient Norman motte. The Avon Gorge Nature Reserve on the west bank of the Avon can be reached across the Clifton Suspension Bridge, a National Trust Property which includes Leigh Woods and an Iron Age hill-fort. Other sites of interest include Dyrham Park, overlooking the Severn Valley, built between 1691 and 1710 for William Blathwayt and is surrounded by 263 acres of ancient parkland with a herd of fallow deer. For the more energetic there is the eight mile Bath Skyline Walk, giving quite superb views across Bath and Dolebury Warren, some 12 miles south from Bristol where an Iron Age fort tops the barren hill, gives the most breathtaking views in the Mendips. The seaside is also well represented in this region by Weston-super-Mare, south west of Bristol, which offers in addition to all the traditional attractions, a glorious sandy bay between two protective headlands.

The region is rich in natural scenery, and such is the quality, colour and texture of the stone that even the most formal buildings seem to blend comfortably into the landscape. To the north of Bristol is the delightful Blaise Hamlet designed by John Nash in 1811 for the owner of Blaise Castle as homes for old retainers. Regarded as the most picturesque medieval hamlet in England, the cottages, each with a unique charm, are built around an undulating green and are well worth a visit. However with so much on offer the traveller is spoilt for choice. Busy days, seaside days, walking days or simply lazy days, what more could you wish for?

PLACES TO VISIT

This is a small selection of interesting places to visit. Many more are listed in our annual guide to Museums, Galleries, Historic Houses & Sites (see page 448)

Bath Abbey
Bath
Britain's last great medieval church with fan vaulting designed by Robert and William Vertue. Its vaults are also open to the public and include Saxon and Norman sculpture.

Bristol Cathedral
College Green, Bristol
A twelfth century Norman chapter house, founded as an Augustinian Abbey but developed into a Cathedral in 1542.

Maritime Heritage Centre
Wapping Wharf, Gas Ferry Road, Bristol
Showing the development of the ship building industry within the last 200 years from wood to iron and modern steel. Also houses the SS Great Britain.

Roman Baths & Pump Room
Stall Street, Bath
Former baths, now a museum with many Roman relics and treasures.

No. 1 Royal Crescent
Bath
A representative of the finest achievements of eighteenth century architecture and the highest point of Palladian architecture in Britain. The house is restored and decorated to how it was in the eighteenth century.

Victoria Art Gallery
Bridge Street, Bath
The gallery houses Bath and North East Somerset's art collection with oil paintings from fifteenth to twentieth century, plus works of artists who lived and worked in the area.

Bath, Bristol &
Northeast Somerset

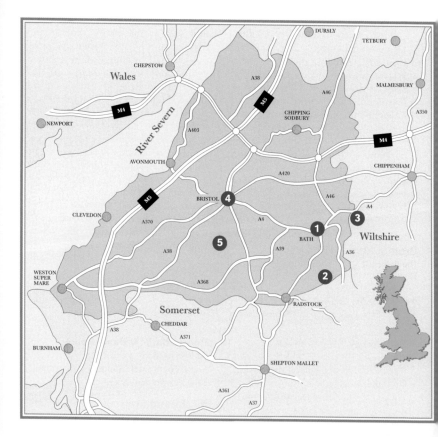

The Blue Map References should be used to locate B & B properties on the pages that follow

Apsley House Hotel 141 Newbridge Hill, Bath BA1 3PT
David & Annie Lanz Tel: 01225 336966 Fax: 01225 425462
Email: info@apsley-house.co.uk Web: www.apsley-house.co.uk

David and Anne Lanz warmly welcome guests into their elegant Georgian house. Beautifully proportioned reception rooms overlook the pretty gardens. Sumptuous decor, fine antiques and oil paintings create a gracious but relaxed atmosphere. Bedrooms are all en-suite, individually furnished and decorated and offer TV, direct dial telephones, hot drinks facilities and hair dryers. Breakfast is a delight with full English and house specialities. Licensed bar. Local information available. Just over 1 mile west of centre. Private car park.

B & B from £32.50pp, Rooms 4 double, 1 four poster, 2 garden rooms, 3 twin, 1 family, Restricted smoking, Children over 5, No dogs, Closed Xmas

9 Bathwick Hill Bath BA2 6EW
Elspeth Bowman
Tel: 01225 460812

Map Ref: 1
On Bathwick Hill

This listed Georgian house stands in a most desirable part of Bath, and there are fine views across the city. It is beautifully furnished, guests are welcome to use the drawing room and the conservatory, also to enjoy the walled garden. A full English breakfast is offered. It is just a short walk to the city centre. This is a friendly family home. Parking is plentiful for guests, there are frequent bus services to the centre. On travelling up Bathwick Hill pass Cleveland Walk on the left, No.9 is on the right.

B & B £25-£28pp, Rooms 2 twin with private bathrooms, No smoking, Children over 12, No dogs, Closed Xmas

Brompton House St John's Road, Bath BA2 6PT
The Selby Family Tel: 01225 420972 Fax: 01225 420505
Email: bromptonhouse@btinternet.com Web: www.bromptonhouse.co.uk

Map Ref: 1
A46

Built as a rectory in 1777, Brompton House is a charming country style Georgian residence set in beautiful secluded gardens with its own free car park. Excellent location only a few minutes level walk from Bath's main attractions. The comfortable en-suite bedrooms are all fully equipped and tastefully furnished. The attractive residents' sitting room is furnished with antiques. A delicious choice of full English or Continental breakfasts are served in the elegant dining room. A strictly no smoking house.

B & B from £30pp, C-Cards MC VS AE, Rooms 2 single, 7 twin, 7 double, 1 family, No smoking, Children over 15, No dogs, Closed Xmas & New Year

Cranleigh 159 Newbridge Hill, Bath BA1 3PX
Tony & Jan Poole Tel: 01225 310197 Fax: 01225 423143
Email: cranleigh@btinternet.com www.cranleighguesthouse.com

Map Ref: 1
A431
see Photo on page 28

Away from traffic and noise, just minutes from the heart of Bath, Cranleigh enjoys lovely views, secluded sunny gardens and private parking. Guest bedrooms are en-suite and exceptionally spacious. Imaginative breakfasts include fresh fruit salad and scrambled eggs with smoked salmon. The Pooles are always happy to help with routes, maps and suggestions. Some ground floor bedrooms are available. This is a no smoking house. Cranleigh is highly regarded and this is an excellent place to stay for exploring Bath. There are reductions for out of season short breaks.

B & B from £33pp, C-Cards MC VS AE, Rooms 2 twin, 4 double, 2 family all en-suite, No smoking, Children over 5, No dogs, Closed Xmas

Cranleigh, Bath

Gainsborough Hotel   Weston Lane, Bath BA1 4AB

Anna Ford   Tel: 01225 311380   Fax: 01225 447411
Email: gainsborough_hotel@compuserve.com   Web: www.gainsboroughhotel.co.uk

Map Ref: 1
A4

A large country house hotel, which stands in its own attractive grounds near botanical gardens, municipal golf course and centre. Both spacious and very comfortable, the Gainsborough welcomes guests to a relaxing and informal atmosphere. The Abbey, Roman Baths and Pump Rooms are all within walking distance via the park. All 17 bedrooms are en-suite with colour and satellite television, tea/coffee making facilities, direct dial telephones and hair dryers. The hotel has a friendly bar, two sun terraces and a large private car park.

B & B £32-£48pp, C-Cards MC VS AE, Rooms 2 single, 12 twin/double, 3 family,
Restricted smoking, Children welcome, No dogs, Closed Xmas & New Year

Holly Lodge   8 Upper Oldfield Park, Bath BA2 3JZ

George Hall   Tel: 01225 424042   Fax: 01225 481138
Email: stay@hollylodge.co.uk   Web: www.hollylodge.co.uk

Map Ref: 1
A367

This charming Victorian town house commands panoramic views of the city and is delightfully furnished with individually designed bedrooms, some with four posters and superb bathrooms. Elegant and stylish, it is owned and operated with meticulous attention to details by George Hall. Superb breakfasts are enjoyed in the appealing breakfast room with the yellow and green decor and white wicker chairs. Furnished with antiques, this immaculate establishment, winner of an 'England for Excellence' award makes a pleasant base for touring Bath and the Cotswolds.

B & B from £40pp, C-Cards MC VS AE DC, Rooms 1 single, 4 double, 2 twin, all en-suite,
No smoking, Children welcome, No dogs, Open all year

Leighton House   139 Wells Road, Bath BA2 3AL

Rhona Sampson   Tel: 01225 314769   Fax: 01225 443079
Email: welcome@leighton-house.co.uk   Web: www.leighton-house.co.uk

Map Ref: 1
A367

Rhona extends a friendly welcome to you at her delightful elegant Victorian home set in beautiful gardens, offering views over the city. With ample private parking, she is only 10 minutes walk from the city centre. The rooms offer every comfort. All have king, queen or twin beds and are tastefully decorated and furnished with en-suite facilities (bath, shower, wc and washbasin), direct dial telephone, hair dryer, television, radio and beverage making facilities. Superb breakfasts served to suit all tastes. Special breaks available at this award winning home.

B & B from £29.50pp, C-Cards MC VS AE, Rooms 4 double, 3 twin, 1 family, all en-suite,
No smoking, Children over 8, No dogs, Open all year

Oakleigh House   19 Upper Oldfield Park, Bath BA2 3JX

Jenny King   Tel: 01225 315698   Fax: 01225 448223
Email: oakleigh@which.net

Map Ref: 1
10 mins walk to centre

Oakleigh House stands in a peaceful location, only ten minutes from the city centre. Victorian elegance is combined with present day comforts. The bedrooms are well equipped and tastefully furnished. They offer en-suite and tea/coffee making facilities. There is colour television, clock radio and a hair dryer. Guests welcome to relax in the lounge where there are books, newspapers and games. Breakfasts are delicious, and the menu is extensive. Private parking is available. Oakleigh House is a good base for touring Glastonbury, Stonehenge, Bristol, Wells, Salisbury and the Cotswolds.

B & B from £34pp, C-Cards MC VS AE DC, Rooms 2 double, 1 twin, all en-suite,
No smoking, No children or dogs, Open all year

Paradise House, Bath

Villa Magdala Hotel, Bath

Paradise House 88 Holloway, Bath BA2 4PX
David & Annie Lanz Tel: 01225 317723 Fax: 01225 482005
Email: info@paradise-house.co.uk www.paradise-house.co.uk

Map Ref: 1
A367
see Photo on page 30

Awarded The 'Which?' 2001 Hotel of the Year 'Brilliant' Award for Bed and Breakfast Accommodation, Paradise House is superbly situated in a quiet location just seven minutes walk from the City Centre. Its half acre gardens at the rear command magnificent panoramic views over the entire city. Bedrooms are all en-suite, many have views and all are individually decorated and furnished to the highest standard. A small personally run hotel where a warm welcome awaits and a sumptuous breakfast is served. The perfect touring base for Bath and the Cotswolds.

B & B from £35pp, Rooms 4 double, 2 four poster, 3 twin, 1 family, all en-suite,
No smoking, Children welcome, No dogs, Closed Xmas

Tasburgh House Hotel Warminster Road, Bath BA2 6SH
David & Susan Keeling Tel: 01225 425096
Email: hotel@bathtasburgh.co.uk Web: www.bathtasburgh.co.uk

Map Ref: 1
M4, A36

Built in 1890, this lovely Victorian mansion provides ideal country comfort in a city setting with spectacular views. The hotel sits in seven acres of beautiful gardens and meadowpark stretching along the Kennet and Avon Canal, with the adjacent canal towpath providing idyllic walks into Bath. The 12 en-suite bedrooms (including four-poster and family rooms) are tastefully furnished, offering many amenities and optimum comfort. Elegant drawing room, dining room and stunning conservatory and terrace. Parking, licensed and evening meals. Every effort is made to ensure a memorable stay.

B & B £41-£56pp, C-Cards MC VS AE DC, Dinner £24, Rooms 1 single, 4 double/twin,
4 four-poster, 3 fam, all en-suite, No smoking, Children welcome, No dogs, Open all year

Villa Magdala Hotel Henrietta Road, Bath BA2 6LX
Roy & Lois Thwaites Tel: 01225 466329 Fax: 01225 483207
Email: office@villamagdala.co.uk Web: www.villamagdala.co.uk

Map Ref: 1
5 mins walk to centre
see Photo on page 31

This gracious Victorian town house hotel stands in its own grounds, overlooking the beautiful Henrietta Park. It is only a few minutes level walk from the Roman Baths and Abbey. All 17 spacious rooms all have ensuite bathrooms, telephone, television and tea/coffee making facilities. There is a comfortable lounge and dining room which enjoy views to the park and where a full English breakfast is offered. The hotel has its own private car park and is an ideal base for exploring Bath and the surrounding countryside.

B & B from £40pp, C-Cards MC VS AE, Rooms 12 double, 3 twin, 3 family, all en-suite,
No smoking, Children over 7, No dogs, Closed Xmas

Pickford House Bath Road, Beckington, Bath BA3 6SJ
Ken & Angela Pritchard Tel / Fax: 01373 830329
Email: AmPritchar@aol.com Web: www.pickfordhouse.com

Map Ref: 1
A36

Pickford House is an elegant Regency style house built in honey coloured Bath stone, it stands on top of the hill overlooking the village of Beckington and surrounding countryside. Some bedrooms are en-suite and all have tea/coffee making facilities and television, all are very comfortable and tastefully decorated. Angela is a talented and enthusiastic cook and offers an excellent 'pot luck' meal, or on request an extensive menu for celebrations. The house is licensed with a large and varied wine list. In summer, visitors may be offered an 'off-the-beaten-track' pre dinner drive.

B & B from £17pp, Dinner from £14, Rooms 1 twin, 1 double,
Children welcome, Dogs by arrangement, Open all year

The Plaine, Norton St Philip, near Bath

The Plaine Bell Hill, Norton St Philip, Bath BA2 7LT

Sarah Priddle & John Webster   Tel: 01373 834723   Fax: 01373 834101
Email: theplaine@easynet.co.uk   Web: www.theplaine.com

Map Ref: 2
A36
see Photo on page 33

A charming family home dating from the 16th century where visitors are welcomed to enjoy beautifully equipped and well presented accommodation including guest lounge. The delightful en-suite double bedrooms each offer four poster beds, colour television, beverage facilities. Located 15 minutes south of Bath, in the historic village of Norton St Philip. Excellent breakfasts are prepared using local produce. Evening meals can be enjoyed at the famous George Inn opposite. An ideal base from which to explore Bath, Wells, Longleat, Stonehenge and the Cotswolds. Private parking.

B & B £29-£36pp, C-Cards MC VS, Rooms 3 double, all en-suite, No smoking, Children welcome, No dogs, Closed Xmas

---

Owl House Lower Kingsdown Road, Kingsdown, Box SN13 8BB

Anne Venus   Tel: 01225 743883   Fax: 01225 744450
Email: venus@zetnet.co.uk   Web: www.owlhouse.co.uk

Map Ref: 3
M4, A4

Owl House may be found just four miles from the centre of Bath. It enjoys gorgeous views across the Avon Valley, the house which is built in traditional Cotswold stone, stands in well tended gardens surrounded by lovely countryside. The bedrooms are comfortable, generously equipped and well furnished. Excellent English breakfasts are offered, and on sunny mornings they may be enjoyed on the terrace which overlooks Bath city. The house is adjacent to the golf course which is surrounded by pleasant walks and good pubs.

B & B £26-£32.50pp, C-Cards MC VS, Rooms 1 single, 1 double, 1 twin, 1 family, all en-suite, No smoking, Children over 8, No dogs, Open all year

---

Box Hedge Farm Coalpit Heath, Bristol BS36 2UW

Marilyn & Bob Downes   Tel / Fax: 01454 250786
Email: marilyn@boxhedgefarmbandb.co.uk   Web: www.boxhedgefarmbandb.co.uk

Map Ref: 4
Westerleigh Road

Box Hedge Farm is set in 200 acres of beautiful rural countryside. Local to the M4/M5, central for Bristol and Bath. An ideal stopping point for the South West and Wales. We offer a warm family atmosphere, with traditional farmhouse cooking. All bedrooms have colour television and tea/coffee making facilities. We also offer self-catering weekend breaks.

B & B £20-£23pp, C-Cards MC VS AE, Rooms 2 single, 2 double, 2 family, some en-suite, Restricted smoking, Open all year

---

Spring Farm The Street, Regil, Winford BS40 8BB

Judy & Roger Gallannaugh   Tel: 01275 472735   Fax: 01275 474445
Email: springfarm@ic24.net

Map Ref: 5
A38, B3130

Set in a pretty country garden, Spring Farm is a cosy Georgian farmhouse with views across the country side to the Mendip Hills. Guests have a private sitting/breakfast room with an open fire in winter, and two double bedrooms with private and en-suite bathrooms. Regil is a quiet farming village in the foothills of the Mendips with villages and fishing lakes close by. There is a good choice of local pubs for evening meals. The beautiful cities of Bath, Bristol and Wells are within easy reach by car.

B & B £22.50-£25pp, Rooms 1 single, 2 double en-suite, No smoking, Children welcome, No dogs, Closed Xmas

Bedfordshire, Berkshire, Buckinghamshire & Hertfordshire

The Home Counties are at the very heart of England, secure in their position around the capital. It was here that the rich and famous built their homes, some of the most spectacular domestic architecture in the country. The great rolling estates, exotic gardens and countryside are cultivated and adapted to enhance the vistas of palaces and manor houses.

Bedfordshire is largely an agricultural area with the River Ouse in the north. Bedford, standing on the river, is the county town famous for its connection with the seventeenth century author of Pilgrim's Progress, John Bunyan. The town's location on the Ouse clothes it with picturesque riverside gardens and walks. Of course, no visitor to this lovely county should miss the Duke of Bedford's palatial mansion Woburn, packed with art treasures and set in its deer park or Woburn Wild Animal Kingdom, Europe's biggest drive-through safari park. Ampthill, a few miles south of Bedford is a charming town of Georgian houses and attractive cottages. Ampthill Park, landscaped by Capability Brown gives fine views over the surrounding countryside.

Luton, in the past a famous hatting town, is Bedfordshire's largest town. It has interesting walks along the River Lee and a path which follows the prehistoric Icknield Way. On the outskirts is the Woodside Farm wildfowl park, and to the south west is one of the National Trust's most unusual properties, the Whipsnade Tree Cathedral. Trees of various species have been planted in the traditional pattern of a cathedral, with grassy avenues representing the nave and transepts.

Like Bedfordshire, Berkshire is renowned for its stately homes, particularly Windsor Castle, the principle home of the Royal Family outside London. The castle houses St George's Chapel, a fine example of Gothic architecture and the Albert Memorial Chapel, commissioned by Queen Victoria after her husband's death. For the children Legoland has to be a must, combining wonderful lego models with fun rides and activities.

The National Trust owns no less than 1,000 acres of Chiltern beech woodland and rolling farmland, as well as most of the lovely village of Bradenham. Aylesbury, the county town is a great centre for exploring Buckinghamshire, as well as being the main market centre for the fertile Vale of Aylesbury. To

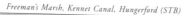
Freeman's Marsh, Kennet Canal, Hungerford (STB)

the south is West Wycombe with its picturesque main street and West Wycombe Park, a fine eighteenth century Palladian mansion, once the home of the famous and flamboyant Sir Francis Dashwood, leader of the Hell-Fire Club. Hidden away in woodland near Kimble is Chequers, the official home of British Prime Ministers. Another spectacular stately home is Waddeson Manor, built in the French style for Baron de Rothschild, containing treasures which include a superb collection of Sevres porcelain. Many visitors will recognise the building as being featured in the TV series 'Howard's Way'.

Hertfordshire's magnificent cathedral of St Albans, which dominates the surrounding countryside, is where England's first recorded Christian martyr is buried. A fine museum houses one of the best Roman collections in the country. The Hertfordshire and Middlesex Wildlife Trust, based here in St Albans is responsible for sterling work in protecting land forms and natural habitats which is threatened by urban development. To the north of Hemel Hempstead the Ashridge Estate runs along the main ridge of the Chilterns and encloses some 4,000 acres of commons and woodlands. At the northern end of the estate the Ivinghoe Hills, an outstanding area of chalk downland are dominated by the Ivinghoe Beacon.

These counties may well cluster around the capital and seem to be increasingly urbanized. However, they stand alone in their variety of stately homes with still a remarkable amount of open space to enchant the visitor.

PLACES TO VISIT

This is a small selection of interesting places to visit. Many more are listed in our annual guide to Museums, Galleries, Historic Houses & Sites (see page 448)

Beale Park
Lower Basildon, Reading,
Berksshire
Situated on the banks of the River Thames the park offers an extraordinary collection of rare birds and animals.

Bekonscot Model Village
Beaconsfield, Buckinghamshire
The oldest model village in the world displaying rural England in the 1930s. The attraction includes, in miniature, landscape gardens, houses, castles, churches and railway stations.

Knebworth House
Knebworth, Hertfordshire
Home of the Lytton family since 1490 and transformed into the Gothic masterpiece it is today in 1843, with a spectacular banquet hall. Its Victorian and Edwardian landscaped gardens also house a maze.

Windsor Castle
Windsor, Berkshire
The official residence of HM The Queen, situated on the River Thames. The State Apartments are furnished with some of the finest works of art in the country. Attractions within the Castle include Queen Mary's Doll House and St George's Chapel.

Woburn Abbey
Woburn, Bedfordshire
The Abbey became the Russell family home in 1619, within a 3,000 acre deer park. Collections of English silver, French and English furniture and art.

Bedfordshire, Berkshire, Buckinghamshire & Hertfordshire

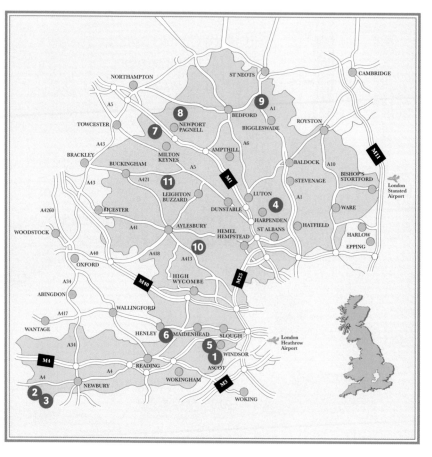

The Blue Map References should be used to locate B & B properties on the pages that follow

Marshgate Cottage Hotel, Hungerford

Lyndrick Guest House The Avenue, Ascot, Berks SL5 7ND

Sue & Graham Chapman Tel: 01344 883520 Fax: 01344 891243
Email: mail@lyndrick.com Web: www.lyndrick.com

Map Ref: 1
M3, M4, M25, A30

A large Victorian house in tree lined avenue. A warm welcome is assured with friendly help and advice on places to visit. Well equipped bedrooms with colour television, radio alarm, hair dryer and tea/coffee making facilities. Enjoy a delicious breakfast in pleasant conservatory overlooking garden. Special diets readily catered for by Sue, an experienced chef. Ideal base for various tourist attractions. Windsor four miles. Close to Ascot Racecourse. Wentworth, Sunningdale, Swinley, Mill Ride, Berkshire Golf Clubs nearby. Easy access by train to London. Ideal for day trips. Heathrow Airport 25 minutes.

B & B from £30pp, C-Cards MC VS, Rooms 1 single, 2 double, 2 twin, most en-suite,
Restricted smoking, No dogs, Open all year

Marshgate Cottage Hotel Marsh Lane, Hungerford, Berks RG17 0QX

Carole Ticehurst Tel: 01488 682307 Fax: 01488 685475
Email: reservations@marshgate.co.uk

Map Ref: 2
M4, A338
see Photo opposite

Marshgate Cottage is tucked away at the end of a quiet country lane just half a mile from Hungerford and four miles from the M4. Guest rooms are in a traditionally designed addition to the original canalside 17th century thatched cottage. All rooms have en-suite shower and toilet, television, phone and tea/coffee making facilities. Guests' lounge and bar. Car park. The town has an abundance of antique and speciality shops, canal trips, pubs and restaurants. Ideal base for touring southern England. Superb walking area.

B & B from £27.50pp, C-Cards MC VS, Rooms 1 single, 2 twin, 5 double, 2 family,
No smoking, Children & dogs welcome, Closed Xmas

Totterdown Lodge Inkpen, Hungerford, Berks RG17 9EA

Louisa Cosgrove Tel: 01488 668590
Email: louisa.cosgrove@btopenworld.com

Map Ref: 3
A4, A338

A delightful period property set in the beautiful Berkshire countryside. This family run home offers all the luxury of a country residence with a relaxed atmosphere. The bedrooms share a private bathroom and have tea/coffee facilities. The guests sitting room has a television and breakfast is served in the dining room in the winter and conservatory in the summer, which offers fabulous rural views. Totterdown Lodge is situated just ten minutes from the M4, driving through the picturesque town of Hungerford, famous for its antique shops. Heathrow only 50 minutes away, London one and a half hours away.

B & B from £30pp, Rooms 1 single, 1 twin, Smoking restrictions, No children,
Dogs by arrangement, Closed Xmas & New Year

Paddock Lodge Porters End, Kimpton, Herts SG4 8ER

Claire van Straubenzee Tel: 01438 832423 Fax: 01438 833527
Email: vanstraubenzee@btinternet.com

Map Ref: 4
M1, A1, B651

Paddock Lodge stands 30 minutes by train from London and only 10 minutes from Luton airport. This is an oasis which is surrounded by cornfields, woods and lovely country views. A large house, furnished with antiques, Paddock Lodge is cosy and very welcoming, guests may be assured of warmth and comfort in bright, informal bedrooms which overlook a spacious, quiet garden. Dinner is by arrangement, Claire's cooking is brilliant, and food is served in a pretty dining room.

B & B from £27.50pp, Dinner from £20, Rooms 1 twin en-suite, 1 twin with private bathroom,
Restricted smoking, Children over 2, Dogs only in car, Closed Xmas & New Year

Burchett's Place Country House   Burchett's Green, Maidenhead, Berks SL6 6QZ

The Hillier Family   Map Ref: 5

Tel: 01628 825023   Fax: 01628 826672   A4

Burchett's Place is set in private grounds offering peace and tranquillity in picturesque unspoilt countryside. The house offers an enchanting combination of country house elegance with a warm homely atmosphere, perfect for relaxation. An ideal base for exploring beautiful Berkshire countryside. Close to Marlow, Henley, Windsor and conveniently situated (20 mins) from Heathrow and less than one hour from London. Bedrooms are spacious and delightfully furnished with beautiful antique furniture. The main drawing room has a magnificent open fire. Full English breakfast is served.

B & B from £30pp, Rooms 1 single, 1 twin, 1 double, 1 family,
No smoking, Children over 12, Open all year

Dumbledore   Warren Row, Maidenhead, Berks RG10 8QS

Lavinia Rashleigh   Tel / Fax: 01628 822723   Map Ref: 6   A4, M4, M40

Email: laviniarashleigh@faxvia.net

This charming part 16th century Tudor country house may be found in the pretty village of Warren Row. It is close to Henley, Marlow and Maidenhead and it has easy access to M4 and M40, Heathrow and Gatwick. The bedrooms are charmingly furnished and they have television and tea and coffee making facilities. Dumbledore is an ideal base for day trips to London from Twyford station. There is a good choice of pubs and restaurants in the area.

B & B £28-£30pp, Rooms 1 single, 1 twin, 1 double, all en-suite,
No smoking, Children over 12, Open all year

Woodpecker Cottage   Warren Row, Maidenhead, Berks RG10 8QS

Michael & Joanna Power   Tel: 01628 822772   Fax: 01628 822125   Map Ref: 6   A4

Email: power@woodpecker.co.uk   www.woodpeckercottage.com   *see Photo opposite*

A tranquil woodland retreat away from crowds and traffic yet within half an hour of Heathrow, Windsor, Henley and Oxford. Set in a delightful garden of about one acre and surrounded by woods where deer abound. The ground floor bedrooms are very well equipped and comfortable, and all have their own bathrooms. There is a cosy sitting room with a wood burning stove in winter. A full English breakfast includes homemade bread and jam made from fruit grown in the garden. Local pubs and restaurants are within easy reach.

B & B £25-£27.50pp, Rooms 1 single, 1 double, both en-suite, 1 twin private bathroom,
No smoking, Children over 8, No dogs, Closed Xmas & New Year

Spinney Lodge Farm   Forest Road, Hanslope, Milton Keynes, Bucks MK19 7DE

Christina Payne   Map Ref: 7

Tel: 01908 510267   M1 J15, A508

Spinney Lodge is an arable, beef and sheep farm. The lovely Victorian farmhouse with its large gardens has en-suite bedrooms with colour television and tea/coffee making facilities. Evening meals are available by arrangement. There are many historic houses and gardens to explore in the area. Woburn, Silverstone, Stowe and Althorp are within an easy drive, as are the well known towns of Northampton and Milton Keynes. Junction 15 of the M1 is only a few minutes drive. Spinney Lodge is ideally placed for those on either business or holiday trips.

B & B £20-£25pp, Dinner from £10, Rooms 1 twin, 4 double,
No smoking, Children over 12, No dogs, Closed Xmas

Woodpecker Cottage, Warren Row, Maidenhead

Clifton Pastures Clifton Reynes, Olney, Bucks MK46 5DW

Andrew & Jane Finn-Kelcey   Tel: 01234 711287   Fax: 01234 711233
Email: finkel@kbnet.co.uk

Map Ref: 8
M1 J14/A509

Clifton Pastures built in 1847, has been home to the Finn-Kelcey family for three generations. The house which stands in its own grounds enjoys wonderful views to the Ouse valley. Very much a family home, the emphasis here is on offering a relaxed and comfortable atmosphere in a country setting. Althorp, Woburn Abbey and many other places of intrigue and interest are nearby. Heathrow Airport is 60 miles away, Oxford and Cambridge just 40. There are plenty of restaurants and pubs in Olney.

B & B £39pp, C-Cards MC VS, Rooms 1 twin en suite, 1 twin private bathroom, No smoking, Children over 12, No dogs, Closed Xmas & New Year

Highfield Farm Great North Road, Sandy, Beds SG19 2AQ

Margaret Codd   Tel: 01767 682332   Fax: 01767 692503
Email: margaret@highfield-farm.co.uk

Map Ref: 9
A1, A421, A14

Highfield Farm may be found in a peaceful location, set back from the A1, yet it has easy access to London. Guests here are certain to receive a very warm welcome to this 300 hundred acre arable farm. Of the seven attractively presented bedrooms, three are on ground floor level, they are in converted stables, and are ideal for those who prefer to avoid the stairs. The gardens are large and there is plenty of safe parking. This is an ideal spot for exploring the area, Cambridge and Bedford are within easy reach.

B & B £25-£45pp, C-Cards MC VS, Rooms 3 double, 4 twin, 1 family, all en-suite, No smoking, Children welcome, No dogs, Open all year

Field Cottage St Leonards, Tring, Herts HP23 6NS

Mike & Sue Jepson
Tel: 01494 837602

Map Ref: 10
A413, B4009

Visitors are assured of a warm welcome to Field Cottage, an award winning bed and breakfast. The house enjoys a pleasant location being situated off a country lane, down a short bridlepath on the very edge of open fields which run right up to the house. There is easy access to the famous Ridgeway. The bedrooms are presented in a pretty cottage style, they have televisions and tea/coffee making facilities. Breakfast is served in a flower filled conservatory which overlooks adjoining fields.

B & B from £27.50pp, Rooms 1 single with pb, 1 double with en-suite, 1 twin with pb, No smoking, Children over 12, No dogs, Closed Xmas & New Year

The Congregational Church 15 Horn Street, Winslow, Bucks MK18 3AP

Mrs Sarah Hood
Tel / Fax: 01296 715717   Mobile: 07711 505031

Map Ref: 11
M1, A41, A413

The Congregational Church, now an intriguing home, was formerly an active Victorian church in the centre of Old Winslow town. Unique in its presentation, each bedroom has its own stained glass window. The sitting room, which has television, used to be the clergy room, and the kitchen/breakfast room was once upon a time the schoolroom. On one side of the aisle are the comfortable bedrooms, and on the other side the bathrooms, one has painted fish swimming round the walls. Breakfasts here are delicious.

B & B from £22.50pp, Rooms 1 single, 1 double, 1 twin, Restricted smoking, Children over 12, No dogs, Open all year

Cambridgeshire & Northamptonshire

Cambridgeshire forms the western march of East Anglia and what this singularly flat county lacks in woodlands it more than makes up for in glorious rivers with the Great Ouse and the Nene. Within Cambridgeshire lies much of the Fen district, a vast area of highly fertile black farmland, once underwater but through many generations drained by cuts and sluices. The last undrained section of the Great Fens is Wicken Fen which now forms the oldest of the county's nature reserves, celebrating its centenary as a National Trust property in 1999. The William Thorpe Visitor Centre admirably explains the history of the Fen's evolution, 600 acres of wetland rich in plant life and displaying a remarkably extensive variety of habitats for birds.

Of course the jewel of the county must be Cambridge, the county town which lies in the chalk downland of the south by the River Cam, known to the Romans as Granta. The ancient college buildings, some founded as far back as the thirteenth century are a great attraction, but the city and university are dominated by the quite magnificent King's College Chapel renowned for its remarkable fan-vaulting and its Rubens painting, 'The Adoration of the Magi'. Beside the thirty or so colleges, the city is packed with interest for the visitor, such as the 'Bridge of Sighs' at St John's, built in 1831, copying its namesake in Venice and the intriguing Mathematical Bridge constructed in wood without using any bolts. Outside the city is

Wimpole Hall, a wonderful eighteenth century house set in an extensive wooded park, Anglesey Abbey, built on the site of an Augustinian priory and dating from 1600, houses the famous Fairhaven collection of paintings and furniture and is set in 99 acres of superb landscaped gardens. The Duxford Air Museum, a part of London's Imperial War Museum, which holds probably Europe's largest collection of historic military aircraft, is also not to be missed.

Until 1965 Peterborough was administered as a separate county known as the Soke of Peterborough and boasts one of the finest Norman cathedrals in Britain, built between 1118 and 1258. The cathedral contains the tomb of Catherine of Aragon, Henry VIII's first wife. Mary Queen of Scots was buried here too but her body was removed to Westminster in 1612. Ely, taking its name from its one time major industry of eeling, is a city of great charm and can also claim a magnificent cathedral, founded in 673 by St Etheldreda. The octagonal tower dominates the flat land

Althorp House and Park

surrounding the city and, standing on an island protected by the treacherous fen, was originally a stronghold during the eleventh century for those resisting William the Conqueror. The city contains some fine medieval and Georgian buildings.

Northamptonshire has always been primarily a farming county, but is also an attractive holiday region. Northampton, the county town was largely destroyed by fire in 1675, and fortunately two of its most spectacular churches survived: the Norman church of St Peter and the remarkable round Holy Sepulchre. The town has at its centre, one of England's largest traditional open market squares. Northampton's museum contains the world's largest collection of boots and shoes, reflecting the town's importance in this industry. Its close neighbour Kettering, also a boot and shoe town,

has a wonderful museum housed in the manor house. To the south of Northampton, at Canons Ashby is the home of the Dryden family, the sixteenth century Canons Ashby House. This National Trust property, set in formal gardens and a seventy acre park, contains some fine Elizabethan wall paintings and Jacobean plasterwork. Lyveden New Bield, near Oundle, is also an excellent day out. This strange incomplete garden house of 1595, constructed in the shape of a cross is inscribed with religious quotations.

Within these two counties is a quite remarkable variation in scenery, ranging from the gently rolling chalk downs south of Cambridge to the bleak and windswept lonely fens, and from the great earthworks of Fleam Dyke, Devil's Dyke and Bran Ditch to the glorious churches and manor houses of Northamptonshire's 'spires and squires'.

PLACES TO VISIT

This is a small selection of interesting places to visit. Many more are listed in our annual guide to Museums, Galleries, Historic Houses & Sites (see page 448)

Althorp
Northampton
Home to the Spencer family for 500 years and the resting place of Diana, The Princess of Wales. An award-winning exhibition commemorates her life and work.

Ely Cathedral
Ely, Cambridgeshire
A fine Cathedral founded by St Etheldreda in 673 AD. The most outstanding feature being the Octagon built to replace the collapsed Norman tower. Also with a stained glass museum.

Kings College Chapel
Cambridge
The oldest Cambridge college, founded

in 1441 by Henry VI. Tours of the impressive architecture and spectacular perpendicular chapel.

Imperial War Museum
Duxford, Cambridgeshire
The centre for historic aviation where many rare aircraft, including Spitfire and Mustang, fly from. Visitors can also see aircraft restoration taking place.

Wimpole Hall
Arrington, Cambridgeshire
The most imposing mansion in Cambridgeshire. The servants quarters are impressive, as are the gardens, re-designed by Bridgeman, Brown and Repton.

Cambridgeshire &
Northamptonshire

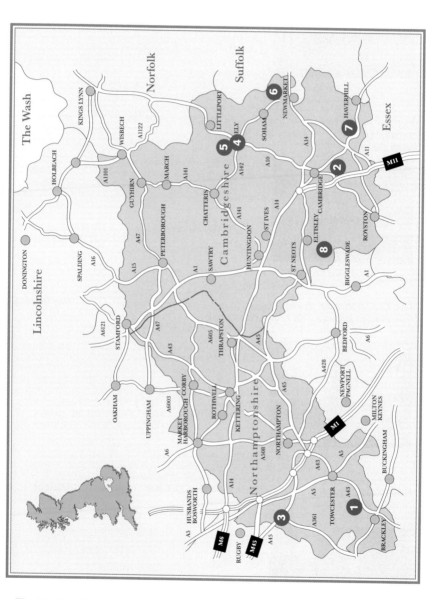

The Blue Map References should be used to locate B & B properties on the pages that follow

Astwell Mill Helmdon, Brackley, Northants NN13 5QU
Phyllis King Tel: 01295 760507 Fax: 01295 768602
Email: astwell01@aol.com

Map Ref: 1
A43, B4525

Converted water mill in open countryside, peacefully situated between two villages. Attractive garden with large lake, stream and waterfalls. Superb views from comfortably furnished bedrooms which all have colour televisions and tea/coffee making facilities. (Hair dryers available). Friendly family atmosphere. Spacious lounge. Interesting country walks and bird life. Off road parking. Astwell Mill is situated between M1 (12 miles) and M40 (10 miles). Local attractions: Silverstone, Stowe, Canons Ashby and Sulgrave Manor. Convenient for Althorp, Blenheim, Warwick, Northampton, Oxford, Banbury and Milton Keynes.

B & B from £22.50pp, Rooms 2 double, 1 en-suite, No smoking,
Children welcome, No dogs, Closed Xmas & New Year

Purlins 12 High Street, Little Shelford, Cambridge, Cambs CB2 5ES
David & Olga Hindley Tel / Fax: 01223 842643
Email: dgallh@ndirect.co.uk

Map Ref: 2
M11, A10

An individually designed country house set in two acres of fields and woodland, in a quiet pretty village on the Cam, four miles south of Cambridge. An ideal centre for visiting colleges, cathedrals and country houses, the Imperial War Museum and also for bird watching. The comfortable en-suite bedrooms (two on the ground floor) all have colour television, radio and tea/coffee making facilities. A conservatory serves as the guests' sitting room and breakfast is provided to suit most tastes. Restaurants are nearby. On drive parking for three cars.

B & B from £24pp, Rooms 2 double, 1 twin, all en-suite, No smoking,
Children over 8, No dogs, Closed mid-Dec to Feb 1

The Old Vicarage Moreton Pinkney, Daventry, Northants NN11 3SQ
Colonel & Mrs Eastwood Tel / Fax: 01295 760057
Email: Tim@tandjeastwood.fsnet.co.uk Web: www.tandjeastwood.fsnet.co.uk

Map Ref: 3
A43, A361

The Old Vicarage is a pretty, ironstone listed 18th century house which stands beside the church in this delightful corner of English countryside. Two comfortably furnished bedrooms are offered to guests, and there is a lovely walled garden which overlooks the church where guests may sit and relax and enjoy meals in summer. Nearby there are a number of public houses with restaurants which serve meals with an interesting menu range to suit all tastes. Guests may enjoy suppers at The Old Vicarage by prior arrangement. A car is essential here.

B & B from £30pp, Dinner from £15, Rooms 1 double, 1 twin, No smoking,
Children by arrangement, Dogs by arrangement, Closed Xmas & New Year

Cathedral House 17 St Marys Street, Ely, Cambs CB7 4ER
Jenny & Robin Farndale Tel / Fax: 01353 662124
Email: farndale@cathedralhouse.co.uk www.cathedralhouse.co.uk

Map Ref: 4
A10
see Photo opposite

Cathedral House is within the shadow of Ely's famous cathedral known as 'The Ship of the Fens', and two minutes walk from Cromwell's house, the museums, shops and restaurants. A Grade II listed house, it retains many original features. The spacious bedrooms are all en-suite and very well appointed. They all overlook the tranquil walled garden. A choice of full English or continental breakfast is served to order at a farmhouse table, by an open fire on chilly days. Ely is an ideal base from which to tour East Anglia by car or rail. Parking.

B & B £25-£37.50pp, Rooms 1 twin, 1 double, 1 family, No smoking,
Children by arrangement, No dogs, Closed Jan

Cathedral House, Ely

Queensberry, Fordham

Hill House Farm 9 Main Street, Coveney, Ely, Cambs CB6 2DJ

Hilary Nix　Tel: 01353 778369

Email: hill_house@madasafish.com

Map Ref: 5

A10, A142

A warm welcome awaits you at this spacious Victorian farmhouse, situated in the quiet village of Coveney, three miles west of the historic cathedral city of Ely. It enjoys open views of the surrounding countryside. The towns of Cambridge, Newmarket and Huntingdon are a few miles away. Ideally placed for touring Cambridgeshire, Norfolk and Suffolk. Wicken Fen and Welney Wildfowl Refuge are nearby. The bedrooms are tastefully furnished, they are warm and well equipped. There is one ground floor bedroom. A first class breakfast is served in the traditional dining room. ETC 4 Diamonds, Gold Award.

B & B from £22pp, C-Cards MC VS, Rooms 1 twin, 2 double, all en-suite,
No smoking, Children over 12, No dogs, Closed Xmas

Queensberry 196 Carter Street, Fordham, Cambs CB7 5JU

Jan & Malcolm Roper

Tel: 01638 720916　Fax: 01638 720233

Map Ref: 6

A14/A142

see Photo opposite

A warm welcome at this very English home, a Georgian house set peacefully in large gardens on edge of the village. 'Queensberry' is the ideal base from which to tour East Anglia; visit the university city of Cambridge; historical cathedral of Ely 'the ship of the Fens', the famous market town of Bury St Edmunds and Newmarket, the horse racing centre of the world. Self-catering converted flint barn in the grounds and ample safe parking. First village off A14 on Newmarket to Ely A142 road. Good restaurants within walking distance.

B & B £25-£30pp, Rooms 1 single, 1 twin, 1 double, 1 en-suite, self contained barn,
No smoking, Children welcome, Dogs by Arrangement, Closed Xmas

---

The Watermill Linton Road, Hildersham, Cambs CB1 6BS

Mr & Mrs Hartland

Tel: 01223 891520

Map Ref: 7

A1307

There is a watermill recorded here in the Domesday Book although the present buildings are 18th and 19th century. Set in six acres of land on the River Granta, the house has views across the garden and water meadows to the village beyond. Meals can be taken in the nearby Pear Tree. The Watermill is well located as it is within easy driving distance from Cambridge, Ely and Saffron Walden, also many other beautiful towns and villages of Suffolk and Essex .

B & B from £22pp, Rooms 1 double/family en-suite, No smoking,
Children welcome, No dogs, Closed Xmas & New Year

Model Farm Longstowe Road, Little Gransden, Cambs SG19 3EA

Mrs Sue Barlow　Tel: 01767 677361　Fax: 01767 677883

Email: bandb@modelfarm.org.uk　Web: modelfarm.org.uk

Map Ref: 8

B1046

Model Farm is a traditional Cambridgeshire farmhouse, situated on a working farm with sheep and crops. Built in the 1870s of local bricks, it retains many of the original features. Guests are provided with comfortable accommodation, the en-suite guest rooms are generously equipped, they have televisions and tea/coffee making facilities. The house enjoys lovely countryside views and a peaceful location, yet it is only 20 minutes from Cambridge. A variety of breakfasts is offered, ranging from a full English to a lighter continental version, plus home produced honey. Several pubs locally.

B & B from £22.50pp, Rooms 3 double with en-suite, No smoking, No children,
Dogs by arrangement, Closed Xmas & New Year

Cheshire, Merseyside & Greater Manchester

Three great cities dominate this area and one could be excused for regarding the region as overwhelmingly industrial and certainly not a holiday venue. However, in contrast to this industrialism are some areas of quite remarkable beauty. Alderley Edge towers six hundred feet over the surrounding countryside, within easy reach of Manchester, giving glorious views across the Cheshire Plain. Bronze Age relics have been discovered here on this heavily wooded sandstone escarpment. Below Alderley Edge is Styal Country Park, an area of glorious woodlands and quiet riverside walks. Here also is the Quarry Bank Cotton Mill, a wonderfully restored Georgian mill where the costumed guides reveal the harrowing lives of the young mill workers of the past.

The Cheshire Plain is a rolling dairy farming region renowned for Cheshire cheese and the remarkable black and white half-timbered architecture. Scattered within this lovely area are some fascinating houses that the holiday maker simply must visit. Little Moreton Hall, regarded as the most perfect example of a timber-framed moated manor

The River Dee (NWTB)

house in the country with musical evenings, suppers and special tours of the splendid wall paintings and knot garden. Tatton Park, the nineteenth century Wyatt house, set in over a thousand acres of deer park is considered to be one of England's most complete historic estates open to visitors. The mansion is a treasure house of china, glass, paintings and furniture, the fifty acres of garden are an absolute joy. Lyme Park, the largest house in the county, was the home of the Legh family for 600 years and houses some magnificent Grinling Gibbons woodcarving as well as Mortlake tapestries and a significant collection of English clocks. This fine house incidentally was 'Pemberley' in the television adaptation of Jane Austen's 'Pride and Prejudice'. Just south of Altrincham is Dunham Massey, a wonderful Georgian house, once the home of the last Earl of Stamford. Set in over 250 acres of wooded deer park, the mansion houses excellent collections of eighteenth century furniture and Huguenot silver.

For the visitors to this region who like their interests centred in one place and who can resist the delights of touring the area, then Chester is undoubtedly the place to be; the city is seeped in history. The Romans built their fort, Deva, here in 79AD as a buttress against the hostile Welsh. When the Romans left in 383AD a prosperous trading centre had been established and continued to develop and prosper through the rule of successive Saxon and Norman overlords. The River Dee gave access to the sea and Chester developed as a port, importing

French wines, Irish linen and Spanish fruits and spices. The Benedictine Abbey, built in 1092 became in 1541 Chester Cathedral with beautiful woodcarvings in the choir stalls. There is much to see in the city, probably the most impressive sight being the Rows, two-tier shopping galleries which date from the Middle Ages. There are many fine buildings including the grand black and white facades. But Chester is by no means a city of the past, it can offer up to the minute entertainment and excellent shopping facilities.

Both Liverpool and Manchester have long histories as great industrial centres and ports. Much of the industrial and commercial life of the north west is centred on these two fine cities, but with the decline in heavy industry there has been a concerted effort to attract holiday visitors. However there is a marked contrast between the industrial buildings and the glorious civic buildings with magnificent museums and art galleries. Both cities can boast spectacular cathedrals, Liverpool has two modern cathedrals in quite distinct styles of ecclesiastical architecture and Manchester cathedral, built in the fifteenth century claims the widest nave in England. Liverpool's Albert Dock waterfront, with its massive warehouses has now become an impressive complex of shops, restaurants and television studios. Similarly Manchester's canal basin of Castlefield has been redeveloped as an urban heritage park and boasts the popular tourist attraction of Granada Studios. Both Manchester and Liverpool can offer theatres, cinemas and nightlife of the highest quality with shopping to match any city in the country. Whatever your holiday requirements, this is a region to suit the most discriminating tastes.

PLACES TO VISIT

This is a small selection of interesting places to visit. Many more are listed in our annual guide to Museums, Galleries, Historic Houses & Sites (see page 448)

Granada Studios
Manchester
A theme park based on Granada produced television programmes with Motion Master where seats move with the action and spectacular 3D effects. Coronation Street, Cracker and Sherlock Homes feature.

Liverpool Cathedral
Liverpool
The largest Anglican Cathedral in Britain with the highest Gothic arches, the largest organ and the heaviest ring of bells. The embroidery exhibition is a unique collection of Victorian and Edwardian embroidery on the triforium gallery.

Liverpool Museum
Liverpool
Important and diverse collections covering archaeology, ethnology and natural and physical sciences. Includes the award-winning Natural History Centre and planetarium.

Lyme Park
Disley, Cheshire
Transformed into an Italianate palace by the Venetian architect Leoni. The State Rooms boast Mortlake tapestries, Grinling Gibbons wood carvings and an important collection of English clocks. It is renowned for being Pemberley in the BBC adaptation of Pride and Prejudice.

Tatton Park
Knutsford, Cheshire
Historic mansion and estate with 2,000 acre deer park, medieval manor house, 50 acre garden and traditional working farm. Fine collections of furniture and paintings.

Cheshire, Merseyside & Greater Manchester

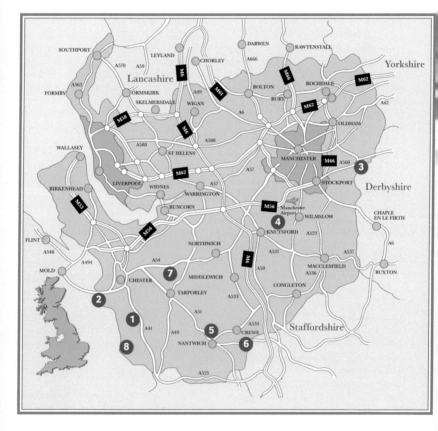

The Blue Map References should be used to locate B & B properties on the pages that follow

Golborne Manor Platts Lane, Hatton Heath, Chester, Cheshire CH3 9AN

Ann Ikin Tel: 01829 770310 Fax: 01829 770370 Mobile: 07774 695268
Web: www.golbornemanor.co.uk

Map Ref: 1
A41, M54

Golborne Manor is an elegant 19th century country residence with glorious views. Renovated to a high standard and set in three and a half acres of grounds and gardens. Beautifully decorated with spacious en-suite bedrooms. Farmhouse breakfast. Tea and coffee in rooms, also colour television. Guest lounge. Croquet and table tennis. Large car park. Easy access to motorway network and North Wales coast. Five and a half miles south of Chester on the A41, turn right a few yards after D.P. Motors (on the left).

B & B from £30pp, Rooms 1 single, 1 double, 1 twin, 1 family, all en-suite,
No smoking, Children welcome, No dogs, Open all year

The Mount Lesters Lane, Higher Kinnerton, Chester, Cheshire CH4 9BQ

Jonathan & Rachel Major Tel / Fax: 01244 660275
Email: major@mountkinnerton.freeserve.co.uk

Map Ref: 2
A55, A5104

The Mount is a Victorian country house with spacious and imaginatively decorated rooms. It is set in 12 acres on the edge of the village of Higher Kinnerton. The gardens have a tennis court and croquet lawn. The bedrooms enjoy countryside views and have television, tea/coffee making facilities. This is an ideal place to relax and explore the North Wales coast and Cheshire. It is six miles from Chester, 45 minutes from Liverpool and Manchester, and one hour from Anglesey. Bodnant Gardens, Port Sunlight, historic Chester, Erdigg, Offas Dyke and Llangollen are all nearby. There is an excellent village pub.

B & B £25-£30pp, Rooms 2 twin, 1 double, all en-suite, No smoking,
Children over 12, Dogs only in car, Closed Xmas

Needhams Farm Uplands Road, Werneth Low, Gee Cross, Hyde, Cheshire SK14 3AG

Mrs C Walsh Tel: 0161 368 4610 Fax: 0161 367 9106
Email: charlotte@needhamsfarm.co.uk Web: www.needhamsfarm.co.uk

Map Ref: 3
A560

Needhams Farm is a non-working farm, being home to cattle and sheep. The farmhouse is 500 years old and it enjoys wonderful views from all the rooms. Log fires welcome in winter, meals are served each evening between seven and nine pm, there is a residential licence. Special suppers may be prepared for children. This welcoming farmhouse is ideally situated for Manchester and the surrounding area including Manchester Airport. The nearest Station is Romiley. There is plenty of parking for guests' cars. The Peak District is just a pleasant drive away.

B & B £20-£45pp, C-Cards MC VS, Dinner from £7, Rooms 1 single, 3 double, 1 twin,
1 family room, all en-suite, Children & dogs welcome, Open all year

Longview Hotel & Restaurant 51/55 Manchester Road, Knutsford, Cheshire WA16 0LX

Pauline & Stephen West Tel: 01565 632119 Fax: 01565 652402
Email: enquiries@longviewhotel.com Web: www.longviewhotel.com

Map Ref: 4
M6, A50

Longview Hotel may be found in the market town of Knutsford, overlooking the common. Many antiques grace this lovely Victorian building and great care has been taken to ensure that whilst the character has been retained, comfort for visitors is also assured. Decoration in the bedrooms reflects the feeling that warmth of hospitality and a relaxed atmosphere are of major importance. All 26 bedrooms radiate this feeling, making this hotel a perfect place to stay whether for business or pleasure.

B & B £33.25-£65pp, C-Cards MC VS AE, Dinner from £12.50, Rooms 6 single, 20 double,
all en-suite, Restricted smoking, Children & dogs welcome, Closed Xmas & New Year

Stoke Grange Farm, Nantwich, Cheshire

Stoke Grange Farm　Chester Road, Nantwich, Cheshire CW5 6BT
Georgina West
Tel / Fax: 01270 625525

Map Ref: 5
M6, A51
see Photo opposite

An attractive Cheshire farmhouse in a picturesque canalside location. Individually styled en-suite rooms with colour television. A four poster bedroom has a balcony overlooking the surrounding countryside. Hearty breakfasts are offered, vegetarians are well catered for. Watch canal boats cruising the Shropshire Union. Relax in the garden with lawns down to the canal. Pets corner and peacocks. Also excellent self catering accommodation is available. Chester and Crewe are not many minutes away. Near to Stapeley Water Gardens, Beeston and Chalmondeley castles, Jodrell Bank, Tatton Park and Chester Zoo.

B & B from £30pp, Rooms 2 double, 1 twin, 1 family, Restricted smoking, Children welcome, No dogs, Open all year

Lea Farm　Wrinehill Road, Wybunbury, Nantwich, Cheshire CW5 7NS
Jean Callwood
Tel / Fax: 01270 841429

Map Ref: 6
A500

Surrounded by rolling countryside, this charming farmhouse is set in landscaped gardens where peacocks roam on a dairy farm. The bedrooms are spacious and there is a luxury lounge which guests are welcome to use. For relaxation there is a pool/snooker table and fishing can be arranged. Leave M6 at Junction 16, go along A500, towards Nantwich, over 2 roundabouts, still heading towards Nantwich, left after railway bridge, go down to T junction, turn left again. Lea Farm is second farm on right. Look for B&B sign.

B & B from £19pp, Rooms 1 double, 1 family, 1 twin, 2 en-suite, No smoking, Children & dogs welcome, Closed Xmas & New Year

Roughlow Farm　Chapel Lane, Willington, Tarporley, Cheshire CW6 0PG
Sally Sutcliffe　Tel / Fax: 01829 751199
Email: sutcliffe@roughlow.freeserve.co.uk　Web: roughlow.freeserve.co.uk

Map Ref: 7
M6, A54

A delightful 18th century converted farmhouse in quiet situation with wonderful views to Shropshire and Wales. Attractive garden with cobbled courtyard and tennis court. Elegantly furnished to a high standard with en-suite facilities, one of the double rooms has a private sitting room. Roughlow Farm is well situated for easy access to Manchester, Chester, Wales, Liverpool and M6. From M6 (J19) take the A556 towards Chester. A54 Kelsall bypass turn left after passing Morreys Nurseries on right hand side, then left again at the pub in Waste Lane, continue bearing right at the next junction. (150 yds on left).

B & B £25-£40pp, Rooms 2 double, 1 twin, all en-suite, No smoking, Children over 6, Dogs only in car, Open all year

Worthenbury Manor　Worthenbury, Wrexham, Cheshire LL13 0AW
Ian & Elizabeth Taylor
Tel: 01948 770342　Fax: 01948 770711

Map Ref: 8
A41, A525, B5069

Worthenbury Manor is a fully restored Grade II listed manor house, surrounded by rolling Cheshire Plains, Welsh Marches and National Trust properties. This is a rural retreat nestling between Wales, Cheshire and Shropshire. Guests may enjoy a country house hospitality, home cooked local produce, freshly baked bread, oak panelling and four poster beds. There is the Georgian styled Captain Rayner's room or the Jacobean Oak room, both rooms are equipped with televisions, hairdryers and bathrobes. This elegant home stands two miles from Bangor on Dee and four miles from Malpas.

B & B £28-£38pp, Dinner from £18, Rooms 2 double, 1 en-suite and 1 with private bathroom, No smoking, Children over 10, No dogs, Closed Nov to Feb

Cornwall

Cornwall is a very special and separate part of Britain since it was isolated from the mainland by the River Tamar. Consequently it retains much of its Celtic character, in fact the name Cornwall comes from the Saxon Cornovii and Wealas meaning Welsh of the west. Historically this is a region of Iron and Bronze Age settlements and monuments, holy wells and ancient churches, a land criss-crossed by the paths of the early

Spectacular Coastline at Land's End (SWT)

saints. The intricate and decidedly rugged coastline of the county being vulnerable to invaders, it is a land of impressive castles. Tintagel Castle, perched on its headland, was claimed by Geoffrey of Monmouth in the twelfth century to be the birthplace of King Arthur and the twin castles of Pendennis and St Mawes were built by Henry VIII to protect the shipping in the River Fol. The wonderfully romantic St Michael's Mount on the rocky island dominating Mount's Bay was

originally the site of a Benedictine chapel established by Edward the Confessor. The mount, joined at low tide to the mainland by a causeway gives magnificent views to Land's End and the Lizard.

The 300 miles of coastline is punctuated by the most enchanting array of quaint and picturesque fishing villages. Today Newlyn is the largest fish-landing station in England and Wales. Not that this county's seafaring activities were always strictly within the law, Cornwall is rich in stories of smuggling, wrecking and pirateering. For the visitor there is everything here to please with the Atlantic coast offering towering cliffs, mountainous seas and glorious sand dunes. In contrast the Cornish Riviera, altogether softer, gives wide golden beaches and mellow fishing villages. The shores of the Helford river, regarded by many as the most beautiful estuary in the country, is protected by the National Trust, as is much of the coastline, including Frenchman's Creek, the location of Daphne du Maurier's novel. The Cornwall Wildlife Trust, founded in 1962 by local people has established forty nature reserves covering over 3,000 acres.

The Cornish hinterland largely grew up around the mining and china clay industry. It is difficult to realise now that Cornwall once dominated the tin and copper markets of the world, but the remnants of the industry, the ruined mine engine houses, are scattered over the landscape. Bodmin Moor covers about a hundred square miles of eastern Cornwall, a bleak, windswept and lonely land of granite Tors and Brown Willy, at 1,377 feet, the county's highest point gives glorious views across the moor. On the edge of the moor, Bodmin, an ancient town established in the sixth century and from 1835 until 1989 the capital of Cornwall, runs steam trains to Bodmin Parkway, with stations for Cardinham Woods and Lanhydrock House, a lovely National Trust property overlooking the River Fowey. Truro, a medieval tin town and principal port for its export can claim the first Anglican cathedral to be built in England since London's St Paul's. The county town, dominated by the three-towered cathedral has a wealth of Regency and Georgian buildings. The centre of Cornwall certainly has a great deal to offer scenically but wherever you are in the county you are never more than twenty miles from the coast and it is the coastal resorts which act as a magnet to the vast majority of holiday makers. Looe, Fowey and

Falmouth, the main seaside resorts on the Riviera coast, offer a dazzling array of seaside activities, enhanced by their glorious garden settings influenced by the warm Gulf Stream. No visitor should leave the county without seeing The Lost Gardens of Heligan, the magnificent gardens of the Tremayne family, wonderfully restored to their pre-First World War beauty, and now attracting over 300,000 visitors each year.

If the visitor to Cornwall should tire of the charms of the familiar resorts, then on the Isles of Scilly they will discover the nature reserve supreme. The five inhabited islands each have their own distinctive character with spectacular beaches, balmy climate and tranquil atmosphere. Tresco, of course is renowned for its sub-tropical Abbey Garden, a blaze of summer colour, but then Cornwall is truly a land for all seasons.

PLACES TO VISIT

This is a small selection of interesting places to visit. Many more are listed in our annual guide to Museums, Galleries, Historic Houses & Sites (see page 448)

The Eden Project
St Austell
The world's largest biodome construction which is home to a giant indoor rainforest and displaying plants found in tropical climates.

Flambards Victorian Village
Helston
A compelling life-size recreation of a lamplit village of bustling streets and alleyways with nearly 60 homes and shops, all authentically equipped and furnished with genuine artefacts.

Jamaica Inn Museum
Bolventor, Bodmin
Cornwall's legendary coaching house with a display of the life and works of

Daphne du Maurier, a theatrical presentation of the history of the Inn and a fine collection of smugglers' relics.

Lost Gardens of Heligan
Pentewan, St Austell
The gardens, created in the nineteenth century were the finest in the country, but they were lost for many years. Now restored, they include 80 acres of pleasure grounds, a complex of walled gardens and a huge vegetable garden.

Tintagel Castle
Tintagel
Set on the North Cornwall Atlantic coastline stands the remains of this thirteenth century castle, supposedly King Arthur's Castle Fortress.

Cornwall

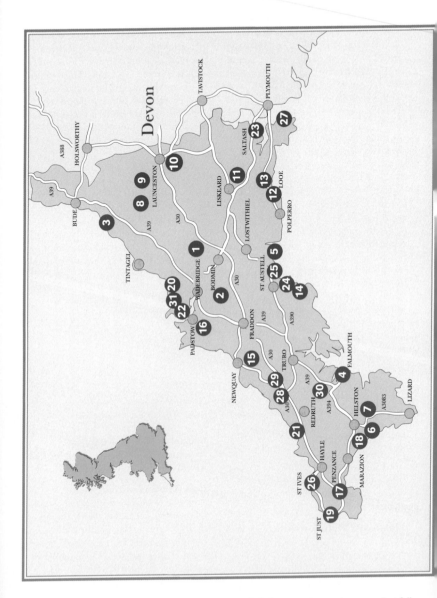

The Blue Map References should be used to locate B & B properties on the pages that follow

Lavethan Blisland, Bodmin PL30 4QG

Christopher & Catherine Hartley　Tel: 01208 850487　Fax: 01208 851387
Email: chrishartley@btconnect.com

Map Ref: 1
A30

This beautiful family home, listed in the Domesday Book, stands in 30 acres of fields and gardens which slope down to a small river. Blisland is one of the prettiest Cornish villages in an area of outstanding natural beauty. Guests' bedrooms are beautifully presented with their own bathrooms and lovely old baths, and the drawing room includes a piano and television. This is a perfect place to stay for golfers, and for those who enjoy riding, the sea and river fishing. A heated outdoor pool is available for guests use.

B & B £35-£40pp, C-Cards MC VS, Dinner from £25, Rooms 2 double, 1 twin, all private bathrooms, No smoking in bedrooms, Children over 10, Dogs only by arrangement, Closed Xmas & New Year

Tregawne Withiel, Bodmin PL30 5NR

David Jackson & Peta, Lady Linlithgow
Tel: 01208 831552　Fax: 01208 832122

Map Ref: 2
A30

Situated in the Ruthern Valley, Tregawne is a lovingly restored 18th century comfortable family farmhouse, furnished with antiques. The accommodation is spacious and elegant with views across the valley. Guests have use of the drawing room and the heated pool. Ideally situated for exploring the coasts, and for wonderful walking on the Saints Way and Camel Trail. Sandy beaches and surfing at Polzeath. Quality golf courses within ten miles. Sea fishing, sailing and riding by arrangement. National Trust houses and gardens to visit. Padstow half an hour. Eden Project 10 minutes.

B & B from £36pp, C-Cards MC VS, Dinner from £22.50, Rooms 2 double en-suite, 1 twin with bathroom, also 3 cottages, Children over 5, Dogs welcome, Open all year

St Gennys House St Gennys, Bude EX23 0NW

Anthony & Jane Farquhar　Tel: 01840 230384　Fax: 01840 230537
Email: ac.farquhar@talk21.com

Map Ref: 3
A39

St Gennys House, a Grade II listed former vicarage, is part 16th century with later Georgian and Edwardian additions. It stands in three acres of grounds, and it has wonderful sea, cliff and farmland views. The bedrooms are fresh and prettily presented, two have spacious, private bathrooms. The drawing room and dining room both overlook the sea and gardens. There are challenging walks from the house, and within easy reach are golf courses, sea fishing, surfing and sandy beaches. A simple supper, or dinner may be pre booked.

B & B £22-£30pp, Dinner from £12, Rooms 1 double, 1 twin, private bathrooms, 1 single, 1 twin, Restricted smoking, Children over 5, No dogs, Closed Xmas

Dolvean Hotel 50 Melvill Road, Falmouth TR11 4DQ

Paul & Carol Crocker　Tel: 01326 313658　Fax: 01326 313995
Email: reservations@dolvean.co.uk　Web: www.dolvean.co.uk

Map Ref: 4
A39

Experience the elegance and comfort of our Victorian home. We have carefully chosen interesting antiques, fine china, and fascinating books to create an ambience where you can relax and feel at home. Each bedroom has its own character. Pretty pictures, and lots of ribbons and lace create an atmosphere that makes you feel special. All bedrooms enjoy en-suite facilities, with fluffy white towels and luxurious toiletries. Thoughtful little extras include mineral water, cookies and chocolates by your bedside. Car park. AA and ETC 5 Diamonds, Silver Award.

B & B £30-£40pp, C-Cards, Rooms 3 single, 4 double, 2 twin, 2 king sized, all en-suite, No smoking, Children over 12, No dogs, Closed Xmas

Trevanion 70 Lostwithiel Street, Fowey PL23 1BQ

Jill & Bob Bullock Tel / Fax: 01726 832602
Email: trefoy@globalnet.co.uk Web: www.users.globalnet.co.uk/~trefoy/fowey.htm

Map Ref: 5
A390, B3269

A warm and friendly welcome awaits you at this comfortable and spacious 16th century Merchants House situated in the historic town of Fowey in the heart of Daphne Du Maurier country. Trevanion makes an ideal base from which to visit the Eden Project, the Lost Gardens of Heligan, National Trust Houses and Gardens, or to explore the beauty of the Cornish Riviera. The rooms are en-suite, and they are well furnished. Facilities include tea/coffee making and colour television. There is some car parking for guests' cars.

*B & B £22.50-£25pp, Rooms 1 double, 1 twin, 1 family, all en-suite,
No smoking, Children over 12, No dogs, Closed Nov to Mar*

The Gardens Tresowes, Ashton, Helston TR13 9SY

Moira & Goff Cattell Tel: 01736 763299
Email: goff.and.moira@amserve.net

Map Ref: 6
A 394

Perhaps this 200 year old granite cottage was home to Cornish miners, as this was two dwellings initially. It retains original features, inglenooks, narrow staircases and low ceilings. The bedrooms are crisp and comfortable, and there is a small sitting room with a wood burner. Supper is available using home grown vegetables and this may be enjoyed in the conservatory overlooking the garden. Within a pleasant drive is the famous St Michael's Mount and the towns of Penzance and St Ives. The Lizard, good beaches, and the Helford River are within easy reach.

*B & B £20-£25pp, Dinner from £13, Rooms 2 double (en-suite), 1 twin/double (with private
bathroom), No smoking, No children or dogs, Closed Xmas & New Year*

The Old Rectory Mawgan, Helston TR12 6AD

Mrs Sue Leith Tel: 01326 221261 Fax: 01326 221797
Email: leith@euphony.net Web: www.oldrectorymawgan.co.uk

Map Ref: 7
A394, A3083, B3293

The Old Rectory stands in the quiet village of Mawgan, on the Lizard Peninsular, England's warmest and most southerly point. The house stands in three acres of valley garden, on the upper reaches of the mystical Helford River. The lovely bedrooms are well proportioned and light, with private bathrooms. Breakfast is served in the large, elegant dining room, there is a choice of English or continental style with fresh fruit. Excellent local country inns and restaurants serve high quality food and wines. Penzance, Falmouth and Truro are half an hour away.

*B & B from £35pp, Rooms 2 double, 2 twin, all with private bathrooms, No smoking,
Children over 12, Dogs by arrangement, Closed Dec to Mar*

The Barton Laneast, near Launceston PL15 8PN

Gilly ffrench Blake Tel: 01566 880104 Fax: 01566 881003
Email: affb@totalise.co.uk

Map Ref: 8
A30, A395

The Barton is a Grade II listed Georgian Farmhouse with 30 acres and fishing on the Inny. The superb accommodation includes a double en-suite with a shower room, a double en-suite closet and a twin opposite the bathroom, all furnished to the highest standard. A private sitting room is also available for guests to relax in after a busy day. The gardens and extensive grounds, including Holy Well, are peaceful with lovely views. It is just five miles off the A30 west of Launceston towards the North Coast and Rock. Secure private parking. Simple dinner, by arrangement.

*B & B £25pp, Dinner available, Rooms 2 double en-suite, 1 twin with private bathroom,
No smoking, Childen over 5, Kennel for dogs, Closed Xmas*

Stenhill Farm, near Launceston

Stenhill Farm North Petherwin, Launceston PL15 8NN

Mr & Mrs E Reddock   Tel / Fax: 01566 785686
Email: e.reddock@btinternet.com   Web: www.stenhill.com

Map Ref: 9
B3254
see Photo on page 61

Stenhill Farm is a 500 year old Cornish longhouse which has been restored to preserve the charm of this lovely Cornish home. There are oak beams, exposed stone walls and granite fireplaces to appreciate. The bedrooms are en-suite, they are delightfully furnished and well equipped. Evening meals are available by arrangement. A former stable, now a self catering cottage with ground floor bedrooms, is available, and enjoys wonderful views to the surrounding countryside and moors. The gardens of Heligan, the Eden Project and National Trust properties are within easy reach.

B & B £21.50-£31.25pp, Dinner from £12.50, Rooms 1 en-suite twin,
No smoking, No children or dogs, Open all year

Hornacott South Petherwin, Launceston PL15 7LH

Jos & Mary Anne Otway-Ruthven   Tel / Fax: 01566 782461
Email: otwayruthven@btinternet.com

Map Ref: 10
B3254

Our 18th century house nestles in a valley with sloping gardens and a stream, in a part of Cornwall's unspoilt countryside. Our guests stay in a suite of twin bedroom with en-suite bathroom and sitting room with television and CD player. Both bed and sitting rooms have French windows facing over our garden. There is a wealth of places to visit within easy reach, National Trust properties, the Eden Project, historic Launceston, the ancient capital of Cornwall, rugged Bodmin Moor and the spectacular coasts. Single available for groups of 3.

B & B from £30pp, Dinner from £18, Rooms 1 en-suite twin, No smoking,
Children welcome, Dogs by arrangement, Closed Xmas & New Year

Tregondale Farm Menheniot, Liskeard PL14 3RG

Mrs Stephanie Rowe   Tel / Fax: 01579 342407
Email: tregondale@connectfree.co.uk   Web: www.tregondalefarm.co.uk

Map Ref: 11
A38

Tregondale Farm is an elegant, charming farmhouse which welcomes guests to enjoy peace and quiet in unspoilt surroundings, it stands in an original walled garden. The delightful bedrooms are well equipped with television and tea/coffee making facilities. Log fires beckon on chilly evenings. Home produce is a speciality of the house, dinner may be arranged. There is much to enjoy here, explore the farm trail through the wooded valley, a paradise for birds, cycle through the countryside, or fish the pond. There is plenty of information for walkers.

B & B £22.50-£25pp, C-Cards MC VS, Dinner from £12.50, Rooms 2 double, 1 twin, all en-suite,
No smoking, Children welcome, No dogs, Open all year

Fieldhead Hotel Portuan Road, Looe PL13 2DR

Gill & Barrie Pipkin   Tel: 01503 262689   Fax: 01503 264114
Email: field.head@virgin.net   Web: www.fieldheadhotel.co.uk

Map Ref: 12
A387

Turn of the century large country house by the sea with spectacular views. Set in beautiful terraced gardens with patios and swimming pool. All rooms en-suite, television, tea/coffee making facilities, tastefully decorated and most with far-reaching sea views. The comfortable lounge, with huge bay windows and candlelit restaurant, serving fresh local produce and seafood, have views across Looe Bay. On site car parking and just an easy stroll along the waterside to the quaint town of Looe with its cobbled streets and pretty cottages.

B & B from £28pp, C-Cards MC VS, Dinner from £22, Rooms 1 single, 8 double, 3 twin, 3 family,
Restricted smoking, Children welcome, Dogs by arrangement, Open all year

Coombe Farm, Widegates, near Looe

Ednovean House, Perranuthnoe, near Penzance

St Aubyn's Marine Drive, Hannafore, Looe PL13 2DH
Peter & Di Bishop   Tel: 01503 264351   Fax: 01503 263670
Email: welcome@staubyns.co.uk   Web: www.staubyns.co.uk

Map Ref: 12
A387

Built in the late 19th century overlooking the sea at Hannafore, St Aubyn's is a fine example of an elegant Victorian home. Guests here are assured of friendly hospitality in spacious accommodation. Both the dining room and guests' lounge have spectacular views over Looe Bay. Most of the lovely bedrooms also enjoy sea views. An extensive breakfast menu is offered, and for suppers, there are a good variety of local restaurants, many of which specialise in locally caught fish. Coastal walking, tennis, bowls, fishing, golf are all available.

B & B £23-£35pp, C-Cards MC VS, Rooms 2 single, 2 double, 4 double/twin, most en-suite, No smoking, Children over 5, No dogs, Closed Nov to Easter

Coombe Farm Widegates, Looe PL13 1QN
Martin & Sylvia Eades   Tel: 01503 240223   Fax: 01503 240895
Email: coombe_farm@hotmail.com   www.coombefarmhotel.co.uk

Map Ref: 13
B3253
see Photo on page 63

Coombe Farm is a perfect place to relax as it enjoys a wonderful setting with superb views down a wooded valley to the sea. Visitors here may enjoy delicious candlelit dinners, log fires, a heated outdoor pool and warm, friendly hospitality. The bedrooms are well equipped and comfortable, with many thoughtful extras to ensure comfort. For those who wish, there is nearby, golf, fishing, tennis, horse riding, glorious walks, beaches and National Trust houses and gardens, and the Eden Project. Sparkling Diamond and Warm Hospitality Awards.

B & B £35-£38pp, C-Cards MC VS AE, Dinner from £17.50, Rooms 2 twin, 5 double, 3 family, all en-suite, No smoking, Children welcome, Dogs by arrangement, Closed Nov to end Feb

Woodlands GH Trewollock, Gorran Haven, Mevagissey PL26 6NS
Dianne Harrison   Tel: 01726 843821
Email: woodlands@gorranhaven.fsbusiness.co.uk   Web: www.woodlandsmevagissey.co.uk

Map Ref: 14
B3273

Woodlands, standing in an acre of south facing gardens with two spring-fed ponds, has magnificent sea views across open fields and adjacent footpath links with the Cornish coastal path (half mile). This family-run guest house offers mostly en-suite accommodation with tea/coffee facilities and televisions. Packed lunches are available to order. It is close to Lost Gardens of Heligan and the Eden Project and an ideal base for visiting the historic sites, gardens, animal sanctuaries and theme parks throughout all of Cornwall. Ample parking is provided.

B & B £20-£30pp, Rooms 1 single, 1 twin, 3 double, 1 family, most en-suite, No smoking, Children welcome, No dogs, Closed Xmas & New Year

Degembris Farmhouse St Newlyn East, Newquay TR8 5HY
Kathy Woodley   Tel: 01872 510555   Fax: 01872 510230
Email: kathy@degembris.co.uk   Web: www.degembris.co.uk

Map Ref: 15
A3058

The original manor house of Degembris was built in the 16th century and is now used as a barn. The present day house surrounded by attractive gardens, was built a mere two hundred years ago, and its slate hung exterior blends well with the rolling countryside over which many of the rooms have extensive views. Each bedroom is tastefully decorated and well equipped. Hearty breakfasts and traditional evening meals are served in the cosy dining room. Take a stroll along the farm trail wandering through woodlands and fields of corn.

B & B £22-£25pp, C-Cards MC VS, Dinner from £12.50, Rooms 1 single, 1 en-suite twin, 1 double, 2 en-suite family, No smoking, Children welcome, No dogs, Closed Xmas

The Old Mill Country House Little Petherick, Padstow PL27 7QT

David & Debbie Walker   Tel: 01841 540388   Fax: 0870 056 9360
Email: dwalker@oldmillbandb.demon.co.uk

Map Ref: 16
A389

The Old Mill House is a 16th century Grade II listed cornmill with waterwheel, set in streamside gardens at the head of Little Petherick creek, a designated area of outstanding natural beauty, two miles from Padstow. Guest bedrooms overlook the garden and stream, they are en-suite with showers, independently heated, have tea/coffee making facilities, hair dryers and toiletries. Free parking in the village car park opposite. Many fine restaurants and pubs in the area. Ideally located for exploring the whole of Cornwall.

B & B £30-£32pp, C-Cards MC VS, Rooms 2 twin, 2 double, all en-suite,
Restricted smoking, Children over 14, No dogs, Closed Nov to Mar

Con Amore 38 Morrab Road, Penzance TR18 4EX

Carol & Keith Richards   Tel / Fax: 01736 363423
Email: KRich30327@aol.com   Web: www.con-amore.co.uk

Map Ref: 17
A30

Highly recommended and family run, Con Amore is ideally situated for just relaxing or for touring the Lands End Peninsula. We are situated opposite sub-tropical gardens and only 100 yards from the promenade and panoramic views over Mounts Bay and St Michael's Mount. All rooms have full central heating, colour television and tea/coffee making facilities. They are all tastefully decorated with their own character. We offer a varied menu, and we cater for all tastes. We offer a reduction for children sharing a room.

B & B from £13pp, C-Cards MC VS, Rooms 1 single, 2 twin, 3 double,
2 family most en-suite, Children & dogs welcome, Open all year

Woodstock House 29 Morrab Road, Penzance TR18 4EZ

Cherry & John Hopkins   Tel / Fax: 01736 369049
Email: WoodstocP@aol.com   Web: www.ivaccommodations.com/woodstock.html

Map Ref: 17
A30

Woodstock is a Victorian guest house situated in central Penzance near the sea front and ideally placed for the Isles of Scilly ferry and heliport, also the railway and bus stations. All rooms have television, radio, hand basins and tea/coffee makers and many rooms have en-suite shower and toilet. A full English breakfast is offered, special diets can be catered for. To find us drive into town past the railway station and along seafront. Turn right into Morrab Road as you approach the Queen's Hotel, 'Woodstock' is 200m on the right.

B & B from £15pp, Rooms 2 single, 3 double (one 4 poster), 3 twin, 1 family,
Children welcome, Open all year

Ednovean House Perranuthnoe, Penzance TR20 9LZ

Clive & Jacqueline Whittington   Tel: 01736 711071
Email: clive@ednoveanhouse.co.uk   www.ednoveanhouse.co.uk

Map Ref: 18
A394, A30
see Photo on page 64

A warm welcome awaits you at our beautifully situated 180 year old country house, offering eight letting rooms, most having en-suite facilities and magnificent sea views. Standing in one acre of lovely gardens, surrounded by farmland and overlooking St Michael's Mount and Mounts Bay, it has one of the finest views in Cornwall. Television lounge, dining room/bar, small library/writing room, putting green and ample parking. A peaceful and tranquil setting with the coast path, village and beach all only a short walk away. AA 4 Diamonds.

B & B £24-£27.50pp, C-Cards MC VS, Rooms 2 single, 4 double, 2 twin, most en-suite,
Restricted smoking, Children over 7, Dogs by arrangement, Closed Xmas & New Year

Boscean Country Hotel, St Just-in-Penwith, Penzance

Quilkyns 1 St Pirans Way, Perranuthnoe, Penzance TR20 9NJ

Paul & Nuala Leeper   Tel: 01736 719141

Email: paul@quilkyns.fsnet.co.uk   Web: www.quilkyns.co.uk

Map Ref: 18
A394, A30

Quilkyns is a family run bed and breakfast in the heart of Perranuthnoe, a small coastal village with a sandy beach. It is also well placed for a visit to St Michael's Mount. Each south facing room has a wash basin, colour television radio and tea/coffee facilities. The bathroom and shower room are close by with access to laundry room if required. Children are welcome if family occupying both rooms. The village pub caters for families and serves excellent food.

B & B from £17pp, Rooms 1 twin, 1 double, No smoking,
Children & dogs welcome, Closed Nov to Feb

Boscean Country Hotel Boswedden Road, St Just-in-Penwith, Penzance TR19 7QP

Dennis & Linda Wilson   Tel: 01736 788748

Email: boscean@aol.com

Map Ref: 19, A3071
see Photo on page 67

Magnificent Country House set in three acres of walled gardens overlooking the sea and surrounding countryside. Centrally heated throughout, log fires when appropriate. Oak panelled television lounge, residents bar. Informal, quiet and relaxing. Boscean Country Hotel has an established reputation for excellent home cooking using fresh, home grown and local produce, unlimited desserts! An ideal base from which to explore West Cornwall and The Lands End Peninsula. Situated close to the coastal footpath. All areas of the Hotel are non-smoking except the bar.

B & B from £23pp, Dinner from £11, Rooms 5 double, 5 twin, 2 family, all en-suite,
Restricted smoking, Children welcome, Dogs by arrangement, Closed Xmas & New Year

Long Cross Hotel & Victorian Gardens Trelights, Port Issac PL29 3TF

Mr & Mrs Crawford   Tel: 01208 880243

Web: www.longcrosshotel.co.uk

Map Ref: 20
B3314

One of Cornwall's most unusual hotels, a character Victorian country house with a unique garden and its own free house tavern. The Long Cross has 12 en-suite rooms all with televisions and tea/coffee facilities. There are some ground floor rooms and some have sea views. The hotel retains many of the original Victorian features and the gardens are open to the public. The free house Tavern is a popular drinking and dining spot with an extensive menu and a famous beer garden. Ideal spot for walkers, near surfing beaches.

B & B from £55 (min 3 nights)pp, Dinner available, Rooms 4 twin, 8 double, 3 family,
Children & dogs welcome, Closed Xmas

Aviary Court Mary's Well, Illogan, Redruth TR16 4QZ

The Studley Family

Tel: 01209 842256 Fax: 01209 843744

Map Ref: 21
A30

This charming country house is set in two acres of secluded well kept gardens, on the edge of Illogan Woods. Aviary Court is ideally located for visiting the coast, which is just five minutes away. St Ives, Tate, the Lost Gardens of Heligan and the Eden project are all within easy reach. There are six well equipped individual bedrooms with tea/coffee making facilities, television and a view of the gardens. The resident family proprietors ensure a personal service offering well cooked varied food that uses as much local Cornish produce as possible.

B & B from £31.50pp, Rooms 1 twin, 4 double, 1 family, Restricted smoking,
Children over 3, No dogs, Open all year

The Old Vicarage St Minver, Rock PL27 6QH

Sarah Tyson Tel: 01208 862951   Fax: 01208 863578
Email: g.tyson@virgin.net

Map Ref: 22
Near Four Ways Inn

A mellow Georgian vicarage sitting on the edge of a delightful hamlet, with views to the fields beyond. The house is one and a half miles from Rock and other sailing and surfing beaches. There are wonderful cliff top walks. The rooms are en-suite, one has a four poster Napoleonic large bed. Breakfasts, with no time limit, include local honey, eggs, bacon and sausages. Within a pleasant drive are the Cornish houses of Pencarrow and Llanhydrock, also the Eden Project is easily found. The market town of Wadebridge is only a few miles.

*B & B £25-£30pp, Rooms 2 double (one 4 poster), 1 twin/childrens room, all en-suite,
No smoking, Children welcome, Dogs by arrangement, Closed Xmas Day*

Lantallack Farm Landrake, Saltash PL12 5AE

Nicky Walker Tel / Fax: 01752 851281
Email: lantallack@ukgateway.net Web: www.lantallack.co.uk

Map Ref: 23
A38

Lantallack Farm is a lovely Grade II Georgian farmhouse which has breathtaking views over undulating countryside, streams and wooded valleys. It is the perfect place for those seeking fun, peace and tranquility. Delicious breakfasts are served in the walled garden on warm summer mornings, and log fires, a good collection of books and two grand pianos provide comfort and entertainment in the winter. There is a choice of good pubs locally for evening meals. A cottage equipped for self catering and with stunning views is available.

*B & B from £27.50pp, Rooms 1 double, 1 twin, both en-suite, No smoking,
Children by arrangement, No dogs, Closed Xmas & New Year*

Anchorage House Nettles Corner, Tregrehan Mills, St Austell PL25 3RH

Jane & Steve Epperson Tel: 01726 814071
Email: stay@anchoragehouse.co.uk Web: www.anchoragehouse.co.uk

Map Ref: 24
A390

Every attention has been paid to the smallest detail in this impressive house, accented with antiques, and featured in a national magazine. Guests are treated to an outdoor heated pool, jacuzzi, satellite television, large beds, conservatory and luxurious, sparklingly clean en-suite rooms equipped with everything to make you happy and very comfortable. Breakfast is worth getting up for. Steven (American) and Jane (English) combine wonderful hospitality and pleasing informality for a special stay. Perfect for visiting historic houses, gardens, Heligan and Eden.

*B & B £35-£39pp, C-Cards MC VS, Dinner £25, Rooms 3 double en-suite,
No smoking, No children or dogs, Closed Dec*

Nanscawen Manor House Prideaux Road, Luxulyan Valley, St Blazey PL24 2SR

Keith & Fiona Martin Tel: 01726 814488
Email: keith@nanscawen.com Web: www.nanscawen.com

Map Ref: 25
A390

This elegant Georgian Manor house may be found in the most glorious country setting. Guests here are certain to be comfortable in the beautifully presented bedrooms which offer either four poster, or six foot double beds. Every extra facility has been added to include colour televisions, hairdryers telephones and a tea/coffee tray. A full English breakfast may be enjoyed, or perhaps some smoked salmon with scrambled eggs, which is a popular option. There is a good selection of local pubs and restaurants. A large swimming pool is available for guests' enjoyment. Eden Project two miles away.

*B & B £40-£45pp, C-Cards MC VS, Rooms 2 double, 1 twin, all en-suite,
No smoking, Children over 12, No dogs, Open all year*

The Grey Mullet, St Ives

The Grey Mullet 2 Bunkers Hill, St Ives TR26 1LJ

Ken Weston Tel: 01736 796635 Email: greymulletguesthouse@lineone.net

Web: www.touristnetuk.com/sw/greymullet

Map Ref: 26

A3074

see Photo opposite

The Grey Mullet is an 18th century Grade II Listed building centrally situated in the old fishing and artists' quarter of St Ives. The house is full of interest and character with oak beams and granite walls hung with paintings and old photographs and offers a warm welcome in homely surroundings. The comfortable en-suite bedrooms, some with four poster beds, have television and tea/coffee making facilities and there is a sitting room with an open fire. Ideal position to enjoy the harbour, beaches, many restaurants and the Tate Gallery.

B & B £23-£26pp, C-Cards MC VS AE DC, Rooms 1 single, 1 twin, 5 double, most en-suite, No smoking, Children over 12, No dogs, Open all year

Old Vicarage Hotel Parc-an-Creet, St Ives TR26 2ES

Mr Jack Sykes and Miss Dianne Sykes Tel: 01736 796124 Fax: 01736 796343

Email: holidays@oldvicaragehotel.com Web: www.oldvicaragehotel.com

Map Ref: 26

B3306

The Old Vicarage, secluded in wooded grounds in a quiet residential area, is a lovingly restored Victorian rectory retaining the period ambience, but with every modern convenience, including full central heating. The lounge has an extensive library, television and video, a well stocked Victorian bar with piano. Large choice of breakfast menu, including vegetarian, served in the elegant blue and gold dining room. Seven bedrooms, all en-suite, all with colour television and tea/coffee facilities. Victorian conservatory massed with plants. Large garden with putting green, badminton, swing and car park.

B & B from £26pp, C-Cards MC VS, Rooms 7 double/twin/family, all en-suite, Restricted smoking, Children & dogs welcome, Closed Oct to Easter

Cliff House Kingsand, Torpoint PL10 1NJ

Ann Heasman Tel: 01752 823110 Fax: 01752 822595

Email: chkingsand@aol.com Web: www.cliffhse.abel.co.uk

Map Ref: 27

A374, B3247

Guests receive a friendly welcome at Cliff House which is a Grade II listed 17th century building, which once was two cottages, and converted into one home 150 years ago. The house stands perched high above the sea and within yards of the south Cornwall coastal path. Although modernised to include en-suite facilities, it still retains many original features. There is a large first floor sitting room, with log fires in winter, and television, cd player and a 1908 refurbished Bluthner boudoir grand piano for guests to use. Excellent home cooked food.

B & B £22-£27.50pp, Dinner from £10, Rooms 2 double, 1 twin, all en-suite, No smoking, By arrangement, No dogs, Open all year

The Old Rectory St John-in-Cornwall, Torpoint PL11 3AW

Clive & Button Poole Tel: 01752 822275 Fax: 01752 823322 Mobile: 07870 509173

Email: clive@oldrectory-stjohn.co.uk

Map Ref: 27

A374

Regency grade II listed country house with subtropical garden and millpond located by tidal creek. Set in a quiet valley of this 'forgotten corner of Cornwall' adjoining Woodland Trust land. Guests have time to reflect and enjoy its understated elegance with its beautifully appointed and romantic bedrooms. A warm welcome, imaginative breakfasts and relaxing drawing room await our guests. Coastal Path walks, beaches, moors, golf, sailing and National Trust properties are close by. Four miles from chain ferry. NB: Water surrounds this property, therefore we cannot accept responsibility for the safety of children.

B & B from £32.50 (min 2 nights)pp, Rooms 1 twin, 2 double, private or en-suite, No smoking, Children by arrangement, Dogs by arrangement, Closed occasionally

Rock Cottage   Blackwater, Truro TR4 8EU

Shirley Wakeling   Tel / Fax: 01872 560252

Email: rockcottage@yahoo.com

Map Ref: 28
A30

Our 18th century beamed cottage was formerly the village schoolmasters home. A haven for non smokers, we offer comfortable, attractive en-suite rooms with central heating, colour television, radio and beverage tray. There is a charming stone walled lounge where guests are always welcome to relax. Breakfast is served in our cosy dining room with its antique Cornish range. Rock Cottage is situated in a countryside village location, just six miles from Truro and only three miles from the ocean. There is ample parking, the gardens are delightful.

B & B from £22pp, C-Cards MC VS, Rooms 1 twin, 2 double, all en-suite,
No smoking, No children or dogs, Closed Xmas & New Year

Ventongimps Mill Barn   Ventongimps, Callestick, Truro TR4 9LH

Mr & Mrs Gibson

Tel: 01872 573275

Map Ref: 29
A3075

Ventongimps Mill Barn is a tastefully converted mill barn of traditional Cornish slate and stone, situated in a quiet hamlet, nestling in a sheltered valley. A stream runs through extensive gardens and lake on our estate of seven acres of fields and woods. Local coastal paths offer breathtaking views and the cathedral city of Truro is just six miles. Evening meals are served in our licensed bar where Portuguese cooking is a speciality. The coastal village of Perranporth with some five miles of sandy beaches is two miles distant.

B & B from £18pp, Dinner from £10.50, Rooms 1 single, 1 twin, 2 double, 4 family,
Restricted smoking, Children welcome, Dogs by arrangement, Open all year

Apple Tree Cottage   Laity Moor, Ponsanooth, Truro TR3 7HR

Ann Tremayne   Tel: 01872 865047

Email: appletreecottage@talk21.com

Map Ref: 30
A39

A warm welcome is assured at Apple Tree Cottage, which is set amidst rolling countryside with delightful gardens and river. The cottage is furnished with country antiques, and the large lounge has a welcoming log fire. Traditional farmhouse breakfasts, cooked on the Aga, may be enjoyed in the sunlit dining room. There are lovely Cornish views from each of the comfortable, well equipped bedrooms. There are several National Trust gardens and the famous Trebah Gardens on the Helford River, just 15 minutes away from this peaceful Cornish cottage.

B & B £23-£25pp, Rooms 2 double, No smoking, Children over 10,
Dogs must be on lead, Closed mid-Dec to mid-Jan

Porteath Barn   St Minver, Wadebridge PL27 6RA

Michael & Jo Bloor   Tel: 01208 863605   Fax: 01208 863954

Email: mbloor@ukonline.co.uk

Map Ref: 31
B3314

Porteath Barn is a fine 19th century building which is set in eight acres of peaceful and secluded valley, with the coast path and Epphaven cove just a few minutes walk away down a private track. Accommodation for guests is in a separate wing. It is an excellent base from which to explore the delights of Cornwall from coast to coast and within easy reach of beaches, surfing, sailing, fishing, also the Camel Trail and the golf courses at St Enodoc and Roserrow. There is a choice of good eating places nearby.

B & B £22.50-£28pp, Rooms 1 double, 2 twin, Restricted smoking,
Children over 12, Dogs by arrangement, Open all year

Cumbria

Consisting of the old counties of Cumberland, Westmorland and a substantial slice of Lancashire, the county of Cumbria is now the second largest of the English counties, containing within its boundaries the Lake District, a region of impressive grandeur. Cumbria attracts vast numbers of visitors at all times of the year to enjoy the climbing, scrambling, sailing, rambling and the joys of the open fells. Magnificent work is done in this area by the National Trust who are responsible for the conservation and management of around a quarter of the Lake District National Park which constitutes about a quarter of the Trust's total holdings in the British Isles.

One of the great delights of the Lake District, is that whatever the season it has its special attractions; spring with its fresh greenery, its snow-capped peaks and of course, Wordsworth's daffodils; summer with its sailing, rambling and lazy days by the lakes; autumn with its richly coloured foliage, its romantic misty scenery; and winter, when the mountains and lakes are seen in their most dramatic garb. The region is undoubtedly popular as a holiday venue but although some of the towns and villages may well be crowded at times, there is space for all who are prepared to take to the many bye-roads and footpaths. The lakes and mountains each have their own particular charm, and one of the great assets of the Lake District is that all this magnificent scenery is packed into a relatively small area

There are sixteen lakes ranging from Windermere, the largest at ten and a half miles in length, to little Brotherswater, only about half a mile long. Windermere is central to the popular holiday pursuits and is alive with activity, such as sailing, water skiing and pleasure boating. However, Ullswater, reached over the steep and winding Kirkstone Pass, is an altogether more peaceful and placid lake. Martindale, consisting of a cluster of valleys, by Ullswater, although only a short distance from the main road is wild and deserted with marvelous views and two interesting churches. By Gowbarrow Park is the lovely Aira Force waterfalls, a highlight of this valley.

The Lake District is undoubtedly Wordsworth country and there must be few corners that have not been lyrically described by the poet and his many writer friends who visited him here. Grasmere in the very centre of the region was his home for some years and Dove Cottage, where

View from Torver towards Dow Cragg and the Old Man of Coniston (CTB)

he and his wife and sister Dorothy lived, is a magnet for William Wordsworth enthusiasts. The poet and members of his family are buried in the beautiful little churchyard in Grasmere, beside one of the most attractive churches in the district. Hawkshead, like Grasmere has close associations with Wordsworth. It was here that the poet attended the grammar school. Another well known resident of this area was Mrs Healis who lived at Near Sawrey. Better known as Beatrix Potter, her home Hill Top Farm attracts huge numbers of visitors each year.

Also nearby is Coniston Water, upon which in 1967 Donald Campbell was killed attempting a new world water speed record. Brantwood, on the eastern shore of the lake was the home of John Ruskin, whose grave in the local churchyard is marked with a fine green slate cross.

No visitor can fail to be enthralled by the history and sheer beauty of the Lake District, but Cumbria has much more to offer, Carlisle is a fine border town with excellent shopping facilities, the ruins of a Norman castle and an impressive cathedral; Kendal, the 'auld grey town' was the home of Henry VIII's sixth wife Catherine Parr and has many interesting museums; Appleby, once the county town of Westmorland is renowned for its June horse fair and gypsy gathering; while Cockermouth in the west was the birthplace of Wordsworth and luckily has not been spoilt by tourism. The far north of the county is rich in the history and folk lore of the border troubles with the south of the county leading conveniently into the glories of the Yorkshire Dales. The western coastline offers wonderful beaches.

PLACES TO VISIT

This is a small selection of interesting places to visit. Many more are listed in our annual guide to Museums, Galleries, Historic Houses & Sites (see page 448)

Carlisle Castle
Carlisle
A medieval fortress where visitors can explore fascinating ancient chambers, stairways, and dungeons and find the legendary 'licking stones'.

Dalemain Historic House & Garden
Penrith
Originally a twelfth century pele tower, the house was continually improved upon, with the Georgian facade added to the Elizabethan part of the house in the eighteenth century. There are three museums within the grounds.

Dove Cottage &
The Wordsworth Museum
Grasmere
The home of William Wordsworth from 1799 to 1808 where visitors are given a guided tour and can view the garden. Opposite is the museum with some of the greatest treasures of the age of Romanticism.

Hill Top
Sawrey, Ambleside
Beatrix Potter wrote many of her famous children's stories in this little seventeenth century stone house. When she died in 1943 she left Hill Top to the National Trust on the proviso that it was kept exactly how she left it, with her own furniture and china.

South Lakes Wild Animal Park
Crossgates, Dalton-in-Furness
The zoo is a world recognised centre for conservation, breeding and education with all of the animals gathered together by the continents they live on.

Cumbria

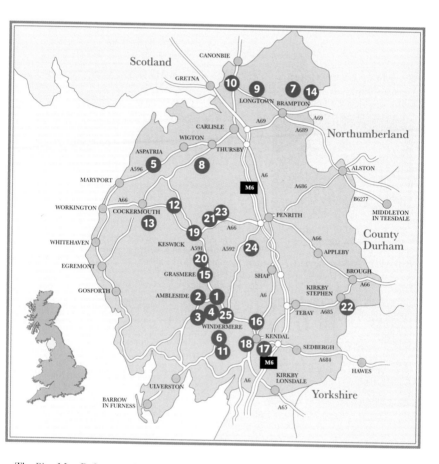

The Blue Map References should be used to locate B & B properties on the pages that follow

2 Swiss Villas Vicarage Road, Ambleside LA22 9AE
David Sowerbutts   Tel: 015394 32691
Email: sowerbutts@tinyworld.co.uk

Map Ref: 1
A591

A Victorian terrace house set off the main road in the centre of Ambleside, near the church, in an elevated position overlooking Wansfell. There is immediate access to the cinema and shops and a variety of restaurants in the town. The bedrooms have been recently refurbished in traditional style. Each room has central heating, tea making facilities and colour television. There is a choice of English or vegetarian breakfast. Open all year round, you are sure of a friendly welcome and good home cooking. Details of a self catering house next door are available.

B & B from £21pp, Rooms 2 double, 1 twin, No smoking,
Children over 11, No dogs, Open all year

Grey Friar Lodge Country Hotel Clappersgate, Ambleside LA22 9NE
Pamela & David Veen   Tel / Fax: 015394 33158
Email: greyfriar@veen.freeserve.co.uk www.cumbria-hotels.co.uk

Map Ref: 2
A593
see Photo opposite

This impressive house was built as a vicarage in 1869. Now it provides the perfect base from which to discover the Lake District. A warm personal welcome is extended to you by Pamela & David Veen in this beautiful old house. Grey Friar Lodge is enhanced by wonderful views and an established reputation for hospitality, comfort and imaginative home cooking. Most of the bedrooms have antique or four poster beds, and they display a collection of pictures and porcelain. This is a special place where guests may relax and enjoy the beauty of the area. Fully licensed.

B & B from £29pp, C-Cards MC VS, Dinner from £19.50, Rooms 2 twin, 6 double, all en-suite,
No smoking, Children over 12, No dogs, Closed mid-Dec to mid-Jan

Borwick Lodge Outgate, Hawkshead, Ambleside LA22 0PU
Rosemary & Colin Haskell   Tel / Fax: 015394 36332
Email: borwicklodge@talk21.com   Web: www.borwicklodge.com

Map Ref: 3
B5286

A leafy driveway entices you to the most enchantingly situated house in the Lake District, a very special 17th century country lodge with magnificent panoramic Lake and mountain views. Quietly secluded in beautiful gardens. Ideally placed in the heart of the Lakes and close to Hawkshead village with its good choice of restaurants and inns. Beautiful en-suite bedrooms include two king size four poster rooms. Rosemary and Colin welcome you to their Award Winning Lodge in this most beautiful corner of England.

B & B £25-£36pp, Rooms 4 double, 1 twin, 1 family, all en-suite,
No smoking, Children over 8, No dogs, Open all year

Bracken Fell Outgate, Ambleside LA22 0NH
Peter & Anne Hart   Tel: 015394 36289
Email: hart.brackenfell@virgin.net   Web: www.brackenfell.com

Map Ref: 4
B5286

A delightful country residence with 2 acres of gardens, situated in beautiful open countryside between Ambleside and Hawkshead in the picturesque hamlet of Outgate. This comfortable home with its lovely accommodation and friendly service is ideally located for exploring the Lake District. Each bedroom has its own private facilities, colour TV, hairdryer, complimentary tea and coffee and super lounge. There is a comfortable lounge, dining room and ample private parking. Two country inns are within walking distance where evening meals are available. Non-smoking.

B & B £24-£27pp, Rooms 3 twin, 4 double, all en-suite,
No smoking, Children over 9, No dogs, Open all year

Grey Friar Lodge Country Hotel
Clappersgate,
near Ambleside

The Fairfield, Bowness-on-Windermere

Aigle Gill Farm Aspatria CA7 2PL
Marjorie Bell   Tel: 016973 20260
Email: marjoriebell77@hotmail.com

Map Ref: 5
A596, M6

Aigle Gill is an attractive whitewashed Cumbrian farmhouse. It is both comfortable and spacious, and visitors here are assured of a warm welcome. The rooms are tastefully decorated. An excellent breakfast is served in the dining room, the perfect start to a day perhaps exploring the delights of this beautiful part of England. We are situated within easy reach of the Northern lakes, Scottish Borders and the Solway coast. There is plenty of parking for guests' cars.

B & B from £18pp, Rooms 1 single, 1 double en-suite, No smoking, Children welcome, No dogs, Closed Nov to Jan

Castlemont Aspatria CA7 2JU
David & Eleanor Lines   Tel: 016973 20205
Email: castlemont@tesco.net

Map Ref: 5
A596

Castlemont is a large Victorian family residence standing in two acres of gardens with unrestricted views of the northern Lakeland Fells and Solway Firth. Built of Lazonby stone, Castlemont combines the best of old world gracious living with benefits of modern facilities. Start your day with a traditional English breakfast or a selected oak smoked kipper, perhaps a poached egg with haddock or ham? Loads of toast, butter and marmalade with pots of tea or coffee, all made on the ever willing Aga.

B & B from £18pp, C-Cards MC VS, Rooms 1 en-suite double, 1 twin, 1 family, No smoking, Children welcome, Open all year

The Fairfield Brantfell Road, Bowness-on-Windermere LA23 3AE
Ray & Barbara Hood   Tel / Fax: 015394 46565
Email: Ray&barb@the-fairfield.co.uk   Web: www.the-fairfield.co.uk

Map Ref: 6
A591
see Photo opposite

Fairfield is a small friendly, family run, 200 year old Lakeland hotel found in a peaceful garden setting. 200 metres from Bowness village, 400 metres from the shores of Lake Windermere and at the end of the Dales Way (81 mile walk from Ilkley to Bowness). The Beatrix Potter exhibition is within easy walking distance. The well appointed and tastefully furnished bedrooms all have colour television, hair dryer, a welcome tray and private shower/bathroom. Breakfasts are a speciality. Leisure facilities available. On site car parking. Genuine hospitality and warm welcome.

B & B from £26pp, C-Cards MC VS, Rooms 1 single, 1 twin, 5 double, 2 family, all en-suite, No smoking, Children welcome, No dogs, Closed Dec to Jan

Lowfell Country House Ferney Green, Bowness-on-Windermere LA23 3ES Map Ref: 6
Stephen & Louise Broughton   Tel: 015394 45612   Fax: 015394 48411   A591, A5074
Email: lowfell@talk21.com   Web: www.low-fell.co.uk

Originally built as a gentleman's residence in the 19th century, this lovely Lakeland house is a five minute walk from the pretty village of Bowness-on-Windermere and the lake. It sits in an acre of wooded garden. The emphasis is on a warm welcome, comfort and good food. Delicious breakfasts from traditional English to fish, a choice of omelettes or aga pancakes, are served in the dining room overlooking the garden. On the second floor a 'hideaway' of two adjoining bedrooms has sloping ceilings and treetop views. Cosy fires and squashy sofas add to the comfort of this delightful home.

B & B £26-£30pp, C-Cards MC, Rooms 1 twin/double, 1 family both en-suite, No smoking, Children welcome, No dogs, Closed Xmas & New Year

Bessiestown Farm Country Guest House, Catlowdy, near Longtown, Carlisle

Cracrop Farm
Kircambeck,
near Brampton

Lakeside, Bassenthwaite Lake, near Cockermouth

Cracrop Farm Kirkcambeck, Brampton CA8 2BW

Marjorie Stobart Tel: 016977 48245 Fax: 016977 48333
Email: cracrop@aol.com

Map Ref: 7
M6, B6318
see Photo on page 81

If you want your holiday to be something special then Cracrop Farm is an excellent choice. A spacious distinguished farm house, sits in a lovely garden on a working farm with breathtaking views. The en-suite guest rooms are tastefully furnished to a high standard each with colour television, central heating and hospitality trays. Breakfasts are a feast. Guests can relax in sauna or spa bath or exercise in gym. There are wonderful places to visit, Hadrian's Wall, Scottish Borders, Carlisle and Lake District. Excellent walking. Farm trail. Wildlife abounds.

B & B from £25pp, Rooms 1 single, 1 twin, 2 double, all en-suite,
No smoking, Children over 12, No dogs, Closed Xmas

Swaledale Watch Whelpo, Caldbeck CA7 8HQ

Arnold & Nan Savage Tel / Fax: 016974 78409
Email: nan.savage@talk21.com

Map Ref: 8
on B5299

Swaledale Watch is a busy sheep farm just outside the picturesque village of Caldbeck, situated within the Lake District National Park. Enjoy great comfort, excellent food, a warm welcome and peaceful unspoilt surroundings. Central for touring, walking or discovering the rolling Northern fells. All rooms have private facilities, are tastefully decorated, have colour television, tea-tray, clean fluffy towels daily and books for every interest in the lounges. Walk into Caldbeck via the Howk, a wooded limestone gorge, guaranteed to be memorable. Your happiness is our priority.

B & B £18-£21pp, Dinner available, Rooms 2 double, 2 triple, all en-suite,
No smoking, Children welcome, No dogs, Closed over Xmas

New Pallyards Hethersgill, Carlisle CA6 6HZ

John & Georgina Elwen Tel / Fax: 01228 577308
Email: info@newpallyards.freeserve.co.uk Web: www.newpallyards.freeserve.co.uk

Map Ref: 9
A7

Whether a one night stop over or a longer visit to explore our wonderful countryside, you may be assured of a warm welcome to our farmhouse. Situated between Carlisle and Gretna Green, the house is just a few minutes from junction 44 of the M6. There are ground floor rooms available for the less able. Dinners are available by arrangement, Georgina has a gold award for cooking. Hadrian's Wall, Northern lakes and Kielder water and forest are within easy reach. Pony trekking and riding are available nearby. Self catering is available also.

B & B £22-£24pp, C-Cards MC VS, Dinner from £13, Rooms 2 twins, 3 double, 1 family,
all en-suite, Restricted smoking, Children welcome, Dogs by arrangement, Open all year

Bessiestown Farm Country GH Catlowdy, Longtown, Carlisle CA6 5QP

Jack & Margaret Sisson Tel: 01228 577219 Fax: 01228 577019
Email: Bestbb2001@cs.com Web: www.bessiestown.co.uk

Map Ref: 10
A7, B6318
see Photo on page 80

One of the nicest farm guest houses offering many of the delights of a small country hotel combined with the relaxed atmosphere of a comfortable family home. Peaceful and quiet. Delightfully decorated public rooms and warm pretty en-suite bedrooms with colour television radio and hostess tray. Delicious traditional home cooking using fresh produce whenever possible. Residential licence. Stop off for England, Scotland and Northern Ireland. The indoor heated swimming pool is open from mid-May to mid-September. Beautiful new honeymoon suite. Family accommodation is in comfortable courtyard cottages.

B & B from £26.50pp, Dinner from £13.50, Rooms 2 double, 1 family, 1 twin,
also 3 Cottages, No smoking, Open all year

Lightwood Farmhouse Country GH Cartmel Fell LA11 6NP

Map Ref: 11
A592

Evelyn Cervetti Tel / Fax: 015395 31454
Email: enquiries@lightwoodguesthouse.co.uk Web: www.lightwoodguesthouse.co.uk

Lightwood is a charming 17th century farmhouse retaining original oak beams and staircase. Standing in two acres of lovely gardens with unspoilt views of the countryside.Two and a half miles from the southern end of Lake Windermere. Excellent fell walking area. All rooms are en-suite, tastefully decorated and furnished with central heating, tea/coffee making facilities and all with colour television . Cosy lounge with log fire and colour television. We serve a good high standard of home cooking with seasonal home grown produce.

*B & B from £24pp, C-Cards MC VS, Dinner from £14, Rooms 2 double, 2 twin, 2 family,
all en-suite, Restricted smoking, Children welcome, No dogs, Closed Xmas*

Lakeside Dubwath, Bassenthwaite Lake, Cockermouth CA13 9YD

Map Ref: 12
A66

Steven Semple   *see Photo on page 82*
Tel: 017687 76358   Fax: 01768 776163

Elegant Edwardian double-fronted house with oak floors and panelled entrance hall, standing in its own garden, overlooking Bassenthwaite Lake. Eight comfortably furnished bedrooms, offering colour television, radio alarm, hair dryer, shoe cleaning and tea/coffee making facilities. Some rooms have lake views. The pleasant lounge overlooks the lake. There is a self contained Lodge within the grounds which sleeps 3/4 and is very popular with families. Keswick and Cumberland are just short drives away and it is a ten minute drive to the glorious Cumbrian valleys, mountains and passes.

*B & B £21-£23pp, Rooms 6 double, 2 twin, most en-suite, No smoking,
Children welcome, No dogs, Open all year*

Link House Bassenthwaite Lake, Cockermouth CA13 9YD

Map Ref: 12
A66

George & Isobel Kerr Tel: 017687 76291   Fax: 017687 76670
Email: linkhouse@lineone.net Web: www.link-house.co.uk

Link House is a warm and friendly family run, late Victorian country house. It is set in the quieter part of the Lake District National Park at the northern end of Lake Bassenthwaite, with stunning views of both the surrounding forests and Fells. The house is conveniently situated, being only minutes from Keswick and Cockermouth. All the attractive bedrooms have en-suite facilities, colour television and tea/coffee making facilities. There is a conservatory bar, lounge and private car park exclusively for guests.

*B & B £27-£29pp, C-Cards MC VS AE, Dinner from £15, Rooms 2 single, 3 double, 2 twin,
1 family, all en-suite, Restricted smoking, Children over 7, Dogs by arrangement, Open all year*

New House Farm Buttermere Valley, Lorton, Cockermouth CA13 9UU

Map Ref: 13
B5289

Hazel Thompson Tel / Fax: 01900 85404
Email: hazel@newhouse-farm.co.uk Web: www.newhouse-farm.co.uk

This is the 'real lakes' with all the peace and beauty of the fells, valleys and lakes but without the crowds. New House Farm is a 17th century Grade II listed farmhouse offering very comfortable accommodation. The bedrooms are all en-suite with many little extras. There are two residents' lounges, both with open fires and a cosy dining room where delicious five course evening meals are served and hearty breakfasts enjoyed in the morning. There are fabulous views from every window. Which? Cumbrian Hotel of the Year award winner.

*B & B from £40pp, C-Cards MC VS AE, Dinner from £22, Rooms 2 twin, 3 double, all en-suite,
No smoking, Children over 6, Dogs by arrangement, Open all year*

Bush Nook Upper Denton, Gilsand CA8 7AF

Paul & Judith Barton Tel: 016977 47194 Fax: 016977 47790

Email: PaulAlBarton@bushnook.freeserve.co.uk Web: www.hadriansway.co.uk

Map Ref: 14
A69

Close to Hadrian's Wall, the North Pennines and Northumberland National Park. Bush Nook is ideally situated to discover and explore this delightful part of England. Surrounded by open countryside, visitors can relax and enjoy peace, tranquillity and traditional home cooking. A full English breakfast is served each morning and in the evening a four course dinner plus coffee is available in our licensed dining room. Colour television, hairdryer and drink making facilities are provided in all rooms. A warm welcome awaits you at Bush Nook.

B & B from £18pp, Dinner from £10, Rooms 1 single, 1 twin, 2 double, most en-suite,
No smoking, Children welcome, Dogs by arrangement, Open all year

Riversdale Grasmere LA22 9RQ

Mariea & Chris Cook Tel: 015394 35619

Email: mariea.cook@tinyworld.co.uk Web: www.riversdalegrasmere.co.uk

Map Ref: 15
B5287 from A591

Quietly situated on the edge of the village of Grasmere, Riversdale overlooks the River Rothay with views beyonds towards the surrounding fells. The three bedrooms are each furnished to a high standard with hospitality trays, hairdryers and toiletries provided, and the house in centrally heated throughout. A private Lounge is available for our guests, with television and a selection of books to help you relax. Breakfast, selected from a varied menu, is served in the delightful Dining Room, and a candlelit evening meal is available upon request.

B & B £25-£30pp, Dinner £15, Rooms 2 double with en-suite shower,
1 twin with private bathroom, No smoking, No children or dogs, Open all year

Ryelands Grasmere LA22 9SU

Lyn & John Kirkbride Tel / Fax: 015394 35076

Email: kirkbride.ryelands@virgin.net Web: www.ryelandsgrasmere.co.uk

Map Ref: 15
A591

Ryelands, a delightful Victorian country house in three acres of peaceful and pleasant gardens on the edge of one of the most beautiful villages in Lakeland. Your friendly, helpful hosts have lovingly restored their home to create elegant, spacious and comfortable rooms for discerning guests, the perfect retreat from which to enjoy the Lake District. You can walk from the house into the beautiful countryside, relax as you row round the Lake or make a pilgrimage to Wordsworth's Homes. Exclusively for non smokers. Brochure available.

B & B £30-£35pp, Rooms 3 double, all en-suite, No smoking,
Children over 10, No dogs, Closed Nov to mid-March

Garnett House Farm Burneside, Kendal LA9 5SF

Mrs Sylvia Beaty

Tel: 01539 724542

Map Ref: 16
A591

Garnett House Farm is a highly acclaimed 15th century farmhouse on a large dairy and sheep farm, just half a mile from the A591 Kendal to Windermere road. All bedrooms are en-suite, they have colour television, radio, tea/coffee facilities. The guests' lounge has four foot thick walls and 16th century oak panelling. Old beams and an old oak spice cupboard are features of the dining room where you are served at separate tables. Good parking, close to village and public transport. Lovely views and walks from the farm. Six miles to Windermere.

B & B from £19pp, Rooms 5 double/family, 5 en-suite, No smoking, No dogs, Closed Xmas

Blaven Homestay   Middleshaw, Old Hutton, Kendal LA8 0LZ

Ms Janet Kaye   Tel: 01539 734894   Fax: 01539 727447   Mobile: 07801 796239
Email: jb@greenarrow.demon.co.uk   www.blavenhomestay.co.uk

Map Ref: 17
B6254
see Photo opposite

This is a lovely Cumbrian house which stands beside a trout stream, close to the village of Old Hutton. It is ideally located for the M6, also for the Lake District and Yorkshire Dales. The garden is delightful and cleverly landscaped with a stream side patio where guests may take aperitifs, or afternoon tea. All bedrooms offer en-suite facilities, they are generously equipped and particularly comfortable. The lounge with a log fire, books and newspapers, is in the 'garden room' which has lovely views. Very special menus with local beef, lamb and trout.

B & B £28.50-£32.50pp, C-Cards MC VS, Dinner from £17.50, Rooms 1 double, 1 family,
all en-suite, No smoking, Children over 10, Dogs by arrangement, Open all year

Tranthwaite Hall   Underbarrow, Kendal LA8 8HG

Mrs D M Swindlehurst   Tel: 015395 68285
Email: tranthwaitehall@hotmail.com

Map Ref: 18
M6, A6

This magnificent farmhouse dates from the 11 century. There are beautiful oak beams, doors and a rare antique black iron fire range. The house is tastefully modernised with full central heating. The pretty, en-suite bedrooms have tea/coffee making facilities, hair dryer and radio. Attractive decor, fabrics and furnishings. This dairy sheep farm has an idyllic setting in a small picturesque village between Kendal and Windermere up an unspoilt country lane where wild flowers, deer and other wildlife can be seen. Many good country pubs and inns nearby.

B & B from £23pp, Rooms 2 double, 1 twin, 1 family room, No smoking, Open all year

Edwardene Hotel   26 Southey Street, Keswick CA12 4EF

Margaret & Derick Holman   Tel: 017687 73586   Fax: 017687 73824
Email: info@edwardenehotel.com   Web: www.edwardenehotel.com

Map Ref: 19
A591

Situated close to the town centre of Keswick yet in a quiet location, the Edwardene Hotel is favoured by artists, politicians and musicians. This 115 year old landmark building is admired for its architecture. Stylishly decorated and full of character, it has a wonderfully restful residents' lounge overlooking Walla Crag. Bedrooms are all en-suite and delightfully furnished in pine. The Edwardene is a licensed hotel, the restaurant is furnished in mahogany. All dietary needs are happily catered for. Other restaurants within walking distance. Keswick is excellent for both in and outdoor entertainment.

B & B from £28pp, C-Cards MC VS AE, Dinner from £13, Rooms 2 single, 6 double,
2 twin, 1 family, all en-suite, No smoking, No dogs, Open all year

Grange Country House   Manor Brow, Keswick CA12 4BA

Duncan & Jane Miller   Tel / Fax: 017687 72500
Email: duncan.miller@btconnect.com

Map Ref: 19
A591

Just a ten minute stroll from the bustling Lake District town of Keswick, stands the elegant Grange Country House, which overlooks Keswick-on-Derwentwater and the surrounding Fell countryside. Your hosts Duncan and Jane Miller take much care to ensure that visitors to their lovely home receive professional service, coupled with quality and style in a relaxed atmosphere. Breakfasts here are to be remembered for their variety, they make for the perfect start to a day spent exploring the wealth of beauty in the Lake District.

B & B £28-£37.50pp, C-Cards MC VS, Rooms 7 double, 3 twin, all en-suite, No smoking,
Children over 7, No dogs, Closed mid Nov to mid Feb

Blaven Homestay, Middleshaw, near Kendal

Thornleigh, Keswick

**Dale Head Hall
Lakeside Hotel**,
Lake Thirlmere,
Keswick

Ravensworth Hotel 29 Station Street, Keswick CA12 5HH
Tony & Tina Russ   Tel: 017687 72476   Fax: 017687 75287
Email: info@ravensworth-hotel.co.uk   Web: www.ravensworth-hotel.co.uk

Map Ref: 19
A591

This Silver Award winning Victorian townhouse offers quality accommodation, a fantastic breakfast and a very warm welcome. When its gardens and window boxes are in bloom during the summer, it presents a delightful vision to those passing. Close to the lake, the theatre and the lower fells, the Ravensworth is the perfect base for an exploration of the town and lakes. All rooms are tastefully furnished and are well equipped with en-suite facilities, colour television, hair dryer, trouser press and beverage tray. The hotel is well known for its extensive breakfast menu and homemade produce.

B & B from £25pp, C-Cards MC VS AE, Rooms 5 double, 2 twin, 1 family, all en-suite,
No smoking, Children welcome, No dogs, Closed Jan

Thornleigh 23 Bank Street, Keswick CA12 5JZ
Jill & Graham Green   Tel: 017687 72863
Email: thornleigh@btinternet.com   www.btinternet.com/~thornleigh

Map Ref: 19
A591
see Photo on page 88

This traditional Lakeland stone-built house is situated in the town of Keswick. The en-suite bedrooms have television and tea/coffee making facilities. They are mainly situated at the rear of the building and with wonderful views over the magnificent mountains and fells surrounding the town. Thornleigh is an idyllic base for walking or touring the Northern Lakes. Your hosts, Jill and Graham, offer a warm welcome and advice on enjoying the aspects of the surrounding area. A delicious English or Continental breakfast will set you up for the day.

B & B from £19pp, C-Cards, Rooms 5 double, 1 twin, all en-suite,
Restricted smoking, Children over 5, No dogs, Open all year

Dale Head Hall Lakeside Hotel Lake Thirlmere, Keswick CA12 4TN
Alan & Shirley Lowe   Tel: 017687 72478   Fax: 017687 71070
onthelakeside@dale-head-hall.co.uk   www.dale-head-hall.co.uk

Map Ref: 20
A591
see Photo on page 89

Alone on the shores of Lake Thirlmere, in acres of mature gardens and woodlands, stands this historic Elizabethan Hall. Now lovingly restored by the resident owners, into one of Lakeland's finest country house hotels. Dale Head Hall offers you a warm welcome, elegant accommodation (including a four poster) and award winning cuisine. Just north of Wordsworth's Grasmere, and the heart of the Lake District, Dale Head Hall is an idyllic starting point for exploring this most beautiful corner of England.

B & B from £32.50pp, C-Cards MC VS AE, Dinner from £32.50, Rooms 11 double, 2 twin,
1 family, all en-suite, Restricted smoking, Children welcome, No dogs, Closed New Year

Scales Farm Country GH Scales, Threlkeld, Keswick CA12 4SY
Chris & Caroline Briggs   Tel / Fax: 017687 79660
Email: scales@scalesfarm.com   Web: www.scalesfarm.com

Map Ref: 21
A66

Chris and Caroline welcome you to stay at Scales farm, a 17th century farmhouse which has been beautifully renovated and converted. The farm is set on the lower slopes of Blencathra, just 10 minutes by car from Keswick and has wonderful open views to the south. All bedrooms are en-suite (three ground floor) and have tea/coffee making facilities, fridge and television. The guests' beamed sitting room has a woodburning stove and a full choice breakfast is served in the attractively decorated dining room. Ample parking space and pretty gardens.

B & B from £26pp, C-Cards MC VS, Rooms 2 twin, 3 double, 1 family/double,
all en-suite, No smoking, Dogs by arrangement, Closed Xmas

Ing Hill Lodge, Mallerstang Dale, near Kirkby Stephen

Beamont, Windermere

Augill Castle Brough, Kirkby Stephen CA17 4DE

Wendy & Simon Bennett Tel: 017683 41937 Fax: 017683 41936
Email: augill@aol.com Web: www.augillcastle.co.uk

Map Ref: 22
A685/A66

Augill Castle stands in open country little changed for centuries. The castle's backdrop is the dramatic North Pennines with gardens opening out to views of the Yorkshire Dales and the Lakeland fells. Built in 1841 as a Victorian gentleman's country residence, the castle has all the fairytale romance of a turreted hideaway. The music room invites guests to enjoy family hospitality, whilst in the Gothic blue dining room dinners of traditionally reared lamb, beef and pork may be enjoyed. The bedrooms are designed to reflect the age and history of this family home.

*B & B £40-£50pp, C-Cards MC VS, Dinner from £22.50, Rooms 2 double, 1 king,
3 super king/twin (all en-suite 4 posters), No smoking, Children welcome, No dogs, Open all year*

Ing Hill Lodge near Outhgill, Mallerstang Dale, Kirkby Stephen CA17 4JT

Tony Sawyer Tel: 017683 71153
Email: IngHill@FSBDial.co.uk

Map Ref: 22
B6259
see Photo on page 91

Unwind in comfort at this small Georgian house in Mallerstang, a little known Dale on the fringe of the National Park. Superb views, quiet and peaceful for your preferred form of relaxation. Excellent en-suite shower rooms, comfortable bedrooms with Sealy beds (most are king-size). Colour television and radio alarm. The Butler's Pantry is popular for making tea and coffee at any time. You get to choose your own breakfast. Lounge with books, maps, open fire and central heating throughout. A warm welcome assured.

*B & B £20-£25pp, Rooms 2 double, 1 twin, all en-suite, Restricted smoking,
No children, Dogs welcome, Closed Jan to Feb*

Near Howe Farm Hotel Mungrisdale, Penrith CA11 0SH

Christine Weightman
Tel / Fax: 017687 79678

Map Ref: 23
A66

A Cumbrian family home which is situated amidst 300 acres of moorland. Five of the seven bedrooms have private facilities and all have tea/coffee making facilities. Meals are served in the comfortable dining room and great care is taken to produce good home cooking with every meal freshly prepared. Comfortable residents' lounge with colour television, games room, smaller lounge with well stocked bar and for the cooler evenings an open log fire. The surrounding area can provide many activities including golf, fishing, pony trekking, boating and walking.

*B & B £19-£24pp, Dinner from £11, Rooms 3 double, 1 twin, 3 family, also 7 bed cottage,
Restricted smoking, Children & dogs welcome, Closed Nov to Mar*

The Old Vicarage Mungrisdale, Penrith CA11 0XR

Gordon & Pauline Bambrough Tel: 017687 79274
Email: oldvic@mungo33.freeserve.co.uk

Map Ref: 23
A66

The Old Vicarage is a spacious late Victorian house of extreme charm and character with full central heating. It is situated in the unspoilt lakeland village of Mungrisdale which nestles at the foot of Souter Fell and Bowscale Fell. A pub and restaurant are near by, also walks to suit everyone from gentle strolls to energetic climbs with an abundance of wild flowers, birds and animals. Bedrooms are equipped with tea/coffee making facilities. There is a pleasant lounge with television where guests may relax.

*B & B from £22pp, Rooms 1 single, 1 twin, 1 double, 1 family,
No smoking, Children welcome, No dogs, Closed Xmas*

Land Ends Country Lodge Watermillock, Ullswater, Penrith CA11 0NB

Tel: 017684 86438   Fax: 017684 86959
Email: infolandends@btinternet.com   Web: www.landends.btinternet.co.uk

Map Ref: 24
A592

Our traditional Cumbrian farmhouse has been tastefully restored to provide comfortable accommodation in clean, bright en-suite rooms in an attractive setting, one mile from Ullswater. Set in 25 acre grounds with a pretty courtyard and fishpond, two private lakes with mown walkways and seats for relaxing, ducks, moorhens and red squirrels, this is the perfect place to enjoy peace and quiet. With superb walking close by and many local attractions this is a central place for exploring the Lakes. Cosy lounge, honesty bar, light evening snacks, packed lunches, drying room, great breakfasts.

B & B from £26pp, Rooms 2 single, 3 double, 2 twin, 1 family, all en-suite,
No smoking, Children welcome, No dogs, Closed Dec to Feb

The Archway 13 College Road, Windermere LA23 1BU

Jonathan & Sarah Harris Tel: 015394 45613 Fax: 015394 45328
Email: archway@btinternet.com Web: www.communiken.com/archway

Map Ref: 25
A591

The Archway is a comfortable Victorian guesthouse which is tastefully furnished and enjoys superb mountain views. A warm welcome and good food are our priority. All rooms are en-suite. A breakfast well worth getting up for offers home-made yoghurt, muesli and granola, a selection of dried and fresh fruits, and a choice of traditional cooked breakfast, pancakes or kippers. A three-course dinner, or packed lunch, is available by arrangement. The house is quietly situated, yet only a short walk from the centre of Windermere.

B & B £20-£30pp, Dinner £15, Rooms 2 twin, 2 double, all en-suite,
No smoking, Children over 10, No dogs, Open all year

Beaumont Thornbarrow Road, Windermere LA23 2DG

Bob & Maureen Theobald Tel: 015394 45521 Fax: 015394 46267
gbb@beaumont-holidays.co.uk www.beaumont-holidays.co.uk

Map Ref: 25
A591
see Photo on page 92

Bob and Maureen Theobald would like to welcome you to Beaumont which has a friendly informal atmosphere within a gracious Victorian house. Ideally located midway between Windermere and Bowness, set in an elevated position in one acre of beautiful landscaped gardens with panoramic views of the surrounding fells. There are five en-suite bedrooms (one with a four poster bed), all have colour television, radio, tea and coffee making facilities. One room is on the ground floor. Guests have free use of private swimming pool/leisure club.

B & B £26-£38.50pp, C-Cards MC VS, Rooms 3 double, 1 twin, 1 family, all en-suite,
No smoking, Children welcome, No dogs, Open all year

The Chestnuts Prince's Road, Windermere LA23 2EF

Peter & Chris Reed Tel / Fax: 015394 46999
Email: peter@chesnuts-hotel.co.uk Web: www.chesnuts-hotel.co.uk

Map Ref: 25
A591

The Chestnuts offers a delightful home from home and a distinctly high standard of comfort and service. The house is a century old, enjoying both lovely gardens and private parking. There is a choice of five elegantly furnished bedrooms each adorned in striking pine, with sumptuous king sized four posters and standard king sized beds, all with either en-suite showers, baths or even luxurious corner baths. There will be a room here to suit you. All our guests have free use of nearby Parklands Leisure Club.

B & B from £25pp, C-Cards, Rooms 5 double, all en-suite,
No smoking, Children & dogs welcome, Open all year

Orrest Head House, Windermere

Kirkwood Guest House Prince's Road, Windermere LA23 2DD

Carol & Neil Cox   Tel / Fax: 015394 43907
Email: neil.cox@kirkwood51.freeserve.co.uk   Web: www.kirkwood51.co.uk

Map Ref: 25
A591

Kirkwood is a large Victorian stone house situated on a quiet corner between Windermere and Bowness ideally situated for exploring the Lake District. All rooms are en-suite with colour television, tea/coffee making facilities and radio. Some rooms have four poster beds, ideal for honeymoons, anniversary, or just a special treat. There is a comfortable lounge in which to relax and for breakfast an extensive menu is offered including vegetarian and special diets. Help with planning walks and drives or choosing a mini bus tour is all part of the personal service.

B & B £24-£28pp, C-Cards, Rooms 3 twin, 3 double, 4 family, all en-suite, No smoking, Children welcome, Dogs by arrangement, Open all year

Orrest Head House Kendal Road, Windermere LA23 1JG

Brenda Butterworth   Tel / Fax: 015394 44315
Email: bjb@orrest.co.uk   Web: www.orrest.co.uk

Map Ref: 25
A591
see Photo on page 95

Orrest Head House, Windermere, is a delightful Cumbrian country house part of which dates back to the 17th century. The atmosphere here is relaxed and homely. The bedrooms are comfortable, they all offer en-suite facilities, and they have colour television, and tea/coffee making facilities. A delicious breakfast is served, a perfect start to a busy day exploring this lovely area. Orrest Head House is set in three acres of garden and woodland, there are far reaching views to the mountains and lake. Both the station and village are closeby.

B & B from £22pp, Rooms 3 double, 2 twin, all en-suite, No smoking, Children over 6, No dogs, Closed Xmas day

Rockside Ambleside Road, Windermere LA23 1QA

Susan Coleman   Tel / Fax: 015394 45343
Email: suecoleman@aol.com   Web: www.rockside-guesthouse.co.uk

Map Ref: 25
A591

This attractive stone house is ideally placed being just 150 yards from the village of Windermere, also near the train and bus station. Rockside offers superb accommodation, all the bedrooms are well equipped, they offer colour television, tea/coffee making facilities and hair dryer. Most rooms are en-suite. There is a good choice of hearty breakfasts to begin the day. Visitors are offered help with planning walks, car routes and activities. There is a large car park.

B & B from £19.50pp, C-Cards MC VS, Rooms 1 single, 2 twin, 4 double, 4 family, most en-suite, Restricted smoking, Children welcome, Small dogs by arrangement, Open all year

Villa Lodge Guest House Cross Street, Windermere LA23 1AE

Mick & Fiona Rooney   Tel: 015394 43318
Email: rooneym@btconnect.com   Web: www.villa-lodge.co.uk

Map Ref: 25
A591

Villa Lodge is a stylish guesthouse hidden away in Cross Street, high up overlooking Windermere village. It boasts magnificent views of the Fells and Lake Windermere. All bedrooms are tastefully decorated and very comfortable, all have colour televisions and tea/coffee making facilities. The full menu breakfast is served in our lovely spacious dining area, special diets are catered for. Evening meal available with residential licence. There is a cosy lounge and sunny conservatory in which to relax. Private car park for guests and we are only two minutes walk from the bus/rail station.

B & B from £23pp, C-Cards MC VS, Dinner from £15, Rooms 2 single, 5 double, 1 twin, all en-suite, Restricted smoking, Children welcome, Dogs by arrangement, Open all year

Derbyshire & Staffordshire

Derbyshire and Staffordshire between them contain a remarkable mix of pastoral and industrial scenery and the two counties share with Yorkshire and Cheshire the impressive Peak District. Kinder Scout, an exposed peat plateau, is the highest point of Derbyshire's Peak District, at the starting point of the Pennine Way National Trail, and gives glorious views across the county. Derbyshire's section of the Peak District covers no less than 555 square miles of the county and affords the visitor fine walking country. Castleton is an ideal holiday centre delightfully situated at the head of the Hope Valley, sheltering under the impressive ruins of Norman Peveril Castle, where the River Noe meets Peaks Hole Water. This is where the ancient craft of Well Dressing, the blessing of the water supply, takes place in June and July of each year. Nearby is the great limestone gorge of Winnats Pass, close to the Blue John mines of Treak Cliff cavern. Blue John is an amethyst-coloured stone, unique to these hills, and since the eighteenth century made into vases and ornaments. This is a region rich in caves with the impressive Speedwell Cavern approached by a mile long underground boat journey and Peak Cavern with its four hundred year old rope walk.

Buxton is an elegant spa town, greatly valued by the Romans who named it Aquae Arnemetiae, once visited by Mary Stuart on the instructions of Queen Elizabeth I. It was the aim of the fifth Duke of Devonshire to make Buxton a town to rival Bath. It never quite succeeded but in 1880 the largest unsupported dome in the world was built here. The town is a delight and houses an excellent museum featuring the Wonders of the Peak District exhibition. Matlock is another fine tourist center, bordering the Peak National Park, and from Matlock Bath, a former spa which occupies an extraordinary site within the deep Derwent Gorge, cable cars give access to the Heights of Abraham. Chatsworth House, home of the Duke and Duchess of Devonshire, is also well worth a visit and often referred to as a treasure house, with beautiful gardens landscaped by Capability Brown.

Derby is very much the product of the Industrial Revolution, although an ancient town established as a trading post at the foot of the Pennines. The eighteenth century growth of the town was largely due to its fine canal network and later it became a major rail centre. The silk, hosiery, cotton and lace industry also thrived here, its diverse skills led to its renown as a rail, aircraft and car manufacturer, notably the Rolls-Royce marque. However, today its fame rests on its high-grade porcelain. The city is an

Higher Tor, Longshaw Estate, Derbyshire (DDDC)

97

important commercial and industrial centre boasting a superb City Museum and Art Gallery, housing paintings by the eighteenth century artist Joseph Wright of Derby.

Staffordshire, although losing much of the Black Country in 1974 to the West Midlands, nevertheless retained the Potteries, Arnold Bennett's 'Five Towns', immortalised in his novels, these five pottery towns became amalgamated to form Stoke-on-Trent in 1910. The presence of all the essential raw materials for pottery manufacture in the region encouraged the development of the industry, but it was the entrepreneurial skills of Wedgwood, Spode and Minton in the eighteenth century that made the potteries internationally famous. Stoke has opened up many of the old factories to visitors and has a wealth of fascinating museums. Just fifteen miles to the east is Alton Towers, Britain's most famous theme park,

built around the ruin of Pugin's Gothic home of the 15th Earl of Shrewsbury. Close by, the National Trust owns ten acres of Toothill Wood which includes Toothill Rock, a glorious viewpoint, and part of the Staffordshire Way, a long distance footpath. Within a short distance of Stoke-on-Trent is lovely Downs Banks, an area of rolling moorland presented to the National Trust in 1946 as a war memorial.

The visitor to this county must not miss Lichfield, a delightful mixture of medieval streets and mellow Regency houses. The cathedral is a fine triple-spired sandstone building dominating its seventeenth and nineteenth century close, separated from the city by the Stowe and Minster Pools and created from the ancient marshes. Despite its industrial history Staffordshire is still very much a farming county and contains a great deal of attractive countryside.

PLACES TO VISIT

This is a small selection of interesting places to visit. Many more are listed in our annual guide to Museums, Galleries, Historic Houses & Sites (see page 448)

Alton Towers
Alton, Staffordshire
Britain's biggest and best-known theme park, occupying a huge site, originally the estate of the Earls of Shrewsbury.

Chatsworth House
Bakewell, Derbyshire
The home of the Duke and Duchess of Devonshire is set in a 1000 acre park with sculptures and fountains. 26 rooms of the house are open to the public displaying magnificent paintings, silver and fine porcelain.

Derby Cathedral
Queen Street, Irongate, Derby
The second highest perpendicular tower in England built between 1510 and 1530. Nave designed by Robert Bakewell with a wrought iron screen so intricate it thatresembles lacework.

Heights of Abraham Cable Cars
Matlock Bath, Derbyshire
A cable car journey across the Derwent Valley to the summit of the hill top country park.

The Potteries Museum & Art Gallery
Hanley, Stoke-on-Trent
The world's finest collection of Staffordshire ceramics. Discover the story of Stoke-on-Trent's people, industry, products and landscapes and explore rich and diverse collections of paintings, drawings, prints, glass and costumes.

Shugborough Estate
Milford, Staffordshire
Eighteenth century mansion house with Grade 1 historic garden and park containing neo-classical monuments.

Derbyshire & Staffordshire

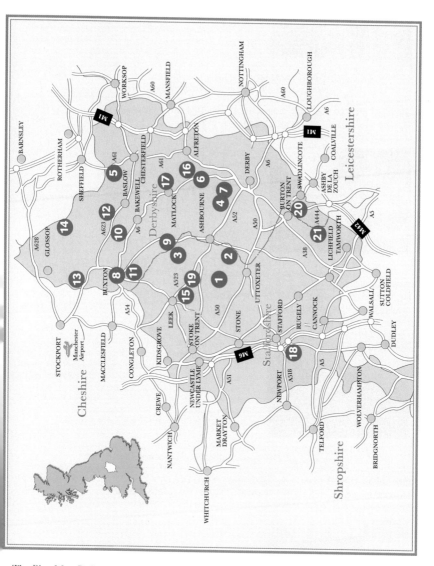

The Blue Map References should be used to locate B & B properties on the pages that follow

Farriers Cottage & Mews Woodhouse Farm, Nabb Lane, Croxden, near Alton, Staffs

ST14 5JB Diana Ball Tel: 01889 507507 Fax: 01889 507282 **Map Ref: 1**
Email: ddeb@lineone.net Web: www.alton-towers.glo.cc Mobile: 07803 530655 **B5030**

Peaceful and secluded, with a warm welcome and relaxed atmosphere, our guests are free to come and go as they please. The Cottage and Mews have their own entrances enhanced with an array of fragrant flowers. All the well equipped bedrooms are presented in a country style with stripped pine, dried flowers and pictures. A peaceful haven offering delicious breakfasts with fresh farm eggs and wholesome local produce, relaxation and stunning views. Step straight from our door to explore the beautiful countryside. Discover the stately homes, historic towns local pubs and restaurants.

B & B from £19pp, C-Cards MC VS, Rooms 3 double, 1 twin, 1 family, all en-suite,
No smoking, Children over 5, No dogs, Open all year

Oldfield House Snelston, Ashbourne, Derbys DE6 2EP

Edmund & Sue Jarvis Tel: 01335 324510 Fax: 01335 324113 **Map Ref: 2**
A515
Email: suejarvis@beeb.net

A fine listed house set in a small tranquil estate village nestling in the glorious Dove valley, three miles south west of Ashbourne. Perfectly situated for exploring the Derbyshire Dales, visiting the host of great houses nearby or just taking the opportunity of relaxing in a peaceful country house. Upon arrival enjoy tea in the drawing room or, weather permitting, in the garden with its herbaceous borders, old roses, scrubs and trees. The comfortable well furnished bedrooms have television and tea/coffee making facilities.

B & B from £32pp, Dinner from £20, Rooms 1 twin, 1 double, en-suite or private facilities,
Restricted smoking, No children or dogs, Closed Xmas & New Year

Rose Cottage Snelston, Ashbourne, Derbys DE6 2DL

Cynthia Moore Tel: 01335 324230 Fax: 01335 324651 **Map Ref: 2**
B5033, A515
Email: pjmoore@beeb.net

Rose Cottage is a 19th century cottage, set in an acre of garden, with five acres of paddocks, making it a peaceful location to stay. The house is on a quiet country lane, a walk away from the pretty village of Snelston, it overlooks the beautiful and unspoiled valley of the River Dove. There are good pubs locally, and restaurants four miles away in the town of Ashbourne. The area has much to offer with wonderful walking and cycling, and there are beautiful properties such as Chatsworth House and Sudbury Hall.

B & B £25-£27pp, Rooms 1 double en-suite, 1 twin, 1 single, private bath,
No smoking, Children over 12, Dogs by arrangement, Closed Xmas

Stanshope Hall Stanshope, Ashbourne, Derbys DE6 2AD

Naomi Chambers & Nick Lourie Tel: 01335 310278 Fax: 01335 310470 **Map Ref: 3**
A515
Email: naomi@stanshope.demon.co.uk Web: www.stanshope.net

Stanshope Hall, dating from the 16th century, stands on the brow of a hill between the Manifold and Dovedale in the Peak District. The hall faces south across rolling landscape. Lovingly restored and retaining many of its original features. All bedrooms are en-suite with direct dial phone and tea/coffee making facilities. There is a guests' drawing room with piano and record player and local information table. Centrally heated throughout. Home cooked dinners with garden and local produce and a residents' licence. Extensive breakfast menu. Brochure available.

B & B £25-£40pp, C-Cards MC VS, Dinner from £21, Rooms 1 twin, 2 double, all en-suite,
Restricted smoking, Children welcome, No dogs, Closed Xmas

Park View Farm
Weston Underwood,
near Ashbourne

Park View Farm   Weston Underwood, Ashbourne, Derbys DE6 4PA

Michael & Linda Adams   Tel / Fax: 01335 360352   Mobile: 07771 573057

Email: enquiries@parkviewfarm.co.uk   www.parkviewfarm.co.uk

Map Ref: 4
A38
see Photo on page 101

Enjoy Country House hospitality in our elegant Victorian farmhouse. It is set in large gardens with lovely views overlooking the park containing the National Trust's magnificent Kedleston Hall. Delightful dining room and lovely drawing room overlooking the south facing terrace. Delicious breakfasts; fresh fruits, homemade bread and new laid eggs. Beautifully furnished romantic en-suite four poster bedrooms. AA Premier 5 Diamonds.

B & B £30-£35pp, Rooms 3 double, all en-suite, No smoking, Children over 5, No dogs, Closed Xmas

Millbrook   Furnace Lane, Monkwood, Barlow, Derbys S18 7SY

Avril Turner

Tel: 0114 2890253   Fax: 0114 2891365   Mobile: 07831 398373

Map Ref: 5
B6051

Millbrook is spacious and comfortably furnished having en-suite facilities, drinks tray, colour television, hairdryer, alarm radio, trouser press and guests' lounge. Attention is paid to detail to make your stay as enjoyable as possible. Situated down a quiet country lane surrounded by lovely countryside with many walks around, yet within easy reach of Sheffield and Chesterfield and on the edge of the Peak District with Chatsworth House and Haddon Hall close by. There are many hostelries serving good pub food nearby. ETC 4 Diamonds, Silver Award.

B & B from £25pp, Rooms 1 double, 1 twin, all en-suite, No smoking, Children welcome, No dogs, Closed Xmas & New Year

Chevin Green Farm   Chevin Road, Belper, Derbys DE56 2UN

Carl & Joan Postles   Tel / Fax: 01773 822328

Email: spostles@globalnet.co.uk   Web: www.chevingreenfarm.co.uk

Map Ref: 6
A6, A517

Take a break, relax and unwind in our 18th century modernised farmhouse set in picturesque hillside scenery 'The Chevin'. The centrally heated rooms are all en-suite with colour televisions and tea/coffee making facilities. Guests own lounge and dining room with separate tables. Generous breakfasts using our own free range eggs: sausage and bacon from local award winning pork butcher. Ideally situated for either holiday makers or business people. Experience the myriad of things to do in Derbyshire like Chatsworth House, Haddon Hall, Dovedale, and the Well dressing celebrations.

B & B £23-£26pp, C-Cards MC VS, Rooms 3 double, 2 twin, 1 family, all en-suite, No smoking, Children welcome, No dogs, Closed Xmas & New Year

Dannah Farm Country House   Bowmans Lane, Shottle, Belper, Derbys DE56 2DR

Martin & Joan Slack   Tel: 01773 550273   Fax: 01773 550590

Email: reservations@dannah.demon.co.uk   Web: www.dannah.co.uk

Map Ref: 7
A517

Dannah Farm is situated a few hundred yards from Shottle Village, part of the Chatsworth estates, and originally a royal deer park. Still very much a working farm with 128 acres which include crops and beef cattle. The 18th century farmhouse is beautifully furnished, and full of character. The bedrooms all with private facilities, are very well equipped, and they look out over green fields and rolling countryside. There are some special rooms with four posters, private sitting rooms and whirlpool baths. Excellent breakfasts are served, and dinners by arrangement.

B & B £37.50-£55pp, C-Cards MC VS, Dinner from £19.50, Rooms 4 double, 2 twin, 1 single, 1 suite, all en-suite, Restricted smoking, Children welcome, No dogs, Closed Xmas

Biggin Hall, Biggin-by-Hartington, near Buxton

Grosvenor House Hotel 1 Broad Walk, Buxton, Derbys SK17 6JE

Graham & Anne Fairbairn Tel / Fax: 01298 72439
Web: www.cressbrook.co.uk/buxton

Map Ref: 8
A6

Privately run, licensed hotel in quiet centre of historic spa town enjoying spectacular views overlooking 23 acres of landscaped gardens and Opera House. Bedrooms, both standard and deluxe are tastefully decorated, en-suite and non-smoking with colour television, radio/alarm and hospitality tray. Our charming lounge and dining room offer a home-from-home atmosphere with panoramic views. An excellent hearty breakfast is offered. Wide choice of good restaurants and pubs within short walking distance. Comfort and hospitality assured. Scenic countryside, Chatsworth and Haddon Hall nearby. ETC, AA 4 Diamonds and 'Which'.

B & B from £25pp, Rooms 5 double, 1 twin, 2 family, all en-suite, Smoking in lounge only, Children over 8, Guide dogs only, Open all year

Biggin Hall Biggin-by-Hartington, Buxton, Derbys SK17 0DH

James Moffett Tel: 01298 84451 Fax: 01298 84681
Email: bigginhall@compuserve.com Web: www.bigginhall.co.uk

Map Ref: 9
A515
see Photo on page 103

Beautifully restored, this stone built house dating from the 17th century, set 1,000 feet up in the Peak District National park, is delightful in every way. Antiques, a log fire, a four poster bed give this home a wealth of charm. The food is outstanding with the owners priding themselves on the use of only the freshest and best produce available. The home baked bread is excellent. Perfect in every way. Easy access to the Spa town of Buxton, Chatsworth House, Haddon Hall, etc. Beautiful uncrowded footpaths from the grounds.

B & B from £30pp, C-Cards MC VS AE, Dinner from £12, Rooms 9 double, 10 twin, all en-suite, Restricted smoking, Children over 11, No dogs in main house, Open all year

Cressbrook Hall & Cottages Cressbrook, near Bakewell, Buxton, Derbys SK17 8SY

Len & Bobby Hull-Bailey Tel: 01298 871289 Fax: 01298 871845
Email: stay@cressbrookhall.co.uk Web: www.cressbrookhall.co.uk

Map Ref: 10
A6, A623

Built in 1835, Cressbrook Hall perches high on the south facing Wye Valley overlooking Cressbrook Mill, adjacent to the beautiful Monsal Dale. Once a mill owner's house, this impressive family residence stands in rural grounds with self catering holiday cottages. Exceptional countryside for walking, with excellent pubs and restaurants very close by. The accommodation is elegant, the bedrooms are well equipped with television and tea/coffee making facilities. Breakfast is served in the exquisite period dining room. Chatsworth House and Haddon Hall are 10 minutes. Colour brochure on request.

B & B from £32.50pp, C-Cards MC VS DC, Dinner from £18.50, Rooms 2 double, 1 twin, 1 family, all en-suite, No smoking, Children welcome, No dogs, Closed mid-Dec to New Year

Staden Grange Country House Staden Lane, Staden, Buxton, Derbys SK17 9RZ

Mrs MacKenzie
Tel: 01298 24965 Fax: 01298 72067

Map Ref: 11
A515

Staden Grange is different, set in open farmland, it is a comfortable country house with a range of accommodation on the outskirts of Buxton. Spacious parking with easy access to Buxton Opera House, Chatsworth and the wonderful walks in the Peak District. Don't forget the Commonwealth Games 25th July to 4th August 2002. Hourly rail link to Manchester Airport. Stay in the countryside but enjoy the city. Comfortable en-suite rooms, some on the ground floor, ideal for the elderly or guests with pets. Four poster or suite available. Come and enjoy.

B & B from £25pp, Rooms 6 double, 4 twin, 1 family, all en-suite, Children & dogs welcome, Closed Xmas & New Year

Delf View House Church Street, Eyam, Derbys S32 5QH

David & Meirlys Lewis   Tel: 01433 631533   Fax: 01433 631972
Email: lewis@delfview.co.uk   Web: www.lewis@delfview.co.uk

Map Ref: 12
A623

Tranquil and relaxing accommodation in an elegant Georgian country House in historic Eyam, centrally located in the magnificent Peak National Park. Antique furniture, original paintings and books provide a wonderful ambience in the three spacious bedrooms as well as in the guests' drawing room where complimentary tea is served on arrival. Superb breakfasts in the 17th century beamed dining room are a splendid start for walking or for visiting stately Chatsworth, Haddon, Hardwick and Eyam Hall. Hospitality trays and television in all bedrooms. Private parking.

B & B from £25pp, Rooms 1 twin, 2 double, 1 en-suite,
No smoking, Children over 12, Open all year

Cote Bank Farm Buxworth, High Peak, Derbys SK23 7NP

Pamela & Nick Broadhurst   Tel / Fax: 01663 750566
Email: cotebank@btinternet.com

Map Ref: 13
A6, B6062

Wake to bird song and views to lift the spirits. Feast on a breakfast of freshly baked bread, homemade preserves and the best of local produce then enjoy a walk either gentle or strenuous across our peaceful sheep farm and the glorious Peak District hills beyond. Relax in our pretty country garden, curl up with a book by the log fire or explore the quaint markets and the stately homes of Derbyshire. En-suite bedrooms have tea making facilities and colour televisions. Safe parking by the door.

B & B from £25pp, Rooms 1 twin, 2 double, all en-suite, No smoking,
Children over 10, No dogs, Closed Nov to Mar

Underleigh House off Edale Road, Hope, Hope Valley, Derbys S33 6RF

Philip & Vivienne Taylor   Tel: 01433 621372   Fax: 01433 621324
Email: underleigh.house@btinternet.com   Web: www.underleighhouse.co.uk

Map Ref: 14
A6187 (formally A625)

Set in an idyllic and peaceful location amidst glorious scenery, this extended cottage and barn conversion (dating from 1873) is the perfect base for exploring the Peak District. Nestling under Lose Hill, Underleigh is in the heart of magnificent walking country. Each bedroom is furnished to a high standard with many thoughtful extras included. Delicious breakfasts in the flagstoned dining hall feature local and home-made specialities. The beamed lounge, with a log fire on chilly evenings, is the perfect place to relax after a delightful day in the Peak National Park.

B & B from £33pp, C-Cards MC VS, Rooms 3 double, 2 twin, 1 suite, all en-suite, No smoking,
Children over 12, Dogs by arrangement, Closed Xmas & New Year

---

Choir Cottage & Choir House Ostlers Lane, Cheddleton, Leek, Staffs ST13 7HS

William & Elaine Sutcliffe   Tel: 01538 360561
Email: enquiries@choircottage.co.uk   Web: www.choircottage.co.uk

Map Ref: 15
A520

Choir Cottage is a 17th century, stone, Staffordshire cottage which was in former times a resting place for weary ostlers. The cottage stands adjacent to Choir House where owners William and Elaine Sutcliffe live. The two bedrooms are beautifully appointed, they offer en-suite facilities, four poster beds and attractive pine furniture. They are centrally heated and have television and a tea/coffee tray. This is a quiet location, yet very convenient for the Peak District, potteries and Alton Towers. Cheddleton and the surrounding area has a wealth of footpaths.

B & B £25-£30pp, Rooms 1 double, 1 family, both en-suite, No smoking,
Children welcome, No dogs, Closed Xmas day & Boxing day

Mount Tabor House Bowns Hill, Crich, Matlock, Derbys DE4 5DG

Fay & Steve Whitehead Tel / Fax: 01773 857008 Mobile: 07977 078266

Email: mountabor@email.msn.com

Map Ref: 16
M1 J26/28,
B5035, A6, A38

Once a chapel, Mount Tabor House enjoys stunning views over the Amber Valley. En-suite bedrooms are well furnished, one offers a king size/twin bed with a large corner bath, both have hospitality tray, power shower, tv/video, radio, hairdryer and garden views. Meals, including vegetarian, are generous and freshly prepared, using quality local and organic produce, they may be enjoyed al fresco on the balcony overlooking garden and countryside. Crich is home to the National Tramway Museum, Crich Pottery and Peak Practice. Nearby Wingfield Manor, Lea Gardens, Chatsworth, Haddon and National Trust properties.

B & B £25-£27.50pp, C-Cards MC VS, Dinner from £17.50, Rooms 1 double/twin/family,
1 twin/double, 1 family, all en-suite, No smoking, Children welcome, No dogs, Closed Xmas & New Year

Hearthstone Farm Riber, Matlock, Derbys DE4 5JW

Joyce & Ian Gilman Tel: 01629 534304 Fax: 01629 534372

Email: bed_and_breakfast@hearthstonefarm.fs.business.co.uk

Map Ref: 17
A6, A615

Situated high on the hill above Matlock on the edge of the small village of Riber whose castle dominates the town of Matlock; this 150-acre family run livestock farm provides organic beef, lamb, pork and eggs for sale through our on-farm outlet. The farmhouse dates back to the 16th century and offers a warm and comfortable environment from which to explore the beautiful Derbyshire Dales and visit local historic sites of interest. All rooms have tea and coffee making facilities and colour television. Meals are prepared using our own produce wherever possible.

B & B from £25pp, Dinner from £12.50, Rooms 1 double with pb, 1 double en-suite,
1 twin en-suite, No smoking, Children welcome, Well behaved dogs, Closed Xmas & New Year

Littlemoor Wood Farm Littlemoor Lane, Riber, Matlock, Derbys DE4 5JS Map Ref: 17

Gilly Groom Tel: 01629 534302 Fax: 01629 534008

Email: gillygroom@ntlworld.com Web: www.aplaceinthecountry.co.uk

A6, A615

This peaceful and informal farmhouse lies at the edge of the Derbyshire Dales and the Peak Park. Set among 20 acres of meadows with wonderful open views it is the perfect place to unwind. Rooms are attractive and comfortable with television and tea/coffee trays. We provide hearty breakfasts including home-produced bacon and sausages, and cater for vegetarian and special diets. Many stately homes including Chatsworth House and other popular places of interest are nearby. Ashbourne, Bakewell and M1 Junction 28 all within 20 minutes.

B & B from £25pp, C-Cards MC VS, Dinner from £12.50, Rooms 1 double, 1 double/twin,
both private facilities, No smoking, Children over 8, No dogs, Closed Xmas & New Year

Chartley Manor Farm Chartley, Stafford, Staffs ST18 0LN

Jeremy & Sarah Allen

Tel / Fax: 01889 270891 Mobile: 07958 304836

Map Ref: 18
A518

Set in its own parkland, opposite Chartley Castle, prison of Mary Queen of Scots, this half timbered manor house with oak panelled bedrooms, four poster beds and log fires, displays exquisite furniture. The gardens are large and formal with tree lined walks. The bedrooms, one with a hidden priest's hole door, are flower filled and comfortably equipped. A full English breakfast is offered, to include Staffordshire oat cakes. Excellent food available locally in award winning pub. The county show ground, Uttoxeter race course and Alton Towers are within easy reach.

B & B £25-£35pp, C-Cards MC VS, Dinner available, Rooms 2 double, 1 twin, all en-suite,
Restricted smoking, Children over 12, Dogs by arrangement, Closed Xmas day

Slab Bridge Cottage Little Onn, Church Eaton, Stafford, Staffs ST20 0AY
Diana and David Walkerdine
Tel: 01785 840220

Map Ref: 18
M6, A5

Slab Bridge Cottage is a 19th century Staffordshire cottage which takes its name from the nearby bridge on the Shropshire Union Canal. It is situated in a quiet, idyllic setting, guests may enjoy breakfasts and dinners on board a canal boat, and enjoy a gentle trip up the canal. The bedrooms are prettily presented, they have televisions and tea/coffee making facilities. The cottage is well placed for the M6, junction 12, it is also convenient for the potteries, Peak District, Alton Towers and North Wales.

B & B from £23pp, Dinner from £15, Rooms 2 double with private facilities, No smoking, Children welcome, Dogs by arrangement, Closed Xmas & New Year

Leehouse Farm Leek Road, Waterstones, Stoke-on-Trent, Staffs ST10 3HW
Josie & Jim Little
Tel: 01538 308439

Map Ref: 19
A523

Josie and Jim welcome you to their lovely Georgian farmhouse, providing excellent accommodation in the centre of a village in the Peak Park. Ideally situated for cycling, walking or touring the beautiful valleys of the Manifold Dove and Churret. Convenient for visiting Stately Homes, Alton Towers and the potteries. The business traveller will find it well situated on the A523, midway between Derby and Manchester. Our spacious bedrooms are centrally heated with television and tea/coffee making facilities. Private parking and secure parking for bicycles. ETC 4 Diamonds, Silver Award.

B & B from £20pp, Rooms 1 twin, 2 double, all en-suite, Restricted smoking, Children over 8, Dogs by arrangement, Closed Xmas

The Old Hall Netherseal, Swadlincote, Derbys DE12 8DF
Clemency Wilkins   Tel: 01283 760258   Fax: 01283 762991
Email: clemencywilkins@hotmail.com

Map Ref: 20
A444/M42 J11

The Old Hall, which is a Grade II listed house dating from 1640, is situated in 18 acres of beautiful lakeside gardens, woodland and open fields. Originally a monastery the house retains its unique character and original features whilst benefiting from all modern conveniences. Bedrooms are quiet, comfortable, spacious and attractively furnished with colour TV and tea/coffee making facilities. Ideally situated for visiting Calke Abbey, Chatsworth, Kedleston and Shugborough. 25 mins from NEC and Castle Donington.

B & B from £26pp, Dinner from £16, Rooms 1 twin, 2 double, en-suite/private bathroom, No smoking, No children or dogs, Closed Xmas & New Year

The Old Rectory Elford, Tamworth, Staffs B79 9DA
Mrs Lawrie Ward
Tel: 01827 383233   Fax: 01827 383630

Map Ref: 21
A513

The Old Rectory is a Grade II listed house standing in an idyllic setting in the small village of Elford with two acres of gardens running down to the River Tame and views of the countryside. A well charted history includes the reported sighting of a friendly ghost. Now a comfortable home after careful restoration, there is character, some period pieces and traditional furnishings to enjoy. Dinner is served in the dining room, or the kitchen which is warmed by the Aga. Elford is well placed for the Cotswolds and the Derbyshire Peaks.

B & B from £32.50pp, Dinner from £19.50, Rooms 1 double en-suite, 1 twin en-suite, Restricted smoking, Children over 5, No dogs, Closed Xmas & New Year

Devon

Devon is a superb holiday region and few counties in England can match its variety of scenery with two contrasting coastlines and some quite spectacular countryside. The northern coast, Devon's longest unspoilt coastline, is an impressive array of high cliffs along the Bristol Channel and a series of great headlands protecting fine broad sandy beaches from the wild Atlantic gales. Here are small resorts of a very special charm including Lynton, an ideal holiday center, adjoining the

Haytor on Dartmoor (SWT)

lovely Valley of the Rocks Visitor Centre. Five hundred feet below is Lynmouth, joined to Lynton by a zig-zag path and a hundred year old cliff railway. It is a romantic and picturesque fishing village, backed by glorious wooded cliffs and the home of the Exmoor National Park. The largest seaside resort of North Devon is Ilfracombe, which until the arrival of the railway at the end of the nineteenth century was only a small fishing town. However its dramatic rocky headlands and quaint sheltered

bays attracted large numbers of holiday makers. The town still retains much of its old character. Further west, the little town of Clovelly needs no introduction being one of the most photographed villages in the country, its steep cobbled single street, picturesque cottages and little harbour has made it a tourist attraction for well over a century. Bideford, a highly successful port on the River Torridge from the seventeenth century, is also a fine holiday center and was in fact the basis for Charles Kingsley's famous novel Westward Ho! It was the great Elizabethan seafarer, Sir Richard Grenville who secured Bideford's first town charter.

Devon's south coast, like its north coast, can claim massive cliffs, but the climate is altogether softer and balmier. This region includes the English Riviera, a wonderful stretch of golden beaches, palm trees and vivid blue seas. Torquay is the largest and most impressive of Devon's resorts and its singularly mild climate ensured its development during the late eighteenth century as a holiday centre. There is much to enjoy here, with its yachting and fishing harbour, fine gardens, sandy beaches and its exotic pavilion. Sidmouth is an elegant resort which, like Torquay, developed from a small fishing village during the eighteenth century and grew in popularity following the visit of the young Princess Victoria in 1819. Now the highlight of the summer season is its folk festival in late July to early August which offers music, dance, street theatre and family shows.

Plymouth, where Drake played his infamous game of bowls, is the largest city in the southwest. Flanked by the estuaries of the Rivers Tamar and Plym, the Hoe, overlooking Plymouth Sound, gives magnificent views across the sea and headlands. Drake's Island, used as a fort from 1860, is in the centre with the mile long breakwater beyond. The centre of Plymouth was largely destroyed during the Second World War, however, there is much to see of historic significance centred around the Barbican, the site of the original town, including a fish market and Tudor and Jacobean buildings. Round the coast is Dartmouth, another ancient port, sheltering in the mouth of the Dart estuary and built up a steep hillside. Dartmouth Castle built in the late fifteenth century stands on rocks at the entrance to the river.

Attractive as the Devon coasts are, the centre of the county holds its own fascination. Exeter, like Plymouth, was severely damaged during the Second World War but still retains a great deal of its character. The magnificent cathedral with its two massive Norman towers thankfully survived the destruction and contains the priceless Exeter Book of Anglo-Saxon poetry. The remarkable thirteenth century underground water system can be explored by guided tours and the Maritime Museum is also a fine visitor attraction, housing over a hundred historic vessels.

The large number of cairns, hut circles and Bronze Age remains suggest that Dartmoor was far from deserted in the distant past, but climatic change ensured that this large area of Devon was to become the largest expanse of wilderness in southern Britain. Massive granite peaks rise over 2,000 feet out of this bleak gorse and heather upland. The Dartmoor National Park covers over 365 square miles and the Exmoor National Park, once a great hunting region, is now an area of glorious scenery, open walking country and the haunt of red deer and wild ponies.

PLACES TO VISIT

This is a small selection of interesting places to visit. Many more are listed in our annual guide to Museums, Galleries, Historic Houses & Sites (see page 448)

Buckland Abbey
Yelverton
A Cistercian monastery that became the home of Sir Francis Drake. Craft workshops, herb garden and estate walks.

Exeter Cathedral
Exeter
A Norman Cathedral built in the twelfth century with impressive vaulted ceiling, medieval stained glass and carved tombs.

National Marine Aquarium
Coxside, Plymouth
State of the art aquarium and as near as you will get to being submerged without

getting wet with a shark theatre, a live coral reef and a wave tank.

Plymouth Dome
The Hoe, Plymouth
Takes the visitor through the centuries in Plymouth from the sights and sounds of Elizabethan times to the Blitz. Audiovisual presentations and reconstructions.

Underground Passages
Exeter
City passages built in medieval times to carry water into the city, the only one of its kind in Britain open to the public.

Devon

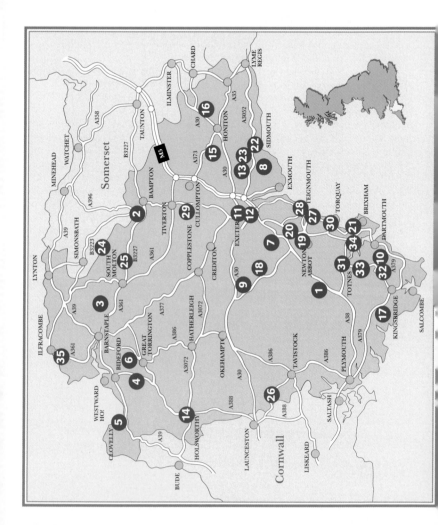

The Blue Map References should be used to locate B & B properties on the pages that follow

Wellpritton Farm Holne, Ashburton TQ13 7RX

David & Susan Grey Tel: 01364 631273

Email: info@wellprittonfarm.com Web: www.wellprittonfarm.com

Map Ref: 1
A38

Relax in a lovely Dartmoor farmhouse with wonderful views set in the heart of the countryside, yet only 3 miles from A38 Express way, half an hour to Exeter/Plymouth/Torbay. Mouth watering food every day as featured in the West country Good Food Guide 1999. Most rooms are en-suite with tea/coffee making facilities and central heating. There is a delightful character residents lounge, an outdoor swimming pool and garden. Pet goats, horses, dogs and chickens abound. Most country pursuits are nearby.

B & B from £20pp, C-Cards MC VS, Dinner from £10, Rooms 2 twin, 2 double, most en-suite, Restricted smoking, Children over 5, Dogs welcome, Closed Xmas & New Year

The Bark House Oakford Bridge, Bampton EX16 9HZ

Alastair Kameen & Justine Hill Tel: 01398 351236

Web: www.barkhouse.co.uk

Map Ref: 2
A396

Enjoy being pampered and spoilt in this charming house. Situated in the beautiful Exe Valley between central Devon and Exmoor, the house stands in one and a quarter acres of woodland and herbaceous gardens. Strong emphasis is placed on West-Country produce in the elegant dining room. Breakfasts are treated seriously too. The cosy lounge has a cheery log fire in all but the hottest weather. Bedrooms are furnished to a high standard - some luxuriously. All have TV and phone. AA 5 Diamonds.

B & B from £39.50pp, Dinner £25, Rooms 3 double, 2 twin, all en-suite/private, Restricted smoking, Closed most Mon/Tue

Huxtable Farm West Buckland, Barnstaple EX32 0SR

Antony & Jackie Payne Tel / Fax: 01598 760254

Email: gbbenquiries@huxtablefarm.co.uk Web: www.huxtablefarm.co.uk

Map Ref: 3
A361

Enjoy a memorable candelit dinner of farm/local produce with complimentary homemade wine in this wonderful mediaeval Devon longhouse (dating back to 1520). Huxtable Farm displays such delights as original oak panelling, beams and bread ovens. This secluded sheep farm with abundant wildlife and panoramic views is ideally situated on the Tarka Trail for exploring Exmoor National Park and North Devon's dramatic coastline. There is a tennis court, sauna, fitness and games room for guests' pleasure. Log fires are to be enjoyed in winter.

B & B £25-£26pp, C-Cards MC VS, Dinner from £16, Rooms 1 twin, 3 double, 2 family, all en-suite/private, Restricted smoking, Children welcome, No dogs, Closed Dec to Jan

Beara Farmhouse Buckland Brewer, Bideford EX39 5EH

Ann & Richard Dorsett

Tel: 01237 451666

Map Ref: 4
A388

Beara Farmhouse is a traditional Devon farmhouse of considerable age, with stone floors, beams and inglenook fireplaces. The farmhouse may be found down a small track, overlooking fields and woods, it enjoys a peaceful location. The family poultry provide entertainment for guests who are invited to relax here. Vegetarians are catered for, the hens providing free range eggs. The local pub in Buckland Brewer serves excellent food. Beara Farmhouse is well placed for interesting visits to places like Clovelly, Rosemoor Gardens, Torrington, the Tarka Trail and the South West coastal path.

B & B from £25pp, Dinner from £12, Rooms 1 double, 1 twin, both en-suite, No smoking, No children or dogs, Closed Mid Dec to 6th Jan

Lower Waytown Horns Cross, near Clovelly, Bideford EX39 5DN

Annette & Colin Penny
Tel: 01237 451787   Fax: 01237 451817

Map Ref: 5
A39
see Photo Opposite

This beautifully converted barn and roundhouse has been transformed into a delightful, spacious home offering superb accommodation. Tastefully furnished with antiques, the unique round beamed guests' sitting room adjoins the attractive dining room where delicious breakfasts are served. Bedrooms are en-suite and equipped for every comfort. Relax in extensive grounds with ponds, waterfowl and black swans. Lower Waytown is situated in unspoilt countryside with spectacular coastal scenery, pretty coves and coastal footpaths nearby, picturesque Clovelly lies five miles westward.

B & B from £26pp, Rooms 1 twin, 2 double, all en-suite, No smoking,
Children over 12, No dogs, Closed Xmas & New Year

Riversdale Weare Gifford, Riversdale, Bideford EX39 4QR

Maggie & Eddie Ellison   Tel: 01237 423676
Email: Riversdale@connectfree.co.uk

Map Ref: 6
A386

Riversdale is a 200 year old country house set beside the River Torridge. Bedrooms are en-suite with television, refreshment tray, fresh flowers, hairdryer, radio and complimentary toiletries. The comfortable beamed sitting room, with its stone fireplace and stove, leads to an elegant dining room where a varied breakfast is served (including porridge, smoked haddock, fruit). Nearby activities include walking, golfing, watersports, cycling the Tarka Trail and fishing our private beat. RHS Rosemoor, Dartington Crystal, Clovelly, Westward Ho! and Arlington Court are all within a short drive.

B & B from £24pp, Rooms 1 twin, 2 double, all en-suite,
No smoking, Children welcome, No dogs, Closed Oct to Mar

Whitstone Farm Bovey Tracey TQ13 9NA

Katie Bunn Tel: 01626 832258   Fax: 01626 836494
Email: katie@reynolds2000.co.uk

Map Ref: 7
A382, A38

A warm welcome awaits you at Whitstone Farm where luxury accommodation is offered in well equipped rooms which have tea/coffee making facilities and television. The farmhouse stands in three acres of grounds, which is home to over 250 specimen trees; the guests' lounge enjoys views to Dartmoor. For those seeking peace and quiet this makes an ideal location, and yet Bovey Tracey is just five minutes away. Well situated for exploring South Devon. National Trust properties, spectacular gardens, steam railways, coastal and moorland walking are all nearby. A three night discount is available.

B & B from £27.50pp, Dinner from £18, Rooms 1 twin, 2 double, all en-suite,
No smoking, Children over 15, No dogs, Closed Xmas & New Year

Lufflands Yettington, Budleigh Salterton EX9 7BP

Brenda & Colin Goode   Tel: 01395 568422   Fax: 01395 568810
Email: lufflands@compuserve.com   Web: www.lufflands.co.uk

Map Ref: 8
B3178

A warm welcome and friendly atmosphere can be found at Lufflands, a 17th century former farmhouse set in the hamlet of Yettington, just three miles from the sea at Budleigh Salterton. It is ideal for a relaxing break with excellent walking nearby, or as a location for touring, with easy access to Exeter and the M5. All rooms are equipped to a very high standard. Your breakfast is freshly cooked to order and served in the original farmhouse kitchen. There is off street parking.

B & B £19-£22pp, C-Cards MC VS, Rooms 1 single, 1 double, 1 family, all en-suite/private,
No smoking, Children welcome, Dogs by arrangement, Open all year

Lower Waytown, Horns Cross, near Clovelly

Parford Well Sandy Park, Chagford TQ13 8JW
T Daniel
Tel: 01647 433353

Parford Well, named after the village well, is a comfortable and stylishly furnished house set in a lovely walled garden within the Dartmoor National Park standing just below Castle Drogo. The attractive bedrooms are well equipped and comfortable. There are wonderful walks on the doorstep - both in the wooded valley of the River Teign and on the open Moor. It's the ideal place for a few days' break if you want to get away from it all and be well looked after. High quality breakfasts freshly prepared using local produce.

B & B from £25pp, Rooms 1 twin, 1 double, both en-suite, 1 private double, No smoking, Children over 8, No dogs, Closed Xmas & New Year

Woodside Cottage B & B Blackawton, Dartmouth TQ9 7BL
Tim & Sally Adams   Tel: 01803 712375
Email: woodside-cottage@lineone.net   Web: www.woodside-cottage-devon.co.uk

Woodside Cottage is an 18th century former gamekeeper's lodge of great character, set in superb unspoilt countryside with stunning views across a beautiful South Hams valley. Reached down a quiet country lane, the house is ideally placed for easy access to all the leisure activities that South Devon has to offer. Within a short walk is the village and two excellent pubs. The house is extremely comfortable and has attractive gardens with magnificent views. Guests are offered home made cakes and tea on arrival. The en-suite bedrooms enjoy wonderful views across the Devon countryside.

B & B from £25pp, Rooms 2 double, 1 twin, all en-suite, No smoking, Children over 12, No dogs, Closed Nov to Feb

Broome Court Broomhill, Dartmouth TQ6 0LD
Tom Boughton & Jan Bird
Tel: 01803 834275   Fax: 01803 833260

Broome Court is tucked into a south facing hill, overlooking 3 copses and surrounded by green, undulating south Devon countryside rich in wildlife. The old farm buildings encircle a paved courtyard abounding with flowers and shrubs, and in the old farmhouse kitchen your hosts will provide the sort of hearty breakfast that dreams are made of. No noise or smell of traffic at Broomhill - nor the hubbub of everyday life - but the peace and tranquillity of the rolling Devon countryside awaiting you.

B & B from £35pp, Rooms 1 twin, 2 double, all en-suite, also family unit, Restricted smoking, Children over 12, Dogs by arrangement, Open all year

Lower Marsh Farm Marsh Green, Exeter EX5 2EX
Sian Wroe   Tel: 01404 822432   Fax: 01404 823330
Email: lowermarshfarm@talk21.com

Lower Marsh Farm is a beautiful 17th century listed farmhouse set in its own extensive grounds of lawns, orchards, ponds, streams, stables and paddocks. It is just on the outskirts of the pretty hamlet of Marsh Green in the peaceful and gently rolling Devonshire countryside. The accommodation offered to guests is both gracious and comfortable, the three bedrooms being generously equipped. There is a charming sitting room which has a log fire for comfort in winter. Breakfasts here are traditional, vegetarians are well catered for. A local pub serves excellent suppers.

B & B £23-£26pp, Rooms 2 double, 1 twin, all en-suite, No smoking, Children welcome, Dogs by arrangement, Open all year

Great Wooston Farm, Moretonhampstead

Raffles 11 Blackall Road, Exeter EX4 4HD

Sue & Richard Hyde   Tel / Fax: 01392 270200
Email: raffleshtl@btinternet.com   Web: www.raffles-exeter.co.uk

Map Ref: 12
Exeter Central

Raffles is a large Victorian town house, furnished with antiques, it provides comfort and style being tastefully decorated although retaining a Victorian quality. There is a delightful walled garden, yet Raffles is only minutes from the city centre. This is the home of Richard and Sue, whose aim is to provide high quality accommodation with friendly personal service. All rooms are en-suite, they have tea and coffee making facilities, colour television and central heating. Secure parking. Raffles is an excellent base from which to explore Devon.

B & B from £25pp, C-Cards MC VS AE, Dinner from £16, Rooms 2 single, 1 twin, 2 double, 2 family, all en-suite, Restricted smoking, Children welcome, Dogs by arrangement, Open all year

---

Wood Barton Farringdon, Exeter EX5 2HY

Jackie Bolt   Tel: 01395 233407   Fax: 01395 227226
Email: jackie_bolt@hotmail.com

Map Ref: 13
A3052

Wood Barton is a 17th century farmhouse in quiet countryside, yet it is only three miles from junction 30 of the M5. Guests can enjoy a traditional English breakfast which is cooked on the Aga. The bedrooms are spacious and well equipped. Each one has an en-suite shower room, they have central heating, hospitality tray, colour television and radio. The city of Exeter is a short drive as are sandy beaches, National Trust houses and golf courses. There is a choice of good local eating places. Easy access.

B & B from £21pp, Rooms 1 twin, 1 double, 1 family, all en-suite, No smoking, Children welcome, No dogs, Closed Xmas & New Year

---

Leworthy Farmhouse Lower Leworthy, near Pyworthy, Holsworthy EX22 6SJ

Pat Jennings
Tel: 01409 259469

Map Ref: 14
A388, A3072

Charming Georgian Farmhouse, nestling in an unspoilt backwater, with lawns, mature orchard, wetlands meadow and carp-fishing lake. A genuinely warm, friendly and discreet, peaceful haven. Beautifully prepared en-suite guest rooms, ample fresh milk, quality teas, pretty china, fresh flowers. Crisp bedlinen, Chintzy curtains, luxury carpet. Peaceful lounge, chiming clocks, books, magazines, comfy old sofas, sparkling old china, Victoriana. Traditional farmhouse breakfast, or porridge, prunes, fresh fruit salad, yogurt, free range eggs, kippers, black pudding. Explore this lovely unspoilt area. Good walking, fishing, cycling.

B & B £20-£22pp, Dinner from £15, Rooms 1 twin, 2 double, 1 family, all en-suite or private bathroom, No smoking, Children welcome, No dogs, Open all year

---

Woodhayes Honiton EX14 4TP

Mr & Mrs Noel Page-Turner   Tel / Fax: 01404 42011   Mobile: 07941 444560
Email: cmpt@inweb.co.uk

Map Ref: 15
A30

Woodhayes, a classical listed Georgian house, is surrounded by 150 acres of woodland and pastureland, and one acre of carefully tended gardens. It is situated in the Blackdown Hills, an area of outstanding natural beauty, bordered by the Dumpdon Celtic hill fort, and the River Otter. The thriving market town of Honiton is a mile away. The house commands superb views from all the windows. The farm and vegetable garden provide much of the ingredients used to create delicious dinners which are enjoyed in the pre 18th century dining room.

B & B from £37pp, C-Cards MC VS, Dinner from £24, Rooms 1 single, 1 double, 1 twin, all en-suite, Restricted smoking, Children welcome, Dogs by arrangement, Closed Feb

Courtmoor Farm Upottery, Honiton EX14 9QA

Rosalind & Bob Buxton Tel: 01404 861565
Email: courtmoor.farm@btinternet.com Web: www.btinternet.com/~courtmoor.farm

Map Ref: 16
A30

Courtmoor Farm is situated on the A30 between Ilminster and Honiton. It is set back a quarter of a mile from the road in 17 acres of grounds and woodlands. Rosalind and Bob Buxton offer a warm welcome and luxury accommodation in peaceful surroundings. Each room has fine views, tea and coffee making facilities and colour television. Evening meals are available by prior arrangement. The premises are licensed. The farmhouse is ideally situated for both North and South coasts, also moorland.

B & B from £20pp, C-Cards MC VS, Dinner from £12, Rooms 1 twin, 1 double, 1 family, all en-suite, No smoking, Children welcome, No dogs, Closed Xmas & New Year

Helliers Farm Ashford, Aveton Gifford, Kingsbridge TQ7 4ND

Mrs C Lancaster Tel / Fax: 01548 550689 Mobile: 07929 382670
Email: helliersfarm@ukonline.co.uk Web: www.helliers.co.uk

Map Ref: 17
A379

Helliers Farm is a small sheep farm set on a hill, overlooking a lovely valley in the South Hams, just one mile from the village of Aveton Gifford and 15 miles from Plymouth. This is an ideal centre to stay for touring the coasts and moors. Golf courses at Bigbury, Thurlestone and Dartmouth are just three in the area. Also within a pleasant drive there are some National Trust houses to visit. The en-suite bedrooms are tastefully appointed. There is a comfortable lounge where guests may relax. Excellent farmhouse breakfasts are served here. ETC 4 Diamonds.

B & B from £23pp, Rooms 1 single, 1 double, 1 twin, 1 family, most en-suite, No smoking, Children welcome, Closed Xmas & New Year

Great Sloncombe Farm Moretonhampstead TQ13 8QF

Trudie Merchant Tel / Fax: 01647 440595
Email: hmerchant@sloncombe.freeserve.co.uk Web: www.greatsloncombefarm.co.uk

Map Ref: 18
A382

Share the magic of Dartmoor all year round whilst staying in our lovely 13th century farmhouse full of interesting historical features. Great Sloncombe is a working dairy farm set amongst peaceful meadows and woodland abundant in wild flowers and animals including badgers, foxes, deer and buzzards. A welcoming and informal place to relax and explore the moors and Devon countryside. The comfortable en-suite rooms have central heating, televisions and coffee/tea making tray. Delicious Devonshire suppers and breakfasts with newly baked bread.

B & B from £23pp, Dinner from £13, Rooms 2 double, 1 twin, No smoking, Children over 8, Dogs by arrangement, Open all year

Great Wooston Farm Moretonhampstead TQ13 8QA

Mary Cuming
Tel / Fax: 01647 440367 Mobile: 07798 670590

Map Ref: 18
A30, B3212
see Photo on page 115

Great Wooston is a peaceful haven, once part of the Manor House estate owned by Lord Hambleton. It is situated high above the Teign Valley in the Dartmoor National Park. There are wonderful views across open moorland and plenty of walks. Golf, fishing and riding may be enjoyed nearby. The farmhouse is surrounded by a delightful and well mananged garden of one acre, with a barbecue and picnic area. The three bedrooms are warm and pleasant, and one has a four poster. Be prepared for some excellent breakfasts and quality accommodation.

B & B £20-£24pp, C-Cards MC VS, Rooms 2 double (1 four poster), both en-suite, 1 twin with pb, No smoking, Children over 8, No dogs, Open all year

Sampsons Farm, Preston, near Newton Abbot

The Thatched Cottage, Kingsteignton, near Newton Abbot

The Thatched Cottage 9 Crossley Moor Road, Kingsteignton, Newton Abbot TQ12 3LE

Janice & Klaus Wiemeyer Tel: 01626 365650
Email: thatched@globalnet.co.uk

Map Ref: 19, A380
see Photo on page 119

The Thatched Cottage Restaurant is a Grade II listed 16th century thatched Devon Longhouse of great charm and character. Our licensed restaurant and cosy cocktail bar, featuring a large open fireplace, is well known locally for its fine food. Fresh local produce is used, and prepared in our own kitchens to order. All of our rooms are fully en-suite, they are well presented and comfortably furnished, they each have central heating, colour television and tea/coffee trays. Guests are welcome to relax in the pretty garden.

B & B from £25pp, C-Cards MC VS, Dinner from £14.50,
Rooms 1 single, 2 king size/twin, No smoking, No dogs, Open all year

Sampsons Thatch Hotel Restaurant Preston, Newton Abbot TQ12 3PP   Map: 20

Nigel Bell Tel / Fax: 01626 354913
Email: nigel@sampsonsfarm.com Web: www.sampsonsfarm.com

A38, A380, B3195, B3193
see Photo on page 118

Our thatched farmhouse is older than Shakespeare! Only five minutes from the A38 and A380, Sampsons Thatch is set in its own grounds in a tiny village. We have a wealth of oak beams, log fires and history. Our award winning restaurant is renowned for serving delicious Devon produce and our hens provide the eggs. We have a range of pretty, en-suite rooms in our barn conversions around the farm courtyard. Also a special disabled en-suite and a luxury ground floor apartment for groups with dogs. There are lovely river and meadow walks and Dartmoor views. Secure parking is offered. AA 4 Diamonds Rosette.

B & B £25-£50pp, C-Cards MC VS, Dinner from £12.50, Rooms 8 double en-suite,
luxury apartment, Restricted smoking, Children welcome, Dogs by arrangement, Open all year

Elberry Farm Broadsands, Paignton TQ4 6HJ

Mandy Tooze Tel / Fax: 01803 842939
Web: www.elberryfarm.co.uk

Map Ref: 21
A379

Elberry Farm is a working farm with beef, poultry and arable production. The farmhouse is between two beaches both within a two minute walk. Broadsands being a safe bathing beach has been awarded the European Blue Flag 1994. As an alternative there is a nine hole pitch and putt golf course opposite, a short drive away is the zoo, town centre and the National park. The comfortable bedrooms have tea/coffee making facilities. Guests are welcome to relax in the lounge; stroll around the secluded garden. Baby sitting available by arrangement.

B & B from £15pp, Dinner from £7, Rooms 1 twin, 2 double/family, 1 en-suite double,
No smoking, Children welcome, Dogs by arrangement, Closed Dec

Cheriton Guest House Vicarage Road, Sidmouth EX10 8UQ

Diana & John Lee
Tel / Fax: 01395 513810

Map Ref: 22
A3052

Cheriton Guest House is a large town house which backs on to the River Sid, with the 'Byes' parkland beyond. There are private parking spaces at the rear. The half mile walk to the sea front, via the town centre, is all on level ground. Cheriton is notorious for its fine cooking and varied menus. There is a comfortable lounge with colour television. Beautiful secluded rear garden for the exclusive use of guests. All bedrooms have central heating, colour television and tea/coffee making facilities and all rooms are en-suite.

B & B from £20pp, Dinner from £10, Rooms 3 single, 5 double/twin, 2 family, all en-suite,
No smoking, Children welcome, Dogs by arrangement, Open all year

Peeks House Harpford, Sidmouth EX10 0NH
Fiona & Brian Rees
Tel / Fax: 01395 567664

Map Ref: 23
A3052

Beautiful Regency house in the conservation Hamlet of Harpford on the banks of the River Otter. Three miles from the Regency town of Sidmouth and the medieval town of Ottery St Mary. Twenty minutes from the M5 it is an area of peace and tranquillity. All rooms are en-suite, have colour television, hairdryers and tea/coffee making facilities. Sumptuous freshly cooked English breakfasts are served. Evening meals are available by prior arrangement. A perfect location for visiting the many attractions in Devon and the West Country.

B & B from £28pp, Dinner from £20, Rooms 2 twin, 2 double, all en-suite, No smoking, Children over 16, No dogs, Closed Nov to Feb

---

Barkham Sandyway, Simonsbath EX36 3LU
John & Penny Adie   Tel / Fax: 01643 831370
Email: adie.exmoor@btinternet.com   Web: www.exmoor-vacations.co.uk

Map Ref: 24
A361

Tucked away in a hidden valley in the heart of the Exmoor National Park you can relax and enjoy the peace and quiet of our lovely old farmhouse.There is a beautiful oak panelled dining room, where you can enjoy delicious candlelit dinners, after which, step out to the patio and watch the sun go down. In winter log fires are lit in the drawing room, an ideal place to while away dark evenings. The bedrooms are pleasant and comfortable. Barkham enjoys wonderful views down the valley with its woods, streams and waterfalls.

B & B £28-£35pp, Dinner from £18, Rooms 1 double en-suite, 1 private single, 1 double en-suite, No smoking, Children over 12, No dogs, Closed Xmas

---

Kerscott Farm Exmoor, South Molton EX36 4QG
Theresa Sampson   Tel: 01769 550262   Fax: 01769 550910
Email: kerscott.farm@virgin.net   Web: www.devon-bandb-kerscott.co.uk

Map Ref: 25
B3227/A361

Enjoy a restful country break at our peaceful Exmoor working farm, mentioned in the Domesday Book (1086), in a central tranquil location. Picturebook 16th century farmhouse has a fascinating interior with many antiques, pictures and china, a rare find. Superb elevated position with extensive beautiful views overlooking Exmoor National Park and surrounding countryside. Pretty, tastefully furnished en-suite bedrooms with colour television. Highly acclaimed, varied home baked food including bread and preserves. Tested pure spring water. The perfect place to enjoy a holiday. ETC 5 Diamonds, Gold Award, AA 5 Diamonds.

B & B £22-£23pp, Dinner from £10, Rooms 1 twin, 2 double, all en-suite, No smoking, No children or dogs, Closed Xmas

---

Beera Farmhouse Milton Abbot, Tavistock PL19 8PL
Hilary Tucker   Tel / Fax: 01822 870216
Email: robert.tucker@farming.co.uk   Web: www.beerafarmbedandbreakfast.com

Map Ref: 26
A30, B3362

Take walks on our beautiful peaceful working farm on the banks of the river Tamar, relax in the garden, visit the north Cornish cost with rugged cliffs, the south coast with quaint fishing villages (go fishing and bring home your catch for me to cook for your supper), national trust properties, family fun parks, golf courses and Tavistock for shopping and history. Beautifully decorated rooms, all are en-suite with tea/coffee, hairdryers and clock/radios. Excellent evening meals by prior arrangement. Brochure available.

B & B from £20pp, C-Cards MC VS, Dinner from £13, Rooms 2 double, 1 twin, all en-suite, No smoking, Children welcome, No dogs, Open all year

Fonthill, Shaldon, near Teignmouth

Fonthill Torquay Road, Shaldon, Teignmouth TQ14 0AX

Jennifer Graeme Tel / Fax: 01626 872344
Email: swanphoto2@aol.com

Map Ref: 27
A379
see Photo opposite

Fonthill is peacefully situated in its own beautiful grounds of 25 acres, close to the pretty coastal village of Shaldon. The three delightful bedrooms have views of the gardens and the River Teign, and the village pubs and restaurants are within easy walking distance. There is a hard tennis court for guests' use, and the coastal path to Torquay is nearby. Dartmoor National Park is within easy reach, also Plymouth, Exeter and several fine National Trust properties. Fonthill has been a Highly Commended establishment for many years.

B & B from £28pp, Rooms 3 twin with private or en-suite bathroom,
No smoking, No dogs, Closed Nov to Mar

Ringmore House Brook Lane, Shaldon, Teignmouth TQ14 0AJ

Robert & Helen Scull Tel: 01626 873323 Fax: 01626 873353
Email: hscull@aol.com Web: www.ringmorehouse.co.uk

Map Ref: 27
A379

Beautiful Grade II listed house within 12 metres of the estuary and set in lovely ancient gardens. It is an easy walk to the village centre and beaches. Guests are brought a tray of tea in bed, and are offered homemade bread and jams, within a huge breakfast menu. Wonderful conservatory and dining room, meals available some evenings. Guests may choose a four poster bed. All rooms are beautifully furnished and include a colour television. Self catering cottage available adjacent to the main house and has views over the gardens, with private walled garden in addition.

B & B from £25pp, Rooms 1 twin, 3 double, some en-suite, No smoking,
Children over 8, No dogs, Closed Xmas

Virginia Cottage Brook Lane, Shaldon, Teignmouth TQ14 0HL

Jennifer & Michael Britton
Tel / Fax: 01626 872634

Map Ref: 27
B3199

Virginia Cottage is a Grade II listed 17th century house set within a partly walled garden, it is a delightful and relaxing place to stay. The pretty bedrooms offer en-suite or private facilities, and tea/coffee makers, they enjoy views across the gardens. There is an attractive sitting room with an inglenook fireplace. A short walk takes you to the village, where there are good pubs and restaurants. This is an ideal location for exploring the Dartmoor National Park, Cathedral city of Exeter and delights of Devon. Car parking in grounds.

B & B from £25pp, Rooms 2 double en-suite, 1 double with private bathroom, No smoking,
Children over 12, No dogs, Closed Dec to Mar

Wytchwood West Buckeridge, Teignmouth TQ14 8NF

Jennifer Richardson Brown Tel: 01626 773482 Mobile: 07971 783454
Email: wytchwood@yahoo.com Web: www.messages.to/wytchwood

Map Ref: 28
B3192

Award Winning Wytchwood has an outstanding reputation for lavish hospitality and traditional home cooking. To stay here is to be truly pampered! Panoramic views, beautiful garden, parking, stylish interior design and the prettiest en-suite bedrooms, all combine to fulfil every expectation. Homemade bread and rolls, jams, preserves, orchard honey and fresh garden produce. Delicious Devonshire cream teas, sponges and cakes. Many culinary awards. Wealth of historic sites and beautiful beaches nearby. Several superb golf courses and good traditional pubs. A warm welcome awaits.

B & B from £25pp, C-Cards MC VS, Rooms 1 twin, 2 double, en-suite/private,
No smoking, No dogs, Open all year

Bickleigh Cottage Hotel Bickleigh, Tiverton EX16 8RJ

R S H & P M Cochrane
Tel: 01884 855230

Map Ref: 29
A396

Situated on the bank of the River Exe near Bickleigh bridge, a landmark famous for its scenic beauty, Bickleigh Cottage Country Hotel has been privately owned by the Cochrane family since 1933. The original cottage was built circa 1640 with additions in the 1970s. All bedrooms are en-suite and have tea/coffee making facilities. The location of Bickleigh makes it a perfect centre for touring Devon. Exeter with its cathedral, Tiverton Castle, Knightshayes Court and Killerton House are all nearby.

B & B from £23.50pp, C-Cards MC VS, Rooms 1 single, 2 twin, 2 double, all en-suite, Restricted smoking, Children over 14, No dogs, Closed Oct to Apr

Kingston House 75 Avenue Road, Torquay TQ2 5LL

Teresa & Giovanni Butto   Tel: 01803 212760
Email: Butto@Kingstonhousehotel.co.uk Web: www.Kingstonehousehotel.co.uk

Map Ref: 30
A380

Teresa and Giovanni assure guests of a warm West Country and Continental welcome to their beautifully maintained Victorian hotel, which offers all modern day comforts in a relaxed and informal atmosphere. Guests are welcome to relax in the lounge, and to enjoy the sunny terrace at the hotel front to watch the world go by! The bedrooms are generously equipped and immaculately presented, two have four poster beds. Kingston House is situated only a short walk from the seafront, Riviera Centre, the harbour and town centre, also Torre Abbey and its beautiful gardens.

B & B £19-£26.50pp, Rooms 2 single, 2 twin, 2 double, No smoking, Children over 8, No dogs, Closed mid-Nov to Mar

Fairmount House Hotel Herbert Road, Chelston, Torquay TQ2 6RW

Shaun & Carole Burke   Tel / Fax: 01803 605446
Email: fairmounthouse@aol.com

Map Ref: 30
A380

Fairmount House was built in 1900 as a five bedroomed family home, complete with servants' quarters and cellars. This family run Hotel now welcomes visitors to enjoy comfortable, well equipped accommodation, with traditional home cooking using local produce. The two ground floor rooms enjoy independent access to the garden, they offer corner baths/shower. Torquay is known as 'the queen of the Riviera' it has miles of beaches and coves, as well as sub tropical plants and of course an excellent range of entertainments. There are within walking distance some interesting attractions.

B & B £28-£33pp, C-Cards MC VS, Dinner from £12, Rooms 1 single, 4 double, 2 family, 1 twin, all en-suite, No smoking, Children & dogs welcome, Closed Xmas & New Year

The Old Forge at Totnes Seymour Place, Totnes TQ9 5AY

David Miller and Christine Hillier
Tel: 01803 862174   Fax: 01803 865385

Map Ref: 31
A381, A384, A38
see Photo opposite

Find a warm welcome in relaxing surroundings all year round in this historic 600 year old stone building with cobbled drive and coach arch leading into the delightful walled garden. It is a rural haven, just four minutes walk from Totnes town centre and riverside. Luxurious and cosy cottage style rooms are all en-suite with CTV, radio-alarms, hair dryer and beverage tray. Licensed. Own Parking. Huge breakfast menu, (traditional, vegetarian, continental and special diets). Conservatory leisure lounge with whirlpool spa. Speciality golf breaks. No smoking indoors. Featured on the Holiday programme (BBC TV).

B & B £27-£48pp, C-Cards MC VS, Rooms 1 single, 2 twin, 2 double, 5 family, all en-suite, No smoking, Children welcome, Guide dogs only, Open all year

The Old Forge at Totnes

Higher Torr Farm East Allington, Totnes TQ9 7QH
Mrs Helen Baker   Tel / Fax: 01548 521248
Email: Helen@hrtorr.freeserve.co.uk

Map Ref: 32
A381

Relax and unwind in a spacious comfortable old farmhouse, set in the South Devon hills, with panoramic views of Dartmoor. Richard and Helen Baker welcome you to their family home. Guests are encouraged to explore the farm and its neighbouring walkways and bridle paths. En-suite bedrooms each have tea/coffee making facilities, clock radio and colour television. Guests served full English breakfast in private lounge/dining room. Ample parking for cars and boats. Central to Dartmouth/Salcombe, sandy beaches and market town of Kingsbridge.

B & B £20-£25pp, Rooms 1 twin, 1 double, both en-suite,
Children welcome, No dogs, Closed Xmas

Orchard House Horner, Halwell, Totnes TQ9 7LB
Helen Worth   Tel: 01548 821448
Web: www.orchard-house-halwell.co.uk

Map Ref: 33
A381

Tucked away in a rural hamlet of the South Hams, between Totnes and Kingsbridge, Orchard House lies beneath an old cider orchard, a fifteen minute drive from the coast and Dartmoor. It offers superb accommodation, all bedrooms are en-suite and spacious with colour television, radio, tea and coffee making facilities and beautiful furnishings. Guests here have their own sitting room with a log fire in winter. Breakfasts are generous and varied using local produce when possible. There is a large mature garden and plenty of parking. ETC 5 Diamonds, Silver Award.

B & B £20-£23pp, Rooms 2 double, 1 twin/family, all en-suite, No smoking,
Children over 3, No dogs, Closed Nov to Feb

The Red Slipper Stoke Gabriel, Totnes TQ9 6RU
Clive & Pam Wigfall
Tel / Fax: 01803 782315

Map Ref: 34
A385

The Red Slipper is a small friendly licensed establishment appointed to a high standard, located in the centre of a picturesque and peaceful village on the River Dart. The attractive en-suite bedrooms (mainly on the ground floor), have remote control colour television, clock/radio, hair dryer, tea/coffee making facilities, and sweets. A sheltered courtyard garden is available all day. Dinner available on request. From Thursday to Saturday an A'la Carte menu is offered using fresh produce. Guests may enjoy traditional Sunday lunches. Parking is available.

B & B from £24.50pp, Dinner from £12.50, Rooms 3 twin, 1 double, 1 family, all en-suite,
Restricted smoking, Children & dogs welcome, Open all year

Sunnycliffe Hotel Chapel Hill, Mortehoe, Woolacombe EX34 7EB
John & Jan Woodward   Tel: 01271 870597
Email: jj@sunnycliffe.freeserve.co.uk

Map Ref: 35
A361

Sunnycliffe Hotel is a small award winning quality hotel set above a picturesque Devon cove on the Heritage coast. All of the bedrooms are en-suite and they have magnificent sea views. They are well equipped with colour television/video, tea/coffee making facilities. A five course dinner with a varied menu prepared from fresh local produce, is offered. There are plenty of lovely walks through hidden valleys, coastal paths where the countryside greets the sea in breathtaking scenic beauty. Regret no children or pets. Brochure available.

B & B from £25pp, C-Cards MC VS, Dinner £15, Rooms 6 double, 2 twin,
Restricted smoking, No children or dogs, Closed Nov to Feb

Dorset

Dorset is largely Hardy's Wessex. There is hardly a part of the county that does not appear, although under a pseudonym, in one of Thomas Hardy's books. In the north of the county a region of sandy heathland stretches from the border with Hampshire to the centre of Dorset, while a range of chalk downs rolls to the east towards Salisbury Plain. In the south, the coast consists of a narrow broken ridge of chalky cliffs, the most easterly known as the Purbeck Hills.

Weymouth to the east lying behind a curving bay, is an elegant resort made famous by George III, who popularized the seaside as a leisure pursuit. The Isle of Portland, not strictly speaking an island, is attached to the mainland of Weymouth by a shingle bank created by the deposition of millions of pebbles through the process of long-shore drift. The bank encloses a lagoon known as the Fleet, a glorious haven for birds and a magnet for anglers. The view from the lighthouse, Portland Bill, is just spectacular, on the very edge of treacherous jagged cliffs.

The Dorset coast is renowned for its fossils, particularly around Lyme Regis, a lovely late Georgian seaside town favoured by the novelist Jane Austen, and the Cobb, the historic harbour wall was also the setting for John Fowles' The French Lieutenant's Woman. Further to the east is West Lulworth famous for Lulworth Cove, a truly enchanting circular bay, virtually surrounded by high cliffs. The whole area around West Lulworth, a picturesque village of thatched cottages, is wonderful walking country. Swanage is a medieval fishing village that developed into a fine seaside holiday resort with the coming of the railway. Its setting is superb against the Purbeck Hills, with the wide sweep of the bay in front. The Purbeck Ridge offers a spectacular panorama of Poole harbour. Poole is set on Britain's largest natural harbour, once the base for smugglers and buccaneers, now the home port of hosts of pleasure craft, particularly yachting. Brownsea Island within Poole harbour is a five hundred acre island of heath and woodland with glorious views of the Dorset coast. The island includes a two hundred acre nature reserve leased to the Dorset Wildlife Trust, a haven for a wide variety of wildlife including the red squirrel. Bournemouth, with a long sandy beach is a fine shopping centre, attracting visitors from a wide area. The public gardens, stretching from the sea into the centre of the town are splendid. Bournemouth is also gaining a reputation among the youth for its varied nightlife, almost to

Dorset's Heritage Coast (STB)

rival Brighton's. Nearby Christchurch is an alternative base from which to explore the area and its beautiful priory with both Norman and Tudor architecture is definitely a site of interest.

The National Trust cares for much of coastal Dorset. The heathland behind Studland beach is a National Nature Reserve, particularly interesting in winter because of its large variety of over-wintering birds. The Studland peninsular is part of the large Corfe Castle estate. The Castle itself is one of the most impressive ruins in the country, strategically placed in the only gap in the chalk ridge which cuts Purbeck off. This important royal castle was besieged twice during the civil war, but seized and destroyed in the second attempt in 1646 by the Parliamentary forces.

The county town of Dorchester is built on the site of a Roman town, with the nearby ancient Neolithic henge, the Maumbury Rings, being used in Roman times as an amphitheatre. The town boasts some fine Georgian buildings and the High Street has a particularly impressive variety of town houses. The Shire Hall preserves the old county court as a memorial to the Tolpuddle Martyrs who were tried here in 1834. Thomas Hardy lived and worked in Dorchester and his novel, The Mayor of Casterbridge, so brilliantly describes life in the town during the nineteenth century. To the north is Cerne Abbas, overlooked by the extraordinary prehistoric hill-carving of the Cerne Giant, a naked man carrying a club, and believed to be associated with pagan fertility rites, although there is still much dispute as to his true origins.

PLACES TO VISIT

This is a small selection of interesting places to visit. Many more are listed in our annual guide to Museums, Galleries, Historic Houses & Sites (see page 448)

Athelhampton House and Gardens
Athelhampton, Dorchester
Thomas Hardy was a frequent visitor here, one of the finest fifteenth century houses in Britain with magnificently furnished rooms and Grade I gardens including the world famous topiary pyramids.

Brewers Quay and Timewalk Journey
Weymouth
Travel back 600 years and discover Weymouth's history with Spanish Galleon and Georgian ballroom with a speciality shopping village and craft centre and Courtyard Restaurant.

Compton Acres Gardens
Poole
Ten seperate world gardens overlooking Poole Harbour, including a Spanish Water Garden, Egyptian Court Garden and now a Sensory Sculpture Garden.

Corfe Castle
Wareham
The castle was built in the eleventh century on a steep hill. Many fine Norman and early English feautures have survived to this day. Visitors can see the remains of the eleventh century enclosure and hall and an early twelfth century great tower.

Dorset County Museum
Dorchester
Winner of Best Museum of Social History Award 1998, displays Dorset's history from the earliest times with wildlife, geography and famous figures.

Dorset

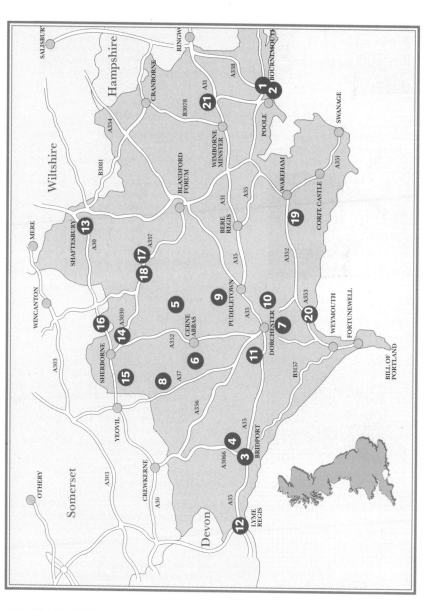

The Blue Map References should be used to locate B & B properties on the pages that follow

Gervis Court Hotel 38 Gervis Road, Bournemouth BH1 3DH

Alan & Jackie Edwards   Tel: 01202 556871   Fax: 01202 467066
Email: enquiries@gerviscourthotel.co.uk   Web: www.gerviscourthotel.co.uk

Map Ref: 1
A338

Gervis Court Hotel is a charming, detached Victorian villa, standing in its own grounds amongst the pine trees. The bedrooms are comfortably furnished and well equipped. For those who prefer to avoid stairs, there are some bedrooms on the ground floor. It is a short walk to the beach, shops, theatres, clubs and conference centre. There is a wide choice of restaurants, pubs and clubs within a few minutes stroll. Gervis Court is ideally located for exploring Bournemouth, Poole, the New Forest and the beautiful Dorset Coast.

B & B £20-£30pp, C-Cards MC VS, Rooms 1 single, 2 family, 2 twin, 8 double,
No smoking, Children welcome, No dogs, Open all year

Rosemount 32 Bryanstone Road, Talbot Woods, Bournemouth BH3 7JF

Mary Barrett   Tel: 01202 462729
Email: rosemount@dandenong32.freeserve.co.uk   Web: www.dandenong32.freeserve.co.uk

Map Ref: 2
A347

Stay a while in this lovely Edwardian house and not only enjoy the warm atmosphere and good food, but also the beautiful sights Dorset has to offer. The seafront and the New Forest National Park are a short drive away and Bournemouth University is within walking distance. We provide holiday makers and business people with a very high standard of cleanliness, decor and modern comfortable furnishings. The bedrooms are fully en-suite with colour television, tea and coffee making facilities available.

B & B from £17.50pp, Rooms 3 single (one en-suite), 1 twin en-suite, 1 double en-suite,
No smoking, Children over 10, No dogs, Closed Xmas day

Britmead House 154 West Bay Road, Bridport DT6 4EG

Alan & Louisa Hardy   Tel: 01308 422941   Fax: 01308 422516
Email: britmead@talk21.com   Web: www.britmeadhouse.co.uk

Map Ref: 3
A35

Britmead House, which may be found in a pleasant location just a short walk from West Bay Harbour, is a licensed hotel with a reputation for friendliness and high standards. The bedrooms are individually styled, and they are well equipped with many extras. The lounge and dining room are both south west facing, and they look across the garden and to the countryside beyond. The famous Chesil Beach and the Dorset Coastal Path are nearby, and for those who wish, there is also swimming, golf, fossil hunting, seafishing and walking. Private car parking.

B & B £22-£32pp, C-Cards MC VS, Rooms 3 double, 2 twin, 2 family, all en-suite,
Restricted smoking, Children welcome, Dogs by arrangement, Open all year

Spray Copse Farm Lee Lane, Bradpole, Bridport DT6 4AP

Stuart & Ginnie Stacey   Tel: 01308 458510   Fax: 01308 421015   Mobile: 07850 300044
Email: spraycopse@lineone.net   Web: www.spraycopsefarm.com

Map Ref: 4
A35

Spray Copse Farm is an attractive house built of local ham Stone in a traditional Dorset style, with beamed ceilings, inglenook fireplaces and wood burning stoves. It is set in peaceful surroundings with 3 acres of gardens, incorporating a lake and the River Asker as well as dovecotes, rare breed chickens and ponies in the paddock. The rooms are large and well equipped with television/Sky Digital and tea/coffee making facilities. Your breakfast/dinner is served in the large conservatory and consists of local produce and free-range eggs together with homemade jam and marmalade.

B & B £25-£30pp, Dinner from £18, Rooms 1 single, 1 double, 1 twin, 1 family,
all en-suite/private, No smoking, Children over 4, Dogs not in bedrooms, Closed Nov to Mar

Lamperts Cottage, Sydling St Nicholas, near Cerne Abbas

Holyleas House Buckland Newton, Dorchester DT2 7DP

Tia Bunkall Tel: 01300 345214 Fax: 01305 264488 Mobile: 07968 341887
Email: tiabunkall@holyleas.fsnet.co.uk

Map Ref: 5
A352

The family Labrador, Holly, will greet you to this warm and friendly country house which stands in lovely walled gardens. Buckland Newton is a peaceful village between Sherborne and Dorchester surrounded by rolling hills. The area is superb for walking, visiting historic houses, gardens and the coastline. The rooms are beautifully decorated with fine views. The guests' sitting room has a log fire in winter where you can relax with a good book. Breakfast includes free range eggs, home made marmalade. Vegetarians catered for. Good pubs nearby for suppers. ETC 4 Diamonds, Silver Award.

B & B from £22.50pp, Rooms 1 single, 1 twin, 1 double, all en-suite/private, No smoking, Children & dogs welcome, Closed Xmas & New Year

Rew Cottage Buckland Newton, Dorchester DT2 7DN

Annette & Rupert McCarthy
Tel / Fax: 01300 345467

Map Ref: 5
A35, A352

Visitors to Rew Cottage are assured of a warm welcome. Peacefully located in the heart of Thomas Hardy country, the cottage is surrounded by farmland with lovely views on all sides. This is an ideal centre for walking or touring, as it is within easy reach of Sherborne, Dorchester and the sea. The bedrooms are comfortably furnished and equipped with television and tea/coffee making facilities, with two adjacent private bathrooms. There is a good choice of breakfasts including traditional, with homemade marmalades and preserves. Nearby are some attractive pubs and restaurants.

B & B £22.50-£26pp, Rooms 1 twin, 1 double, Restricted smoking, Children by arrangement, Dogs by arrangement, Closed mid-Dec to mid-Jan

Lamperts Cottage Sydling St Nicholas, Cerne Abbas, Dorchester DT2 9NU

Nicky Willis Tel: 01300 341659 Fax: 01300 341699
Email: nickywillis@teso.net

Map Ref: 6
A37
see Photo on page 131

A stream runs in front of this 16th century thatched listed cottage. It is situated in a peaceful village in the beautiful Sydling Valley. The bedrooms are prettily decorated with dormer windows under the eaves. Central heating and tea/coffee makers. Breakfast is served in the dining room which has an Inglenook fireplace, bread oven and beams. West Dorset is an ideal touring centre with beaches. The countryside is excellent for walking with footpaths over chalk hills and through hidden valleys. This is the perfect place for those seeking peace and tranquility.

B & B from £21pp, C-Cards, Rooms 1 twin, 1 double, 1 family, Restricted smoking, Children over 8, Dogs by arrangement, Open all year

Higher Came Farm House Higher Came, Dorchester DT2 8NR

Lisa Bowden Tel / Fax: 01305 268908
Email: highercame@eurolink.ltd.net

Map Ref: 7
A354

This is a beautiful 17th century farmhouse peacefully nestling in the heart of Dorset's Hardy country. It is within easy reach of Dorchester, Weymouth and Bridport. The walking here is superb, as is fishing, sailing and sight seeing. This traditional farmhouse has spacious attractively furnished bedrooms, an en-suite family room, and two double rooms with private bathrooms. All have television tea/coffee making facilities and hairdryers. We offer home cooked breakfast using local produce. Relax in our comfortable residents lounge or stroll in the large gardens. We are open all year. ETC 4 Diamonds.

B & B £25-£32pp, C-Cards MC VS, Rooms 1 double/twin en-suite, 1 double/twin, 1 double, both pb, Restricted smoking, Children welcome, Dogs by arrangement, Open all year

Brambles Woolcombe, Melbury Bubb, Dorchester DT2 0NJ
Anita & Andre Millorit
Tel: 01935 83672   Fax: 01935 83003

Map Ref: **8**
A37
see Photo on page 135

Brambles is a delightful thatched cottage set in peaceful countryside near the historic towns of Dorchester and Sherborne, and a short drive to the coast. Beautifully appointed and well equipped, it offers every comfort, and a friendly welcome. The pretty bedrooms always have fresh flowers, also colour television and tea/coffee making facilities. There is a wide choice of breakfast, including traditional, continental, vegetarian or fruit platter. There are many places of interest to visit and walks to explore. Parking within the grounds. Special rates for longer stays.

B & B £20-£25pp, Dinner available, Rooms 2 single, 1 twin en-suite, 1 double en-suite, No smoking, Children welcome, No dogs, Closed Xmas & New Year

Muston Manor Piddlehinton, Dorchester DT2 7SY
Mr & Mrs O B N Paine
Tel: 01305 848242

Map Ref: **9**
B3143

Originally built in 1609 by the Churchill family, Muston Manor remained in their ownership until bought by the present owners, the Paine family in 1975. The house stands in five acres, surrounded by farmland in the peaceful valley of Piddle. Here there are many good pubs serving excellent food. The bedrooms are large warm and comfortable, and well furnished. They are centrally heated and they provide tea/coffee making facilities. For guests' enjoyment, there is a heated swimming pool in Summer. For those who like walking, there is an excellent network of footpaths.

B & B from £22pp, Rooms 2 double, 1 en-suite, No smoking, Children over 10, Dogs by arrangement, Closed Nov to Feb

Lower Lewell Farmhouse West Stafford, Dorchester DT2 8AP
Marian Tomblin
Tel: 01305 267169

Map Ref: **10**
A35, A352

A 17th century farmhouse authentically improved and situated among a patchwork of fields in rolling Dorset countryside. Reputed to be Talbothays Dairy from Thomas Hardy's 'Tess of the D'Urbervilles'. Built in Portland stone under a red tiled roof with a Victorian brick and slate extension, this is a homely farmhouse with beams, log fires and plenty of space. Hearty breakfasts from the farmhouse kitchen are served at separate tables in the dining room with inglenook fireplace. There are good local pubs offering snacks and restaurant meals.

B & B from £20pp, Rooms 1 twin, 1 double, 1 family, Open all year

Churchview Guest House Winterbourne Abbas, Dorchester DT2 9LS
Michael & Jane Deller   Tel / Fax: 01305 889296
Email: stay@churchview.co.uk   Web: www.churchview.co.uk

Map Ref: **11**
A35

Our 17th century Guest House noted for warm, friendly hospitality, traditional breakfasts and delicious evening meals, makes an ideal base for exploring beautiful West Dorset. Our character bedrooms are comfortable, well appointed and include televisions and hospitality trays. Meals taken in our period dining room feature local produce, cream and cheeses. Relaxation is provided by two attractive lounges and licenced bar. Your hosts will give every assistance with local information on attractions, walks and touring to ensure you of a memorable stay.

B & B £24-£31pp, C-Cards MC VS, Dinner from £14, Rooms 1 single, 3 twin, 4 double, 1 family, all en-suite/private, No smoking, Children over 5, Dogs welcome, Closed Xmas & New Year

Rashwood Lodge Clappentail Lane, Lyme Regis DT7 3LZ

Mrs Diana Lake
Tel: 01297 445700

Map Ref: 12
A35, A3052

Rashwood Lodge is an unusual octagonal house located on the Western hillside with views over Lyme Bay. Just a short walk away is the coastal footpath and Ware Cliff famed for its part in 'The French Lieutenant's Woman'. The bedrooms have their own private facilities. There is an additional twin room for extra family members. The rooms each have colour television and tea/coffee making facilities, they enjoy their south facing aspect, overlooking a large and colourful garden which is set in peaceful surroundings. A golf course is one mile away.

B & B £23-£27pp, Rooms 2 double, 1 twin, 1 en-suite, 2 private bathrooms, No smoking, Children over 4, Dogs by arrangement, Closed Nov to Feb

The Red House Sidmouth Road, Lyme Regis DT7 3ES

Tony & Vicky Norman Tel / Fax: 01297 442055
Email: red.house@virgin.net Web: www.SmoothHound.co.uk/hotels.redhous2.html

Map Ref: 12
A35, A3052, B3165

The Red House was built in 1928 for a famous maritime inventor, it commands wonderful views along the Dorset Coast over Golden Cap. Set in mature grounds and adjacent to open countryside, it is within walking distance of the town centre and harbour. The well appointed bedrooms have en-suite facilities, central heating, shaver points, television, radio, fridge and tea/coffee making facilities. Lyme Regis, with its ancient Cobb harbour, remains unspoilt, yet it offers a wide range of activities. The rich scenery and pretty villages make touring a delight.

B & B £20-£27pp, C-Cards MC VS, Rooms 1 double, 2 twin, all en-suite, No smoking, Children over 8, No dogs, Closed November to March

Cliff House Breach Lane, Shaftesbury SP7 8LF

Diana & David Pow Tel / Fax: 01747 852548 Mobile: 07990 574849
Email: dianaepow@aol.com Web: cliff-house.co.uk

Map Ref: 13
A30, A350

Cliff House is a fine example of a spacious Grade II listed property. It stands in an acre of walled, mature gardens, and it is within pleasant walking distance of the ancient Saxon hilltop town of Shaftesbury. A good choice of delicious English breakfasts is offered, which include homemade jams using fruit from the garden. The bedrooms are peaceful, they have large en-suite bathrooms, televisions and tea/coffee making facilities. An ideal position for touring the countryside and country houses. There are good pubs and restaurants locally.

B & B £27.50-£30pp, Rooms 2 twin, all en-suite, No smoking, Children over 5, No dogs, Closed Xmas

Munden House Mundens Lane, Alweston, Sherborne DT9 5HU

Sylvia & Joe Benjamin Tel: 01963 23150 Fax: 01963 23153 Mobile: 07971 846246
Email: sylvia@mundenhouse.demon.co.uk Web: www.mundenhouse.demon.co.uk

Map Ref: 14
A3030

Originally Mundens was a small complex of stone cottages, dating back more than 300 years, and it was converted around 1850 into a farmhouse. The bedrooms all have their own character. They are generously equipped, and display some appealing antique pieces which compliment the individual themes. A light, airy drawing room has outstanding views over the Blackmore Vale leads into the dining room with its lofty beamed ceiling, original walls and 300 year old fireplace. In the heart of Thomas Hardy country, Munden House is the perfect base from which to explore Dorset.

B & B £32.50-£45pp, C-Cards MC VS, Rooms 4 double, 2 twin, 1 family, all en-suite, No smoking, Children welcome, No dogs, Open all year

Brambles, near Dorchester

Heartsease Cottage North Street, Bradford Abbas, Sherborne DT9 6SA
Robin & Wendy Dann Tel / Fax: 01935 475480   Mobile: 07929 717019
Email: heartsease@talk21.com

Map Ref: 15
A30

'Heartsease' describes our cottage better than any brochure. This delightful cottage, in old honey coloured stone and slate, dates back to 1750. There is a huge conservatory which looks out onto an idyllic garden and a beautiful Dorset village lane. Guests here have their own sitting room. The bedrooms are individually themed, Victorian, Farmhouse and Nautical. There is a large choice of breakfasts and dinners, the kind that you would love to have at home but never have enough time.

B & B from £22pp, Dinner from £13, Rooms 1 double, 2 twin, en-suite or private bathroom, Restricted smoking, Children over 8, No dogs, Open all year

The Old Vicarage Sherborne Road, Milborne Port, Sherborne DT9 5AT
Jorgen Kunath and Anthony Ma Tel: 01963 251117 Fax: 01963 251515
Email: theoldvicarage@milborneport.freeserve.co.uk Web: www.milborneport.freeserve.co.uk

Map Ref: 16
A30

Built by the Lord of The Manor, the Old Vicarage may be found situated on the edge of the village. It overlooks open country, towards the Sherborne Castle Estate. The historic town of Sherborne is intriguing, so are the many houses and gardens in the area. It's ideal for hiking, cycling, golf and walking. The Old Vicarage is spacious and elegantly furnished with antiques. At weekends the former owners of a highly acclaimed London restaurant serve delicious food, ask for sample menu. There is an excellent pub/restaurant a stroll away.

B & B from £29pp, C-Cards MC VS AE, Dinner from £22, Rooms 1 single, 3 double, 2 twin, 1 family, all en-suite, Restricted smoking, Children over 5, Dogs in coach house, Closed Jan

Fiddleford Millhouse Fiddleford, Sturminster Newton DT10 2BX
Jennifer & Anthony Ingleton
Tel: 01258 472786

Map Ref: 17
A357

Fiddleford Millhouse is a magical Grade I listed mill/manor house of great architectural interest with a lovely garden running down to the river Stour in a secluded location. It is a beautifully furnished and decorated home. There are three large bedrooms for guests, one with a half tester bed and 16th century moulded plaster ceiling and its own bathroom, one large bedroom with a king size four poster and one pretty double bedroom. Central heating, television and tea/coffee in all bedrooms. Nearby are good pubs. Ideally situated for beautiful walks.

B & B from £20pp, Rooms 3 double, 1 en-suite, No smoking, Children over 12, Dogs by arrangement, Open all year

Stourcastle Lodge Goughs Close, Sturminster Newton DT10 1BU
Jill & Ken Hookham-Bassett Tel: 01258 472320   Fax: 01258 473381
Email: enquiries@stourcastle-lodge.co.uk Web: www.stourcastle-lodge.co.uk

Map Ref: 18
B3092

Built in 1732 this residence offers very high standards and quality throughout. The bedrooms have impressive Victorian bedsteads, stencilled borders, antique furniture and modern well equipped bathrooms some with whirlpool baths. Peacefully situated down a lane yet moments from the town centre. Oak beams, log fires and views of the lovely garden from every room. Jill is a gold medalist chef, so with dishes like baked poussin with creamy curry sauce followed by boozy bread and butter pudding, this is an excellent place to both stay and eat.

B & B £32-£39pp, C-Cards MC VS, Dinner from £19.50, Rooms 1 twin, 4 doubles, all en-suite, Restricted smoking, No children or dogs, Open all year

West Coombe Farmhouse Coombe Keynes, Wareham BH20 5PS
Rachel & Peter Brachi Tel: 01929 462889 Fax: 01929 405863
Email: west.coombe.farmhouse@barclays.net Web: www.westcoombefarmhouse.co.uk

Map Ref: 19
B3071

West Coombe Farmhouse is a restored Georgian farmhouse, it stands in the delightful Dorset village of Coombe Keynes which is close to Lulworth Cove. The coastline is beautiful and there are many lovely walks to enjoy. There is a wealth of historic houses to visit, beautiful gardens and pretty villages to explore. In Summer unwind in the garden, in winter, linger by the open fire in the sitting room. There are three attractively presented bedrooms for guests. Some excellent country pubs and restaurants closeby serve delicious suppers.

B & B £20-£27.50pp, Rooms 1 single, 1 twin, 1 double, most en-suite,
No smoking, Children over 12, No dogs, Closed Xmas

Long Coppice Bindon Lane, East Stoke, Wareham BH20 6AS
Sarah Lowman Tel: 01929 463123
Email: Sarah@long-coppice.freeserve.co.uk

Map Ref: 19
A352

Long Coppice is situated in a peaceful country lane one and a half miles from the village of Wool. We are ideally situated for those who wish to relax in rural surroundings, and are within easy reach of local attractions, beaches, coastal path and cycle routes. We have eight acres of garden, woodlands and meadows, a haven for wildlife, and many species of birds visit us. Our rooms are spacious and comfortably furnished, the family room has direct access to the garden. For evening meals there are good pubs nearby.

B & B from £20pp, Rooms 1 twin, 1 family, both en-suite, No smoking,
Children welcome, Dogs by arrangement, Closed Xmas

Dingle Dell Church Lane, Osmington, Weymouth DT3 6EW
Joyce & Bill Norman Tel / Fax: 01305 832378
Email: Norman.dingledell@btinternet.com

Map Ref: 20
A353

Dingle Dell lies down a quiet lane at the edge of this charming village, a mile from the coast. Set back among old apple trees in its own lovely garden, with roses covering the mellow stone walls, it provides a peaceful spot to relax, and a pleasant base from which to explore the many local attractions, including beautiful coastal and country footpaths. Large, attractive rooms overlook gardens and countryside, providing comfort, colour television and tea/coffee facilities. Generous English breakfasts, or special diets by request. A warm personal welcome guaranteed.

B & B from £21pp, Rooms 1 twin, 1 double en-suite, No smoking,
No children or dogs, Closed Nov to Feb

Thornhill Holt, Wimborne BH21 7DJ
John & Sara Turnbull Tel: 01202 889434
Email: sct@gardener.com

Map Ref: 21
A31

Built in the 1930s Thornhill is a very attractive thatched family home. You are certain to receive a warm welcome here. The house is set in peaceful, rural surroundings, it has a large garden and hard tennis court which guests may use. The house is situated three and a half miles from Wimborne. It lies well away from the road and the location is ideal for exploring the coast, New Forest and Salisbury area. There are plenty of local pubs offering good food.

B & B from £22pp, Rooms 1 single, 1 twin, 1 double, No smoking,
Children over 14, No dogs, Open all year

Essex

To experience the real Essex, the visitor has to get away from the main roads. The southwest of the county has been, and is still being, slowly but surely swallowed up by London, and much of the county not yet consumed is nevertheless heavily influenced by the capital. The north bank of the Thames and the southern border of Essex from Tilbury to Southend-on-Sea is a complex array of container ports, oil and gas installations and industry of all descriptions, and yet six thousand acres of Epping Forest survives, all that is left of a sixty thousand acre royal hunting ground. At Hatfield Forest, near Bishop's Stortford, lies over a thousand acres of ancient woodland, remains of more of Essex's royal forests. This historic landscape has been designated a Site of Special Scientific Interest. There is a wealth of pollarded hornbeams and oaks supporting a wide variety of wildlife, wonderful walking country and coarse fishing on two lakes.

Colchester is a great centre for the holiday visitor and claims to be Britain's oldest town, and certainly it was there before the Romans established their legionary base and capital in 43AD. The Normans built a castle here in 1076, with Europe's largest Norman keep, which now houses an excellent museum. The town in fact possesses a number of first class museums including the intriguing Hollytrees Museum of toys and curios. For lovers of zoos, the Colchester Zoo covers over forty acres and houses many endangered species. At Halstead to the west is a magnificent eighteenth century weatherboarded watermill. Further west is Saffron Walden, a wonderful old market town with a wealth of historical and architectural interest, with many fascinating houses clustering round the largest parish church in Essex, the church of St Mary the Virgin, which was beautifully rebuilt in the 1500s. From medieval times until the eighteenth century this was the centre for growing the saffron crocus, hence the town's name. English Heritage cares for the magnificent Jacobean mansion at Audley End, just a mile from Saffron Walden. The house, completed in

Colchester Castle Museum seen from the park

1616, stands in glorious parkland landscaped by Capability Brown and includes an Adam bridge and temple. To the south is Great Dunmow, a pleasant old town with the strange tradition of awarding each leap year the Dunmow Flitch of bacon to idyllically married couples.

The county town of Chelmsford is based upon a town planned by the Bishop of London in 1199, although there was a much earlier settlement here, established on the Roman road between Colchester and London. With the development of the railway in 1843 the town swiftly grew as an industrial centre. The county can also boast two highly popular seaside resorts; Clacton-on-Sea has a seven mile stretch of sandy beach and a large number of holiday attractions, including the Living Ocean Aquarium with its sharks, rays and sealions, the Magic City indoor play centre for children and a pier. Southend-on-Sea, at the southern end of the coast, began life as a humble seaside village, only to blossom into an important resort with the arrival of the railway. The bracing sea air and comparatively low rainfall attracted hosts of daytrippers from London and there is much to do with parks, museums, all-the-fun-of-the-fair, restaurants, theatres and night clubs, plus excellent shopping.

However, the Essex coast is far from being just a bucket and spade region; Maldon, renowned for its barges grew prosperous on its barge traffic to London and now stages barge races. Goggeshal is a lovely old cloth and lace town and can claim in Paycocke's House probably the finest half-timbered house in England. Danbury, Essex's second highest spot gives spectacular views across the emotive Blackwater Estuary and Northey Island, a bird reserve and site for saltmarsh plants within the Estuary.

Essex is a bustling county of high activity, but there is much to attract the holiday maker. There is a wide choice of things to see and do and for the less active there are some lovely areas of quiet calm.

PLACES TO VISIT

This is a small selection of interesting places to visit. Many more are listed in our annual guide to Museums, Galleries, Historic Houses & Sites (see page 448)

Audley End House and Gardens
Audley End, Saffron Walden,
Built by the first Earl of Suffolk this Jacobean house has gardens designed by Capability Brown and a magnificent Great Hall with seventeenth century plaster ceilings, and furniture by Robert Adam.

Colchester Castle Museum
Colchester
The largest Norman Castle Keep in Europe with fascinating archaeological collections and an illustration of Colchester's early history.

Hedingham Castle
Halstead
A majestic Norman Castle built in 1140, home of the de Veres and visited by many famous monarchs of the past. A splendid banqueting hall and minstrels gallery.

Sir Alfred Munnings Art Museum
Dedham, Colchester
The home, studios and grounds where Sir Alfred Munnings KCVO lived and painted for 40 years. A large collection representing his life's work.

Essex

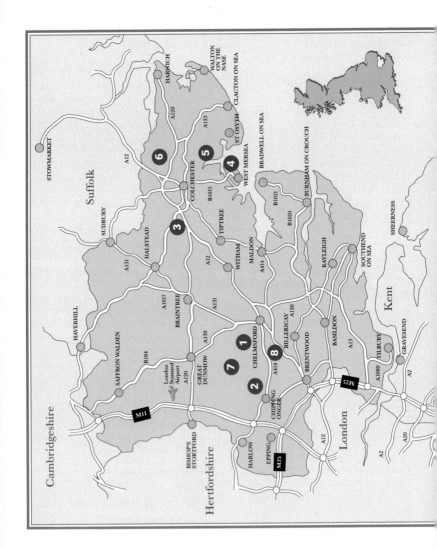

The Blue Map References should be used to locate B & B properties on the pages that follow

Fitzjohns Farmhouse Mashbury Road, Great Waltham, Chelmsford CM3 1EJ
Roslyn Renwick   Tel: 01245 360204/361224   Fax: 01245 361724   **Map Ref: 1**
Mobile: 07808 078834   Email: rosrenwick@aol.com   **A130**

This 13th century farmhouse is to be found surrounded by countryside, yet only 20 minutes drive from Stansted Airport. A timber framed home, with uneven floors and oak beams add to the charm of this lovely Essex Hall. Breakfast is served in the warmth of the kitchen, homemade bread and free range speckled eggs are on offer. There is a tennis court and a lovely garden with a pond for guests to enjoy. Suppers and lifts to the airport are offered by arrangement. This is a good area for walking, riding and fishing.

B & B £28-£35pp, Dinner from £12.50, Rooms 1 twin, 1 double, private bathroom,
No smoking, Children welcome, No dogs, Open all year

Diggins Farm Fyfield, Chipping Ongar CM5 0PP
Margaret Frost   **Map Ref: 2**
Tel: 01277 899303   Fax: 01277 899015   **M11, B184**

Diggins Farm is a fine, 16th century Grade II listed Essex farmhouse. It stands in 440 acres of arable land in a peaceful location, overlooking the Roding Valley. There are oak beams, and spacious, well equipped and tastefully decorated bedrooms. The farmhouse is well placed being convenient for Stansted Airport, mainline train and underground transport links. There are two golf courses and four fishing lakes nearby. For suppers, there are two good local pubs. Visitors to Diggins Farm may be assured of a warm welcome.

B & B from £25pp, Rooms 1 double, 1 twin, 1 family, most en-suite, No smoking,
Children over 12, No dogs, Closed Xmas & New Year

Old House Fordstreet, Aldham, Colchester CO6 3PH
Mrs Patricia Mitchell   **Map Ref: 3**
Tel / Fax: 01206 240456   **A12, A1124**

Old House dates from the 14th century, it has a long and varied history. There are oak beams, welcoming log fires, a two acre garden and ample parking. This comfortable family home provides well equipped accommodation, bedrooms have electric blankets, televisions and tea/coffee making facilities. Old House is only five miles west of Colchester, Britain's oldest recorded town with Roman walls, a Norman castle and museums. Harwich Ferry is just half an hour away. There are three pubs from which to choose within 150 yards.

B & B from £22.50pp, C-Cards MC VS, Rooms 1 single, 1 twin, 1 family, 1 en-suite,
2 private bathroom, Restricted smoking, Children welcome, No dogs, Open all year

Bromans Farm East Mersea, Colchester CO5 8UE
Ruth Dence   **Map Ref: 4**
Tel / Fax: 01206 383235   **B1025**

This 14th century farmhouse is just five minutes walk from the sea. Bromans Farm is a beautifully sunny house where guests may relax in the conservatory which overlooks the secluded garden. In winter, the log fire in the book lined sitting room is the perfect place to rest. Home baked bread is served at breakfast, which is perhaps followed by a day of wild walking, watching and listening to the Brent geese as they wheel through the Constable skies. There is a local restaurant and a pub ten minutes walk away.

B & B from £25pp, Rooms 1 double, 1 twin, both with private bathroom facilities,
Restricted smoking, Children welcome, Dogs by arrangement, Open all year

Garnish Hall, Margaret Roding, near Dunmow

Live & Let Live 2 Alma Street, Wivenhoe, Colchester CO7 9DL
Mrs Linda Tritton Tel: 01206 823100 Mobile: 07976 246082
Email: lindatritton@hotmail.com

Map Ref: 5
A133, A12

This is a Grade II listed early Victorian house, set in the heart of a conservation area, within yards of the quayside and a beautiful river walk. Your hostess is a keen cook and offers a comprehensive breakfast menu. Charming meals, available on request, are a speciality, or there are excellent pubs nearby. Tea making facilities and television are provided, and guests have use of a sitting room overlooking the river. The local car park is nearby. Beth Chattos Gardens and historic town of Colchester close by.

B & B from £23pp, Dinner from £12.50, Rooms 1 single, 1 twin, Restricted smoking, Children over 10, No dogs, Closed Xmas & New Year

May's Barn Farm May's Lane, off Long Road West, Dedham CO7 6EW
Mrs Jean Freeman Tel: 01206 323191
Email: maysbarn@talk21.com Web: www.mays.barn.btinternet.co.uk

Map Ref: 6
B1029

May's Barn Farm is the perfect place for those seeking absolute quiet and seclusion. The house is reached by a long track off the main road. It stands in 300 acres of farmland, with wonderful views across Dedham Vale, immortalised by the artist John Constable who was born nearby in the village of East Bergholt. The rooms are large, comfortable and traditionally furnished, a cosy sitting room warmed by a log fire invites guests to relax, the attractive walled garden may also be enjoyed. A full English breakfast is served.

B & B £21-£22.50pp, Rooms 1 double, 1 twin, 1 en-suite, 1 private, Restricted smoking, Children over 10, No dogs, Open all year

Garnish Hall Margaret Roding, Dunmow CM6 1QL
Anna Pitt Tel: 01245 231209 Fax: 01245 231224 Mobile: 07773 024415
Email: anna@garnishhallfsnet.co.uk

Map Ref: 7
A1060
see Photo opposite

Garnish Hall is a sixteenth century manor house which in former times was moated. Parts of the house were built in the 13th century. Situated on the A1060, the house is well placed for the Reid Rooms and Punch Bowl. There is a lecture room and a dining room to seat up to a dozen guests. The grounds include an Elizabethan walled garden where black swans, peacocks, geese and ducks wander freely. There is a hard tennis court with lights for guests' enjoyment, the property stands adjacent to a beautiful Norman church.

B & B from £27.50pp, Dinner from £15, Rooms 2 double, 1 family, all en-suite, No smoking, Children & dogs welcome, Closed Xmas

Yew Tree House Mill Green Road, Fryerning, Ingatestone CM4 0HS
Elizabeth & Tony Dickinson
Tel: 01277 352580

Map Ref: 8
M25, A12, B1002

The house nestles behind Yew hedges in peaceful countryside. Guests have their own lounge, with television, looking on to a secluded walled garden. Bedrooms are luxurious and beautifully decorated with tea/coffee making facilities. Elizabeth is a trained cook and enjoys serving interesting evening meals in the dining room which reflects her enthusiasm for cooking. Yew Tree House is five miles from the M25, and London is 30 minutes by train. Local places to visit include Ingatestone Hall, Hyde Hall, RHS Garden and other interesting nurseries and gardens.

B & B from £35pp, Dinner from £15, Rooms 2 double en-suite/private bathroom, Restricted smoking, Children over 12, No dogs, Closed Xmas & New Year

Gloucestershire

Few counties can compete with Gloucestershire in scenic beauty and entrancing small towns and villages, but then few counties can claim such attributes as the Cotswold Hills, the Forest of Dean and the Vales of Severn and Berkeley. The rolling grasslands of the Cotswolds, ideal for sheep farming, covers the glorious golden limestone which has been extensively quarried for centuries, providing the building material that has made the landscape so attractive. Dover's Hill, to the north of Chipping Campden, forms a natural amphitheatre on a spur of the Cotswolds, where the 'Cotswold Olympic Games' are held each June. The games established in 1612 by Robert Dover were revived in 1951. Chipping Campden itself is a fine town of impressive stone buildings, probably the grandest being the fourteenth century home of William Grevel, a prosperous wool merchant. Cirencester has arguably the finest 'wool' church in the Cotswolds, its ideal setting at the crossing of the Fosse Way and Ermin Way ensured its prominence and prosperity from Roman times.

To the west lies the Forest of Dean, probably the wildest part of Gloucestershire and an area exploited for iron and coal since Roman times, the whole region being a fine expanse of open heath and woodland criss-crossed with paths. The Dean Heritage Centre is well worth a visit with the Clearwell Caves, a network of miners tunnels, open to visitors. The world's largest collection of wildfowl covering over one hundred and fifty different species can be seen at Slimbridge Wildfowl and Wetlands Trust, which was founded by artist and naturalist Peter Scott in 1946. On the eastern bank of the River Severn lies the Vale of Berkeley, thousands of acres of low-lying land, a region of lovely lanes and hump-backed bridges overlooked by Berkeley Castle where Edward II was murdered in 1327.

Of course two great towns dominate the county: Gloucester and Cheltenham. Gloucester is a city of contrasts, from its fascinating medieval centre to its revitalised nineteenth century docks. The docks, once linked to the sea by the Gloucester-Sharpness Canal, now form an attractive business and leisure complex which includes the National Waterways Museum. It also boasts a magnificent Gothic Cathedral, built in 1089. Based upon a Norman abbey, its massive piers contrast with the delicate fourteenth century vaulting of the choir, which houses the largest stained glass window in England. This fine city has interest for everyone, and is one of the locations of the Three Choirs Festival, the oldest music festival in Europe. Gloucester's neighbour, Chelt-

Bibury in the Cotswolds (STB)

enham, is an elegant Regency spa and was transformed from a small spa village into a fashionable centre through the patronage of George III. The mineral spring was discovered here in 1715 by, according to legend, a flock of pigeons, on the site which is now Ladies College. Visitors are still able to taste the healing waters, now housed by the Pittville Pump Room. The Promenade and Montpellier Street are excellent shopping centres and the town can claim superb open spaces and gardens including Pittville Park, the Imperial Gardens and Montpellier Gardens. Nearby is Prestbury, the most haunted village in Britain, and also the location of Cheltenham Race Course. To the north is Tewksbury, a handsome medieval town with an abbey church, one of England's finest examples of Norman ecclesiastical architecture. The town is rich in lovely timber-framed buildings with a long and fascinating history and was the site of a decisive battle during the War of the Roses. Therefore the impressive town museum in Barton Street with details of all of the history is well worth a visit.

This is also a county of never to be forgotten gardens, including Rosemary Verey's Barnsley House, with its knot and herb gardens and world famous potager, an inspiration all year round. Hidcote Manor Garden near Chipping Campden must be one of the most delightful gardens in England, an 'Arts and Crafts' masterpiece created by the horticulturist Major Lawrence Johnston. Of a quite different character is Chedworth Roman Villa which was excavated in 1864 and is set in a glorious wooded combe. Alternatively is Westbury Court Garden, a formal water garden, the earliest of its kind in the country.

PLACES TO VISIT

This is a small selection of interesting places to visit. Many more are listed in our annual guide to Museums, Galleries, Historic Houses & Sites (see page 448)

Berkeley Castle
Berkeley
Home of the Berkeley family for 850 years and particularly famous for the dungeon where Edward II was gruesomely murdered in 1327.

Clearwell Caves Ancient Iron Mines
Royal Forest of Dean, Coleford
Iron ore has been mined here for over 3,000 years to form an incredible system of underground tunnels and chambers. Eight caverns are now open to the public with geological and mining displays.

Gloucester Cathedral
Gloucester
This Gothic Cathedral is the focus of the city with its perpendicular style and a Great Cloister with the oldest fan vaulting in the country.

National Waterways Museum
Gloucestershire Docks, Gloucester
A fascinating museum based within Gloucester Docks with a passenger boat taking visitors for both short and long trips down the canal.

Slimbridge Wildfowl and Wetlands Trust
Slimbridge

Set in 800 acres of varied wetland habitat where wildfowl can be observed in their natural environment with over 2,300 birds from 200 species.

Gloucestershire

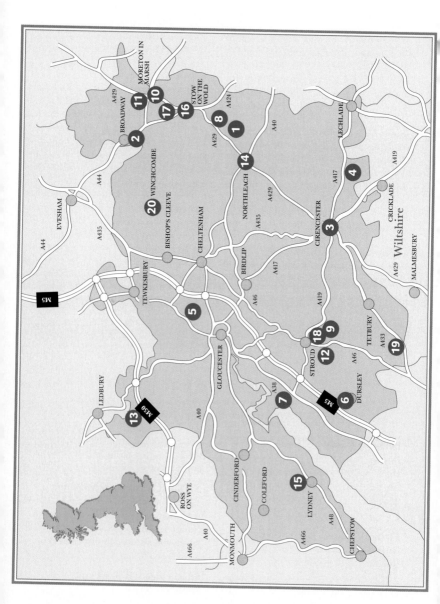

The Blue Map References should be used to locate B & B properties on the pages that follow

Church House Clapton-on-the-Hill, Bourton-on-the-Water GL54 2LG
Mrs Caroline Nesbitt
Tel: 01451 822532 Fax: 01451 822472

Map Ref: 1
A40, A429

Church House is a completely restored 17th century Cotswold stone family home in the hamlet of Clapton-on-the-Hill. It offers seclusion and privacy to visitors here, whilst commanding wonderful views across the Windrush Valley and to the tiny 12th century church of St James. There are beamed bedrooms with sloping ceilings, and guests enjoy a private drawing room, and a dining room which is open right to the eaves. There are good local pubs, and Church House is well located for visiting the attractions of the Cotswolds, Bath, Cheltenham and Stratford.

B & B £30-£35pp, Rooms 1 double, 1 twin, both en-suite, Restricted smoking, Children welcome, Dogs by arrangement, Closed Xmas

Upper Farm Clapton-on-the-Hill, Bourton-on-the-Water GL54 2LG
Helen Adams
Tel: 01451 820453 Fax: 01451 810185

Map Ref: 1
A429

A working family farm of 140 acres in a peaceful undiscovered Cotswold village two miles from the famous village of Bourton-on-the-Water. The listed 17th century farmhouse has been tastefully restored and offers a warm and friendly welcome with exceptional accommodation and hearty farmhouse fayre. The heated bedrooms are of individual character, some are en-suite with television and one is on the ground floor. From its hill position, Upper Farm enjoys panoramic views of the surrounding countryside, it makes an ideal base for touring, walking or simply relaxing. Brochure available.

B & B from £20pp, Rooms 3 double, 1 family, 1 twin, some en-suite, No smoking, Children over 5, Closed Dec to Feb

Burhill Farm Buckland, Broadway WR12 7LY
Pam Hutcheon Tel / Fax: 01386 858171
Email: burhillfarm@yahoo.co.uk Web: www.burhillfarm.co.uk

Map Ref: 2
B4632

A warm welcome awaits our guests at our mainly grass farm lying in the folds of the Cotswolds. Burhill Farm is just two miles south of Broadway. Both guests' rooms are en-suite and have television, hospitality trays and hairdryers. The Cotswold Way runs through the middle of the farm providing beautiful walks with much interest. There are many pretty, well known villages to visit nearby and Stratford-upon-Avon is about half an hour's drive. Come and enjoy the peace and quiet with breakfast on the patio if the weather is fine.

B & B from £22.50pp, Rooms 2 double, both en-suite, No smoking, Children welcome, No dogs, Closed Xmas

Ashwood House Snowshill, Broadway WR12 7JU
Jon & Sue Collett
Tel: 01386 853678

Map Ref: 2
A44

Enjoying spectacular views Ashwood House stands in a unique position at the head of the Snowshill valley. Jon and Sue Collett enjoy welcoming guests to this beautiful rural setting on the outskirts of the picturesque Cotswold village of Snowshill. The spacious double en-suite room is comfortably furnished and has television, radio, refrigerator and tea facilities. There is a separate staircase enabling guests to come and go as they please. Restaurants abound in nearby Broadway or the Snowshill Arms offers good bar meals and local ales.

B & B from £25pp, Rooms 1 double en-suite, No smoking, Children welcome, No dogs, Closed Xmas

Old Court Coxwell Street, Cirencester GL7 2BQ

Stephen & Anna Langton   Tel: 01285 653164   Fax: 01285 642803
Email: langton@cripps.f9.co.uk

Map Ref: 3
A419, A417, A429

Old Court was built for a rich wool-merchant in the early 18th century, in a quiet street behind the church in this delightful market town. Guests will find an old fashioned atmosphere, and are served breakfast in a panelled dining room, with a jacobean fireplace. A wide easy-to-climb staircase leads up to the four large guest bedrooms on the first floor. Elegant curtains and antique furniture create the comfort and style of a past era. Four cars may park in the private yard. Bath, Oxford and Stratford are about an hour's drive.

B & B from £32.50pp, C-Cards MC VS AE, Rooms 2 twin, 2 double (1 fourposter), all en-suite shower or bath, No smoking, Children & dogs welcome, Closed Xmas & New Year

The Masons Arms Meysey Hampton, Cirencester GL7 5JT

Andrew & Jane O'Dell   Tel / Fax: 01285 850164
Email: Jane@themasonsarms.freeserve.co.uk

Map Ref: 4
A417

Dating from the 17th century, The Masons Arms is situated on the southern fringe of the Cotswolds. It provides a haven for the traveller seeking peace. The bedrooms are comfortable and individually decorated, some with exposed stonework or beams, all are en-suite with tea/coffee, colour television and direct dial telephone. Ideal for visits to Cheltenham, Bath, Oxford and local beauty spots, with fishing, cycling and walks nearby. The heart of the Masons, is the bar, where local guests enjoy a convivial atmosphere. Excellent home cooked food with a varied menu with daily specials.

B & B from £30pp, Dinner from £8.95, Rooms 9 singles, 3 twin, 6 double, 2 family, all en-suite, Children welcome, Dogs by arrangement, Open all year

Frogfurlong Cottage Frogfurlong Lane, Down Hatherley GL2 9QE

Clive & Anna Rooke
Tel / Fax: 01452 730430

Map Ref: 5
A38

At Frogfurlong Cottage we have two self-contained suites offering tranquility and a truly 'get away from it all' break. The accommodation comprises a double en-suite with jacuzzi and direct access to the 30ft indoor heated swimming pool, and a twin/kingsize en-suite with shower. Both have colour television and tea/coffee tray facilities. The 18th century cottage, surrounded by fields, is situated in the green-belt area within the triangle formed by Cheltenham, Gloucester and Tewkesbury. Local attractions include the Cotswolds, the Malverns and the Forest of Dean.

B & B from £22pp, Dinner from £14.50, Rooms 2 double en-suite, No smoking, No children or dogs, Closed Xmas

Drakestone House Stinchcombe, Dursley GL11 6AS

Hugh & Crystal St John-Mildmay
Tel / Fax: 01453 542140

Map Ref: 6
M5, A38, B4060

Drakestone House stands in a beautiful and protected area of the glorious Cotswolds. The house is a fine example of an arts and crafts building, it is fascinating and furnished with beautiful pieces. There are log fires to welcome you, and gardens which are slowly being restored to enjoy. The atmosphere here is relaxed and informal whilst providing a warm comfort. Hugh and Crystal offer you generous hospitality and an enjoyable stay. There are plenty of lovely walks to enjoy and many places of interest nearby.

B & B from £31.50pp, Dinner from £17.50, Rooms 1 double with pb, 2 twin with 1 pb, No smoking, Children welcome, Dogs not in house, Closed Dec to Feb

Hunters Lodge, Minchinhampton

The Old School House Whittles Lane, Frampton-on-Severn GL2 7EB

Mrs Carol Alexander   Tel: 01452 740457   Fax: 01452 741721
Email: theoldies@f-o-s.freeserve.co.uk

Map Ref: 7
M5 J15

The Old School House is a charming, late 18th century house situated down a quiet lane off the village green which is the longest in England. The house with its beams, beautiful garden and orchards beyond is a most peaceful place to stay. The bedrooms in this comfortable home are delightfully presented and invite guests to sleep well. There are many famous attractions locally, the famous Slimbridge Wildfowl Trust, the ancient and beautiful Berkeley Castle, Gloucester Docks, the Spa town of Cheltenham, Roman Bath and Bristol. A choice of good eating places nearby.

B & B from £26.50pp, Rooms 1 double, 1 twin, both en-suite, Restricted smoking, Children over 10, Dogs by arrangement, Closed Xmas & New Year

Stepping Stone Rectory Lane, Great Rissington GL54 2LL

Roger & Sandra Freeman   Tel: 01451 821385   Fax: 01451 821008
Email: ststbandb@aol.com

Map Ref: 8
A424

Stepping Stone offers peace, tranquillity, country views and good walking. Set in a large garden at the edge of the picturesque village of Great Rissington. It is just three miles from the well known village of Bourton-on-the-Water and 200 metres from the Lamb Inn. There are two self contained units which offer quiet, comfortable accommodation with a sitting area, fridge and shower room. All the bedrooms have tea and coffee facilities, colour television and central heating. The house is well placed for exploring the Cotswolds.

B & B from £27.50pp, C-Cards MC VS, Rooms 1 single, 1 twin, 3 double en-suite, No smoking, Children over 12, Dogs by arrangement, Closed Xmas

Hunters Lodge Dr Browns Road, Minchinhampton GL6 9BT

Margaret & Peter Helm
Tel: 01453 883588   Fax: 01453 731449

Map Ref: 9
A419, A46
see Photo on page 149

Hunters Lodge is a beautifully furnished old Cotswold Stone house situated 650ft up in South Cotswolds on the edge of 600 acres of National Trust land - Minchinhampton Common. The spacious bedrooms have either en-suite or private bathrooms, colour television, tea/coffee making facilities. There is a separate lounge for guests, which leads into a delightful conservatory and large garden. This is an ideal centre for walking and touring the lovely Cotswold towns. A selection of local menus, maps and brochures is available, we can help to plan your daily itinerary. AA 5 Diamonds.

B & B £23-£25pp, Rooms 1 twin, 2 double/twin, all en-suite/private, No smoking, Children over 10, No dogs, Closed Xmas

Treetops Guest House London Road, Moreton-in-Marsh GL56 0HE

Elizabeth & Brian Dean   Tel / Fax: 01608 651036
Email: treetops1@talk21

Map Ref: 10
A44

A beautiful family home offering traditional bed and breakfast. There are six attractive bedrooms all have en-suite facilities, and two of them are on the ground floor and therefore suitable for disabled persons or wheelchair users. All rooms are comfortably furnished with either sofas or armchairs, television, radio, hair dryer and tea/coffee facilities. There is a sun lounge and a delightful secluded garden where guests are welcome to relax. Cots and high chair available. Ideally situated for exploring the Cotswolds. A warm and homely atmosphere awaits you here.

B & B £22.50-£25pp, C-Cards MC VS, Rooms 4 double, 2 twin, all en-suite, No smoking, Children & dogs welcome, Closed Xmas

New Farm Dorn, Moreton-in-Marsh GL56 9NS

Catherine Righton Tel: 01608 650782 Fax: 01608 652704 Mobile: 07712 919849
Email: cath.righton@amserve.net

Map Ref: 11
A429

Old farm house in hamlet one mile from Moreton-in-Marsh. Offering first class accommodation, very competitive terms. Lovely four poster and very pretty twin rooms, all spacious and en-suite, colour television, tea/coffee tray. Dining room has impressive fire place. Breakfast is served with hot crispy bread. There is a menu. Parking off road. Ideal for touring Cotswolds. Stratford 14 miles, Oxford 25 miles, Cheltenham 16 miles. Moreton has plenty of eating places for evening meals.

B & B from £20pp, Rooms 2 double, 1 twin, 1 family, all en-suite,
No smoking, Children over 8, No dogs, Open all year

The Laurels Inchbrook, Nailsworth GL5 5HA

Lesley Williams-Allen Tel / Fax: 01453 834021
Email: laurels@inchrook.fsnet.co.uk

Map Ref: 12
A46

The Laurels is a rambling old house with a warm atmosphere. Relax beside an open fire in the panelled study, play snooker or board games in the beamed lounge or take advantage of the licensed dining room where excellent home cooked meals are served. Enjoy the wildlife in the garden - many types of birds and other creatures which come to the feeding station by the stream. All bedrooms are en-suite, with television and tea/coffee making facilities. There is an outdoor heated swimming pool for guests' enjoyment. Self catering cottage available.

B & B from £20pp, Dinner from £12, Rooms 2 double, 2 twin, 3 family, all en-suite,
No smoking, Children & dogs welcome, Open all year

The Old Winery Welsh House Lane, Dymock, Newent GL18 1LR

Michael & Jo Kingham
Tel / Fax: 01531 890824

Map Ref: 13
M50 J2

The Old Winery, stands in a beautiful part of the country where the counties of Gloucestershire, Herefordshire and Worcestershire meet. The house enjoys fine views of undulating hills and vineyards, this is a perfect area for those who love country walks. Guests may sit out on the terrace, which is candlelit in the evenings, and enjoy the peace and quiet of this lovely location. The bedrooms here are very pretty, comfortable and well maintained, and are located in the converted grain barn. Much to see and do nearby.

B & B £30-£32pp, Dinner from £18, Rooms 1 twin en-suite,
No smoking, Children welcome, No dogs, Closed Xmas & New Year

Cotteswold House Market Place, Northleach GL54 3EG

Pauline & Frank Powell Tel / Fax: 01451 860493
Email: cotteswoldhouse@talk21.com Web: www.cotteswoldhouse.com

Map Ref: 14
A40, A429

Cotteswold House is a Grade II listed 400 year old Cotswold stone wealthy wool merchant's home with beamed ceilings, original panelling and Tudor archway. Relax in a luxury private suite or double or twin rooms each with private bathroom. All the rooms are spacious, elegant and well equipped. Enjoy traditional English food and a friendly welcome. Find us in the centre of this ancient market town of Northleach in the heart of the Cotswolds. Our house makes an ideal base from which to explore this lovely area.

B & B £25-£37.50pp, C-Cards MC VS, Rooms 1 luxury double suite, 1 double, 1 twin, all with pb,
No smoking, No children or dogs, Closed Xmas & New Year

Hope Cottage, Box, near Stroud

Northfield Cirencester Road, Northleach GL54 3JL

Pauline Loving   Tel / Fax: 01451 860427
Email: nrthfieldO@aol.com

Map Ref: 14
A429, A40

Detached family house in the country close to all services in the small market town of Northleach with its magnificent church, musical and countryside museums. Excellent centre for visiting lovely Cotswold villages. Easily reached by car are Cheltenham, Oxford, Cirencester, Stratford, Burford Wildlife Park, local golf course, fishing, Cotswold walks and horse riding. All rooms are en-suite, with central heating, television and tea/coffee trays and there is a log fire in the lounge. Large gardens to relax in or to enjoy a selection of freshly prepared evening meals. Brochure available on request.

B & B from £25pp, C-Cards MC VS, Dinner from £8, Rooms 2 double, 1 twin/family, all en-suite, No smoking, Children welcome, No dogs, Closed Xmas & New Year

Edale House Folly Road, Parkend, near Lydney, Royal Forest of Dean GL15 4JF

Christine & Alan Parkes   Tel: 01594 562835   Fax: 01594 564488
Email: edale@lineone.net   Web: www.edalehouse.co.uk

Map Ref: 15
A48, B4234

Edale House is a fine Georgian residence facing the cricket green in the village of Parkend at the heart of the Royal Forest of Dean. Once the home of local GP, Bill Tandy, author of 'A Doctor in the Forest'. The house has been tastefully restored to provide comfortable en-suite accommodation with every facility including tea/coffee equipment, television and hair dryer. Enjoy delicious, imaginative cuisine prepared by your Hosts and served in the attractive dining room. Within easy reach of Wye Valley. Riding, cycling, canoeing, walking, are all close to hand.

B & B £23-£28.50pp, C-Cards MC VS, Dinner from £13.50, Rooms 1 twin, 4 double, all en-suite, Restricted smoking, Children by arrangement, Dogs by arrangement, Closed New Year

The Limes Evesham Road, Stow-on-the-Wold GL54 1EJ

Helen & Graham Keyte
Tel / Fax: 01451 830034/831056

Map Ref: 16
A424

The Limes is a large Victorian, family house, established as bed and breakfast accommodation for over 30 years. It is pleasantly situated, with views over the fields and the attractive garden with an ornamental pool. The lovely bedrooms are spacious and are equipped with radio/alarms, tea/coffee making facilities and digital television. It is just a few minutes walk to the town centre. Car parking available. A choice of breakfast is offered, and vegetarian diets are catered for. Many guests from home and abroad return each year.

B & B from £21.50pp, Rooms 3 double, 1 family, 1 twin, 4 en-suite, 1 private, Children welcome, Dogs by arrangement, Closed Xmas

Windy Ridge Longborough, Stow-on-the-Wold GL56 0QY

Cecil J Williams   Tel: 01451 832328/830465   Fax: 01451 831489
Email: nick@windy-ridge.co.uk   Web: www.windy-ridge.co.uk

Map Ref: 17
A424

Windy Ridge is a small country estate, situated high in the Cotswold hills, overlooking the Evenlode Valley. This beautiful family home displays some wonderful features, mullioned windows, gables and Norfolk reed thatched roofs. Visitors here are offered generously furnished bedrooms and a large pine-panelled sitting room. The house is set in a prize winning garden. There is an outdoor heated swimming pool, tennis court, billiard/snooker room and a 10 acre arboretum, for guests' enjoyment. This is a wonderful area for exploration. There is a super pub a two minute walk away.

B & B from £40pp, Rooms 2 double, both en-suite, 1 double, with private bathroom, No smoking in bedrooms, Children over 15, No dogs, Open all year

Hope Cottage Box, Stroud GL6 9HD

Sheila & Garth Brunsdon   Tel: 01453 832076
Email: garth.brunsdon@virgin.net

Map Ref: 18
A46, A419
see Photo on page 152

For peace and tranquillity, this charming undiscovered village of Box ten miles from Cirencester is unrivalled. Hope Cottage is in an area of outstanding natural beauty and enjoys glorious Cotswold views. Here, you can savour the charm of this delightful country house, set in three acres with landscaped gardens and an outdoor heated pool for guests use in the summer. Very comfortable en-suite rooms all with king-size bed, settee, colour television and hospitality tray. Sumptuous traditional English breakfast. Excellent local restaurants and pubs. Strategic base for walking and touring.

B & B from £25pp, Rooms 2 double, 1 twin, all en-suite,
No smoking, Children welcome, No dogs, Closed Dec

Tavern House Willesley, Tetbury GL8 8QU

Mrs V Kingston   Tel: 01666 880444   Fax: 01666 880254
Email: tavernhousehotel@ukbusiness.com

Map Ref: 19
A433
see Photo opposite

Delightfully situated 17th century former Cotswold coaching inn, only 1 mile from Westonbirt Arboretum. Superb luxury bed & breakfast. All rooms en-suite with direct dial phone, colour TV, tea maker, hair dryer, trouser press, etc. Guests lounge. Charming secluded walled garden. Ample parking. Convenient for visiting Bath, Bristol, Gloucester, Cheltenham, Bourton-on-the-Water, Castle Combe. English Tourist Board Silver award winner for excellence. Bed & Breakfast of the year 1993. Colour brochure on request.

B & B from £32.50pp, Rooms 1 twin, 3 double, all en-suite,
Restricted smoking, Children over 10, No dogs, Open all year

Gower House 16 North Street, Winchcombe GL54 5LH

Sally & Mick Simmonds
Tel: 01242 602616   Mobile: 07811 387495

Map Ref: 20
B4632

Gower House, a 17th century town house, is conveniently situated close to the centre of Winchcombe, a small picturesque country town on the 'Cotswold Way'. It makes an ideal base for exploring the Cotswolds. Ramblers, cyclists and motorists all receive a warm welcome here. The three comfortable bedrooms have colour television, radio, tea/coffee making facilities and full central heating. There is also a lounge area with television and a secluded garden available for guests' use. Off street parking at the rear includes two garages.

B & B from £22.50pp, Rooms 2 twin/double en-suite, 1 double private bathroom,
Restricted smoking, No dogs, Closed Xmas & New Years Eve

Wesley House High Street, Winchcombe GL54 5LJ

Matthew Brown
Tel: 01242 602366   Fax: 01242 609046

Map Ref: 20
A46

This charming, half timbered house was built around 1435. Once a merchant's residence it has been restored, and now provides every comfort for guests who come here, yet it has lost none of the character of this medieval building. The cosy bedrooms are individually designed. The log fire in the lounge offers a warm welcome to those who choose to relax after a dinner in our renowned restaurant. The food here is exciting and innovative, with an emphasis on freshness of produce and clarity of taste. Ideal location for exploring the Cotswolds.

B & B £35-£40pp, Dinner from £15.50, Rooms 1 single, 2 twin, 4 double, all en-suite,
No smoking, Children welcome, No dogs, Open all year

Tavern House, Willesley, near Tetbury

Hampshire & The Isle of Wight

Hampshire is a county of remarkable scenic variations. The best is arguably in the east around Selborne and the far west in the New Forest region. The water meadows with its rivers providing some of the finest fly fishing in Britain and between the rolling chalk downs in the north and the gloriously scenic South Downs lies rich and fertile farm land. The coast is of course dominated by the two great ports, Southampton and Portsmouth. Southampton has a busy container and passenger port and its unique tidal system made it the premier port for the great 'Queens' liners. The Romans had a military port here, and in 1620 the Pilgrim Fathers set sail for the New World from Southampton, before putting in at Plymouth. Despite considerable bombing damage, much of the charming medieval town remains. The city is a thriving shopping centre and possesses some extremely good aviation and maritime museums. Portsmouth, a few miles along the coast, is a fascinating naval town which grew enormously during the eighteenth century. The Point, at the narrow entrance to the harbour is singularly picturesque and is a fine place to view the ships. Nelson's flagship 'Victory' is in dry dock at the entrance to the Royal Dockyard. The dockyard also contains the excellent Royal Navy Museum as well as the 'Mary Rose', Henry VIII's warship, raised from the seabed in 1982, the Mary Rose Museum, and the restored HMS Warrior, the first iron-clad warship, built in 1860.

The New Forest, the largest of William the Conqueror's hunting forests to survive, is a mixture of woodland, heath and open grazing. In the fifteenth century much of the timber from the forest was used in the building of ships for the navy. The National Trust controls 1,400 acres of Bramshaw Commons and Manorial Wastes, together with land at Hale Purliew and Hightown Common, all grazed by commoner's stock. This is splendid territory for walking, camping and picnics as there are no major hills with wild ponies and red deer having the right of way as they graze. The Ornamental Drive at Bolderwood is a perfect place to enjoy the woodland and see the deer from observation platforms. The New Forest Museum at Lyndhurst is well worth a visit with the town still retaining its ancient Verder's Court dealing with forest rights.

Selbourne, in the east of Hampshire, is a lovely holiday location for exploring the glorious hills and valleys and Selbourne Common, covering 240 acres and is an area of outstanding natural beauty. At the centre of Hampshire is Winchester, the capital of Wessex from

New Forest Ponies (STB)

the time of Alfred the Great, and the capital of England from the tenth century up until the Norman Conquest. Winchester became the main religious and commercial centre in medieval times, and the cathedral, the longest Gothic cathedral in Europe, has an outstanding Norman crypt and contains the finest set of medieval chantry chapels in the country, plus the grave of Jane Austen. The city is crammed with buildings of style and interest, many built with Georgian brick, the Royal Hampshire Regiment Museum being one of the most attractive. The thirteenth century great hall is the only surviving part of the castle and displays King Arthur's round table, an early medieval fake. To travel the length of the River Test, one of England's finest trout rivers is a joy. The Test valley contains a wealth of picturesque villages including the three Wallops, Over, Middle and Nether, renowned for their thatched cottages and lovely churches.

The Isle of Wight, reached by ferry either from Southampton, Portsmouth or Lymington is very much geared to attract the holiday visitor. There is much to see, the green whaleback hills on the south coast offer superb views, and at the western end of Tennyson Down are the spectacular chalk pinnacles known as The Needles. Yarmouth is a pretty port of whitewashed cottages, once an important medieval port and one of the numerous Solent Forts built by Henry VIII. Cowes, Shanklin, Sandown and Bembridge are all resorts with an individual character. The island has a distinctive Victorian atmosphere, and of course no visitor should leave without seeing Osborne House, Queen Victoria's retreat.

PLACES TO VISIT

This is a small selection of interesting places to visit. Many more are listed in our annual guide to Museums, Galleries, Historic Houses & Sites (see page 448)

Beaulieu Motor Museum
Beaulieu, Brockenhurst
Over 250 exhibits showing the history of motoring from 1896 within 75 acres of grounds, plus abbey ruins and a display of monastic life.

Breamore House
Breamore, Fordingbridge
Elizabethan manor house with fine collections, also Breamore Countryside Museum depicting the days when the village was self-sufficient.

Flagship Portsmouth
Portsmouth
This is home to some of the country's greatest flagships, such as King Henry VIII's Mary Rose, Lord Nelson's HMS Victory and mighty HMS Warrior.

Highclere Castle and Gardens
Highclere
A Victorian mansion, home to the Carnarvons, designed by Sir Charles Barry, set in parkland by 'Capability' Brown.

Jane Austen's House
Chawton
The house where Jane Austen wrote most of her work is now a museum dedicated to her life and works.

Winchester Cathedral
Winchester
A Norman Cathedral largely redesigned in the fourteenth century with the longest nave in Europe and superbly carved choir stalls. Also the burial place of many Saxon Kings.

Hampshire & The Isle of Wight

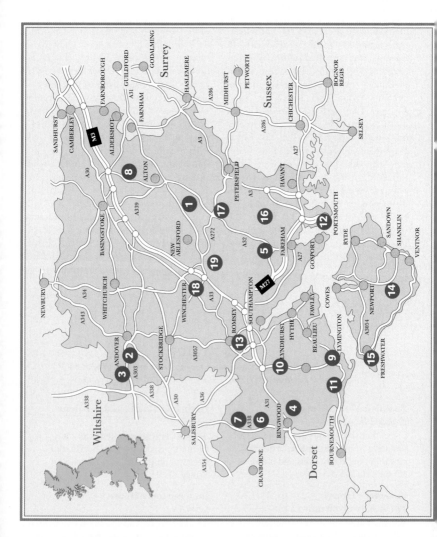

The Blue Map References should be used to locate B & B properties on the pages that follow

Thickets Swelling Hill, Ropley, Alresford SO24 0DA

David & Sue Lloyd-Evans
Tel: 01962 772467

Map Ref: 1
A31

Thickets is a spacious country house surrounded by a two acre garden, it has fine views across the rolling Hampshire countryside. There are two comfortable twin bedded rooms with private bath or shower room, tea/coffee making facilities are available. Guests have their own sitting room with television. A full English breakfast is served. Within a few minutes drive is Jane Austen's House, Winchester with its fine cathedral is just twenty minutes away. Salisbury, Chichester and The New Forest are all within easy reach. Heathrow Airport is one hour.

B & B from £22.50pp, Rooms 2 twin, both with private facilities, Restricted smoking,
Children over 10, No dogs, Closed Xmas & New Year

Broadwater Amport, Andover SP11 8AY

Carolyn Mallam   Tel / Fax: 01264 772240
Email: carolyn@dmac.co.uk Web: www.dmac.co.uk/carolyn

Map Ref: 2
A303

Broadwater is a delightful 17th century thatched cottage, set in a pretty garden in a peaceful village setting. Visitors here are offered quiet and cosy accommodation in a relaxed and friendly atmosphere. There is a private sitting room for guests' use, it has colour television, oak beams and a traditional fireplace. At breakfast home made bread is offered. Amport is ideally located being close to Stonehenge, also the A303, and it has easy access to airports and ferries. There is a flat which sleeps two or three, self catering or B&B.

B & B £25-£30pp, C-Cards MC VS, Rooms 2 twin en-suite,
No smoking in bedrooms, Children over 8, No dogs, Open all year

May Cottage Thruxton, Andover SP11 8LZ

Tom & Fiona Biddolph
Tel: 01264 771241   Fax: 01264 771770   Mobile: 07768 242166

Map Ref: 3
A303
see Photo on page 161

May Cottage dates back to 1740 and it is situated in the heart of this picturesque and tranquil village with an old Inn. It is a most comfortably furnished home, the bedrooms all offer en-suite/private bathrooms, colour television radio, and tea/coffee trays. Guests have their own sitting and dining rooms. This is an ideal base for visiting ancient cities, stately homes and gardens yet within easy reach of ports and airports. Parking facilities.

B & B from £27.50pp, Rooms 1 single, 2 twin, 1 double, most en-suite,
No smoking, Children over 6, No dogs, Closed Xmas

Holmans Bisterne Close, Burley BH24 4AZ

Robin & Mary Ford
Tel / Fax: 01425 402307

Map Ref: 4
A31, A35

Holmans is a charming country house, it can be found in the heart of the New Forest. Set in four acres of land, it has stabling which is available for guests' own horses. A warm friendly welcome is assured here, the bedrooms are en-suite tastefully furnished and very well equipped, to include tea and coffee making facilities. There is a colour television in the guests' lounge, which has an adjoining orangery. Log fires add to the cosy atmosphere in winter. Superb walking, horse riding and carriage driving. Golf nearby.

B & B from £27.50pp, Rooms 1 twin, 2 double, all en-suite, No smoking,
Children welcome, No dogs in bedrooms, Closed Xmas

Chiphall Acre Droxford Road (A32), Wickham, Fareham PO17 5AY

Mr & Mrs Stevens Tel / Fax: 01329 833188
Email: mavis.stevens@zoom.co.uk Web: www.chiphallacre.co.uk

Map Ref: 5
M27, M3

Chiphall Acre provides that priceless asset - a quiet room for a peaceful sleep. The light airy ground floor rooms, overlook the garden. They are attractively presented, are well equipped with beverage trays, towelling robes, hair dryer, radio and central heating. There is a sun porch and a comfortable dining room/lounge with television and video. Chiphall Acre is situated in a private lane overlooking Bere Forest in the Meon Valley. It is conveniently ten minutes from the M27, 20 minutes from the M3, and near Winchester Cathedral City, Portsmouth and Southampton Channel Ports.

B & B from £26pp, Rooms 1 twin, 1 double, 1 family en-suite,
No smoking, Children welcome, No dogs, Open all year

Green Patch Furzehill, Fordingbridge SP6 2PS

Meg Mulcahy
Tel: 01425 652387 Fax: 01425 656594

Map Ref: 6
A338

You are assured of a very warm welcome to Green Patch which is an elegant house in a beautiful setting of eight acres. It has wonderful views and direct access onto the New Forest. All the rooms are spacious, with television, tea and coffee making facilities. A wide choice of breakfasts is served in the lovely oak panelled dining room or on the terrace. Huge conservatory and garden for guests' enjoyment. Easy reach of Bournemouth, Southampton, Salisbury, Winchester, Portsmouth. Much to see and do. Good eating places nearby.

B & B £22-£27.50pp, Rooms 1 twin, 1 double, 1 family, 1 en-suite, 2 private,
No smoking, Children over 5, No dogs, Open all year

Cottage Crest Castle Hill, Woodgreen, Fordingbridge SP6 2AX

Mrs G Cadman
Tel: 01725 512009

Map Ref: 7
A338

Cottage Crest is situated in a delightful spot on the edge of the New Forest, set in its own 4 acres of garden surrounded by ancient and ornamental forest with superb views of the River Avon in the Valley. The en-suite bedrooms are spacious, decorated to very high standard and have TV and tea/coffee making facilities. A short walk takes one into the village with its local pub which serves excellent meals, Within easy reach of the coast and Isle of Wight. It is the ideal place to either relax, in the peaceful surroundings, or visit the many interesting places in the area.

B & B £23-£24pp, Rooms 1 twin, 2 double, all en-suite, Children over 10, No dogs, Closed Xmas

Street Farmhouse Alton Road, South Warnborough, Hook RG29 1RS

Colin & Wendy Turner
Tel / Fax: 01256 862225

Map Ref: 8
M3 J5, B3349

Attractive 16th century farmhouse on the edge of old Hampshire village. Sympathetically restored, with beamed ceilings, walls, large inglenook fireplace, and other original features. Pretty, light and warm bedrooms with televisions and tea trays. Superb breakfasts in an elegant dining room. Interesting large garden with outdoor heated swimming pool in season. Chawton village (home of Jane Austen) 6 miles away. Excellent pubs nearby. Street Farmhouse makes an ideal base to explore Southern England. Conveniently located for Winchester, Southampton, Portsmouth, the New Forest and London, 1 hour. M3 (junction 5) 4 miles.

B & B from £17pp, C-Cards MC VS, Dinner from £16, Rooms 2 twin, 1 en-suite,
Restricted smoking, Children welcome, No dogs, Open all year

May Cottage, Thruxton, near Andover

Jevington 47 Waterford Lane, Lymington SO41 3PT

Ian & Jane Carruthers Tel / Fax: 01590 672148
Email: jevingtonbb@lineone.net Web: www.caruthers.co.uk

Map Ref: 9
A337

This comfortable family home is situated in a quiet lane midway between the High Street and Marinas. It makes an ideal base for the New Forest, Solent coastline walks. It is just a ten minute drive to Isle of Wight ferry, ten minutes walk to the ancient market town. A good selection of pubs and restaurants. Tea/coffee making facilities, television, off street parking. Children welcome. Places of interest to visit include Beaulieu, Winchester, Stonehenge, Portsmouth, Bournemouth and Southampton. Bike hire, riding, sailing and nature walks in the New Forest can all be arranged.

B & B from £23pp, Rooms 1 twin, 1 double, 1 family, all en-suite,
No smoking, Children & dogs welcome, Open all year

West Lodge 40 Southampton Road, Lymington SO41 9GG

Josephine & David Jeffcock Tel: 01590 672237 Fax: 01590 673592
Email: Jeffcock@amserve.net.

Map Ref: 9
A337, B3054

This pleasant Edwardian town house stands on a main road, but it is quiet. Beautifully presented, the house is well furnished, there is a deep red dining room, family portraits and books to enjoy. The bedrooms are traditionally furnished, they have television, tea and coffee making facilities. There are numerous cafes, restaurants and inns within a stroll away, Josephine and David are happy to direct you to the nicest of these. There is parking behind the house and a garden to enjoy. Within easy reach of the sea, interesting towns, houses and gardens.

B & B £25-£30pp, Rooms 1 single, 1 double, 1 twin, all en-suite,
No smoking, Children over 8, No dogs, Closed Xmas & New Year

The Penny Farthing Hotel Romsey Road, Lyndhurst SO43 7AA

Mike and Joan Tel: 023 8028 4422 Fax: 023 8028 4488
Email: stay@pennyfarthinghotel.co.uk Web: www.pennyfarthinghotel.co.uk

Map Ref: 10
A337

Ideally situated in Lyndhurst village centre, The Penny Farthing Hotel offers smart en-suite rooms with remote control colour television and tea/coffee making facilities. There is also a residents' lounge with bar, a lock up cycle store and a large private car park to the rear. A new cottage annexe is now available with four extra bedrooms, which is ideal for groups. Lyndhurst village has a good selection of pubs, restaurants, cafes and shops. The New Forest Visitor Centre and Museum, both provide a wealth of interest for the visitor.

B & B £29.50-£45pp, C-Cards MC VS AE, Rooms 1 single, 2 twin, 6 double, 2 family,
Restricted smoking, Children welcome, No dogs, Closed Xmas

Yew Tree Farm Bashley Common Road, New Milton BH25 5SH

Mrs Daphne Matthews
Tel / Fax: 01425 611041

Map Ref: 11
A35
see Photo opposite

Total relaxation in two lovely spacious bed sitting rooms marvellously comfortable, with double or twin beds and both with own bathroom, in a traditional, cosy, thatched farm house on the edge of the New Forest. An extensive breakfast may be enjoyed in the bedroom, homemade dinners by arrangement, using top quality produce. Private entrance and ample parking. Very easily located. Turn off the A35 between Lyndhurst and Christchurch onto the B3058. Yew Tree Farm is a small holding with nine acres of grassland.

B & B £35-£45pp, Dinner from £20, Rooms 1 twin private bathroom, 1 double en-suite,
No smoking, No children or dogs, Closed occasionally

Yew Tree Farm, New Milton

Fortitude Cottage 51 Broad Street, Portsmouth PO1 2JD
Maggie & Mike Hall   Tel / Fax: 023 9282 3748
Email: fortcott@aol.com   Web: www.fortitudecottage.co.uk

Map Ref: 12
at Southern End of A3

A charming unusual town house overlooking the quayside in the heart of Old Portsmouth. Built on the site of a 16th century cottage destroyed during the second war and named after an 18th century warship. The immaculately maintained bedrooms and bathrooms are decorated in delicate pastel shades and needlepoint pictures and flowers abound. Breakfast is served on pine tables in a beamed room with views over the water. Fortitude Cottage has won 'Britain in Bloom' awards for her window boxes and hanging baskets; and 'Heartbeat' for healthy food choices.

B & B from £25pp, C-Cards MC VS AE, Rooms 1 double en-suite, 2 twin en-suite/private bathroom, No smoking, Children over 10, No dogs, Closed Xmas

Ranvilles Farm House Romsey SO51 6AA
Bill & Anthea Hughes
Tel / Fax: 02380 814481

Map Ref: 13
M27

Ranvilles Farm House dates from the 15th Century when Richard de Ranville came from Normandy and settled with his family, now this Grade II listed house provides a peaceful setting surrounded by five acres of gardens and paddock. All rooms are attractively decorated and furnished with antiques, and each has its own en-suite bathroom. The spacious dining room overlooks the barnyard. Ranvilles Farm House is three miles from the New Forest and just over a mile from Romsey, a small town equi-distant from the Cathedral cities of Winchester and Salisbury.

B & B from £25pp, Rooms 1 single, 1 twin, 2 double, 1 family, all en-suite, No smoking, Children & dogs welcome, Closed Xmas & New Year

North Court Shorwell, Isle of Wight PO30 3JG
Mrs Christine Harrison   Tel: 01983 740415   Fax: 01983 740409
Email: john@north-court.demon.co.uk   Web: www.wightfarmholidays.co.uk/northcourt

Map Ref: 14
B3323, B3399

North Court is a fine, imposing Jacobean mansion set amongst the rolling Downs in a small village. Built in 1615, the house stands in magnificent gardens of 15 acres, which are home to exotic and sub-tropical flowers. There is a walled garden, a stream, a sunken rose garden, mediterranean terraces and a tennis court. A walk through these fascinating grounds provides a new interest at every turn. The rooms here are lovely, very spacious and with beautiful views. The Crown Inn, which is just a stroll away through the gardens, serves evening meals.

B & B £24-£30pp, Rooms 1 single, 3 double, 3 twin, all en-suite, No smoking, Children welcome, Dogs by arrangement, Closed Xmas & New Year

Strang Hall Uplands, Totland Bay, Isle of Wight PO39 0DZ
Vera F McMullan
Tel / Fax: 01983 753189

Map Ref: 15
B3322

Strang Hall is an Edwardian family home, set peacefully in the hills above Totland Bay. It enjoys wonderful views over the Downs and the Solent. The house was built in the Arts and Craft style, and having been modernised, it now offers comfortable accommodation. The house stands in two acres of gardens with an orchard. The beaches of Totland Bay and Colwell Bay are within walking distance, as is the Totland Church and village post office. Freshwater is one mile away, here is a library, medical centre and an indoor swimming pool.

B & B from £25pp, Dinner from £20, Rooms 1 single, 1 twin, 1 double, 1 family, some en-suite, Restricted smoking, Children welcome, No dogs, Closed Xmas & New Year

Cams Hambledon, Waterlooville PO7 4SP
Julian & Valerie Fawcett
Tel: 023 9263 2865   Fax: 023 9263 2691

Map Ref: 16
B2150, A3

Cams is a beautiful Grade II Listed house with Jacobean origins. Accommodation comprises two twin-bedded, one en-suite, two double bedrooms, one en-suite. All have basins, televisions, tea/coffee facilities. Breakfast is served in a 17th century panelled dining room with French windows onto the lawn. There is a large garden with fine trees, tennis court and ample parking. Cams is well situated for Winchester, Chichester with its theatre and Portsmouth with its historic ships. There is a good pub within walking distance serving excellent food.

B & B from £24pp, Rooms 2 double, 2 twin, some en-suite, No smoking,
Children welcome, Dogs by arrangement, Closed Xmas & New Year

Home Paddocks West Meon GU32 1NA
Raye & Simon Ward   Tel: 01730 829241   Fax: 01730 829577
Email: homepaddocks@compuserve.com

Map Ref: 17
A32, A272

Home Paddocks is the cherished home of the Ward family. On the outskirts of West Meon it is set in a large garden with tennis court and croquet lawn. Dating back to the 1560s, there is a Victorian conservatory. The comfortable bedrooms with garden views, have private facilities. Guests have the use of the drawing room and dining room. Ideal for visiting Winchester, Southampton, the New Forest and many places of interest along the South Coast. A good selection of pubs, restaurants, golf courses and gardens to visit in the area.

B & B from £22.50pp, Dinner from £15, Rooms 2 en-suite twin, Restricted smoking,
Children by arrangement, Dogs by arrangement, Closed Xmas

Brymer House 29-30 St Faith's Road, St Cross, Winchester SO23 9QD
Fizzy & Guy Warren   Tel: 01962 867428   Fax: 01962 868624
Email: brymerhouse@aol.com

Map Ref: 18
A303, M3, M27

Brymer House offers quiet and comfortable accommodation in your own half of a beautifully furnished and decorated town house within a short walk of the Cathedral city centre and water meadows. The en-suite bedrooms with tea/coffee making facilities and TV are small and cosy. There is an 'honesty box' in the dining room for drinks, open fire in the sitting room, fresh flowers, choice of delicious breakfasts, easy parking and a very warm welcome.

B & B £25-£30pp, Rooms 1 double, 1 twin, both en-suite,
Restricted smoking, Children over 7, No dogs, Closed Xmas

Great Hunts Place Owslebury, Winchester SO21 1JL
Tim & Sue Torrington   Tel: 01962 777234   Fax: 01962 777242
Email: tt@byngs.freeserve.co.uk   Web: www.byngs.freeserve.co.uk

Map Ref: 19
M3, A34, A272

Originally two Edwardian cottages, Great Hunts Place was converted and 'Georgianised' in the 1970s. The house sits in 15 acres of its own land, and enjoys views over the surrounding countryside. There is a swimming pool and tennis court for guests' use. This traditionally furnished house may be found on the Pilgrim's way, it makes it an ideal location for those who enjoy walking. The historic town of Winchester is six miles away, and Salisbury, Oxford, Portsmouth and Chichester are within an easy drive. There is an excellent pub within five minutes walk.

B & B £25-£30pp, Rooms 1 twin en suite, 1 twin with private bathroom,
Children over 10, No dogs, Closed Xmas & New Year

Herefordshire & Worcestershire

These two counties, joined in 1974, share the dramatic Malvern Hills which lie along the Severn Plain, separating the low plains of Herefordshire from the glorious Vale of Evesham. This jagged ridge was exploited as a defensive site by Iron Age man, who built their ancient forts at Worcestershire Beacon and Herefordshire Beacon from which there are wonderful views to the hills of the Welsh Marches and to the Cotswold escarpment. Great Malvern, at the centre of this lovely area, is an ideal base for the holidaymaker. The town developed as a spa during the nineteenth century and is renowned for its crystal clear water, its Victorian character and the fine fifteenth century priory tower which dominates the district. Sir Edward Elgar, whose 'Pomp and Circumstance' marches were inspired by the Malverns, was born at Lower Broadheath in 1857 and his works are annually performed as part of the Malvern and Worcester Music Festivals. Worcester, famous for its manufacture of porcelain since 1862, was made a diocese in 680AD and its present cathedral, begun in the eleventh century has an impressive Norman crypt. The city possesses some quite remarkable examples of domestic architecture including The

Commandery, once a hospice for travellers in the eleventh century and the headquarters of Charles II during the Battle of Worcester, now is a museum of local history. The battles of the Civil War are recalled in nearby Ledbury where Ledbury Park, which dates from 1600, was the Royalist headquarters during the local skirmishes. The town is an ancient market town with its seventeenth century market hall still retaining its original wooden pillars. The church of St Michael and All Angels has a fine detached bell tower with a slender spire. To the west at Brockhampton, the National Trust owns almost 1,700 acres of wonderful woodlands and parkland open to the public with waymarked footpaths to follow and superb views. Lower Brockhampton boasts the interesting ruins of a twelfth century chapel and a splendid late fourteenth century moated manor house with an unusual half-timbered gatehouse.

Hereford, the ancient capital of West Mercia, stands in a commanding position over the River Wye. It was founded in the seventh century as an outpost on the border with Celtic Wales. The glorious cathedral contains the Mappa Mundi, a circular map of

Severn Valley Railway crossing the River Severn (WCC)

166

the world painted on vellum and showing Jerusalem at the centre of the world, believed to have been completed in 1290. The cathedral also contains a remarkable library of 1,500 chained books. The area benefits from the cider industry and Hereford is the home of the largest Cider Maker in the world with the Cider Museum and King Offa Distillery celebrating this important trade.

The River Wye meanders in wide loops through the county on its course from Plynlimon to Chepstow. It is really spectacular at many locations, but few quite as superb as at Symond's Yat where the Wye passes through a deep gorge protected by massive cliffs giving spectacular panoramic views. Ross-on-Wye is a charming market town standing on a sandstone bluff overlooking the Wye. It is a town with lovely public gardens, and some fine half-timbered and Georgian houses. Leominster in the north, wonderfully located at the junction of Pinsley

Brook and the River Lugg amongst cider-apple orchards and hopfields, is yet another town full of fascinating buildings, with an excellent folk museum. Its priory is a gem, but the timber-framed Grange, once the market hall, is Herefordshire's most elaborately carved building and a very rare surviving example of the work of John Abel, the king's carpenter.

The Vale of Evesham is a picture in the spring when the fruit trees are in blossom. The town of Evesham, at the centre of the fruit growing area, developed around the now ruined Benedictine abbey whose bell tower of 1539 dominates the delightful riverside gardens. The interesting obelisk on Green Hill is a memorial to Simon de Montfort, the father of the House of Commons, who died in battle in 1265. No visitor should leave this part of the county without visiting Broadway, one of the prettiest small towns in the region and the gateway to the Cotswolds.

PLACES TO VISIT

This is a small selection of interesting places to visit. Many more are listed in our annual guide to Museums, Galleries, Historic Houses & Sites (see page 448)

Hanbury Hall
Hanbury, Droitwich, Worcestershire
A William & Mary style house with fine collections of porcelain and Dutch flower paintings, as well as recreated eighteenth century formal gardens.

Eastnor Castle
Eastnor, Ledbury, Herefordshire
A magnificent Georgian castle, home to the Hervey-Bathurst family and set in a large deer park. There are many outdoor activities and within the house, tapestries, fine art and armour.

Severn Valley Railway
Bewdley, Worcestershire
Preserved standard gauge steam railway, services operating through 16 scenic miles along the River Severn. One of the largest collections of locomotives and rolling stock in the country.

Worcester Cathedral
College Green, Worcester
This Norman Cathedral was founded in 679 AD with an impressive bell-tower, completed in 1374. It houses King John's tomb and Prince Arthur's Chantry.

Herefordshire & Worcestershire

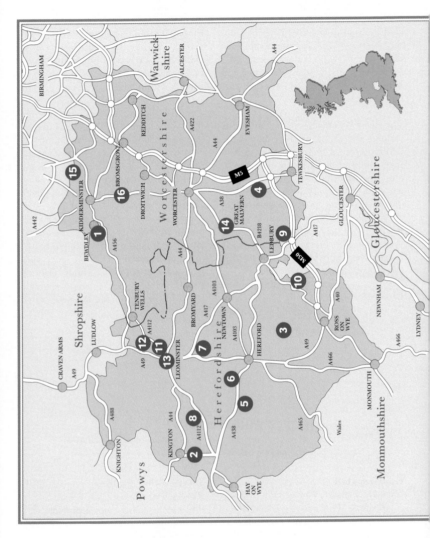

The Blue Map References should be used to locate B & B properties on the pages that follow

Tarn Long Bank, Bewdley, Worcs DY12 2QT
Topsy Beves
Tel: 01299 402243

Map Ref: 1
A456

This is an attractive country house with a library, set in 17 acres of gardens and fields with spectacular views, in a tranquil area by an ancient coppice. All bedrooms have basins and there is one bathroom and two shower rooms. Excellent breakfasts with home baked rolls are served in the elegant dining room. Conveniently situated for Worcestershire Way Walk (guests can be collected), Wyre Forest, River Severn (fishing), Midland Safari Park, Severn Valley Steam Railway, gardens, stately homes, golf. Two miles west of Georgian Bewdley on A456. There is ample parking.

B & B from £18pp, Rooms 2 single, 2 twin, No smoking,
Children welcome, No dogs, Closed Nov to Feb

Bollingham House Eardisley, Herefs HR5 3LE
John & Stephanie Grant Tel: 01544 327326   Fax: 01544 327880
Email: bollhouse@bigfoot.com

Map Ref: 2
A4111

Quite breathtaking. This Georgian gentleman's residence overlooks one of the finest views in England. The rooms are gracious with welcoming log fires, spacious bedrooms, fresh cut flowers and an interesting English garden to wander around. The extensive gardens include terracing, ponds and a walled garden with a special rose walk, and just outside the dining room window is a Victorian chapel. Bollingham House is conveniently situated for the Welsh Marches, Offa's Dyke, the well known book town Hay-on-Wye, Hereford Cathederal and golf at the famous Kington Golf Club.

B & B from £25pp, Dinner from £14.50, Rooms 1 twin, 2 double, all private bathrooms,
Restricted smoking, Children welcome, Dogs by arrangement, Closed Xmas & New Year

The Bowens Country House Fownhope, Hereford, Herefs HR1 4PS
Carol Hart Tel / Fax: 01432 860430
Email: Thebowenshotel@aol.com Web: www.thebowenshotel.co.uk

Map Ref: 3
B4224

Peacefully situated opposite the church on the edge of the village in the Wye Valley, midway between Hereford and Ross-on-Wye. Ideal for touring, walking and exploring the Welsh Borders, Malverns, Cotswolds, Brecon Beacons and the wooded countryside of Herefordshire. Tastefully restored 17th century country house set in two acres of gardens. Comfortable, well appointed bedrooms, all fully en-suite each with television, telephone, central heating and tea/coffee facilities. Oak beamed lounge with inglenook fireplace. Superb home-cooked meals, including vegetarian dishes, using local/home produce.

B & B £25-£32.50pp, C-Cards MC VS, Dinner from £15, Rooms 2 single, 6 double/twin, 2 family,
all en-suite, Restricted smoking, Children welcome, Dogs by arrangement, Open all year

Old Parsonage Farm Hanley Castle, Worcs WR8 0BU
Ann Addison Tel / Fax: 01684 310124
Email: OPWines@aol.com

Map Ref: 4
M5 & M50, B4209
see Photo on page 170

Old Parsonage Farm, built in 1777, sits on the edge of the historic village of Hanley Castle, and commands wonderful views over the Malvern Hills from the delightful garden which plays host to visiting wildlife. It is surrounded by farmland, and enjoys access to footpaths. The house has retained many interesting features, a hall with a vaulted ceiling, a dining room with inglenook and a bread oven. The Addisons specialise in food and wine. The highlight of the day is a memorable four course dinner, with a choice of over 90 wines from around the world to accompany it.

B & B £22.50-£28.50pp, Dinner £16.90, Rooms 2 double, 1 double/twin/family, 2 en-suite,
Restricted smoking, Children over 12, Dogs by arrangement, Closed Mid-Dec to Mid-Jan

Old Parsonage Farm, Hanley Castle

The Old Rectory Byford, Hereford, Herefs HR4 7LD

Charles & Audrey Mayson Tel: 01981 590218 Fax: 01981 590499
Email: info@cm-Ltd.com

Map Ref: 5
A438

Byford is a hamlet in beautiful rural Herefordshire close to the River Wye on the Wye Valley walk. Our home is Georgian, the rooms are elegant and spacious, the dining room has three ceiling to floor windows with panelled pine shutters and doors. A magnificent cedar tree dominates the garden and herbaceous borders. The bedrooms are large with views of parkland and hills, they have sofas, books, television, tea/coffee and lovely en-suite facilities. Visit delightful villages, churches, mountains and gardens too many to list.

B & B from £21.50pp, Dinner from £12.50, Rooms 1 twin, 2 double, all en-suite, No smoking, Children welcome, No dogs in house, Closed Nov to Feb

Appletree Cottage Mansell Lacy, Hereford, Herefs HR4 7HH

Monica Barker Tel: 01981 590688
Email: monica.barker@tesco.net

Map Ref: 6
A480

Appletree cottage was originally one cottage, and then it became a cider house, and eventually two converted farm cottages. One cottage was built in 1450, and the more modern one was built during the late 16th century. Both bedrooms have tea/coffee making trays, and the house is fully centrally heated. The open plan sitting room has a wood burning stove which ensures a cosy warmth throughout the house. English country breakfasts are served in the dining room. We are surrounded by many places of interest, Hereford, and the famous village of Weobley are a short drive away. Both bedrooms have tea/coffee making trays.

B & B £17-£22pp, Rooms 2 twin (1 en-suite), No smoking, No children or dogs, Open all year

The Vauld Farm The Vauld, Marden, Hereford, Herefs HR1 3HA

Jean Bengry
Tel: 01568 797898

Map Ref: 7
A49

The perfect accommodation for relaxing and discovering the delights of Herefordshire. The Vauld Farm is a 16th century Elizabethan manor with spacious en-suite bedrooms, including a four poster. All of them have private lounge areas with television and tea/coffee facilities, they overlook the duck pond and open countryside. Breakfast and optional evening meals are served in the dining room which has a large open fire, massive oak beams overhead and flagstone floor. Guests are welcome to bring their own wine etc. Quiet location with ample parking. Hereford 8 miles.

B & B from £25pp, Dinner from £20, Rooms 1 twin, 2 double, 1 family, all en-suite, Restricted smoking, Children over 12, No dogs, Open all year

Upper Newton Farmhouse Kinnersley, Herefs HR3 6QB

Jon & Pearl Taylor Tel / Fax: 01544 327727
Email: jtaylor@click.kc3.co.uk Web: www.uppernewton.herefordshire.com

Map Ref: 8
A4112, A438

AA Landlady of the year 2000 mainly because of our attention to detail and provision of delicious local, seasonal food. The Stable accommodation provides a suite of rooms for guests to relax in. Beautifully decorated, totally equipped with luxurious extras. Information about local walks, farm diary, local attractions, long distance paths are all provided. Pearl delights in helping guests get the most out of their stay. Lovely, developing and established gardens, stunning views make Upper Newton a haven to retreat to.

B & B from £25pp, Rooms 1 twin, 2 double, all en-suite, No smoking, No children or dogs, Open all year

Grove House Bromsberrow Heath, Ledbury, Herefs HR8 1PE
Michael & Ellen Ross Tel: 01531 650584 Mobile: 07960 166903
Email: rossgrovehouse@amserve.net

Map Ref: 9
M50, A417

Grove House is a 15th century grade II listed home standing in 13 acres of fields and garden, near the southern end of the Malvern Hills. The Cotswolds, Wales, Stratford, Cheltenham and Worcester are all within easy driving distance. There are beams, panelling and open log fires to enjoy, they provide the perfect back drop for gleaming antiques and fresh flowers. The spacious bedrooms with four poster beds, bowls of fresh fruit and homemade biscuits have televisions and tea trays. A hard tennis court and a neighbour's pool are available to guests.

B & B from £36.50pp, Dinner from £23.50, Rooms 2 double, 1 twin, 1 family, all en-suite, Restricted smoking, Children welcome, Dogs not in bedrooms, Closed Xmas & New Year

Hallend Kynaston, Much Marcle, Ledbury, Herefs HR8 2PD
Mrs Angela Jefferson Tel: 01531 670225 Fax: 01531 670747
Mobile: 07774 269910 Email: khjefferson@hallend91.freeserve.co.uk

Map Ref: 10
A449, A4172

Hallend is a fine listed Georgian farmhouse, surrounded by 400 acres of beautiful countryside, and with views over its own park and farmland. Hugh and Angela have spent much time renovating this lovely home, now the gardens and ponds have been replanted. The prettily presented bedrooms are decorated in a classic English style, dinner is served in the dining room with its collection of marine paintings; guests may bring their own wine. Summer breakfasts are served in the geranium filled conservatory by the outdoor heated pool. There are many wonderful walks to enjoy.

B & B from £37.50pp, C-Cards VS, Dinner from £22.50, Rooms 2 double, 1 twin, all en-suite, No smoking, Children over 12, No dogs, Closed Xmas & New Year

Lower Bache House Kimbolton, Leominster, Herefs HR6 0ER
Rose & Leslie Wiles Tel: 01568 750304
Email: leslie.wiles@care4free.net

Map Ref: 11
A4112

This award winning seventeenth century country house, set in fourteen acres of private nature reserve nestling in a tiny tranquil valley, provides four self-contained suites, each with its own private sitting room. Water colours, original prints, plants, books and ornaments create an atmosphere of quality and comfort. A renowned cuisine, using locally produced organic meat and vegetables complete the hallmarks of peace, privacy and fine food of this charming country retreat. An unsurpassed opportunity to savour rural England at its very best.

B & B from £29.50pp, Dinner from £15.50, Rooms 2 twin, 2 double, all en-suite, No smoking, Children over 8, No dogs, Open all year

The Hills Farm Leysters, Leominster, Herefs HR6 0HP
Peter & Jane Conolly Tel: 01568 750205 Fax: 01568 750306
Email: conolly@bigwig.net

Map Ref: 12
A4112

The Hills Farm dates back to the 16th century. Jane, the AA Landlady of the Year 1999, and Peter provide exceptionally comfortable accommodation. They offer three bedrooms in individual barn conversions, and two in the main house. All the rooms are en-suite with colour television tea/coffee facilities and panoramic views. In the guests' sitting room there are local maps, books and magazines to peruse. A scrumptious dinner, when prebooked, is served at 7pm, at individual tables, and guests are encouraged to bring their own wine.

B & B from £28pp, C-Cards MC VS, Dinner from £19, Rooms 2 twin, 3 double, all en-suite, No smoking, No children or dogs, Closed Nov to Mar

Wyche Keep, Malvern

Highfield Newtown, Ivington Road, Leominster, Herefs HR6 8QD
Catherine & Marguerite Fothergill   Tel: 01568 613216
Email: info@stay-at-highfield.co.uk   Web: www.stay-at-highfield.co.uk

Map Ref: 13
A44, A49

Highfield stands in a large garden with unspoilt views of open farmland and distant mountains and enjoys a pleasant rural situation just one and a half miles from the old market town of Leominster. The house was built in Edwardian times and accommodation is elegant and comfortable with a friendly relaxed atmosphere. Meals are carefully prepared from good fresh ingredients and are served in the charming dining room. All gastronomic needs and desires are catered for and a modest wine list is available. Groups are welcome. ETC 4 Diamonds.

B & B from £20pp, Dinner from £13.50, Rooms 1 double, 2 twin en-suite/private,
Restricted smoking, No children or dogs, Closed Nov to Feb

Wyche Keep 22 Wyche Road, Malvern, Worcs WR14 4EG
Judith & Jon Williams   Tel: 01684 567018   Fax: 01684 892304
Email: wychekeep@aol.com   Web: www.jks.org/wychekeep

Map Ref: 14
B4218
see Photo on page 173

Wyche Keep is a unique arts and crafts castle style house, perched high on the Malvern Hills. It was built by the family of Sir Stanley Baldwin, Prime Minister, to enjoy the spectacular 60 mile views, and has a long history of elegant entertaining. Three large luxury double suites, including four poster. Traditional English cooking is a speciality and guests can savour memorable four course candlelit dinners, served in a 'house party' atmosphere in front of a log fire. Fully licensed. Magical setting with private parking.

B & B £30-£35pp, Dinner from £20, Rooms 2 twin, 1 double, all en-suite, No smoking,
No children or dogs, Open all year

St Elisabeth's Cottage Woodman Lane, Clent, Stourbridge, Worcs DY9 9PX
Sheila Blankstone   Tel: 01562 883883   Fax: 01562 885034
Email: st_elizabeth_cot@btconnect.com

Map Ref: 15
A491

This beautiful country cottage is set in a tranquil setting with six acres of landscaped gardens with an outdoor heated swimming pool. There are lovely country walks. The accommodation includes television in all rooms plus coffee and tea making facilities. A residents' lounge is available. There are plenty of pubs and restaurants nearby. Easy access to M5, M6, M42 and M40. 25 minutes from NEC and Birmingham Airport. Destinations within easy reach include, Symphony Hall and Convention Centre in Birmingham, Black Country Museum, Dudley, Stourbridge Crystal Factories, Severn Valley Railway.

B & B from £30pp, Rooms 1 twin, 2 double, all en-suite,
No smoking, Children & dogs welcome, Open all year

Garden Cottages Crossway Green, Hartlebury, Worcester, Worcs DY13 9SL
Pauline Terry   Tel / Fax: 01299 250626
Email: accommodation@mamod.co.uk   Web: www.gardencottages.co.uk

Map Ref: 16
A449

Situated in a quiet rural position but close to the main A449 Worcester/Kidderminster road, and within easy reach of Birmingham and the M5, half an hour from Stratford-upon-Avon and the Cotswolds. This L shaped cottage has attractive grounds, a wealth of oak beams and ample parking space. The single and double bedrooms are en-suite. There is a sitting room and sun lounge which guests are welcome to enjoy. An evening meal is available if booked in advance, or there are a good selection of pubs and restaurants in the area, some within walking distance.

B & B from £25pp, Rooms 1 single, 1 double, 1 twin, 1 family,
Restricted smoking, Children welcome, No dogs, Closed Xmas

Kent

Kent is without doubt the 'Garden of England', the soil is remarkably fertile and the county is crowded with orchards, market gardens, fields of vegetables and some hop fields, although not so many as there used to be. Being the closest part of England to mainland Europe, Kent has been the main route between London and the Continent since Julius Caesar landed here in 55BC, to be followed by St Augustine and his missionaries from Rome in 597AD, and the Saxons four centuries later. This is a county of great activity and greatly contrasting scenery with the North Downs cutting through the whole of Kent and culminating in the spectacular White Cliffs of Dover. The Romney Marshes, once renowned for smuggling, are a low lying and windswept region where the sea has receded, leaving the drained marshes grazed by Romney sheep. Here the Royal Military Canal, built as a defence during the Napoleonic Wars, runs through Hythe, one of the Cinque Ports and terminus of the Romney, Hythe and Dymchurch Railway.

Folkstone has probably seen more upheaval than most towns, not least during the Second World War. However, the old town still thankfully retains much of its charm, including the fine Victorian section and The Leas, a wonderful cliff-top Promenade. Folkstone's major change in recent years has been the on-going development around the landfall point of the Channel Tunnel. Its near neighbour, Dover, an important cross-Channel port since Roman times, despite much destruction during World War Two, still offers the visitor some interesting architecture and of course the castle, one of Europe's most impressive medieval fortresses. The White Cliffs Experience is an interactive view of Dover's history, a fascinating tunnel system which is open to the public. Margate, Ramsgate, and Broadstairs, on the north eastern tip of Kent, each with their own particular character, present a delightful seaside holiday region. Margate, one of England's earliest coastal resorts, has over nine miles of sandy beach with safe swimming and a pier built in 1810 and Ramsgate, a busy cross-Channel terminal has its attractive Royal Esplanade, amusement parks and Pavilion with a splendid 500 berth marina. Broadstairs, very much a family resort still retains its village atmosphere and was popular with Charles Dickens who had several holiday homes here. Its Annual Folk Festival Week in August is one of the leading folk festivals in southern England.

Maidstone, the county town which stands on the rivers Medway and Len, is a perfect centre for visitors exploring the delights of the valley of the Medway. There are glorious river

Penshurst Place Gardens (SEETB)

walks, gardens, boating and excellent fishing. Positioned close to Cranbrook is Sissinghurst Castle Garden, the magnificent five and a half acre connoisseur's garden created by Vita Sackville-West and her husband. Just four miles from Maidstone is the wonderfully romantic Leeds Castle, built in the eleventh century on two islands in a lake, upon which black swans swim. Canterbury, on the River Stour, like so many of the cities in this part of England suffered greatly in the bombings of the Second World War, but miraculously the lovely cathedral was spared. Built in Caen limestone, along with Bell Harry, its great central tower, the cathedral includes an outstanding collection of twelfth and thirteenth century stained glass. Here the shrine of Thomas a Becket, murdered on the steps of the cathedral in 1170, became an important place of pilgrimage in the Middle Ages. This prompted Geoffrey Chaucer to write his colourful catelogue of pilgrims in his "Canterbury Tales", now dramatized in a disused church on St Margaret's Street.

Kent is renowned for its spectacular stately homes. Knowle at Sevenoaks in a magnificent deer park is the largest private house in England, dating from 1456, it was enlarged by the 1st Earl of Dorset, to whom it was granted by Elizabeth I. It was the history of this house upon which Virginia Woolf, a frequent visitor, based her novel Orlando. Penshurst Place is an outstanding example of fourteenth century domestic architecture, while nearby Hever Castle, a fine moated Tudor house was the birthplace of Anne Boleyn. Another attraction to this lovely county is Chartwell near Westerham, the home of Sir Winston Churchill from 1924 until his death in 1965. The house is filled with mementoes of the great man.

PLACES TO VISIT

This is a small selection of interesting places to visit. Many more are listed in our annual guide to Museums, Galleries, Historic Houses & Sites (see page 448)

Canterbury Cathedral
Canterbury
Dominating the skyline at 557 feet the Cathedral has held pilgrimage status since 1170 when Thomas Becket was martyred. The earliest part of the Cathedral is the Romanesque crypt circa 1100.

Dover Castle
Dover
Magnificent medieval fortress with Anglo-Saxon church and Roman lighthouse. Discover the top secret World War II wartime tunnels, deep in the White Cliffs of Dover.

Leeds Castle
Maidstone, Kent
Shrouded in mist, mystery and legend, Leeds Castle, dubbed the loveliest Castle in the world, rises from its own lake. Built in 857 AD the Castle has been home to six medieval queens of England.

Penshurst Place and Gardens
Penshurst, Tonbridge
One of England's greatest family owned stately homes. A medieval manor home with fine collections of paintings, tapestries and furniture. Tudor gardens and an adventure playground.

Kent

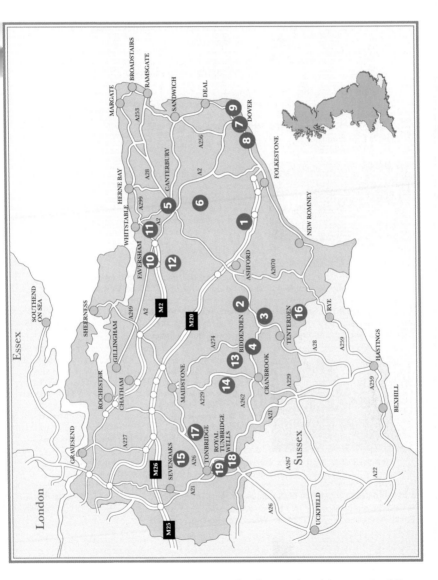

The Blue Map References should be used to locate B & B properties on the pages that follow

Bulltown Farmhouse Bulltown Lane, West Brabourne, Ashford TN25 5NB

Lilly Wilton   Tel: 01233 813505   Fax: 01227 709544
Email: wiltons@bulltown.fsnet.co.uk

Map Ref: 1
M20

Bulltown Farmhouse is an attractively restored 15th Century Kentish farmhouse. It is a large timber framed medieval building, and is located on the south west side of the North Downs and Pilgrim's Way. The countryside here is unspoiled, the walks are wonderful. The house is set in one acre of cottage gardens and it is surrounded by quiet farmland. The rooms are all large, period furnished and have unspoiled outlooks. The Channel Tunnel is only ten minutes away, with Canterbury and the Channel port 10 and 15 miles respectively. Excellent inns nearby.

B & B from £22.50pp, Rooms 1 double, 1 twin, 1 family, all en-suite, No smoking,
Children welcome, No dogs, Open all year

The Coach House Oakmead Farm, Bethersden, Ashford TN26 3DU

Bernard & Else Broad
Tel / Fax: 01233 820583

Map Ref: 2
A28

Guests are welcomed at the Coach House, a comfortable family home set off the road in five acres of gardens and paddocks. Bethersden Village is a mile away and has a selection of country pubs. Breakfast of your choice is cooked using local produce and is served in the dining room or conservatory which guests may use as a sitting room. The house is one mile from the village and is central for ferries, tunnel, Eurostar. Within easy reach is Canterbury, Leeds Castle and Sissinghurst. Dutch is spoken here.

B & B from £20pp, Rooms 1 twin, 1 double, 1 family, all en-suite/private,
Restricted smoking, Children welcome, No dogs, Closed Oct to Mar

Little Hodgeham Smarden Road, Bethersden, Ashford TN26 3HE

Anne & Mark Bradbury   Tel: 01233 850323   Fax: 01233 850006
Email: little.hodgeham@virgin.net   Web: www.littlehodgeham.co.uk

Map Ref: 2
M20/A28

Little Hodgeham is a 16th century Kent cottage which is set in mature landscaped gardens, yet only minutes from the M20 motorway and Ashford International Station. This charming cottage has been sympathetically restored, and it provides stylishly decorated accommodation with full en-suite facilities in a peaceful location. A King size four poster, a galleried ceiling, a wealth of beams, both bedrooms enjoy delightful views over the gardens and farmland. A large sitting room, a cosy dining room, the perfect setting for weekend dinner parties, and English breakfasts. Wonderful garden, 24 foot pool.

B & B £30-£32.50pp, Dinner from £18, Rooms 1 twin, 1 suite with King size 4 poster,
both en-suite, No smoking, Children welcome, Open all year

Lion House Church Hill, High Halden, Ashford TN26 3LS

Gerald & Caroline Mullins   Tel / Fax: 01233 850446
Email: lionhouse@tinyworld.co.uk   Web: www.lionhouse.org.uk

Map Ref: 3
A28

Situated on the village green with pub, village shop, historic church; Lion House is a listed Queen Anne farmhouse set in a large mature garden. Caroline and Gerald offer a friendly welcome, comfortable centrally heated accommodation with en-suite bath and shower, television, tea/coffee making facilities and trouser press. There is a private dining room and sitting room. Within easy reach of Sissinghurst and Leeds castles, Canterbury, channel tunnel and ports. Early departures and late arrivals catered for. Supper or dinner by arrangement.

B & B from £20pp, Dinner from £15, Rooms 1 single, 1 twin, 1 family, all en-suite,
Restricted smoking, Children welcome, No dogs, Closed Xmas

Bishopsdale Oast Cranbrook Road, Biddenden TN27 8DR

Iain & Jane Drysdale Tel: 01580 291027 Fax: 01580 292321
Email: drysdale@bishopsdaleoast.co.uk Web: www.bishopsdaleoast.co.uk

Map Ref: 4
A28

Bishopsdale Oast until 1963 was a working oast house, for drying hops used in making beer. Certain features are there to acknowledge, the sitting room still has the original fireplace, the largest bedroom was where the hops were dried, a ground floor bedroom opens onto the garden. The house stands in a quiet secluded area in the heart of the Weald of Kent, in four acres of wild and cultivated gardens. It offers a relaxed atmosphere with log fires, lovely walks and views. Guests can enjoy meals in the dining room or on the terrace.

B & B £27.50-£30pp, C-Cards MC VS, Dinner from £22, Rooms 2 double, 2 twin, 1 family, all en-suite, Restricted smoking, Children over 12, No dogs, Closed Xmas

Clare Ellen Guest House 9 Victoria Road, Canterbury CT1 3SG

Loraine Williams Tel: 01227 760205 Fax: 01227 784482
Email: loraine.williams@clareellenguesthouse.co.uk Web: www.clareellenguesthouse.co.uk

Map Ref: 5
A28

A warm welcome and bed and breakfast in style. Large quiet elegant en-suite rooms all with colour television, clock/radio, hair dryer and tea/coffee facilities. Ironing centre with trouser press for guests' convenience. Full English breakfast, vegetarians and special diets catered for, on request. Numerous restaurants/pubs close by. Six minutes walk to City centre, Cathedral, Marlow Theatre and Canterbury bus station. Four minutes walk to Canterbury East railway station. Close proximity to cricket ground and University. Private car park and garage available.

B & B £24.50-£27pp, C-Cards MC VS, Rooms 1 single, 2 double, 2 twin, 1 family, all en-suite, Restricted smoking, Children welcome, No dogs, Open all year

Maynard Cottage 106 Wincheap, Canterbury CT1 3RS

Fiona Ely Tel: 07951 496836
Email: fionaely@onetel.net.uk Web: www.SmoothHound.co.uk/hotels/maynard.html

Map Ref: 5
A28

Maynard Cottage is a late 17th century cottage dating back to 1695. We have one bedroom, newly decorated to a high standard with soft furnishings to match.The room offers en-suite facilities with modern amenities. A hairdryer and toiletries are provided for guests' use. Tea, coffee facilities with biscuits and home made cakes are offered. There are easy chairs to sit and relax, also colour television and radio alarm. Hearty breakfasts. Evening meals from Monday to Thursday. A six minute walk to the City centre. Station is three minutes. A relaxed and friendly atmosphere in a cosy cottage.

B & B £22.50-£30pp, C-Cards MC VS AE, Dinner from £16, Rooms 1 twin/family/double en-suite, No smoking, Children welcome, No dogs, Open all year

Sylvan Cottage Nackington Road, Canterbury CT4 7AY

Chris & Jac Bray Tel: 01227 765307 Fax: 01227 478411
Email: jac@sylvan5.fsnet.co.uk Web: www.sylvancottage.co.uk

Map Ref: 5
A2, B2068

Enjoy sharing our 17th century cottage, complete with beams and inglenooks. Great semi-rural location for walkers, cyclists, channel-hoppers, and families. A pleasant twenty minute walk from the city and close to the County Cricket ground. Cotton bed-linen, modern bathrooms and book filled sitting room opening into a garden surrounded by woods and fields. Off road parking, or we'll pick-up guests from the stations, just ask. Walk across the fields to the pub, or join us for dinner/supper - bring your own wine.

B & B from £20pp, Dinner £10, Rooms 1 twin, 1 double, 1 double/family, all en-suite, No smoking, Children welcome, No dogs, Closed occasionally

Thanington Hotel 140 Wincheap, Canterbury CT1 3RY

Jill & David Jenkins Tel: 01227 453227 Fax: 01227 453225

Email: thanington@lineone.net Web: www.thanington-hotel.co.uk

Map Ref: 5
A28

Spacious Georgian bed & breakfast hotel, ideally situated, only a 10 minute stroll from the city centre. 15 en-suite bedrooms, beautifully decorated and furnished, all in immaculate condition with modern day extras. King size four poster beds, antique bedsteads and two large family rooms. Walled garden with patio, indoor swimming pool, intimate bar, guest lounge and snooker/games room. Delicious breakfasts served in the elegant dining room. Secure private car park. An oasis in a busy tourist city, convenient for channel ports, tunnel and historic houses of Kent. Gatwick 60 minutes.

B & B from £34pp, C-Cards MC VS AE DC, Rooms 10 double 3 twin 2 family,
Restricted smoking, Small dogs welcome, Open all year

Zan Stel Lodge 140 Old Dover Road, Canterbury CT1 3NX

Zandra & Ron Stedman

Tel: 01227 453654

Map Ref: 5
B2068, A2
see Photo opposite

Gracious Edwardian house with many original features, offering high standards of cleanliness and service in a smoke free atmosphere. Individually styled bedrooms include colour TV, beverage making facilities and little niceties that usually meet with guests approval. The elegant dining room overlooks a delightful cottage garden extending onto a walled garden with fishponds which helps to complete the ambience of a relaxing stay. Ten minute walk to city/railway/coach station, thirty minute drive to Channel Tunnel and ferry ports, Private car park. Which? Good B&B Recommended, ETC 4 Diamonds, Silver Award.

B & B from £23pp, Rooms 2 double, 1 twin, 1 family, 2 en-suite, No smoking, Open all year

Upper Ansdore Duckpit Lane, Petham, Canterbury CT4 5QB

Roger & Susan Linch Tel: 01227 700672 Fax: 01227 700840

upperansdore@hotels-activebooking.com www.smoothhound.co.uk/hotels/upperans.html

Map Ref: 6
B2068, A2

Upper Ansdore is a medieval farmhouse, and is located in a very quiet secluded valley, with beautiful views. Once the home of the Lord Mayor of London, it overlooks a Kent nature reserve. Take a short break or a longer stay, and sample over 600 years of history. Breakfast is served in the oak beamed dining room with Tudor inglenook fireplace and furnished with antiques. Canterbury is just 15 minutes and Dover 30 minutes. SAE please for a colour brochure.

B & B £21-£22.50pp, C-Cards MC VS, Rooms 1 twin, 3 double, 1 family, all en-suite,
No smoking, Children over 5, Dogs welcome, Closed Xmas

Castle House 10 Castle Hill Road, Dover CT16 1QW

Rodney & Elizabeth Dimech Tel: 01304 201656 Fax: 01304 210197

Email: Dimechr@aol.com Web: www.castle-guesthouse.co.uk

Map Ref: 7
A2/M2 and A20/M20

Castle House is ideally situated being just below Dover Castle and close to the Town Centre, Ferries, Hoverport and Cruise Liner Terminal. It is just ten minutes from the Channel Tunnel. Good food, comfortable accommodation and genuine hospitality is offered by hosts Rodney & Elizabeth. All the rooms are well equipped to include colour television, hospitality trays and alarm clock. A hearty breakfast is served to ensure an excellent start to the day, particularly for those continuing a journey. Off street parking.

B & B £20-£25pp, C-Cards MC VS AE, Rooms 4 double, 1 twin, 1 single.,
No smoking, Open all year

Zan Stel Lodge, Canterbury

The Old Vicarage, Hougham

The Old Vicarage Chilverton Elms, Hougham, Dover CT15 7AS
Judy Evison Tel: 01304 210668 Fax: 01304 225118
Email: vicarage@csi.com

Map Ref: 8
A20
see Photo opposite

Guests are welcomed in a warm and relaxed style by Judy and Bryan, the owners of this award winning country guest house. Enjoying an outstanding position, set in wooded gardens with open views over the Elms Vale, it is hard to believe that The Old Vicarage is only two miles from the bustle of the port of Dover. Many visitors come back time and again for a short break holiday, to share the elegance, peace and quiet, and to enjoy the pubs, restaurants and attractions of east Kent

B & B £35-£40pp, C-Cards MC VS, Rooms 1 double en-suite, 1 double private, 1 family private, Not in bedrooms, Children welcome, No dogs, Closed Xmas & New Year

Wallett's Court Country House Hotel West Cliffe, St Margaret's, Dover CT15 6EW
The Oakley Family Tel: 01304 852424 Fax: 01304 853430
Email: stay@wallettscourt.com Web: www.wallettscourt.com

Map Ref: 9
A258, A2

Relaxed and secluded, yet only three miles from Dover in The Heart of White Cliffs Country, this 17th century manor house hotel with restaurant and spa is simply beautiful. Luxurious bedrooms have antique four-poster beds, vaulted beamed ceilings and some rooms afford distant views of the English Channel. The restaurant noteworthy in its own right is mentioned in many major food guides and serves some of the finest cuisine in Kent. The spa, a haven of relaxation, houses an indoor pool, sauna, steam room and jacuzzi.

B & B from £45pp, C-Cards MC VS AE, Dinner from £20, Rooms 2 twin, 10 double, 4 four poster/suite, all en-suite, Restricted smoking, Children welcome, No dogs, Open all year

Preston Lea Canterbury Road, Faversham ME13 8XA
Alan & Catherine Turner Tel: 01795 535266 Fax: 01795 533388
Email: preston.lea@which.net Web: http://homepages.which.net/~alan.turner10

Map Ref: 10
A2

Preston Lea is a beautiful and elegant private house which stands in secluded gardens on the edge of the town of Faversham. Visitors here will receive a warm welcome and tea on arrival. The bedrooms which enjoy sunshine and garden views, are well equipped and spacious. They are furnished with antiques they offer every comfort. Guests are welcome to relax in the drawing rooms, the panelled dining room or the gardens. A delicious breakfast is offered and for supper there is a choice of restaurants nearby. Beaches and places of interest closeby.

B & B £28-£30pp, C-Cards MC VS, Rooms 2 double, 1 twin, all en-suite, No smoking, Children welcome, No dogs, Open all year

Tenterden House 209 The Street, Boughton, Faversham ME13 9BL
Prudence Latham
Tel: 01227 751593

Map Ref: 11
M2, A2

The renovated gardener's cottage of this listed Tudor house, provides two en-suite bedrooms (one double, one twin) which can be used separately or together for families or friends. Each room offers tea/coffee facilities and television. Situated in the village, close to Canterbury, the ferry ports and Euro Tunnel, it makes an ideal base for day trips to France and for touring rural and historic Kent. A full English breakfast is served in the main house and a choice of excellent pub or restaurant food is within easy walking distance. Off road parking is provided.

B & B from £20pp, Rooms 1 twin, 1 double, both en-suite, Children welcome, No dogs, Closed Xmas

Leaveland Court Leaveland, Faversham ME13 0NP

Corrine Scutt   Tel: 01233 740596   Fax: 01233 740015
Email: leaveland@mail.com

15th Century Leaveland Court is an enchanting timber framed farmhouse with adjoining granary and stables. In a quiet rural setting the house nestles between 13th century Leaveland Church and woodlands and retains its true character as the heart of a 500 acre working downland farm. Offering a high standard of accommodation and cuisine, a warm welcome is always assured. All bedrooms are en-suite and have tea/coffee making facilities. Guests are invited to use the heated outdoor swimming pool set in secluded and attractive gardens.

*B & B from £25pp, Rooms 1 twin, 2 double, all en-suite, No smoking,
Children welcome, Dogs by arrangement, Closed Nov to Feb*

Maplehurst Mill Mill Lane, Frittenden TN17 2DT

Kenneth & Heather Parker   Tel: 01580 852203   Fax: 01580 852117
Email: maplehurst@clara.net   Web: www.home.clara.net/maplehurst

In their romantic watermill near Sissinghurst, Heather and Kenneth make you feel a welcome friend, whilst giving you all the comforts of tastefully decorated en-suite bedrooms, a cosy drawing room which straddles the millstream, and delicious imaginative breakfasts and candlelit dinners using home produced vegetables, fruit and eggs supplemented by a good wine list. Wildlife and flowers abound in their 11 acres of water meadows and landscaped gardens, which also contain a heated swimming pool. No wonder the mill has featured in many national magazine articles.

*B & B from £38pp, C-Cards MC VS, Dinner from £24, Rooms 2 twin, 3 double, all en-suite,
No smoking, Children over 12, No dogs, Closed Xmas & New Year*

Merzie Meadows Hunton Road, Marden, Maidstone TN12 9SL

Pamela & Rodney Mumford   Tel / Fax: 01622 820500   Mobile: 07762 713077
Web: www.smoothound.co.uk/hotels/merzie.html

Merzie Meadows is a country home individually designed with water fowl and horse paddocks. It enjoys tranquil surroundings and is central for much historical interest including Leeds, Sissinghurst Castle and London. Set in 20 acres the gardens are beautiful, they display an all year round interest. Traditional elegance is combined with modern comforts. The spacious rooms are decorated to a high standard and include a guest wing with sitting room, study and terrace. The rooms here overlook landscaped gardens with a pool. Near good eating places, convenient for London. AA Premier Collection, 5 Diamonds.

*B & B £25-£30pp, Rooms 2 double, guest wing triple, all en-suite, Restricted smoking,
Children over 14, No dogs, Closed mid-Dec to mid-Feb*

Jordans Sheet Hill, Plaxtol, Sevenoaks TN15 0PU

Mrs Jo Lindsay
Tel / Fax: 01732 810379

An exquisite picture postcard 15th century Tudor house situated in the picturesque village of Plaxtol among orchards and parkland. Jordans, awarded a historic building of Kent plaque, has an enchanting English cottage garden with winding paths, rambler roses and espalier trees. There are oak beams, inglenook fireplaces, leaded windows, it is beautifully furnished with antiques and paintings many by Mrs Lindsay, who is also a Blue Badge Guide and can help in planning your tour. Jordans is close to Ightham Mote, Hever, Chartwell, Penshurst Place, Knole, Leeds Castle and Great Comp Garden.

*B & B from £33pp, Rooms 2 double/single, 2 en-suite, No smoking,
Children over 12, No dogs, Closed mid-Dec to mid-Jan*

Jordans, Plaxtol, near Sevenoaks

Oxney Farm Moons Green, Wittersham, Tenterden TN30 7PS

Eve Burnett Tel: 01797 270558 Fax: 01797 270958

Email: oxneyf@globalnet.co.uk Web: www.users.globalnet.co.uk/~oxneyf

Map Ref: 16
B2082

A warm welcome from Kent Hospitality Award winner awaits you at Oxney Farm. It is convenient for the Channel Tunnel and ferry ports. The spacious well furnished comfortable farmhouse, with a luxurious indoor pool, lies in peaceful rural surroundings. The area is steeped in history, scenery and culture. The miniature ponies add their charm to the friendly country house atmosphere. Directions: from Tenterden or Rye, B2082 to Wittersham, at Swan Inn turn into Swan Street, Oxney Farm is 1.3 miles along on the left.

B & B £25-£30pp, C-Cards MC VS, Rooms 1 twin, 2 double, all en-suite,
No smoking, No children or dogs, Open all year

Leavers Oast Stanford Lane, Hadlow, Tonbridge TN11 0JN

Anne & Denis Turner Tel / Fax: 01732 850924 Mobile: 07771 663250

Email: denis@leavers-oast.freeserve.co.uk

Map Ref: 17
A26

A warm welcome awaits you at Leavers Oast. An excellent base for touring the many historic buildings including Leeds and Hever Castles, Chartwell and Sissinghurst. Built circa 1880, Anne and Denis have modernised the accommodation and created a very attractive garden. They have many interests including antiques, art and travel. Two bedrooms are in roundels, the other in the barn. All are spacious and comfortably furnished with television and coffee and tea making facilities. There are many good places to eat or by prior arrangement excellent evening meals are available.

B & B from £27.50pp, Dinner from £22, Rooms 1 twin, 2 double, 1 en-suite,
No smoking, Children from 12, No dogs, Open all year

40 York Road Tunbridge Wells TN1 1JY

Patricia Lobo

Tel / Fax: 01892 531342

Map Ref: 18
M25/A21/A26

40 York Road is an attractive Regency house which stands in the centre of Tunbridge Wells, it has a delightful enclosed courtyard garden. Hostess Patricia Lobo is a professional cook, she is happy to cater for vegetarians and other requests by arrangement. Bedroom one offers a balconied bay window, bedrooom two enjoys a lovely view to the garden. A good local variety of shops and restaurants. So much to see and do, Hever, Scotney, Leeds Castles. Within walking distance of mainline station for London. Gatwick and the Channel Ports are within easy reach.

B & B from £27pp, Dinner from £18, Rooms 2 double/twin en-suite, No smoking in bedrooms,
Children over 12, No dogs, Closed Xmas & New Year

Number Ten Modest Corner, Southborough, Tunbridge Wells TN4 0LS

Anneke Leemhuis Tel / Fax: 01892 522450 Mobile: 07966 190102

Email: modestanneke@lineone.net

Map Ref: 19
A26, A21

Situated in a quiet hamlet with beautiful views and lovely walks, Number Ten is a stone's throw away from Royal Tunbridge Wells and Tonbridge railway station, where frequent trains take you into London within the hour. Tea/coffee and television in all of the rooms. Excellent showers in the bathrooms. A unique welcoming atmosphere and so tranquil that only the birds wake you in the morning. A full English breakfast is served, and may be enjoyed in the garden, weather permitting. Dutch, German and a little French spoken.

B & B £22.50-£25pp, Dinner from £15, Rooms 2 twin, 1 double en-suite, Restricted smoking,
Children & dogs welcome, Closed Xmas & New Year

Lancashire

To many, Lancashire is L.S. Lowry country, a county of vast clattering mills, long lines of millworkers' terraced houses, dirt, smoke and noise. Certainly this was once the case, after all it was the coal, iron-ore, damp climate and swiftly flowing water that firmly established the Industrial Revolution in this rich region. Towns expanded, and with the growing cotton industry fortunes were made and great municipal buildings and private houses were constructed, reflecting the personal and public pride in the new prosperity. Therefore with the ever expanding towns there was a great need for close resorts to cater for the all too short breaks from toil. The result was that Lancashire is now blessed with some of the finest seaside resorts in the country. Blackpool with its 518 feet high imitation of the Eiffel Tower must be the Queen of English holiday resorts. Once the destination for a Victorian day-out for the millworkers of the cotton towns, the resort is now famed internationally, the season having been considerably lengthened by the spectacular Illuminations. This wonderful blaze of colour stretches for miles along the seafront and lasts from August until November. There is everything here that the holiday maker could wish for; amusement arcades line the pavements of the Golden Mile and the Pleasure Beach claims the world's highest and fastest rollercoaster. But behind the brash face of Blackpool is a resort of fine gardens, parks and lovely surrounding countryside.

In the north of the county, Morecambe, once known as Bradford-by-the-Sea for obvious reasons, swiftly developed when the railway brought hoards of day trippers to the resort. Never as popular as its sister Blackpool, the town can nevertheless offer many attractions, which include the tasty Morecambe Bay shrimps. Preston at the head of the Ribble estuary, is now the administrative centre of Lancashire, and was the home of Sir Richard Arkwright who invented the spinning frame that revolutionised the textile industry. The town also has some excellent architecture reflecting Preston's prosperity during the Industrial Revolution, of which The Harris Museum and Art Gallery, built in the Classical style, is a fine example. Lancaster, dominated by its medieval castle of John of Gaunt, Duke of Lancaster, is an ancient city with a formidable history. The House of Lancaster provided kings of England for 62 years until Henry VI was deposed during the War of the Roses.

Within a very short distance of the great cities of this region is some glorious countryside. The Trough of Bowland, the largest area of unspoiled and remote countryside in the county, gives exhilarating views across the Fylde and the Wyre valley. North of Bury is the Stubbins Estate,

The Ribble Valley (NWTB)

187

436 acres of woodland and fields owned by the National Trust, giving access from Rossendale Valley to Holcombe Moor, a bleak area of rough grassland and heath, notable especially for its numerous bird species. The Martin Mere Wildlife and Wetlands Trust acquired in 1972 is 363 acres of marshland and internationally renowned as a wildfowl centre. It was originally one of England's largest lakes until drained in the eighteenth century. The area was allowed to revert to wetland and now attracts up to a tenth of the world's population of pink-footed geese in the winter. Parbold Beacon is the highest point in the south of the county and gives wonderful views across the Lancashire Plain.

The east of the county contains some fine cotton towns with Clitheroe, an ancient town with a Norman keep, one of the earliest stone buildings in the county. Just four miles away is mysterious Pendle Hill, a superb view point but most famous for the Witches of Pendle, who in the early seventeenth century lived in villages along the lower slopes of the hill until their execution at Lancaster Castle in 1612. It was at Burnley where the textile industry in this region really began, with the invention of the fulling mill and the Leeds and Liverpool Canal, which runs through the town, brought prosperity to Burnley during the Industrial Revolution. Burnley Mechanics Arts and Entertainments Centre is well known nationally as a jazz and blues venue. Chorley in the west has a unique 'Flat Iron' market and nearby Duxbury Park is a haunt of red squirrel, foxes and herons.

PLACES TO VISIT

This is a small selection of interesting places to visit. Many more are listed in our annual guide to Museums, Galleries, Historic Houses & Sites (see page 448)

Astley Hall Museum and Art Gallery
Astley Park, Chorley
The Hall dates back to Elizabethan times with the Art Gallery playing host to temporary exhibitions. The collections range from 18th century creamware to the first Rugby League Cup.

Blackpool Tower
The Promenade, Blackpool
Proud Victorian landmark, over 100 years old, offering a variety of family attractions from the children's Jungle Jim to tea dances in the famous Tower Ballroom.

Lancaster Castle
Lancaster
King John has said to have held court at this Castle where many trials and executions have taken place. There is a large display of miniature coats of arms in the Shire Hall.

Rufford Old Hall
Rufford, Ormskirk
One of the finest sixteenth century buildings in Lancashire where Shakespeare is said to have performed for the owner. It houses a magnificent hall with an intricately carved moveable wooden screen.

Lancashire

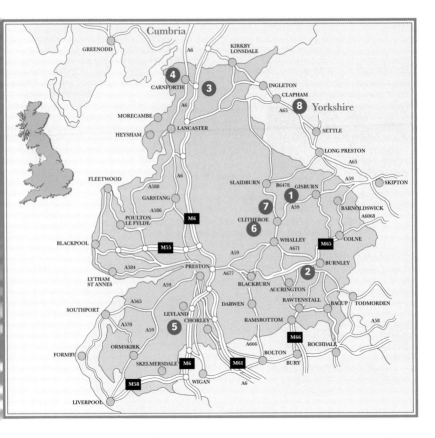

The Blue Map References should be used to locate B & B properties on the pages that follow

Middle Flass Lodge Settle Road, Bolton-by-Bowland BB7 4NY

Joan M Simpson and Nigel E Quayle   Tel: 01200 447259   Fax: 01200 447300
Email: info@middleflasslodge.fsnet.co.uk   Web: www.mflodge.freeservers.com

Map Ref: 1
A59

In former times Middle Flass Lodge was a barn and cow byre, the conversion was completed in 1996. The lodge stands in the peaceful Ribble Valley, surrounded by beautiful, open countryside abundant with birds and wildlife, this is an ideal place for country lovers to relax and enjoy a break. The bedrooms are neat, cosy and well presented with excellent views. Nigel is a former head chef, he creates imaginative meals using fresh produce, Joan also has a catering background. The restaurant is licensed, there is a comfortable lounge to enjoy.

B & B £23-£30pp, C-Cards MC VS, Dinner from £18, Rooms 2 double, 2 twin, 1 family, all en-suite, No smoking, Children welcome, Dogs not in house,

Eaves Barn Farm Hapton, Burnley BB12 7LP

Mrs M Butler   Tel / Fax: 01282 771591   Mobile: 07798 836005
Web: www.eavesbarnfarm.co.uk

Map Ref: 2
A679, M65
see Photo opposite

Eaves Barn is a working farm with a spacious cottage attached to the main house offering luxurious facilities. The elegant guests' lounge has an open log fire and is traditionally furnished including antiques. Individually designed bedrooms with colour television and en-suite facilities. A full English breakfast is served in the Victorian style conservatory. 'Best Bed & Breakfast' in Lancashire 1992. Situated within easy reach of the Ribble Valley and Fylde Coast, Lake District, Yorkshire Dales and the Lancashire hills. Burnley, Blackburn, Preston and Manchester Airport can be reached using the motorway network.

B & B £25-£30pp, Dinner from £14, Rooms 1 single, 1 double, 1 twin, all en-suite, Restricted smoking, Children over 12, No dogs, Closed Xmas & New Year

New Capernwray Farm Capernwray, Carnforth LA6 1AD

Peter & Sally Townend   Tel / Fax: 01524 734284
Email: newcapfarm@aol.com   Web: www.newcapfarm.co.uk

Map Ref: 3
M6 J35

New Capernwray Farm is a welcoming 17th century former farmhouse, set in beautiful Lancashire countryside, and ideal stop-over to Scotland. The atmosphere here is wonderfully relaxed and very friendly. The house is full of character, it offers superb accommodation in luxuriously equipped king, queen and twin bedrooms with en-suite or private facilities. Renowned for its excellent, four course candle-lit dinners, guests may bring their own wines. Detailed help is available with routes and individually printed maps. The farmhouse has received many awards.

B & B £33-£39pp, C-Cards MC VS, Dinner from £19.50, Rooms 1 double, 1 twin, both en-suite, 1 double private showerroom, No smoking, Children over 10, Dogs by arrangement, Closed Nov to Apr

The Bower Yealand Conyers, Carnforth LA5 9SF

Michael & Sally-Ann Rothwell   Tel: 01524 734585   Fax: 01524 730710
Email: info@thebower.co.uk   Web: www.thebower.co.uk

Map Ref: 4
M6, A6

This is a beautiful, small Georgian country house, set in the Arnside and Silverdale Area of Outstanding Natural Beauty, at the northern most tip of Lancashire. It is an ideal base from which to explore the Lake District and Yorkshire Dales National Parks. The Bower is in the small, picturesque village of Yealand Conyers, with extensive views of Ingleborough and surrounding hills. The Rothwells are keen bridge players and love classical music. The lovely bedrooms are generously equipped, delicious home cooked four course dinners are offered. Very peaceful, an ideal stop-over to Scotland.

B & B £28.50-£33.50pp, C-Cards MC VS, Dinner from £13, Rooms 1 double/twin en-suite, 1 double private bathroom, No smoking, Children over 12, No dogs, Open all year

Eaves Barn Farm, Hapton, near Burnley

Parr Hall Farm Parr Lane, Eccleston, Chorley PR7 5SL

Mrs & Mrs Motley Tel: 01257 451917 Fax: 01257 453749

Email: parrhall@talk21.com

Map Ref: 5
M6, A49, B5250

Parr Hall, an 18th century farmhouse set in extensive mature gardens, is peacefully situated in the village of Eccleston. It is within walking distance of good pubs and restaurants. In the 19th century a rear wing was added as a harness room to service horse-drawn buses. Since the present owners have purchased the property, it has been extensively modernised. The bedrooms are furnished to a high standard, they are spacious, and well equipped. Martin Mere, Rufford Old Hall, the Lancashire coast and West Penine Moors are within easy driving distance.

B & B from £25pp, C-Cards MC VS, Rooms 1 single, 2 double, 1 twin, 1 family, most en-suite,
No smoking, Children welcome, No dogs, Open all year

Alden Cottage Kemple End, Birdy Brow, Stonyhurst, Clitheroe BB7 9QY

Brenda Carpenter Tel / Fax: 01254 826468

Email: carpenter@aldencottage.f9.co.uk

Map Ref: 6
M6 J31, A59

Alden Cottage is a charming country cottage, it stands in an Area of Outstanding Natural Beauty, overlooking the Ribble and Hodder valleys. Delightfully furnished rooms display all modern comforts, also fresh flowers, chocolates and a jacuzzi shower and bath. This is a perfect place for a peaceful, relaxing holiday. Alden Cottage is a winner of several awards, including ETC 4 Diamonds plus Gold Award, and Ribble Valley Civic Design and Conservation Award. There is parking for six cars.

B & B from £24.50pp, Rooms 2 double, 1 twin, all en-suite or private bathroom,
No smoking, Children welcome, No dogs, Open all year

Peter Barn Country House Cross Lane, Waddington, Clitheroe BB7 3JH

Jean & Gordon Smith Tel: 01200 428585 Mobile: 07970 826370

Email: jean@peterbarn.fsnet.co.uk

Map Ref: 7
A59, B6478

Award winning Lancashire hospitality is offered in our charmingly restored stone built Tithe Barn on the edge of the Forest of Bowland. Oak beams, squashy sofas and log fires in guests' sitting room with wonderful views of Ribble Valley. Three tastefully furnished bedrooms with all comforts. An acre of impressive gardens with stream and ponds. Jean's home made muesli and marmalade is legendry. Excellent walking, good eating nearby, easy reach of the M6, coast and Lake District. Queen Mother's Award (Environmental), ETC 4 Diamonds, Highly Recommended, Sunday Observer Top 20 B&Bs in Great Britain.

B & B £25-£26pp, Rooms 2 double, 1 twin, all en-suite, No smoking,
Children over 8, No dogs, Closed Xmas & New Year

Woodview Guest House The Green, Austwick, Lancaster LA2 8BB

Mrs Jenny Suri

Tel / Fax: 015242 51268

Map Ref: 8
A65

Woodview is one of Austwick's oldest farmhouses (circa 1700), it is an elegant Grade II listed building which stands on the village green. Having been sympathetically refurbished with great attention to detail, the property retains many of its original features. The bedrooms are furnished to a high standard and they are well equipped with modern comforts. There is a charming, beamed guests' lounge with an open fire, the dining room has a relaxed and friendly atmosphere, here traditional breakfasts and evening meals are offered. An ideal base for exploring, by car or on foot.

B & B £50-£64pp, C-Cards MC VS, Rooms 3 double, 1 twin, 2 family, all en-suite, No smoking,
Children welcome, Dogs by arrangement, Closed Xmas & New Year

Leicestershire, Nottinghamshire & Rutland

Leicestershire, a county at the very heart of England, is endowed with some of the country's largest and most impressive estates. A largely agricultural county on the eastern side with the industrial East Midlands on the western side. The City of Leicester, situated on the River Soar, is the county town and a major commercial and industrial centre. It has a magnificent museum overlooking the site of the Roman baths and the half-timbered medieval Guildhall in Castle Park, the scene of a great banquet celebrating the defeat of the Spanish Armada. The de Montfort Hall recalls Simon de Montfort, the first Earl of Leicester, a great benefactor of the city, who led the revolt against his brother-in-law, Henry III, and set the pattern for future parliamentary government. Leicester is an excellent centre for touring the region, displayed by the statue outside the railway station, of travel pioneer Thomas Cook, who organised his first tour from here in 1841. To the north of the city is Loughborough where Cook brought that first excursion to a temperance meeting. The town is an important educational centre and a fine holiday base, being surrounded by Charnwood Forest. A wonderful area of high undulating country-side punctuated by rocky granite outcrops and scattered with lovely grey-stone villages. It was right here at Bradgate House, surrounded by glorious parkland and open heath that the tragic queen-for-nine-days, Lady Jane Grey lived. To the east is Melton Mowbray, famous for its cheese and pork pies, with its wolds presenting wonderful walking country. Much of the countryside here is planted with small coverts for the breeding of foxes, the land being hunted by the Quorn, Cottesmore and Belvoir Hunts. The kennels of the Belvoir Hunt are housed at Belvoir Castle, a fairytale castle, seat of the Dukes of Rutland since the days of Henry VIII. However the present handsome building is a Gothic revival structure built in 1816 by Wyatt, with lovely gardens, overlooking the beautiful Vale of Belvoir. In the west is Ashby-de-la-Zouch, a former spa with some fine Georgian buildings. Its fifteenth century manor of Lord Hastings was reputedly the setting for Sir Walter Scott's 'Ivanhoe' and the Staunton Harold church here is one of the very few churches to be built during the Commonwealth.

Rutland became a part of Leicestershire with the 1974 reorganisation, and not without considerable opposition. A mere fifteen miles in length and eleven in width, it was England's smallest county, and with a history going back to before the twelfth century. A large

Stanford Hall, Lutterworth, Leicestershire

part of the county now lies beneath Rutland Water, one of the largest man-made lakes in Europe, providing major recreational facilities, including fishing, sailing and pleasure cruises, as well as drinking water for the East Midlands.

Nottinghamshire, lying on the low ground of the Trent basin is renowned as the county of Robin Hood, the outlaw who roamed this region and lived in Sherwood Forest, a royal hunting forest which once covered over 160 square miles. Sherwood Forest County Park contains the ancient Major Oak, reputedly the home of Robin, while Edwinstowe Church is claimed to be the scene of his marriage to Maid Marion. The historic city of Nottingham is a fine shopping centre, its old market square was the location of the ancient Goose Fair, now moved to the Forest area. The seventeenth century castle became a museum in 1878 but below the castle is the intriguing Trip To Jerusalem Inn, said to have been established in the days of the Crusades. Clumber Park, the former estate of the Dukes of Newcastle is a glorious 3,800 acres of parkland, farmland, lake and woodlands and includes the largest double lime avenue in Europe as well as an 80 acre lake. Clumber's walled garden includes a Victorian Apiary and Vineries and Tools exhibition. Southwell, to the north of Nottingham can claim one of the most delightful cathedrals in the country. Its Chapter House, begun in 1292, contains some remarkable stone carving depicting the oak, maple, vine and ivy leaves of Sherwood Forest. Eastwood is the birthplace of D.H.Lawrence, the author of 'Sons and Lovers', and celebrates his life with his miner's terraced house having since been converted into a museum.

PLACES TO VISIT

This is a small selection of interesting places to visit. Many more are listed in our annual guide to Museums, Galleries, Historic Houses & Sites (see page 448)

Belvoir Castle
near Grantham
Home of the Duke and Duchess of Rutland, the castle has a notable collection of art treasures and also houses the Queen's Royal Lancers' Museum.

Newstead Abbey
Ravenshead, Nottinghamshire
The birthplace of Lord Byron where you can see his own apartments as well as the elegant Salon and the Baronial Great Hall. Set in I gardens with waterfalls, lakes, themed gardens and ponds..

Bosworth Battlefield Visitor Centre
Market Bosworth, Leicestershire
An interpretation of the Battle of Bosworth 1485 through a film theatre, exhibitions and models.

Southwell Minster
Southwell, Nottinghamshire
Originally a monastery founded in the 10th century or earlier, the church begun in 1108, was raised to cathedral status in the late 19th century. Famous for its carved foliage decoration.

Stanford Hall
Lutterworth, Leicestershire
Built in the 1690s for Sir Roger Cave, home to his descendants with exquisite architecture, a library with over 5,000 books and a motorcycle museum.

Leicestershire,
Nottinghamshire & Rutland

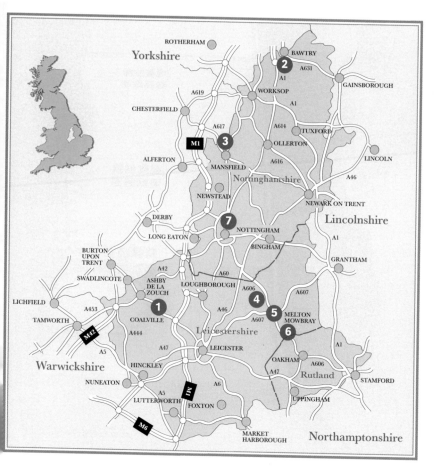

The Blue Map References should be used to locate B & B properties on the pages that follow

Gorse House, Grimston, Melton Mowbray

Abbots Oak Country House Warren Hills Road, Greenhill, Coalville, Leics LE67 4UY

Mrs Carolyn Voce
Tel / Fax: 01530 832328

Map Ref: 1
M1 J22, A511

Abbots Oak Country House is a beautiful Grade II listed home which stands in mature gardens and woodlands, with natural granite out-crops. The house displays a wealth of carved oak panelling including a three storey staircase which reputedly is from Nell Gwynn's townhouse. The delightful bedrooms all have either en-suite or private bathroom. Open fires on cool evenings create a relaxed and friendly atmosphere, superb dinners are served in the candlelit dining room. Guests may play tennis or relax in the gardens. Stratford, Belvoir Castle and Rutland Water are within pleasant driving distance.

*B & B £30-£45pp, Dinner from £20, Rooms 3 double, 1 twin, all en-suite,
Restricted smoking, Children & dogs welcome, Open all year*

The Old George Dragon Scrooby, near Bawtry, Doncaster, Notts DN10 6AU

John & Georgina Smithers
Tel: 01302 711840

Map Ref: 2
A638, A1M

A warm welcome awaits you at this attractive 18th century cottage. It is situated in the picturesque village of Scrooby, internationally known for its links with the Pilgrim Fathers and Robin Hood country, which is easily reached. The accommodation is tastefully furnished, it has retained many of its original features. The bedrooms which comprise two double rooms and one twin room, all have either en-suite or private facilities, colour television and a tea and coffee tray. The Old George Dragon is two miles from the A1 M, it is not a pub.

B & B from £20pp, Rooms 1 twin, 2 double, all en-suite, Open all year

Titchfield GH 300/302 Chesterfield Road North, Pleasley, Mansfield, Notts NG19 7QU

Betty Hinchley
Tel: 01623 810921   Fax: 01623 810356

Map Ref: 3
M1, A617

Titchfield is two houses converted into one family run guest house offering eight comfortable rooms. Guests have a lounge with television, a kitchen for making hot drinks, a bathroom and shower. It also has an adjoining garage. Titchfield is near to Mansfield which is a busy market town. The well known Sherwood Forest and the Peak District are easily accessible. We are very handy for touring this lovely area and for those wishing to continue their travels. A warm and friendly welcome is assured here at all times.

*B & B from £18pp, C-Cards MC VS, Rooms 4 single, 2 twin, 1 double, 1 family,
Restricted smoking, Children welcome, Dogs by arrangement, Closed Xmas*

Gorse House 33 Main Street, Grimston, Melton Mowbray, Leics LE14 3BZ

Lyn & Richard Cowdell   Tel / Fax: 01664 813537   Mobile: 07768 341848
Email: cowdell@gorsehouse.co.uk   Web: www.gorsehouse.co.uk

Map Ref: 4
M1, A46
see Photo opposite

Convenient for both Nottingham and Leicester (just two miles from the A46), this extended 17th century cottage is situated in the pretty conservation village of Grimston where life is peaceful and unhurried. Set in an attractive garden and with light and airy rooms, Gorse House provides comfort and relaxation. Beautiful countryside for walking, riding (stables available) and touring. Ragdale Hall Health Hydro close by and good pub food in the Black Horse within 100 yards walk.

*B & B £20-£25pp, Rooms 2 double/twin en-suite, No smoking,
Children over 12, No dogs, Open all year*

Sulney Fields Colonel's Lane, Melton Mowbray, Notts LE14 3BD

Hilary Collinson Tel: 01664 822204 Fax: 01664 823976
Email: hillyc@talk21.com

Map Ref: 5
A606, A607

Sulney Fields is a large family house which looks out onto lawns and rose beds, it is situated in a quiet position and enjoys stunning views, the Vale of Belvoir is close at hand. Most of the bedrooms have private facilities, they are all well equipped with tea and coffee making facilities, all rooms have a television. A comfortable sitting room is available for guests' use. There are many good local pubs from which to choose, one is within walking distance.

B & B £20-£22.50pp, Rooms 1 single, 2 double with 1 pb, 2 twin with 1 pb, No smoking, Children & dogs welcome, Closed Xmas & New Year

The Grange New Road, Burton Lazars, Melton Mowbray, Leics LE14 2UU

Pam & Ralph Holden
Tel / Fax: 01664 560775

Map Ref: 6
A606

This beautiful country house surrounds you with elegance, comfort and friendly care. Outstanding views and lovely formal garden of two and a half acres. Formerly a hunting lodge, it now provides attractive accommodation. Each bedroom is en-suite with telephone, television and tea/coffee making facilities. The drawing room is furnished with antiques and has an open log burning fire. Dinner is served in a spacious dining room. Only one and a half miles to Melton Mowbray and close to Rutland Water and Belvoir Castle.

B & B from £22.25pp, C-Cards MC VS, Rooms 1 single, 1 twin, 1 double, 1 family, all en-suite, Restricted smoking, Children welcome, No dogs, Open all year

Hillside House 27 Melton Road, Burton Lazars, Melton Mowbray, Leics LE14 2UR

Sue & Peter Goodwin Tel: 01664 566312 Fax: 01664 501819
Email: sue&peter@hillside-house.co.uk Web: www.hillside-house.co.uk

Map Ref: 6
A606

Hillside House is a charmingly converted old farm building overlooking rolling countryside. It stands in the small village of Burton Lazars. Comfortable accommodation is offered in three bedrooms which have either en-suite or private facilities. All the bedrooms are well equipped with television, hospitality trays, central heating, radio alarms and hair dryers. The house is centrally heated throughout. There is a pleasant garden for guests to enjoy. Hillside House is situated within easy reach of Burghley House, Belvoir Castle, Stamford and Rutland Water - also beautiful villages and countryside.

B & B £19-£22pp, Rooms 1 double en-suite, 1 twin en-suite, 1 twin private bathroom, Restricted smoking, Children over 10, No dogs, Closed Xmas & New Year

Greenwood Lodge City GH Third Avenue, Sherwood Rise, Nottingham, Notts NG7 6JH

Michael & Sheila Spratt Tel / Fax: 0115 9621206
Email: coolspratt@aol.com

Map Ref: 7
A60 Mansfield Rd

Greenwood Lodge City Guest House is less than a mile from the centre of Nottingham. Just off the A60 Mansfield Road, situated in a quiet area and is the home of Sheila and Michael Spratt who offer superior accommodation, all en-suite with hospitality tray, trouser press, TV, hair dryer and fine four poster. Magnificent conservatory dining room in elegant gardens. Ample off-street parking. The only guest house in Nottinghamshire to receive an ETC Gold Award. Within short distance of Newstead Abbey, Chatsworth House, Sherwood Forest, Belvoir Castle.

B & B from £28pp, Rooms 1 single, 1 twin, 2 double, 2 four-poster, all en-suite, No smoking, Children welcome, Dogs by arrangement, Open all year

Lincolnshire

Lincolnshire may well be flat, but dull it certainly is not. The county radiates from the flat shores of the North Sea, north to Yorkshire and west to the Midlands. The land is particularly flat where it joins the Wash and the Fens in the south but cutting through the centre is the Lincolnshire Edge, a ridge of chalk, upon which stands Lincoln, its triple towered cathedral gloriously dominating all the surrounding countryside. Lincoln cathedral is exceptional indeed, one of England's finest, largely rebuilt during the thirteenth and fourteenth centuries following an earthquake in 1185. The cathedral is renowned for its decagonal chapter house with its magnificent intricately carved Angel Choir, and the famous Lincolnshire Imp, a stone carving with the story that the imp was caught chatting up the angels and so was turned to stone. The historic city of Lincoln has much to attract the visitor with the Norman castle walls walk, the Jew's House, St Mary's Guild Hall, the Usher Gallery and the fine Georgian and medieval houses in Minster Yard. The statue of Lord Tennyson the poet, who was a great lover of this county, stands outside the cathedral. His poem, 'Maud', of 'come into the garden' fame is said to be linked to the lovely gardens of Harrington Hall in the Lincolnshire Wolds. These uplands, though only about 500 feet, are designated as an Area of Outstanding Natural Beauty and stretch from Dorset to Yorkshire containing the prehistoric ridge top routes and give fine views across the county.

The Holland region in the southwest is in effect a continuation of the Cambridgeshire fen country, drained in the seventeenth century and renowned for its flower bulb industry. Spalding is the hub of this area and holds a Flower Parade every May, surely the greatest free pageant of colour in the country, when over three million tulips are used to decorate floats, and accompanied by bands parade the streets. On the southern rim of Lincolnshire, within the flood plain of the River Welland, are the Deepings, Market Deeping and Deeping St James, with its lovely church and rare Georgian tower. Nearby, Stamford, designated England's first conservation area in 1967, contains a remarkable number of excellent buildings in the lovely local stone. The Church of St Martin houses the alabaster monument to Lord Burghley, whose palatial mansion, Burghley House, stands on the outskirts of the town in its Capability Brown landscaped park. Built for William Cecil, chief minister to Elizabeth I, the house contains some remarkable Italian plaster work.

Lincoln Castle from Cathedral (LCC)

To the north is Boston, once England's second most important port. The historic market town is dominated by the magnificent Church of St Botolph, England's largest parish church, known as the Boston Stump, where from its tower a third of Lincolnshire can be seen. It was, incidentally, from Boston that the main group of the 'Pilgrim Fathers' embarked in the 'Mayflower'.

For the visitor interested in the rich history of this region there is more than enough to satisfy the most inquiring mind, but for the visitor intent upon the pleasures of the seaside there is Skegness with its wide sandy beaches. From the early nineteenth century the little fishing village was attracting holiday visitors, but with the arrival of the railway and with the innovative planning of the Earl of Scarborough, the main landowner, the town swiftly developed into what it is today, a first class holiday resort. To the north, its sister resort Mablethorpe, has miles of golden sands as well as an animal and bird garden with a seal sanctuary.

Of course the Plain of Lincolnshire was renowned during the Second World War for its RAF airfields. Scampton was the home base of 617 Squadron, the 'Dambusters', and at Coningsby the Battle of Britain's Memorial Flight has its home with its display of Spitfires, a Hurricane and a Lancaster. Horncastle, north of Coningsby, standing between the Wolds and the Fens, was a Roman settlement and an important medieval trading center. Today the town is a fascinating mixture of styles. Further north, Louth, another Area of Outstanding Natural Beauty, is ideal for exploring the Lincolnshire Wolds and the exceptionally attractive Hubbards Hills valley.

PLACES TO VISIT

This is a small selection of interesting places to visit. Many more are listed in our annual guide to Museums, Galleries, Historic Houses & Sites (see page 448)

Belton House, Park and Gardens
Belton, Grantham
Built in 1685 for Sir John Brownlow, with alterations by James Wyatt in the 1770s. Fine collections and gardens with an orangery.

Burghley House
Stamford
The largest and grandest house of the first Elizabethan Age, completed by William Cecil, Lord Burghley, in 1587. 18 state rooms are open with fine art, furniture and paintings and grounds designed by 'Capability' Brown.

Lincoln Castle
Lincoln
A medieval castle with grassy lawns inside the walls, a Magna Carta exhibition and old Victorian Prison. Reconstructed Westgate and popular events throughout the summer.

Lincoln Cathedral
Lincoln
One of the largest churches in England and inside the visitor can find two famous stained glass windows, the Dean's Eye and the Bishop's Eye, as well as the famous Lincoln Imp.

Lincolnshire

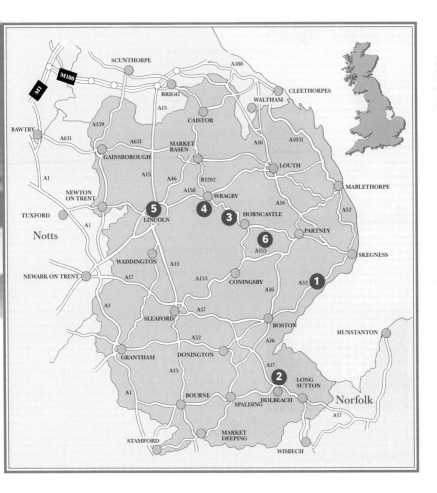

The Blue Map References should be used to locate B & B properties on the pages that follow

The Old Vicarage Church Lane, Wrangle, Boston PE22 9EP
Michael & Julia Brotherton Tel: 01205 870688 Fax: 01205 871857
Email: jb141@aol.com Mobile: 07867 893665

Map Ref: 1
A52

This fine, imposing vicarage which may be found opposite the church, was built in local, handmade, mellow red brick, it is a listed Queen Anne building. Standing in the village of Wrangle, it enjoys a glorious setting. The house dispays a wealth of panelling which lends an air of history and intrigue, the sitting room is panelled, as is the stone flagged hall, square in dimension, and leads to a red pine staircase, also panelled. Dinner including wine, is available, hosts Michael and Julia love cooking, the fruits and vegetables are home grown.

B & B from £27.50pp, Dinner from £24.50, Rooms 1 double, 1 twin, No smoking, Children welcome, No dogs, Closed Xmas & New Year

Cackle Hill House Cackle Hill Lane, Holbeach PE12 8BS
Maureen Biggadike Tel: 01406 426721 Fax: 01406 424659
Email: cacklehill2@netscapeonline.co.uk

Map Ref: 2
A17

A warm friendly welcome awaits you at our comfortable home set in a rural position. All the rooms are tastefully furnished, have en-suite/private facilities and hospitality trays. There is an attractive guests' lounge with a colour television. For those who wish to explore this intriguing county, Cackle Hill House is ideally situated. There are many attractions, from museums and monuments to miles of golden sands. The counties of Norfolk and Cambridgshire are within a pleasant drive.

B & B from £20pp, Rooms 1 double en-suite, 1 twin en-suite, 1 twin pb, No smoking, Children over 10, Dogs by arrangement, Closed Xmas & New Year

Pipwell Manor Washway Road, Saracen's Head, Holbeach PE12 8AL
Lesley Honnor Tel / Fax: 01406 423119
Email: honnor@pipwellmanor.freeserve.co.uk

Map Ref: 2
A17

This Georgian house was built around 1740 and is a Grade II listed building. It has been tastefully restored and redecorated in the appropriate style and retains many of its original features. All 4 bedrooms are attractive and well furnished and have tea/coffee making facilities. Parking is available and guests are welcomed with home made cakes and tea. Pipwell Manor stands amid gardens and paddocks in a small village just off the A17 in the Lincolnshire Fens. A lovely place to stay. 'Country Living' Highly Recommended.

B & B from £23pp, Rooms 2 double, 1 twin, all en-suite/private, No smoking, No children or dogs, Closed Xmas & New Year

Baumber Park Baumber, Horncastle LN9 5NE
Mrs C Harrison
Tel: 01507 578235 Fax: 01507 578417 Mobile: 07977 722776

Map Ref: 3
A158
see Photo opposite

Baumber Park is a spacious, elegant farmhouse of character in a quiet parkland setting on a mixed farm. Large gardens, wildlife pond, grass tennis court. Fine bedrooms with lovely views, period furniture, log fires and books. Close to the Lincolnshire Wolds, this rolling countryside is little known and quite unspoilt. Bridleways and lanes ideal for walking, cycling or riding: stabling for horses available. Two championship golf courses at nearby Woodhall Spa, well located for historic Lincoln, interesting market towns and many antiques shops. A warm welcome awaits.

B & B from £22.50pp, Dinner from £10, Rooms 1 double, 1 twin, all en-suite/private, Restricted smoking, Children welcome, Dogs by arrangement, Closed Xmas & New Year

Baumber Park, Baumber, near Horncastle

Greenfield Farm Mill Lane/Cow Lane, Minting, Horncastle LN9 5PJ

Judy & Hugh Bankes Price   Tel / Fax: 01507 578457   Mobile: 07768 368829

Email: greenfieldfarm@farming.co.uk

Map Ref: 4
A158

Enjoy a quiet stay in our lovely spacious home, surrounded by extensive grounds and dominated by a wonderful wildlife pond. Centrally placed and easy to find, Lincoln Cathedral is 15 minutes away and the sleepy Lincolnshire Wolds five minutes. We are close to the aviation trails, antique centres and Cadwell Park. The bedrooms have modern en-suite shower rooms with heated towel rails, tea/coffee making and wonderful views. A typical farmhouse breakfast is served, you must try the Lincolnshire sausages and homemade marmalade. Plenty of parking, traditional pub one mile.

B & B from £22pp, Rooms 2 double, 1 twin, all en-suite/private, No smoking, Children over 10, No dogs, Closed mid-Dec to mid-Jan

Minster Lodge Hotel 3 Church Lane, Lincoln LN2 1QJ

John & Margaret Baumber   Tel / Fax: 01522 513220

Email: info@minsterlodge.co.uk   Web: www.minsterlodge.co.uk

Map Ref: 5
A15, A46

Enjoy the unique Minister Lodge experience for warmth of welcome, comfort and hospitality. This impressive family owned Victorian residence, has been refurbished to a high standard, and is now your personal 'Home away from Home'. It is in a premier situation, being within walking distance to the magnificent Cathedral, castle, museum, university, Usher Gallery and Lawn Exhibition Centre. There is an excellent selection of restaurants and tourist shops. 'A lovely place with extra-ordinary hospitality' Philip Lader, US Ambassador, London. 'A superb experience in every way!' Carlo Curley, International Concert Organist.

B & B from £35pp, C-Cards MC VS AE, Rooms 6 single, 3 twin, 6 double, 2 family, all en-suite, No smoking, Children welcome, No dogs, Open all year

Orchard House 119 Yarborough Road, Lincoln LN1 1HR

June Williams   Tel: 01522 528795   Mobile: 07939 548742

Email: orchardhouse50@hotmail.com   Web: orchardhouselincoln.com

Map Ref: 5
A15, A57, A158

Orchard House, a pleasant red brick Edwardian guest house, may be found close to the Cathedral and shopping centre. It is small and friendly, and stands in 1/3 of an acre of immaculate gardens, it has ample private parking. All the well presented bedrooms offer en-suite facilities, colour television and tea/coffee making facilities. A superb full English breakfast is served in the light and bright dining room, the eggs are provided by our own hens. Dinners are available by arrangement.

B & B from £20pp, Rooms 1 double, 1 twin, 1 family, all en-suite, Restricted smoking, Children over 5, No dogs, Open all year

White Oak Grange Hagworthingham, Spilsby PE23 4LX

Mrs Jan Morris-Holmes   Tel: 01507 588376   Fax: 01507 588377

Web: www.whiteoakgrange.com

Map Ref: 6
A158

White Oak Grange is a fine country house, it stands in six acres of beautiful gardens, which enjoy spectacular views over the glorious Lincolnshire Wolds. Guests here are assured of a warm welcome and generous hospitality, open log fires help to create a relaxed atmosphere. Home cooking is a speciality, vegetables from the garden and fresh local produce are used whenever possible. The house is licensed. Private trout fishing is available, and the area is renowned for its wonderful walks through Tennyson country. Four Diamonds, Silver Award.

B & B from £25pp, Dinner from £15, Rooms 2 double, 1 twin, 3 en-suite, No smoking, Children over 10, No dogs, Closed Xmas & New Year

Norfolk

The fact that the National Trust owns so much of Norfolk indicates just what an attractive county this is. Of course, the Norwich School of English Landscape Painters appreciated the wide panoramic skies, the wonderful cloud formations and the glorious seascapes many years before the Trust took an interest. However, one of the great advantages of this fine county is that there are still parts relatively unexplored. The north Norfolk coast has so much to offer the holiday visitor, the naturalist in particular, holding the largest saltmarshes in Europe. Blakeney Point, the three and a half mile long sand and shingle spit is the summer home for over eleven species of seabird, and winter home for large flocks of brent geese. Common seals also breed off the point of the spit.

To the south, King's Lynn, known as Bishop's Lynn until confiscated by Henry VIII, was a powerful and prosperous member of the Hanseatic League, the North European Merchants Group. The town is a delightful cluster of medieval lanes around the waterfront and the fifteenth century St George's Guildhall of 1420 is thought to be the oldest guildhall in England. Just outside King's Lynn is situated the country retreat of the Queen and the Duke of Edinburgh, Sandringham. It houses a grand collection of guns and armour brought back from the far east in 1876 plus a fascinating museum in the old coach and stable block.

This region is an ideal holiday centre with so much to see, including 2,000 acres of beach and four miles of tidal foreshore with sand dunes and saltmarshes, which include the site of the Roman fort of Branodunum. Visitors can also visit the National Nature Reserve on Scolt Head Island, an important breeding site for tern. Nobody could leave this northern coast without sampling the delights of Cromer and its crabs and Little Walsingham, a centre of pilgrimage for nine hundred years. Nearby is Wells-next-the-Sea which is not only famous for its whelks but is also home to Holkham Hall a majestic stately home in 3000 acre deer park with the interesting Bygones Museum.

Burnham Mill (EETB)

Great Yarmouth, with one of the most attractive waterfronts in England, protected from the rages of the North Sea behind its spit of land, has for over a thousand years been an important port but then during the nineteenth century was 'discovered' by the Victorians. Now five miles of promenade, golden beaches and a spectacular pleasure beach make Great Yarmouth one of the country's major seaside resorts. The visitor must not miss South Quay, a sixteenth century building with a nineteenth century facade, now a fascinating museum of domestic life.

The Norfolk Broads is a triangular area of the county which stretches from Stalham in the north to Norwich in the west and Lowestoft in the southeast, attracting thousands of visitors each year with its lakes and waterways offering glorious leisurely sailing. The Rivers Ant, Chet, Thurne, Bure, Yare and Waveney link the Broads and are jam-packed with pleasure craft. If you want to avoid the crowds there are still many streams and rivulets giving peace and tranquillity. Without doubt, to fully appreciate this wonderful region it must be enjoyed from a boat, and Wroxham and Hoveton are at the very heart of the Broads scene with boatyards and river craft of every description.

Norwich is the queen of this lovely county and the perfect base to explore the whole area. A university city with antique and speciality shops galore, also offering some fine buildings, Elm Hill, Colegate and Bridewell Alley. The city can boast thirty-three medieval churches, but without doubt the gem is the eleventh century cathedral. It displays some of the best Gothic architecture in Britain with its spire being second in height to Salisbury. Whatever you wish to learn about the lovely county of Norfolk is contained within the quite splendid museums of Norwich, including the Bridewell Museum in Bridewell Alley, which explains the trades, industries and daily life of Norwich over the last two hundred years. The Castle Museum is also not to be missed, with its celebrated paintings by the Norwich School, so aptly encapsulating the very spirit of the county.

PLACES TO VISIT

This is a small selection of interesting places to visit. Many more are listed in our annual guide to Museums, Galleries, Historic Houses & Sites (see page 448)

Blickling Hall
Blickling, Norwich
One of England's great Jacobean houses with fine collections of pictures, furniture and tapestries. The grounds include an extensive formal garden, a crescent shaped lake, and an orangery and temple built by the Ivorys

Holkham Hall
Wells-next-the-Sea, Norfolk
An eighteenth century Palladian-style mansion set in a great agricultural estate and a living treasure house of artistic and architectural history.

Norfolk Lavender
Heacham, King's Lynn
A family enterprise and the oldest established lavender farm in England. Lavender is distilled from the flowers and the oil made into a wide range of gifts.

Norwich Cathedral
The Close, Norwich
The Norman Cathedral was begun in 1096, made of Caen stone with a 315 foot high spire. The stone vaulting roof replaced the existing wooden one in the 14th century and tells the story of the Bible.

Sandringham House and Museum
Sandringham, King's Lynn
The country retreat of HM Queen Elizabeth was built in 1870 by the Prince and Princess of Wales and stands in 60 acres of grounds and lakes, with important royal collections on display.

Thursford Collection
Thursford, Fakenham
A splendid collection of old road engines and mechanical organs, all richly decorated and engraved with regular musical evenings.

Norfolk

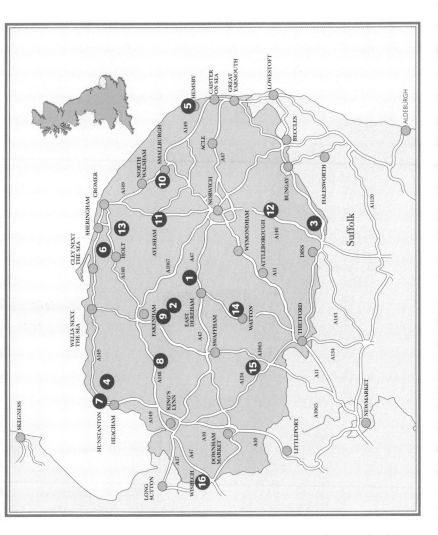

The Blue Map References should be used to locate B & B properties on the pages that follow

Peacock House, Old Beetley, near Dereham

Bartles Lodge Church Street, Elsing, Dereham NR20 3EA
David & Annie Bartlett
Tel: 01362 637177

Map Ref: 1
A47, A1067

If you would like a peaceful stay in the heart of Norfolk's beautiful country yet only a short drive to some of England's finest beaches, then Bartles Lodge could be the place for you. All rooms are tastefully decorated in country style, and they have full en-suite facilities. Bartles Lodge overlooks 12 acres of landscaped meadows with its own private fishing lakes. Although the lodge is fully licensed, the local village inn is 100 yards away. Why not telephone David or Annie so that we can tell you about our lovely home.

B & B from £23pp, Rooms 4 double, 3 twin, Open all year

Peacock House Peacock Lane, Old Beetley, Dereham NR20 4DG
Peter & Jenny Bell   Tel: 01362 860371   Mobile: 07979 013258
PeakH@aol.com   www.smoothhound.co.uk/hotels.peacockh.html

Map Ref: 2
B1110
see Photo opposite

Peacock House is a lovely old farmhouse, peacefully situated, offering excellent accommodation. All the guest rooms are en-suite and beautifully furnished in traditional country style, with colour televisions and hospitality trays. Guests have their own attractive sitting room and are welcome to enjoy the garden. Norwich, which is a university city, with antique and speciality shops, also is home to some wonderful buildings the finest perhaps being the 11th century Cathedral. Spectacular Norfolk beaches, Sandringham, National Trust houses and numerous places of interest are within easy reach. Off road parking.

B & B from £22.50pp, Rooms 1 twin, 1 double, 1 family, all en-suite, No smoking, Children welcome, Dogs by arrangement, Open all year

Grove Thorpe Grove Road, Brockdish, Diss IP21 4JR
Angela & John Morrish   Tel / Fax: 01379 668305
Email: b-b@grovethorpe.freeserve.co.uk   Web: www.grovethorpe.co.uk

Map Ref: 3
A143

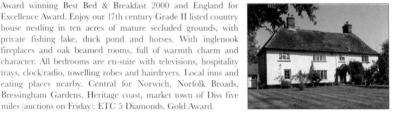

Award winning Best Bed & Breakfast 2000 and England for Excellence Award. Enjoy our 17th century Grade II listed country house nestling in ten acres of mature secluded grounds, with private fishing lake, duck pond and horses. With inglenook fireplaces and oak beamed rooms, full of warmth charm and character. All bedrooms are en-suite with televisions, hospitality trays, clock/radio, towelling robes and hairdryers. Local inns and eating places nearby. Central for Norwich, Norfolk Broads, Bressingham Gardens, Heritage coast, market town of Diss five miles (auctions on Friday). ETC 5 Diamonds, Gold Award.

B & B £26-£35pp, Rooms 3 double/twin, all en-suite, 1 ground floor, No smoking, Children over 12, No dogs, Closed Xmas & New Year

North Farmhouse Station Road, Docking PE31 8LS
Helen & Roger Roberts   Tel: 01485 518493
Email: northfarmhouse@aol.com

Map Ref: 4
A149

North farmhouse is an attractive typical Norfolk Flint and Brick building standing in an acre. It is at least 300 years old and has accommodation for four people. We have one twin bedroom and one double bedroom both with their own facilities. We are excellently situated for anyone wishing to visit the North West Norfolk area and Sandringham, and fairly central for Kings Lynn, Wells, Fakenham and Hunstanton. The area is superb for walking, bird watching, cycling, golf and beaches.

B & B £18-£25pp, Rooms 1 double, 1 twin, both with pb, 1 family en-suite, No smoking, Children & dogs welcome, Closed Xmas & New Year

Tower Cottage Black Street, Winterton-on-Sea, Great Yarmouth NR29 4AP

Alan & Muriel Webster

Tel: 01493 394053

Map Ref: 5
Black Street

This charming flint cottage with many original features, stands in a pretty village, opposite the 14th century church. Two attractive bedrooms are located on the ground floor and have beverage trays, colour television and wash hand basins. One double is in a small converted barn with en-suite facilities and its own sitting area. Generous breakfasts including homemade preserves are served amongst the grapevines in the conservatory in summer. A beautiful, unspoilt sandy beach and traditional village pub serving good food, are a few minutes walk away. The Norfolk broads are two miles, Norwich 19 miles.

*B & B £19-£21pp, Rooms 1 twin own bathroom, 1 double shower/wc, 1 double en-suite,
Restricted smoking, Children over 8, No dogs, Open all year*

Rosedale Farm Guesthouse Holt Road, Weybourne, Holt NR25 7ST

Charles & Pauline Lacoste   Tel: 01263 588778

Email: rosedale.lacoste@tinyworld.co.uk

Map Ref: 6
A149 Coast Road

Ideally set for getting away, Rosedale is a traditional flint and brick farmhouse and situated within its own walled gardens on the Norfolk coastline, equi-distant from Cley-Next-The-Sea and Cromer. Whether sight-seeing or rambling no one will be short of places to visit with Sheringham Park and Kelling Heath on the doorstep and the Shire Horse Centre, Felbrigg, Blickling Holkham Hall and Thursford Museum all nearby. Excellent cuisine awaits you at Rosedale, residents' own sitting room and large comfortable bedrooms. Licensed. Cycle hire available. Heated swimming pool. Self catering cottage also available.

*B & B from £27.50pp, Dinner from £16, Rooms 1 twin, 2 double, 1 family, all en-suite,
Restricted smoking, Children welcome, Dogs small extra charge, Closed Xmas*

Fieldsend 26 Homefields Road, Hunstanton PE36 5HL

Sheila & John Tweedy Smith

Tel / Fax: 01485 532593

Map Ref: 7
A149
see Photo opposite

Come and stay at Fieldsend and enjoy the comfort of a large Edwardian carrstone house, which is close to the Town Centre and the sea, with Panoramic views over the Wash. Guests have a choice of three rooms, two en-suite and one with a private bathroom, all individually decorated by the owner who specialises in rag rolling, making the drapes and pelmets as well as upholstery and collecting coloured glass. One bedroom has a four poster. Delicious breakfasts are served by a Cordon Bleu cook. Parking in the grounds.

*B & B from £22.50pp, Rooms 1 twin, 2 double, all en-suite/private,
Children welcome, No dogs, Open all year*

Lower Farm Harpley, Kings Lynn PE31 6TU

Amanda Case

Tel: 01485 520240   Fax: 01845 520240

Map Ref: 8
A148

Lower Farm is a large family home, set in delightful countryside and off the beaten track. It is comfortable and hospitable, there are family dogs and horses, and there is stabling for visitors' use. The bedrooms have views over the lovely gardens and offer space with some welcome extras including a tea and coffee tray and a fridge. The house is south east of Sandringham, one and a half miles from Peddars Way, and 20 minutes from the coast. There is an excellent pub in the village. Parking is available.

*B & B £20-£25pp, Rooms 1 twin private bathroom, 2 double en-suite, No smoking,
Children over 12, Dogs in stables, Open all year*

Fieldsend, Hunstanton

Manor House Farm Wellingham, Kings Lynn PE32 2TH
Elisabeth Ellis
Tel: 01328 838227 Fax: 01328 838348

Map Ref: 9
A1065

Tucked away in the heart of rural Norfolk surrounded by lovely gardens next to tiny 13th century church. Conservation award winning farm. Beautifully converted old stables. Two en-suite double bedrooms, spacious sitting room and small kitchen. The emphasis here is charm and comfort. Antiques, lovely rugs, cushions and artefacts complete the restful ambience. A delicious breakfast, using home produced fruit, eggs, bacon and sausages, is served in dining room of main house. 20 minutes coast, close to Sandringham, golf courses and many places of interest. Wheelchair friendly.

B & B from £25pp, Rooms 1 twin, 1 double, both en-suite, Restricted smoking,
Children over 10, Dogs by arrangement, Open all year

Holly Grove Worstead, North Walsham NR28 9RQ
Michael & Bibby Horwood Tel: 01692 535546 Mobile: 07770 963055
Email: michaelhorwood@freenetname.co.uk Web: Broadland.com/Hollygrove

Map Ref: 10
A149

Holly Grove is a peaceful place to stay. Built in 1810, the house is a delightful mix of Georgian charm and modern comforts. During the Summer there is a heated swimming pool to enjoy. The large, comfortable bedrooms are furnished in traditional, country house style. Home made bread is just one speciality offered at breakfast time, Bibby is a Cordon Bleu cook and tailormade packed lunches are a speciality. The local village pub serves suppers, there are also other pubs nearby. The natural beauty of North Norfolk may be found on the doorstep of this lovely home.

B & B £23-£25pp, Rooms 1 double/family en-suite, 1 twin with private shower, No smoking,
Children welcome, No dogs, Closed Xmas & New Year & Crufts

The Old Pump House Holman Road, Aylsham, Norwich NR11 6BY
Tony & Lynda Richardson
Tel / Fax: 01263 733789

Map Ref: 11
A140

The Old Pump House is a lovely old Georgian farmhouse with a warm, welcoming atmosphere and much character, situated near the edge of the town, yet only a step away from the fine church and market place. Six attractive, nicely furnished rooms, four with en-suite, all with television, tea and coffee making facilities. Breakfast is served in the pine shuttered Red Room, overlooking the tranquil garden. Off road parking for six cars. Nearby are the Broads, numerous stately houses and gardens, the coast, delightful Norwich and two steam railways.

B & B from £24pp, C-Cards MC VS, Rooms 1 single, 2 double, 2 twin, 1 family, most en-suite,
No smoking, Well behaved children, No dogs, Closed Xmas & New Year

Greenacres Farmhouse Woodgreen, Long Stratton, Norwich NR15 2RR
Joanna Douglas Tel / Fax: 01508 530261
Email: greenacresfarm@tinyworld.co.uk

Map Ref: 12
A140

A 17th century farmhouse on a 30 acre common with ponds and wildlife, ten miles from Norwich. All bedrooms are tastefully furnished to compliment the oak beams and period furniture, with tea/coffee facilities and television. The beamed sitting room with inglenook fireplaces invites you to relax. A sunny dining room encourages you to enjoy a leisurely breakfast. Snooker table and all-weather tennis court. Jo is trained in therapeutic massage, aromatherapy and reflexology and will gladly offer this service to guests. Enjoy the peace of this charming home.

B & B from £22.50pp, Rooms 1 twin, 2 double, all private/en-suite,
No smoking, No children or dogs, Open all year

Westwood Barn Crabgate Lane South, Wood Dalling, Norwich NR11 6SW

Mrs Sentinella
Tel: 01263 584108

Map Ref: 13
B1149

Westwood Barn offers outstanding accommodation all on ground floor level. All rooms have en-suite bathroom, television and tea and coffee making facilities. Magnificent rooms with original beams. Beautiful four poster bedded room. This is an idyllic rural location for discovering the charms and tranquillity of north Norfolk. The picturesque village of Heydon which has been the location of many films, is just two miles away. National Trust properties, the historic city of Norwich, the coast and Broads are within a twelve mile radius. Illustrated brochure on request.

B & B from £23pp, Rooms 1 twin, 2 double, all en-suite, 1 four poster, Children welcome, No dogs, Open all year

White Hall Carbrooke, near Watton, Thetford IP25 6SG

Mrs S Carr   Tel: 01953 885950   Fax: 01953 884420
Email: shirleycarr@whitehall.uk.net

Map Ref: 14
B1108

White Hall is an elegant listed Georgian house standing in delightful grounds of three acres with a large natural pond, surrounded by fields and providing a haven of peace. Spacious accommodation, full central heating, log fires on chilly evenings, early morning tea and evening drinks ensure your stay is enjoyable and relaxing. Situated on the edge of Carbrooke village and in the centre of the interesting and attractive area of Breckland, we are ideally situated for the many attractions in both Norfolk and north Suffolk. Good choice of local eating places.

B & B from £21pp, Rooms 1 double en-suite, 1 twin, 1 double, Restricted smoking, Children welcome, Dogs by arrangement, Open all year

Old Bottle House Cranwich, Mundford, Thetford IP26 5JL

Marion Ford
Tel: 01842 878012

Map Ref: 15
A134

A warm welcome is assured at The Old Bottle House. This is a 275 year old former coaching inn, which has a lovely garden and rural views. The house is set in a wonderful position on the edge of Thetford Forest. The spacious colour co-ordinated bedrooms have tea and coffee making facilities, and colour television. Delicious meals are served in the dining room which has an inglenook fireplace. There is a pleasant seating area on a galleried landing where guests may relax after a busy day.

B & B from £22.50pp, Dinner from £14, Rooms 2 twin, 1 double/family, No smoking, Children over 5, No dogs, Closed Xmas & New Year

Somerville House Church Road, Terrington St John, Wisbech PE14 7RY

Colin & Mibette Sussams   Tel / Fax: 01945 880952
Email: somervillemc@hotmail.com   Web: www.somervillehouse.co.uk

Map Ref: 16
A47, A17

Somerville House, which dates back 300 years, stands in two acres of mature gardens on the edge of the Fens, and just six miles from Kings Lynn and the Fenland town of Wisbech. The spacious en-suite bedrooms are well equipped and comfortable. A full English or Continental breakfast is served in the attractive restaurant, which is where guests may also enjoy delicious dinners, selected from a carefully compiled menu offering dishes made from local produce and foods in season. The comfortable lounge is the perfect place to enjoy a pre-dinner drink.

B & B from £25pp, C-Cards MC VS, Dinner from £13.50, Rooms 1 single, 1 double, 1 twin, 2 en-suite, Restricted smoking, Children welcome, No dogs, Closed Xmas

Northumbria

The most northerly of the English counties can indeed justifiably claim to have everything that the holiday maker could desire, and certainly no brief visit could possibly give anything but the smallest indication of what is on offer. The coastline is magnificent with its mile upon mile of wide sandy beaches, links and dunes, nature reserves, picturesque rocky offshore islands and sturdy squat spectacular castles. Bamburgh, once the Saxon capital of the region, has a superb castle, built in the twelfth century. The castle looks out over the Farne Islands, twenty-eight dolerite rock islands, famous as a bird sanctuary and the breeding ground for grey seal. The lighthouse on Longstone was manned by Grace Darling and her father. Grace Darling was a local heroine who rowed out to rescue the crew of a ship which had struck the rocks and the Grace Darling Museum at Bamburgh records her life and heroism, her tomb is in the churchyard. Then to the north, Lindisfarne Castle stands on Holy Island, accessible by a narrow causeway. The castle, built in 1550, dominates the little island where St Cuthbert lived and died. Nearby is Newton Pool, a fresh water lake behind the dunes, a nature reserve, home to breeding birds including blackheaded gulls, mute swans and reed bunting. Whitley Bay and Tynmouth boast award winning beaches while Saltburn-by-the-Sea, a little Victorian seaside resort has a fascinating Smugglers Heritage Centre. The Lifeboat Museum at Redcar, another seaside resort, contains the 'Zetland', the world's oldest surviving lifeboat.

The visitor to this region could be excused for never leaving the coast, such is the wealth of interest, but this would be a mistake as inland there are just as many delights. The City of Durham is an attraction not to be resisted, the cradle of Christianity in England and the historic capital of the northeast. The history and tradition of the region is centred on the magnificent Norman cathedral and its adjacent castle. The cathedral contains the shrine of St Cuthbert and that of the Venerable Bede. However, even though the castle is now used as university accommodation, visitors are still invited to explore it, developed from a Norman motte and bailey.

Because of its remoteness the Northumberland National Park is one of the least visited parks. The vast Kielder Forest spreads over a large section of western Northumberland, the home of red squirrels and deer. Kielder Water is the largest man-made reservoir in

Hadrian's Wall, Northumberland (NTB)

Europe and offers water sports and activities of every description. The southern part of the national park holds the largest Roman monument in Great Britain, Hadrian's Wall. Stretching from Newcastle on the northeast coast to the Solway Firth on the coast of Cumbria, this great fortification at the northern most point of the Roman empire was planned in 122AD by the Roman Emperor Hadrian to separate the Britons from the Picts. To walk the wall is a wonderful experience, and the views from the Great Whin Sill, the hard rock base of so much of the wall, are spectacular. To obtain a potted history of the whole of this remarkable region the holiday visitor must call at the North of England Open Air Museum at Beamish. Here the award-winning museum tells the social history of the North of England. A northern industrial village of the early 1900s is evocatively re-created, complete with colliers' cottages and even trams.

There is so much impressive scenery and architecture to see that it is all too easy to miss the smaller gems, such as the lovely gardens of Howick Hall built in 1782, the home of the second Earl Grey after whom the tea was named and the Cragside House and gardens near Morpeth, the first house in the world to be lit by hydro-electric power. Gibside, near Burnopfield, has a beautiful park designed by Capability Brown and the Palladian-style chapel within the grounds was the Bowes family mausoleum. No visitor should leave this region without visiting the Bowes Museum by the small market town of Barnard Castle on the banks of the River Tees. The museum contains a fine collection of furniture, ceramics and paintings and the famous mechanical Silver Swan by John Cox.

PLACES TO VISIT

This is a small selection of interesting places to visit. Many more are listed in our annual guide to Museums, Galleries, Historic Houses & Sites (see page 448)

Alnwick Castle
Alnwick, Northumberland
The seat of Duke of Northumberland whose family, the Percys, have lived here since 1309. A treasure trove of fine furniture and paintings.

Auckland Castle
Bishop Auckland, County Durham
Home of the Bishops of Durham for over 800 years, set in delightful rural countryside. Attractions are the Magnificent Chapel, Throne Room and Long Dining Room.

Captain Cook Birthplace Museum
Middlesbrough
Near the site of the cottage where Captain James Cook was born in 1728. Displays depict his life from his time in Great Ayton to his employment at Staines and Whitby.

Durham Cathedral
Durham
The Cathedral building, dating back 900 years, is widely regarded as one of the most complete and perfect examples of Romanesque architecture in existence. It is the final resting place of St Cuthbert, the greatest of the early English saints.

North of England Open Air Museum
Beamish, County Durham
Living, working experience of life as it was in the Great North in the early 1800s and 1900s, set in 300 acres of beautiful countryside and winner of British Museum of the Year.

Northumbria

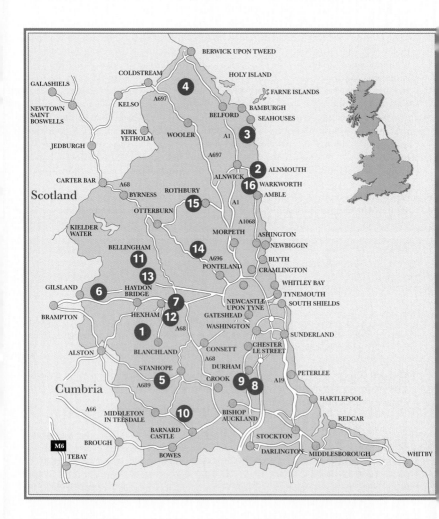

The Blue Map References should be used to locate B & B properties on the pages that follow

Thornley House Allendale NE47 9NH
E Finn Tel: 01434 683255
Email: e.finn@ukonline.co.uk Web: www.ukonline.co.uk/e.finn

Map Ref: 1
B6303

A beautiful country house in spacious and peaceful grounds surrounded by fields and woodland. One mile out of Allendale. Relaxed comfortable accommodation, three roomy light bedrooms, two en-suite, one with a private bathroom next door. All have tea and coffee facilities. Two lounges, one with television, one with a Steinway grand piano, ample books, games, maps, good food and home baking. Bring your own wine. Marvellous walks (guided sometimes available) and bird watching. Hadrian's Wall, Stately homes, Kielder Forest nearby. Vegetarian meals and packed lunches on request. Brochure available.

B & B from £20.50pp, Dinner from £13, Rooms 1 twin, 2 double, all en-suite, No smoking, Children over 10, Dogs by arrangement, Open all year

Marine House Private Hotel Alnmouth NE66 2RW
John & Christina Tanney Tel: 01665 830349
Email: tanney@marinehouse.freeserve.co.uk

Map Ref: 2
A1

Relax in the friendly atmosphere of this 200 year old listed building. Marine House Hotel is charming, it may be found on the edge of the village golf links, enjoying wonderful sea views. There are ten individually appointed bedrooms, some with tester/crown drapes; all are en-suite with colour television and a hospitality tray. Four course gourmet candlelit dinners by our resident chef. Cocktail bar, spacious seafront lounge. Visit the Farne Islands or Alnwick Gardens. Discover the Roman Wall, impressive border fortresses, romantic ruins and elegant stately homes.

B & B from £28pp, Dinner from £14, Rooms 2 twin, 6 double, 2 family all en-suite, Restricted smoking, Children over 7, Dogs welcome, Open all year

North Charlton Farm Chathill, Alnwick NE67 5HP
Mrs Sylvia Armstrong Tel: 01665 579443 Fax: 01665 579407 Mobile: 07812 696050
Email: ncharlton@agric.snowgoose

Map Ref: 3
A1

Come and visit us and have tea in our homely yet luxurious and spacious, farmhouse. Furnished to a very high standard with tea/coffee making facilities and televisions in our large bedrooms with fantastic views to the sea. We offer home cooking and a warm welcome when you arrive. An ideal base for exploring Northumberland - the Roman Wall, many stately homes, the Farne Islands are all within easy reach. We also have 2 self-catering houses.

B & B from £30pp, Rooms 2 double en-suite, 1 twin with private bathroom, Restricted smoking, Children over 10, No dogs, Open all year

The Old Manse 5 Cheviot View, Lowick, Berwick Upon Tweed TD15 2TY
Mrs Barbara Huddart Tel: 01289 388264 Mobile: 07980 850394
Email: glenc99@aol.com

Map Ref: 4
A1

This Grade II Georgian church manse was built in 1823, it stands in the peaceful village of Lowick, eight miles from Berwick-upon-Tweed. It is beautifully furnished with antiques which enhance the original charm, though every modern comfort is offered. There is a choice of two en-suite rooms, both are well equipped. On arrival, guests are welcomed with tea and home baking in the drawing room in front of an open fire. Locally smoked kippers are a choice at breakfast, all preserves are homemade. Packed lunches are available. Barbara Huddart will assist you with travel plans.

B & B £25-£27.50pp, Rooms 1 double, 1 twin, both en-suite, No smoking, Children welcome, No dogs, Closed Xmas & New Year

Lands Farm Westgate-in-Weardale, Bishop Auckland DL13 1SN

Mrs B Reed
Tel / Fax: 01388 517210   Mobile: 07803 054819

Map Ref: 5
A689

You will be warmly welcome to Lands Farm an old stone-built farmhouse within walking distance of Westgate village. Relax in the conservatory over looking the large garden and listen to the gentle trickle of Swinhope burn as it meanders by. Accommodation is offered in centrally heated double and family rooms with luxury en-suite facilities, television and tea/coffee making. Full English breakfast or continental alternative is served in an attractive dining room. This is an ideal base for walkers and for touring Durham, Hadrian's Wall and Beamish Museum.

B & B from £23pp, Rooms 1 double, 1 family, both en-suite,
Children welcome, No dogs, Open all year

Holmhead GH on Thirlwall Castle Farm, Hadrians Wall, Greenhead, Brampton CA8 7HY

Brian & Pauline Staff   Tel / Fax: 016977 47402
Holmhead@hadrianswall.freeserve.co.uk   www.bandbhadrianswall.com

Map Ref: 6, M6 J43, A69, B6318
see Photo opposite

Enjoy fine food and hospitality with a personal touch, in a smoke free atmosphere. This lovely old farmhouse is built with Hadrians Wall stones, near the most spectacular remains. Four cosy bedrooms with en-suite shower/wc. Quality home cooking using fresh produce, guests dine together at candlelit table in dinner party style. Speciality list of organically grown/produced wines featuring world award winners. Small cocktail bar and television, books, maps and guides in the lounge. Your host is a former Northumbria Tour Guide and is an expert on Hadrian's Wall. Special breaks arranged.

B & B from £28pp, C-Cards MC VS, Dinner from £19.50, Rooms 2 twin, 1 double, 1 family,
all en-suite, No smoking, Children welcome, No dogs, Closed Xmas & New Year

Clive House Appletree Lane, Corbridge NE45 5DN

Ann Hodgson   Tel: 01434 632617   Mobile: 07949 766143
Email: atclive@supanet.com

Map Ref: 7
A68, A69

Originally built in 1840 as part of Corbridge village school, Clive House has been tastefully converted to provide four lovely bedrooms, one of which has a four-poster. All the rooms are en-suite with tea and coffee making facilities, colour television, hair dryer and telephone. The village centre with many speciality shops and eating places is only a few minutes walk away. At the centre of Hadrian's Wall country, historic Corbridge is an ideal base for exploring Northumberland and a convenient break between York and Edinburgh. Which Recommended, ETB 4 Diamonds.

B & B from £28pp, Rooms 3 double, 1 single, all en-suite,
No smoking, No children or dogs, Closed Xmas

Ash House 24 The Green, Cornforth DL17 9JH

Delia Slack   Tel: 01740 654654   Mobile: 07711 133547
Email: delden@easicom.com

Map Ref: 8
A1M, A167, A688

Built in the mid 19th century, Ash House is a beautifully appointed period house combining a delicate mixture of homeliness and Victorian flair. Elegant rooms, individually and tastefully decorated, combining antique furnishings, beautiful fabrics, carved four posters and modern fittings. Spacious, graceful and filled with character, Ash House offers a warm welcome to both the road-weary traveller and those wishing merely to unwind in the quiet elegance of this charming home on the village green. Private parking. Well placed between York and Edinburgh. Adjacent A1(M) motorway.

B & B from £20pp, Rooms 1 twin, 1 double, 1 family, Restricted smoking,
Children over 8, Dogs welcome, Closed Xmas & New Year

Holmhead Guest House, Greenhead, near Brampton

Idsley House
4 Green Lane, Spennymoor, Durham DL16 6HD

Joan, David Dartnall

Tel: 01388 814237

Map Ref: 9

A167, A688

Idsley House is a long established guest house run by Joan and David Dartnall. It is a large detached house in a quiet area, just off the A167/A688 and eight minutes from Durham City. All the rooms are spacious and furnished to a high standard. Double, twin and family rooms are en-suite and have television and welcome trays. Breakfast is served in a pleasant conservatory overlooking a mature garden. There is a large quiet lounge for guests to relax in. Ample safe car parking in walled garden. Evening meals by arrangement.

B & B from £24pp, C-Cards MC VS AE, Rooms 1 single, 1 double, 2 twin, 1 family, all en-suite, Restricted smoking, Children & dogs welcome, Closed Xmas & New Year

Cloud High
Barnard Castle, Eggleston DL12 0AU

Frank & Eileen Bell   Tel / Fax: 01833 650644

Email: cloudhigh@btinternet.com   Web: www.cloudhigh-teesdale.co.uk

Map Ref: 10

B6278

Idyllically situated at 1000' in peaceful, secluded countryside, Cloud High commands magnificent unrivalled views of Teesdale and surrounding dales. Here the emphasis is on comfort, luxury and relaxation with every amenity in the three lovely en-suite bedrooms (one with balcony) and private lounge. Breakfasts, taken in the conservatory overlooking the garden and with a backdrop of the Pennines, are our speciality with a choice of traditional or interesting alternatives. The perfect base for exploring this historical, cultural and scenic area.

B & B £23-£26pp, Rooms 1 twin, 2 double, all en-suite, No smoking, Children over 12, No dogs, Closed Xmas & New Year

Westfield Guest House
Bellingham, Hexham NE48 2DP

Barbara Lockhart   Tel: 01434 220340   Fax: 01434 220356

Email: barbaralockhart@hotmail.com   Web: www.westfield-house.net

Map Ref: 11

B6320

Westfield is a truly hospitable home. It was built as an elegant, but cosy Victorian gentleman's residence, with nearly an acre of gardens. The bedrooms are comfortable, with more than a touch of luxury. Tea trays in all rooms. Breakfast and dinner are superb, with both traditional and international cooking at its best. Ideal touring spot with wonderful countryside, Roman wall, castles and National Trust properties. Safe car parking. Licensed. Stay awhile and be spoilt.

B & B from £28pp, C-Cards MC VS, Dinner from £16, Rooms 1 twin, 1 four poster, 1 family, all en-suite., No smoking, Children welcome, No dogs, Closed Xmas & New Year

Rye Hill Farm
Slaley, Hexham NE47 0AH

Elizabeth Courage   Tel / Fax: 01434 673259

Email: enquiries@consult-courage.co.uk   www.ryehillfarm.co.uk

Map Ref: 12

A68, A69, B6306

see Photo opposite

Rye Hill Farm invites you to enjoy the pleasures of Northumberland throughout the year whilst living in the pleasant family atmosphere of a cosy farmhouse adapted especially to receive holidaymakers. Bedrooms are all en-suite, centrally heated and have large bath towels. A full English breakfast and an optional three course evening meal are served in the dining room with an open log fire and a table licence. Pay phone and tourist information in the reception lounge. Guests are invited to use the games room and look around the farm.

B & B £22.50-£28pp, C-Cards MC VS, Dinner from £14, Rooms 3 double, 1 twin, 2 family, Restricted smoking, Children & dogs welcome, Open all year

Rye Hill Farm, Slaley, near Hexham

The Hermitage Swinburne, Hexham NE48 4DG
Simon & Kate Stewart
Tel: 01434 681248   Fax: 01434 681110

Map Ref: 13
A6079

The Hermitage is an elegant and comfortable house. It is furnished with antiques and old family pictures. The rooms are spacious and beautifully decorated. There is a large well kept garden, a terrace to sit out on in the evenings and a tennis court. All the bedrooms have tea and coffee making facilities. The drawing room has an open fire, which is lit on cooler evenings and a television. There is total peace and quiet. The house is very convenient for the Roman Wall and Northumberland castles and mansions. Ample parking.

B & B from £30pp, Rooms 1 single, 2 twin, 1 double, all en-suite/private, Restricted smoking, Children over 10, Dogs by arrangement, Closed Oct to Mar

Shieldhall Wallington by Kirkharle, Morpeth NE61 4AQ
Stephen & Celia Gay   Tel: 01830 540387   Fax: 01830 540490
Email: Robinson.Gay@btinternet.com

Map Ref: 14
B6342, A696

Shieldhall is set in the heart of the Northumbrian Borders and nestles into rolling landscape overlooking the National Trust's estate of Wallington. Once home to the family of Capability Brown, this 17th house has been charmingly restored, and lends itself well to being a country guest house. Every bedroom is furnished individually, and has its own entrance into the central courtyard. Dinners may be ordered in advance, and are served in a candlelit dining room. There are many heritage sites such as Hadrian's Wall within easy driving distance of Shieldhall.

B & B £22.50-£28.50pp, C-Cards MC VS, Dinner available, Rooms 2 double, 1 twin, No smoking, No children, Dogs by arrangement, Closed Nov-Mar

Thropton Demesne Farmhouse Thropton, Rothbury NE65 7LT
Kris Rogerson
Tel: 01669 620196

Map Ref: 15
B6341

Well off the road, this old stone farmhouse surveys the Coquet River and Cheviot hills. All three bedrooms have their own bathrooms, colour television, tea and coffee making facilities and hairdryer. The guests' sitting room has log fires and outside is a pretty garden. Kris provides light evening meals on request; also packed lunches. The Northumberland National Park is on the doorstep and Rothbury with its National Park Information Centre, Cragside House and gardens (National Trust) and historic Brinkburn Priory (English Heritage) is only three miles away.

B & B from £23pp, Dinner from £8.50, Rooms 1 twin, 2 double, all en-suite, No smoking, Children by arrangement, No dogs, Open all year

North Cottage Birling, Warkworth NE65 0EX
John & Edith Howliston   Tel: 01665 711263
Email: edithandjohn@another.com   Web: www.accta.co.uk/north

Map Ref: 16
A1068

Dating back to the 17th century, North Cottage has a cosy home from home atmosphere. Substantial full English breakfasts are served in the dining room. Afternoon tea is served free, on arrival, or when required. The bedrooms, which are all on the ground floor, are comfortable and well furnished with tea and coffee making facilities, electric blanket, clock radio, colour television and the beds have either a duvet or blankets. The double and twin rooms are en-suite and the single has a wash hand basin.

B & B £22-£24pp, Rooms 2 double, 1 twin, 1 single, most en-suite, No smoking, Children welcome, No dogs, Closed Xmas & New Year

Oxfordshire

Lying midway between the Thames estuary and the River Severn, with the glorious Cotswolds to the north, the chalk hills of the Chilterns in the south and with the basins of the Thames and Cherwell forming the central plain, Oxfordshire must be one of England's most attractive counties. The Oxfordshire Chilterns is a wonderful area of beechwoods and chalk, here the Ridgeway, a pre-Roman track follows the western escarpment and runs to the Vale of the White Horse with its spectacular Iron Age hill figure known as the White Horse of Uffington. Here the Buscot and Coleshill estates, some 7,500 acres of farmland and woodland which includes Badbury Hill, belong to the National Trust. The Iron-Age hill-fort gives spectacular views over the upper Thames Valley and south to the Berkshire Downs. To the southeast of Watlington with its Elizabethan cottages and fine Georgian inn, the 'Hare and Hounds', on an escarpment of the Chilterns, Watlington Hill, at 700 feet, gives splendid views over much of the county. The hill is skirted by the Upper Icknield Way, a superb region for walkers and for the naturalist the area is a fascinating district of lovely yew forests, whitebeam, dogwood and hawthorn.

The Oxfordshire Cotswolds are a delight, offering the visitor excellent walking, through a countryside of honey-coloured limestone villages, cottage gardens and rich russet-coloured fields hemmed with their drystone walls. Chipping Norton, a wonderful old wool town with its fine fifteenth century church and handsome stone buildings is a great centre from which to explore the area. Burford is also an excellent holiday centre, rich in fine buildings indicating its prosperity as a wool town, it boasts a magnificent church and a picturesque medieval bridge across the Windrush. Further south is the Cotswold Wildlife Park, 120 acres of gardens surrounding a Gothic style manor house with a variety of animals and wildlife in spacious enclosures, including white rhinos and tigers. Nearby is Minster Lovell, one of this county's prettiest villages, a long cottage lined street with Minster Lovell Hall, a quite fascinating medieval fortified manor house, a ruin steeped in legend. Banbury, in the north of the county, is an interesting centre renowned for its cross, which was destroyed by Puritans in 1602, later to be replaced by the Victorians. The town is famous also for its mouth-watering Banbury cakes, made to a 350 year old recipe. To the south is the town of Bicester, an ancient town of Roman origin and a noted hunting centre, with some extremely attractive buildings in Market End and Sheep Street. To the west at Woodstock is Blenheim Palace, a vast and sumptuous treasure

Blenheim Palace from the East (STB)

house, built to the design of John Vanbrugh for John Churchill the first Duke of Malborough, as a gift from Queen Anne in recognition of his victory at Blenheim in 1704. The palace was the birthplace in 1874 of Winston Churchill, the great war leader and stands in a great park laid out by Henry Wise and modified later by 'Capability' Brown.

At the centre of this glorious county lies Oxford with its stunning heritage of historic buildings. Delightfully situated on the Thames or Isis, with large swathes of greenery it is easy to forget that Oxford is an important industrial, commercial and residential city. Oxford can offer all that one would expect of a modern city, fine shops, excellent cinemas and theatres. There are sightseeing buses touring the city at regular intervals and boating on the Thames and Cherwell. From the twelfth century the city has been an important centre of learning. The most famous of its colleges, Christ Church, known as 'The House', was founded by Cardinal Wolsey. Each of the colleges, set in cloistered seclusion behind high walls has its own distinctive charm and treasures. Christ Church has in its picture gallery, works by Durer and Michelangelo and New College has in its chapel a statue of Lazarus by Jacob Epstein. Alongside these Oxford colleges have developed some remarkable public buildings, the Sheldonian Theatre built in 1664, the Radcliffe Camera, the Bodleian Library with over five and a half million volumes and the Ashmolean Museum, a treasure house of art and antiquities including a ninth century brooch made for King Alfred.

PLACES TO VISIT

This is a small selection of interesting places to visit. Many more are listed in our annual guide to Museums, Galleries, Historic Houses & Sites (see page 448)

Blenheim Palace
Woodstock
The home of the 11th Duke of Marlborough and birthplace of Winston Churchill. The park consists of over 2,000 acres, landscaped by 'Capability' Brown, a lake, Vanbrugh's Grand Bridge and Column of Victory.

Cotswold Wildlife Park
Burford, Oxford
This 200 acre landscaped parkland surrounds a Gothic-style manor house and has a varied collection of animals from all over the world.

Didcot Railway Centre
Didcot
A unique collection of Great Western Railway steam engines, coaches, wagons, buildings and artefacts.

The Oxford Story
6 Broad Street, Oxford
An excellent introduction to Oxford with 900 years of University history told in one hour. From scientists to poets, astronomers to comedians.

River and Rowing Museum
Mill Meadows, Henley-on-Thames
A spectacular journey through over 250,000 years of life on the river with three main galleries dedicated to the River Thames, the international sport of rowing and the town of Henley.

Stonor
Henley-on-Thames
Home of Lord and Lady Camoys and the Stonor family for over 800 years. Contains a fine collection of items from Britain, Europe and America. Extensive gardens and park

Oxfordshire

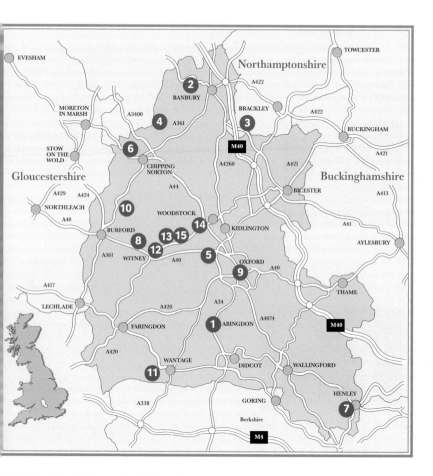

The Blue Map References should be used to locate B & B properties on the pages that follow

22 East St Helen Street Abingdon OX14 5EB
Mrs Howard Tel: 01235 550979 Fax: 01235 533278
Email: srhoward@talk21.com

Map Ref: 1
A34, A415

This attractive, comfortable 18th century house is situated in a quiet charming street in the centre of town close to the river and 20 minutes from Oxford. Breakfast, which is served in the flag stoned dining room, is as organic and wholesome as possible. It includes fresh and stewed fruit, home made muesli and marmalade and wholemeal bread. A speciality is scrambled eggs with ham or smoked salmon and mushrooms, (no fry-ups). Overflow guests can stay in a nearby house where William III stayed during the glorious Revolution.

B & B £26-£32pp, Rooms 3 single, 1 twin, 2 double, 1 en-suite, No smoking,
Children welcome, Guide Dogs only, Closed Xmas, New Year & Easter

Swallows Barn Shutford Road, Balscote, Banbury OX15 6JJ
Stephen & Marypen Wills Tel: 01295 738325 Fax: 01295 738314
Email: s.wills@swallowsbarn.freeserve.co.uk

Map Ref: 2
A422
see Photo opposite

Swallows still dart among the eaves where once a farm barn stood in this idyllic Cotswold village. Our spacious honey stone house has been blended into the rural scene, the old stone wall a backdrop to the waterfall and charming tiered garden. The guest room is very large, sunny and comfortable with elegant chintz furnishing, country antiques, sofa, tea and television. We can accommodate extra family. Breakfast is taken at the Georgian table, or on the terrace. Walks abound and Oxford, Stratford-upon-Avon and Warwick are within an easy drive.

B & B from £25pp, Rooms 1 double/twin or family en-suite, Restricted smoking,
Children welcome, Dogs by arrangement, Closed Mid-Dec to Mid-Jan

Home Farmhouse Charlton, Banbury OX17 3DR
Col & Mrs Grove-White Tel / Fax: 01295 811683
Email: grovewhite@lineone.net Web: www.homefarmhouse.co.uk

Map Ref: 3
M40
see Photo on page 229

Home Farmhouse, over 400 years old, is a charming house, warm and welcoming, with exposed beams, winding staircases and inglenook fireplaces. Rosemary has used her experience as an interior designer to furnish the house in harmony with its age, but with the emphasis on comfort. One hour from Heathrow, it is an ideal base from which to spend days visiting Oxford, Stratford-upon-Avon, Warwick Castle, the Cotswolds and famous houses and gardens including Blenheim, Woburn, Waddesdon, Hidcote, Kiftgate and Sezincote. Also close to Bicester Village.

B & B from £31pp, C-Cards MC VS, Dinner from £25, Rooms 2 twin/double, 1 double,
all en-suite/private, No smoking, Children over 12, Dogs by arrangement, Closed Xmas

Mine Hill House Lower Brailes, Banbury OX15 5BJ
Hester & Edward Sale
Tel: 01608 685594

Map Ref: 4
B4035

Mine Hill House which was built in 1733, is situated on top of a hill with stunning views over miles of unspoilt countryside. It is a Cotswold farmhouse full of wonderful paintings, flagstone floors and open log fires. Hester is a highly trained cook and is delighted to cook dinner on request. It is a superb location to explore the Cotswolds, Stratford, Oxford, Blenheim Palace and the famous gardens of Hidcote and Kiftgate, all are within a 20 mile radius. There is also a golf course at the bottom of Mine Hill.

B & B from £25pp, Dinner from £20, Rooms 1 twin, 1 double, both en-suite/private,
Restricted smoking, Children welcome, Dogs by arrangement, Closed Xmas

Swallows Barn, Balscote,
near Banbury

Burleigh Farm Bladon Road, Cassington OX29 4EA

Jane Cook Tel: 01865 881352

Email: jcook@farmline.com

Map Ref: 5
A40, A4095

Burleigh Farm is a listed stone farmhouse in a quiet position. This is a working farm on the Duke of Marlborough's Blenheim Estate. The comfortable bedrooms have either private or en-suite facilities and they all have television and coffee/tea making facilities. There is a relaxing garden for guests' use. The farmhouse is conveniently placed for visits to the beautiful Blenheim Palace, the University City of Oxford and the Cotswolds. The pleasant towns of Burford, Bibury and Chipping Norton are within an easy drive away.

B & B from £22.50pp, Rooms 1 twin, 1 family/double, both en-suite, No smoking, Open all year

Rectory Farm Salford, Chipping Norton OX7 5YZ

Nigel & Elizabeth Colston Tel / Fax: 01608 643209 Mobile: 07866 834208

Email: colston@rectoryfarm75.freeserve.co.uk

Map Ref: 6
A44

Rectory Farm is a 200 hundred year old, creeper-clad working farm, standing in 450 peaceful acres of beautiful North Cotswold country. A mature garden leads down to two trout lakes, where fishing is available for guests. The family have lived here all their lives, they are willing to share their local knowledge with visitors. Very much a traditional family home, the rooms are large and light filled. This is the ideal base from which to explore the Cotswolds and many of the historic towns which are all within a pleasant drive.

B & B from £34pp, Dinner from £14, Rooms 1 double en-suite, 1 double, 1 twin both private bathroom, Restricted smoking, Children welcome, Dogs by arrangement, Closed Dec & Jan

Slater's Farm Peppard Common, Henley on Thames RG9 5JL

Mrs Penny Howden

Tel / Fax: 01491 628675

Map Ref: 7
B481

A warm and friendly home, Slater's Farm is a quietly situated, attractive Georgian country house with an acre of lovely garden including a hard tennis court, which guests are welcome to use. All the bedrooms are attractively furnished for the comfort of our guests. Traditional pubs, within a few hundred yards, serve good evening meals. Lovely walks through unspoilt countryside. The Chilterns, Windsor, Oxford, Cotswolds all within easy driving distance. Heathrow can be reached in under one hour. French and German are spoken.

B & B from £24pp, Dinner from £16, Rooms 2 twin, 1 double, 2 private, Restricted smoking, Children welcome, No dogs, Closed Xmas & New Year

The Old Vicarage Minster Lovell OX8 5RR

Bridget Geddes Tel: 01993 775630 Fax: 01993 772534

Email: ageddes@lix.compulink.co.uk

Map Ref: 8
A40

The Old Vicarage and Garden House were built in the 19th century, the River Windrush trickles through the garden. The church and ruins of Minster Lovell Hall stand closeby. The Garden House, with its own kitchen, sitting room and bathroom is ideal for those preferring a self-catering arrangement. There is a four poster bed in the bedroom in the main house. Within walking distance is the village pub. This lovely home is an easy drive from Stratford, Burford, Cirencester and Oxford. A wonderful location for those wishing to explore the Cotswolds.

B & B from £37.50pp, Rooms 2 double, with private bath, No smoking in bedrooms, Children over 6, No dogs, Closed Xmas & Easter

Home Farmhouse, Charlton, near Banbury

Shipton Grange House, Shipton-under-Wychwood

Green Gables 326 Abingdon Road, Oxford OX1 4TE

Parvesh & Narinder Bhella   Tel: 01865 725870   Fax: 01865 723115
Email: green.gables@virgin.net

Map ,
A4

Green Gables was built in 1914 for a local toy merchant, and this Edwardian house displays much character. It is well placed whether for business or pleasure, as the house stands only one mile from the city centre, also being on a frequent bus route. A pleasant riverside walk beside the Thames also takes you to the centre. The bedrooms are light, bright and spacious. There is one ground floor room which is suitable for disabled guests. There is ample private parking.

B & B from £27pp, Rooms 1 single, 2 twin, 4 double, 2 family, all en-suite,
No smoking, No dogs, Closed Xmas & New Year

Pine Castle Hotel 290/292 Iffley Road, Oxford OX4 4AE

Mrs S Pavlovic
Tel: 01865 241497   Fax: 01865 727230

Map Ref: 9
A4158

Pine Castle is a home from home for guests. The comfortable rooms are well-furnished and have en-suite bathrooms, colour televisions, direct-dial telephones, hair driers and a selection of reading material. All bedrooms are non-smoking, as is the breakfast room but smokers are welcome to use the lounge were there is also a small bar. Well situated midway between Ring Road and city centre and served by an excellent local bus service. River walk close by.

B & B from £32.50pp, Rooms 2 twin, 5 double, 1 family, all en-suite,
Restricted smoking, Children welcome, No dogs, Closed Xmas & New Year

Shipton Grange House Shipton-under-Wychwood OX7 6DG

Veronica Hill
Tel: 01993 831298   Fax: 01993 832082   Mobile: 07971 426843

Map Ref: 10
A361
see Photo opposite

Shipton Grange House is a unique conversion of a Georgian Coach House and stabling, situated in the former grounds of Shipton Court. The house is secluded in its own walled garden and is approached by a gated archway. There are three elegantly furnished guest bedrooms each with an en-suite or private bathroom, colour television and tea and coffee facilities. Shipton Grange House is delightful, and it is ideal for visiting Blenheim Palace, Oxford, Stratford, Warwick and many beautiful and well known gardens. There are some excellent restaurants within walking distance.

B & B from £29pp, Rooms 1 twin, 2 double, all en-suite/private,
No smoking, Children over 12, No dogs, Closed Xmas

Ridgeway House West Street, Childrey, Wantage OX12 9UL

Maxine Roberts
Tel: 01235 751538

Map Ref: 11
B4507

Ridgeway House is set in the beautiful village of Childrey, which is close to the market town of Wantage. It is an ideal base for exploring Oxford, the Cotswolds, White Horse Hill, and for walking the Ridgeway. All the rooms with their fresh fruit and flowers, offer en-suite facilities, they have beautiful views, colour television, beverage tray and fridge. There is a delicious breakfast choice, to include homemade bread and jams. A private car park is available for guests' cars.

B & B from £22.50pp, Rooms 2 single, 2 twin, 2 double, 2 family, all en-suite,
No smoking, Children welcome, Dogs by arrangement, Open all year

od Green, Witney OX28 1DE
Tel: 01993 705485   Mobile: 07768 614347
etcomuk.co.uk   Web: www.netcomuk.co.uk/~kearse/index.html

Map Ref: 12
A40, A4095

Field View is an attractive Cotswold stone house set in two acres. It is situated on picturesque Wood Green, midway between Oxford University and the Cotswolds. The setting here is peaceful and guests are assured of being welcomed to a warm and friendly atmosphere. It is an ideal centre for touring, and yet the lively market town of Witney is only eight minutes walk from the house. There are three comfortable en-suite rooms. Each one has a colour television, tea/coffee making facilities, radio and hairdryer.

B & B from £24pp, Rooms 2 twin, 1 double, all en-suite, No smoking,
No children or dogs, Closed Xmas & New Year

Gorselands Hall Boddington Lane, North Leigh, Witney OX29 6PU

Mr & Mrs N Hamilton   Tel: 01993 882292   Fax: 01993 883629
Email: hamilton@gorselandshall.com   Web: www.gorselandshall.com

Map Ref: 13
A4095/A40

This lovely Cotswold stone country house built on the Blenheim Estate, c.1900, stands about halfway between Witney and Woodstock. It enjoys the peacefulness of the countryside, yet Oxford is an easy journey by road or rail. Gorselands Hall stands in an acre of secluded gardens and features flagstone floors and exposed beams. Guests have their own comfortable sitting room with a snooker table. There is also a grass tennis court. Bedrooms are attractively presented, well equipped and enjoy garden views. Ground floor accommodation available. A wonderful touring and cycling area. Excellent pubs locally.

B & B £22.50-£25pp, C-Cards MC VS AE, Rooms 1 twin, 4 double, 1 family, all en-suite,
No smoking, Children welcome, Dogs by arrangement, Open all year

Manor Farmhouse Manor Road, Bladon, Woodstock OX20 1RU

Helen Stevenson   Tel / Fax: 01993 812168
Email: helstevenson@hotmail.com   Web: www.oxlink.co.uk/woodstock/manor-farmhouse/

Map Ref: 14
A4095

Listed Cotswold stone house (1720) in quiet conservation area of Bladon village, within walking distance of two pubs and one mile from Blenheim Palace and historic Woodstock. Ideal for exploring Oxford and the Cotswolds. The large double room featured in a Laura Ashley catalogue. The small twin room is approached by a spiral staircase, so is not for the unsprightly. Both rooms have colour TV's and tea/coffee making facilities. They share a shower room, so are ideal for families or 4 people travelling together.

B & B from £24pp, Rooms 1 twin, 1 double, No smoking, Children welcome,
Dogs by arrangement, Closed Xmas & New Year

Wynford House 79 Main Road, Long Hanborough, Woodstock OX29 8JX

Mrs Carol Ellis
Tel: 01993 881402   Fax: 01993 883661

Map Ref: 15
A4095, A44

Wynford House is situated in the village of Long Hanborough only one mile from Bladon, final resting place of Sir Winston Churchill and three miles from famous Woodstock and Blenheim Palace. There is a warm welcome, excellent food and comfortable accommodation. All the bedrooms, one of which is en-suite, have colour television and coffee/tea making making facilities. The house is ideally situated for the Cotswolds. The City of Oxford is 12 miles away. There are several local pubs and restaurants within walking distance.

B & B from £22pp, Rooms 1 family, 1 twin, 1 double, 1 en-suite, No smoking,
Children welcome, Dogs by arrangement, Closed Xmas & New Year

Shropshire

Strangely enough, this rich agricultural county was the cradle of the Industrial Revolution, but then Shropshire is a county of intriguing contrasts. Only fifty miles in length and forty miles wide the county is virtually cut in two by the River Severn which flows across the county from the Welsh border in the west to Shrewsbury. The Shropshire Plain, which stretches from Whitchurch in the north to Church Stretton in the southwest is dominated by the Wrekin, a long, domed hill of volcanic rock, the oldest in England, heavily wooded and with a steep promontory overlooking the Severn Valley. In the southwest of the county are the rugged Stiperstones, and in the south the Clee Hills. Between the Clee Hills and Wenlock Edge lies the glorious valley of the Corve, leading to Ludlow, one of England's best preserved medieval and Georgian towns. Broad Street is the most celebrated of the town's thoroughfares, a wonderful mixture of timber-framed Tudor buildings and seventeenth to nineteenth century brick facades. The cathedral-like Church of St Lawrence is renowned for its wonderful fifteenth century carved misericords. The poet AE Housman, whose poetry, and in particular his 'A Shropshire Lad' effectively depicts this wonderful rural county, is buried in the churchyard. Ludlow Castle, built in 1085 by Roger Montgomery, Earl of Shrewsbury, holds in its inner bailey, outdoor performances of Shakespeare plays during the Ludlow Festival in June and July. The town is ideal for exploring the Welsh Marches and the South Shropshire Hills. In the southwest lies The Long Mynd, an area of high and lonely moorland and splendid walking country. The National Trust owns almost six thousand acres of this heather covered upland. To enjoy this region a good starting point is the Carding Mill Valley from which radiate paths leading to a number of prehistoric remains, hill forts and burial grounds and to the ancient Port Way track which traverses the hill. The Trust owns some 550 acres of Wenlock Edge, the thick wooded limestone escarpment running from Craven Arms to Ironbridge is internationally famous for its coral reef exposures.

In the north of the county are the lovely Shropshire meres with Ellesmere being the attractive capital of the region. A former canal town, Ellesmere has a wealth of charming timber-framed and Georgian houses bordering The Mere, a haven for water fowl and the largest of the town's nine lakes. Ellesmere is a fine holiday centre and a magnet for lovers of small boats. Oswestry, to the west and very Welsh in character, can claim some

Iron Bridge near Telford (ST)

233

fine nineteenth century buildings, witness to the town's prosperity when in 1860 it became the headquarters of the Cambrian Railway. The town is also the birthplace of the composer, Walford Davies.

Shrewsbury, the county town and a perfect base to explore the county, is wonderfully situated within a tight loop of the meandering Severn. The town became strategically important soon after the Norman Conquest when William the Conqueror entrusted Roger de Montgomery to build his castle. The castle was converted to a house during the eighteenth century and the church of the abbey founded here by the same Roger de Montgomery was made famous by Ellis Peters in The Brother Cadfael novels. The town prospered during the Tudor period and possesses some remarkably fine timber-framed houses. Its prosperity continued, thanks to the rich trade in wool, resulting in Owen's

Mansion and Ireland's Mansion. Shrewsbury's later popularity among fashionable society produced a magnificent selection of Georgian houses. The town's museums are well worth a visit, Rowley House Museum displays an excellent interpretation of the early history of Shrewsbury.

Attractive and seductive as rural Shropshire is, no visitor should leave the county without visiting the Ironbridge Gorge. Here the Industrial Revolution was born and England established as the first industrial nation. Here also we saw the precursor of change to the whole country, particularly the Midlands and northern England. The Iron Bridge itself is merely the centre of a complex of fascinating sites. The outstanding Ironbridge Gorge Museum skilfully brings to life the story of this region, while at Blists Hill Open Air Museum a working Victorian town is recreated in forty-two acres of woodland.

PLACES TO VISIT

This is a small selection of interesting places to visit. Many more are listed in our annual guide to Museums, Galleries, Historic Houses & Sites (see page 448)

Ironbridge Gorge Museums
Ironbridge, Telford
The history of the world's first cast-iron bridge. It is home to nine superb attractions.

Hawkstone Park
Weston-under-Redcastle, Shrewsbury
Created in the eighteenth century by the Hill family, this Grade I listed park offers visitors a magical world of caves, cliffs, hidden pathways, grottos and nearly 100 acres of hilly terrain.

Ludlow Castle
Castle Square, Ludlow
Built between 1086 to 1094 to maintain the English Kingdom of William the

Conqueror and was later enlarged as a palace. Once home to the princes in the tower and Prince Arthur and his bride, Catherine of Aragon.

The Shrewsbury Quest
Abbey Foregate, Shrewsbury
A twelfth century visitor attraction where you can solve mysteries, create illuminated manuscripts, play medieval games and relax in the beautiful herb garden.

Wroxeter Roman City Museum
Wroxeter, Shrewsbury
Once the forth largest city in Roman Britain, the city depicts life as it was, using excavations of Roman relics, paintings and drawings

Shropshire

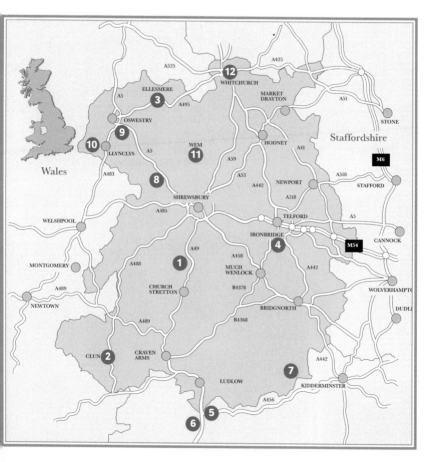

The Blue Map References should be used to locate B & B properties on the pages that follow

The Severn Trow, Jackfield, near Ironbridge

Jinlye Castle Hill, All Stretton, Church Stretton SY6 6JP
Janet Tory   Tel / Fax: 01694 723243
Email: info@jinlye.co.uk

Map Ref: 1
A49, B4370

An award-winning guest house set in 15 acres of grounds and nestling amidst the Shropshire Highlands where a stroll from the house can provide some of the most stunning views in England. Once a crofter's cottage dating back at least 200 years and now extended to provide luxurious and peaceful accommodation, there are Inglenook fireplaces, beamed ceilings and spacious lounges with comfortable sofas and easy chairs. The conservatory overlooks the garden, full of rare plants. The spacious en-suite bedrooms all have magnificent views and ground floor rooms are also available.

B & B £27-£35pp, Rooms 4 twin, 4 double, all en-suite, Restricted smoking, Children over 12, Dogs welcome, Open all year

New House Farm Clun SY7 8NJ
Miriam Ellison   Tel: 01588 638314
Email: sarah@bishopscastle.co.uk   Web: www.new-house-clun.co.uk

Map Ref: 2
A488, A489

Remote and very peaceful 18th century farmhouse set high in Clun Hills near Welsh border, a hill farm which includes an Iron Age Hill Fort. Walks from the doorstep include Offa's Dyke, Shropshire Way and Kerry Ridgeway. Accommodation is spacious with scenic views. Tea and coffee facilities, television and period furnished to a high standard. Books and more books to browse in a large country garden. 'I can however recommend the magnificently isolated New House Farm' Financial Times. Please ring for brochure.

B & B £25-£27.50pp, Rooms 1 family, 1 twin, both en-suite/private, No smoking, Children over 10, Dogs by arrangement, Closed Nov to Mar

Greenbanks Coptiviney, Ellesmere SY12 0ND
Christopher & Tanda Wilson-Clarke   Tel / Fax: 01691 623420   Mobile: 07967 605124
Email: wilson.clarke@ukonline.co.uk   Web: www.wolseylodges.co.uk

Map Ref: 3
A495

Visitors to Greenbanks are welcomed to warm hospitality in a friendly atmosphere. This attractive Victorian house stands peacefully situated in a tranquil, unspoiled area, within view of the magnificent Welsh Hills. It is well placed for Shrewsbury, Oswestry, Wrexham and Chester which are nearby. There is a wildlife pond and a lovely woodland walk to enjoy through the extensive gardens. Guests may use the synthetic grass tennis court. Within easy reach are the great houses and gardens of Attingham, Bodnant, Chirk, Erddig and Powis.

B & B from £35pp, Dinner from £20, Rooms 1 double, 1 twin, both en-suite, No smoking, Children over 12, Dogs only outside, Closed Xmas & New Year

The Severn Trow Church Road, Jackfield, Ironbridge TF8 7ND
Pauline Hanningan   Tel: 01952 883551
Email: paulineseverntrow@lineone.net   www.theseverntrow.fsnet.co.uk

Map Ref: 4
M54, A442
see Photo opposite

For centuries, travellers to the area have enjoyed the hospitality and comfort of The Severn Trow, a former ale house, lodgings and brothel, catering for boatmen of the river. Today, more discerning visitors are able to enjoy luxurious four poster beds. The bedrooms have television, all have tea/coffee making facilities. A superb English breakfast is served, vegetarian or special diets may be prepared by request. There is accommodation for guests of limited mobility. A lounge with television is available for guests' use. Ample car parking space.

B & B £23-£28pp, Rooms 3 double en-suite, No smoking, Children by arrangement, Dogs by arrangement, Closed Nov to Dec

The Marcle   Brimfield, Ludlow SY8 4NE
Patricia Jones   Tel / Fax: 01584 711459   Mobile: 07968 491458
Email: marcle@supanet.com   Web: www.marcle.com

Map Ref: 5
A456, A49

This delightful 16th century house lies in the centre of this pretty village. Extensively renovated by the present owners, exposed beams, timbered walls and other features abound. The elegantly furnished lounge and other areas are impeccably maintained and decorated. There are just three bedrooms, decorated with pretty wallpapers and equipped with modern facilities. Well tended lawns and gardens surround the house and hospitality from the Jones family is warm and welcoming. AA 4 Diamonds, Selected. ETB 2 Crowns Highly Commended.

B & B from £27pp, Dinner from £15, Rooms 1 twin, 2 double, all en-suite,
No smoking, Children over 12, No dogs, Closed Jan to Mar

Shortgrove   Brimfield Common, Ludlow SY8 4NZ
Beryl Maxwell
Tel: 01584 711418

Map Ref: 6
A49
see Photo opposite

Shortgrove is a Grade two listed Elizabethan timber framed house with gardens and grounds of three and a half acres on a gated common, in absolute peace and quiet. The whole house is exceptional inside and out with every comfort to make a stay here memorable. Food is to an extremely high standard, Beryl is a cookery tutor. Nearby are castles, National Trust houses, antiques shops, Hereford with its Cathedral and mappa Mundi, beautiful Ludlow, black and white villages, Hay on Wye for book buffs, Mortimer Forest for walking and riding.

B & B from £28pp, Dinner from £22, Rooms 1 en-suite twin, 1 private double,
No smoking, No children or dogs, Closed Oct to Easter

Cleeton Court   Cleeton St Mary, Ludlow DY14 0QZ
Mrs Ros Woodward   Tel / Fax: 01584 823379   Mobile: 07778 903136
Email: jk.stranghan@talk21.com   Web: www.cleetoncourt.co.uk

Map Ref: 7
A4117

This attractive, part 14th century old farmhouse was completely renovated in 1997, and is now a comfortable family home with views over meadows and heathland. The accommodation offered to visitors is prettily presented, there is a four poster bedroom with a huge bathroom, plenty of character and comfort to match. Breakfast is served in a sunny, oak beamed dining room, there is a beautiful drawing room where guests may relax in front of a log fire. Good local pubs, and there are many excellent restaurants in Ludlow which is eight miles away.

B & B £27.50-£32.50pp, Rooms 1 double, 1 twin, both en-suite, Restricted smoking,
Children over 5, No dogs, Closed Xmas & New Year

Top Farmhouse   Knockin, Oswestry SY10 8HN
Pam Morrissey   Tel: 01691 682582   Fax: 01691 682070
Email: p.a.m@knockin.freeserve.co.uk   Web: www.topfarmknockin.co.uk

Map Ref: 8
A5

Lovely black and white 16th century house offering old fashioned hospitality and modern comforts. All rooms en-suite with tea and coffee making facilities, trouser press, colour television and hairdryers. There is a comfortable chair and room to move around. Hearty breakfasts are served in an elegant dining room overlooking the garden. There is an attractive guests' drawing room with a grand piano. The house is situated in the picturesque village of Knockin, within walking distance of good pub food. Convenient for Wales, Chester, Shrewsbury, Oswestry. Chirk and Powis Castle close by.

B & B from £23pp, C-Cards, Rooms 1 twin, 1 double, 1 family, all en-suite,
No smoking in dining room, Children over 12, Dogs welcome, Open all year

Shortgrove, Brimfield Common, near Ludlow

Ashfield Farmhouse Maesbury, Oswestry SY10 8JH
Mrs Margaret Jones Tel / Fax: 01691 653589   Mobile: 07989 477414
Email: marg@ashfieldfarmhouse.co.uk Web: www.ashfieldfarmhouse.co.uk

Map Ref: 9
A5, A483

Old roses and scarlet creepers ramble this lovely 16th century coach house and Georgian farmhouse in Welsh Borders. One mile Oswestry, A5, A483, a true English/Welsh mix. Scented gardens, lovely views, excellent hospitality, inviting home with original period features. Exceptionally pretty, comfortable en-suite rooms, cottagey, spacious, fully equipped. Parking. Five minutes walk canalside Inn, restaurant and boathire. Chester, Llangollen, Shrewsbury and Ironbridge closeby. North Wales, castles, lakes, hidden valleys on our doorstep plus Sugar and Spice our Shetland ponies too. ETC 4 Diamonds, Silver Award.

B & B from £20pp, C-Cards MC VS AE, Rooms 3 double/single/twin/family, 2 family, 2 en-suite,
1 private, Restricted smoking, Children & dogs welcome, Open all year

Four Gables Nantmawr, Oswestry SY10 9HH
June & Bill Braddick
Tel: 01691 828708

Map Ref: 10
A5

June and Bill offer you a warm and friendly welcome and good home cooked food at their country home, set in a small hamlet on the borders of Wales. The guest lounge overlooks five acres of landscaped gardens, which are abundant with wildlife, birds and butterflies. Excellent for bird watchers. The garden and two large coarse fishing pools have been featured on BBC Midlands television. The countryside is unspoilt and near to horse riding and Offa's Dyke footpaths. We are licensed to sell alcohol to our guests.

B & B from £25pp, Dinner from £10, Rooms 1 twin, 2 double, all en-suite,
Children welcome,No dogs, Closed Xmas & New Year

Brownhill House Ruyton XI Towns, Shrewsbury SY4 1LR
Yoland & Roger Brown Tel: 01939 261121 Fax: 01939 260626
Email: brownhill@eleventowns.co.uk Web: www.eleventowns.co.uk

Map Ref: 11
A5, B4397

Brownhill House offers impeccable standards, modern facilities and a relaxed atmosphere in historic Ruyton XI Towns. The unique two acre garden 'has to be seen to believed' and has beautiful views. There is easy access to the historic and countryside attractions of Shropshire and North Wales, Ironbridge, Snowdonia, Chester to Ludlow. There are local pubs within walking distance. An extensive breakfast menu is offered and dinners are available using local and home grown produce. Do bring your own wine. Good restaurants are within easy reach. Tea and coffee is always available.

B & B £17.50-£24pp, C-Cards MC VS, Dinner from £14, Rooms 1 single, 1 twin, 1 double,
all en-suite, Restricted smoking, Children welcome, No dogs, Open all year

Dearnford Hall Tilstock Road, Whitchurch SY13 3JJ
Charles & Jane Bebbington Tel: 01948 662319 Fax: 01948 666670
Email: dearnford_hall@yahoo.com Web: www.dearnfordhall.com

Map Ref: 12
B5476

Once home to the High Sheriff of Shropshire, Dearnford Hall combines 18th century elegance with 20th century comfort. King-sized en-suite bedrooms are bright and sunny, with rich fabrics, deep mattresses, fat duvets and fine linen. Bathrooms have power showers and baths. Breakfast is served in the dining room and is a feast of fresh local produce. Enjoy a game of croquet on the lawn, wander through this 'conservation rich' farm to the trout lake where you can fish. Jane can arrange fly-fishing tuition. Wonderful gardens, towns and the Welsh borders are nearby.

B & B £35-£50pp, C-Cards MC VS, Rooms 1 double/twin, 1 twin, all en-suite,
No smoking, Children over 12, Dogs by arrangement, Closed Xmas

Somerset

There is no doubt that Somerset is a holiday county; there is so much to enjoy here that one visit could never suffice. The diversity of scenery to the northwest is the high heather-clad moorland plateau of Exmoor bordering the Bristol Channel, giving England's highest sea cliffs. This was once wild and windswept hunting country, changed somewhat during the nineteenth century by a rich ironmaster who converted some 15,000 acres of the moor into farmland and in the process planted miles of beech hedges, many surviving today. This is a glorious region of wild ponies, red deer and lovely combes, an area of prehistoric sites and ancient packhorse bridges. The National Trust owns the vast Holnicote Estate which includes the high tors of Dunkery and Selworthy Beacons that offer staggering views in all directions. Not to be missed by those who enjoy walking in superb scenery is Oare, a pretty and remote hamlet in a wooded valley on the very edge of Exmoor. Its little church was the setting for the wedding of Lorna Doone in R.D.Blackmore's novel. The small harbour of Minehead, developed as a seaside resort during the Victorian era and still retaining much of its Victorian atmosphere, is a grand centre for touring this district. The West Somerset Steam Railway, the longest privately run railway in the country meanders the twenty miles from Minehead to Bishops Lydeard and just two miles from Minehead is the gloriously picturesque and much visited town of Dunster with its fine sixteenth century Yarn Market. Dunster Castle, which is part medieval, part Victorian and the fortified home of the Luttrell family for 600 years, is set in a 28 acre park.

In the east are the Mendips, a range of limestone hills running from Weston-Super-Mare across the county to Frome. Over the centuries the limestone has been deeply eroded producing a large number of underground caves and gorges. The Cheddar Gorge and its associated caves are a great attraction. A road weaves between spectacular cliffs over 400 feet high. Nearby is Wookey Hole, illuminated caverns carved out by the River Axe, housing the famous Wookey Witch. Also within the same area is a 400 year old papermill. The Ebbor Gorge gives wonderful views of the Somerset Levels and in this woodland region badgers are plentiful and buzzards and sparrowhawk may be seen. The Black Rock Nature Reserve is a lovely walking area with plantations, natural woodland, limestone scree

Wells Magnificent Cathedral (SWT)

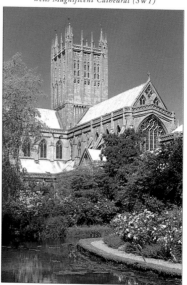

and dramatic rock faces. At the eastern end of the Mendips stands Wells, England's smallest city, its spectacular limestone streets dwarfed by its magnificent cathedral. The city is an historical and architectural treasure and the wells and springs that give the city its name are in the gardens of the bishop's palace. The Quantock Hills, stretching from near Taunton to the Bristol Channel, at Quantockhead provide the perfect region for the serious walker. The most dramatic parts are Beacon and Bicknoller Hills east of Williton, 630 acres of moorland which includes the ancient monument, Trendle Ring, an Iron Age fort. From the Quantocks are magnificent views over the Bristol Channel, The Vale of Taunton Deane and Exmoor.

At the centre of the county are the Somerset Levels, low-lying flat land. Here the town of Glastonbury, a center of both Christian and atheist beliefs, clusters around the base of the green hillock of Glastonbury Tor, which some say was the Isle of Avalon in the King Arthur legend, crowned with the tower of St Michael's Chapel, visible from far around. The ancient abbey has long been a place of pilgrimage as legend tells that it was here that Joseph of Arimathea buried the chalice used at the Last Supper.

Taunton, the county town of Somerset, has been an important centre of trade and administration since Saxon times. It was in Taunton in 1685 that the Duke of Monmouth was proclaimed king causing the local people to rebel and it was in the Great Hall of Taunton Castle that Judge Jeffreys held his Bloody Assizes in the aftermath of the rebellion. But there is a wealth of interest in this lovely town, much recorded in the excellent Somerset County Museum.

PLACES TO VISIT

This is a small selection of interesting places to visit. Many more are listed in our annual guide to Museums, Galleries, Historic Houses & Sites (see page 448)

Cheddar Caves and Gorge
Cheddar
Two stunning showcaves, Gough's Cave and Cox's cave are both illuminated. The caves were occupied by stone age man 40,000 years ago and there is also a heritage centre with a reconstruction of the dwellings.

Glastonbury Abbey
Glastonbury
Surrounded in myth and legend this is a modern day pilgrimage site set in 36 peaceful acres with the chapel, with its holy water vessel, stone altar and sacred Thorn Tree.

Montacute House
Montacute
This fine Elizabethan house was built by Sir Edward Philips, Speaker of the House of Commons, in 1588. Filled with treasures, especially the Long Gallery, it is set in suitably formal gardens.

Wells Cathedral
Wells
The Cathedral was built incorporating several Gothic styles but it is most famous for its west front, a magnificent sculpture gallery, and its 600 year old clock.

Somerset

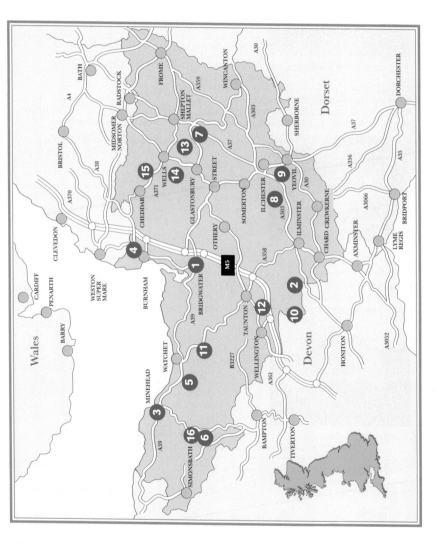

The Blue Map References should be used to locate B & B properties on the pages that follow

Friarn Cottage Over Stowey, Bridgwater TA5 1HW
Penny & Michael Taylor-Young
Tel / Fax: 01278 732870

Map Ref: 1
A39

A warm welcome is extended to guests at Friarn Cottage, over 500 feet up on the Quantock Hills amid beautiful Somerset countryside. Visitors have a self contained wing, a sitting room complete with videos, a fire, plus central heating. Breakfast may be served in the garden which is pretty all year round. The bedroom has wonderful views with blankets or duvets to suit. For nature lovers this is a joy. Ponies, sheep, ravens, buzzards and deer abound. Wonderful for bird watching. Nether Stowey is nearby, Taunton and Bridgwater a drive away. Dinner by arrangement.

B & B from £28.50pp, Dinner from £10, Rooms double/twin en-suite, No smoking, No children, Dogs in car, Open all year

Hawthorne House Bishopswood, Chard TA20 3RS
Roger & Sarah Newman-Coburn   Tel: 01460 234482   Fax: 01460 255059
Mobile: 07710 255059   Email: info@roger-sarah.com   Web: www.roger-sarah.co.uk

Map Ref: 2
A303, B3170

Hawthorne House is situated in the scenic Blackdown Hills just 1 mile off the A303, ideal for overnight stops for Cornwall or the Plymouth Ferries. The coast, Exmoor and at least six National Trust Properties are reached within the hour. Guests have unrestricted access to their rooms, the garden and a comfortable lounge with colour television. The dining room overlooks the terraces and has panoramic views over the garden down to the wildlife pond and over the surrounding hills. Short breaks available.

B & B from £22.50pp, Dinner from £12.50, Rooms 1 twin, 2 double, both en-suite/private, No smoking, Children over 12, Dogs welcome, Open all year

Conygar House 2A The Ball, Dunster TA24 6SD
Mrs B Bale   Tel / Fax: 01643 821872
Email: bale.dunster@virgin.net   Web: http://homepage.virgin.net/bale.dunster

Map Ref: 3
A39

Conygar House is situated in a quiet road a step away from the main street of the delightful medieval town of Dunster. From here are wonderful views of Dunster Castle, and to Exmoor beyond. Visitors are invited to enjoy the garden, and also to relax on the patio. There are restaurants, bars and shops just a minute's walk away. Dunster beach, and the town of Minehead and of course Porlock are all within easy reach. Conygar is an ideal base from which to explore Exmoor and the surrounding villages. ETC 4 Diamonds, Silver Award.

B & B £22.50-£25pp, Rooms 2 double en-suite, 1 twin with private bathroom, No smoking, Children welcome, No dogs, Closed 1st Dec to 1st Feb

Knoll Lodge Church Road, East Brent TA9 4HZ
Jaqui & Tony Collins
Tel: 01278 760294

Map Ref: 4
M5, A38, A370

Knoll Lodge is a 19th century Somerset house set in an acre of old orchard at the foot of Brent Knoll in the quiet Sedgemoor village of East Brent. Two and a half miles from the M5 and three miles from the coast, it is an ideal centre for visiting Axbridge, Cheddar, Wookey Hole, Wells, Bath and the Somerset Levels. There is ample parking, a guest lounge and conservatory; and all rooms have colour television, tea and coffee, hairdryer and American patchwork quilts. Highly Recommended for good food.

B & B from £22pp, Dinner £12, Rooms 2 double en-suite, 1 twin with private bathroom, No smoking, Children over 12, No dogs, Closed Xmas

Wood Advent Farm, Roadwater in Exmoor National Park

Wood Advent Farm Roadwater, Exmoor National Park TA23 0RR

John & Diana Brewer Tel / Fax: 01984 640920
Email: jddibrewer@aol.com Web: www.woodadventfarm.co.uk

Map Ref: 5
A39
see Photo on page 245

Wood Advent Farm is an attractive 19th century listed Somerset farmhouse and working farm. Peace and tranquillity are offered here in the beautiful Exmoor countryside. Well marked foot paths go for miles. The en-suite bedrooms with television and hospitality trays, have delightful views to enjoy. Two large reception rooms with log fires, dining room where delicious Exmoor dishes are served with good wine. Relax by the pool, and enjoy afternoon tea in the garden. Truly a wonderful base for visiting the West Country. We look forward to welcoming you to Wood Advent.

B & B from £23pp, C-Cards MC VS, Dinner from £15, Rooms 2 twin, 2 double, 1 family, all en-suite/private, No smoking in bedrooms, Children over 8, Dogs in kennel or car, Closed Xmas

Larcombe Foot Winsford, Exmoor National Park, Minehead TA24 7HS

Mrs Val Vicary Tel / Fax: 01643 851306
Email: larcombefoot@talk21.com

Map Ref: 6
A396

Larcombe Foot is a charming period house set in its own grounds overlooking the beautiful, tranquil upper Exe Valley, with footpath access to the moor from the doorstep. The house is one mile from the pretty village of Winsford with its thatched 12th century pub. Comfort here is paramount, with the pleasantly furnished rooms facing south with valley views. They have private bathrooms and tea/coffee makers. There is a cosy guests' sitting room with a log fire and television. Delicious home cooked dinners available. Perfect area for walking, riding, fishing and simply relaxing.

B & B from £23pp, Dinner from £12.50, Rooms 1 single, 1 double, 1 twin, all en-suite, Children over 6, Dogs welcome, Closed Dec to Mar

Pennard House East Pennard, Shepton Mallet BA4 6TP

Susie & Martin Dearden Tel / Fax: 01749 860266
Email: m.dearden@ukonline.co.uk

Map Ref: 7
A37

Pennard House is a beautiful Georgian home situated on the last south facing slope of the Mendip Hills. It stands in secluded gardens, surrounded by meadows, woodlands and cider orchards. There is a grass tennis court and Victorian spring-fed swimming pool. The house is furnished with antiques. Television and tea/coffee making facilities are available. 'Pennard House Antiques' are run from the rear of the house. The house is ideally situated for visiting Glastonbury, Wells, Bath and the historic houses and gardens of Stourhead, Longleat, Montacute, Hadspen and many others. Nearby golf and riding are available.

B & B from £30pp, C-Cards MC VS, Rooms 1 single, 2 twin (1 en-suite, 1 private), 1 double en-suite, Restricted smoking, Children welcome, No dogs, Closed Xmas & New Year

East Lambrook Farm East Lambrook, South Petherton TA13 5HH

Mrs Eeles Tel / Fax: 01460 240064
Email: nicolaeeles@supanet.com

Map Ref: 8
A303

East Lambrook Farm is a 17th century farmhouse in a quiet position in the village, with a pub nearby. The house is warm and comfortable with central heating and wood-burning stoves, antique furniture, coffee and tea making facilities in the bedrooms, and a sitting room with television. Guests are welcome to enjoy the large garden and tennis court. There are many gardens to visit in the area, namely Montacute, Tintinhull, Barrington Court (National Trust properties). Also bicycle routes, River Parrett trail and pretty villages.

B & B £23-£25pp, Dinner from £15, Rooms 1 twin, 2 double, 2 private bathrooms, No smoking, Children welcome, No dogs, Closed Xmas & New Year

Courtfield Norton-sub-Hamdon, Stoke-sub-Hamdon TA14 6SG

Richard & Valerie Constable   Tel: 01935 881246

Email: courtfield@hotmail.com

Map Ref: 9
A303, A356

A Grade II listed family home standing in the centre of the delightful Somerset village of Norton-sub-Hamdon. The house enjoys a pleasant walled garden setting, there is a tennis court for visitors to enjoy. The large, charming bedrooms have handbasins, televisions, sofas and an upstairs kitchen. There is a lovely conservatory where breakfast and candlelit dinners are served, it has views to the gardens and church. The pub serves excellent food and is three minutes walk away. This is ideal countryside for walking, and for visiting the many stately homes and gardens nearby.

B & B from £28pp, Dinner from £18, Rooms 1 double, 1 twin, both private bathroom, No smoking, Children over 8, Dogs by arrangement, Closed Xmas & New Year

Pear Tree Cottage Stapley, Churchstanton, Taunton TA3 7QA

Pam Parry   Tel / Fax: 01823 601224

Email: colvin.parry@virgin.net

Map Ref: 10
M5, A303, A30

Charming south facing thatched country cottage in an idyllic rural location, near Somerset/Devon border in an Area of Outstanding Natural Beauty. Picturesque countryside with winding lanes of flora and fauna. Wildlife abounds. Centrally placed for North and South coasts of Somerset/Devon/Dorset. Exmoor, Dartmoor, Torbay and even Cornwall reachable for day trips. Wealth of National Trust and other famous gardens encircle. Traditional cottage garden with lawns, borders, vegetable raised beds, approximately one acre leading to two and a half acre arboretum. Televisions, beverages in all rooms.

B & B from £15pp, Dinner from £10, Rooms 1 single, 1 double, with pb, 1 family/twin en-suite, No smoking, Children welcome, Dogs by arrangement, Open all year

Northam Mill Water Lane, Stogumber, Taunton TA4 3TT

Richard Spicer and Kate Butler   Tel: 01984 656916   Fax: 01984 656144

Mobile: 07836 752235   Email: bmsspicercaol.com   Web: www.northam-mill.co.uk

Map Ref: 11
A358

Northam Mill is hidden in a delightfully peaceful valley between the Quantock and Brendon Hills in glorious West Somerset. This 300 year old corn mill is home to Richard and Kate who enjoy welcoming guests to share the charm of their home. It is an adults' oasis, there are no children here. The beamed library where guests enjoy breakfasts and delicious five course dinners, is a pleasant place for relaxing after a day exploring, on foot or by car. Well equipped bedrooms are beautifully presented, there is a three bedroomed self contained apartment.

B & B £25.50-£37.50pp, C-Cards MC VS AE, Dinner from £22.50, Rooms 1 single, 3 double, 2 twin, most en-suite, Restricted smoking, No children, Dogs in heated kennels, Open all year

Causeway Cottage West Buckland, Wellington TA21 9JZ

Lesley Orr   Tel / Fax: 01823 663458

Email: orrs@westbuckland.freeserve.co.uk   Web: www.welcome.to/causeway-cottage

Map Ref: 12
M5 J26

This 200 year old cottage may be found at the foot of the Blackdown Hills on the Devon/Somerset border. It has lovely gardens, an apple orchard and views across the fields to the village church. The freshly presented bedrooms are en-suite, centrally heated and furnished with antique pine. The smell of homemade bread wafts through the cottage, Lesley runs cookery courses and she will happily prepare a delicious supper. Many famous attractions are easily reached by car, Dartmoor, Exmoor, Wells Cathedral and Glastonbury are just a pleasant drive away.

B & B from £25pp, Dinner from £12, Rooms 2 double en-suite, No smoking, Children over 10, No dogs, Closed Xmas & New Year

Riverside Grange Tanyard Lane, North Wootton, Wells BA4 4AE

Pat English
Tel: 01749 890761

Map Ref: 13
A39

Built in 1853, Riverside Grange is a charming converted tannery quietly situated on the river edge overlooking cider orchards. Peacefully situated, it is set in an area of outstanding natural beauty. The rooms are tastefully furnished to a high standard and include tea and coffee making facilities and colour televisions. North Wootton is a short drive from both Wells and Glastonbury, and the famous factory shopping outlet 'Clarks Village' in Street. There is a village Inn serving good food within a short walk.

B & B £22.50pp, Rooms 1 twin, 1 double, No smoking,
No children or dogs, Closed Xmas & New Year

Southway Farm Polsham, Wells BA5 1RW

Naomi Frost   Tel: 01749 673396   Fax: 01749 670373   Mobile: 07971 694650
Email: southwayfarm@ukonline.co.uk   Web: southwayfarm.co.uk

Map Ref: 14
A39

Southway Farm is an attractive creeper clad, Grade II listed Georgian farmhouse, situated halfway between Glastonbury and Wells. The large, comfortable, attractively presented bedrooms with wonderful countryside views are equipped with tea/coffee making facilities, televisions and radio alarm clocks. A delicious full English breakfast and homemade bread is served, although vegetarians are also catered for. Guests may relax in the cosy lounge with television, or in the pretty, tranquil garden. This is an ideal location for a restful holiday, or for touring the glorious West Country.

B & B from £22pp, Rooms 2 double, 1 twin, all en-suite,
No smoking, Children welcome, No dogs,

Stoneleigh House Westbury-sub-Mendip, Wells BA5 1HF

Wendy & Tony Thompson   Tel / Fax: 01749 870668
Email: stoneleigh@dail.pipex.com   Web: www.stoneleigh.dial.pipex.com

Map Ref: 15
A371

A beautiful 18th century farmhouse (flagstone floors, beams, crooked walls) situated between Wells and Cheddar. Wonderful southerly views over unspoilt countryside to Glastonbury Tor from the bedrooms and guests lounge. The bedrooms are prettily furnished with country antiques, and the en-suite bath/shower rooms work properly! Round this off with a delicious breakfast, Wendy's decorative needlework, Tony's classic cars, the old forge, a cottagey garden and friendly cats. Large car park. Excellent pubs nearby.

B & B £27-£29pp, Rooms 2 double, 1 twin, 2 en-suite, 1 private bathroom,
Strictly no smoking, Children over 10, No dogs, Closed Xmas

Cutthorne Luckwell Bridge, Wheddon Cross TA24 7EW

Ann Durbin   Tel / Fax: 01643 831255
Email: durbin@cutthorne.co.uk   Web: www.cutthorne.co.uk

Map Ref: 16
B3224

Cutthorne is a country house tucked away in the heart of beautiful Exmoor. It is 'off the beaten track,' one can ride and walk in glorious countryside. Exmoor ponies, sheep and maybe some red deer can be spied from the saddle. The beautiful Bluebell Valley is a step away. Visitors here are welcome to picnic by the trout pond or wander in the fields. Beautifully presented bedrooms, a four poster, an antique French bed and far reaching views. English breakfasts, with many choices. Candlelit fireside dinners. Close to Dunster, Tarr Steps, Lynton and Lynmouth.

B & B £25-£34pp, Dinner from £16, Rooms 1 twin, 1 double, 1 four poster, all en-suite,
No smoking, Children over 12, Dogs welcome, Open all year

Suffolk

Suffolk is a delightful county of softly undulating rural landscape, of slow-flowing streams, picturesque villages and the open heath country of the Breckland. The coastline, under constant attack from the eroding sea, nevertheless offers lovely shingle shores, sandy beaches and low cliffs. Dunwich Heath, one of Suffolk's most important conservation areas covers over 200 acres of Sandlings heathland with sandy cliffs and a mile of lovely beach, adjacent is the Minsmere nature reserve run by the RSPB, a refuge for migrating and resident birds.

The glories of this county have been captured on canvas by John Constable and Thomas Gainsborough and the holiday visitor would be well rewarded for following in the footsteps of Constable through a countryside little changed from his day. Sudbury, Gainsborough's birthplace and once one of the largest East Anglian woollen towns is an excellent starting point. Gainsborough's house, an elegant Tudor building with an added Regency facade is now a museum. The narrow twisting streets and medieval houses surround the fine fifteenth century church of St James which contains Constable's painting of 'Christ's Blessing of the Bread and Wine'. Dedham to the east was a favourite subject of Constable, and little wonder, its fine High Street of Tudor and Georgian houses is a delight. Further east at East Bergholt is the birthplace of Constable and a great attraction for tourists, as both Flatford Mill and Willy Lot's Cottage, popular subjects of the master's paintings, are close by.

Lavenham, a medieval wool town is a popular place for tourists who wish to visit the beautiful black and white timbered buildings on market square. Also worth visiting is the fifteenth century Guildhall which has a complete history of Lavenham's wool trade. Lowestoft in the north offers a contrasting variety of pleasures with Lowestoft Ness, the most easterly point of the British Isles, a wild and windswept sanctuary for birds, and Oulton Broad is a popular site for many watersports. There is also Pleasurewood Hills American Theme Park with 50 acres of rides and attractions. Lowestoft was a centre for fishing from the fourteenth century and the fish market is still very much in evidence. South is Aldeburgh, boasting some fine medieval buildings. Much of its ancient history has been devoured by the voracious sea, in fact the handsome sixteenth century Moot Hall, once in the centre of the town, is

Framlingham Castle (EETB)

now at the water's edge. The town is the birthplace of George Crabbe, the eighteenth century writer whose poem, 'The Borough' was adapted by Benjamin Britten to become his opera, 'Peter Grimes', an evocation of life on the Suffolk coast. Aldeburgh is renowned for its music festival held at nearby Snape with the Maltings Proms, venue of the festival, founded by Benjamin Britten.

Ipswich, the county town and inland port on the River Orwell can boast no less than twelve medieval churches and the handsome sixteenth century Christchurch Mansion with its excellent collection of Suffolk antiques and paintings. Cardinal Wolsey was born here, his Tudor brick gate still stands in Fore Street. Bury St Edmunds was once the town of Beodericsworth, a Saxon settlement when the bones of Edmund, the last king of East Anglia who was killed by the Danes for refusing to deny Christianity, were brought for burial. The settlement changed its name to St Edmundsbury and became an important place of pilgrimage. Except for its two gateways the fourteenth century abbey is in ruins. It was in 1214, at the altar of an earlier abbey on this site that the Barons swore to force King John to honour the Magna Carta. Of course to the west of Bury St Edmunds is Newmarket, the home of the Jockey Club and the historic centre of English horseracing. Before leaving, you must visit the Theatre Royal in Westgate Street, built in 1819 it is a very rare example of a Georgian playhouse boasting a national reputation attracting the foremost touring companies in the country. Also well worth a visit is the eccentric Ickworth House built by the Earl of Bristol in 1795, it is surrounded by a glorious Italianate garden and Capability Brown park,. and contains a superb collection of works by Titian, Gainsborough and Velasquez.

PLACES TO VISIT

This is a small selection of interesting places to visit. Many more are listed in our annual guide to Museums, Galleries, Historic Houses & Sites (see page 448)

Framlingham Castle
Framlingham
One of the first castles to have a curtain wall and several towers instead of one central keep. Mary Tudor spent the summer here waiting to find out if she or Lady Jane Grey was to be declared Queen.

Ickworth House
Horringer, Bury St Edmunds
Discover the Italianate wonders of the house and gardens, an immense oval Rotunda with two large wings with curving corridors, collections of Georgian silver and paintings by Titian and Velasquez.

Kentwell Hall
Long Melford, Sudbury
A mellow red-brick Tudor manor house surrounded by a moat and extensive woodlands. The house has been interestingly restored with Tudor costumes and a mosaic rose maze. The gardens are a delight.

National Horseracing Museums and Tours
Newmarket, Suffolk
A museum displaying the development of horse-racing. There is a display of sporting art and five galleries of loans from major museums and private collections.

Suffolk

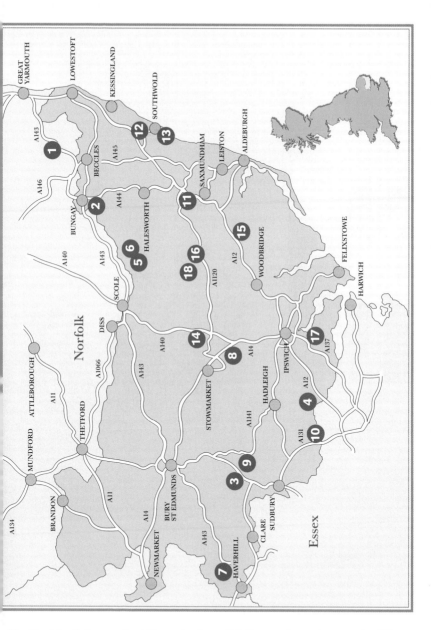

The Blue Map References should be used to locate B & B properties on the pages that follow

The Hatch, Hartest, near Bury St Edmunds

The Elms Toft Monks, Beccles NR34 0EJ

Richard & Teena Freeland Tel: 01502 677380 Fax: 01502 677362
Email: richardfreeland@btconnect.com Web: www.freelandenterprises.co.uk

Map Ref: 1
A143

Built in 1720, originally a Flax weaver's residence, this beautiful family home welcomes guests to enjoy a stunning moated garden, rose walks, lawns and a tennis court. Drinks may be enjoyed on the terrace before dinner, featuring local produce including fish, game and poultry. Handsome fireplaces, huge sash windows and cast iron baths all contribute to the splendour and style of this traditional Suffolk house. The Elms is close to Southwold and other interesting local coastal towns. There is spectacular local coarse fishing and farm walks, also golf, tennis and riding.

B & B £35-£65pp, Dinner from £22, Rooms 1 twin en-suite, 2 double, 1 private bathroom 1 en-suite, No smoking, Children over 5, No dogs, Closed occasionally

Earsham Park Farm Harleston Road, Earsham, Bungay NR35 2AQ

Bobbie Watchorn Tel / Fax: 01986 892180 Mobile: 07798 728936
Email: bobbie@earsham-parkfarm.co.uk Web: www.earsham-parkfarm.co.uk

Map Ref: 2
A143,A144

Surrounded by countryside. This family run delightful quiet and friendly farmhouse is set in a superb location overlooking the Waveney Valley. The rooms are spacious and elegantly furnished, but with comfort as a priority. They have extensive facilities including television, a tea-tray, easy chairs, and a four poster is available. The towels are thick, and the linen embroidered. Visitors are welcome to enjoy the gardens here, and to do some interesting farm walks. Delicious local food. There are many places to to visit, Norwich and the coast are a pleasant drive. ETC 4 Diamonds, Silver Award.

B & B from £24pp, C-Cards MC VS, Dinner available, Rooms 2 double, 1 twin, all en-suite, No smoking, Children welcome, Dogs by arrangement, Open all year

The Hatch Pilgrims Lane, Cross Green, Hartest, Bury St Edmunds IP29 4ED

Bridget & Robin Oaten
Tel / Fax: 01284 830226

Map Ref: 3
B1066
see Photo opposite

The Hatch is a gorgeous thatched timber framed listed 15th century house, situated outside the attractive High Suffolk village of Hartest. Surrounded by farmland, the house is very comfortably furnished with fine fabrics and antiques. Guests have the use of the delightful drawing and sitting rooms, both with inglenook fireplaces and log fires for cooler evenings. Bedrooms have very comfortable beds, goose down duvets, bottled water, decanter of sherry, sweets, fresh flowers. There is a lovely garden for guests to enjoy. Hartest is an ideal centre for visiting West Suffolk, Cambridgeshire and Ely. Good walking and cycling.

B & B from £30pp, Rooms 1 twin, 1 double, No smoking, Children over 9, Closed occasionally

Old Vicarage Higham, Colchester CO7 6JY

Meg Parker Tel: 01206 337248
Email: oldvic.higham@bushinternet.com

Map Ref: 4
A12

This charming detached 16th century house is situated in a beautiful Suffolk village. The fields of the Old Vic go down to the river Brets and Stour where there are boats to see. Facilities include a swimming pool and a tennis court. There is much to do visiting the famous villages of Lavenham and Sudbury showing many Gainsborough pictures. The sea is half an hour away. The house has three bedrooms with television and tea making facilities. A fine drawing room overlooks the garden, which guests are welcome to enjoy.

B & B £25-£30pp, Rooms 1 twin, 1 double, 1 family, 2 en-suite, Restricted smoking, Children & dogs welcome, Open all year

Gables Farm Earsham Street, Wingfield, Diss IP21 5RH
Michael & Sue Harvey Tel: 01379 586355 Fax: 01379 588058
Email: gables-farm@ntlworld.com Web: www.gablesfarm.co.uk

Map Ref: 5
B1118 or A143

Gables Farm is a 16th Century timbered farmhouse set in moated gardens. Wingfield is a quiet village in the heart of East Anglia, it is convenient for Norwich, Bury St Edmunds and coast and many places of interest. Ideal for cycling and walking, fishing two miles away. The bedrooms, of which two are double and one a twin, are all en-suite. They have a colour television, and a hospitality tray. A full English breakfast with free range eggs is served, and where possible, local produce is used. A leaflet is available by request.

B & B from £22pp, Rooms 1 twin, 2 double, all en-suite, No smoking, Children welcome, Dogs by arrangement, Closed Xmas & New Year

Priory House Priory Road, Fressingfield, Eye IP21 5PH
Rosemary Willis
Tel: 01379 586254

Map Ref: 6
B1116

A warm welcome awaits visitors to this lovely 16th century farmhouse, set in secluded lawns and gardens. The comfortable bedrooms have tea/coffee facilities, two rooms have private bathrooms, all are centrally heated. The house has exposed beams, and is furnished with antique furniture. There is a guests' lounge and a pleasant dining room, with access throughout the day. Fressingfield is ideal for a peaceful holiday and as touring base for Norwich, Bury St Edmunds, the Broads, historic buildings and gardens. Excellent local pub in the village, a few minutes walk.

B & B from £26pp, Rooms 1 twin, 2 double, private bathrooms, Restricted smoking, Children over 10, Dogs by arrangement, Closed Xmas & New Year

The Old Vicarage Great Thurlow, Haverhill CB9 7LE
Jane Sheppard
Tel: 01440 783209 Fax: 01638 667270

Map Ref: 7
A1307, A143

Set in mature grounds and woodlands this delightful Old Vicarage has a friendly family atmosphere. Complete peace and comfort are assured with wonderful views of the Suffolk countryside. Open log fires welcome you in winter. Guests are welcome to use the large garden and there is ample parking space. Perfectly situated for Newmarket, Cambridge, Long Melford and Constable Country, the attractively furnished bedrooms have en-suite or private facilities. Tea and coffee trays are provided in all rooms. Evening meals are available with prior notice.

B & B from £28pp, Dinner from £18, Rooms 1 single, 1 twin, 1 double, all en-suite, Restricted smoking, Children over 7, Dogs by arrangement, Closed Xmas

Pipps Ford Needham Market, Ipswich IP6 8LJ
Raewyn Hackett-Jones Tel: 01449 760208 Fax: 01449 760561
Email: b&b@pippsford.co.uk Web: www.pippsford.co.uk

Map Ref: 8
A14, A140

Pipps Ford is a fine and beautiful, long, low, black and white timbered house, parts of which date from 1540. It stands in a pretty, old fashioned garden by the Gipping river. It is a house with sloping floors, beams, inglenooks with log fires, and historic associations. The cottagey sitting rooms are filled with antique furniture and china collections, they have a wonderful atmosphere. The bedrooms are attractive with en-suite bathrooms and they have tea/coffee making facilities, radio/clock alarms, and hair dryers. There are more bedrooms in the stables. Excellent, imaginative evening meals are offered.

B & B £28-£37.50pp, C-Cards MC VS AE, Dinner from £19.50, Rooms 4 double, 3 twin, Restricted smoking, Children over 5, Dogs by arrangement, Closed Xmas & New Year

Lavenham Priory Water Street, Lavenham, Sudbury CO10 9RW
Tim & Gilli Pitt Tel: 01787 247404 Fax: 01787 248472
Email: mail@lavenhampriory.co.uk Web: www.lavenhampriory.co.uk

Map Ref: **9**
B1115, A1141

Lavenham Priory, a Grade I listed house provides an unforgettable experience. Bed chambers feature crown posts, Elizabethan wall paintings and oak floors, with four-poster, lit bureau and polonaise beds. Lavenham is one of the finest medieval villages in England with its historic buildings and streets. Within easy walking distance of The Priory are the National Trust Guildhall, art galleries, antique shops and the magnificent Wool Church of St Peter and St Paul. Winner of the AA guest accommodation of the year award for England and the EETB's regional best B & B.

B & B £39-£54pp, C-Cards MC VS, Rooms 5 double, 1 twin, all en-suite, No smoking,
Children over 10, No dogs, Closed From Xmas to New Year

Wood Hall Little Waldingfield, Lavenham, Sudbury CO10 0SY
Susan T del C Nisbett Tel: 01787 247362 Fax: 01787 248326
Email: nisbett@nisbett.enta.net Web: www.nisbett.enta.net

Map Ref: **9**
B1115

Wood Hall, a Tudor House, was modernised in the Georgian period. It has large windows and a brick facade which hides the richly beamed original. The house is full of antiques, and it has a lovely walled garden for guests to enjoy. There are two light and airy bedrooms for guests, both are well equipped. Wood Hall is ideally placed for visiting Lavenham and the surrounding medieval villages and Churches. Thomas Gainsborough's house may be found in Sudbury, the area is known as Constable country. Cambridge is less than one hour away.

B & B from £30pp, Dinner from £15, Rooms 1 double, 1 twin, both en-suite,
No smoking, Children over 10, No dogs, Closed Xmas

Hill House Gravel Hill, Nayland CO6 4JB
Mrs P Heigham Tel: 01206 262782
Email: heigham.hillhouse@rdplus.net

Map Ref: **10**
A134

Hill House is a comfortable 16th century timber framed 'Hall House' full of beams and inglenooks. It is set on edge of 'Constable' village in a quiet location. The garden is secluded with views over the valley. All the bedrooms are comfortably furnished with colour television, radio, tea/coffee trays. This a good base from which to explore and walk. The golf course is just one mile away. Excellent restaurants and good pub food locally. Easy access to A12, convenient for Lavenham, Dedham, Flatford Mill and Harwich.

B & B from £23pp, Rooms 1 single, 1 double en-suite, 1 twin en-suite, No smoking,
Children over 10, No dogs, Closed Xmas & New Year

Church Farm Yoxford Road, Sibton, Saxmundham IP17 2LX
Elizabeth Dixon Tel: 01728 660101 Fax: 01728 660102
Email: dixons@church-farmhouse.demon.co.uk Web: www.church-farmhouse.demon.co.uk

Map Ref: **11**
A1120

Surrounded by glorious countryside this spacious 17th century house is ideal for exploring the Suffolk heritage coast. The bedrooms at Church Farm are elegant, comfortable, light and exceptionally well appointed with central heating, colour television, video, mini hi-fi, hairdryer and hospitality tray. The two doubles are en-suite, the twin with private bathroom. The guest dining room has a wealth of beams whilst the lounge has deep sofas and a wood burning stove. Both overlook the attractive front garden. A warm and friendly welcome awaits you. ETC 5 Diamonds, Silver Award.

B & B £25-£30pp, Rooms 1 twin, 2 double, all en-suite/private, No smoking,
Children over 6, No dogs, Closed Xmas

Church Farmhouse, Uggeshall, near Southwold

Poplar Hall Frostenden Corner, Frostenden, Southwold NR34 7JA
Anna & John Garwood
Tel: 01502 578549

Map Ref: 12
A12

Peaceful and quiet, yet only minutes from the lovely seaside town of Southwold, Poplar Hall is a 16th century thatched house in a one and a half acre garden. Wonderful walks in the area, either coastal or country. Walberswick, Dunwich, Aldburgh, Snape are a short distance. Poplar Hall offers luxury accommodation with television, tea/coffee making facilities and vanity units in all rooms. Guests' library, sitting and dining rooms are a pleasure to be in, here you may enjoy our famed breakfast of fresh fruit, local fish, sausage, bacon and home made preserves.

B & B from £25pp, Rooms 1 single, 2 double, cot available, 1 en-suite, No smoking, Children welcome, No dogs, Closed Xmas

Church Farmhouse Uggeshall, Southwold NR34 8BD
Sarah Jupp Tel: 01502 578532 Fax: 01953 888306 Mobile: 07748 801418
Email: sarahjupp@compuserve.com

Map Ref: 12
A12
see Photo opposite

This lovely 17th century listed farmhouse, set in three acres of garden and orchard, next to a thatched church, makes a wonderful base from which to discover this unspoilt part of Suffolk. Sympathetically restored, with lovely fabrics, fresh flowers and cotton sheets. It is all very relaxed and peaceful here - let Sara cook a wonderful dinner for you; this she does excellently from her Aga-warm kitchen. Southwold is four miles away and there are lovely walks, birds, lots of art and music nearby and Sarah has a wealth of local knowledge.

B & B £30-£35pp, Dinner from £20, Rooms 1 single, 1 double, 1 twin, most en-suite, No smoking, Children over 12, No dogs, Closed Xmas day

Ferry House Walberswick, Southwold IP18 6TH
Cathryn Simpson Tel / Fax: 01502 723384
Email: ferryhouse.walberswick@virgin.net Web: www.ferryhouse-walberswick.com

Map Ref: 13
A12

Ferry House is just 200 metres from the River Blyth, and close to the seashore. Walberswick is a delightful artists village, and this house was built to an unusual design for a playwright's summer residence. The fireplace surround in the dining room depicts scenes believed to be from one of his plays. Now this charming home offers a warm welcome with stylish, well provided guest accommodation. Snape Maltings, Minsmere Bird Reserve and Regency town of Southwold are within easy reach. Good pubs serving food are well within walking distance.

B & B from £20pp, Rooms 2 single, 1 double, No smoking, Children over 10, No dogs, Closed Xmas & New Year

Cherry Tree Farm Mendlesham Green, Stowmarket IP14 5RQ
Martin & Diana Ridsdale
Tel: 01449 766376

Map Ref: 14
A140

Cherry Tree Farm is a traditional timber framed farmhouse situated in the heart of rural Suffolk, where guests are welcomed to warm hospitality. Accommodation is in three en-suite bedrooms. The guests lounge has an inglenook fireplace with a woodburning stove for cool evenings. Great care is taken in the preparation of meals which are served around a refectory table, bread is home baked and seasonal vegetables are garden fresh, traditional puddings are a speciality. Licensed, with a wine list containing a unique selection of East Anglian wines.

B & B from £27pp, Dinner from £17, Rooms 3 double en-suite, No smoking, No children or dogs, Closed Dec to Feb

The Old Rectory Campsea Ashe, Woodbridge IP13 0PU
Stewart Bassett
Tel / Fax: 01728 746524

Map Ref: 15
A12
see Photo opposite

Peaceful Georgian rectory set in mature gardens with a relaxed and homely atmosphere. There are log fires in drawing rooms and dining room, and a spacious conservatory. All bedrooms are en-suite with tea/coffee making facilities. Delicious home cooked food in the licensed restaurant, to which outside diners are welcome. Local home-made bread, and a variety of home-made marmalade, jam and local honey is a speciality. Television and games in the drawing room. Well placed for Snape, Woodbridge and coastal areas. Brochure is available on request. Children are welcome.

B & B from £30pp, C-Cards VS AE DC, Dinner from £18.50, Rooms 1 single, 4 double, 2 twin, all en-suite, Restricted smoking, Well behaved children, Dogs welcome, Closed Xmas

Grange Farm Dennington, Woodbridge IP13 8BT
Mrs E Hickson   Tel: 01986 798388   Mobile: 07774 182835
Web: www.framlingham.com/grangefarm

Map Ref: 16
A1120

Grange Farm is a moated medieval farmhouse, set in spacious grounds in a peaceful part of Suffolk. The garden has a wealth of birds to enjoy, including woodpeckers, linnets, kingfishers and owls at night. A superb all weather tennis court is there for guests' enjoyment. There is an excellent variety of restaurants and pubs locally, including a Thai restaurant. There are many places of interest, the Heritage coast being not far away, also Snape Maltings concert hall, Ickworth House, Sutton Hoo burial ground and more. This is the land of churches.

B & B £22pp, Dinner from £12, Rooms 1/2 double or 1/3 twin (let as single) shared bathroom, No smoking, Children over 12, No dogs, Closed Dec to Jan

Woolverstone House Mannings Lane, Woolverstone, Ispwich IP9 1AN
Mrs Jane Cook   Tel: 01473 780940   Fax: 01473 780959
Email: cooks@enterprise.net

Map Ref: 17
A12, A14

This fascinating Suffolk home, designed by Sir Edwin Lutyens, was built in 1901 as a retreat for East End nuns of the order of Saint Peter, the present drawing room was once a chapel. The house features a charming Gertrude Jekyll garden, a cool shady courtyard and a wealth of architectural interest. This unique house offers much intrigue, it is presented in a style to enhance the Lutyens design. Surrounded by beautiful countryside on the Shotley Peninsula, it is convenient for Woodbridge, Ipswich, Harwich, Orford and Constable country. Sailing, walking and birdwatching are nearby.

B & B £35-£55pp, Dinner from £17.50, Rooms 2 double, both en-suite, 1 twin, private bathroom, No smoking, Children over 12, No dogs, Closed Xmas & New Year

Guildhall Church Street, Worlingworth IP13 7NS
Mrs Penfold
Tel / Fax: 01728 628057

Map Ref: 18
A140, A1120

Guildhall is 16th century thatched and Grade II listed. Set in countryside, ideal for bird watching, walking and painting. The Heritage coast is approx 30 minutes. Southwold, Minsmere, historic Framlingham, Eye, or Diss a short drive. Rooms are heavily beamed, beautifully furnished and centrally heated. Tea and coffee facilities. Separate television guest lounge with inglenook. Full English breakfast (dinner by previous arrangement) served in a charming dining room or conservatory. Large mature gardens with summer house at your disposal.

B & B £22-£24pp, Dinner from £12, Rooms 2 double, en-suite/private, No smoking, No children or dogs, Closed Oct to mid-Mar

The Old Rectory, Campsea Ashe, near Woodbridge

Surrey

Surrey still remains Britain's most wooded county and is crossed from east to west by the North Downs, whose chalk slopes are broken by the lovely Rivers Wey, Mole and Darent. Its steep scarp slope which faces south is cut by interesting wooded combes ablaze with wildflowers. Box Hill, a highly popular beauty spot, made famous by Jane Austen's Emma, rises four hundred feet from the River Mole on the very edge of the North Downs. This glorious country park consists of over a thousand acres of woods and chalk downland with quite superb views to the South Downs. To the east is a range of sandy hills with Leith Hill being the highest point in south east England. Here the National Trust own the large countryside property which includes a tower dating from 1766 which gives magnificent views across the Surrey Weald and it is claimed that from this tower, 1,029 feet above sea level, you can, on a clear day see no less than eleven counties. Reigate, once an important coaching town, is an ideal centre for exploring this lovely region. The attractive old market town clustered around its Norman castle boasts some fine old houses. To the east near Dorking where the River Mole cuts through the chalk downs is Polesden Lacey, a wonderfully elegant Regency villa set in extensive grounds with a fine walled rose garden and tree-lined walks. The house contains a fascinating collection of paintings, furniture, silver and porcelain and it was here that the Queen Mother and King George VI spent part of their honeymoon.

In the south west corner of Surrey, in the Wey Valley is Frensham Common, now part of a country park managed by Waverley Borough Council. The area is famed for its ponds, Frensham Great and Little Ponds which were dug during the Middle Ages and are the largest in the county. The area is very popular with holiday visitors, having safe sandy beaches, sailing and a wealth of wildlife including wildfowl. To the south at Hindhead are over 1,400 acres of open heathland and woodland covering delightful valleys and sandstone ridges, a great walking region.

Guildford, Surrey's ancient capital, is beautifully sited at the ford where the

Loseley Park, Guildford (SEETB)

River Wey cuts through the North Downs. The town was first mentioned in the will of Alfred the Great, back in 899AD, but its importance was established with the building of its castle (now a ruin), in the twelfth century by Henry II. An important weaving town in Tudor times, today Guildford is a university town, with excellent shopping and a fine venue for the holiday visitor. Dapdune Wharf is being conserved as a focal point for the history of boat building on the River Wey. The Wey is one of the earliest historic waterways in the country. Built in 1651 the waterway was eventually extended by Godalming Navigation to reach the Thames at Weybridge. The eighteenth century watermill on the Tillingbourne at Shalford and Oakhurst Cottage, a small sixteenth century timber-framed cottage wonderfully restored, with its cottage garden, are well worth a visit. To the north of Guildford at West Clandon is Clandon Park, a fine Palladian house with a magnificent two-storeyed marble hall. Clandon is a treasure house of antiques and contains the Ivo Forde collection of Meissen Italian comedy figures.

On the edge of Windsor Great Park, in the north of the county, lies Virginia Water, an artificial lake one-and-a-half miles long, created in the middle of the eighteenth century for the first Duke of Cumberland and contained within four hundred acres of lovely public gardens. At nearby Egham are 188 acres of the historic meadows of Runnymede where in 1215 King John signed the Magna Carta. The American Bar Association built the impressive Magna Carta Memorial, a domed classical temple at the foot of Cooper's Hill. Overlooking the memorial at the top of the hill is the Air Forces Memorial and the John F Kennedy Memorial, an acre of ground given by the people of Great Britain to the people of America as a memorial to their president.

PLACES TO VISIT

This is a small selection of interesting places to visit. Many more are listed in our annual guide to Museums, Galleries, Historic Houses & Sites (see page 448)

Chessington World of Adventures
Leatherhead Road, Chessington
A family theme park, well known for its zoo with penguins, gorillas, tigers and monkeys.

Claremont Landscape Gardens
Portsmouth Road, Esher
Early eighteenth century landscape garden with lake, island, grotto, amphitheatre and views.

Denbies Wine Estate
Dorking
England's largest wine estate set in 265 acres. A tour is provided featuring a 3D time lapse film of vine growing with a tasting in the cellars.

Hampton Court Palace
East Molesey
In peaceful surroundings on the banks of the River Thames, Hampton Court Palace spans 400 years of history and was home to Henry VIII and William III.

Loseley Park
Guildford
A fine example of Elizabethan architecture set in magnificent parkland. Interesting collections of furniture and Christian pictures. Walled garden.

Thorpe Park
Staines Lane, Chertsey
Much to offer for fun seekers of all ages including Europe's highest water ride.

Surrey

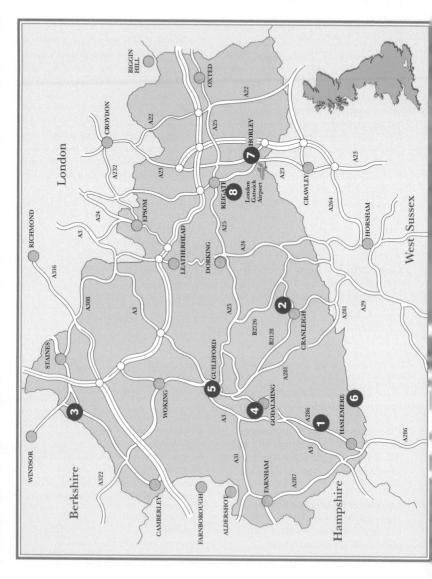

The Blue Map References should be used to locate B & B properties on the pages that follow

Greenaway Pickhurst Road, Chiddingfold GU8 4TS

Sheila Marsh   Tel: 01428 682920   Fax: 01428 685078   Mobile: 07785 534199
Email: jfvmarsh@nildram.co.uk   Web: greenaway.nildram.co.uk

Map Ref: 1
A283

Greenaway is a charming 16th century Surrey home which stands close to the centre of the picturesque village of Chiddingfold. It looks out onto a glorious, well tended English cottage garden and a large dovecote. The interior is delightful, an inglenook fireplace, low-ceilinged, beamed rooms, each presenting their own character. Breakfast is served in the antique filled dining room, and suppers may be enjoyed at a choice of local pubs within walking distance of the house. Petworth House, Bignor Roman villa, Chichester and Portsmouth are within an easy drive.

B & B £35-£40pp, C-Cards MC VS, Rooms 2 double, 1 twin, 1 en-suite, No smoking, Children welcome, Dogs by arrangement, Closed Xmas & New Year

High Edser Shere Road, Ewhurst, Cranleigh GU6 7PQ

Carol Franklin-Adams   Tel: 01483 278214   Fax: 01483 278200   Mobile: 0777 5865125
Email: franklinadams@highedser.demon.co.uk

Map Ref: 2
A25

High Edser is an early 16th century farmhouse set in an area of outstanding natural beauty surrounded by its own land. A tennis court is available for guests' use. There is a guests' lounge with television and all rooms have tea/coffee making facilities. Within easy reach of Guildford, Dorking and Horsham. Many National Trust properties and other places of interest are close by. Gatwick and Heathrow are approximately 30 minutes drive. We welcome children and dogs by prior arrangement.

B & B £25-£30pp, Rooms 1 twin, 2 double, No smoking, Children welcome, Kennel for dogs, Closed Xmas & Easter

The Old Parsonage Parsonage Road, Englefield Green TW20 0JW

Peter & Sandi Clark   Tel / Fax: 01784 436706
Email: the.old.parsonage@talk21.com   Web: www.theoldparsonage.com

Map Ref: 3
A30

The Old Parsonage is a late Georgian house set in a pretty village on the edge of Windsor Great Park. Guest accommodation is traditionally furnished and overlooks the old fashioned gardens. Bedrooms are equipped with television and coffee/tea making facilities. All meals are freshly prepared to order and wine is available. Local facilities include a beauty salon, swimming, golf and horse riding. Conveniently situated for Heathrow (20 minutes), M25, M4, M3, Windsor Ascot, Wisley Gardens and Egham mainline station (Waterloo 30 minutes).

B & B from £25pp, Dinner from £18, Rooms 1 single, 1 twin, 3 double, 1 family, most en-suite, No smoking, Children welcome, No dogs, Closed Xmas

Lower Eashing Farmhouse Eashing, Godalming GU7 2QF

Gillian & David Swinburn   Tel / Fax: 01483 421436
Email: davidswinburn@hotmail.com

Map Ref: 4
A3

Lower Eashing Farmhouse which is a part 16th, 18th and 19th century Grade II listed building, stands in the small, pretty village of Eashing set in a beautiful part of Surrey. The accommodation offered to guests includes a large sitting room with a cosy log fire, television and a piano. Guests are welcome to sit in the lovely walled garden. There are plenty of pubs and restaurants nearby. In addition to London and Portsmouth, many places of historic and cultural interest are within easy reach, including Windsor, Hampton Court, Winchester, Arundel and Petworth.

B & B £27.50-£35pp, Rooms 2 single, 2 twin - 1 en-suite, 1 private, No smoking, Children welcome, No dogs, Closed Xmas & New Year

Barn Cottage, Leigh, near Reigate

Littlefield Manor Littlefield Common, Guildford GU3 3HJ

John Tangye
Tel: 01483 233068 Fax: 01483 233686 Mobile: 07860 947439

Map Ref: 5
A3

Built in the 1550's, Littlefield Manor is a lovely old house isolated in 400 acres of farmland, yet it is only 35 miles from central London, making it the perfect place for business and holiday visitors. The bedrooms all offer en-suite facilities, they are equipped with televisions and tea/coffee making facilities. The house happily retains many of its original fascinating features, to include wooden floors, open fires, beamed ceilings, church panel doors, deep baths and wonderful views. The house has a traditional rose garden, and two acres of well tended lawns.

B & B from £30pp, C-Cards, Rooms 1 double en-suite, 1 twin with private bathroom, Children welcome, No dogs, Closed Xmas & New Year

Deerfell Blackdown Park, Fernden Lane, Haslemere GU27 3LA

Elisabeth Carmichael Tel: 01428 653409 Fax: 01428 656106
Email: deerfell@tesco.net

Map Ref: 6
A286, A3

Deerfell lies secluded on the south west side of National Trust Blackdown Hill, with wonderful views towards the South Downs and coast. Rooms are peaceful and comfortable with en-suite bath/shower, tea/coffee making facilities and a television - one double with separate bath/shower. Guests have the use of a comfortable sitting room with open fire, and breakfast is served in the attractive dining room. Many places of interest are within easy reach, and London is accessible from nearby Haslemere station only 4 miles away.

B & B from £22pp, Rooms 1 single, 1 twin, 1 double, 1 family, most en-suite, No smoking, Children over 6, Dogs restricted, Closed mid-Dec to mid-Jan

The Lawn Guest House 30 Massetts Road, Horley RH6 7DE

Carole & Adrian Grinsted Tel: 01293 775751 Fax: 01293 821803
Email: info@lawnguesthouse.co.uk Web: www.lawnguesthouse.co.uk

Map Ref: 7
A23

The Lawn Guest House, a totally non-smoking establishment, is an attractive Victorian house set in pretty gardens just one and a half miles from Gatwick airport and two minutes walk from Horley where there are pubs, restaurants, shops and a main line railway to London. The comfortable bedrooms are all en-suite with colour/text television, tea and coffee facilities, hair dryers and direct dial phones. A full English breakfast is served, or a healthy alternative consisting of fruit, yoghurt and muesli. There is plenty of holiday and overnight parking on site.

B & B from £27.50pp, C-Cards MC VS AE, Rooms 3 double, 3 twin, 3 triple, 3 family, all en-suite, No smoking, Children & dogs welcome, Open all year

Barn Cottage Church Road, Leigh, Reigate RH2 8RF

Pat & Mike Corner
Tel: 01306 611347

Map Ref: 8
A25
see Photo opposite

Barn Cottage is a converted 17th century barn furnished with antiques, set in a large garden with tennis court and swimming pool. We have television and tea/coffee making facilities in both rooms. Leigh is a pretty village, the Plough Pub is 100 yards away. We provide transport to Gatwick (15 minutes) and Redhill Station (30 minutes to London, 30 minutes to Brighton). Dorking, famous for antiques is five miles away. There are National Trust properties within reach, including Hever Castle and Chartwell (Churchill's House). Introduction to Walton Heath Golf Club available.

B & B from £28pp, Rooms 1 twin, 1 double, 1 with bathroom, Restricted smoking, Children welcome, Dogs by arrangement, Closed Xmas

Sussex

One could be excused for regarding Sussex as very much a seaside county, certainly Rudyard Kipling saw the county as 'Sussex by the sea', but there is considerably more to Sussex than its undoubtedly glorious coastline. The South Downs, that ancient chalk ridge, runs from east to west separating the Sussex Weald from the English Channel, eventually arriving dramatically in the towering form of Beachy Head, the highest cliff on the south coast, and needless to say giving superb views. To explore this area there could be no better starting point than the ancient city of Chichester, although holiday visitors may find it extremely difficult to drag themselves away from the attractions of this fair city! Chichester was a Roman town and there is still evidence of its Roman grid plan, the interesting early sixteenth century market cross indicates the crossing of four of the city's main streets. The Cathedral, early Norman with early English additions, is magnificent, as indeed is its tapestry by John Piper, its painting by Graham Sutherland and its glass by Chagall. The city is blessed with some handsome Georgian houses and an excellent Festival Theatre, plus Chichester Harbour, a fine yachting centre. Nearby is Fishbourne Roman Palace, built for King Cogidubnus, a Roman ally with reconstructed gardens and the original mosaic flooring of the palace, plus the first underground heating system. Petworth House lies to the south, a magnificent seventeenth century palace renowned for its Grinling Gibbons carvings and fine furniture. William Turner worked here for many years during the nineteenth century and a number of his paintings are on exhibition. The house is set in a spectacular 700 acre deer park landscaped by Capability Brown. The glories of Petworth Park are matched by the wonderful Nymans Garden to the east near Haywards Heath, stocked with collections of rare and beautiful plants, trees and shrubs from all over the world. Here is a delightful hidden sunken garden, a walled garden, laurel walk, even romantic ruins! But Sussex is wonderfully endowed with spectacular gardens, in particular Sheffield Park Garden, a hundred acres of landscaped garden with five lakes linked by picturesque waterfalls and cascades. Another Capability Brown masterpiece, and superb whatever the season visited.

Bodiam, in the Rother Valley is an attractive village with a romantic moated castle built in 1385. The castle is extremely popular with children, having a wealth of spiral staircases and battlemented turrets with glorious views from the battlements. To the west of Bodiam is Bateman's, the home of Rudyard Kipling from 1902-36, who loved this county. The house is well worth a visit, the rooms

Great Dixter House & Gardens, Northiam, Rye (SEETB)

and his study are just as they were during the great man's lifetime.

The pride and joy of Sussex however must be its coast, with glorious Brighton at the very centre. The largest town in the county, Brighton was in fact mentioned in the Domesday Book, but it was in 1782 that the Prince of Wales, later to become King George IV arrived, that the town really prospered. The fashionable and famous flocked to Brighton in the wake of the Prince, who built his flamboyant 'Marine Pavilion' here. By 1841 the railway had reached the town and the 'Brighton Belle' brought London to the seaside. Today Brighton offers a delightful warren of narrow pedestrianised streets known as the Lanes, fine shops, restaurants, theatres, the Brighton

Festival in May and of course in November the renowned London to Brighton Veteran Car Run. To the east is Brighton's sister resort Eastbourne, developed extensively in 1851 by the Duke of Devonshire to rival Brighton. Here the Eastbourne Sovereign Centre, a massive indoor water leisure complex is a popular attraction, as is the Butterfly Centre on Royal Parade. Hastings, of course holds a special place in the hearts of all Englishmen and was a thriving port even before William the Conqueror arrived. To the north is the attractive town of Battle which grew up around Battle Abbey. The Abbey's high altar marks the spot where Harold is said to have fallen, pierced in the eye with a Frenchman's arrow. There is a fascinating battle-field trail and audiovisual display detailing the whole story of the battle.

PLACES TO VISIT

This is a small selection of interesting places to visit. Many more are listed in our annual guide to Museums, Galleries, Historic Houses & Sites (see page 448)

Arundel Castle
Arundel
Home of the Dukes of Norfolk, the great castle dates from the Norman conquest, containing a very fine collection of furniture and paintings.

Bluebell Railway
Sheffield Park, Uckfield
Bluebell Railway runs standard gauge steam trains through 9 miles of Sussex countryside and has a large collection of railwayana.

Chichester Cathedral
Chichester
The Cathedral was consecrated in 1108 and later much rebuilt and

restored. It has the only cathedral spire in England visible from the sea.

Great Dixter House & Gardens
Northiam, Rye
A fifteenth century manor house owned by gardening writer Christopher Lloyd. Lutyens restored both the house and gardens in 1910.

Royal Pavilion
Brighton
Set in restored Regency Gardens, the Royal Pavilion, formerly the seaside residence of King George IV, is an exotically beautiful building with magnificent decorations and furnishings.

Sussex

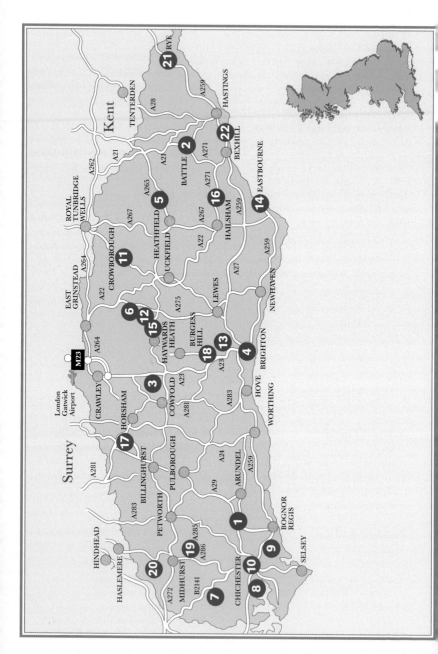

The Blue Map References should be used to locate B & B properties on the pages that follow

Woodacre Arundel Road, Fontwell, Arundel, W Sussex BN18 0QP

Vicki Richards   Tel: 01243 814301   Fax: 01243 814344
Email: wacrebb@aol.com   Web: www.woodacre.co.uk

Map Ref: 1
A27
see Photo on page 271

Woodacre offers hospitality in a traditional family house with guest accommodation in a separate cottage, joined to the main house. The rooms are well presented and spacious, each one has a television and tea/coffee making facilities. Our guests are welcome to use the garden. We have plenty of parking space. We are easy to find from the A27 and conveniently located for Chichester, Arundel, Goodwood and Bognor Regis.

B & B from £22.50pp, C-Cards MC VS, Rooms 2 twin, 1 en-suite double, 1 family, Restricted smoking, Children & dogs welcome, Open all year

Fox Hole Farm Kane Hythe Road, Battle, E Sussex TN33 9QU

Paul & Pauline Collins
Tel: 01424 772053   Fax: 01424 773771

Map Ref: 2
B2096

Fox Hole Farm is a beautiful and secluded 18th century woodcutter's cottage nestling in over 40 acres of its own rolling lush East Sussex land. The farmhouse retains many of its original features and it is heavily beamed with a large inglenook fireplace featuring a woodburning stove. It has been carefully converted to offer three traditionally furnished and well appointed double rooms, all with en-suite bathrooms, television and tea making facilities. There is a large country garden containing many species of flowers, shrubs, trees and a natural pond.

B & B from £24.50pp, Rooms 3 double en-suite, No smoking, Children over 10, Dogs by arrangement, Closed Xmas & New Year

Timbers Edge Longhouse Lane, off Spronketts Lane, Warninglid, Bolney,

E Sussex RH17 5TE   Geoffrey & Sally Earlam   Tel: 01444 461456
Fax: 01444 461813   Email: Gearlam@aol.com

Map Ref: 3
A272,A23

This beautiful Sussex country house is set in over two acres of formal gardens, surrounded by woodlands. Breakfast is served in the spacious conservatory overlooking the pool. Timbers Edge is located within easy reach of Gatwick (15 mins), Brighton (20 mins) and Ardingly the South of England Showground (20 mins). The beautiful gardens of Nymans and Leonardslee (10 mins), Hickstead Show Jumping Ground (10 mins). All the bedrooms have television and beverage making facilities.

B & B from £25pp, Rooms 2 twin, No smoking, No dogs, Open all year

Adelaide Hotel 51 Regency Square, Brighton, E Sussex BN1 2FF

Paula Hamblin   Tel: 01273 205286   Fax: 01273 220904
Email: adelaide@pavilion.co.uk

Map Ref: 4
A259

A warm welcome, friendly service, comfort and delicious food are the hallmarks of this elegant Grade II listed Regency Town House Hotel, modernised but retaining the charm of yester year. Centrally situated in Brighton's Premier sea-front square with NCP underground car park. There are 12 peaceful en-suite bedrooms, individually designed and furnished with co-ordinating decor, and equipped with telephone and colour television . A beautiful four poster bedroom is available. Easy access to A23, 30 minutes to Gatwick. Discounts available when staying two nights or more.

B & B £35-£46pp, C-Cards MC VS AE, Rooms 3 single, 1 twin, 7 double, 1 family, all en-suite, Restricted smoking, Children over 12, No dogs, Closed Xmas day

Trouville Hotel 11 New Steine, Brighton, E Sussex BN2 1PB
John & Daphne Hansell
Tel: 01273 697384

Map Ref: 4
A23/A259

The Trouville is a Grade II listed regency townhouse tastefully restored to a high standard, and situated in a delightful seafront square. The Marina Pavilion Lanes Conference Centre and many restaurants are all within walking distance. Accommodation is in eight attractive rooms each with colour television and tea/coffee making facilities. En-suite and four poster rooms are available. There are many places of interest in this area including National Trust Properties and gardens, beautiful Downland villages and countryside and historic towns and castle.

B & B from £29pp, C-Cards MC VS AE, Rooms 2 single, 1 twin, 3 double, 2 family, most en-suite, Restricted smoking, Children welcome, No dogs, Closed Xmas & Jan

Ashlands Cottage Burwash, E Sussex TN19 7HS
Nesta Harmer
Tel: 01435 882207

Map Ref: 5
A265

This pretty period cottage may be found in quiet Wealden farmland within designated area of outstanding natural beauty. The views are glorious, and there are beautiful gardens and picnic spots. Kipling's 'Batemans' is only 5 minutes walk across the fields and many more places of interest nearby. Ashlands Cottage is an ideal location for those who enjoy walking and touring. The bedrooms are comfortable and welcoming and there is a sitting room where guests may relax.

B & B from £17pp, Rooms 2 twin, Restricted smoking, Children over 12, Dogs by arrangement, Open all year

Judins Heathfield Road, Burwash, E Sussex TN19 7LA
Sandra Jolly Tel: 01435 882455 Fax: 01435 883775
Email: sandra.jolly@virgin.net

Map Ref: 5
A265

Judins is a delightful 300 year old country house with outstanding views over Rother Valley and 1066 countryside. My guests can relax in beautiful gardens, linger under the Weeping Willow, or swim in the heated pool. Walk through open fields to Batemans, former home of Rudyard Kipling. At home enjoy the spacious conservatory with sunken fish pond and waterfall. Memorable breakfasts are served in the beamed dining room. Each bedroom has its own charm with Sky television, radio and hostess tray. Rain or shine you'll always enjoy the special atmosphere at Judins.

B & B from £30pp, C-Cards MC VS, Rooms 3 double en-suite, Restricted smoking, Children welcome, No dogs, Open all year

Holly House Beaconsfield Road, Chelwood Gate, E Sussex RH17 7LF
Deidre & Keith Birchell Tel: 01825 740484 Fax: 01825 740172
Email: db@hollyhousebnb.demon.co.uk

Map Ref: 6
A275

On the edge of Ashdown Forest in a rural village setting, stands Holly House a 130 year old forest farmhouse. Now converted to form a comfortable family home which has seen Chelwood Gate change from a hamlet to a pleasant village with a Church, two pubs and a well stocked village shop. We offer guests here a warm welcome with an inviting lounge, comfortable beds and memorable breakfasts served in the conservatory overlooking the interesting garden. Guests may use the heated swimming pool in summer.

B & B from £25pp, Dinner from £14, Rooms 1 single, 2 twin, 2 double, some en-suite, Children & dogs welcome, Open all year

Woodacre, Fontwell, near Arundel

Abelands Barn, Chichester   Barn Main House (above)   The Cow Shed (below)

The Flint House, East Lavant, near Chichester

The Providence Compton, Chichester, W Sussex PO18 9HD   Map Ref: 7
Juliet & John Diamond Tel: 02392 631880
Email: julietjohn@diamond63.freeserve.co.uk

Quaint Victorian Grade II listed cottage with pretty garden and orchard. The two rooms with bathroom in between are only let to same party. Lone visitors are welcome. Sitting room with television, tea and coffee available. Compton lies between Petersfield and Chichester in the Downs and close to the South Downs Way, Uppark and many other places of interest. Lovely walking and riding country. Field available for visiting horses at £10 per horse per day. Pub for meals and shop in village. On bus route.

B & B £20-£25pp, Rooms 1 double, 1 twin, shared bathroom, No smoking, Children welcome, No dogs, Closed Xmas & New Year

The Flint House Pook Lane, East Lavant, Chichester, W Sussex PO18 0AS   Map Ref: 8
Tim & Vivien Read Tel: 01243 773482   A286
Email: theflinthouse@ukonline.co.uk   *see Photo on page 273*

This 19th century house, which was built by Napoleonic prisoners of war, may be found in a peaceful, rural location on the edge of the South Downs, between Lavant and Goodwood, famous for its wonderful racecourse. For those who prefer to avoid stairs, the two large bedrooms are on the ground floor. The area is particularly favoured for walking, and there are excellent pubs closeby. A twenty minute drive takes one to the sea, and the well known historic town of Chichester is within easy reach.

B & B £27.50-£35pp, Rooms 1 king size double & 1 twin, both en-suite, No smoking, Children welcome, No dogs, Closed Xmas

Abelands Barn Merston, Chichester, W Sussex PO20 6DY   Map Ref: 9
Mike & Gaile Richardson   A259
Tel: 01243 533826 Fax: 01243 555533   *see Photo on page 272*

A traditional 1850 Sussex Barn converted in to a beautiful, interesting family home. It provides spacious and flexible accommodation, with all facilities. A period, flint outbuilding contains large, en-suite bedroom, and the imposing main Barn offers a ground floor 'family' suite of two bedrooms, bathroom and 'snug'. Attractive gardens overlook the lovely South Downs, and a courtyard offers secure, overnight, parking. Abelands Barn is situated two miles from Chichester, with many local attractions including Goodwood, Arundel, the coast and prestigious Festival Theatre.

B & B £25-£35pp, C-Cards MC VS AE, Rooms 1 twin, 2 double, 1 family, en-suite, Children welcome, No dogs, Closed Xmas & New Year

Chichester Lodge Oakwood, Chichester, W Sussex PO18 9AL   Map Ref: 10
Mr & Mrs Dridge   A27, B2178
Tel: 01243 786560

Chichester Lodge is a charming 1840 Gothic Lodge with wonderful interior design and antique furnishings. Lots of flag stone floors, polished wood, beautiful Gothic windows, every attention to detail. Wood burning stove in hall way. There are two acres of very pretty garden with hedges and honeysuckle and hidden corners. The en-suite bedrooms are comfortable with nice decorations and furnishings and all rooms have television. There is also a garden room with awood burning stove for winter evenings. Nearby activities include fishing, golf, theatre and Goodwood.

B & B from £25pp, Rooms 2 double, all en-suite, No smoking, No children or dogs, Open all year

England *Sussex*

Hatpins Bosham Lane, Old Bosham, Chichester, W Sussex PO18 8HG
Mary Waller Tel / Fax: 01243 572644 Mobile: 07778 452156
Email: mary@hatpins.co.uk Web: www.hatpins.co.uk

Map Ref: 8
A259
see Photo on page 277

Mary Waller, a former designer of hats and wedding dresses, has combined her talents with a flair for decorating to transform her home into delightful bed and breakfast accommodation. Enhancing the decor is the warmth of Mary's hospitality. Bosham is an appealing town and Old Bosham brims with charm and it is fun to wander to the waterfront and explore the lanes. Nearby, is Portsmouth and the city of Chichester with its lovely harbour. A few miles inland is Downland Museum a collection of old cottages and buildings. Honeymoon couples welcome.

B & B £25-£45pp, Rooms 5 en-suite/private bathrooms, No smoking, Children over 10, No dogs, Open all year

White Barn Crede Lane, Old Bosham, Chichester, W Sussex PO18 8NX
Christine Reeves & Terry Strudwick Tel / Fax: 01243 573113
Email: whitebarn@compuserve.com

Map Ref: 8
A259

An architecturally unique single storey house, peacefully situated in the beautiful Saxon harbour village of Bosham. Our three en-suite rooms are privately located within the property and furnished to give home from home comforts. An ideal base for visiting Portsmouth and its historic ships, Chichester and the famous Festival Theatre, Goodwood, the South Downs, beaches and marinas. We look forward to welcoming you to our home.

B & B from £28pp, C-Cards MC VS, Dinner from £20, Rooms 2 double, 1 twin, all en-suite, No smoking, Children over 12, No dogs, Open all year

Hope Court Rannoch Road, Crowborough, E Sussex TN6 1RA
Mrs N L Backhouse Tel: 01892 654017 Mobile: 07710 289138
Web: www.visitbritain.com/search

Map Ref: 11
A26

Hope Court is a comfortable country house situated in an area of outstanding beauty, facing south over Ashdown Forest. It is a good touring location for National Trust gardens, castles and the south coast. The accommodation offers one double bedroom with private bathroom, one twin bedroom with en-suite shower with clock radios, tea/coffee making facilities. There is private parking in drive. Guests have their own lounge with Sky television and video. There is a patio door to the garden, and log fires on chilly days. Good restaurants and inns are close by.

B & B from £25pp, Rooms 1 double private bathroom, 1 twin en-suite, No smoking, Children over 10, No dogs, Closed Xmas & New Year

Sliders Farm Furners Green, Danehill, E Sussex TN22 3RT
David & Jean Salmon Tel / Fax: 01825 790258
Email: jean&davidsalmon@sliders.co.uk

Map Ref: 12
A275

Sliders Farm is quietly situated, surrounded by fields and woodland within walking distance of Sheffield Park Gardens. The Bluebell Railway and Ashdown Forest. Gatwick, Ardingly Showground, Glyndebourne and Brighton are easily accessible. London 45 minutes by train. The 30 acres of grounds and gardens contain a swimming pool, tennis court and fishing lakes. All the bedrooms have television and tea/coffee making facilities. The guests' lounge and oak panelled dining room both have large inglenook fireplaces. A 400 year old barn contains two self-catering units. Plenty of parking.

B & B from £27.50pp, Rooms 1 twin, 2 double, 1 family, all en-suite, Restricted smoking, Children welcome, No dogs, Closed Xmas & Boxing Day

Cleavers Lyng Country Hotel, Herstmonceux, near Hailsham

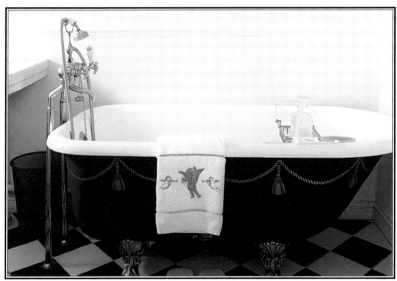

Hatpins, Old Bosham,
near Chichester

South Cottage The Drove, Ditchling, E Sussex BN6 8TR
Sonia Stock   Tel: 01273 846636   Mobile: 07788 486315
Email: sonia.stock@amserve.net

Map Ref: 13
M23, M27

This is a traditional country cottage with a pretty garden down a private lane. It is surrounded by fields, yet is only minutes from the historic village of Ditchling and its three pubs. The cottage is warm and comfortable with tea making facilities and television in each room, it has far-reaching views across fields to Ditchling Beacon and the South Downs. It is convenient for Gatwick, Newhaven, Brighton and Glyndebourne and is only a mile from the South Downs Way for walkers and cyclists.

B & B from £25pp, Rooms 1 single, 1 twin with wash basin, 1 double, private bathroom, No smoking, Children & dogs welcome, Closed Xmas & New Year

Brayscroft Hotel 13 South Cliff Avenue, Eastbourne, E Sussex BN20 7AH
Gerry Crawshaw   Tel: 01323 647005   Fax: 01323 720705   Mobile: 07960 187531
Email: brayscroft@hotmail.com   Web: www.brayscrofthotel.co.uk

Map Ref: 14
A259

Brayscroft is a small, award-winning hotel personally managed with style and flair by travel writer and author Gerry Crawshaw. It is superbly situated in an attractive tree-lined avenue of Edwardian houses, a minute from the seafront and a few minutes walk from the Bandstand, Western Lawns, Theatres, and the Devonshire Park, in one of Eastbourne's most fashionable areas. Elegantly appointed guest rooms have superb modern en-suite facilities, televisions, radio alarms and well-stocked hospitality trays. For outdoor lovers, the walks around Beachy Head and the South Downs Way are close by.

B & B from £27pp, C-Cards MC VS, Dinner from £12, Rooms 1 single, 2 double, 2 twin, all en-suite, No smoking, Children over 14, Dogs in bedrooms only, Open all year

The Pilstyes 106-108 High Street, Lindfield, Haywards Heath, W Sussex RH16 2HS
Roy & Carol Pontifex   Tel: 01444 484101   Fax: 01444 484100
Email: bnbuk@pavilion.co.uk

Map Ref: 15
B2028

Quintessential English 16th Century cottage everyone dreams about in an enviable position close to all Lindfield's amenities. Let as B&B (Roy and Carol live in the adjoining cottage) or self catering basis, whichever you prefer. Romantic four poster bedroom suitable for honeymooners or a special occasion. Gatwick Airport 15 miles away. London 45 minutes by train. Picturesque Lindfield which is well known for its variety of period houses has brick pavements and grass verges interspersed with lime trees. Pubs, tearooms, shops, village pond with ducks are all nearby.

B & B from £37.50pp, C-Cards MC VS AE, Rooms 1 twin, 1 double, No smoking, Children over 8, No dogs, Open all year

Cleavers Lyng Country Hotel Church Road, Herstmonceux,
E Sussex BN27 1QJ   Tel: 01323 833131   Fax: 01323 833617
Email: scil@supanet.com   Web: www.cleaverslyng.co.uk

Map Ref: 16
A271
see Photo on page 276

Photogenic Cleavers Lyng is a small family run hotel adjacent to the west gate of Herstmonceux Castle dating from 1577 with oak beams and inglenook fireplace. There are wonderful panoramic views. Guests can enjoy good home cooking in a traditional English style and a full English breakfast. The hotel is fully licensed with a lounge bar serving fine wines and draught beers. There is a television lounge. All the bedrooms are fully en-suite, centrally heated and have tea/coffee making facilities, colour televisions and direct dial telephones with modem points. Special attraction - badger watch!

B & B from £30pp, C-Cards MC VS, Dinner from £14.95, Rooms 4 double, 3 twin, Non smoking restaurant, Children & dogs welcome, Closed Xmas & New Year

Amberfold, Heyshott, near Midhurst

Wartling Place Wartling, Herstmonceux, E Sussex BN27 1RY
Barry & Rowena Gittoes Tel: 01323 832590 Fax: 01323 831558
Email: accom@wartlingplace.prestel.co.uk Web: www.countryhouseaccommodation.co.uk

Map Ref: 16
A259, A27

Wartling Place is a superb Georgian Grade II listed country house set within three acres of secluded gardens, surrounded by magnificent shrubs and trees. The house has been splendidly restored and refurbished, and two of the luxuriously appointed bedrooms offer romantic kingsize four poster beds for those special occasions. Closeby are some of the finest restaurants and country pubs which East Sussex has to offer. There is a wealth of stately homes and National Trust gardens within easy reach, Sissinghurst, Great Dixter, Hever and Pashley Manor to name but a few.

B & B £35-£47.50pp, C-Cards MC VS AE, Dinner from £25, Rooms 2 double/king 4 posters, 1 king double/twin, all en-suite, No smoking, Children welcome, No dogs, Open all year

Glebe End Church Street, Warnham, Horsham, W Sussex RH12 3QW
Liz & Chris Cox Tel: 01403 261711 Fax: 01403 257572
Email: CoxesWarnham@aol.com

Map Ref: 17
A24

Glebe End is a fascinating medieval house with a secluded, sunny walled garden in Warnham village. Its original features include heavy flagstones, curving ships' timbers and an inglenook fireplace. Four: single, twin and king-sized en-suite rooms, charmingly furnished with antiques plus television and hot drinks trays. Liz Cox is an excellent cook; breakfasts are delicious with home made marmelade. Tennis, swimming, golf and health club nearby. 20 minutes to Gatwick. Children welcome. Animals by arrangement. Two excellent Inns within five minutes walk. Off street parking.

B & B from £25pp, Dinner available, Rooms 1 single, 1 double, 1 twin, 1 family, most en-suite, Restricted smoking, Children welcome, Dogs by arrangement, Open all year

Clayton Wickham Farmhouse Belmont Lane, Hurstpierpoint, W Sussex BN6 9EP
Mike & Susie Skinner Tel: 01273 845698 Fax: 01273 841970
Email: susie@cwfbandb.fsnet.co.uk

Map Ref: 18
A23

A warm welcome awaits you in this beautifully restored 16th century farmhouse with masses of beams and huge inglenook in the drawing room. Set in three acres of splendid gardens with tennis court and lovely views. Enviably quiet and secluded, yet conveniently situated for all transport facilities and places of interest. Rooms, including one four poster en-suite, are generously equipped. Thereis the offer of room service for early morning tea. The genial hosts serve truly delicious food with a wide breakfast choice. An excellent candlelit dinner, or simpler meal, available on prior request.

B & B from £35pp, Rooms 2 twin/double, 1 double four-poster en suite, 1 single, Restricted smoking, Children welcome, Dogs by arrangement, Open all year

Amberfold Heyshott, Midhurst, W Sussex GU29 0DA
Alex & Annabelle Costaras
Tel: 01730 812385 Fax: 01730 812842

Map Ref: 19
A286
see Photo on page 279

Amberfold, situated in the scenic hamlet of Heyshott, dates back to Tudor times. Miles of unspoiled woodland walks start on your doorstep. An ideal hideaway for nature lovers, yet only five minutes drive from historic Midhurst and local attractions of Goodwood, Chichester and coast. Accommodation comprises: two private self-contained annexe, with access all day. Double bedroom, shower room, toilet, central heating and television. In addition, electric kettle, cafetiere, toaster. A fridge, lavishly replenished daily with selection of food, is provided for self-service continental breakfast.

B & B from £27.50pp, Rooms 2 en-suite double, No smoking, No children or dogs, Open all year

Filsham Farm House, St Leonards on Sea

Redford Cottage Redford, Midhurst, W Sussex GU29 0QF
Caroline Angela
Tel / Fax: 01428 741242

Map Ref: 20
A272, A3, A286

You are certain of a warm welcome in an attractive country house dating back to the 16th century in an area of outstanding natural beauty. Comfortable rooms include a self-contained garden suite with its own beamed sitting room and en-suite facilities. Rates include full English breakfast and tea/coffee making facilities, television provided in bedrooms and drawing room. Convenient to Midhurst, Petworth, Goodwood, Chichester and South Downs. There are excellent walks and National Trust Properties within easy reach. An ideal retreat for a peaceful stay.

B & B from £35pp, Rooms 3 double/twin, all en-suite, No smoking,
Children welcome, No dogs in bedrooms, Closed Xmas & New Year

Little Orchard House West Street, Rye, E Sussex TN31 7ES
Sara Brinkhurst Tel / Fax: 01797 223831
Web: www.littleorchardhouse.com

Map Ref: 21
A259, A268

Little Orchard House is centrally situated in peaceful surroundings. Rebuilt in 1745, the house has been lovingly renovated over the years and retains it original fascinating character. Both bedrooms are en-suite with a four poster. There are personal antiques, paintings, books and bears throughout the house, with a peaceful book room and a sitting room with open fire. The generous breakfast provides as much as can be eaten at a time to suit you. Large walled garden available for guests' use. Off street parking available.

B & B £32-£45pp, C-Cards MC VS, Rooms 2 double, No smoking,
Children over 12, No dogs, Open all year

Filsham Farm House 111 Harley Shute Road, St Leonards on Sea, E Sussex TN38 8BY
Barbara Yorke Tel: 01424 433109 Fax: 01424 461061
filshamfarmhouse@talk21.com www.filshamfarmhouse.co.uk

Map Ref: 22, A21, A27
see Photo on page 281

Filsham Farm House is an historic 17th century listed Sussex farm house, with old beams and a large inglenook fireplace, where a log fire burns at breakfast time in the winter months. The house is within easy reach of the town centre, sea and the surrounding countryside. It is furnished with an interesting collection of antiques to provide a high standard of accommodation. All rooms have television sets and tea/coffee making facilities and there is ample parking space at the rear of the house.

B & B from £20pp, Rooms 1 twin, 2 double, 1 family, most en-suite,
Restricted smoking, Dogs welcome, Open all year

The Old Oast Underhill, Maresfield, Uckfield, E Sussex TN22 3AY
Mr & Mrs D A Wadsworth
Tel: 01825 768886

Map Ref: 23
A22

This beautiful oast house stands in three acres of secluded garden and woodland, in an area of outstanding natural beauty. The house has been carefully restored and now offers a very high level of hospitality. The bedrooms are luxurious, generously equipped, and one is in the roundel of the Oast. Guests are welcome to relax in the comfort of the sitting room, with its Inglenook fireplace. The heated swimming pool is available in summer.

B & B from £30pp, Rooms 1 double, 2 twin, Children & dogs welcome, Open all year

Warwick & West Midlands

The West Midlands region was once the centre of a vast and complicated canal system, but is now the hub of an equally complicated motorway network. This is one of the most important industrial and manufacturing regions and despite Charles Dickens' description of 'an industrialised realisation of hell', the so called Black Country, Birmingham and Coventry have much to offer the holiday visitor. The towns and cities of the West Midlands provide excellent shopping, theatre, galleries and exhibitions. Brindleyplace is an urban development by the old canal system and contains many shops, bars and restaurants. Birmingham is also the home of the renowned City of Birmingham Symphony Orchestra and the Birmingham Royal Ballet, formally the Sadler's Wells Company, with the City Museum and Art Gallery holding the world's finest collection of pre-Raphaelite paintings. Nearby is Cadbury World, the centre dedicated to the history and making of chocolate, guiding visitors through the discovery by the Aztecs to the origins of the Cadbury family in Bournville.

Nearby Coventry, despite all the appalling bomb damage of 1940, boasts some fine buildings including the medieval Guildhall of St Mary in Bayley Lane, and of course the wonderfully innovative Cathedral of St Michael by Sir Basil Spence, containing Graham Sutherland's enormous tapestry 'Christ in Majesty'. The cathedral was destroyed in 1940 and the ruins left as a reminder with the present cathedral built within the structure. Just five miles south west of Coventry stands the glorious massive sandstone ruin of Kenilworth Castle built by Geoffrey de Clinton, chamberlain to Henry I in 1125 and later owned by John of Gaunt.

Walsall, to the north of Birmingham and once the nineteenth century, 'town of a hundred trades' is fascinating, dominated by its parish church perched on a steep limestone hill. Its large open-air markets on Tuesdays and Saturdays attract crowds of shoppers. The birthplace of the humourist Jerome K Jerome whose house is now a museum is only one of the many attractions of a town with a fine country park, arboretum and impressive open spaces. Nearby is Wightwick Manor, a late nineteenth century house much influenced by William Morris, set in a delightful Victorian/Edwardian garden of topiary and yew hedges.

Warwickshire is the quintessential England, one of the country's smallest counties, it is a region rich in history and blessed with some of the country's loveliest scenery. Stratford upon Avon is of course a magnet to the thousands of pilgrims who flock to see the birth and death place of William

Warwick Castle (HETB)

Shakespeare. The town with its many half-timbered buildings is a shrine to The Bard with the Shakespeare Birthplace Trust maintaining five buildings associated with Shakespeare, including Hall's Croft, the home of Shakespeare's daughter Susanna and her husband. Just out of town at Shottery is Anne Hathaway's Cottage, the home of Shakespeare's wife before her marriage and at Wilmcote is Mary Arden's House, once the childhood home of Shakespeare's mother and now a farm and countryside museum. Gloriously sited on the bank of the River Avon is the Shakespeare Memorial Theatre, home of the distinguished Royal Shakespeare Company. Close to Stratford upon Avon is Charlecote Park, the home of the Lucy family since 1247. The present house was built in 1550 and visited by Queen Elizabeth I. It is also claimed that the young Shakespeare poached deer here.

For sheer spectacle little can match wondrous Warwick Castle, one of Britain's most visited stately homes. For centuries it was the grand home of the Earls of Warwick, now brought to life with waxworks depicting the history of the family that lived there. In the summer there are many events, including jousting and other medieval entertainment. The centre of the city of Warwick was rebuilt following a disastrous fire in 1694 and possesses some fine buildings particularly around High Street and Northgate Street. Not to be missed is Leycester's Hospital and the stunning view of the castle from Castle Bridge, where the spectacular castle walls are reflected in the still waters of the Avon. Royal Leamington Spa which is adjacent to Warwick was designated a Royal Spa by Queen Victoria following a visit in 1838. It is a beautiful regency town with the Royal Pump Rooms housing a fascinating museum and art gallery.

PLACES TO VISIT

This is a small selection of interesting places to visit. Many more are listed in our annual guide to Museums, Galleries, Historic Houses & Sites (see page 448)

Birmingham Museum & Art Gallery
Birmingham
Major collections of the fine and decorative arts, archaeology and ethnography, natural history and social history in the Midlands.

Heritage Motor Centre
Gaydon, Warwick
The history of the British motor industry is portrayed from the 1880's to date including rallying, racing and record breaking vehicles.

Shakespeare's Birthplace
Stratford-upon-Avon
Where Shakespeare was born in 1564, a fascinating insight into what life was like when Shakespeare was a child. The Shakespeare exhibition provides an introduction to his life and background.

Upton House
Banbury
An important collection of paintings and porcelain and an outstanding garden, of interest throughout the season.

Warwick Castle
Warwick
Staterooms, dungeons, torture chambers, armoury are to be viewed. Warwick Castle holds over a thousand years of secrets.

Warwick & West Midlands

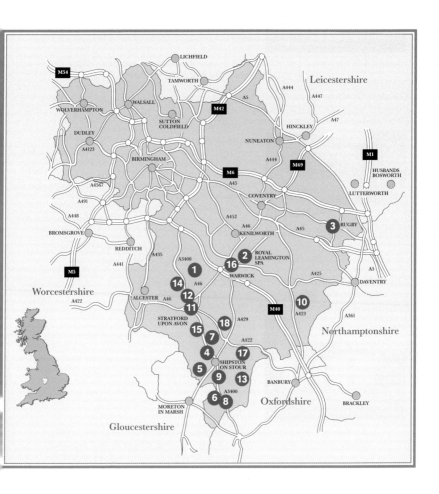

The Blue Map References should be used to locate B & B properties on the pages that follow

Woodside Langley Road, Claverdon CV35 8PJ

Doreen Bromilow Tel: 01926 842446 Fax: 01926 843697
Email: ABO21@dial.Pipex.com

Map Ref: 1
A4189

Woodside is set in 22 acres of conservation woodland and garden. All bedrooms are spacious, furnished in a cottage style with antiques and period furniture. They have tea and coffee making facilities, television and radio. Lovely outlook over woodland and garden. Downstairs bedrooms are ideal for disabled visitors. Full central heating, large log fire with television and video in comfortable lounge makes for a relaxed evening after a busy day. A home cooked dinner is served to order. Perhaps visit one of the interesting eating places locally. Doreen and her dogs will give you a warm welcome.

B & B £25-£28pp, Dinner from £15, Rooms 2 single/double/family en-suite, 1 double pb, 2 twin, Restricted smoking, Children welcome, Dogs by arrangement, Closed Xmas

Garden Cottage 52 Kenilworth Road, Leamington Spa CV32 6JW

Christine Jenkin Tel / Fax: 01926 338477
Email: christine@gardencottage.fsworld.co.uk

Map Ref: 2
A452

A warm welcome awaits you in this charming and quiet converted coach house which is situated on the A452, just five minutes from the town centre. Garden Cottage is close to Stratford-upon-Avon, Kenilworth, Warwick, the Royal Agricultural Centre and the Birmingham NEC and Airport. The accommodation comprises one spacious twin bedded room with an adjoining conservatory and private bathroom, and one double with large a en-suite shower room. Television and coffee/tea making facilities are provided. Excellent home cooked breakfasts. Off road parking. Garden.

B & B from £22pp, Rooms 1 twin, 1 double, Restricted smoking, Children welcome, Dogs by arrangement, Open all year

Lawford Hill Farm Lawford Heath Lane, Rugby CV23 9HG

Don & Susan Moses Tel: 01788 542001 Fax: 01788 537880
Email: lawford.hill@talk21.com Web: www.lawfordhill.co.uk

Map Ref: 3
A428

We invite you to relax and enjoy our Georgian home set in a picturesque garden. Lawford Hill has much character, it is spacious for those seeking solitude, yet sufficiently small and informal for those who wish to enjoy the company of their fellow guests. Our bedrooms, three in the main house and three in our converted stables, are charmingly decorated and comfortably furnished. Some en-suite, colour television and all with coffee/tea making facilities. Perfectly placed for touring Stratford, Warwick and the lovely Cotswolds.

B & B from £21.50pp, C-Cards MC VS, Rooms 1 single, 1 twin, 3 double, 1 family, some en-suite, No smoking, Children & dogs welcome, Closed Xmas & New Year

Blackwell Grange Blackwell, Shipston-on-Stour CV36 4PF

Liz Vernon Miller Tel: 01608 682357 Fax: 01608 682856
Email: staying@blackwellgrange.co.uk Web: www.blackwellgrange.co.uk

Map Ref: 4
A3400/A429

This Grade II listed farmhouse, part of which dates from 1603, is situated on the edge of a peaceful village with an attractive garden and views of the Ilmigton Hills. The spacious bedrooms are en-suite and have tea and coffee making facilities, and one ground floor bedroom is suitable for guests with disabilities. A stone flagged dining room with inglenook fireplace and guests drawing room with a log fire in winter and deep sofas, make this a very relaxing place to stay.

B & B £30-£40pp, C-Cards MC VS AE, Dinner from £15, Rooms 1 single, 1 twin, 2 double, all en-suite, Restricted smoking, Children over 12, No dogs, Closed Xmas day

Lower Farm Darlingscott, Shipston-on-Stour CV36 4PN

Jackie Smith　Tel / Fax: 01608 682750
Email: lowerfarmbb@beeb.net　Web: www.cotswoldbandb.co.uk

Map Ref: 5
A429

Darlingscott is a pretty, unspoilt hamlet close to the famous Fosseway. Here may be found Lower Farm which is an historic 18th century farmhouse where guests are offered warm hospitality. A fine collection of prints and interesting pictures are displayed throughout the house. Visitors are welcome to enjoy the garden and to relax on the patio. Lower Farm is a perfect location from which to visit the Cotswold town of Chipping Campden. The magnificent gardens of Hidcote and Kiftsgate, also the famous towns of Stratford-upon-Avon and Warwick are within easy reach.

B & B £22.50-£25pp, Rooms 2 double, 1 twin, all en-suite,
No smoking, Children over 8, No dogs, Closed Xmas

Lower Farm Barn Great Wolford, Shipston-on-Stour CV36 5NQ

Rebecca & Fred Mawle　Tel: 01608 674435　Mobile: 07932 043111
Email: rebecca@greatwolford.freeserve.co.uk

Map Ref: 6
A44, A3400

This lovely 100 year old converted barn stands in the small, peaceful Warwickshire village of Great Wolford. The property retains much of its original form including exposed beams and ancient stonework. It is now modernised and very comfortable. The beautifully furnished bedrooms have tea and coffee making facilities. A warm welcoming, sitting room with television, is for guests' use. Great Wolford has a lovely old pub, only five minutes walk from Lower Farm Barn, where traditional home made food is served. Convenient for Warwick and Stratford-upon-Avon.

B & B from £21pp, Rooms 2 double, 1 en-suite (or family room), Restricted smoking,
Children welcome, No dogs, Open all year

The Old Manor House Halford, Shipston-on-Stour CV36 5BT

Jane & William Pusey　Tel: 01789 740264　Fax: 01789 740609
Email: wpusey@st-philips.co.uk

Map Ref: 7
A429/A3400

The Old Manor House is situated eight miles south of Stratford-upon-Avon, and on the edge of the Cotswolds. Dating from the 18th century, the house stands in three acres of landscaped gardens, which lead gently to the River Stour. Fishing is available, also tennis. A self contained wing has its own drawing room and dining room, whilst the main house displays ancient beams and oak furniture. A cordon bleu dinner may be enjoyed by arrangement. There is an excellent choice of restaurants locally and there are many good Cotswold pubs.

B & B from £30pp, Dinner available, Rooms 1 double, 1 twin, Restricted smoking,
Children welcome, Dogs by arrangement, Closed Xmas

Ashby House Long Compton, Shipston-on-Stour CV36 5LB

Paul & Charlotte Field　Tel / Fax: 01608 684286
Email: e.p.field@fieldashby.demon.co.uk

Map Ref: 8
A3400

Offering a quiet, comfortable and friendly stay, Ashby House is ideally located for visiting Shakespeare's Stratford, Oxford, Blenheim Palace, Warwick Castle and all the Cotswold villages. The bedrooms and pretty bathrooms are spacious and well equipped for all your needs. Breakfast with homemade preserves, and delicious dinners are served in the 19th century dining room. There is a good village pub within easy walking distance and the well-known Whichford Pottery is a few miles away. Good safe parking.

B & B £19-£23pp, Dinner from £12, Rooms 1 twin, 1 double, 1 family, all private bathrooms,
No smoking, Children welcome, No dogs, Closed Xmas

Glebe Farm Home, Loxley, Stratford-upon-Avon

Wolford Fields Shipston-on-Stour CV36 5LT

Map Ref: 9
A44, A3400

Richard Mawle Tel: 01608 661301 Mobile: 07958 649306
Email: richard.wolfordfield@bush.intent.net

Wolford Fields is a large Cotswold farmhouse with gardens, which was built by Lord Campendown in 1857 and has been farmed by the Mawle family since 1901. The three comfortable bedrooms, with colour televisions and tea making facilities, share two warmly decorated bathrooms which are fitted with power showers. Guests may relax in the pleasant television lounge where tea, coffee and chocolate making facilities are available. Also, guests may stroll in the large garden. Space is available for car parking. Wolford Fields is conveniently situated for Stratford-upon-Avon and the Cotswolds, 4km south of Shipston.

B & B from £17.50pp, Rooms 2 double, 1 twin, No smoking, Open all year

Crandon House Avon Dassett, Southam CV47 2AA

Map Ref: 10
B4100,A423,M40 J12

Deborah Lea Tel: 01295 770652 Fax: 01295 770632
Email: crandonhouse@talk21.com Web: www.crandonhouse.co.uk

Beautiful country home in peaceful location, offering luxury accommodation. Set in 20 acres with lovely views over unspoilt countryside. The attractive bedrooms all have private or en-suite facilities and are generously equipped. Guests' have their own dining room and two comfortable sitting rooms one with colour television and woodburning stove. Excellent breakfast menu with an interesting variety to include traditional farmhouse fare. Good pubs and restaurants nearby. Situated in South Warwickshire within easy reach of Stratford, Warwick, Heritage Motor Centre and National Herb Centre.

B & B £20-£26pp, C-Cards MC VS, Rooms 3 double, 2 en-suite, 2 twin en-suite,
Restricted smoking, Children over 8, No dogs, Closed Xmas

The White House Burton Dassett, Southam CV47 2AB

Map Ref: 10
B4100

Lisa Foxwell Tel / Fax: 01295 770143 Mobile: 07767 458314
Email: lisa@whitehouse10.freeserve.co.uk

A large country house situated at the top of the Burton Dassett Hills, a well known land mark, central to Banbury, Leamington Spa, Stratford-upon-Avon, the NEC and the Cotswolds. The White House was originally built in 1938 as a farm cottage and is set in a rural position enjoying magnificent views over the Warwickshire and Oxfordshire countryside. Homely, friendly and welcoming. Non-smoking en-suite rooms with colour television, tea and coffee making facilities. Brochure available on request.

B & B from £22.50pp, Rooms 2 double, 1 twin, all en-suite, No smoking,
Children welcome, No dogs, Open all year

Wormleighton Hall Wormleighton, Southam CV47 2XQ

Map Ref: 10
A423

Mrs Nicola Burton Tel / Fax: 01295 770234 Mobile: 07778 991527
Email: wormleightonhall@farming.co.uk

Located in the historic conservation village of Wormleighton, this stone farmhouse may be found at the end of a tree lined drive set in its own extensive and secluded grounds with panoramic views across the rolling countryside. All bedrooms are spacious and furnished to a high standard, televisions and hostess trays included. Guests can enjoy the sun lounge, swimming pool, tranquil gardens and traditional home cooking including dinner by arrangement. The house is centrally located for easy access to Stratford, Warwick, Oxford, NEC, NAC and M40 (10 minutes.) Stabling is available.

B & B £25-£35pp, Dinner from £15, Rooms 1 double en-suite, 1 double/twin, 1 single,
both private, Smoking in sunroom only, Children over 8, Dogs by arrangement, Open all year

Penshurst Guest House 34 Evesham Place, Stratford-upon-Avon CV37 6HT

Karen Cauvin Tel: 01789 205259 Fax: 01789 295322   Map Ref: 11
Email: penhurst@cwcom.net Web: www.penhurst.net   A439

You'll get an exceptionally warm welcome from Karen and Yannick at this prettily refurbished, totally non-smoking, Victorian townhouse, situated just five minutes walk from the town centre. The bedrooms have been individually decorated and are well equipped with many little extras apart from the usual television and beverages. Perhaps you'd like a lie-in while on holiday? No problem! Delicious English or Continental breakfasts are served from 7.00am right up until 10.30am. Home-cooked evening meals by arrangement. Facilities for disabled. Brochure available.

B & B from £16pp, Rooms 1 single, 2 twin, 2 double, 2 family, some en-suite, No smoking, Open all year

Burton Farm Bishopston, Stratford-upon-Avon CV37 0RW   Map Ref: 12

Eileen & Tony Crook Tel: 01789 293338 Fax: 01789 262877   A46
Email: tony.crook@ukonline.co.uk Web: www.stratford-upon-avon/burtonfarm.htm

Burton Farm is a 140 acre working farm, approximately 2 miles from Stratford. The farmhouse and barns date from Tudor time, and are steeped in the character for which the area is world famous. The accommodation, all of which has en-suite facilities, enjoys an environment of colourful gardens and pools which support wildlife and a collection of unusual birds and plants. The friendly atmosphere and quiet retreat will ensure a pleasant stay. Antique furniture enhances this charming home.

B & B from £25pp, Rooms 2 double, 2 twin, 3 with 4 poster, 1 family, all en-suite, No smoking, Children welcome, No dogs, Closed Xmas

Glebe Farm House Loxley, Stratford-upon-Avon CV35 9JW   Map Ref: 13

Kate McGovern Tel: 01789 842501 Fax: 01789 841194   A429, A422
Email: scorpiolimited@msn.com Web: www.glebefarmhouse.com   *see Photo on page 288*

Glebe Farm is an 18th century, fine, large country house set in 30 acres of wonderful Warwickshire countryside. It is ideally placed being only two miles from Stratford-upon-Avon, and ten minutes from the famous Warwick Castle. All the generously appointed rooms have four poster beds, en-suite bathrooms with lovely garden and countryside views. There is a stone inglenook and a comfortable lounge where guests may enjoy a drink before dinner, which is taken in the candlelit conservatory. This is a fully organic farm, and home to some Hebridean sheep.

B & B from £47.50pp, C-Cards MC VS, Dinner from £22.50, Rooms 4 double en-suite, No smoking, Children over 12, No dogs, Open all year

Holly Tree Cottage Pathlow, Stratford-upon-Avon CV37 0ES   Map Ref: 14

John & Julia Downie Tel / Fax: 01789 204461   A3400
Email: john@hollytree-cottage.co.uk Web: www.hollytree-cottage.co.uk

Period cottage dating back to 17th century, with beams, antiques, tasteful furnishings and friendly atmosphere. Large picturesque gardens with extensive views over open countryside. Situated three miles north of Stratford towards Henley-in-Arden on A3400, convenient for overnight stops or longer stays, ideal for threatre visits. Excellent base for touring Shakespeare country, Heart of England, Cotswolds, Warwick Castle and Blenheim Palace. Well situated for National Exhibition Centre. Television and tea and coffee in all rooms. Full English, continental or vegetarian breakfasts. Pubs and restaurants nearby.

B & B from £25pp, Rooms 1 twin, 1 double, 1 family, all en-suite, No smoking, Children & dogs welcome, Open all year

Nolands Farm, Oxhill, near Warwick

The Green, Upper Quinton, Stratford-upon-Avon CV37 8SX   Map Ref: 15
1789 720500   Mobile: 07831 485483   B4632, A3400
nhouse.com

Built in 1856, Winton House is a historic Victorian farmhouse, situated in an area of natural beauty, six miles from Stratford-upon-Avon and the well known towns and villages of the Cotswolds. The charming bedrooms have four poster beds, with hand made quilts and en-suite bathrooms. Delicious, 'Heartbeat award' winning breakfasts with organic fruit from our nearby orchard. Log fires to warm in winter, cycles are available for hire. There are excellent local pubs and restaurant. A lovely spot for walking and touring. Hidcote Gardens and other National Trust properties are close by.

B & B £30-£37.50pp, Rooms 2 double, 1 twin, 1 family 2 en-suite, 2 private,
No smoking, Children welcome, No dogs, Closed Xmas

Forth House 44 High Street, Warwick CV34 4AX
Elizabeth Draisey   Tel: 01926 401512   Fax: 01926 490809
Email: info@forthhouseuk.co.uk   Web: www.forthhouseuk.co.uk

Map Ref: 16
A429

Our rambling Georgian family home within the old town walls of Warwick provides two peaceful guest suites hidden away at the back of the house. One family ground floor suite opens onto the garden whilst the other suite enjoys views across it. Both suites have private sitting and dining rooms. They are well equipped with television, fridge, hot and cold drink facilities. Ideally situated for holidays or business. Stratford, Oxford, Birmingham and Cotswold villages within easy reach. Breakfasts, English or continental at an agreed time. J15 of M40 two miles.

B & B from £30pp, C-Cards MC VS, Rooms 1 double/twin, 1 family, both en-suite,
No smoking, Children welcome, Guide dogs only, Closed occasionally

---

Nolands Farm Oxhill, Warwick CV35 0RJ
Sue Hutsby   Tel: 01926 640309   Fax: 01926 641662
Email: inthecountry@nolandsfarm.co.uk   www.nolandsfarm.co.uk

Map Ref: 17
A422
see Photo on page 291

Nolands Farm is situated in a tranquil valley with fields, woods and wildlife. A working arable farm, it offers the country lover a happy relaxing stay. The en-suite bedrooms, with television and hostess trays are mostly on the ground floor in tastefully restored annexed converted stables. There are romantic 4 poster bedrooms with bathroom. A licensed bar adjoins the garden conservatory. Fly and coarse fishing, clay pigeon shooting and hot air ballooning are available. Cycles for hire and riding nearby. Ample parking. Stratford 8 miles, Warwick 12 miles. Dinner by arrangement.

B & B from £22pp, C-Cards MC VS, Dinner from £19.95, Rooms 1 single, 4 four posters,
2 double, 1 family 2 twin, Restricted smoking, Children over 7, Guide dogs only, Open all year

---

Docker's Barn Farm Oxhill Bridle Road, Pillerton Hersey, Warwick CV35 0QB
Carolyn Howard
Tel: 01926 640475   Fax: 01926 641747

Map Ref: 18
A422

Docker's Barn is an idyllically situated old barn conversion surrounded by its own land. Its location makes it handy for Warwick, Stratford, NEC, NAC, the Cotswolds and the Heritage Motor Centre. Junction 12 of the M40 is just six miles. The attractive, beamed en-suite bedrooms have hospitality trays and colour television, and the four poster suite has its own front door. Wildlife abounds and lovely walks lead from the Barn. We keep horses and hens. The service here is friendly and attentive. French and Spanish are spoken.

B & B from £21pp, Rooms 1 twin, 2 double, all en-suite,
No smoking, Children over 8, Dogs by arrangement, Closed Xmas

---

Wiltshire

Following a dispute between the occupants of the royal castle and the cathedral, or more probably because of its bleak, windy and waterless location, the monks of Old Sarum vacated their ancient cathedral, and in the early thirteenth century moved down the valley and built their new cathedral in the pleasant watermeadows where the three rivers, the Avon, Bourne and Nadder meet. And what a building Salisbury Cathedral is! Built between 1220 and 1260 it is the only early English cathedral to be built all in one style and the graceful spire, added in the middle of the fourteenth century is 123 metres higher than any other in the country. The Chapter House contains the best preserved of the four manuscripts of the Magna Carta. The cathedral close, England's largest, is contained within walls with medieval gateways and one of the finest houses in the close is Mompesson House, containing the important Turnbull collection of eighteenth century English drinking glasses. Salisbury is packed with interest and is a glorious mixture of inns, churches and fine buildings. The Iron Age hill-fort of

Figsbury Ring lies to the north-east giving glorious views of the cathedral and city, as does the seventeenth century folly, a curious octagonal tower on Pepper Box Hill in the south east.

Wiltshire is dominated by the central high chalk plateau of Salisbury Plain, twenty miles by twelve miles, an area of grassy downland from prehistoric times until World War I when large tracts were ploughed. Stonehenge, the country's most famous prehistoric stone circle and a World Heritage Site, attracts visitors from all over the world with the significance of the henge puzzling archaeologists for generations. This impressive monument consists of Sarsen stones from Wiltshire and stones from the Preseli Hills of Wales. It is believed to have been remodeled during the Bronze Age (1600BC) when enormous lintels were added. The National Trust owns 1,450 acres of land surrounding the monument including interesting Bronze Age barrow groups. At Avebury, one of the most important megalithic monuments in Europe, the Trust manages a 28 acre site with stone circles enclosed by a ditch. The site includes the Alexander Keiller Museum and the Wiltshire Life Society's display of Wiltshire rural life in the Great Barn. Just a mile from Avebury is Silbury Hill, the largest prehistoric mound in Europe and remarkably, it has been calculated that it would have taken seven hundred men over ten years to build.

In the south of the county by Warminster are the colourful delights of Stourhead, a

Stonehenge, Wiltshire (SWT)

garden regarded as one of the highest achievements of English landscape gardening. The garden was laid out between 1741 and 1780 with lakes, classical temples, rare trees and plants, inspired by a Grand Tour of Europe by Henry Hoare II, the son of a wealthy banker. The house, built in 1721 by Colen Campbell was one of England's first Palladian mansions with King Alfred's Tower, the red-brick folly built at the edge of the estate in 1772, at 160 feet giving superb views. However, no-one can leave this lovely county without visiting that extravagant palace Longleat, built for John Thynne in 1580 and greatly embellished by the fourth Marquess of Bath on returning from a grand tour. As well as the wonderful grounds landscaped by 'Capability' Brown there is the world's largest maze and the hugely popular safari park.

Malmesbury in the north of the county can boast some of the finest Norman architecture in the country. The ancient settlement grew around its abbey, established in the seventh century, developing in size and importance as a place of pilgrimage to the shrine of St Aldhelm. Marlborough to the south is renowned for its fine wide High Street, and is an excellent centre for exploring the rolling Marlborough Downs and Savernake Forest, at one time a medieval hunting forest, now a glorious walking region. No visitor in this region should miss Lacock Abbey founded in 1232 and converted into a country house some time after 1539. This was the nineteenth century home of William Henry Fox Talbot who invented photography. A museum commemorating his achievement is in Lacock village, one of the prettiest villages in the country.

PLACES TO VISIT

This is a small selection of interesting places to visit. Many more are listed in our annual guide to Museums, Galleries, Historic Houses & Sites (see page 448)

Avebury Stone Circle
Avebury, Marlborough
The site includes the Alexander Keiller Museum which houses one of the most important prehistoric collections of artefacts in Britain

Bowood House
Calne
A Georgian House in a beautiful parkland setting landscaped by 'Capability' Brown. Interesting collections of costumes, watercolours, miniatures and jewellery.

Longleat
Warminster
A great Elizabethan house which includes

many treasures - paintings, tapestries, murals, furniture. Also renowned for its Safari park.

Salisbury Cathedral
Salisbury
The cathedral is unique amongst English medieval cathedrals in that it was designed as a single unit and finished in 1280. It has the tallest spire in England (404ft high) which was added in 1334.

Wilton House
Wilton, Salisbury
Classic example of Palladium style architecture. One of the finest art collections in Europe with over 230 original paintings on display.

Wiltshire

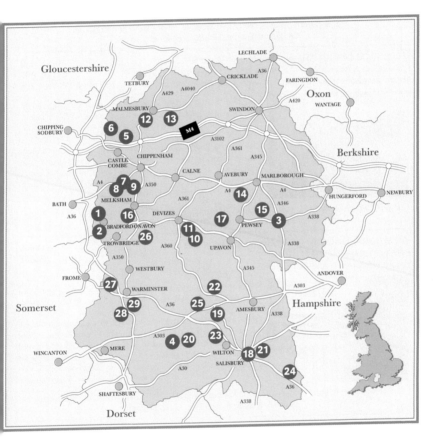

The Blue Map References should be used to locate B & B properties on the pages that follow

Fern Cottage Monkton Farleigh, Bradford-on-Avon BA15 2QJ

Christopher & Jenny Valentine Tel: 01225 859412 Fax: 01225 859018
Email: enquiries@fern-cottage.co.uk Web: www.fern-cottage.co.uk

Map Ref: 1
A363

Delightful stone cottage dating from 1680, in a quiet conservation Village. Original oak beams, open fire, antiques and family heirlooms. Three beautifully appointed bedrooms with private bath/shower, colour television, tea/coffee facilities. Traditional English breakfast is served at a large attractively arranged table and there is a lovely conservatory where guests may relax and look out over a well maintained garden. The local Inn, 100 yards away, serves excellent fare. There are many places of interest within a few minutes drive. Ample parking.

B & B from £30pp, Rooms 3 double, all en-suite, No smoking,
Children welcome, No dogs, Open all year

Burghope Manor Winsley, Bradford-on-Avon BA15 2LA

Elizabeth & John Denning Tel: 01225 723557 Fax: 01225 723113
Email: burghope.manor@virgin.net www.burghopemanor.co.uk

Map Ref: 2
B3108, A36
see Photo on page 298

Burghope Manor is a classic example of a medieval manor house. It stands in beautiful countryside on the edge of the village of Winsley, only five miles from Bath and one and a half miles from Bradford-on-Avon. Although steeped in history, it is first and foremost a living family home which has been carefully modernised so that the wealth of historical features may compliment the present day comforts which include full central heating and en-suite bathrooms. There is a good selection of pubs all within easy walking and driving distance.

B & B £42.50-£50pp, C-Cards MC VS AE, Rooms 2 double, 3 twin, all en-suite, No smoking,
Children over 10, No dogs, Closed Xmas & New Year

Westcourt Bottom 165 Westcourt, Burbage SN8 3BW

Felicity Mather Tel: 01672 810924
Email: westcourt.b-and-b@virgin.net

Map Ref: 3
B3087

Westcourt Bottom is a large 17th century thatched cottage which may be found five miles south of Marlborough in quiet Wiltshire countryside. The beautifully styled bedrooms are well equipped, they offer coffee, tea and biscuits. Some rooms are half timbered, a cosy sitting room with a log fire and television for guests' relaxation. There is a sunken Italianate garden and a heated swimming pool for everyone to use. The house is central for Stonehenge, Avebury, Savernake Forest, Ridgeway and Kennet and Avon Canal. There is an excellent pub nearby. Ample parking.

B & B from £28pp, Dinner from £15, Rooms 2 double, 1 en-suite, 1 twin, No smoking,
Children welcome, No dogs, Open all year

The Old Rectory Chilmark SP3 5AT

Scarlet & Edward Leatham Tel: 01722 716263 Fax: 01722 716159
Email: leathamschilmark@talk21.com

Map Ref: 4
A303 (2 miles)
see Photo opposite

Built in Chilmark stone, this 13th century house is in the main street of the village, standing in its own grounds of 20 acres, visitors can relax in complete quiet in the heart of the countryside. There is a library and drawing room with log fires to enjoy. Dine by candlelight in the spectacular dining room, where the food served features locally produced meat and fish, the vegetables and soft fruit are mostly from the kitchen garden. The famous gardens of Stourhead and Heale are close by and it is ideally located for visits to Stonehenge, Salisbury and Bath.

B & B £38pp, C-Cards MC VS, Dinner £25, Rooms 2 twin, 1 en-suite, 1 private bathroom,
Restricted smoking, Children over 10, Dogs by arrangement, Closed Xmas & New Year

The Old Rectory, Chilmark

Burghope Manor, Winsley, near Bradford-on-Avon

Church House Grittleton, Chippenham SN14 6AP
Anna Moore Tel: 01249 782562 Fax: 01249 782546
Email: moore@flydoc.fsbusiness.co.uk

Map Ref: 5
M4 J17

Once a Georgian Rectory and now 'home from home' to many returning guests who enjoy our garden, copper beeches, heated pool, croquet and sheep! A short drive to the M4, we are the 'Gateway to the West' offering the delights of historic Wiltshire and nearby Bath and Malmesbury. Grittleton has a live church, pub and cricket club, with riding, golf and tennis nearby. Bedrooms have television, tea/coffee making facilities. There is a large drawing room. Dinner by arrangement - 4 courses plus half a bottle of wine per person. Ample off-road parking.

B & B from £30pp, Dinner from £20, Rooms 2 twin, 1 double, 1 family, Restricted smoking, Children under 2/over 12, No dogs, Open all year

Manor Farm Alderton, Chippenham SN14 6NL
Jeffrey & Victoria Lippiatt Tel / Fax: 01666 840271 Mobile: 07421 415824
Email: j.lippiatt@farmline.com Web: www.themanorfarm.co.uk

Map Ref: 6
B4040
see Photo on page 300

This is a beautiful 17th century Cotswold family home. It stands in the charming village of Alderton, near Castle Combe. The house offers warmth and comfort, there are always log fires on chilly days, the drawing room being the perfect place to relax. Visitors are welcome to enjoy the garden and also the farm. Breakfasts are delicious, traditional farmhouse fare, or maybe Scottish smoked salmon and scrambled eggs with home baked bread. This is an ideal place to stay for exploring the city of Bath. The dogs here are smiley.

B & B from £30pp, Dinner available, Rooms 2 double, 1 twin, all en-suite, Restricted smoking, Children over 12, Dogs by arrangement, Closed Xmas & New Year

Church Farm Hartham, Corsham, SN13 0PU
Mrs Kate Jones Tel: 01249 715180 Fax: 01249 715572 Mobile: 07977 910775
Email: kmjbandb@aol.com Web: www.churchfarm.cjb.net.

Map Ref: 7
A4

Church Farm is a Cotswold farmhouse on a working farm offering wonderful countryside views. Plenty of wildlife close by, also cycle ways and marked walks. Accommodation is for up to six people. All the bedrooms have television tea and coffee making facilities, central heating and super views. Local produce used where possible. Lots of secure parking and stabling can also be arranged. Close to Bath, Castle Combe and Lacock. Good road/rail links. Plenty to visit locally e.g. Stonehenge, Avebury, Bowood, Kennet and Avon Canal. Idyllic rural situation and ideal holiday base.

B & B £22.50-£25pp, Rooms 1 single, 1 double, 1 family, most en-suite, No smoking, Children over 6 months, No dogs, Closed Xmas & New Year

Pickwick Lodge Farm Guyers Lane, Corsham SN13 0PS
Gill Stafford Tel: 01249 712207 Fax: 01249 701904
Email: b&b@pickwickfarm.freeserve.co.uk

Map Ref: 7
M4 J17, A4

Enjoy a stay at our beautiful home set in wonderful countryside where you can take a short stroll or longer walk and see rabbits, pheasant and occasional deer, or relax in our garden, just only 15 minutes drive from Bath. Ideally situated to visit Lacock, Castle Combe, Avebury, Stonehenge, many National Trust properties or explore some of the idyllic villages and have lunch or supper at a quaint pub. Two well appointed and tastefully furnished bedrooms, refreshment trays with home-made biscuits. Start the day with a hearty delicious breakfast using local produce.

B & B from £22.50pp, Rooms 1 twin, 2 double, 2 en-suite, 1 private, No smoking, Children welcome, No dogs, Closed Xmas & New Year

Manor Farm, Alderton, near Chippenham

Hatt Farm Old Jockey, Box, Corsham SN13 8DJ
Carol & Michael Pope   Tel: 01225 742989   Fax: 01225 742779
Email: hattfarm@netlineuk.net

Hatt Farm is an extremely comfortable Georgian farmhouse set in peaceful surroundings, far from the madding crowd. A scrumptious breakfast is served overlooking beautiful views of the rolling Wiltshire countryside. What can be nicer than sitting by a log fire in winter or enjoying the spacious garden in summer? Lovely walks and good golfing nearby. Ideally situated for touring the Cotswolds or visiting the endless delights of the relatively undiscovered county of Wiltshire. All this yet only 15 minutes away is the city of Bath.

B & B from £22.50pp, Rooms 1 twin en-suite, 1 double/family with private bathroom, Restricted smoking, Children welcome, No dogs, Closed Xmas & New Year

Heatherly Cottage Ladbrook lane, Gastard, Corsham SN13 9PE
Peter & Jenny Daniel   Tel: 01249 701402   Fax: 01249 701412
Email: ladbrook1@aol.com   Web: www.smoothhound.co.uk/hotels/heather3.html

Delightful 17th century cottage in a quiet country lane with two acres and ample parking, overlooking open countryside. The accommodation, with a separate entrance, has three well appointed and tastefully furnished bedrooms with colour television and tea/coffee making facilities. The cottage is located eight miles from the M4 and nine miles from Bath. It is ideal for visiting Avebury, Stonehenge, the National Trust village of Lacock and Lacock Abbey, Castle Combe, Bowood House, Corsham and Corsham Court and other historic places of interest. Excellent pubs nearby for evening meals.

B & B from £24pp, Rooms 1 twin en-suite, 2 double en-suite, No smoking, Children over 7, No dogs, Closed Xmas & New Year

Eastcott Manor Easterton, Devizes SN10 4PL
Mrs Janet Firth
Tel: 01380 813313

Eastcott Manor is a 16th century Manor House in a tranquil setting between the north edge of Salisbury Plain and Devizes. Television and tea/coffee making facilities in all rooms, guest lounge. Parking for six cars. Dinner by arrangement with home grown fruit and vegetables. Convenient for Bath, Salisbury, Stonehenge, Avebury, Longleat, Wilton house and National Trust properties such as Stourhead and Lacock Abbey. Children welcome and well behaved dogs by arrangement. Excellent country for walking and riding and convenient for Kennet and Avon Canal.

B & B from £23pp, Dinner from £20, Rooms 2 single, 1 double, 1 twin, all en-suite/private, Restricted smoking, Children & dogs welcome, Closed Xmas & New Year

Hill House Stert, Devizes SN10 3JB
Mrs Carol Mitchell   Tel / Fax: 01380 722356
Email: caminteriors@yahoo.co.uk

A modern house set in one of the prettiest villages in Wiltshire. Hill House was built by the owner with comfort in mind with a pretty garden overlooking corn fields and a hill fort. The cosy bedrooms under the eaves have been designed with a 'house and garden' feel. There is a small sitting room with television and books for guests to enjoy. Dinner, using home grown vegetables is available by arrangement, and there are good pubs nearby. Walking, National Trust properties and gardens are within easy reach. Andover, the M3, the M4, Bath, Marlborough and Salisbury are all only 20 minutes away.

B & B from £25pp, Dinner from £12.50, Rooms 1 double, 1 twin, both with private bathrooms, No smoking, Children over 12, No dogs, Closed mid-Dec to mid-Jan

Clatford Park Farm, Clatford, near Marlborough

Manor Farm Corston, Malmesbury SN16 0HF

Mrs Ross Eavis Tel: 01666 822148 Fax: 01666 826565
Email: ross@manorfarmbandb.fsnet.co.uk Web: www.manorfarmbandb.co.uk

Map Ref: 12
A429

Relax and unwind in this charming award winning 17th century farmhouse on a working dairy arable farm. Six tastefully furnished bedrooms, four en-suite, all with tea/coffee making facilities, radio and television. A beautiful lounge with inglenook fireplace as well as a secluded garden for guests' use. Meals are available in the local pub within walking distance. Manor Farm is an ideal base for one night or longer stays for exploring the Cotswolds, Bath, Stonehenge, Avebury, Lacock and many stately homes. Children over 10 years.

B & B from £23pp, C-Cards, Rooms 1 single, 1 twin, 3 double, 1 family, 4 en-suite, No smoking, Children over 10, No dogs, Closed Xmas & New Year

Stonehill Farm Charlton, Malmesbury SN16 9DY

Edna Edwards Tel: 01666 823310
Email: johnedna@stonehillfarm.fsnet.co.uk

Map Ref: 12
B4040

STOP! You've found us!!! Stonehill Farm is a 15th century Cotswold stone farmhouse on a family run dairy farm in lush rolling countryside on the Wiltshire/Gloucestershire border. There are three pretty rooms, one en-suite, all with hospitality trays. Wonderful breakfasts, friendly welcome and pets can come too. Ideal for one night, or several days. Oxford, Bath, Stratford-upon-Avon, Stonehenge and the delightful Cotswold hills and villages are all within easy reach by car. Hope to see you soon.

B & B from £22pp, Rooms 2 double, 1 twin, Restricted smoking, Children & dogs welcome, Open all year

Winkworth Farm Lea, Malmesbury SN16 9NH

Tony & Doi Newman Tel: 01666 823267
Email: doinewman@winkworth89.freeserve.co.uk

Map Ref: 13
A429, B4042

A friendly, welcoming 17th century Cotswold stone farmhouse set in a delightfully secluded walled garden. The pleasantly decorated spacious and comfortable bedrooms have country views and fresh flowers, they are equipped with tea/coffee making facilities and televisions. There are a number of good country pubs and restaurants locally, and Malmesbury Town, said to be the oldest borough in England, is a short drive away. The farmhouse is ideally based for a quiet, relaxing holiday or as a touring base. It is within easy reach of Cirencester, Cheltenham and Bath.

B & B from £25pp, Rooms 2 double with en-suite, 1 family with private bathroom, No smoking, Children & dogs welcome, Closed Xmas & New Year

Clatford Park Farm Clatford, Marlborough SN8 4DZ

Christopher & Elizabeth Morgan-Smith
Tel: 01672 861646

Map Ref: 14
A4, A345
see Photo opposite

This is an attractive 18th century mellow red brick farmhouse, three miles south west of Marlborough, and six miles from Avebury. The house stands on a quiet road, surrounded by fields and the largest bluebell woods in the country. This is a small farm with sheep, horses, chickens and ducks. There is a garden, and also a sitting room with a wood burning stove and television. Home grown vegetables, free range eggs and homemade bread are offered here. There are good pubs and restaurants locally. Horses are welcome, marvellous riding over the Marlborough Downs.

B & B £22-£26pp, Rooms 1 double en-suite, 1 double with private bathroom, No smoking, Children welcome, Dogs by arrangement, Open all year

Clench Farmhouse, Clench, near Marlborough

Clench Farmhouse Clench, Marlborough SN8 4NT

Clarissa Roe Tel: 01672 810264 Fax: 01672 811458 Mobile: 07774 784601
Email: clarissaroe@btinternet.com www.clenchfarmhouse.co.uk

Map Ref: 15
A345, A346
see Photo opposite

Attractive 18th century farmhouse in its own grounds with lovely views and surrounded by farmland. There are three double bedrooms each with their own bathroom (two of which are en-suite). The house has a happy and relaxed atmosphere and a warm welcome awaits guests. There is a tennis court, heated pool and croquet lawn for guests use. Delicious dinners are offered by prior arrangement. We also have a two bedroom and two bathroom self catering cottage. Lovely walks and within easy reach of Avebury, Stonehenge, Oxford, Salisbury and Bath.

B & B from £30pp, Dinner from £20, Rooms 1 double, 1 twin/double, 1 twin, 2 en-suite, Restricted smoking, Children welcome, Dogs by arrangement, Open all year

Frying Pan Farm Broughton Gifford, Melksham SN12 8LL

Ralph & Barbara Pullen Tel: 01225 702343 Fax: 01225 793652
Email: fr@dial.pipex.com Web: www.fryingpanfarm.dial.pipex.com

Map Ref: 16
A350, B3107

Frying Pan Farm is a cosy 17th century farmhouse, it overlooks the spacious garden and meadowland. There is ample parking for guests' cars. The accommodation is tastefully furnished, the en-suite rooms have colour television, tea and coffee making facilities. Guests have their own lounge and they are welcome to browse through the well stocked book case. The farm is situated to the east of Bath. Ideal situation for visiting Lacock, Bradford on Avon, Caen Hill, Flight of canal locks, also many National Trust Properties. Good pub in the village one mile away.

B & B from £22pp, Rooms 1 twin, 1 double, both en-suite, No smoking, Children over 2, No dogs, Closed Xmas & New Year

St Cross Woodborough, Pewsey SN9 5PL

Serena Gore
Tel / Fax: 01672 851346

Map Ref: 17
A4, A345, A342

Standing in the quiet village of Woodborough, which is close to the famous Kennet and Avon Canal, stands St Cross. It is a charming 17th century thatched cottage, which extends warmth and friendliness to visitors here. The cottage is decorated and presented to a high standard, the two bedrooms are comfortable and well equipped. The breakfasts here are delicious and dinner may be enjoyed, by arrangement. There are however, some good pubs in the village serving excellent suppers. This is an ideal base from which to explore the area. Dogs are welcomed here.

B & B from £30pp, C-Cards, Dinner from £12.50, Rooms 1 double, 1 twin, with private bathroom, No smoking in bedrooms, Children over 5, Well behaved dogs, Open all year

Farthings 9 Swaynes Close, Salisbury SP1 3AE

Gill Rodwell Tel / Fax: 01722 330749
Email: farthings@shammer.freeserve.co.uk Web: www.shammer.freeserve.co.uk

Map Ref: 18
A30

Farthings is a central but very quiet townhouse. It is the charming home of Mrs Gill Rodwell, it's just a pleasant stroll away from the city centre, where the famous Cathedral is one of Salisbury's main attractions. Parking is no problem in this peaceful Close. The comfortable, nicely furnished, bedrooms all have tea/coffee making facilities, and there is a good choice of breakfast. The breakfast room, with its interesting collection of old family photos, opens onto a delightful garden. An ideal base for visiting this old market town and the surrounding area.

B & B from £22pp, Rooms 2 single, 1 en-suite twin, 1 en-suite double, No smoking, Children over 12, No dogs, Open all year

The Mill House Berwick St James, near Salisbury SP3 4TS

Diana Gifford Mead
Tel / Fax: 01722 790331

Map Ref: 19
A303, A36, B3083
see Photo opposite

Stonehenge three miles, Diana welcomes you to the Mill House set in acres of nature reserve. An island paradise with the River Till running through the working mill and beautiful garden. Diana's old fashioned roses long to see you as do the lovely walks. Built by the miller in 1785, the bedrooms with tea/coffee making facilities, and television, command magnificent views. Fishing or swimming in the mill pool. Golf and riding nearby. Attention to healthy and organic food. Sample superb cuisine at the Boot Inn, Berwick St James.

B & B £25-£35pp, Rooms 2 single, 2 twin, 4 en-suite double,
Children over 5, No dogs, Open all year

Morris' Farm House Baverstock, Dinton, Salisbury SP3 5EL

Martin & Judith Marriott   Tel / Fax: 01722 716874
Email: marriott@waitrose.com

Map Ref: 20
Hindon Road

100 year old farmhouse with attractive garden set in open countryside. It is peaceful, with a homely and friendly atmosphere. There is a small guest sitting room with television, and breakfast is served in a south facing conservatory. Tea, coffee and hot chocolate making facilities are in each room, an excellent pub is two minutes walk for evening meals. Local attractions include Wilton House and Wilton carpet factory four miles; Salisbury with Cathedral and Museum seven miles; Old Sarum nine miles; Stonehenge, Stourhead and Longleat Safari Park are between 12 and 15 miles.

B & B from £20pp, Rooms 1 double, 1 twin, shared bathroom, No smoking,
Children & dogs welcome, Closed Xmas

Wyndham Cottage St Marys Road, Dinton, Salisbury SP3 5HH

Ian & Rosie Robertson
Tel: 01722 716343   Mobile: 077 699 116600

Map Ref: 20
A303, A36, B3089

A charming 18th century thatched stone cottage, lovingly restored and set in magnificent National Trust countryside, on edge of picturesque village. Bluebells, lambs and calves in Spring, delightful walks with marvellous views of the surrounding area. The cottage garden has many interesting plants, plus the old favourites. Excellent pubs nearby. Ideally situated for several days sightseeing at some wonderful historic places, cities and gardens. Stonehenge, Avebury, Salisbury, Bath, Wells, Wilton House, Stourhead, Longleat and many more. Tea/coffee facilities and colour television.

B & B from £25pp, Rooms 2 double en-suite, No smoking,
Children over 12, No dogs, Closed Nov to Mar

1 Riverside Close Laverstock, Salisbury SP1 1QW

Mary Tucker   Tel / Fax: 01722 320287
Email: marytucker2001@yahoo.com

Map Ref: 21
A30

This charming, well appointed home, may be found in a quiet area just one and a half miles from Salisbury Cathedral. The tastefully furnished suites complete with their own en-suite bath or shower room, television and drink making facilities. Salisbury is the centre of an area steeped in antiquity, rich in natural beauty, with many places of outstanding historical interest. Your hosts take endless care to ensure the well being of their guests, they are happy to plan itineraries for them.

B & B from £25pp, Dinner from £12, Rooms 1 double, 1 family, No smoking,
Children & dogs welcome, Open all year

The Mill House, Berwick St James, near Salisbury

Newton Farm House, Whiteparish, near Salisbury

Maddington House   Maddington Street, Shrewton, Salisbury SP3 4JD

Dick & Joan Robathan   Tel / Fax: 01980 620406
Email: rsrobathan@freenet.co.uk

Map Ref: 22
A360

Maddington House is the family home of Dick and Joan Robathan. An elegant 17th century Grade II listed house with a period hall and dining room, it is in the centre of the pretty village of Shrewton - about two and a half miles from Stonehenge and ten miles from Salisbury. There are three attractive guest rooms all of which have colour television and tea/coffee facilities. The village has three pubs within walking distance. This is a delightful home and the perfect base for a relaxing break.

B & B from £22.50pp, Rooms 1 twin, 1 double, 1 family, all en-suite, Restricted smoking, Children over 7, No dogs, Closed Xmas & New Year

Elm Tree Cottage   Chain Hill, Stapleford, Salisbury SP3 4LH

Chris & Joe Sykes   Tel: 01722 790507
Email: jaw.sykes@virgin.net

Map Ref: 23
A36, A303

This 17th century cottage with inglenook is set in a picturesque village. The attractively decorated bedrooms have en-suite/private bathrooms, television and tea/coffee making facilities. A two storey self-contained unit with a kitchen is available for families and longer staying guests. It has use of a garden room and may be used on a self catering basis to sleep up to six or seven people. Breakfast is served as required. Guests may enjoy the flower garden. Good walking with spectacular views, and also central to Salisbury, Bath, Wilton, Stonehenge, Avebury and Stourhead.

B & B from £25pp, Rooms 2 double, 1 family, all en-suite, Restricted smoking, Children welcome, Dogs by arrangement, Closed Dec to Feb

Newton Farmhouse   Southampton Road, Whiteparish, Salisbury SP5 2QL

Suzi & John Lanham   Tel / Fax: 01794 884416
enquiries@newtonfarmhouse.co.uk   www.newtonfarmhouse.co.uk

Map Ref: 24
A36
see Photo opposite

Historic listed 16th century farmhouse bordering the New Forest and originally part of the Trafalgar Estate. Convenient for Salisbury, Stonehenge, Romsey, Winchester, Portsmouth and Bournemouth. Delightful bedrooms, all with pretty en-suite facilities, five with genuine period four poster beds. Beamed dining room with flagstone floor and fireplace with bread oven and collection of Nelson memorabilia and antiques. Superb breakfast complimented by fresh fruits, home made breads, preserves and free range eggs. Swimming pool idyllically set in extensive grounds. AA, ETC 5 Diamonds, Silver Award.

B & B £25-£30pp, Dinner from £20, Rooms 2 twin, 3 double, 3 family, all en-suite, No smoking, Children welcome, No dogs, Open all year

Scotland Lodge Farm   Winterbourne Stoke, Salisbury SP3 4TF

Catherine Lockwood   Tel: 01980 621199   Fax: 01980 621188
Email: william.lockwood@bigwig.net

Map Ref: 25
A303

A warm welcome awaits you at this family run Competition Yard set in 46 acres. Dogs and horses are welcome. Lovely views with Stonehenge and Salisbury nearby. Conservatory for guests' use, with travel cot and highchair available. Rooms have colour television and tea/coffee making facilities, good local pubs. French, German and Italian spoken. Wilton House, Longleat, Stourhead, Heale Gardens all nearby. Bournemouth, Winchester, Bath within an hour. On A303 west out of Winterbourne Stoke, past turning on left to Berwick St James, and on right immediately after Scotland Lodge. Automatic entry gate.

B & B from £24pp, Rooms 2 double, 1 twin/triple, private bathrooms, No smoking, Children & dogs welcome, Open all year

Spiers Piece Farm Steeple Ashton, Trowbridge BA14 6HG

Jill Awdry
Tel / Fax: 01380 870266

Map Ref: 26
A361

Try our 'home away from home' farmhouse bed and breakfast in the heart of the Wiltshire countryside. Spiers Piece Farm is a spacious Georgian farmhouse with a large garden, great views and peace and tranquillity. It may be found adjacent to an historical, picturesque village. There are many tourist attractions within easy reach, including Bath and Stonehenge. All rooms have tea/coffee making facilities and washbasins. Guests have their own luxury bathroom, sitting room with colour television and dining room. Great breakfasts are offered to last you all day.

*B & B from £18pp, Rooms 2 double with TV, 1 twin, Restricted smoking,
Children welcome, Dogs by arrangement, Closed Nov to Feb*

Sturford Mead Farm Corsley, Warminster BA12 7QU

Lynn Corp   Tel / Fax: 01373 832213
Email: lynn_sturford.bed@virgin.net

Map Ref: 27
A362

Sturford Mead Farm is on the A362 between Frome and Warminster, nestling under the historic monument of Cley Hill (National Trust) and opposite Longleat with its safari park, lake and grounds. Stourhead, Cheddar Gorge, Wookey Hole and the prettiest English village of Castle Combe are close by. The Cathedral cities of Wells and Salisbury are within easy distance as is Bath. The comfortable bedrooms, all with private facilities, have tea/coffee makers, and television.

*B & B from £24pp, Rooms 2 twin, 1 double, all en-suite/private, No smoking,
Children welcome, No dogs, Open all year*

Springfield House Crockerton, Warminster BA12 8AU

Rachel & Colin Singer
Tel / Fax: 01985 213696

Map Ref: 28
A36 A350

Situated in the beautiful Wylye Valley and on the edge of the famous Longleat Estate, this is a charming and welcoming village house dating from the 17th century. Guests enjoy tastefully furnished rooms with lovely garden and woodland views. Grass tennis court. The cities of Salisbury, Wells and Bath are easily reached, with Stonehenge, Stourhead Gardens, Stately homes and castles nearby. There are endless walks through woodland or over Salisbury Plain, and two adjacent golf courses. Excellent village pub and lakeside restaurant just a few minutes walk.

*B & B from £27pp, Rooms 2 double, 1 twin, en-suite/private,
No smoking, Children & dogs welcome, Open all year*

Deverill End Deverill Road, Sutton Veny, Warminster BA12 7BY

Joy Greathead   Tel: 01985 840356   Email: riversgreathead@amserve.net
Web: www.suttonveny.co.uk/ForSaleTraders/LocalTraders.htm

Map Ref: 29
A36

Deverill End has a magnificent southern view over pastures which border the garden. Accommodation consists of two double rooms and one twin; all en-suite with colour television and tea/coffee making facilities. Parking is off road. The garden is lovely and full of interesting plants and shrubs. Ducks wander freely, whilst bantams, guinea fowl and a few laying hens have free range within the orchard. Halfway between the Georgian City of Bath and Salisbury, we are an ideal base for visiting Stonehenge, Stourhead's landscaped gardens, the Elizabethan splendour of Longleat and other historical attractions.

*B & B £23-£25pp, Rooms 1 twin, 2 double, all en-suite, No smoking,
Children over 10, No dogs, Open all year*

Yorkshire

Yorkshire is by far Britain's largest county with a vast variation in scenery ranging from the pretty and picturesque to the awe-inspiring and majestic. There is open space aplenty with seaside resorts to suit every possible taste, magnificent stately homes, gardens and parkland of incomparable beauty and history, folklore and legend to entrance the most curious of visitor. This is depicted particularly in York, the city which encapsulates the very essence of Yorkshire. No other city can offer such a concentration of medieval and other historic treasures. The Minster, built between 1240 and 1475 is the largest Gothic cathedral in Britain and contains amongst its many wonders some of the nation's most magnificent stained glass, some dating from 1150. The buildings of this city are a delight with high storeys adjacent to Georgian houses bound together by narrow cobbled roads. York also contains a wide selection of superb museums which between them tell the story of the ancient city and county. The Castle Museum, displaying everyday Victorian and Edwardian life, the Jorvik Viking Centre, a recreation of the ninth century Viking settlement, and the National Railway Museum are all popular tourist attractions.

Near to York is the splendid Castle Howard, recognizable as 'Brideshead' in the television adaptation of Brideshead Revisited. It is the eighteenth century home of the Howard family and is set in 1000 acres of parkland, including a beautiful Rose Garden. This grand manor house also contains a collection of rare china, Felix Kelly murals and an extensive picture gallery.

The grey-white limestone peaks of the Pennine Range, reaching 2,000 feet in places, form the backbone of the county with the Yorkshire Dales National Park covering a vast area of fine walking country. Airedale, with its curious limestone scenery around Malham boasts glorious Gordale Scar waterfall as well as the proud fortress town of Skipton, home of the quite remarkable Lady Anne Clifford who in the seventeenth century restored or built many important buildings. Swaledale is home to the impressive Norman castle at Richmond and the lovely ruin of Easby Abbey with Hardraw Force nearby, the tallest waterfall in England. The Settle to Carlisle railway crosses the high Pennines passing over the spectacular Ribblehead Viaduct in the shadow of

East Window, York Minster (YTB)

Whernside and along the Eden Valley giving memorable views of the Dales landscape. Here the 'Three Peaks', Whernside, Ingleborough and Pen-y-Ghent are a popular challenge to serious walkers. Ingleton is the centre for pot-holers, the whole area being riddled with caves and pot-holes with Gaping Gill renowned as being large enough to contain St Paul's Cathedral.

The North Yorkshire Moors, the largest expanse of moorland in England became a National Park in 1952, including much of the North Yorkshire coastline. Whitby, where Bram Stoker wrote Dracula, was also the point where Captain James Cook set off and is a lovely seaside town with the spectacular monastic site of Whitby Abbey. Staithes, Robin Hood's Bay and Runswick Bay are also resorts of endearing charm and history.

The Vale of York, a magnet to holiday visitors offers a wide variety of attractions. Fountains Abbey and Studley Royal Water Gardens must be one of the most remarkable sites in Europe. A World Heritage Site it encompasses the spectacular ruin of a twelfth century Cistercian Abbey, a Jacobean Mansion and one of the finest surviving examples of a Georgian Green Water Garden. Sheltered in a quiet secluded valley near the historic city of Ripon, there are lakes, avenues, cascades and classical temples. Another sight not to be missed is Rievaulx Terrace and Temples to the north east of Fountains Abbey, two mid-eighteenth century temples on a grass-covered terrace with impressive vistas over Rievaulx Abbey and the Rye Valley to the Hambleton Hills. Harrogate, as well as being a charming town is in its own right an ideal centre for touring the whole Plain of York, with easy access over the Buttertubs Pass to the Yorkshire Dales in the west, and the coastal resorts in the east. Harrogate is a town of elegant Victorian buildings, fine tree-lined avenues, excellent shopping and beautiful municipal gardens, as indeed befits the home of Harlow Carr Botanical Gardens, the headquarters of the Northern Horticultural Society.

PLACES TO VISIT

This is a small selection of interesting places to visit. Many more are listed in our annual guide to Museums, Galleries, Historic Houses & Sites (see page 448)

Castle Howard
Castle Howard, York
This impressive mansion has collections of fabulous paintings, fine furniture, porcelain and sculpture. The gardens are substantial, the walled rose garden must be seen.

Harewood House
Hardwood, Leeds
A fine country mansion with an outstanding art collection, chippendale furniture, and porcelain.

Nostell Priory
Wakefield
The Priory contains one of England's finest collections of Chippendale furniture and an exceptional art collection.

Skipton Castle
Skipton
The last stronghold of the Royalists in the North, one of the most complete and well preserved medieval castles in England.

York Minster
York
The largest Gothic cathedral in England, dating from the 13th century, including a display of a large collection of diocesan church plate.

Yorkshire

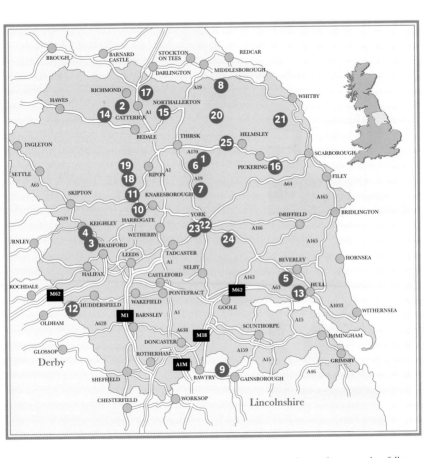

The Blue Map References should be used to locate B & B properties on the pages that follow

Shallowdale House West End, Ampleforth YO62 4DY

Phillip Gill & Anton Van Der Horst   Tel: 01439 788325   Fax: 01439 788885
Email: stay@shallowdalehouse.demon.co.uk   Web: www.shallowdalehouse.demon.co.uk

Map Ref: 1
A170

Situated on the southern edge of the North York Moors National Park, all the rooms at Shallowdale House command sublime views of unspoilt English countryside. The bedrooms are stylish and spacious, with tea/coffee making facilities and television, baths and showers. As well as comfort and caring service, there is a strong emphasis on imaginative, freshly cooked food, and the house is licensed. An ideal centre for touring, and visiting the abbeys, castles and stately homes of North Yorkshire. Delightful gardens.

B & B £32.50-£40pp, C-Cards MC VS, Dinner £22.50, Rooms 2 kingsized/twin, 1 double, all en-suite/private, No smoking, Children over 12, No dogs, Closed Xmas & New Year

Elmfield Country House Arrathorne, Bedale DL8 1NE

Jim & Edith Lillie   Tel: 01677 450558   Fax: 01677 450557   Mobile: 07802 730027
Email: stay@elmfieldhouse.freeserve.co.uk   Web: www.countryhouseyorkshire.co.uk

Map Ref: 2
A684

Large country house set in lovely rolling countryside at the gateway to the Yorkshire Dales. All bedrooms are spacious, comfortable with en-suite facilities. A delightful four poster room is available and all rooms include direct dial telephones, colour television with separate movie channel, radio alarms and coffee/tea facilities. Two rooms are designed specifically for disabled guests. Full English breakfast is served with home cooked dinner in the evening. Lounge bar, conservatory lounge, games room and solarium. Also on site is private fishing lake and secure parking.

B & B from £25pp, Dinner from £15, Rooms 3 twin, 4 double, 2 family, all en-suite, Restricted smoking, Children welcome, No dogs, Open all year

Five Rise Locks Hotel Beck Lane, Bingley BD16 4DD

Pat & William Oxley   Tel: 01274 565296   Fax: 01274 568828
Email: info@five-rise-locks.co.uk   Web: www.five-rise-locks.co.uk

Map Ref: 3
A650

Welcome to an hotel of charm and character, where each en-suite bedroom is as individual as you - from the seclusion of the Turret Rooms, the panoramic views from the Studio - each has the same extraordinary peacefulness. Award winning restaurant open daily offering excellent selection of English and European dishes complimented by a well chosen wine list. Whether you intend to tour the Dales, Haworth, Saltaire, mill shopping, or relax - stroll along the Canal and admire the engineering feat of the Five Rise Locks.

B & B £29-£32.50pp, C-Cards MC VS, Dinner from £13, Rooms 1 single, 3 twin, 5 double, 2 double/family, all en-suite, Restricted smoking, Children & dogs welcome, Open all year

March Cote Farm Cottingley, Bingley BD16 1UB

George & Jean Warin   Tel: 01274 487433   Fax: 01274 561074   Mobile: 07889 162257
jean.warin@nevisuk.net   www.yorkshirenet.co.uk/accgde/marchcote

Map Ref: 4
A650
see Photo opposite

Friendly atmosphere awaits you in our 17th century farmhouse, fully modernised with central heating and a high standard of furnishings and decor. Character still maintained with original oak beams and mullion windows. Top quality farmhouse cooking, served in guests' dining room. Colour television and tea/coffee making facilities in all rooms. Many places of interest within comfortable travelling distance - Moors, Dales, museums and National Trust properties. Pretty garden. Many repeat bookings. Professional, business and tourist guests all welcome. Plenty of car parking. Also holiday cottages.

B & B from £22pp, Dinner from £10, Rooms 2 double, 1 family suite, all en-suite/private, Restricted smoking, Children welcome, No dogs, Closed Xmas

March Cote Farm, Cottingley, near Bingley

Rudstone Walk
South Cave, Beverley, Brough HU15 2AH
Laura & Charlie Greenwood Tel: 01430 422230 Fax: 01430 424552
Email: admin@rudstone-walk.co.uk Web: www.rudstone-walk.co.uk

Map Ref: 5
B1230, A1034, M62

A unique country house set in its own acres on the edge of the unspoilt Yorkshire Wolds, with magnificent views over the Vale of York and Humber Estuary. Luxurious en-suite bed and breakfast accommodation is provided in a courtyard garden development surrounding the 400 year old Farmhouse, where delicious home-cooked meals are served. If you prefer, self-catering accommodation is available, sleeping one to six people. An ideal location for exploring the historic towns of York and Beverley, the surrounding countryside and the heritage coastline, all within easy reach of us.

B & B from £29.50pp, C-Cards MC VS AE DC, Dinner from £18, Rooms 6 twin, 7 double, 1 family, all en-suite, Restricted smoking, Children welcome, Dogs by arrangement, Closed Xmas week

Oldstead Grange
Oldstead, Coxwold, YO61 4BJ
Mrs Anne Banks Tel: 01347 868634
Email: anne@yorkshireuk.com Web: www.yorkshireuk.com

Map Ref: 6
A19

Oldstead Grange blends traditional 17th century features with superb comfort and luxury in a beautiful quiet situation amidst our 160 acres of fields, woods and valleys near Byland Abbey in the Moors National Park. Spacious en-suite bedrooms with really comfortable king-size beds, colour television, warm towels and robes, fresh flowers and refreshment tray with homemade chocolates and biscuits. Special four poster suite. Breakfast choice of teas, coffees, fruit and freshly prepared traditional and speciality dishes. Renowned eating places in local picturesque villages. Colour brochure. ETC 5 Diamonds, Gold Award.

B & B £28-£35pp, C-Cards MC VS, Rooms 1 twin, 2 double, all en-suite, No smoking, Children over 10, No dogs, Open all year

Alderside
Thirsk Road, Easingwold YO61 3HJ
Daphne Tanner Smith Tel / Fax: 01347 822132
Email: john.TSmith@tinyonline.co.uk

Map Ref: 7
A19

Alderside is a comfortable Edwardian family home quietly situated in its own large gardens, secluded, yet it is only ten minutes walk from Easingwold market place and within easy reach of York, the Moors and coast. The two double bedrooms each have a private or en-suite bathroom, colour television, clock radios and tea/coffee making facilities. There is an additional room for accompanying relatives or friends. Traditional English breakfast is served using local produce and home made preserves. There are excellent eating places nearby. Private parking.

B & B from £21pp, Rooms 2 double en-suite/private, No smoking, Children over 10, No dogs, Closed Nov to Apr

Manor House Farm
Ingleby Greenhow, Great Ayton TS9 6RB
Margaret & Martin Bloom Tel: 01642 722384
Email: mbloom@globalnet.co.uk

Map Ref: 8
A172

Delightful farmhouse (part 1760) built of Yorkshire stone, set in 164 acres of park and woodlands at the foot of the Cleveland hills in the North York Moors National Park. Environment is tranquil and secluded. Ideal for nature lovers, relaxing, touring and walking. Accommodation is attractive with exposed beams and interior stonework. Atmosphere is warm and welcoming. Guests have separate entrance, lounge and dining room. Fine evening dinners, special diets if required, excellent wines. Brochure available. Credit and debit cards accepted.

Dinner B & B from £45pp, C-Cards, Dinner available, Rooms 2 twin, 1 double, all en-suite/private, No smoking, Children over 12, Dogs by arrangement, Closed Xmas

Gringley Hall Gringley on the Hill DN10 4QT

Ian & Dulce Threlfall　Tel: 01777 817262　Fax: 01777 816824
Email: dulce@gringleyhall.fsnet.co.uk

Map Ref: 9
A631

Gringley Hall stands in one of the most picturesque villages in North Nottinghamshire, close to Clumber Park, Sherwood Forest and the Dukeries. Built in the early 1800s, the Hall was also a children's convalescent home. After many years of careful restoration, the accommodation presented to guests is spacious and comfortable, the bedrooms have kingsize beds and en-suite bathrooms. Breakfast is an experience not to be missed with delicious fresh fruits, organically produced bacon, sausage and eggs. Dinners and light suppers using home grown produce wherever possible, are available by arrangement.

B & B £30-£35pp, Dinner from £22.50, Rooms 3 single, 3 double, 3 twin, 3 family, all en-suite, Restricted smoking, Children & dogs welcome, Open all year

---

Acacia Lodge 21 Ripon Road, Harrogate HG1 2JL

Dee & Peter Bateson　Tel: 01423 560752　Fax: 01423 503725
Web: www.smoothhound.co.uk/hotels/acacialodge.html

Map Ref: 10
A61

This highly Commended, warm, lovingly restored family run Victorian hotel with pretty gardens stands in a select central conservation area. Acacia Lodge is a short stroll from Harrogate's fashionable shops, many restaurants and conference/exhibition facilities. The house retains its original character with fine furnishings, antiques and paintings. All the bedrooms are luxuriously en-suite with every comfort and facility. Award winning breakfasts are served in the oak furnished dining room. There is a beautiful lounge with an open fire and a library of books. Private floodlit parking for all guests. Brochure on request.

B & B from £29pp, Rooms 2 twin, 2 double, 2 triple, all en-suite, No smoking, Children over 10, No dogs, Closed Xmas & New Year

---

Ashley House Hotel 36-40 Franklin Road, Harrogate HG1 5EE

Ron & Linda Thomas　Tel: 01423 507474　Fax: 01423 560858
Email: ashleyhousehotel@btinternet.com

Map Ref: 10
A1

Ron and Linda Thomas offer you a cheery welcome and value for money in quality bedrooms, all en-suite with colour television and hospitality tray. Sample our generous breakfast before walking into the town centre or Valley Gardens. Drive through the Yorkshire Dales or Moors, visit Fountains Abbey or Harewood House or take the train to Knaresborough, York or Leeds. Harrogate has some 60 restaurants, most within walking distance of the hotel. Visit our cosy bar for a pre-dinner drink or nightcap - over 100 whiskies to choose from.

B & B from £30pp, Rooms 5 single, 5 twin, 5 double, 2 family, all en-suite, Children & dogs welcome, Open all year

---

Franklin View 19 Grove Road, Harrogate HG1 5EW

Jennifer Mackay　Tel: 01423 541388　Fax: 01423 547872
Email: jennifer@franklinview.com　Web: franklinview.com

Map Ref: 10
A59/A1/M1

This Edwardian family home may be found in a tree lined avenue in the heart of Harrogate. Careful preservation has ensured that the original features including the Gothic windows still remain. Each room displays an individual appeal, and they are all presented to suit the style of the house. Guests may choose either a traditional breakfast or a healthy alternative to suit. Within a short walk is a selection of well recommended international restaurants. Harrogate town has beautiful parks and nearby, there are wonderful well known places to visit.

B & B £24-£27pp, C-Cards MC VS, Rooms 2 double, 1 twin, all en-suite, No smoking, No children or dogs, Open all year

High Winsley Cottage Burnt Yates, Harrogate HG3 3EP

Clive & Gill King
Tel: 01423 770662

Map Ref: 11
A61/B6165

High Winsley Cottage is a traditional Dales stone cottage in Nidderdale. It stands away from the road in peaceful countryside, with lovely views.The cottage is ideally placed for town and country visiting. A warm welcome, good food and comfort are assured. The bedrooms are en-suite and well equipped. Guests have the choice of two sitting rooms with television, books, magazines, guides and maps. Great care is taken with meals, fresh fruit and vegetables from the garden, free range eggs and home baked bread are all on offer.

B & B from £24pp, Dinner from £13.50, Rooms 2 double, 2 twin, all en-suite, No smoking, Children over 11, Closed Jan to Feb

Forest Farm Guest House Mount Road, Marsden, Huddersfield HD7 6NN

May & Ted Fussey Tel / Fax: 01484 842687
Email: mayandted@aol

Map Ref: 12
A62

In the heart of 'Last of the Summer Wine' country, Forest Farm is situated on the edge of the village of Marsden 1,000ft above sea level overlooking the golf course and moorland. It is over 200 years old, a former weavers cottage constructed in stone. It has been restored retaining much of it's original character. Forest Farm offers evening meals, bed and breakfast and packed lunches. Television room. Car parking. We can boast spring water, free range eggs: special diets available with prior arrangement. Come as a guest and leave as a friend!

B & B from £18pp, C-Cards, Dinner from £7, Rooms 1 twin, 1 double, 1 family, Restricted smoking, Children welcome, Dogs by arrangement, Closed Xmas

Box Cottage 2 Hogg Lane, Kirk Ella, Hull HU10 7NU

Martin & Stephanie Hornby Tel / Fax: 01482 658852
Email: Boxcottage2@aol.com

Map Ref: 13
A164

Box Cottage is set within the Kirk Ella conservation area and tucked away with a delightful enclosed garden. The house is imaginatively decorated and furnished with lots of pictures, photos and flowers. Food is of a high standard. Bedrooms have televisions, tea/coffee facilities, books and magazines. Guests are most welcome to use the sitting room and garden. Kirk Ella gives easy access to North Sea ferries, The Yorkshire Wolds, Beverley and York. An ideal base for business people visiting Hull.

B & B £28pp, Dinner £18, Rooms 1 double with private bathroom, 1 single (for same party), No smoking, Children over 8, No dogs, Open all year

Rookery Cottage 1 East Witton, Leyburn DL8 4SN

Ursula Bussey Tel / Fax: 01969 622918
Email: ursulabussey@aol.com Web: www.rookerycottage.co.uk

Map Ref: 14
A6108

Converted 15 years ago from 17th century almshouses, Rookery Cottage is one of the prettiest houses in the village. It was the village Post Office and before that the tailor's house. The south facing bedrooms enjoy views to the garden. There are wonderful beams everywhere, even in the bathroom. The bedrooms each have a painted basin, they are beautifully presented. Breakfasts here are superb. The area is the centre of horse training, and has much to offer in walking, field sports, famous towns and abbeys. Dine at the pub across the road - one of the North Country's finest.

B & B £22.50-£28pp, Rooms 1 twin, 1 double, sharing luxury bathroom, No smoking, Children & dogs welcome, Open all year

Mallard Grange, Aldfield, near Fountains Abbey, Ripon

Porch House High Street, Northallerton DL7 8EG
Janet Beardow Tel: 01609 779831 Fax: 01609 778603
Web: www.smoothhound.co.uk/hotels/porchhouse1.html

Map Ref: 15
A684

Porch House was built in 1584 and took its name from the porch that still frames the entrance. Throughout its history Porch House has offered comfort and shelter to travellers including royalty - James (VI of Scotland I of England) and Charles I. All bedrooms (one ground floor) are en-suite with shower, tea/coffee making facilities, colour television. Traditional English/vegetarian breakfast is cooked to order. Original fireplaces and beams, walled garden, private parking, central position with excellent shopping, and ideal for discovering the Yorkshire Dales, Moors and coast. AA, ETC 4 Diamonds, Gold Award.

B & B from £26pp, C-Cards MC VS, Rooms 4 double, 2 twin, all en-suite, No smoking, No children or dogs, Closed Xmas & New Year

Allerston Manor House near Thornton-Le-Dale, Pickering YO18 7PF
Tess & Rupert Chetwynd Tel / Fax: 01723 850112
Email: red@allerston-manor.com Web: www.allerston-manor.com

Map Ref: 16
A64, A170

Allerston Manor House is quietly placed on the edge of the village bordering the National Park with lovely distant views. Reconstructed around a 14th century Kinghts' Templar Hall it has been carefully restored preserving old features and adding modern comforts. A warm and friendly home, well positioned to explore the many famous sights and only 35 minutes to York. Meals are carefully prepared using free-range meats and home grown produce where possible. Wonderful walks on the Heritage coast and the moors; steam railway, many historic houses and castles.

B & B £35-£42.50pp, C-Cards MC VS, Dinner from £20, Rooms 2 double, 1 double/twin, all en-suite, No smoking, Children over 12, No dogs, Open all year

Brook House Middleton Tyas, Richmond DL10 6RP
Mr & Mrs John Harrop
Tel / Fax: 01325 377713

Map Ref: 17
A1

Brook House is a Georgian period former farmhouse surrounded by mature oaks, tranquil pastures and secluded game coverts. The well proportioned rooms are elegantly furnished, there are log fires to welcome, supported by central heating. Delicious British and French cooking is served in the candlelit dining room, whilst breakfasts are served in the open kitchen. The house is well placed for the A1, it is near Richmond and Barnard Castle, ideal for exploring the Yorkshire Dales and Moors, plus the Cathedral cities of Durham, Ripon and York. A peaceful stop on the journey to Scotland.

B & B from £35pp, Dinner from £25, Rooms 1 double, 1 twin, both en-suite, Restricted smoking, Children over 16, Dogs by arrangement, Closed Xmas & New Year

Mallard Grange Aldfield, near Fountains Abbey, Ripon HG4 3BE
Maggie Johnson Tel / Fax: 01765 620242 Mobile: 07720 295918
Email: mallard.grange@btinternet.com

Map Ref: 18
B6265
see Photo on page 319

Rambling 16th century farmhouse full of character and charm in glorious countryside near Fountains Abbey. Offering superb quality and comfort, spacious rooms furnished with care and some lovely antique pieces. En-suite bedrooms have large comfortable beds, warm towels, colour television, hairdryer and refreshments tray. Delicious breakfasts with homemade preserves. Pretty walled garden. Safe parking. A wonderful place to relax, ideally placed for York, Harrogate, Yorkshire Dales, North Yorkshire Moors and a wealth of historic houses, castles and gardens. Excellent evening meals available locally.

B & B £27.50-£30pp, C-Cards MC VS, Rooms 2 double, 2 twin, all en-suite, No smoking, Children over 12, No dogs, Closed Xmas & New Year

St George's Court, Grantley, near Ripon

Barbican House, York

St George's Court Old Home Farm, Grantley, Ripon HG4 3EU

Sandra Gordon   Tel / Fax: 01765 620618
Email: stgeorgescourt@bronco.co.uk

Map Ref: 19
B6265
see Photo on page 321

Enjoy the friendly welcome and warm hospitality of St George's Court, a listed farmhouse, situated in the beautiful Yorkshire Dales, near Fountains Abbey in 20 acres of peaceful farmland. Our en-suite rooms which are in a renovated farm building, offer comfort and all modern facilities - television and tea/coffee making facilities, whilst retaining character and charm. Delicious breakfasts are served in the lovely farmhouse, guests may enjoy breakfast with a view in a charming conservatory dining room. Lots of parking. Peace and tranquillity are our passwords. AA 4 Diamonds.

B & B £25-£27.50pp, C-Cards MC VS, Rooms 1 twin, 3 double, 1 family, all en-suite,
Restricted smoking, Children & dogs welcome, Closed Xmas

Laskill Farm Hawnby, Thirsk YO62 5NB

Mrs S Smith   Tel / Fax: 01439 798268
Email: suesmith@laskillfarm.fsnet.co.uk

Map Ref: 20
B1257

Charming, warm country farmhouse on 600 acre farm in the north Yorkshire National Park in the heart of James Herriot and Heartbeat country. All rooms are lovingly cared for and are well equipped. Lovely garden with its own lake, peace and tranquillity. Many places of historical interest and stately houses nearby. York only 45 minutes away. Generous cuisine of a high standard using fresh produce. Natural spring water. A walker's paradise. Featured on 1998 BBC 'Holiday' programme, recommended in Sunday Times and 'Which' magazine.

B & B from £28.50pp, Dinner from £13.50, Rooms 1 single, 3 double,
2 twin, most en-suite, Open all year

Whitfield House Hotel Darnholm, Goathland, Whitby YO22 5LA

Adrian & Sue Caulder
Tel: 01947 896215

Map Ref: 21
A169

Quietly situated in the heart of the North York Moors National Park. Once a 17th century farmhouse, Whitfield House has been carefully modernised to provide every comfort whilst retaining its old world charm. We have nine en-suite bedrooms, (non smoking), each having colour television, telephone, tea-makers, radio and hairdryer. Superb country cooking using fresh produce. Personal attention and a warm friendly atmosphere. Licensed. The ideal base for walking or touring the North York Moors, steam railway and the coast. Goathland is 'Aidensfield' in Yorkshire TV's 'Heartbeat'.

B & B from £31pp, Dinner from £12.95, Rooms 1 single, 2 twin, 6 double, all en-suite,
Restricted smoking, Children over 5, Dogs by arrangement, Open all year

---

Barbican House 20 Barbican Road, York YO10 5AA

Michael & Juliet Morgan   Tel: 01904 627617   Fax: 01904 647140
Email: info@barbicanhouse.com   Web: www.barbicanhouse.com

Map Ref: 22
A19
see Photo opposite

Friendly northern welcome in this delightful Victorian residence with lots of charm and character. Carefully restored to retain many of its original features. All bedrooms are en-suite and have television and tea/coffee making facilities. One room is at ground floor level. A traditional English breakfast or a vegetarian breakfast is served, as well as a fresh fruit platter, scones, muffins and yoghurt. Central York is only a five minute walk and the Barbican Leisure centre a 100 yards. A private car park is situated at the rear of the hotel.

B & B from £28pp, C-Cards MC VS, Rooms 1 twin, 6 double, all en-suite,
No smoking, Children over 12, No dogs, Closed Xmas & New Year

The Hazelwood, York

Dairy Guest House 3 Scarcroft Road, York YO23 1ND

Map Ref: 22
A64

Phillip Hunt & Chris Andrade
Tel: 01904 639367

Once the local dairy, and now a beautifully appointed Victorian town house, Dairy Guest House features a flower filled enclosed courtyard. The rooms are well equipped in a cottage style. They are prettily presented, and one room has a four poster bed. Some rooms offer en-suite facilities. Guests are offered either a traditional English, or wholefood vegetarian breakfast There is a relaxed, informal atmosphere here. Dairy Guest House is within walking distance of the city centre, and just 200 yards from the medieval city walls. Please phone for colour brochure.

B & B from £20pp, Rooms 1 single, 1 twin, 2 double, 1 family, some en-suite, Children welcome, Dogs by arrangement, Closed mid-Dec to Jan

The Hazelwood 24/25 Portland Street, York YO31 7EH

Map Ref: 22
Gillygate
see Photo opposite

Tel: 01904 626548 Fax: 01904 628032
Web: www.thehazelwoodyork.com

ETC 4 Diamonds, Silver Award, RAC Sparkling Diamond. Situated in the very heart of York only 400 yards from York Minster, yet in an extremely quiet residential area, the Hazelwood is an elegant Victorian townhouse with its own car park. Our individually styled bedrooms are furnished to the highest standards using designer fabrics. All the rooms have en-suite bathrooms, which are well equipped and imaginatively lit. Our high quality breakfasts cater for all tastes including vegetarian and range from traditional English to croissants and Danish pastries. Completely non-smoking.

B & B £35-£50pp, C-Cards MC VS, Rooms 1 single, 3 twin, 8 double, 2 family, all en-suite, No smoking, Children over 8, No dogs, Open all year

Holmwood House Hotel 114 Holgate Road, York YO24 4BB

Map Ref: 22
A59

Rosie Blanksby & Bill Pitts Tel: 01904 626183 Fax: 01904 670899
Email: holmwood.house@dial.pipex.com Web: www.holmwoodhousehotel.co.uk

Holmwood House Hotel was built as two private houses in the 19th century, backing onto one of the prettiest squares in York. The two listed buildings have been lovingly restored to retain the ambience of a private home and provide peaceful elegant rooms. Bedrooms have en-suite facilities with shower, bath or even spa-bath, television, tea/coffee making facilities and direct dial telephone. There is a car park, and we are only 7-8 minutes walk from the City Walls, with the railway station and city centre 15 minutes walk away.

B & B £32.50 to £52.50pp, C-Cards MC VS, Rooms 3 twin, 8 double, family suites, all en-suite,No smoking, Children over 8, No dogs, Open all year

Nunmill House 85 Bishopthorpe Road, York YO23 1NX

Map Ref: 22
A59/A64

Russell & Cherry Whitbourn-Hammond Tel: 01904 634047 Fax: 01904 655879
Email: info@nunmill.co.uk Web: www.nunmill.co.uk

Nunmill House is an elegant Victorian House, it has been sympathetically restored and now displays many of the original architectural features. The house enjoys a perfect location for those wishing to explore the interest of this exciting city, as it is within walking distance of all the major attractions. York is home to the famous York Minster, museums, galleries, the York racecourse and endless history. The accommodation here is well presented, the rooms being individually styled, comfortable and well equipped. A full English or continental breakfast is offered.

B & B £27-£35pp, Rooms 1 twin, 6 double, 1 family, 7 en-suite, 1 private bathroom, No smoking, Children welcome, No dogs, Closed Dec to Jan

St George's Hotel 6 St George's Place, York YO24 1DR

Brian & Kristine Livingstone   Tel: 01904 625056   Fax: 01904 625009

Email: sixstgeorg@aol.com   Web: www.members.aol.com/sixstgeorg/

Map Ref: 22
A1036, A64

St. Goerge's Hotel is a ten bedroomed Victorian house in a quiet cul-de-sac by York's beautiful racecourse. The comfortably furnished bedrooms are en-suite and have television and tea/coffee trays. There is excellent access from the A64 from the south and A19 from the north, so it is well placed for Castle Howard, Scarborough, Herriot country, the North Yorkshire Moors and the historic places in York. We are just a ten minute walk to the City walls. All pets very welcome. There is private enclosed car parking.

B & B from £24pp, C-Cards MC VS AE DC, Dinner from £7, Rooms 5 double (2 four posters), 5 family, all en-suite, Children & dogs welcome, Open all year

Alcuin Lodge 15 Sycamore Place, Bootham, York YO30 7DW

Susan Taylor   Tel: 01904 632222   Fax: 01904 626630

Email: alcuinlodg@aol.com

Map Ref: 22
A19

Alcuin Lodge is a fine old Edwardian House situated in a quiet cul de sac overlooking a bowling green, yet only five minutes walk through the beautiful Museum Gardens to the heart of our historic city. A warm welcome is assured here. Alcuin Lodge is within walking distance of York train station. The rooms are twin and double en-suite, with tea/coffee facilities and central heating. Guests have access to rooms at all times. There is ample car parking. Just telephone for a comfortable and memorable stay.

B & B from £20pp, C-Cards MC VS DC, Rooms 1 twin, 3 double, 1 family, all en-suite, No smoking, Children over 12, No dogs, Closed Xmas

Arnot House 17 Grosvenor Terrace, Bootham, York YO30 7AG

Kim & Ann Sluter-Robbins   Tel / Fax: 01904 641966

Email: kim.robbins@virgin.net   Web: www.arnothouseyork.co.uk

Map Ref: 22
A19
see Photo opposite

Built in the 1880's, Arnot House is a family run guest house, which stands overlooking Bootham Park, just five minutes walk from York Minster. The four guest bedrooms are furnished in a Victorian style with antiques and paintings, brass or wooden beds. They have colour television, alarm clock, radio, hair dryer and hospitality tray. Breakfast includes cereals, fruit juices, fresh fruit salad, English or vegetarian breakfast or even scrambled eggs with smoked salmon! Car parking available.

B & B from £25pp, C-Cards MC VS, Dinner available, Rooms 1 twin, 3 double, all en-suite, No smoking, Children over 12, No dogs, Closed Xmas & Jan

Grange Lodge 52 Bootham Crescent, Bootham, York YO3 7AH

Jenny Robinson   Tel: 01904 621137

Email: grangeldg@aol.com

Map Ref: 22
A19

The Grange Lodge offers a warm and friendly welcome to all who stay. Accommodation is offered in a choice of seven comfortable and attractively furnished bedrooms, many of which have en-suite facilities. They are all well equipped with television and a tea/coffee making tray. The guest house is conveniently located for all of York's attractions, and it is only ten minutes away from York Minster. This is an ideal place for touring this most beautiful region. Major credit cards are accepted.

B & B £18-£25pp, C-Cards, Dinner from £8, Rooms 3 double, 2 family, 1 twin, 1 single, most en-suite, Children welcome, No dogs, Open all year

Arnot House, Bootham, near York

Curzon Lodge & Stable Cottages 23 Tadcaster Road, Dringhouses, York YO24 1QG

Richard & Wendy Wood   Map Ref: 23
Tel / Fax: 01904 703157   A64, A1036

A charming early 17th century former farmhouse and stables within a city conservation area and overlooking York Racecourse. Once a home of the Terry 'chocolate' family, guests are now invited to share the relaxed atmosphere in ten comfortably furnished, well equipped en-suite rooms, some with four-poster or brass beds. Country antiques, rugs, prints, books, fresh flowers and complimentary sherry in the cosy sitting room lend traditional ambience. Curzon Lodge is a friendly and informal home . Delicious English breakfasts. Enclosed parking in the grounds. Restaurants just one minute's walk. ETC AA RAC 4 Diamonds, Which? Highly Recommended.

B & B £25-£35pp, C-Cards MC VS, Rooms 1 single, 5 double, 3 twin, 1 family, all en-suite,
No smoking, Children welcome, No dogs, Closed Xmas

Fifth Milestone Cottage Hull Road, Dunnington, York YO19 5LR   Map Ref: 24

Karen & Alan Jackson   A1079
Tel: 01904 489361

Fifth Milestone Cottage is situated in the countryside yet close to York city. Three spacious rooms, two with en-suite, one with private bathroom, all have colour television, hospitality tray and central heating. All the rooms are in ground floor converted stables with an antiques theme, you can unwind after a day's business or pleasure in our conservatory or landscape gardens. Private car park to the rear. We are also a convenient base from which to tour 'James Herriot's Yorkshire Dales, Heartbeats North York Moors and the Heritage coast with historic Whitby.

B & B from £16.50pp, Rooms 1 twin, 1 double en-suite, 1 family en-suite,
Restricted smoking, Children & dogs welcome, Open all year

Plumpton Court High Street, Nawton, Helmsley, York YO62 7TT   Map Ref: 25

Chris & Sarah Braithwaite Tel / Fax: 01439 771223   A170
Email: chrisandsarah@plumptoncourt.com Web: www.plumptoncourt.com

Built during the 17th century, Plumpton Court is situated in the village of Nawton, which lies between Helmsley and Kirkbymoorside in the foothills of the North York Moors. Visitors are invited to relax by a real fire in the lounge, before enjoying home cooked local food. The bedrooms are well equipped with en-suite facilities, a ground floor room is also available. There is a private, secure car park and a secluded garden to enjoy. Castle Howard, Nunnington Hall, Rievaulx Abbey, and the historic city of York are within a pleasant drive.

B & B £21-£26pp, Dinner from £14.50, Rooms 4 double, 3 twin, all en-suite,
No smoking, Children over 12, No dogs, Closed Xmas

West View Cottage Pockley, near Helmsley, York YO62 7TE   Map Ref: 25

Mrs Valerie Lack   A170
Tel: 01439 770526 Mobile: 07811 829112

Experience staying in our enchanting 17th century, cruck framed thatched Yorkshire long house, situated in a picturesque village on the edge of the North Yorkshire Moors National Park, just outside Helmsley. For our guests we offer cosy lounge and dining room where we serve breakfast, and evening meal by arrangement. The south facing garden and summerhouse are for your enjoyment and use, there is also private car parking. Ideally situated for touring Moors, Coast, Ryedale, Castle Howard, Rievaulx, North York Moors Railway and York. Excellent choice of pubs and restaurants in the area.

B & B from £25pp, Dinner from £15, Rooms 1 double en-suite, 1 twin private bathroom,
No smoking, Children over 12, No dogs, Open all year

Scotland

The regions of Scotland have through the centuries maintained their differences, the Highlanders, largely Gaelic speaking were mobile cattle farmers, while the Lowlanders, English speaking, were firmly planted arable farmers. The Lowlands is the most densely populated region, an area of impressive castles, palaces and medieval burghs. Edinburgh is a stunning city renowned for its castle, which represents the origin of the city where from the battlements the whole city can be seen. Greyfriars historic church stands not far from the castle, with the most famous memorial of a canine, Greyfriars Bobby, who when his owner died in 1858 followed his master to his grave where he then refused to leave for the next 14 years, becoming a popular tourist attraction. Edinburgh is also renowned for its festival in August where people come from all over the world to join in with the fringe. The architecture of the city is displayed at its best in New Town, the most impressive area of Georgian architecture in the whole of Europe. Glasgow has gradually become the second favourite city to visit in the whole of Britain. The cathedral is the central point of the oldest part of the city, founded by St Mungo, patron saint of Scotland and displaying spectacular pre-Reformation Gothic architecture.

The Southern Uplands consist of the wild western hills of Dumfries and Galloway and the Borders, a region that has experienced turmoil and conflict since Roman times and now a glorious place of rolling hills, bracing moors and fine border towns. Ayrshire is a holiday region with two parts, North Ayrshire with its rugged coastlines and South Ayrshire with its rolling pastures and small villages. However, Ayrshire is most known for being the birthplace of Robert Burns in 1759 at Alloway. Thanks to the Burns National Heritage Park visitors to this area are able to almost walk in his very footsteps with many buildings which were associated with him now turned into museums. Nearby is Culzean Castle, the most visited property belonging to the National Trust of Scotland. It was built by Robert Adams in 1777 and houses a stunning oval staircase and circular saloon. Stirling Castle is also a popular place for tourists and has been the site of many infamous battles including at Stirling Bridge where William Wallace beat the English in 1297 and Robert the Bruce who fought at Bannockburn in 1314.

The boundary between the Lowlands and Highlands is emphasised by The Great Glen, a series of interlinked lochs representing a geological fault zone. The lochs of Linnhe, Lochy, Oich and Ness make up the Caledonian Canal of which Loch Ness is the most famous, being the

Head of Loch Shiel, Glenn Finnan (SCTB)

legendary home of the Loch Ness Monster. The loch sinks down to 800 feet and in its murky depths is said to contain many underground caverns where Nessie resides. The first sighting stretches back to 1871, but the legend was at its most popular in the thirties when the loch became the tourist attraction that it is today. The Highlands and Islands present a back cloth of awesome mountains and majestic coastal scenery. The perfect example of this is Fort William, an excellent site for exploring Ben Nevis, the highest mountain in Britain at 4406 feet with its name meaning 'cloudy mountain'.

The Jacobite Rebellions of the 'Fifteens' and the 'Forty-fives' resulted in the loss of the power of the Clan Chiefs and the accompanying highland way of life. One might associate the Scottish islands with remoteness but these days they are easily accessible; the Western Isles are a 130 mile long chain of islands rich in culture. There are long sandy beaches to enjoy in the height of summer and is an area of unspoilt natural beauty with nature reserves and the famous Standing Stones of Calanais. The Shetland Islands, though renowned for unpredictable weather and scenery can offer either a peaceful holiday or an action packed adventure. The wildlife cannot be surpassed with a variety of migratory birds and regular sightings of whales and dolphins. There are several Neolithic sites in the Scottish Isles but the most impressive is that of Skara Brae on the Orkney Islands, the remains of a Stone Age fishing village preserved from 3000BC.

PLACES TO VISIT

This is a small selection of interesting places to visit. Many more are listed in our annual guide to Museums, Galleries, Historic Houses & Sites (see page 448)

Blair Castle
Pitlochry, Perthshire
A picture of Scottish life from the 16th century to date with fine collections of furniture, paintings, arms and armour, china, embroidery and other treasures. Set in extensive parkland.

Bowhill House and Country Park
Bowhill, Selkirk
Internationally renowned art collection, superb French furniture, silver, porcelain and tapestries. Relics of the Duke of Monmouth, Queen Victoria and Sir Walter Scott.

Gallery of Modern Art
Queen Street, Glasgow
The gallery is on four floors each themed on one of the elements - fire, water, earth and air. Collection of predominantly living artists.

Inveraray Castle
Inveraray, Argyll
Home of the Duke and Duchess of Argyll, built in the late 18th century in French chateau-style, the great hall, armoury and staterooms are open to view.

The National Gallery of Scotland
The Mound, Edinburgh
Outstanding collection of paintings, drawings and prints by the greatest artists from the Renaissance to Post-Impressionism shown alongside the National Collection of Scottish Art.

Scotland

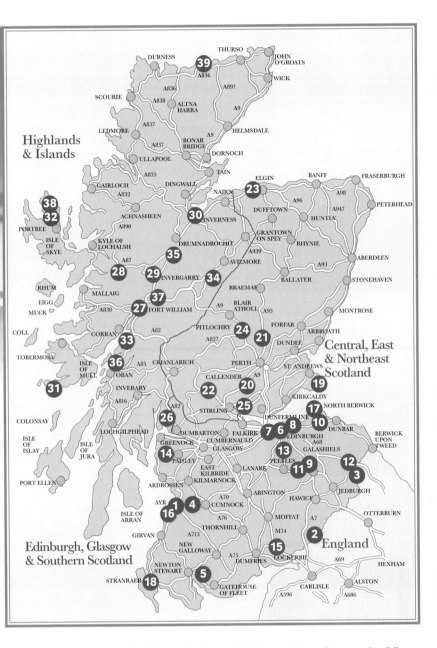

The Blue Map References should be used to locate B & B properties on the pages that follow

The Crescent 26 Bellevue Crescent, Ayr KA7 2DR

Map Ref: 1

Caroline McDonald Tel: 01292 287329 Fax: 01292 286779 Mobile: 07808 778690 A77, A719
Email: carrie@26crescent.freeserve.co.uk Web: www.26crescent.freeserve.co.uk

A warm Scottish welcome awaits you at The Crescent, a Victorian terrace house situated in the heart of Ayr. Built in the height of Victorian splendour it lies amidst an impressive row of imposing terraced houses. Individually styled bedrooms offer the guest every luxury and one room has a four poster bed. Its location allows guest complete peace and quiet and yet close to Ayr's busy shopping centre and seafront. Golf, Culzean Castle and Burns Heritage nearby. 50 minutes drive from Glasgow Airport and 10 minutes drive from Prestwick.

B & B from £25pp, C-Cards MC VS, Rooms 4 double, 2 twin, all en-suite, No smoking,
Children welcome, No dogs, Closed Jan to Feb

Doonbrae 40 Alloway, Ayr KA7 4PQ

Map Ref: 1

Mr & Mrs John Pollok-Morris Tel / Fax: 01292 442511   B7024
Email: doonbrae@aol.com Web: aboutscotland.com

This fine, imposing house built in 1810, stands on the banks of the River Doon, and is surrounded by a two acre garden, in the heart of the famous Burns country. The house is filled with character, the drawing room is half-panelled, oak abounds, there are bay windows with shutters. The attractively presented bedrooms display light, fresh decor, the atmosphere here is happy and relaxed. Doonbrae has been in the family since 1920, it carries much family history. The championship golf courses of Turnberry, Troon and Prestwick are nearby. Evening meals are by arrangement.

B & B from £35pp, Rooms 1 double with private facilities, 1 twin en-suite, No smoking,
Children over 12, No dogs, Closed Xmas & New Year

Dunduff House Dunure, Ayr KA7 4LH

Map Ref: 1

John & Agnes Gemmell Tel: 01292 500225 Fax: 01292 500222   A719
Email: gemmelldunduff@aol.com Web: www.gemmelldunduff.co.uk

Dunduff Farm, is the perfect place for relaxing and unwinding. It is situated just south of Ayr in the coastal village of Dunure. This location is ideal for picturesque walks, for visiting Culzean Castle, Burns Cottage, Turnberry, Galloway Forest, and many more places of interest. The accommodation offered is presented to a high standard. The bedrooms have panoramic, coastal views and they are well equipped. Breakfast has something for all appetites, try our Dunduff Grand to set you up for the day, and our home baked soda bread and locally smoked kippers.

B & B from £20pp, Rooms 1 twin, 2 double, 1 family, all en-suite, No smoking,
Children over 10, No dogs, Closed Nov to Feb

Kirklands Canonbie DG14 0RA

Map Ref: 2

Archie & Elizabeth Findlay Tel: 01387 371769 Fax: 01387 371784   B6357 Just off A7
Email: irvineho@aol.com Web: www.aboutscotland.com/south/kirklands.html

Kirklands is a Georgian House of great charm in a secluded position on the banks of the border Esk river, beside the pretty village of Canobie. The rooms are spacious and elegant with open views to the south. There are pleasant riverside and woodland walks nearby. Kirklands is ideally situated for an over night stop on North/South journeys. The bedrooms have en-suite or private facilities. They are light and sunny with extensive views. Dinner is available. Good pub food available locally. An excellent location for exploring Dumfries and Galloway.

B & B £30-£35pp, C-Cards MC VS, Dinner from £20, Rooms 1 double en-suite, 1 single en-suite,
1 double/twin, No smoking, Children over 8, No dogs in the house, Closed Xmas & Easter

Ruthven House Coldstream TD12 4JU

Elizabeth & Francis Gradidge　Tel: 01890 840771　Fax: 01890 840680
Email: gradidge@gradidge.worldonline.co.uk　Web: www.bordersovernight.co.uk

Map Ref: 3
A1/A698

Ruthven House is a fine Victorian residence which stands just three miles north of the historic town of Coldstream. It is south facing and is set in grounds amidst beautiful countryside with stunning views to the Cheviot Hills. An ideal place to stay as a half way house between the South of England and the North of Scotland. The house offers hospitality and accommodation to fishing, golfing or shooting parties. This is an area of fascinating historical interest, there is much to see and wonderful places to visit.

B & B from £29pp, Dinner from £20, Rooms 3 twin, private bathrooms, No smoking in bedrooms, Children welcome, Dogs by arrangement, Open all year

Low Coylton House Manse Road, Coylton KA6 6LE

Anne & George Hay　Tel / Fax: 01292 570615
Email: xy122@dial.pipex.com

Map Ref: 4
A70

Low Coylton House is a spacious, very comfortable and quiet country house (Old Manse 1820) set in an attractive garden. The well equipped bedrooms offer television and tea/coffee making facilities. They all have a private bathroom. Here is a golfer's paradise, there are several courses nearby, including Ayr, Troon and Turnberry. Ayr is just five miles. Only six miles away are safe, sandy beaches. Visitors may go hill walking which is 15 miles away. Culzean Castle (National Trust) and Glasgow 35 miles. Edinburgh 70 miles.

B & B from £25pp, Rooms 2 twin, 1 double, all private/en-suite, Well behaved children, Well behaved dogs, Closed Xmas & New Year

Auchenskeoch Lodge Dalbeattie DG5 4PG

Christopher & Mary Broom-Smith　Tel / Fax: 01387 780277
Email: brmsmth@aol.com　Web: www.auchenskeochlodge.com

Map Ref: 5
B793

Auchenskeoch Lodge, formerly a Victorian shooting lodge, stands peacefully in 20 acres of grounds which include woodland walks, a croquet lawn, a maze and a little loch. Two spacious bedrooms offer a sitting area, one may be used as an extra bedroom. The house displays charm and character, it is beautifully furnished with antiques, period furniture, books, paintings and sculptures. A large ground floor room is well presented for disabled or elderly guests. A four course candlelit dinner may be enjoyed in house party style, using much home grown produce.

B & B £28-£33pp, C-Cards MC VS, Dinner from £17.50, Rooms 2 double, 1 twin, all en-suite, Restricted smoking, Children over 12, Dogs not in public rooms, Closed Nov to Easter

1 Albert Terrace Churchill, Edinburgh EH10 5EA

Clarissa Notley
Tel: 0131 447 4491

Map Ref: 6
A702

1 Albert Terrace is an elegant private house, which has views to the Pentland Hills. It may be found on a quiet street near to bus routes into the city centre. Alternatively, it is about a 20 minute walk. The bedrooms are en-suite and the double room is attractively furnished and boasts an American four poster bed. Guests have the use of a study/television room and the peace of a beautiful back garden. Excellent restaurants are near at hand and of course Edinburgh offers much of interest in the Arts and History.

B & B £30-£40pp, Rooms 2 double, 1 en-suite, No smoking, Children welcome, No dogs, Closed Xmas

The Avenue Hotel 4 Murrayfield Avenue, Edinburgh EH12 6AX

Adrian & Jackie Hayes
Tel: 0131 346 7270 Fax: 0131 337 9733

Map Ref: 6
A8

Located in a quiet tree lined avenue, is The Avenue Hotel. It is an imposing Victorian villa, situated west of and just minutes from the city centre. It is ideal for both the business traveller and the tourist, as it has easy access to the motorway links to both the north and west of Scotland. All nine individually designed rooms are en-suite with television, direct dial telephone, hair dryer and tea/coffee making facilities. Ample free parking. Full Scottish breakfast is included.

B & B from £30pp, Rooms 2 single, 2 twin, 3 double, 2 family, all en-suite,
Children & dogs welcome, Closed Xmas

Ben Cruachan 17 McDonald Road, Edinburgh EH7 4LX

Nan & Eden Stark Tel: 0131 556 3709
Email: nan@bencruachan.com Web: www.bencruachan.com

Map Ref: 6
A1

A most friendly welcome awaits you here at Ben Cruachan. The house is centrally located, and it offers a high standard of accommodation. It is within walking distance of the Castle, the Royal Mile, Holyrood Palace and Princes Street, one of Britain's most picturesque shopping venues. There are many varied restaurants within a five minute walk. The en-suite rooms are tastefully decorated, have television, central heating and tea/coffee making facilities. An excellent breakfast is served. There is unrestricted street parking.

B & B from £25pp, Rooms 1 twin, 1 double, 1 family, all en-suite, No smoking,
Children over 10, No dogs, Closed Nov to Mar

Ellesmere House 11 Glengyle Terrace, Edinburgh EH3 9LN

Celia & Tommy Leishman Tel: 0131 229 4823 Fax: 0131 229 5285
Email: celia@edinburghbandb.co.uk www.edinburghbandb.co.uk

Map Ref: 6
A702
see Photo opposite

An attractive and comfortable house Centrally located in a residential area and facing south over a park. The castle, Royal Mile (Edinburgh's old historic town) and Princes Street (one of Britain's best shopping venues) are all within very easy reach. Close to International Conference Centre. Rooms are spacious, individually decorated and well equipped with television, heating and tea/coffee making facilities. All rooms are en-suite and a four poster bed is available. There are many varied restaurants and pubs locally.

B & B £28-£38pp, Rooms 1 single, 2 twin, 2 double, 1 family, all en-suite,
Children over 10, Dogs welcome, Open all year

27 Heriot Row Edinburgh EH3 6EN

Andrea & Gene Targett Adams Tel: 0131 225 9474 Fax: 0131 220 1699
Email: t.a@blueyonder.co.uk

Map Ref: 6
Heriot Row

Built in 1804, 27 Heriot Row is in Edinburgh's premier residential street and although only three streets away from Princes Street and the world famous Edinburgh Castle, your stay here will not only be luxurious but it will also be quiet and relaxing. Each room is furnished to the highest deluxe standard with en-suite bath and shower facilities, direct dial telephone, hair dryer, television and tea/coffee making facilities. Your hosts will be delighted to help plan your sightseeing. French, German and Spanish are spoken.

B & B from £45pp, Rooms 1 single, 1 twin, 1 double, all en-suite,
No smoking, Children welcome, No dogs, Open all year

Ellesmere House, Edinburgh

Hopetoun 15 Mayfield Road, Edinburgh EH9 2NG

Rhoda Mitchell Tel: 0131 667 7691 Fax: 0131 466 1691
Email: hopetoun@aol.com Web: http://members.aol.com/hopetoun

Map Ref: 6
City by-pass

Hopetoun is a small, friendly, family run guest house close to Edinburgh university. One and a half miles south of Princes Street, with an excellent bus service into city. Very comfortable accommodation is offered in a completely smoke free environment. Having only three guest bedrooms, and now offering private facilities, the owner prides herself in ensuring personal attention to all guests in a friendly, informal atmosphere. All rooms have central heating, wash basins, colour television and tea/coffee facilities. Parking is also available.

B & B £20-£30pp, C-Cards MC VS, Rooms 1 twin, 1 double, 1 family, 2 en-suite, No smoking, Children welcome, No dogs, Closed Xmas

International Guest House 37 Mayfield Gardens, Edinburgh EH9 2BX

Mrs Niven Tel: 0131 6672511 Fax: 0131 667 1112
Email: intergh@easynet.co.uk Web: www.accommodation-edinburgh.com

Map Ref: 6
A701

Attractive stone built Victorian house situated one and a half miles south of Princes Street on the main A701. Private parking. Luxury bedrooms with en-suite facilities, colour television, telephone and tea/coffee makers. Magnificent views across the extinct volcano of Arthur's Seat. Full Scottish breakfast served on the finest bone china. International has received many accolades for its quality and level of hospitality. A 19th century setting with 21st century facilities. ' In Britain' magazine has rated the International as their 'find' in all Edinburgh. Ground floor room for guests with limited disability.

B & B £20-£45pp, C-Cards MC VS, Rooms 3 single, 2 double, 1 twin, 3 family, all en-suite, Restricted smoking, Children welcome, No dogs, Open all year

The Lodge Hotel 6 Hampton Terrace, West Coates, Edinburgh EH12 5JD

George & Linda Jarron Tel: 0131 3373682 Fax: 0131 3131700
Email: thelodgehotel@btconnect.com Web: www.thelodgehotel.co.uk

Map Ref: 6
A8

The Lodge Hotel is an elegant family run hotel situated one mile from the city centre and all the major tourist attractions. All our en-suite rooms are beautifully furnished throughout, each with many personal touches for our guests' comfort. Relax in the cosy cocktail bar or lounge after a day exploring Scotlands' capital. Our choice of menu offers well prepared dishes with a good selection of wines. Car parking is available with a good bus service from outside the hotel.

B & B £30-£45pp, C-Cards MC VS AE, Dinner from £16.50, Rooms 1 single, 2 twin, 6 double, all en-suite, Restricted smoking, Children welcome, Guide dogs only, Closed most of Dec

Rowan Guest House 13 Glenorchy Terrace, Edinburgh EH9 2DQ

Alan & Angela Vidler Tel / Fax: 0131 667 2463
Email: angela@rowan-house.co.uk Web: www.rowan-house.co.uk

Map Ref: 6
A701, A7

Rowan Guest House is an elegant 19th century Victorian home in a quiet, leafy conservation area. It has free parking and it is only a ten minute bus ride to the centre. The castle, Royal Mile, Holyrood Palace, University, Theatres, restaurants and other amenities are easily reached. The bedrooms are charmingly decorated and have television, tea/coffee and biscuits. A hearty Scottish breakfast is served including porridge and freshly baked scones. Alan and Angela will make every effort to ensure visitors have an enjoyable stay.

B & B £23-£35pp, Rooms 3 single, 2 twin, 3 double, 1 family, some en-suite, Restricted smoking, Children welcome, Dogs by arrangement, Closed Xmas

Spylaw Bank House 2 Spylaw Avenue, Colinton, Edinburgh EH13 0LR

David & Angela Martin Tel: 0131 441 5022

Email: angela@spylawbank.freeserve.co.uk Web: www.spylawbank.freeserve.co.uk

Map Ref: 6
A70

This is an elegant Georigan family home, situated in secluded and spacious grounds three miles from Edinburgh centre. There are luxuriously appointed en-suite rooms with many extra facilities. Guests here have sole use of the original drawing and dining rooms with open fires and period furnishings. Fifteen minutes to city centre with frequent bus services. The house is ideally situated for touring the Borders, Fife, Perthshire and Glasgow. Close to city by-pass and five miles from airport. There is ample parking. Local restaurants and pubs within walking distance.

B & B £25-£35pp, C-Cards MC VS, Rooms 1 twin, 2 double, all en-suite,
No smoking, Children welcome, No dogs, Closed Xmas

The Town House 65 Gilmore Place, Edinburgh EH3 9NU

Susan Virtue Tel: 0131 2291985

Email: susan@thetownhouse.com Web: www.thetownhouse.com

Map Ref: 6
A702, A1
see Photo on page 339

The Town House is an attractive, privately owned Victorian house, located in the city centre. Theatres and restaurants are only a few minutes walk away. The Town House has been fully restored and tastefully decorated, retaining many original architectural features. The bedrooms are individually furnished and decorated, all have en-suite bath or shower and toilet, central heating, radio alarm, colour television, hair dryer and tea/coffee tray. As well as a full Scottish breakfast, there is porridge, kippers and smoked salmon fishcakes. Our private parking is situated to the rear of the house. STB 4 Star.

B & B £28-£38pp, Rooms 1 single, 1 twin, 3 double, all en-suite, No smoking,
Children over 10, No dogs, Closed Xmas

Tudorbank Lodge 18 St John's Road, Corstorphine, Edinburgh EH12 6NY

William & Eleanor Clark Tel: 0131 334 7845 Fax: 0131 334 5386

Email: tudorbank@yahoo.co.uk Web: www.tudorbanklodge.co.uk

Map Ref: 6
A8

This Tudor-style Edinburgh house which, for its architectural interest is listed as an historic listed building, is ideally located for many of the attractions, either leisure or business in this famous city. The Edinburgh festival, fringe and tattoo are all within easy reach. Also, it is near to Murrayfield, which is home to Scottish rugby. Breakfasts here are quite a feature, being freshly cooked to order, with vegetarians being offered ample choice. Tudorbank Lodge is set in private gardens, and there is plenty of parking for guests' cars.

B & B from £25pp, C-Cards MC VS, Rooms 1 single, 2 twin, 2 double, 2 family,
some en-suite, Children welcome, No dogs, Open all year

Craigbrae Kirkliston, Edinburgh EH29 9EL

Michael & Louise Westmacott Tel: 0131 331 1205 Fax: 0131 319 1476

Email: westmacott@compuserve.com Web: www.aboutscotland.com/central/craigbrae

Map Ref: 7
A90

Craigbrae Farmhouse is a family run B&B in an 18th century stone house set in beautiful countryside near Dalmeny village. The bedrooms are pretty and comfortable, each having a basin. The reception rooms have family paintings and country views and you will enjoy a log fire and satellite television in the drawing room. Craigbrae is welcoming and well located in Scotland's central belt for touring and golfing. The Forth Bridge and South Queensferry are closeby with restaurants and pubs, also Dalmeny train station two miles away saves Edinburgh parking hassles.

B & B £25-£30pp, C-Cards MC VS, Rooms 1 double, 2 double/twin, No smoking,
Children welcome, No dogs in house, Closed Xmas

Delta House 16 Carberry Road, Inveresk, Musselburgh, Edinburgh EH21 7TN   Map Ref: 8
Judith & Harper Cuthbert   Tel: 0131 665 2107   Fax: 0131 665 2175   A1, A720
Mobile: 07809 044774   Email: Karmarcla@aol.com

A beautiful Victorian stone built house situated in a quiet conservation village seven miles east of central Edinburgh. It overlooks fields and is close to lovely river walks and the seaside with a harbour. There are buses from door to city, it is near the sports centre with swimming pool and within easy reach of several golf courses. Spacious accommodation with central heating, colour television and tea/coffee making facilities. Two large bathrooms adjacent. Full cooked breakfast included. Parking in a quiet side road or within the large walled garden, by arrangement.

*B & B £18-£25pp, Rooms 3 double, 1 family, 2 en-suite, No smoking,
Children over 7, No dogs, Closed Xmas & New Year*

Ratho Hall 51 Baird Road, Ratho, Edinburgh EH28 8QY   Map Ref: 7
Janet & Freddie Small   Tel: 0131 335 3333   Fax: 0131 335 3035   M8, M9, A8
Email: ratho.hall@btinternet.com   Web: www.countrymansions.com

Ratho Hall, a fine classical Georgian mansion, was built in 1798, it stands proudly in 22 acres of gardens and paddocks, there is a croquet lawn and a tennis court to enjoy. The well proportioned rooms display many interesting period features, an Adam fireplace, ornate plasterwork and lovely mahogany furniture. The bedrooms are delightfully presented, there is a four poster room, they all are equipped with en-suite or private bathrooms. Ratho Hall is 20 minutes from the centre of Edinburgh and five minutes from the International Airport.

*B & B £45-£50pp, C-Cards MC VS, Dinner from £20, Rooms 1 double ensuite, 2 twin/Kingsize,
1 pb, 1 en-suite, No smoking, Children welcome, Dogs by arrangement, Closed Xmas*

Over Langshaw Langshaw, Galashiels TD1 2PE   Map Ref: 9
Sheila Bergius   Tel / Fax: 01896 860244   A7, A68
Email: bergius@overlangshaw.fs.net.co.uk

Escape to the Borders. Enjoy the charm of our lovely farmhouse in this beautiful rural area. Cows and sheep are the mainstay of the farm. Log fires and hearty breakfasts to sustain you on your exploration of the surrounding area. Melrose is delightful and Edinburgh a must. Find Traquair or walk part of the 'Southern Upland Way'. From A7 1 mile north of Galashiels take Langshaw road, and follow the signs. Over Langshaw is the white house on the hill. Two pretty bedrooms with every comfort.

*B & B from £22pp, Rooms 1 double, 1 family, both en-suite, No smoking,
Children welcome, Dogs by arrangement, Open all year*

Abbey Mains Haddington EH41 3SB   Map Ref: 10
David & Joyce Playfair   A1
Tel: 01620 823286   Fax: 01620 826348

This large stone farmhouse, owned by the Playfair family for several generations, stands in the beautiful farmland of East Lothian enjoying superb views of the Lammermuir Hills. Abbey Mains is just two miles from the historic town of Haddington, and 35 minutes from Edinburgh. Within East Lothian there are a number of excellent golf courses, and the beaches are only a ten minute drive away. Other local places of interest include a bird sanctuary, the Scottish Seabird Centre, the Museum of Flight and Glenkinchie, the only Lowland distillery. A superb base for many interests.

*B & B from £40pp, Rooms 2 double, 1 twin, all en-suite, No smoking,
Children welcome, Dogs by arrangement, Closed Xmas & New Year*

The Town House, Edinburgh

Traquair House Innerleithen EH44 6PW

Catherine Maxwell Stuart   Tel: 01896 830323   Fax: 01896 830639
Email: enquiries@traquair.co.uk   Web: www.traquair.co.uk

Map Ref: 11
A72

Visited by 27 kings, this is the oldest inhabited house in Scotland. There is a private chapel, an intriguing old laundry, wonderfully spacious en-suite bedrooms, furnished with antiques. On arrival, guests are invited to a tour of the house, and in the evening, they are welcome to relax in the lower drawing room. There is a maze, seven feet high and a quarter of a mile long! Dinner is available by arrangement, there is also a good local hotel in Innerleithen. This is the place for walking, fishing and relaxation.

B & B from £75pp, C-Cards MC VS, Dinner from £35, Rooms 2 double, both en-suite,
No smoking in bedrooms, Children welcome, Dogs by arrangement, Closed Xmas & New Year

Whitehill Farm Nenthorn, Kelso TD5 7RZ

Betty Smith   Tel / Fax: 01573 470203
Email: besmith@whitehillfarm.freeserve.co.uk   Web: www.whitehillfarm.freeserve.co.uk

Map Ref: 12
A6089

Whitehill is an early Victorian farmhouse on a mixed farm in a wonderful location with marvellous views of the Cheviot Hills. It has been carefully renovated to provide a comfortable, homely, peaceful atmosphere in which to unwind and relax. A sitting room is available to guests with a log fire on cooler evenings. An area with a wealth of history, Abbeys, historic houses, golf, walking, fishing and the coast within easy reach. Edinburgh is approximately one hour away. Four pretty bedrooms with one twin en-suite, and one twin sharing bathroom with two single rooms.

B & B from £22pp, Dinner from £14, Rooms 2 single, 2 twin, 1 en-suite,
Restricted smoking, Children & dogs welcome, Closed Xmas & New Year

Highfield House Kirknewton EH27 8DD

Jill & Hugh Hunter Gordon   Tel: 01506 881489   Fax: 01506 885384
Email: HHunterGordon@compuserve.com   Web: highfield-h.co.uk

Map Ref: 13
A71

Highfield offers its guests a tranquil and comfortable stay. Dating from the 1600's the house is a former Scottish Manse furnished in traditional style and set in its own lovely gardens with room for parking. The en-suite bedrooms are spacious and well appointed. The full Scottish breakfast is taken around the large table in the elegant dining room. Ideally situated for visiting Edinburgh, a train station only five minutes walk. Stirling Castle, Border country, St Andrews and the Trossachs are also all within easy reach.

B & B £25-£30pp, C-Cards MC VS, Rooms 3 double/twin, all en-suite or private bathroom,
No smoking, Children welcome, No dogs, Closed Xmas & New Year

East Lochhead Largs Road, Lochwinnoch PA12 4DX

Janet Anderson   Tel / Fax: 01505 842610
Email: eastlochhead@aol.com   Web: www.eastlochhead.co.uk

Map Ref: 14
A760

Janet Anderson guarantees you a warm welcome at East Lochhead where you will find every home comfort. The one hundred year old farmhouse has spectacular views over Barr Loch and the Renfrewshire hills. You can wander around the landscaped gardens or explore the Paisley/Irvine cycle track which passes close to the house. Janet is an enthusiastic cook and would be delighted to prepare you an evening meal with prior notice. All rooms are en-suite, beautifully furnished and have colour television and tea/coffee making facilities.

B & B from £32pp, C-Cards MC VS AE, Dinner from £18, Rooms 2 double, 1 twin, all en-suite,
Restricted smoking, Children welcome, Dogs by arrangement, Open all year

Knockhill Hoddom, Lockerbie DG11 1AW
Rupert & Yda Morgan   Tel: 01576 300232   Fax: 01576 300818
Email: morganbellows@yahoo.co.uk

Map Ref: 15
M74

Knockhill is a handsome, architecturally impressive Georgian house which lives up to the motto inscribed over the front door through which Robert Burns entered when he went to stay, 'too small for envy, for contempt too great.' This is a friendly house, there are stone stairs, carved oak furniture, rugs and clocks which play their part in creating a comfortable country house ambience. The food is excellent, and there is a variety of nearby restaurants from which to choose. There is golf locally, this is a perfect stop-over en-route to the Highlands.

B & B £25-£30pp, C-Cards MC VS, Dinner from £18, Rooms 2 twin, both with private facilities, Restricted smoking, Children welcome, Dogs by arrangement, Closed Xmas & New Year

The Eisenhower Apartment Culzean Castle, Maybole KA19 8LE
Jonathan & Susan Cardale   Tel: 01655 884455   Fax: 01655 884503
Email: culzean@nts.org.uk   Web: www.culzeancastle.net

Map Ref: 16
A719

Culzean Castle, Robert Adam's final masterpiece, perched on a cliff edge with superb sea views to Arran and Kintyre, is not your average bed and breakfast. The Eisenhower Apartment in the top floor of the castle was given to Eisenhower in 1945 as a thank you from Scotland. It now offers self-contained country house accommodation in six double or twin bedrooms each with private bathroom, a charming round sitting room and the best of Scottish food in an elegant little dining room. Price includes afternoon tea and drinks. House party/corporate bookings only during winter months.

B & B from £100pp, C-Cards MC VS AE, Dinner inc wine £45, Rooms 4 twin, 2 double, all en-suite, No smoking, Children over 10, No dogs, Closed Nov to Mar

The Glebe House Law Road, North Berwick EH39 4PL
Jake & Gwen Scott   Tel / Fax: 01620 892608
Email: J.A.Scott@tesco.net   Web: www.aboutscotland.com/glebe/house

Map Ref: 17
A1, A198

The Glebe House is a beautiful listed Georgian manse built in 1780, it stands in secluded grounds yet it is in the centre of the historic town of North Berwick. The house is elegantly furnished to compliment the many original features. All the well appointed bedrooms are beautifully decorated, one room has a four poster bed. Breakfasts are tasty, potato scones are on the menu! The city of Edinburgh is half an hour away, the sea is only a two minute walk from the house, and there are 18 golf courses within easy reach.

B & B £30-£40pp, Rooms 2 double, 1 twin, all en-suite, Restricted smoking, Children welcome, Dogs not in house, Closed Xmas & New Year

Chlenry Farmhouse Castle Kennedy, Stranraer DG9 8SL
Ginny Wolseley Brinton   Tel: 01776 705316   Fax: 01776 889488
Mobile: 07718 049910   Email: WolseleyBrinton@aol.com

Map Ref: 18
A75, A77

Situated in a private Glen in the heart of Galloway, Chlenry Farmhouse welcomes visitors to enjoy warm hospitality. Both comfortable bedrooms offer tea trays with delicious biscuits, fresh fruit and flowers. A delicious four course dinner with wine is available, or just a simple walkers' supper and picnic lunches may suit. Guests are welcome to wander in the delightful garden, where they may play croquet or simply sit and relax. Delightful golf courses, beautiful gardens and spectacular walks are all within easy reach, and with the beach nearby this is a most peaceful place to stay.

B & B from £27.50pp, Dinner from £23.50, Rooms 1 double, 1 twin, both with private bathroom, Restricted smoking, Children welcome, Dogs in car or kennel, Closed Xmas & New Year

Dunearn House, Auchterarder

Beaumont Lodge Guest House 43 Pittenweem Road, Anstruther KY10 3DT

Julia Anderson   Tel / Fax: 01333 310315   Map Ref: 19
Email: reservations@beau-lodge.demon.co.uk   Web: www.beaumontlodge.co.uk   A917

Beaumont Lodge Guest House is an immaculately maintained home, situated just a two minute walk from the shoreline and Anstruther's nine hole golf course. St Andrews is only nine miles away. This quiet family run guest house offers affordable excellence and guests here are assured of a warm hospitality. The en-suite rooms are spacious, tastefully decorated and have many thoughtful extras which you would only expect to find in the best of hotels. Your host is a keen and accomplished cook. No children. Private parking.

B & B from £25pp, C-Cards MC VS, Dinner from £15, Rooms 2 twin, 2 double, all en-suite,
No smoking, Children over 4, No dogs, Open all year

The Spindrift Pittenweem Road, Anstruther KY10 3DT

Map Ref: 19
Ken & Christine Lawson Tel / Fax: 01333 310573   A917
Email: info@thespindrift.co.uk Web: www.thespindrift.co.uk

The Spindrift is an imposing, stone-built Victorian home. Many original internal features have been carefully restored. Elegantly furnished public rooms. The bedrooms are generously proportioned, individually and tastefully furnished with en-suite bathroom, colour television, direct dial telephone, hospitality tray and a host of other extras to help make your stay a pleasant one. The cuisine is freshly prepared using the best of local produce with a variety of fine wines to complement your meal. The area boasts a wide variety of activities and interests, including golf, boat trips and surfing.

B & B £26.50-£31pp, C-Cards MC VS, Dinner from £13.50, Rooms 4 double, 4 twin, all en-suite,
No smoking, Children over 9, Dogs by arrangement, Closed Xmas

Dunearn House High Street, Auchterarder PH3 1DB

Map Ref: 20
June & Gerrard Elrick Tel: 01764 664774   Fax: 01764 663242   A9
Email: dunearnhouse@talk21.co.uk   *see Photo opposite*

'The Perthshire Experience', hidden behind the High Street you will find a Victorian country house hotel. Quiet and peaceful, sympathetically restored throughout, with spectacular views and a wide variety of outdoor pursuits. Gleneagles and many other stunning golf courses are on the doorstep. All rooms en-suite with colour television, hair dryer, telephone and courtesy tray. Fully licensed with restaurant, cosy lounge and bar. We are well used to caring for your needs and we are able to provide a relaxing environment for you to unwind in.

B & B from £35pp, C-Cards MC VS, Dinner from £7, Rooms 2 single, 1 twin, 3 double, 1 family,
all en-suite, No smoking in bedrooms, Children welcome, No dogs, Open all year

Marlee House Kinloch, Blairgowrie PH10 6SD

Map Ref: 21
Kenneth & Nicolette Lumsden   A923
Tel: 01250 884216

Marlee House is a charming and very pretty Perthshire manor house which stands in extensive gardens and grounds by Marlee Loch, a 170 acre private loch with wonderful bird and fish life. Warm hospitality is extended to guests who can relax in an informal country house atmosphere, with log fires on chilly days. The bedrooms are charming and extremely comfortable, they have televisions and en-suite bathrooms. There are excellent restaurants nearby, this is an ideal base for golf, fishing and skiing, or just for relaxing in comfortable and elegant surroundings.

B & B £35-£45pp, Rooms 1 double, 1 twin, both en-suite, Restricted smoking,
Children over 12, Dogs by arrangement, Closed Xmas & New Year

Leny House   Leny Estate, Callander FK17 8HA

Mrs F Roebuck   Tel / Fax: 01877 331078

Email: res@lenyestate.com   Web: www.lenyestate.com

Map Ref: 22
A84

Leny House is a spacious country mansion steeped in history, dating back to 1513, originally built as a fortalice it was prominent in activities during the Jacobite rebellion, when it was used for arms storage and clandestine meetings. The luxury en-suite bedrooms have four poster beds, antiques and tapestries. There is a grand piano to compliment these baronial surroundings, and open fires throughout the house. There is a pub, a restaurant and ceilidh music to enjoy on the estate. It is a tranquil retreat in which to unwind. Excellent self catering also available.

B & B £50-£55pp, C-Cards MC VS, Dinner from £8, Rooms 3 double, 1 twin, all en-suite, No smoking, Children over 12, No dogs, Closed Nov to Mar

Brough House   Milton Brodie, Forres IV36 2UA

Mrs Rosemary Lawson

Tel / Fax: 01343 850617   Mobile: 07740 681816

Map Ref: 23
A96

Situated in the beautiful Scottish countryside, only 40 minutes from Inverness, this superbly furnished and comfortable home offers tranquility and seclusion. Rosemary's cooking is lovely, based on traditional Scottish recipes with local game, fish from the quayside of Lossiemouth and fruit and vegetables from the garden. It is within east reach of Brodie and Cawdor Castles, The Malt Whisky Trail and the beautiful Spey Valley.

B & B from £30pp, Dinner from £15, Rooms 1 double, 2 twin, all en-suite, Restricted smoking, Children welcome, No dogs, Closed Xmas & New Year

Easter Dunfallandy Country House   Logierait Road, Pitlochry PH16 5NA

Sue Mathieson   Tel: 01796 474128   Mobile: 07990 524219

Email: sue@dunfallandy.co.uk   Web: www.dunfallandy.co.uk

Map Ref: 24
A9, A924

Easter Dunfallandy is a fine Victorian house which enjoys an elevated position commanding wonderful views over Highland Perthshire. It is an oasis of peace and quiet in some of the most spectacular scenery in Scotland, just two miles south of Pitlochry. All three bedrooms have en-suite bath or shower rooms with complimentary toiletries, they are tastefully appointed to reflect the unique character of the house. A gourmet Scottish breakfast is offered to include porridge, Scottish smoked salmon and creamy scrambled eggs. A perfect base from which to explore the Central Highlands.

B & B £25-£29pp, C-Cards MC VS, Dinner from £20, Rooms 1 double, 2 twin, all en-suite, No smoking, Children over 8, No dogs, Open all year

Westbourne House B & B   10 Dollar Road, Tillicoultry, Stirling FK13 6PA

Jane & Adrian O'Dell   Tel: 01259 750314   Fax: 01259 750642

Email: odellwestbourne@compuserve.com   Web: www.westbournehouse.co.uk

Map Ref: 25
A91

A fascinating Victorian mill owner's mansion set within wooded grounds, beneath the Ochil Hills. The atmosphere at Westbourne is warm and friendly with log fires on cool evenings and a croquet lawn. Off the road parking is available. Located amid glorious countryside in central Scotland, with The Trossachs, Loch Lomond, Edinburgh and Glasgow just one hour away. Motorway connections are within 15 miles. A wide range of activities is available nearby: sight seeing in historic Stirling, numerous golf courses, fishing and hill walking in Braveheart country.

B & B from £22pp, Rooms 2 double en-suite, 1 family, No smoking, Children welcome, Dogs by arrangement, Closed Xmas & New Year

Kirkton House Darleith Road, Cardross, Dumbarton G82 5EZ

Stewart & Gillian Macdonald Tel: 01389 841951 Fax: 01389 841868
Email: GBBB@kirktonhouse.co.uk Web: www.kirktonhouse.co.uk

Map Ref: 26
A814

Kirkton House is a 18/19th century converted farmstead, in a tranquil country setting, commanding panoramic views of the Clyde. Loch Lomond, Glasgow city or Airport and the main West Highland routes are easily accessible. The guest lounge and dining areas have original stone walls. Rooms have full hotel amenities, bath/shower, television, telephone, tea/coffee tray, desk and hair dryer. Wines, draught beer and spirits available. Dine by oil lamplight. Extensive daily menu for home cooked dinners. Guest comment, 'One of the finest places we have stayed.'

B & B from £30.50pp, C-Cards MC VS AE DC, Dinner from £16.25, Rooms 2 twin, 4 family, all en-suite, Restricted smoking, Children & dogs welcome, Closed Dec to Jan

Ashburn House Achintore Road, Fort William PH33 6RQ

Alexandra Henderson Tel: 01397 706000 Fax: 01397 702024
Email: ashburn.house@tinyworld.co.uk Web: www.highland5star.co.uk

Map Ref: 27
A82

Overlooking Loch Linnhe, Ashburne is a most relaxing Bed and breakfast. The Highland owners pay every attention to detail but do not impose on your privacy, even separate tables in the Victorian corniced breakfast room. The house has achieved all the highest accolades and commendations. All the bedrooms are en-suite with 6 feet wide super king beds, centrally heated and with television. There is free off road parking. The house has a full fire certificate. An excellent centre to tour the magical Highlands and Skye. Discount for week booking. Colour brochure available.

B & B £30-£40pp, C-Cards MC VS, Rooms 3 single, 4 double, all en-suite, No smoking, Children welcome, No dogs, Closed Nov to Feb

Duich House Letterfearn, Glenshiel IV40 8HS

Anne Kempthorne Tel / Fax: 01599 555259
Email: duich@cwcom.net Web: www.milford.co.uk/go/duich.html

Map Ref: 28
A87

Duich House built in 1830, is a well presented, finely furnished home which commands spectacular views across Loch Duich to the mountains of Kintail. Wildlife abounds, one may see seals and otters pine marten and deer, maybe a dolphin, and the birdlife is fascinating. There are two beautifully appointed bedrooms, with some thoughtful little extras, spring water, fresh fruit and biscuits. Breakfasts here are serious, and dinners are equally impressive with seafood, and Scottish beef being delicious specialities. This is certainly a true taste of Scotland. Wonderful walking everywhere.

B & B £34-£40pp, Dinner from £30, Rooms 2 double with private facilities, No smoking, Children over 16, No dogs, Closed Oct to Mar

Craigard House Invergarry PH35 4HG

Robert & Barbara Withers Tel / Fax: 01809 501258
Email: bob@craigard.saltire.org Web: www.craigard.saltire.org

Map Ref: 29
A87

Set in the breathtaking splendour of the Highlands, Craigard, a large country house on the western outskirts of the village of Invergarry is the perfect base for a relaxing and varied holiday. Four of the well furnished bedrooms have a washbasin and tea/coffee making facilities. Guests can enjoy a quiet drink in the relaxed atmosphere of the residents' lounge and on cooler evenings pull up to a roaring log fire. There is television in all bedrooms. The magnificent scenery surrounding Craigard makes it an ideal point for touring.

B & B from £18pp, C-Cards MC VS, Dinner from £15, Rooms 1 single, 5 double, 1 twin, shower and bathroom, No smoking, Children over 12, No dogs, Open all year

Skiary Loch Hourn, Invergarry PH35 4HD

John & Christina Everett
Tel: 01809 511214

Map Ref: 29
A87

Enjoying a location away from the outside world, Skiary, originally a fisherman's cottage offers the traveller to the wilds of Loch Hourn, a cosy, safe haven, heated by log fires and lit by oil lamps. The backdrop to this tiny little pine lined cottage are mountains and waterfalls inhabited by unhurried otters and deer. The greenhouse dining room on the loch side is the perfect venue to savour delicious dinners prepared by enthusiastic hosts who know how to appeal to all appetites. John provides a ferry service across the loch. No access by road, collected by boat. Accommodation is full board.

Dinner B & B £80pp, Rooms 3 twin (1 shared bathroom), Restricted smoking,
No children, Dogs by arrangement, Closed Oct to Mar

Ballindarroch Aldourie, Inverness IV2 6EL

Alison Parsons & Philip Alvy Tel: 01463 751348 Fax: 01463 751372
Email: ali.phil@ntlworld.com www.milford.co.uk/go/ballindarroch.html

Map Ref: 30
B862
see Photo opposite

Originally built as a shooting lodge circa 1850, Ballindarroch stands in ten acres of woodland gardens above the Caledonian Canal. The house offers peace and relaxation, and the animals here, including sheep, a pony, dogs and a cat, help to create a family atmosphere. Views of the garden and surrounding woodland may be enjoyed from the very spacious bedrooms. A generous breakfast may include natural smoked kippers, finnan haddock and white pudding. As well as numerous golf courses there are many wonderful local attractions for those seeking beauty and history.

B & B £20-£30pp, Rooms 1 family, 1 double, 1 twin, 1 single, 2 private bathrooms,
Restricted smoking, Children & dogs welcome, Open all year

Red Bay Cottage Deargphort, Fionnphort, Isle of Mull PA66 6BP

John & Eleanor Wagstaff
Tel: 01681 700396

Map Ref: 31
A849

Red Bay Cottage is a modern house built on the shoreline of the south west coast of Mull. John and Eleanor have built up a very good reputation for the quality of food in their adjoining restaurant and guests can eat in the pleasant dining room, overlooking Iona Sound and the white sands of Iona. An ideal base for touring Mull, Iona and the Treshnish Isles. Eleanor is a qualified practising silversmith so why not enjoy a winter break. Send for details of residential silversmithing courses.

B & B from £16.50pp, Dinner from £7.50, Rooms 2 twin, 1 double, Restricted smoking,
Children welcome, Dogs by arrangement, Open all year

Lyndale House Edinbane, Isle of Skye IV51 9PX

Linda & Marcus Ridsdill-Smith Tel: 01470 582329
Email: linda@lyndale.free-online.co.uk

Map Ref: 32
A850
see Photo on page 348

This wonderfully elegant 300 year old house enjoys a secluded position as it may be found at the end of a long wooded driveway with views across the sea. After careful restoration it is now a beautiful family home offering total tranquility and seclusion, but with all the benefits of modern comforts, the bedrooms are luxuriously appointed, they have fresh flowers, bathrobes and there is a heated shower room floor. The sunsets here are unforgettable, and Lyndale House is ideally placed for exploring the rest of the island. Excellent meals are available locally.

B & B from £40pp, Rooms 1 double en-suite, 1 twin with private bathroom, No smoking,
Children welcome, Dogs by arrangement, Closed Xmas & New Year

Ballindarroch, Aldourie, Inverness

Lyndale House, Edinbane, Isle of Skye

Ardsheal Home Farm Kentallen, Duror in Appin PA38 4BZ

Flavia MacArthur
Tel / Fax: 01631 740229

Map Ref: 33
A828

Ardsheal Home Farm is a charming Scottish hill farm of 1,000 acres, surrounded by breath taking views. It may be found on the shores of Loch Linnhe, overlooking the Morven Hills. A warm welcome is assured from the friendly hosts here. There are three attractive bedrooms, they are comfortable and well furnished - with electric blankets and tea/coffee making facilities. The farm is convenient for touring the inner Isles. There is a private one mile beach with spectacular sunsets.

B & B £18-£19pp, Dinner from £13.50, Rooms 1 twin, 1 double, 1 private bathroom,
No smoking, Children welcome, Guide dogs only, Closed Oct to Mar

Ardsheal House Kentallen of Appin PA38 4BX

Mr & Mrs Neil Sutherland   Tel: 01631 740227   Fax: 01631 740342
Email: info@ardsheal.co.uk   Web: www.ardsheal.co.uk

Map Ref: 33
A828

Ardsheal House was built in the 16th century, it was later destroyed by fire and rebuilt around 1760. To the north is Ben nevis, north west, the Isle of Skye, to the south is Oban and the island of Mull. Steeped in history, the accommodation is luxurious with fabulous views over Loch Linnhe and the mountains of Morven. The food at Ardsheal is innovative country house cooking using fresh produce from the house garden and home baked bread. After exploring the 800 acre estate, guests can enjoy a stroll to the loch side.

B & B from £50pp, C-Cards MC VS AE, Dinner from £27, Rooms 1 single, 5 double, 1 twin,
1 family, all en-suite, Restricted smoking, Children & dogs welcome, Closed Xmas

Balcraggan House Feshiebridge, Kincraig PH21 1NG

Helen Gillies
Tel: 01540 651488

Map Ref: 34
A9, B970

Balcraggan House is situated in the foothills of Glenfeshie, where pine marten, buzzard, osprey, roe deer and red squirrel abound, with a badger sett nearby. Miles of cycle routes and walks go straight from the front door, or use your car to explore the magnificent Highlands. The bedrooms are generously sized and they are tastefully furnished. There are log and peat fires in the drawing and dining rooms, the perfect place to relax after a day exploring this wonderful area.

B & B from £25pp, Dinner from £15, Rooms 1 twin, 1 double, both en-suite,
No smoking, Children over 10, No dogs, Open all year

Foyers Bay House Lower Foyers, Loch Ness

Mr & Mrs O E Panciroli   Tel: 01456 486624   Fax: 01456 486337
Email: panciroli@foyersbay.freeserve.co.uk   Web: www.foyersbay.freeserve.co.uk

Map Ref: 35
A82, A9

In its own magnificent grounds of wooded pine slopes, abundant rhododendrons and apple orchard with fabulous view of Loch Ness, nestles the splendid Victorian villa of Foyers Bay House. The grounds are set amid beautiful forest, nature trails and adjoin the famous Falls of Foyers. The villa is tastefully refurbished. Rooms have telephone, television and en-suite bath or shower room, tea/coffee making facilities, fresh fruit and bath/shower gel, compliments of your hosts Otto & Carol Panciroli. The guest house has a table licence.

B & B from £23pp, C-Cards MC VS AE, Dinner from £10.50, Rooms 3 double, 2 twin,
No smoking in bedrooms, Children welcome, No dogs, Open all year

Hawthorn 5 Keil Crofts, Benderloch, Oban PA37 1QS

Will & June Currie Tel: 01631 720452 Fax: 01631 720240

Email: junecurrie@hotmail.com Web: www.hawthorncottages.co.uk

Map Ref: 36
A828

A warm welcome awaits you on our family run croft where highland cattle are bred and graze. Our comfortable bungalow is furnished to a high standard with supreme en-suite bedrooms with a small lounge area attractively colour co-ordinated with many extras, television, tea/coffee facilities. Peacefully located 15 minutes from Oban, gateway to the Highlands. An ideal base for touring the West Coast. Daily sailings to Mull and Iona. Wonderful for hill walking, fishing, sailing, pony trekking, Sea Life Centre and Rare Breeds Park nearby. Dinner available, delicious home cooking is a speciality.

B & B £18-£21pp, C-Cards MC VS, Dinner from £10, Rooms 1 twin, 1 double, 1 family, all en-suite, Restricted smoking, Children over 3, No dogs, Open all year

Invergloy House Spean Bridge PH34 4DY

Mrs Margaret Cairns Tel: 01397 712681

Email: cairns@invergloy-house.co.uk Web: www.invergloy-house.co.uk

Map Ref: 37
A82

Invergloy House welcomes non smokers. This is a converted coach house and stables set in 50 acres of attractive wooded grounds. Guests have their own large sitting room with magnificent views over Loch Lochy and mountains. All rooms are tastefully and traditionally furnished. Bedrooms have en-suite facilities. The house lies five and a half miles north of Spean Bridge on the main road to Inverness and Island of Skye. Overlooking Loch Lochy where free fishing is available from a private shingle beach, reached by footpath. SAE for details.

B & B £23-£25pp, Rooms 3 twin, all en-suite, No smoking, Children over 8, No dogs, Open all year

Glenview Inn & Restaurant Culnacnoc, Staffin IV51 9JH

Paul & Cathie Booth Tel: 01470 562248 Fax: 01470 562211

Email: enquiries@glenview-skye.co.uk Web: www.glenview-skye.co.uk

Map Ref: 38
A855

This is a charming inn, and it may be found nestling between the mountains and sea. It is ideally situated for exploring the magnificent scenery of North Skye. We have pretty country style bedrooms with private facilities and tea/coffee making trays. The cosy lounge has a television and an open peat fire. A lovely place to relax after supper in our restaurant which is fully licensed and is much acclaimed. It offers the best of fresh Skye seafood, as well as traditional, ethnic and vegetarian specialities.

B & B £20-£30pp, C-Cards MC VS, Dinner from £12.95, Rooms 1 twin, 3 double, 1 family, all en-suite, Restricted smoking, Children & dogs welcome, Closed Nov to Feb

Catalina Aultivullin, Strathy Point, Sutherland KW14 7RY

Jane & Peter Salisbury Tel: 01641 541395 Fax: 0870 124 7960

Email: jane@catalina72.freeserve.co.uk

Map Ref: 39
A836

The Good Guide to Britain publishes us as 'an outstanding place to stay'. The Automobile Association said we were 'unique'. Our two guests (maximum) have their own private suite comprising a twin bedroom, shower room/wc, lounge and dining room. Total privacy and peace assured. Situated between John O'Groats and Cape Wrath - an ideal base to explore the whole of the Far North. A fabulous walking area. Our menu: Scottish venison, Scottish salmon, chicken in white wine sauce plus vegetarian and other dishes. AA 4 Diamonds, Which? Rosette winner 1998.

B & B from £17pp, Dinner from £9, Rooms 1 en-suite twin, No smoking, No children or dogs, Open all year

Wales

A proud and independent nation where the Welsh language is the first language of many, particularly in the north and west. There is a strong tradition here of choral singing, and the Welsh love of music in all its forms. Literature and poetry is also manifest in the large number of eisteddfods. The decline in the Welsh mining industry has now resulted in the most important industry being tourism.

The land bordering on England, known as the Marches and formed by the gorge of the lower Wye gives a glorious introduction to South Wales. The coastline improves as you proceed westwards with the Gower Peninsular jutting fourteen miles out into Carmarthen Bay,

declared in 1956 the first official Area of Outstanding Beauty, and Pembrokeshire, an old favourite destination of seaside holiday makers. Mid Wales represents glorious unspoilt border country with little traffic and was described in the Times as "one of the last wildernesses of Britain". It is relatively unknown to the holiday visitor offers the glorious Brecon Beacons National Park, the Black Mountains, a wild ridge to the west rising to 2,630 feet at Fan Brycheiniog, and the Cambrian Mountains. North Wales contains the Snowdonia National Park including the highest mountains in England and Wales. The north coast boasts the 'Queen of the Welsh Resorts', Llandudno, gloriously situated between the

Lake Vyrnwy, Powys, Mid-Wales (WTB)

Cwmystwyth, Ceredigion, Mid-Wales (WTB)

Great Orme and the Little Orme. The town retains much of its Victorian charm

The Isle of Anglesey is a delight, with fine beaches and a remarkable number of neolithic remains. The Menai Strait between the island and the mainland is spanned by Telford's suspension bridge.

Wales is a country of spectacular sights, of magnificent National Parks and wonderful mountain scenery with well over a hundred medieval castles. In 1284 at Caernarfon Castle, Edward I presented his son to the Welsh people as Prince of Wales. HRH Prince Charles was similarly invested in 1969.

PLACES TO VISIT

This is a small selection of interesting places to visit. Many more are listed in our annual guide to Museums, Galleries, Historic Houses & Sites (see page 448)

Caernarfon Castle
Caernarfon
The castle was begun by Edward I in 1283, and is the most famous and one of the most impressive castles in Wales. Prince Charles was invested here in 1969.

Glynn Vivian Art Gallery
Swansea
Swansea porcelain and pottery, works by Welsh and UK artists, glass including time paperweights, European and Oriental china.

National Museum and Gallery
Cardiff
Founded in 1907 to preserve Welsh heritage, the museum's collections include works of major impressionists, national sciences, archaeology and geology.

Powis Castle and Garden
Welshpool
The medieval castle contains one of the finest collections of paintings and furniture in Wales. The garden is famous for its clipped yew trees and herbaceous borders.

St Davids Bishop's Palace and Cathedral
St Davids, Dyfed
The 12th to 14th century cathedral is one of Britain's finest. Nearby is the 14th century Bishop's Palace, unoccupied for the past 300 years.

Wales

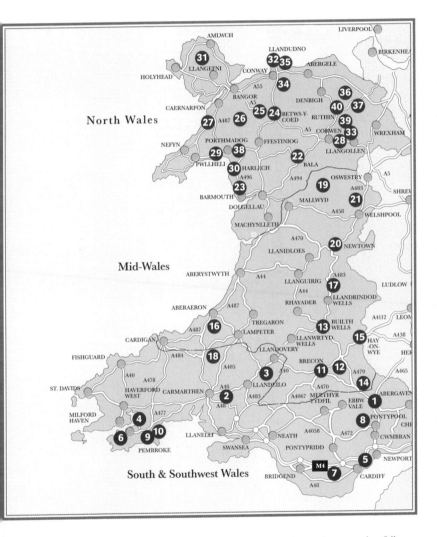

The Blue Map References should be used to locate B & B properties on the pages that follow

Mount Pleasant Farm, Llanwrda

The Wenallt Abergavenny NP7 0HP

B L Harris Tel / Fax: 01873 830694
Email: wenallt@ukworld.net Web: www.ukworld.net.wenallt

Map Ref: 1
A465

This historic 15th century longhouse, Wenallt, nestles in the rolling hills of the Brecon Beacons. It has been described by some guests as the perfect peace and tranquillity. The small quiet hotel offers comfort, personal service and excellent home cooking. This is the ideal location for enjoying country walks, breathtaking views or for just relaxing on the spacious lawns. If you are an artist or a photographer, then this is the ideal base with its panoramic views. The bedrooms are en-suite. Inglenook log fires to warm in Winter. Restaurant licensed.

B & B from £19.50pp, Dinner from £12, Rooms 4 single, 1 twin, 5 double, 1 family, all en-suite, Restricted smoking, Children welcome, Dogs by arrangement, Open all year

Llanwenarth House Gofilon, Abergavenny NP7 9SF

Mrs A R Weatherill Tel: 01873 830289 Fax: 01873 832199
Email: amanda.bbdq@welsh-hotel.co.uk Web: www.welsh-hotel.co.uk

Map Ref: 1
A465

King Charles is said to have kept reserve horses and arms at this beautiful 16th century Welsh manor house, now home to the Weatherill family who welcome guests to enjoy warm hospitality in comfortable, beautifully furnished rooms. The spacious, generously equipped, centrally heated bedrooms enjoy countryside and mountain views, they have en-suite bath or shower rooms. Dinner is served by candlelight, Amanda is a Cordon Bleu cook, she makes full use of local game and fish, home produced meat, poultry and garden vegetables. The house overlooks the Usk Valley and is three miles from Abergavenny.

B & B £42-£45pp, Dinner from £25, Rooms 4 double, 1 twin, all en-suite, Restricted smoking, Children over 8, Dogs by arrangement, Closed Xmas & Feb

Plas Alltyferin Pontargothi, Nantgaredig, Carmarthen SA32 7PF

Charlotte & Gerard Dent Tel: 01267 290662 Fax: 01267 290919
Email: dent@altyferin.fsnet.co.uk

Map Ref: 2
A40

Plas Alltyferin is a classic Georgian country house lying in the hills above the beautiful Towy Valley, overlooking a Norman hillfort, the River Cothi, famous for salmon and sea trout, and its own private cricket pitch. There are two spacious twin bedrooms, each with private bathroom and stunning views, for guests who are welcomed as friends of the family. Antique furniture, log fires and excellent local pubs and restaurants. Marvellous touring country for castles, beaches and Welsh speaking Wales. Total peace but under four hours from London.

B & B from £25pp, Rooms 1 twin en-suite, 1 twin private bathroom, Children over 12, Dogs by arrangement, Closed Xmas & New Year

Mount Pleasant Farm Llanwrda SA19 8AN

Sue & Nick Thompson
Tel / Fax: 01550 777537 Mobile: 07770 993588

Map Ref: 3
A40, A482
see Photo opposite

If you want to completely relax, come to Mount Pleasant Farm, a 200 year old farmhouse with its amazing views and large comfortable beds in beautifully furnished bedrooms. Sue, an interior decorator, loves cooking and is happy to share her recipes, so bring that notebook! She uses mainly organic and local produce which are particularly noticeable in her vegetarian dishes. There are many lovely walks, and the house is within half an hour from Aberglasney Gardens and the Botanical Gardens of Wales. The seaside and coastal walks are only an hour away.

B & B from £25pp, Dinner from £12.50, Rooms 1 single, 2 double/twin, all en-suite, No smoking, Children over 12, No dogs, Closed Xmas

The Peacock Guest House Hoarstone, Martletwy, Narberth SA67 8AZ   Map Ref: 4

Mrs R E Mooney   Tel / Fax: 01834 891707   A40, A477, A4075
Email: ros@peacockguesthouse.co.uk   Web: www.peacockguesthouse.co.uk

Visitors here can be assured of peaceful nights and warm hospitality. This attractive house is set in the beautiful Pembrokeshire Coast National Park. The gardens here in a tree lined glade are home to some peacocks, there are tables and chairs where guests are welcome to relax and enjoy the gentle atmosphere. The individually styled bedrooms are named and with lovely views. Large choice of breakfasts. It is possible to enjoy picnics, packed lunches and dinners by arrangement. The house is ideally placed for exploring the beauty of Pembrokeshire. Fishing, horse riding, bike hike available.

B & B £20-£25pp, C-Cards MC VS, Dinner available, Rooms 1 double en-suite,
1 twin with private bathroom, Restricted Smoking, Children over 12, No dogs, Closed Oct to Mar

West Usk Lighthouse St Brides, Wentloog, Newport NP1 9SF   Map Ref: 5

Frank & Danielle Sheahan   Tel: 01633 810126/815860   B4239, M4 J28
Email: lighthouse1@tesco.net   Web: www.westusklighthouse.co.uk

Grade II listed, this is a real lighthouse built in 1821 to a unique design. Rooms are wedge shaped within a circular structure. The hall is slate bedded and leads to a stone spiral staircase and the collecting well! Wonderful views from the roof patio. All the bedrooms are en-suite and have been individually furnished to include a king size waterbed and a four poster bed. Guests can try the flotation tank for deep relaxation also other therapies. Most amenities are close by and the area is full of interest. Rolls Royce drive to local restaurant.

B & B from £40pp, C-Cards MC VS AE DC, Rooms 3 double en-suite, No smoking,
Children welcome, Dogs by arrangement, Open all year

Cresswell House Cresswell Quay, Pembroke SA68 0TE   Map Ref: 6

Philip Wight   Tel: 01646 651435   A4075
Email: phil@cresswellhouse.co.uk   Web: www.cresswellhouse.co.uk

In former times this Georgian house was home to the Quay Master on the Cleodale Estuary. Sitting snugly on the estuary bank, all the rooms enjoy views to the river abundant with interesting birdlife. Guests here are treated to imaginative and memorable food at both breakfast and dinner, or if they wish, there is a fine old fashioned inn just 50 yards away. Cresswell House is situated within an eight mile radius of Tenby, Pembroke, historic castles and the coastal path.

B & B £25-£30pp, Dinner from £25, Rooms 2 double, 1 twin, all en-suite, Restricted smoking,
Children over 7, No dogs, Closed Xmas & New Year

Llanerch Vineyard Hensol, Pendoylan, Cardiff CF72 8JU   Map Ref: 7

Peter & Diana Andrews   Tel: 01443 225877   Fax: 01443 225546   M4 J34
Email: enquiries@llanerch-vineyard.co.uk   Web: www.llanerch-vineyard.co.uk

Recently featured on the BBC, television 'Holidays Out' programme, this beautifully converted and fully modernised farmhouse overlooks the six acre vineyard and the Vale of Glamorgan's rich farmland. All rooms are en-suite with central heating, tea-making facilities and televisions. Guests can tour the vineyard and winery, taste the award winning wines and follow trails through acres of protected farm woodland and lakes. Ideal location for touring South Wales, fifteen minutes from Cardiff. Ample parking. Golf, fishing and riding nearby. One of Wales 'Great Little Places.' A non-smoking establishment.

B & B from £25pp, C-Cards MC VS, Rooms 2 twin, 1 double, all en-suite,
self contained double suite, No smoking, Children over 8, No dogs, Closed Xmas & New Year

Ty'r Ywen Farm Lasgarn Lane, Mamhilad, via Trevethin, Pontypool NP4 8TT

Map Ref: 8
A472

Susan Armitage Tel / Fax: 01495 785200
Email: susan.armitage@virgin.net http://freespace.virgin.net/susan.armitage/webpage3.htm

Ty'r Ywen Farm is a remote 16th century Welsh longhouse. It may be found high on the Gwent Ridgeway in the Brecon Beacons National Park. It has breathtaking views down the Usk Valley and across the Bristol Channel. The house retains many original features, there are inglenook fireplaces, and comfortable bedrooms. One room has a four poster bed, it also has its own jacuzzi. All pets are welcome. We have two loose boxes and grazing for horses. 30,000 acres of upland moor crossed by numerous bridleways.

B & B £20-£30pp, C-Cards MC VS, Rooms 3 double (4 poster beds), 1 twin, all en-suite, No smoking, Children over 14, Dogs welcome, Closed Xmas & New Year

Fernley Lodge Manorbier, Tenby

Map Ref: 9
B4585

Jane Cowper Tel: 01834 871226
Email: fernleylodge@yahoo.com

Fernley Lodge is in the centre of the beautiful coastal village of Manorbier. The Pembrokeshire coastal path and superb beach, which are overlooked by the church and Norman castle, are just a quarter of a mile away. The imposing house is a wonderfully restored property, it is classically decorated with antique furnishings. All rooms have television and tea making facilities. The guests' drawing room overlooks the croquet and tennis lawn.There is an open fire in this lovely room on cooler evenings.

B & B £20-£25pp, Rooms 2 double, 1 en-suite family, No smoking, Children & dogs welcome, Closed Xmas

The Old Vicarage Manorbier, Tenby SA70 7TN

Map Ref: 9
A4139

Jill McHugh Tel / Fax: 01834 871452 Mobile: 07974 109877
Email: old_vic@manorbier@yahoo.com

Situated in the village of Manorbier with its castle and beaches, the Old Vicarage offers gracious accommodation with glimpses of Barafundle Bay. Guests are free to enjoy the gardens or log fire in the drawing room. Both spacious bedrooms are furnished with antiques and have tea/coffee making facilities. For the more energetic, the Pembrokeshire coastal path passes through the village. The old servants' quarters are available as a two bedroomed self-catering unit for longer stays. Irish ferries from Pembroke and Fishguard. Beaches a five minute walk. Absolutely no smoking.

B & B from £22.50pp, Rooms 1 twin, 1 double, en-suite, No smoking, No children or dogs, Closed Xmas

Wychwood House Penally, Tenby SA70 7PE

Map Ref: 10
A4139

Lee & Mherly Ravenscroft Tel: 01834 844387 Mobile: 07815 678812
Email: wychwoodbb@aol.com

A large country house enjoying sea views. The well equipped bedrooms are elegant and spacious, some have a sun balcony. Dine by candle light and enjoy Lee's interesting and freshly cooked four course menu of the day. Open fires to welcome you. Two miles south of Tenby, Penally lies a quarter of a mile off the A4139 and is situated between two golf courses. The ancient walled town of Tenby may be reached by walking along a nearby beach. Boat trips can be arranged to visit the monastic Island of Caldey.

B & B from £25pp, C-Cards MC VS, Dinner from £17.50, Rooms 2 double (4 poster beds), 1 family, all en-suite, No smoking, Children welcome, Dogs by arrangement, Open all year

The Beacons 16 Bridge Street, Brecon LD3 8AH

Mr & Mrs P E Jackson Tel: 01874 623339
Email: beacons@brecon.co.uk

Map Ref: 11
A40, A470
See Photo opposite

The Beacons is a recently restored 17th/18th century house. It still retains many original features such as moulded ceilings, low doors, sloping floors, beams and fireplaces. Guests may choose from a variety of well-appointed standard, en-suite or luxury period rooms. Relax with a drink in the original meat cellar (complete with hooks) or in a comfortable armchair in front of the fire. Enjoy excellent food and fine wines in the candlelit restaurant (five nights). Please ring Peter or Barbara Jackson for more information. Private car park and bike store.

B & B from £18pp, Dinner from £9.95, Rooms 1 single, 3 twin, 4 double, 6 family, most en-suite, Restricted smoking, Children & dogs welcome, Closed Xmas

Trefecca Fawr Brecon LD3 0PW

Miles & Patricia Park Tel: 01874 712 195 Fax: 01874 712 196
Email: lodge@trefecca.zx3.net Web: www.trefeccafawr.co.uk

Map Ref: 11
A40, B4560

Without doubt the most comfortable and well appointed private country house accommodation in the National Park, set in 20 lush acres of landscaped gardens with views to the mountains. The Grade I listed medieval and 17th century house with fine plaster ceilings is perfect for a short break among the lakes and mountains of mid-Wales. Hay-on-Wye, book lovers paradise, is nearby; ancient castles, priories and gardens abound with plenty of local restaurants. The house is in glorious unspoilt border country, described in the Times as 'one of the last wildernesses of Britain'.

B & B £38-£48pp, C-Cards MC VS, Rooms 2 double, 1 twin, all en-suite, No smoking, Children over 12, No dogs, Closed Dec to Feb

Dolycoed Talyllyn, Brecon LD3 7SY

Mary Cole
Tel: 01874 658666

Map Ref: 12
A40

Dolycoed is an attractive Edwardian house, it stands in a sheltered spot in the Brecon Beacons National Park, just five miles from the town of Brecon. There are mature gardens for guests to enjoy, the house offers warmth and good home comforts. Disabled guests are welcome. Directions to Dolycoed are: from Brecon A40/A470 take the A40 for Abergavenny, left onto the B4558 to Llangorse, first right and next right, the house is on the right at the next junction.

B & B from £20pp, Rooms 1 twin, 1 double with shower, Children & dogs welcome, Closed Xmas

Trericket Mill Vegetarian Guesthouse Erwood, Builth Wells LD2 3TQ

Nicky & Alistair Legge Tel: 01982 560312 Fax: 01982 560768
Email: mail@trericket.co.uk Web: www.trericket.co.uk

Map Ref: 13
A470

Trericket Mill Vegetarian Guesthouse has a unique, informal and historic atmosphere. It offers a range of accommodation overlooking the River Wye in the heart of Wales, from camping and bunkroom with optional bedding and breakfast, to en-suite bed and wholesome breakfast in this Grade II listed water corn mill. Guests may enjoy the original milling machinery, log fires, books, games and a riverside garden. Catering is vegetarian using wholefoods wherever possible. The bedrooms are accessed via a wooden spiral staircase, they have original fireplaces, handcrafted beds and views across the River Wye.

B & B £21-£24pp, Dinner from £12.75, Rooms 2 double, 1 twin, all en-suite, No smoking, Children welcome, No dogs, Closed Xmas

The Beacons, Brecon

Glangrwyney Court, Crickhowell

Glangrwyney Court Crickhowell NP8 1ES

Christina Jackson Tel: 01873 811288 Fax: 01873 810317
Email: glangrwyne@aol.com www.walescountryhousebandb.com

Map Ref: 14
A40

See Photo opposite

Glangrwyney Court is a Grade II listed Georgian mansion set in four acres of garden, surrounded by parkland. The house is fully centrally heated with log fires in winter and all the bedrooms have television and tea/coffee making facilities. The house is furnished with antiques and there is a residents' lounge with television and video. Ample car parking is available and there is tennis, croquet and bowls. Golf and pony trekking can be arranged and hill walking in the Brecon Beacons National Park is only minutes away.

B & B from £22.50pp, C-Cards, Dinner from £20, Rooms 1 single, 2 twin, 2 double, 1 family, all en-suite, Restricted smoking, Children & dogs welcome, Open all year

York House Hardwicke Road, Cusop, Hay-on-Wye HR3 5QX

Peter & Olwen Roberts Tel / Fax: 01497 820705
Email: roberts@yorkhouse59.fsnet.co.uk

Map Ref: 15
B4348

York House is a traditional Victorian guest house which may be found quietly situated at the edge of Hay-on-Wye, which is a small but ancient town full of history and fascinating little shops. Standing in a well tended south facing garden with views to the Black Mountains, the house now lovingly restored, welcomes guests to enjoy comfort and convenience, whilst appreciating the charm of many original features. The beautifully appointed, named bedrooms each display an individual style. There is a comfortable guests' lounge, traditional dinners are usually served at 7.30pm.

B & B £27-£29pp, C-Cards MC VS AE, Dinner from £16, Rooms 1 double, 3 double/twin, all en-suite, No smoking, Children over 8, Dogs by arrangement, Closed Xmas

Gwynfryn Llanarth, Ceredigion SA47 0PA

Paul & Delyth Wilson and Peter Grey-Hughes Tel: 01545 580837 Fax: 01545 580212
Email: delyth.wilson@virgin.net Web: www.privateprincipality

Map Ref: 16
A487

Gwynfryn is a handsome family home standing in five acres of gardens, it is well placed for lovely walks along the coastal paths, and for visits to the attractive fishing villages of Cardigan Bay, as well as the beautiful mountains of mid-Wales. Originally built for a retiring bishop, it is a typical house of the time, it retains the charm of this bygone era. The house is decorated with traditional furnishings, fine paintings and antique furniture, it offers every comfort, guests are made to feel immediately at home. Excellent dinners are offered using local produce.

B & B from £40pp, Dinner from £23, Rooms 1 double, 1 twin, both en-suite, No smoking, No children or dogs, Closed Dec to Feb

Guidfa House Crossgates, Llandrindod Wells LD1 6RF

Tony & Anne Millan Tel: 01597 851241 Fax: 01597 851875
Email: guidfa@globalnet.co.uk Web: www.guidfa-house.co.uk

Map Ref: 17
A44, A483

This stylish Georgian guest house has earned an enviable reputation for its comfort, good food and service. It offers superior en-suite accommodation including a ground floor room. Relax in the elegant sitting room with its open log fireplace and discreet corner bar. Enjoy the imaginative meals prepared by 'Cordon Bleu' trained Anne complemented by an excellent wine list. With notice, special diets can be catered for. Set in the very heart of Wales, 3 miles north of Llandrindod Wells, Guidfa House is an excellent base for touring the wonderful local countryside.

B & B from £26.50pp, C-Cards MC VS, Dinner from £17.50, Rooms 1 single, 3 double, 2 twin, all en-suite, Restricted smoking, Children over 12, Only guide dogs, Open all year

Broniwan Rhydlewis, Llandysul SA44 5PF

Mrs Carole Jacobs Tel / Fax: 01239 851261
Email: broniwan@compuserve.com

Map Ref: 18
A486, B4334

A small, peaceful farm in Ceredigion, just 10 minutes from the coast, and with wonderful views of the Preseli Hills. This grey stone house was built for the local doctor in 1867. Birdlife abounds in this unhurried, gentle place where daffodils in spring carpet the drive to the terraced lawn where guests may relax, and enjoy tea. The bedrooms are cosy and comfortable, and the sitting room is furnished with country antiques, paintings, books and flowers. Meals are varied and include vegetarian, using home produced eggs, beef, fruit and vegetables. Close to the wonderful Cardiganshire coast.

B & B from £25pp, Dinner from £17, Rooms 1 single, 2 double with en-suite, No smoking, Children over 11, Dogs by arrangement, Open all year

Bron Heulog Waterfall Street, Llanrhaeadr YM Mochnant SY10 0JX

Karon & Ken Raines Tel: 01691 780521
Email: kraines@enta.net Web: www.kraines.enta.net

Map Ref: 19
B4396, A483

Built in 1861, this beautiful Victorian house stands in a two acre garden which is home to a 140 year old weeping ash. Now fully restored, the house features a magnificent curved staircase, there are original fireplaces in every room. The bedrooms, Orchid, Bluebell and Sunflower, enjoy views to the garden with a pond and waterfall, or to the mountains or village which offers good general amenities. Here there are good places to eat, plus general stores. This is the perfect location for those who enjoy birdwatching, cycling, and other outdoor pursuits.

B & B £22-£25pp, C-Cards MC VS, Rooms 2 double, 1 twin, all en-suite, No smoking, Children welcome, Dogs must sleep in car, Open all year

Dyffryn Farmhouse Aberhafesp, Newtown SY16 3JD

Dave & Sue Jones Tel: 01686 688817 Fax: 01686 688324
Email: daveandsue@clara.net

Map Ref: 20
B4568

Come and stay in our lovingly restored 17th century farmhouse, which is set in the heart of a 200 acre working sheep and beef farm. There is an abundance of wildlife and flowers along the stream outside the door, with woodland and lakes nearby. Close to golf, fishing and glorious walks. Luxury en-suite rooms with full central heating. Traditional farmhouse fare including vegetarian specialities and totally non smoking. Garden and banks of stream for guests to sit by. Come and enjoy life on a Welsh hill farm. You might want to stay!

B & B from £25pp, Dinner from £12, Rooms 1 twin, 2 double, 1 family, all en-suite, No smoking, Children welcome, No dogs, Closed Xmas & New Year

Lower Trelydan Farmhouse Guilsfield, Welshpool SY21 9PH

Graham and Sue Jones Tel / Fax: 01938 553105
Email: stay@lowertrelydan.com Web: www.lowertrelydan.com

Map Ref: 21
A490, B4392

Graham and Sue welcome you to their beautiful listed house on this working farm. It was built in the 16th century and was once the home to John Gwyn, diarist of the Civil War. Attractive en-suite rooms freshly decorated, with colour television, licensed bar and beverage tray. Delicious cuisine served every night in elegant beamed dining room. Relax afterwards in the beamed and panelled lounge and enjoy quiet luxury in a relaxed, friendly family atmosphere. Lovely situation with Welshpool only two miles away with a weekly market. Powis Castle, the Canal boats and Llanfair Light Railway also nearby.

B & B from £26pp, Dinner from £14, Rooms 1 single, 2 double, 1 twin, 1 family, all en-suite, No smoking, Children welcome, No dogs, Closed Xmas & New Year

Fron Heulog Country House, Betws-y-Coed

Fronddderw Guest House Stryd-y-Fron, Bala LL23 7YD

Norman & Janet Jones Tel: 01678 520301

Email: GB&B@thefron.co.uk Web: www.thefron.co.uk

Map Ref: 22
A494

Whilst the occasional owl may break the silence, the peace and tranquility of this magnificent 16th century mansion will captivate you. With spectacular views across to the Berwyn Mountains and the North end of Bala Lake, this is the perfect setting for a relaxed break. An ideal centre for touring North and Mid Wales, walking, cycling and local sports. Only five minutes walk from Bala town centre. A warm welcome is assured from Janet and Norman. Colour television in all rooms.

B & B from £21pp, C-Cards MC VS, Dinner from £14, Rooms 1 single, 2 twin, 2 double, 3 family, most en-suite, No smoking, Children welcome, No dogs, Closed Dec to Feb

Llwyndu Farmhouse Llanaber, Barmouth LL42 1RR

Peter & Paula Thompson Tel: 01341 280144 Fax: 01341 281236

Email: Intouch@llwyndu-farmhouse.co.uk Web: www.llwyndu-farmhouse.co.uk

Map Ref: 23
A496

Llwyndu Farmhouse is a delightful 16th century house which nestles in a spectacular location with panoramic views over Cardigan Bay, just north of Barmouth. Here Peter and Paula Thompson have created a very special place for you to stop and relax for a few days. A real historic farmhouse with inglenooks, oak beams, nooks and crannies. Seven very comfortable en-suite bedrooms, a fully licensed restaurant and imaginative cuisine by candlelight make a stay here one to remember. A very beautiful area to explore. For more details, ring Peter or Paula.

B & B from £32pp, C-Cards MC VS, Dinner from £14.95, Rooms 1 twin, 4 double, 2 family, all en-suite, No smoking, Children welcome, Dogs by arrangement, Closed Xmas

Fron Heulog Country House Betws-y-Coed LL24 0BL

Jean & Peter Whittingham Tel: 01690 710736 Fax: 01690 710920

Email: jean&peter@fronheulog.co.uk Web: www.fronheulog.co.uk

Map Ref: 24
A5, A470, B5106
see Photo on page 363

'The Country House in the Village', Fron Heulog offers the warm welcome for which Wales is famous. This stone-built house of Victorian charm has excellent standards of comfort, food and modern amenities, with hosts' personal hospitality and local knowledge in a friendly atmosphere. There are three well appointed, attractively presented bedrooms. Turn off the busy A5 road over picturesque Pont-y-Pair Bridge (B5106), immediately turn left between shop and river. Fron Heulog is up ahead 150 metres from the bridge, on a quiet, peaceful, wooded riverside, with private parking. Longer stay - lower rate

B & B £22-£28pp, Rooms 2 double, 1 twin, all en-suite, No smoking, No small children, No dogs, Open all year

Tan-Y-Foel Country House Capel Garmon, Betws-y-Coed LL26 0RE

Mr & Mrs Pitman Tel: 01690 710507 Fax: 01690 710681

Email: enquiries@tyfhotel.co.uk Web: www.tyfhotel.co.uk

Map Ref: 25
A5/A470

Snowdonia's only 5 Star Country House, dating from the 17th century, built in Welsh stone, beautifully decorated in traditional modern style providing visitors with outstanding accommodation and cuisine. Set high in the hillside just outside Betws-y-Coed with magnificent views of the Conwy Valley. No traffic or busy clamour, relaxing, romantic location. Perfect base to explore Snowdonia's National Park attractions.

B & B £45-£75pp, C-Cards MC VS AE DC, Dinner from £30, Rooms 4 double/twin, 2 king/double, all en-suite, No smoking, Children over 7, No dogs, Closed Xmas & some of Jan

Cwm Caeth Nantmor, Beddgelert, Caernarfon LL55 4YH

Map Ref: 26
A498, A4085

Gay & Tim Harvey Tel: 01766 890408
Email: timharvey@ukonline.co.uk

Cwm Caeth is a charming south facing farmhouse situated in the heart of Snowdonia just outside the village, it has magnificent mountain views. Part of the film 'The Inn of Sixth Happiness' was filmed here. The house displays some friendly, familiar signs of its age, low ceilings, cosy rooms and cottagey walls. Mount Snowdon, the sea, wonderful Welsh castles, copper and slate mines are all close by. Meals are available locally. Cwm Caeth, a typical Welsh farmhouse, is noted for its peaceful location and warm hospitality. WTB 3 Stars.

B & B from £20pp, Rooms 1 double en-suite, Children over 8,
Dogs by arrangement, Closed Dec to Feb

The White House Llanfaglan, Caernarfon LL54 5RA

Map Ref: 27
A487

Richard Bayles Tel: 01286 673003
Email: rwbayles@sjms.co.uk

A comfortably appointed modern country house enjoying splendid views of the Menai Straits and Snowdonia. A haven for bird watchers and walkers. An outdoor swimming pool is available for guests. Caernarfon Golf Club is only two miles away. Access to The White House is via the A487 Caernarfon/Porthmadog, on leaving Caernarfon, across roundabout then turn right for Saron/Llanfaglan. Set mileometer to zero and proceed for 1.6 miles and turn right signposted to Sea shore. The White House is on the left, last house before the sea.

B & B £20-£22pp, Rooms 2 double, 2 twin, all en-suite/private, Restricted smoking,
Children welcome, Dogs by arrangement, Closed Nov to Mar

Rhagatt Hall Carrog, Corwen LL21 9HY

Map Ref: 28
A5

John & Frances Bradshaw Tel: 01490 412308 Fax: 01490 413388
Email: fjcb01@aol.com

This attractive Georgian mansion, was built in mellow stone it stands on a hillside overlooking the River Dee and the Berwyn Mountains. Surrounded by mature trees and spacious gardens, there are beautiful walks through bluebell woods to the river. The bedrooms are spacious and enjoy views to the gardens. The sitting room has a log fire and french windows to the terrace. Frances has a Cordon Bleu Diploma, there is the Grouse pub a mile away. Local places of interest can be reached from here via the steam railway from Carrog.

B & B from £34pp, C-Cards MC VS, Dinner from £12, Rooms 1 double, 1 twin, all en-suite,
No smoking in bedrooms, Children over 12, No dogs, Closed Xmas & New Year

Min-Y-Gaer Hotel Porthmadog Road, Criccieth LL52 0HP

Map Ref: 29
A497

Mrs Rita Murray Tel: 01766 522151 Fax: 01766 523540
Email: info@minygaerhotel.co.uk Web: www.minygaerhotel.co.uk

Min-Y-Gaer Hotel is a pleasant Victorian house, conveniently situated overlooking the sea and close to the beach. The hotel has delightful views of Criccieth Castle and the beautiful Cardigan Bay Coastline. There are ten comfortable, centrally heated rooms, all with colour television and tea/coffee making facilities. They are all non smoking. A lounge and licensed bar are available for guests and there is a private car park on the premises. An ideal base for touring Snowdonia and the Llyn Peninsula.

B & B £22-£26pp, C-Cards MC VS AE, Rooms 1 single, 2 twin, 4 double, 3 family, all en-suite,
No smoking in bedrooms, Children welcome, No dogs, Closed Nov to Feb

Firs Cottage, Maenan, Llanrwst

Noddfa Guest House Ffordd Newydd, Harlech LL46 2UB

Jane & Richard Salter Tel: 01766 780043
Email: noddfa@welshnet.co.uk Web: www.noddfa.welshnet.co.uk

Map Ref: 30
A496

Noddfa overlooks the Royal St David's Golf Course, with splendid views of the Snowdon mountain range and Tremadog Bay. Noddfa means 'refuge' and was protected by Harlech castle in the 18th century. Extensively rebuilt in 1850 it provides comfortable bedrooms with en-suite or private bathrooms. The historic town of Harlech offers restaurants, swimming pool, theatre and spectacular sandy beach. Central for the attractions of Wales. Residential licence, evening meals on request. Jane and Richard Salter invite you to enjoy the hospitality of their home.

*B & B from £24pp, C-Cards, Rooms 1 single, 5 double, some en-suite,
Restricted smoking, Children over 5, No dogs, Open all year*

Drws Y Coed Farm Llannerch-Y-Medd, Isle of Anglesey LL71 8AD

Jane Bown
Tel / Fax: 01248 470473 Mobile: 07971 827184

Map Ref: 31
A55, A5, A5025

With wonderful panoramic views of Snowdonia and unspoilt countryside, enjoy peace and tranquillity at this beautifully appointed farmhouse on a 550 acre working beef, sheep and arable farm. It's centrally situated to explore Anglesey. Tastefully decorated and furnished superb en-suite bedrooms with all facilities. Excellent breakfasts are served in the cosy dining room, and there is an inviting spacious lounge with antiques and a log fire. Full central heating. Games room. Historic farmstead with lovely private walks. Warm welcome assured from Tom and Jane. 25 minutes to Holyhead for Irish Sea crossings.

*B & B £23-£25pp, C-Cards MC VS, Rooms 1 twin, 1 double, 1 family, all en-suite,
No smoking, Children welcome, No dogs, Closed Xmas day*

White Lodge Hotel Central Promenade, Llandudno LL30 1AT

John Knight
Tel: 01492 877713

Map Ref: 32
A470, B5115

White Lodge Hotel is in an excellent position on the promenade and has retained the character of the Victorian period. A well kept hotel with a friendly and relaxing atmosphere. The en-suite bedrooms are all spacious and individually decorated, with tea/coffee making facilities and colour television. Breakfast and dinner are served in the pleasant dining room. Guests may relax in the lounge, enjoy a drink in the licensed bar and have use of the nearby swimming pool. There is a private car park. Well situated for Llandudno's many attractions.

*B & B from £27pp, Dinner from £9, Rooms 4 twin, 6 double, 2 family, all en-suite,
Children over 5, No dogs, Closed Dec to Feb*

Lympley Lodge Colwyn Road, Craigside, Llandudno LL30 3AL

Patricia Richards Tel: 01492 549304 Fax: 0870 138 3370
Email: clive@lympleylodge.co.uk Web: www.lympleylodge.co.uk

Map Ref: 32
B5115

Lympley Lodge is a beautiful Victorian House set beneath the headland known as Little Orme, and it overlooks the sweep of Llandudno bay. Each bedroom has a character of its own, from the Orme room with its own elegance, to the Marina with its Medtierranean charm. All bedrooms are very well equipped. Guests are offered a variety of both fresh and preserved fruits, locally cured bacon, sausages and free range eggs. There is an excellent choice of restaurants and bistros. Llandudno is the perfect base from which to explore North Wales. WTB 5 Stars.

*B & B £27.50-£30pp, Rooms 3 double, all en-suite, No smoking,
Children over 12, No dogs, Closed mid-Dec to mid-Jan*

Dee Farm Rhewl, Llangollen LL20 7YT

Mrs Mary Harman   Tel / Fax: 01978 861598

Email: harman@activelives.co.uk

Map Ref: 33

A5, A542

Just a field away from the River Dee, this 200 year old long stone farmhouse was once a miners' Inn. The small pretty garden enjoys views across the fields, down to the river and beyond. The family hens and ducks provide free range eggs for the morning, and vegetables for dinner are home grown. The Sun Inn serves excellent food and is only 500 yards away, whereas in Llangollen, there are numerous restaurants from which to choose. There are plenty of walks to enjoy and the area is home to several National Trust properties.

B & B £21-£24pp, Dinner from £12, Rooms 1 single, 2 twin with en-suite, No smoking,
Children welcome, Dogs by arrangement, Closed Nov to Mar

Firs Cottage Maenan, Llanrwst LL26 0YR

Jack & Mary Marrow

Tel: 01492 660244   Mobile: 0775 1058051

Map Ref: 34

A470

see Photo on page 366

Our 17th century Welsh cottage is a comfortable family home, situated in the Conway Valley, and enjoying wonderful views to the hills. The cottage stands away from the A470, in a quiet area with a beautiful garden and patio where guests may relax and plan visits to the many places of interest. Bodnant Garden, Conwy Castle, Llandudno and Snowdon are all within easy reach. There is a good choice of places to eat. We offer three well furnished cottage bedrooms and a full Welsh breakfast with homemade bread jams and marmalades.

B & B from £17.50pp, Rooms 2 twin/double, 1 double, Restricted smoking,
Children welcome, Dogs by arrangement, Closed Xmas

The Old Rectory Country House Llanrwst Rd, Llansanffraid Glan Conwy LL28 5LF

Michael & Wendy Vaughan   Tel: 01492 580611   Fax: 01492 584555

Email: info@oldrectorycountryhouse.co.uk   www.oldrectorycountryhouse.co.uk

Map Ref: 35

A470

This idyllic country house stands in large gardens overlooking Snowdonia, the Conwy estuary and Conwy Castle. Wendy is a 'Master Chef of Great Britain' and she features in all of Britain's premier good food guides. Welsh mountain lamb, Welsh Black beef and locally landed fish are on her menu. An award winning wine list complements her cuisine. The house displays a sense of elegance coupled with a delight in old paintings, antiques and opulent furnishings. The bedrooms are luxuriously appointed and generously equipped. Three golf courses within ten minutes.

B & B £49.90-£84.90pp, C-Cards MC VS, Dinner from £29.90, Rooms 4 double, 2 twin,
all en-suite, No smoking, Children over 5, Dogs in coach house only, Closed Dec to Jan

Plas Penucha Caerwys, Mold CH7 5BH

Nest Price

Tel: 01352 720210   Fax: 01352 720881

Map Ref: 36

A55, B5122, A541

Welcome to the 16th century farmhouse altered over succeeding generations, but retaining a sense of history in comfortable surroundings. The house has been in the family for 450 years. It displays many of the original marks of history, to include some Elizabethan panelling in the dining room. The large gardens overlook the Clwydian Hills. There is a spacious lounge and library, and the bedrooms are well equipped. Full central heating and log fires. Ideal for walking and exploring countryside. All North Wales and Chester in easy reach, two miles from A55 Expressway.

B & B £21-£25pp, Dinner from £11.50, Rooms 2 twin, 2 double, some en-suite,
Restricted smoking, Children welcome, Dogs by arrangement, Open all year

Pentre Cerrig Mawr, Maeshafn, near Mold

Pentre Cerrig Mawr Maeshafn, Mold CH7 5LU

Ted & Charmian Spencer Tel / Fax: 01352 810607
charmian.sunbeam@care4free.net www.pentrecerrigmawr.com

Map Ref: 37
A494
see Photo on page 369

This beautiful Elizabethan house, set in two acres of walled garden is peaceful and cosy with beams and open fires in the principal rooms. The comfortable bedrooms and guest lounge have spectacular views across the valley. Perfect for touring Snowdonia, the Welsh National park, the coast, the medieval towns of Ruthin and Chester, just 40 minutes from Manchester and Liverpool and en-route for Holyhead. Ted and Charmian enjoy welcoming guests to their home to make this a truly relaxing break with interesting pubs, lovely walks, trips, theatre, etc.

B & B from £37pp, C-Cards MC VS, Dinner from £25, Rooms 2 double, 1 double/twin, all en-suite, No smoking, Children over 8, Dogs by arrangement, Closed occasionally

Y Wern Llanfrothen, Penrhyndeudraeth LL48 6LX

Tony Bayley Tel / Fax: 01766 770556
Email: bbwern@btinternet.com

Map Ref: 38
A4085, B4410

'Y Wern' was built in the 16th century. It is a stone built farmhouse situated in beautiful countryside within the Snowdonia National Park. 'Wern' abounds with oak beams and inglenook fireplaces, and the large comfortable bedrooms have delightful views over glorious countryside. They are well equipped with beverage making facilities. This is an excellent centre for walking, and it is well placed for several beaches. There are also some famous attractions such as Portmerion, castles, the slate mines and the Ffestiniog Railway. Dinner is available by arrangement.

B & B from £19pp, Dinner from £12.50, Rooms 2 twin, 2 double, all en-suite/private, No smoking, Children over 5, No dogs, Closed part Dec

Eyarth Station Llanfair D C, Ruthin LL15 2EE

Jen & Bert Spencer Tel: 01824 703643 Fax: 01824 707464
Email: eyarthstation@amserve.net Web: www.smoothhound.co.uk/hotels/eyarth

Map Ref: 39
A525

In 1964 the line closed to passing trains here. Eyarth Station has been converted into an elegant country house, where guests see the delights of a working station. The bedrooms have country views over an area of outstanding natural beauty. Visitors are invited to use the sun terrace and the heated pool. One and a half miles away is the medieval town of Ruthin, which hosts banquets at the castle. This is a walker's paradise and the wonders of Snowdonia, Shrewsbury, Chester and the North Wales coast, are all within a pleasant drive.

B & B £23-£25pp, C-Cards MC VS, Dinner from £12, Rooms 2 twin, 2 double, 2 family, all en-suite, Restricted smoking, Children & dogs welcome, Closed Nov, Jan & Feb

The Old Barn Esgairlygain, Llangynhafal, Ruthin LL15 1RT

Mrs I Henderson
Tel: 01824 704047/704993 Fax: 01824 704047

Map Ref: 40
B5429

Sleep in the haylofts, breakfast in the Shippon where the cows used to be milked. Our stone barn has been sensitively converted for guests keeping the low sloping ceilings and beams. There are lovely views to be enjoyed over the Vale of Clwyd, with spectacular sunsets, and direct access to Clwydian Hills, Offa's Dyke and mountain bike tracks. Horse riding is available nearby. Central for Llangollen, Chester, Snowdonia, Castles and coast with a wealth of National Trust properties. Refreshments on arrival and a warm welcome is assured.

B & B from £20pp, Rooms 1 double, 1 family, both en-suite, Restricted smoking, Children & dogs welcome, Closed Nov to Feb

Ireland

Ireland

Ireland is known for being a country with a unique history with cultural areas in music and literature. The clean air with unpolluted lakes and mountain scenery make sure that a visit to Ireland is one to be remembered. The South West region is one of natural rural beauty with one of the most famous sites in Ireland, Blarney Castle, just north of Cork, which is renowned for the Blarney Stone on the high battlements with those who kiss the stone supposedly blessed with the gift of eloquence. Cork is an important seaport where the River Lee runs through from two directions, hence the number of bridges in the city. The Lakes of Killarney in County Kerry is a beautiful spot, made up of three lakes and containing a wealth of salmon and brown trout. The lakes take up a quarter of Killarney National Park with its unique ecology, rich in wildlife and a cross-section of birds.

Dublin, the capital city, is a thriving university town with a growing cosmopolitan influence. This is especially apparent at Temple Bar, the cultural quarter of Dublin, developed in the nineteenth century with its narrow cobbled streets containing many small galleries, unique shops and of course a wealth of bars and restaurants. Dublin Castle stands at the meeting of the River Liffey and the Poddle and is worth visiting for its really magnificent State Apartments, where the inauguration of the Irish Presidents is held. The North West of Ireland is commonly known for Sligo, Yeats' Country, where the poet was inspired by his childhood spent in the area. Much of the region can be recognised within his poetry and his burial place is situated at Drumcliffe. Sligo is also the site of the greatest concentration of megalithic tombs; in particular Maeve's Cairn on Knocknarea is a sight worth seeing. Slieve League, part of Donegal's 200 miles coastline, is the highest sea cliff in Europe with a 300 metre drop into the treacherous Atlantic. There are excellent walks here with breathtaking scenery, but the area can be dangerous. The West of the country is a delightful region of unspoilt countryside with scenic Connemara in County Galway, a rocky mountain range and a beautiful wild landscape. Galway itself is a roaring university city, famous for its festivals and the popular Galway Races every July. Nearby is Ceide Fields, at 24 square miles the most extensive Stone Age site in the world and is thought to be over 5000 years old. The neighbouring county of Mayo is a centre of pilgrimage, where apparitions of the Virgin Mary has appeared to the people of Knock since 1879.

The region of Shannon is named after its river, the longest in the British Isles and home of the airport. Bordering the river is

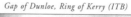
Gap of Dunloe, Ring of Kerry (ITB)

the city of Limerick with a city charter even older than London's and traces of human settlement going back over 5000 years. The city, with the publishing of Frank McCourt's Angela's Ashes and the subsequent film is experiencing a resurgence, also offering a walking tour of the sights in the novel. Nearby is Bunratty Castle and Folk Park in County Clare, within 26 acres. The castle is renowned for its medieval origins with the fascinating Folk Park recreating nineteenth century Ireland. County Clare is not only known for its involvement with traditional Irish music but also the spectacular Cliffs of Moher which span a five mile stretch with puffins, cormorants and rare fossils.

The East Midlands is well known for its diverse landscape and cultural heritage including Bru na Boinne, the monuments of Newgrange and Knowth, in County Meath with its Stone Age Passage Graves. They are thought to date from 3200BC, older than both the Pyramids of Egypt and Stonehenge. Just south of the monument is Clonmacnoise, in County Offaly, a monastery founded 1500 years ago by St Ciaran which attracted scholars from all over Europe. It was recently restored and houses an interesting museum explaining the history of the monastery and the surrounding area. The South East is known as the Sunshine Region with the best sandy beaches and resorts. On the southern coastline is Waterford, the oldest city in Ireland, renowned for its glassworks and the Waterford Crystal Factory and nearby Kilkenny, famous for its dark black marble.

Northern Ireland is a country steeped in history and the most magnificent natural sites. One must start with the city of Belfast in County Antrim, and its beautiful sandstone Castle, completed in 1860, overlooking the city. Near to Belfast is the Giant's Causeway, a dramatic rock formation evolved from the

volcanic activity on the land 60 million years ago.

To the west is County Derry with its popular beaches, in particular Benone Strand, Ireland's longest beach. Londonderry is encircled by a stone wall, built in the seventeenth century as a defence from Gaelic chieftains, that is still intact and considered the best preserved fortification in Europe. The 'wild' County of Tyrone has a variety of mountains, rivers, moorlands and outstanding landscapes. Within Omagh are interesting museum and heritage sites including the unmissable Ulster-American Folk Park.

County Fermanagh is the 'Lakeland County' with the domination of Lough Erne with its 200 islands including Devenish Island with its sixth century monastery. To the east is County Armagh, known as the 'Garden of Ulster' due to the beautiful landscape and the striking appearance of Armagh itself. One of the most important sites of Armagh is the Navan Fort which was the first capital of Ulster and became the crowning place of the Kings of Ulster.

County Down is a region of outstanding mountain views with the Mourne Mountains rising above 2,000 feet. The region also has 200 miles of coastline and cannot be rivalled for its history and wildlife.

Carrick-a-rede Rope Bridge, Co Antrim (NITB)

Northern Ireland

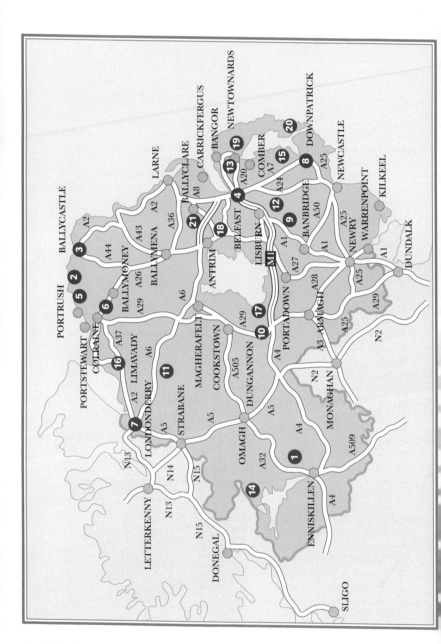

The Blue Map References should be used to locate B & B properties on the pages that follow

Rossfad House   Killadeas, Ballinamallard, Co Fermanagh BT94 2LS
John & Lois Williams
Tel: 028 66388505

Map Ref: 1
B82

Rossfad is a Georgian Country house on the shores of Lower Lough Erne. Built in 1776, the house lends itself well to families and friends travelling in groups, as there is a Victorian guest wing with its own access, south facing guest rooms, and views extending to the garden, trees, lakes and mountains. The bedrooms are large, simply furnished and comfortable. Log fires are lit for chilly nights, and the sun floods the sitting room at breakfast time. There are several lakeside restaurants locally, and the county town of Enniskillen is five miles away. Wonderful for sailing, fishing, surfing, canoeing, golfing and riding.

B & B £17.50-£25pp, Rooms 1 double, 1 double/family, 1 en-suite, 1 pb, No smoking, Children welcome, No dogs, Closed Nov to Feb

Whitepark House   150 Whitepark Road, Whitepark Bay, Ballintoy, Co Antrim BT54 6NH
Bob & Siobhan Isles   Tel: 028 2073 1482
Email: bob@whiteparkhouse.com   Web: www.whiteparkhouse.com

Map Ref: 2
A2

This unique country house built in 1735, stands on the Antrim coast road between The Giant's Causeway and Carrick-a-Rede Rope Bridge. The house is full of character, it stands in mature gardens, and it displays interesting collections from the Far East. A warm welcome awaits guests here, who are offered tea and homebaked cakes on arrival to be enjoyed by the fire. Bedrooms are individually decorated and well presented, with views to the garden and sea. Breakfasts are hearty and vegetarians are well catered for. There are good local pubs. Beaches and Glens are nearby.

B & B from £25pp, C-Cards MC VS, Rooms 2 double, 1 twin, Restricted smoking, Children over 10, No dogs, Open all year

Colliers Hall   50 Cushendall Road, Ballycastle, Co Antrim BT54 6QR
Gerard & Maureen McCarry   Tel: 028 2076 2531   Fax: 028 2076 2842
Mobile: 07748 353593   Email: droughinlea@anna12.fs.co.uk   Web: www.colliershall.com

Map Ref: 3
A2

Colliers Hall, an 18th century farmhouse situated on the scenic north Antrim coast. Irish hospitality is offered in a relaxed homely atmosphere. Choice of breakfasts, home cooking a priority. Three bedrooms en-suite, tastefully decorated with antique furnishings with tea/coffee facilities. Television, video and piano in spacious guest lounge. Colliers Hall is a working farm with sheep, cattle and horses, visitors can walk around fields and gardens. Ideal base for hill coastal walking, bird watching, fishing, pony trekking and cycling. Boat trips to Rathlin Island. Giants Causeway and Glens of Antrim.

B & B from £18pp, C-Cards MC VS, Rooms 2 double, 1 twin, all en-suite, No smoking, Children welcome, No dogs, Closed Sep to Apr

Greenwood House   25 Park Road, Belfast, Co Antrim BT7 2FW
Jason & Mary Harris   Tel: 028 9020 2525   Fax: 028 9020 2530
Email: info@greenwoodguesthouse.com   Web: www.greenwoodguesthouse.com

Map Ref: 4
A24

This Victorian red brick guest house was an Ulster guest house of the year 2000 finalist. Retaining much of its Victorian charm, the house displays a warm, contemporary style, coupled with quality comfort. The bedrooms are well appointed, beds and baths are comfortable, they have handmade furniture, deep baths and power showers. Breakfasts are interesting and varied, they include homemade breads, fruit compotes and conserves, vegetarians are catered for. The city centre with sight seeing and shopping is nearby. Well placed for the North Coast, Mourne Mountains and Fermanagh lakes.

B & B from £27.50pp, C-Cards MC VS, Rooms 2 single, 2 double, 2 twin, 1 family, all en-suite, No smoking, Children welcome, No dogs, Closed Xmas & New Year

The Bushmills Inn 9 Dunluce Road, Bushmills, Co Antrim BT57 8QG

Stella Minogue Tel: 028 2073 2339 Fax: 028 2073 2048

Email: greatbritish@bushmillsinn.com Web: www.bushmillsinn.com

Map Ref: 5
A2

'A living museum of Ulster hospitality.' At the home of the world's oldest distillery, between the Giant's Causeway and Royal Portrush Golf Club, this award winning hotel and restaurant has been outstandingly successful in recreating its origins as an old coaching inn. Turf fires, gas lights and pitched pine set the tone in the public rooms, whilst the spacious bedrooms of the river facing Mill House, each with their own sitting area, compliment the smaller rooms of the original Coaching Inn overlooking the village.

B & B £44-£64pp, C-Cards MC VS AE, Dinner from £25, Rooms 4 singles, 4 double, 21 twin/double, 3 family, all en-suite, Restricted smoking, Children welcome, Guide dogs only, Open all year

Craig Park Country House 24 Carnbore Road, Bushmills, Co Antrim BT57 8YF

Jan & David Cheal Tel: 028 2073 2496 Fax: 028 2073 2479

Mobile: 07801 808840 Email: jan@craigpark.co.uk Web: www.craigpark.co.uk

Map Ref: 5
B66, B17

Craig Park is a beautifully renovated 18th century farmhouse, the three lovely bedrooms are all en-suite, with television and tea/coffee facilities. The hosts have travelled extensively and love meeting other travellers. There are incredible sweeping views to the west to the mountains of Donegal. Craig Park is perfectly located for Northern Ireland's most famous touris attraction the Giants Causeway. Close to Rathlin Island and wonderful beaches. Awarded Guest House of the year in the area for three years running. AA 4 Diamonds.

B & B from £27.50pp, C-Cards MC VS, Rooms 1 double, 1 twin, 1 family, No smoking, Children welcome, Guide dogs only, Closed Xmas & New Year

Killens Restaurant 28 Ballyclough Road, Bushmills, Co Antrim BT57 8UZ

Peter Lafferty Tel: 028 207 41536 Fax: 028 2074 1070

Email: peter@killlens.com Web: www.killens.com

Map Ref: 5
B17, B67

Killen's restaurant with rooms, stands in the midst of lush north Antrim farmland. A perfect place for those seeking peace and quiet. The lounge is a warm and welcoming room where guests may enjoy tea by the open fire. It is the place to enjoy coffee after dinner with friends. The impressive dinner menu takes inspiration from the seasons, classic flavours with contemporary style, complemented with an appealing wine list. A suite offers a four poster bed, sitting area and a sunken bath. There's a heated swimming pool and sauna.

B & B £25-£35pp, C-Cards MC VS, Dinner from £19, Rooms 5 double, 1 family, all en-suite, Restricted smoking, Children welcome, Dogs by arrangement, Closed Xmas & New Year

Camus House 27 Curragh Road, Castleroe, Co Londonderry BT51 3RY

Jo King

Tel: 028 7034 2982 Mobile: 077303 86104

Map Ref: 6
A54
see Photo opposite

Built in 1685, it is believed that Camus House was built on the site of an old monastery. The house is the oldest in the area and it stands in wonderfully peaceful surroundings overlooking the River Bann with salmon fishing, permits are available for guests. The accommodation here is warm, friendly and very comfortable, a log fire in the sitting room greets visitors in winter. Mrs King is a member of the Healthy Eating Circle Galtee Breakfast Awards, she is also an enthusiastic fisher woman. The bedrooms are warmly equipped with electric blankets and tea/coffee trays.

B & B from £22.50pp, Rooms 1 single, 1 twin, 1 double en-suite, 1 family, Restricted smoking, Children welcome, No dogs, Open all year

Camus House, Castleroe, Co Londonderry

Sylvan Hill House, Dromore, Co Down

The Merchant's House 16 Queen Street, Derry, Co Londonderry BT48 7EQ Map Ref: 7
Joan & Peter Pyne   Tel: 028 7126 9691   Fax: 028 7126 6913   A2
Email: saddlershouse@btinternet.com   Web: www.the saddlershouse.com

An award winning restored Georgian town house, situated in a conservation area. The property is of architectural and historical interest. It is the most centrally located bed and breakfast in the city. It is close to all amenities and tourist attractions of Londonderry, as well as being an hour's drive from the Giant's Causeway. Donegal is close by.

B & B £22.50-£25pp, C-Cards MC VS, Rooms 2 single, 1 double, 1 double en-suite, 2 twin,
No smoking, No children, Dogs welcome, Open all year

The Saddlers House 36 Great James Street, Derry, Co Londonderry BT48 7DB
Joan and Peter Pyne   Tel: 028 7126 9691   Fax: 028 7126 6913   Map Ref: 7
Email: saddlershouse@btinternet.com   Web: www.thesaddlershouse.com   A6, N15, A5

The Saddlers House is a mid 19th century townhouse, in a conservation area. The house is the most centrally located B&B in the city, being close to the city walls, excellent restaurants, galleries and shops. The town of Donegal is on the doorstep. The bedrooms are well appointed, they offer comfortable furniture, television, books and tea and coffee trays. This is the only completely intact walled city in Ireland. There is much to see, including the Millennium Forum theatre, museums, the verbal arts centre, Saint Columb's Cathedral to name a few.

B & B £20-£22.50pp, C-Cards MC VS, Rooms 1 single, 4 double, 2 twin,
No smoking, Children & dogs welcome, Open all year

Tyrella House Downpatrick, Co Down BT30 8SU   Map Ref: 8
David & Sally Corbett   Tel / Fax: 028 4485 1422   Mobile: 07714 9540   A25
Email: tyrella.corbett@virgin.net

Hidden away under the Mourne Mountains and sheltered from the sea breezes by tall beech woods, Tyrella's grasslands sweep down to a private sandy beach. After a day of fresh sea air, Tyrella is a wonderful place to relax and enjoy delicious dinners, perhaps of home grown lamb and vegetables from the garden. Guests can ride over one of Tyrella's cross country courses or gallop on the sandy beach that stretches for miles in either direction. For garden and architecture lovers there are the National Trust houses at Mountstewart, Castleward and Rowallane. Fishing can be arranged. Tyrellas has a polo ground.

B & B from £45pp, C-Cards MC VS AE, Dinner from £22, Rooms 1 double, 1 twin, 1 family,
all en-suite, No smoking, Children over 8, No dogs, Closed Dec to Feb

Sylvan Hill House 76 Kilntown Road, Dromore, Co Down BT25 1HS   Map Ref: 9
Elise Coburn   A1
Tel / Fax: 028 9269 2321   *see Photo opposite*

Sylvan Hill house has that essential ingredient that ensures that guests return again and again - welcoming hosts, Elise and Jmmy Coburn. Elise and Jimmy began taking guests into their delightful home as a means of paying for the installation of a very expensive damp course and they discovered that they loved taking guests from all over the world and all walks of life. The bedrooms consist of a spacious double-bedded room with en-suite bathroom, while a snug twin-bedded room has it shower cubicle in the room and an adjacent toilet. A third bedroom is available for families who wish to have children share the bathroom with them.

B & B from £28pp, Dinner from £16, Rooms 1 double with pb, 2 twin with shower,
Restricted smoking, Well behaved children, Dogs welcome, Open all year

Grange Lodge 7 Grange Road, Dungannon, Co Tyrone BT71 7EJ
Norah & Ralph Brown   Tel: 028 8778 4212   Fax: 028 8778 4313
Email: grangelodge@nireland.com

Map Ref: 10
M1 J15, A29

Grange Lodge is a lovely old Georgian house whose origins trace back to 1698. It stands in 20 acres of gardens and grounds and is one mile from M1 junction 15 on the A29. This family home generates a welcome atmosphere of peace and gracious living. The individually styled bedrooms are decoratively finished and overlook the pretty gardens. There are fresh flowers and little extras to ensure a comfortable stay. A large drawing room or cosy 'den' is where guests may relax. Within a ten minute drive, there is an excellent variety of attractions. AA 5 Diamonds.

B & B from £39pp, C-Cards MC VS, Dinner from £25, Rooms 1 single, 3 double, 1 twin, all en-suite, No smoking, Children over 12, No dogs in house, Closed Xmas & New Year

Drumcovitt House 704 Feeny Road, Feeny, Co Londonderry BT47 4SU
Florence Sloan   Tel / Fax: 028 7778 1224
Email: drumcovitt.feeny@btinternet.com   Web: www.drumcovitt.com

Map Ref: 11
A6, B74

More than 300 years ago, Drumcovitt House was built on land owned by the Fishmongers Company. A later Georgian addition ensures the main bedrooms have magnificent views down a wooded valley to Benbraddagh. The beech trees in the garden and on the farm are home to birds, bats and butterflies. The house is always warm, being centrally heated, also a log fire in the drawing room provides a welcome. The individually named bedrooms are generously equipped, Azalea room offers a king size and a single bed. Three pubs in the village.

B & B £20-£24pp, C-Cards MC VS AE, Rooms 1 double, 1 twin, 1 family, 2 bathrooms, Children welcome, Guide dogs only, Open all year

Fortwilliam Country House 210 Ballynahinch Road, Hillsborough,
Co Down BT26 6BH   Terry & Mavis Dunlop   Tel: 02892 682255   Fax: 02892 689608
Email: fortwilliam.country.house@ukgateway.net   Web: www.fortwilliamcountryhouse.com

Map Ref: 12
B177,A1

Fortwilliam set in the heart of the country, is an Ulster Guest House of the Year Winner. The house is over 300 hundred years old and is decorated and furnished to reflect the character and charm of this appealing home. The bedrooms are spacious and comfortable and enjoy views across the countryside. The snug sitting room often has a welcoming log fire, on sunny days, guests may sit in the walled garden and enjoy views to the hills. Hearty 'Ulster' breakfasts are offered, perfect before a day of sightseeing, golfing walking, or just relaxing.

B & B from £27.50pp, C-Cards MC VS, Rooms 1 twin, 2 double, No smoking, Children welcome, By arrangement, Closed Xmas

Beech Hill Country House 23 Ballymoney Road, Craigantlet, Holywood,
Co Down BT23 4TG   Victoria Brann   Tel / Fax: 028 9042 5892
Email: beech.hill@btinternet.com   Web: www.beech-hill.net

Map Ref: 13
A2

A stunning home in the peaceful Holywood Hills. 15 minutes from Belfast City airport and ferries, Bangor and Newtownards. 19 golf courses locally. A wonderful, friendly home brimming with style, the perfect base for business or holiday. The bedrooms all offer en-suite facilities, direct dial telephone, television and tea and coffee trays. All ground floor bedrooms are suitable for partially disabled. Guests are welcome to use the large drawing room and conservatory. There is a lovely garden and private parking. Many excellent local restaurants, National Trust properties and museums.

B & B from £30pp, C-Cards MC VS, Rooms 1 double, 1 king, 1 twin/superking, all en-suite, Restricted smoking, Children over 12, Dogs by arrangement, Open all year

Ardess House Kesh, Co Fermanagh BT93 1NX

Dorothy Pendry   Tel / Fax: 028 6863 1267
Email: ardess@lineone.net   Web: www.fermanaghcraft.com/ardesscraft

Map Ref: 14
B72

Ardess House is a restored Georgian rectory, built in 1780. It stands in secluded grounds deep in the Fermanagh countryside, close to Lower Lough Erne. Relax in the gardens, or the secluded courtyard. Walk in the grounds and admire the Jacob sheep, the basis of Dorothy's spinning and weaving. You could join in an activity in Ardess Craft Centre. The guest bedrooms are spacious and comfortable. Guests may enjoy dinner in the red dining room, the organic produce from the kitchen garden being the basis of traditional and vegetarian dishes.

B & B from £27.50pp, C-Cards MC VS AE, Dinner from £15, Rooms 3 double, 1 twin, all en-suite, No smoking, Children welcome, Dogs by arrangement, Closed Dec and Jan

Dufferin Coaching Inn 31 High Street, Killyleagh, Co Down BT30 9QF

Morris Crawford & Kitty Stewart   Tel: 028 44828229   Fax: 028 44828755
Mobile: 07799 718922   Email: dufferin@dial.pipex.com   Web: www.dufferincoachinginn.co.uk

Map Ref: 15
A7

The Inn dates from the 1800's and is on the shores of Strangford Lough in the shadows of Killyleagh Castle. Some of the rooms have four-poster beds and are decorated in a country manor house style. The award winning Dufferin Arms pub and restaurant is adjacent and has a traditional bar 120 years old, a cellar restaurant specialising in fish and local produce and music. It is renowned for its atmosphere, good food and warm welcome. Attractions include sailing, horse-riding, fishing, walking the Ulster way, the historical town of Downpatrick and golf. It is a haven for both tourists and the business traveller.

B & B from £32.50pp, C-Cards MC VS AE, Dinner from £15, Rooms 4 double, 2 twin, all en-suite, No smoking, Children welcome, No dogs, Open all year

Streeve Hill 25 Downland Road, Limavady, Co Londonderry BT49 0HP

Peter & June Welsh
Tel: 028 77766563   Fax: 028 77768285

Map Ref: 16
A2

Streeve Hill, built by Conolly McCausland in 1730, stands within the demesne of Drenagh. It has a Palladian facade of rose brick and enjoys fine views over parkland to the distant Sperrin Mountains. Recent renovations have combined contemporary comforts with 18th century charm. The gardens of Drenagh are nearby with their fine Italian terraces and enchanting Moon Garden. Streeve Hill is renowned for its gourmet dinners and irresistible breakfasts. It is ideally placed for visits to Downhill, the Giant's Causeway and Donegal. Golf, tennis, riding, shooting and fishing are all available nearby.

B & B £40-£50pp, C-Cards MC AE, Dinner from £25, Rooms 2 double, 1 twin, 1 family, all en-suite, Restricted smoking, Children welcome, No dogs, Closed Dec to Mar

Charlemont House 4 The Square, Moy, Co Tyrone BT71 7SG

Laurence & Margaret McNeice
Tel: 028 8778 4755   Fax: 028 8778 4895

Map Ref: 17
M1

Charlemont House, the most imposing residence of the square, was built in 1760. It still retains all the mystery and intrigue of a bygone era, coupled with warmth and hospitality and an inviting relaxation. The bedrooms are en-suite and comfortably furnished, well presented and generously equipped. Guests here can enjoy an integration of leisure and grace with every modern facility. Breakfasts are satisfying, true Irish fare is offered each morning. From the house one can stroll to the library, riding school, bank, hairdresser, numerous shops and lively local pubs.

B & B from £20pp, C-Cards VS, Rooms 6 double, 3 twin, all en-suite, Restricted smoking, Children welcome, Dogs by arrangement, Open all year

The Beeches Country House 10 Dunadry Road, Muckamore, Co Antrim BT41 2RR

Marigold Allen   Tel: 028 9443 3161   Fax: 028 9443 2227   **Map Ref: 18**
Email: reception@thebeeches.org   Web: www.thebeeches.org   **M2, A6**

The Beeches Country House is a detached Edwardian residence situated in its own mature landscaped ground. This quiet and secluded family run house offers a high standard of accommodation and secure car parking facilities. The personal touch provides the house with a friendly atmosphere in the peaceful locality of Dunadry. Each room is well equipped, all en-suite, with direct dial telephone and television. There is a range of cooked breakfasts and four course evening meals are available on request, using fresh home grown or local organic produce. There is golf, fresh water fishing and river cruises locally.

B & B from £30pp, C-Cards MC VS AE, Dinner from £15, Rooms 2 single, 3 double, all en-suite,
No smoking, Children welcome, No dogs,

Edenvale House 130 Portaferry Road, Newtownards, Co Down BT22 2AH   Map Ref: 19

Diane & Gordon Whyte   Tel: 028 9181 4881   Fax: 028 9182 6192   Mobile: 07798 741790   **A20**
Email: edenvalehouse@hotmail.com   Web: www.edenvalehouse.com

This pretty Georgian house is peacefully situated on the shores of Strangford Lough with spectacular views to the Mourne mountains. It stands surrounded by seven acres of garden and paddocks, with the beautiful gardens of the National Trust, and Mountstewart nearby. The bedrooms, one with a four poster, are large and gracious, they have televisions and hospitality trays, and they enjoy views over Strangford Lough. Breakfasts are memorable, as well as 'the Ulster fry,' there is home made bread, fruit compote and cream, a favourite speciality. Afternoon tea is served in the garden. 10 golf courses nearby.

B & B from £27.50pp, C-Cards MC VS, Rooms 1 double, 1 twin, 1 family, all en-suite,
Restricted smoking, Children & dogs welcome, Closed Xmas

The Narrows 8 Shore Road, Portaferry, Co Down BT22 1JY

Will Brown and James Brown   Tel: 028 4272 8148   Fax: 028 4272 8105   **Map Ref: 20**
Email: info@narrows.co.uk   Web: www.narrows.co.uk   **A20**
see Photo opposite

The Narrows occupies a stunning location overlooking Strangford Lough, in Portaferry. It comprises two buildings separated by a coach entrance opening to a courtyard, outbuildings and a charming walled garden. The bedrooms are en-suite, with uninterrupted views of the lough, most are fully accessible to wheelchair users. The restaurant has two AA rosettes, seafood and other ingredients being cooked to perfection. The lough is a Marine Nature Reserve offering wonderful excursions by car, foot or boat. The NationalTrust properties of Castleward and Mount Stewart are nearby. Nine golf courses are within 30 miles.

B & B from £42.50pp, C-Cards MC VS AE, Dinner from £20, Rooms 1 single, 6 double, 5 twin,
1 family, Restricted smoking, Children welcome, No dogs, Open all year

The Moat Inn 12 Donegore Hill, Templepatrick, Co Antrim BT41 2HW   Map Ref: 21

Robert & Rachel Thompson   Tel: 028 9443 3659   Fax: 028 9443 3726   **A57**
Email: themoatinn@talk21.com

The Moat Inn dates from around 1740. Originally a Coaching Inn, it has now been turned into a comfortable country home with real fires, antiques and our well-stocked library. Although surrounded by quiet countryside, we are convenient to Belfast, Ballymena, Larne and the spectacular North Antrim Coast. Free transfers are available to Belfast International Airport. We have been awarded by 'A Taste of Ulster' for our inventive home cooking and are recommended by the 'Bridgestone Guide to the 100 Best Places to Stay in Ireland'. The perfect retreat!

B & B from £30pp, C-Cards MC VS, Dinner from £20, Rooms 2 double, 1 twin, all en-suite,
Restricted smoking, Children welcome, No dogs, Open all year

The Narrows, Portaferry, Co Down

Dublin & The East

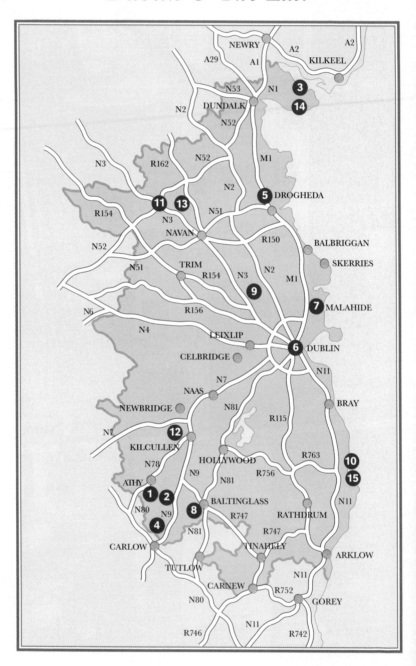

The Blue Map References should be used to locate B & B properties on the pages that follow

Tonlegee House & Restaurant Athy, Co Kildare

Map Ref: 1
N78

Marjorie Molloy Tel / Fax: +353 507 31473
Email: marjorie@tonlegeehouse.com www.tonlegeehouse.com

see Photo on page 386

Tonlegee House is a lovingly restored Georgian house standing in its own grounds a mile from the town of Athy. The house is beautifully furnished and presented in a style to complement this gracious era. The traditionally furnished bedrooms have en-suite facilities, multi channel television and direct dial telephone. The restaurant is intimate and cosy, guests may enjoy country house cooking at its best, with delights such as quail in pastry with wild mushroom sauce. There is racing at the Curragh and Punchestown, the National Stud and Japanese gardens are within easy reach.

B & B from €55pp, C-Cards MC VS AE, Dinner from €30, Rooms 2 single, 8 double, 2 double/twin, all en-suite, Children welcome, Dogs by arrangement, Closed Xmas & New Year

Griesemount Ballitore, Co Kildare

Map Ref: 2
N9

Carolyn & Robert Ashe Tel: +353 507 23158 Fax: +353 503 40687
Mobile: +353 8683 08676 Email: griesemount@eircom.net

Griesemount was built by Quakers in 1817 and now offers its guests a chance to stay in a peaceful and relaxed country house. Between Dublin and Kilkenny, near Ferries, airport, superb golf, racecourses, historic houses, gardens and mountains. Fly-fishing nearby. Some quotes from the visitors book: 'warm welcome', 'could not have chosen a better place', 'beauty at every turn', 'wonderful views', 'best spot of our holiday', 'superb nights sleep', 'terrific breakfast', 'would love to stay longer', 'home from home', 'hate to leave', 'best stay of our holiday', 'will be back'.

B & B €40-€45pp, Dinner from €25, Rooms 2 double, 1 twin, 2 with pb, 1 en-suite, Restricted smoking, Children & dogs welcome, Closed Xmas & New Year

Jordans Townhouse, Bar & Restaurant Newry Street, Carlingford, Co Louth

Ambrose and Marion Ferguson Tel: +353 42 937 3223 Fax: +353 42 937 3875 Map Ref: 3
N1

Email: jordans@iol.ie Web: www.jordans-townhouse.ie

Formerly a row of fishermen's cottages in the 16th century, Jordans has to be one of the most elegant townhouses of any village. The five en-suite guest bedrooms are huge with spectacular views of Carlingford Lough. Jordans restaurant has won many ratings and awards and offers the best of seasonal local produce. The newly opened bar with its comfortable surroundings and traditional sessions has also proved to be a great attraction. Tranquil Carlingford is a heritage village. Medieval treasures include King John's Castle, The Mint, Taafees's Castle and Thosel Old Town Hall.

B & B €45-€70pp, C-Cards MC VS AE DC, Dinner from €17, Rooms 5 single/double/twin/family, all en-suite, Children welcome, No dogs, Open all year

Kilkea Lodge Farm Kilkea, Castledermot, Co Kildare

Map Ref: 4
N9, R418

Godfrey & Marion Greene Tel / Fax: +353 503 45112
Web: www.dirl.com/kildare/kilkea-lodgefarm.htm

Kilkea Lodge Farm is a family farmhouse with a 'home from home' emphasis. The house is suited to artistic friendly guests who enjoy walking, open spaces, painting, music, horses, dogs and gardens. The well equippped bedrooms offer either en-suite or private facilities. There is an attractive sitting room with an open fire for guests' relaxation. The farmhouse is approached down a long drive, off the Castledermot Athy Road. This is the ideal spot from which to sight see the Wicklow Mountains. Within easy reach is the National Stud, and several well known racecourses.

B & B from €45pp, C-Cards, Dinner available, Rooms 2 double en-suite, 1 double, 1 twin, 1 family, all with pb, Children & dogs welcome,

Tonlegee House & Restaurant, Athy, Co Kildare

Tullyesker Country House N1 Road, Monasterboice, Drogheda, Co Louth
Map Ref: 5
N1
Eobhain & Cepta McDonnell Tel: +353 41 9830430 Fax: +353 41 9832624
Email: mcdonnellfamily@ireland.com Web: www.bestirishbandb.com

Tullyesker Country House officially graded Premier Select 5 Diamonds Bed and Breakfast. One of only 44 in all of Ireland. Three acre garden, panoramic views over the Boyne Valley. Bedrooms with tea/coffee facilities, muti-television, hairdryer, electric blankets, Orthopedic beds. Breakfast menu. Secure private parking. Beside Drogheda on the N1 road at Monasterboice with its High Crosses, Newgrange and Knowth's Neolithic Tombs, five miles away. Easy reach of the Hill of Tara, Trim Castle, Slane Castle and Kells. For sightseeing and shopping in Dublin City centre take a £7 return bus.

B & B from €23pp, Rooms 3 double, 1 twin, 1 family, all en-suite, Restricted smoking, Children over 10, No dogs, Closed Dec to Jan

Aberdeen Lodge 53/55 Park Avenue, Ballsbridge, Dublin 4
Map Ref: 6
Pat Halpin Tel: +353 1 2838155 Fax: +353 1 2837877
Email: aberdeen@iol.ie Web: www.halpinsprivatehotels.com

Aberdeen Lodge is an elegant Edwardian property, situated in Dublin's prestigious embassy district. The spacious, comfortable bedrooms are tastefully furnished to a very high standard and offer every modern comfort including some suites with a jacuzzi and executive facilities. This graceful lodge offers excellent cuisine and impeccable service in the beautifully furnished dining room, which overlooks the extensive, landscaped gardens. Minutes by DART to the centre of Dublin city, Aberdeen Lodge is the perfect base from which to explore the city sights, and the Wicklow Mountains to the south.

B & B from €45pp, C-Cards MC VS DC, Rooms 2 single, 6 twin, 10 double, 2 family, Children welcome, No dogs, Open all year

Blakes Townhouse 50 Merrion Road, Ballsbridge, Dublin 4
Map Ref: 6
R105
Pat Halpin Tel: +353 1 6688324 Fax: +353 1 6684280
Email: blakestownhouse@iol.ie Web: www.halpinsprivatehotels.com

Blakes Townhouse is a grand two storey Edwardian house which stands next door to the embassies in the exclusive Ballsbridge district of Dublin. The house provides a serene atmosphere, coupled with privacy and seclusion for guests, yet it is only a short stroll from the city centre. All of the bedrooms are individually designed and traditionally decorated, each one has a full private bathroom, and is equipped to please the discerning traveller, whether staying in Dublin for business or pleasure, an ideal four star property.

B & B €45-€90pp, C-Cards MC VS DC, Rooms 2 single, 3 twin, 7 double, 2 family, all en-suite, Children welcome, No dogs, Open all year

Cedar Lodge 98 Merrion Road, Dublin 4
Map Ref: 6
Gerard & Mary Doody Tel: +353 1 668 4410 Fax: +353 1 668 4533
Email: info@cedarlodge.ie Web: www.cedarlodge.ie

Cedar Lodge is a luxurious alternative to a hotel. Modern comforts and Edwardian style combine to create a truly unique experience. Our beautifully furnished en-suite bedrooms are presented to an International standard. There is a comfortable lounge and a spacious dining room. This jewel among guesthouses is located in leafy Ballsbridge, and is adjacent to the RDS, the British Embassy and the Four Seasons Hotel. Cedar Lodge is just 10 minutes from the city centre, it is close to the airport and car ferries. There is a private car park.

B & B €45-€82pp, C-Cards MC VS AE, Rooms 6 twin, 7 double, 2 family, all en-suite, No smoking, Children over 5, No dogs, Closed Xmas

Glenogra House 64 Merrion Road, Ballsbridge, Dublin 4

Seamus & Cherry McNamee Tel: +353 1 668 3661   Fax: +353 1 668 3698
Email: glenogra@indigo.ie   Web: www.glenogra.com

Map Ref: 6

Located opposite the RDS and Four Seasons Hotel, Glenogra House stands close to the city centre, bus and train stations, embassies, restaurants and car ferries. Glenogra provides luxury and elegance in a personalised family run enviroment. The cosy drawing room is perfect for a restoring cup of tea. En-suite bedrooms are decorated in harmony with a period residence, all are equipped with telephone, television and tea/coffee making facilities. Private parking is available for guests' cars. Directions to Glenogra on request.

B & B from €50pp, C-Cards MC VS AE DC, Rooms 1 single, 3 twin, 10 double, all en-suite, No smoking, Children welcome, No dogs, Closed Xmas & New Year

Merrion Hall 54/56 Merrion Road, Dublin 4

Mr Pat Halpin Tel: +353 1 668 1426   Fax: +353 1 668 4280
Email: merrionhall@iol.ie   Web: www.halpinsprivatehotels.com

Map Ref: 6

Merrion Hall is a small exclusively styled property located in the Embassy district of Dublin city offering peace and tranquility, yet within minutes of the city centre. All the rooms are with full private bathroom and air conditioning, they offer every modern comfort for the discerning traveller, all that one would expect of a private hotel. There are five four poster rooms and two suites with period furniture and whirlpool spas. The drawing rooms and library provide an ideal relaxation area for residents to unwind during their visit to this vibrant city.

B & B €45-€90pp, C-Cards MC VS DC, Rooms 3 single, 7 twin, 12 double, 2 family, all en-suite, Children welcome, No dogs, Open all year

Simmonstown House 2 Sydenham Road, Ballsbridge, Dublin 4

Finola & James Curry Tel: +353 1 6607260   Fax: +353 1 6607341
Email: info@simmonstownhouse.com   Web: www.simmonstownhouse.com

Map Ref: 6

Simmonstown House is a delightful Victorian town house in Ballsbridge, Dublin's most elegant residential district. It was fully restored in period style and modernised by Finola and James Curry in 1988 and houses all the family antiques, paintings and silverware. Simmonstown has a deserved reputation for its ample and innovative breakfasts, served in the family dining room. The house is within walking distance of the city centre and close to main bus and train services. Top quality restaurants are but a short walk away.

B & B from €64pp, C-Cards MC VS AE, Rooms 2 double, 1 twin, 1 family, all en-suite, No smoking, Children welcome, No dogs, Closed Xmas & New Year

Belcamp Hutchinson Carrs Lane, Malahide Rd, Balgriffin, Dublin 17

Doreen Gleeson and Karl Waldburg Tel: +353 1 846 0843   Fax: +353 1 848 5703
belcamphutchinson@eircom.net   www.belcamphutchinson.com

Map Ref: 7

see Photo opposite

Belcamp Hutchinson is a Georgian house built in 1786. Only 20 minutes from Dublin City, 15 minutes from Dublin Airport and five minutes from one of Irelands prettiest villages Malahide. During its recent refurbishment great care was taken to ensure that work was carried out uniting the old elegance of the house with modern amenities. We are proud to offer guests the most up-to-date facilities in a setting unspoilt by the passage of time.

B & B from €65pp, C-Cards MC VS, Rooms 1 single, 8 double, 3 twin, all en-suite, Restricted smoking, Children over 10, Dogs welcome, Closed Xmas & New Year

Belcamp Hutchinson, Balgriffin, Dublin 17

Boltown House, Kells, Co Meath

Rathsallagh House Dunlavin, Co Wicklow
Joe & Kay O'Flynn   Tel: +353 45 403112   Fax: +353 45 403343
Email: info@rathsallagh.com   Web: www.rathsallagh.com

Map Ref: 8
N9

Winner of the prestigious Country House of the Year Award 2000, the National Breakfast Award four times and a member of Irelands Blue Book. Rathsallagh was converted from a Queen Anne stable block in 1798. It has its own 18 hole Championship Golf Course and is set in a peaceful oasis of 530 acres of rolling parkland with thousands of mature trees, lakes and streams. On the West side of the Wicklow mountains close to Puchestown and the Curragh racecourses, yet only one hour from Dublin airport.

B & B €115-€135pp, C-Cards MC VS AE, Dinner from €50, Rooms 29 double, all en-suite, Restricted smoking, Children over 12, Dogs by arrangement, Closed Xmas

The Old Workhouse Dunshaughlin, Co Meath
Niamh Colgan   Tel / Fax: +353 1 825 9251
Email: comfort@a-vip.com   Web: www.travelto/oldworkhouse.com

Map Ref: 9
N3,M50

This 1840's listed building was restored in 1988 to create a welcoming bed and breakfast, which now has a big reputation in Ireland. Niamh, (pronounced Neeve) is a friendly professional who ensures that her guests will want to return. The comfortable bedrooms have many thoughtful extras such as jelly beans and a decanter of sherry, the ground floor suite has a Victorian double bed, a large bathroom and a claw tub. Neeve holds the title for the Best Breakfast in Ireland, locally cured ham, home baked soda bread and poached fruit are some of the delights.

B & B €50-€76pp, C-Cards MC VS, Rooms 1 twin, 4 double, Restricted smoking, No children, Dogs by arrangement, Closed Xmas & New Year

Pinewood Lodge Glendalough, Co Wicklow
Michael & Mary Cullen   Tel: +353 404 45437/45950   Fax: +353 404 45437
Email: pwlodge@gofree.indigo.ie

Map Ref: 10
R756

This spacious dormer bungalow is set in one acre and is bordered by forests. Pinewood Lodge is situated on the Wicklow Way in Ireland's garden county. The area abounds with pretty villages, country houses and wonderful scenery. Guests may be assured of a warm welcome to this family home. The bedrooms are spacious attractively presented, they offer tea/coffee making facilities. There is a comfortable lounge, and in the breakfast room guests may select from an interesting menu. It is only a five minute walk to a nearby pub and restaurants.

B & B €26-€30pp, C-Cards MC VS, Rooms 2 double, 2 twin, 2 family, all en-suite, No smoking, Children over 4, Dogs by arrangement, Open all year

Boltown House Kells, Co Meath
Jean & Susan Wilson   Tel: +353 46 43605   Fax: +353 46 43036
Email: boltown@eircom.net

Map Ref: 11
N3, N52
see photo opposite

Built in the mid 18th century, Boltown House is set in 100 acres of rolling farmland. With pleasant gardens and a charming atmosphere, the house offers a peaceful refuge just an hour from Dublin. The bedrooms are large and very comfortable with views to the garden. There are many archaeological sites nearby, including Newgrange and Trim. Guests may also visit the wonderful gardens at Butterstream, Lakeview and Ballinlough Castle. Golf can be played nearby, and fishing is available on the Blackwater. Dinner is delicious and carefully prepared using the best of local ingredients.

B & B €50-€60pp, C-Cards MC VS AE, Dinner from €30, Rooms 3 double/twin, all en-suite, Restricted smoking, Children welcome, No dogs in bedrooms, Closed Xmas & New Year

Martinstown House The Curragh, Kildare, Co Kildare

Meryl Long   Tel: +353 45 441269   Fax: +353 45 441208
Email: info@martinstownhouse.com   Web: www.martinstownhouse.com

Map Ref: 12
M9, M7, N78

Martinstown offers the discerning traveller peace and tranquility, yet it is situated within one hour of Dublin Airport and City, and one and a half hours from ferry ports, Rosslare is two hours away. Built as a cottage orne by the famous architect Decimus Burton in the 1830's it is a most charming house, set in beautiful parkland. The old fashioned walled garden provides flowers, fruit and vegetables in season. On the farm are cattle, sheep, a pony and foal and a donkey and proper free-range hens. The food is delicious, visitors appear to enjoy everying!

B & B from €95pp, C-Cards MC VS AE, Dinner from €40, Rooms 3 double, 1 twin, all en-suite, Restricted smoking, Children over 12, No dogs, Closed Xmas & New Year

Mountainstown House Castletown-Kilpatrick, Navan, Co Meath

John & Diana Pollock   Tel / Fax: +353 46 54154
Email: pollock@oceanfree.net

Map Ref: 13
N3, R163

Beautifully restored Dutch Wren and early Georgian house, it is bright, sunny and warm. The house was owned by Samuel Gibbons from 1727 until 1796 when it was bought by John Pollock. This is a beautiful sporting estate and working farm. There is an 18th century courtyard, spring wells, carriage wash, parkland, horses and donkeys, poultry and peacocks are free roaming. The bedrooms are south facing, there is a fabulous four poster master bedroom. The house is perfect for honeymooners, it is available for wedding receptions. Beautiful Catholic and Protestant churches within a few miles.

B & B €45-€70pp, Dinner from €32, Rooms 1 single, 4 double, 1 twin/family, most en-suite, Restricted smoking, Children welcome, Dogs by arrangement, Closed Xmas & New Year

Cooley Lodge Nr Carlingford, Riverstown, Co Louth

Geraldine & Freeman Lynn   Tel: +353 42 9376201
Email: cooley1@gofree.indigo.ie

Map Ref: 14
R173

A unique stone building discreetly converted into first class accommodation. The bedrooms are spacious and comfortable, individually styled with tasteful decor and furnishings, many with idyllic mountain views. An elegant sitting room boasting splendid antiques and paintings with a blazing turf fire in autumn evenings. The south-facing conservatory adjoins the 25m indoor heated swimming pool, both having incomparable mountain views. Breakfast is taken in the delightful galleried dining-room, flooded with early morning light. Cooley Lodge is ideally situated to tour the North East coast of Ireland.

B & B from €45pp, C-Cards MC VS AE DC, Rooms 7 double, 3 twin, 1 family, all en-suite, Children welcome, No dogs, Closed Nov to Apr

Lissadell House Ashtown Lane, Wicklow, Co Wicklow

Patricia Klaue   Tel: +353 404 67458
Email: lissadellhse@eircom.net   Web: www.geocities.com/lissadellhse

Map Ref: 15

Lissadell House is an imposing part Georgian house which stands in its own grounds in scenic Wicklow countryside, yet it is just one and a half kms from the county town of Wicklow. The house is surrounded by golf clubs and nature walks. There are some wonderful sandy beaches only a short drive away, and for those who enjoy horses, riding can be arranged. This well recommended house is only 45 minutes from the city of Dublin. A warm welcome awaits all who come to stay.

B & B €30-€34pp, No smoking, Children welcome, Guide dogs only, Closed Dec to Feb

The South & Southeast

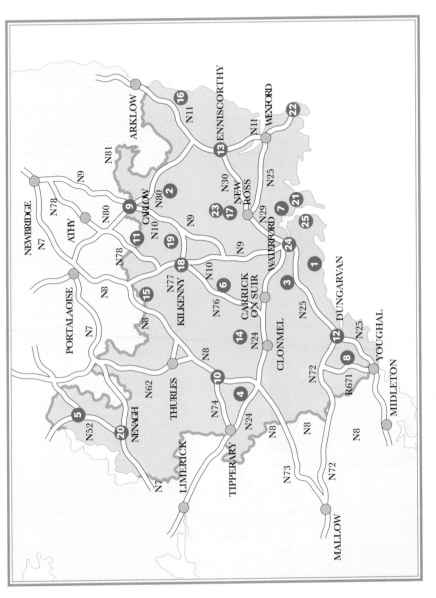

The Blue Map References should be used to locate B & B properties on the pages that follow

Annestown House Annestown, Co Waterford
John & Pippa Galloway Tel: +353 51 396160 Fax: +353 51 396474
Email: relax@annestown.com Web: www.annestown.com

Map Ref: 1
R675

The house stands in its own grounds overlooking a bay on the rugged Copper Coast of Co Waterford. An easygoing rambling home, it has a billiard room and two sitting rooms inside and croquet and tennis lawns outside, as well as the paths that lead down to the beach. The area is attractively undeveloped and peppered with archaeological and geological features, as well as varieties of living nature. Unusually the village has no pub, but within a couple of miles there are two 'locals' and places to eat.

B & B €47.50-€52.50pp, C-Cards MC VS AE, Dinner from €30, Rooms 3 double, 1 twin, 1 family, all en-suite, No smoking in bedrooms, No dogs, Closed Nov to Feb

Lorum Old Rectory Kilgreaney, Bagenalstown, Co Carlow
Bobbie & Don Smith Tel: +353 503 75282 Fax: +353 503 75455
Email: bobbie@lorum.com Web: www.lorum.com

Map Ref: 2
N9

A warm welcome is assured at Lorum. Set Beneath Mt. Leinster in the tranquil Barrow Valley, the Rectory, built in 1863 of cut granite, is filled with pleasant conversation and the exciting aroma of freshly baked bread. This family run home has built a reputation for its warmth of welcome and imaginative home cooking, using locally produced organic ingredients wherever possible. Whatever their requirements, guests at Lorum are spoiled for choice. You will enjoy your stay at Lorum with Bobbie and Don.

B & B from €50pp, C-Cards MC VS, Dinner from €35, Rooms 4 double, 1 twin, all en-suite, No smoking, Children over 12, Dogs by arrangement, Closed Xmas & New Year

Sherwood Park House Kilbride, Ballon, Co Carlow
Patrick & Maureen Owens Tel: +353 503 59117 Fax: +353 503 59355
Email: info@sherwoodparkhouse.ie Web: www.sherwoodparkhouse.ie

Map Ref: 2
N80, N81

Sherwood Park House is listed built in 1730, set in rolling parklands and tranquil countryside in Slaney valley, beside Altamont Gardens. Good salmon fishing river. Magnificent views from the house, Wicklow mountains to the front and Blackstairs Mountains to the back of the House. Set in large gardens, laid to lawn. All bedrooms furnished with old antique beds - 4 poster, half tester and brass - and have both bath tub and shower facilities. All meals are prepared from either home or locally grown produce. Homemade bread, scones and jams. There is golf and horse racing locally.

B & B €40pp, C-Cards MC VS AE, Dinner €35, Rooms 2 double, 3 triple, Restricted smoking, Children welcome, Dogs by arrangement, Open all year

Glasha Farmhouse Glasha, Ballymacarbry, Co Waterford
Paddy & Olive O'Gorman Tel / Fax: +353 52 36108 Mobile: +353 8624 43255
Email: glasha@eircom.net Web: www.glashafarmhouse

Map Ref: 3
R671

Multi award winning luxury family farmhouse set in between the Comeragh and Knockmealdown Moutains. All rooms en-suite, including some with jacuzzi baths. All have television, radio, tea/coffee making facilities, snack bars, etc. Luxury guest room available, also conservatory and patio area containing a magnificent water-feature. Beautiful gardens. Ideally suited for walking, golfing, horse riding and touring. Very friendly and homely atmosphere. Wonderful breakfast menu. Good local restaurants and pubs.

B & B €30-€35pp, C-Cards MC VS, Rooms 1 single, 2 double/twin, 3 twin, 2 family, all en-suite, No smoking, Children over 10, No dogs, Closed Nov to Feb

Bansha Castle Bansha, Co Tipperary

Teresa & John Russell   Tel: +353 62 54187   Fax: +353 62 54294
Email: johnrus@iol.ie   Web: www.tipp.ie/bansha-castle.htm

Map Ref: 4
N24

Beautiful old country house, built in the 1700's, in lovely wooded grounds and gardens. A warm welcome and superb food make this gracious house your ideal base. Snooker room. Though specialising in relaxation, golf, walking, fishing and horse riding can be arranged locally. Children welcome. Dinner 7.30 p.m. Advance booking recommended. Available for rental.

B & B from €32pp, Dinner from €23, Rooms 2 double, 3 twin, 1 family, all en-suite, Children welcome, No dogs, Open all year

Ballycormac House Aglish, Roscrea, near Borrisokane, Co Tipperary

John & Cherylynn Lang   Tel: +353 67 21129   Fax: +353 67 21200
Email: ballyc@indigo.ie   Web: www.ballyc.com

Map Ref: 5
N52
see Photo on page 396

Ballycormac House is a 350 year old Irish farmhouse cottage, set in the middle of North Tipperary countryside. The genial hosts ensure that everyone is made to feel at home. The freshly prepared four course set dinner is served around a large table in the dining room, using home grown produce. The bedrooms are cosy and comfortably furnished, there is a honeymoon suite with four poster bed available for romantics. Nestle down in the relaxing atmosphere of the farmhouse sitting room, with its open turf fire. Ballycormac House offers horse riding holidays. Golf, go-carting, shooting and fishing available locally.

B & B €32-€58pp, C-Cards MC VS, Dinner from €28, Rooms 1 single, 3 double, 1 twin, all en-suite, No smoking, Children & dogs welcome, Open all year

Ballaghtobin Callan, Co Kilkenny

Mrs Catherine Gabbett   Tel: +353 56 25227   Fax: +353 56 25712
Email: catherine@ballaghtobin.com   Web: www.ballaghtobin.com

Map Ref: 6
N76

Ballaghtobin is set in parkland in the middle of a 500 acre working farm. This is a wonderfully peaceful location from which to explore the south east of Ireland, which is steeped in history. The medieval city of Kilkenny is only thirteen miles away. A hard tennis court, testing croquet lawn and ruined Norman Church complete the garden which is available for guests to enjoy. All the bedrooms are en-suite, they are furnished with antiques and have tea/coffee trays and reading material.

B & B €45-€55pp, C-Cards VS, Rooms 1 double, 1 double/twin, 1 family, all en-suite, Restricted smoking, Children over 12, Dogs welcome, Closed Dec to Jan

Kilmokea Country Manor and Gardens Great Island, Campile, Co Wexford

Mark & Emma Hewlet   Tel: +353 51 388109   Fax: +353 51 388776
Email: kilmokea@indigo.ie   Web: www.kilmokea.com

Map Ref: 7
R733

This is a fine 18th century Georgian rectory, set amidst seven acres of fantastic tropical gardens which are renowned world wide. Nestled on the banks of the River barrow, nine miles from Waterford City, guests can experience Irish country life at its best. The bedrooms have wonderful garden views and are individually decorated. The magnolia room has a beautifully dressed four poster and the Rose room a 6'6" bateau lit! There is a baby grand piano, and aromatherapy treatments are available. The area offers golf, beaches, coastal walking, riding, art, heritage and birdlife.

B & B €60-€100pp, C-Cards MC VS, Dinner from €35, Rooms 5 double, 1 twin, all en-suite, Restricted smoking, Children & dogs welcome, Closed Nov to Mar

Ballycormac House, Roscrea, near Borrisokane, Co Tipperary

Richmond House Cappoquin, Co Waterford

Paul & Claire Deevy Tel: +353 58 54278 Fax: +353 58 54988
Email: info@richmondhouse.net Web: www.richmondhouse.net

This is a delightful 18th century Georgian country house with a fully licensed, award-winning restaurant, standing in 12 acres of private parkland. Relax in total tranquility in front of a log fire, or treat yourself to a sumptuous meal in our restaurant. Each of our rooms combines Georgian elegance with modern comforts for the discerning traveller. All the bedrooms are en-suite, well equipped and furnished with antiques. The restaurant offers such temptations as seared scallops on a fresh herb rissotto, prawn ravioli and champagne sauce. Richmond House is well placed for interesting day visits.

B & B €64-€88pp, C-Cards MC VS AE DC, Dinner from €43, Rooms 1 single, 6 double, 2 twin, all en-suite, Restricted smoking, Children welcome, No dogs, Closed Xmas & New Year

Barrowville Town House Kilkenny Road, Carlow, Co Carlow

Randal & Marie Dempsey Tel: +353 503 43324 Fax: +353 503 41953
Web: www.barrowvillehouse.com

Barrowville enjoys a lovely location in its own grounds on the exclusive Kilkenny Road. Just four minutes walk to the town centre. Antique furnishings with well appointed bedrooms, all en-suite and all facilities, most overlooking semi-formal gardens. Breakfast is traditional or buffet, served in an elegant conservatory which overlooks the gardens. Ideal location for touring south-east Wicklow and Kilkenny. Excellent golf courses within 30 minutes drive. Private car park. Recommended by most good guide books.

B & B from €35pp, C-Cards MC VS AE, Rooms 1 single, 3 double, 3 twin, all en-suite, Restricted smoking, Children over 15, No dogs, Closed Xmas & New Year

Dualla House Dualla, Cashel, Co Tipperary

Mairead Power Tel / Fax: +353 62 61487 Mobile: +353 86 8370738
Email: duallahse@eircom.net Web: www.tipp.ie/dualla-house.htm

This elegant Georgian manor dates from 1790, it stands in the Golden Vale of Tipperaray. The location is peaceful with views to rolling parkland and the mountains. This is a 300 acre sheep and grain farm, with a large garden. The rooms are spacious, they have antique furnishings, orthopedic beds, tea/coffee facilities, hairdryers and televisions. The drawing room is large with a welcoming peat fire. Breakfasts are delicious, they include homemade breads, preserves and local cheeses. A wonderful area to explore, the Rock of Cashel, Holycross Abbey, Kilkenny Castle, racing, golf and fishing are nearby.

B & B €30-€40pp, C-Cards MC VS, Rooms 1 double, 1 twin, 2 family, all en-suite, No smoking, Children welcome, Dogs not in house, Closed mid-Nov to mid-Mar

Wandesforde House Castlecomer, Co Kilkenny

Michael & Anna McDonald
Tel: +353 56 42441 Mobile: +353 87678 6208

Built in 1824 by the Duchess of Ormonde as a school for the children on the estate, now a charming guest house, twenty minutes from Kilkenny and five minutes from Castlecomer. All the bedrooms are en-suite, with original high beds and furniture. The magnificent drawing room features an open log fire, antique furniture and a baby grand piano. Guests are welcomed with tea, coffee and home baking. Truly, this is a wonderful base for visiting Kilkenny and the south east. Come and relax in a warm stress-free atmosphere of old fashioned hospitality and charm.

B & B from €35pp, C-Cards MC VS, Dinner from €22, Rooms 2 single, 1 twin, 3 double, all en-suite, No smoking, Children welcome, Dogs outside only, Closed mid-Dec to early Jan

Gortnadiha House Ring, Dungarvan, Co Waterford

Eileen Harty Tel: +353 58 46142 Fax: +353 58 46444
Email: ringcheese@tinet.ie

Map Ref: 12
N25

This gracious country home with woodland gardens is a working dairy farm, enjoying superb views to the sea. Bedrooms are large and spacious with fresh flowers and antique furniture. Guests will enjoy hand made soaps and creams, current literature and books. Fresh fruit and chilled water, freshly squeezed juices, free range eggs, scrambled with smoked salmon, smoked herrings, local black pudding and fruit compotes are there to enjoy. This is the home of the renowned Ring Farmhouse Cheese. There are wonderful walks, gardens and potteries, a whisky distillery and a heritage centre.

B & B €30-€38pp, C-Cards MC VS, Rooms 2 double en-suite, 1 twin private bathroom, Restricted smoking, Children & dogs welcome, Closed mid-Nov to mid-Mar

Salville House Enniscorthy, Co Wexford

Gordon & Jane Parker Tel / Fax: +353 54 35252
Email: info@salvillehouse.com Web: www.salvillehouse.com

Map Ref: 13
N11

Standing in seven acres of grounds, Salville House sits on a hilltop a few miles outside the cathedral town of Enniscorthy and overlooking the River Slaney. Salville House is ideally located for those independant travellers seeking relaxation off the well beaten track. The bedrooms are tastefully furnished with stunning views. All rooms have tea/coffee making facilities, no television. The dining room is, for many guests, the focal point of their stay. Dinner is served at the long table before an open fire and guests may bring their own wine. After dinnr relax in the comfortable surroundings of the drawing room.

B & B €35-€45pp, Dinner from €30, Rooms 2 double en-suite, 1 double with private bathroom, Restricted smoking, Children welcome, Dogs by arrangement, Open all year

Mobarnane House Knockbrit, Fethard, Co Tipperary

Richard & Sandra Craik-White Tel / Fax: +353 52 31962
Email: info@mobarnanehouse.com www.mobarnanehouse.com

Map Ref: 14
R692
see photo opposite

Hidden in the Golden Vale of Tipperary, Morbarnane is a listed, historic, Georgian house set in 60 acres of parkland with an ornamental lake. Recently restored to a high standard, the lovely bedrooms have telephones, televisions and tea/coffee making facilities. Two bedrooms are suites with their own sitting rooms. A four course dinner is available at 24 hours' notice. Tipperary is renowned for arts and crafts, golf courses, mountain scenery, castles and cathedrals; also for the breeding and training of world class race horses. Mobarnane House provides relaxed luxury in a peaceful setting.

B & B €70-€83pp, C-Cards MC VS, Dinner from €35, Rooms 2 double, 2 twin, all en-suite, Restricted smoking, Children over 5, Dogs by arrangement, Open all year

Kilrush House Freshford, Co Kilkenny

Richard & Sally St George Tel: +353 56 32236 Fax: +353 56 32588
Mobile: +353 86 8240028 Email: stgeorg@gofree.indigo.ie

Map Ref: 15
R693, R694

This handsome early 19th century house, has been home to the St George family for over 300 years. It now enjoys a pleasing combination of gracious tradition with modern comfort, this is especially so in the bedrooms where guests will find space and wonderful views to green pastures. The beautiful dining and drawing rooms contain a family collection of furniture and portraits. Guests may walk through the gardens to the fields to see the thoroughbred mares and foals. There is also a hard tennis court for guests' enjoyment. Cashel and Kilkenny are within easy reach.

B & B from €59pp, C-Cards MC VS, Dinner from €25, Rooms 1 double, 2 twin, all en-suite, Restricted smoking, Children over 8, Dogs not in house, Closed Oct to April

Mobarnane House, Knockbrit, near Fethard, Co Tipperary

Woodlands Country House Killinierin, Gorey, Co Wexford   Map Ref: 16, N11

Philomena O'Sullivan Tel: +353 402 37125 Fax: +353 40237133 Mobile: +353 87 6736118
Email: info@woodlandscountryhouse.com Web: www.woodlandscountryhouse.com

Built in 1836, this award-winning house is set in one and a half acres of mature gardens and a courtyard of old stone buildings. The bedrooms are furnished with antiques, they all have television, radio and tea/coffee facilities. Three rooms have balconies overlooking the gardens, this is a charming, intimate place to relax. Fine food and wines. Period furnishings are matched by warm and impeccable service. Guests are welcome to stroll around our gardens, and to enjoy the tennis court and pool table. There are some good restaurants locally. Just one hour from Dublin.

B & B €35-€42pp, C-Cards MC VS, Rooms 1 single, 2 double, 1 twin, 1 family, all en-suite, No smoking, Children welcome, Dogs not in house, Closed Oct to Mar

Cullintra House The Rower, Inistioge, Co Kilkenny   Map Ref: 17

Patricia Cantlon Tel: +353 51 423614   R700
Email: cullhse@indigo.ie Web: http://indigo.ie/~cullhse

Cullintra House stands at the foot of Mount Brandon on 230 acres of wood and hill land with wonderful views and magical walks. A cat lover's paradise and foxes come to dinner each evening in the garden. The pace is leisurely, the atmosphere convivial, and guests are treated to generous hospitality from Patricia an accomplished artist and cook who has created a very special place to stay. Renowned for excellent cuisine, candlelit dinners and breakfasts, lasting to midday, promote a feeling of peace and relaxation. There is a conservatory studio, and galleried rooms created from a barn, all contribute to make this a uniquely memorable stay.

B & B €30-€40pp, Dinner €25, Rooms 6,3 en-suite, Open all year

Butler House Patrick Street, Kilkenny, Co Kilkenny   Map Ref: 18

Mrs Gabrielle Hickey Tel: +353 56 65707/22828 Fax: +353 56 65626   N10
Email: res@butler.ie Web: www.butler.ie

Sweeping staircases, magnificent plastered ceilings, marble fireplaces and a walled garden are features of this notable Georgian town house. Although secluded and quiet, Butler House is located in the heart of the city, close to the castle. The house was restored in the early 1970s, and combines contemporary design with period elegance, to provide the visitor with a unique and interesting experience. There is a suite and three superior rooms which have large bow windows which overlook the walled garden and Kilkenny Castle. There are within walking distance, fine restaurants and pubs.

B & B €57-€114pp, C-Cards MC VS AE DC, Rooms 4 double, 7 double/twin, 1 twin, 1 suite, all en-suite, Children welcome, No dogs, Closed Xmas

Danville House New Ross Road, Kilkenny, Co Kilkenny   Map Ref: 18

Kitty Stallard Tel / Fax: +353 56 21512   N10
Email: treecc@iol.ie

Danville House is two hundred years old, set in a peaceful location among mature trees, situated 1km from Kilkenny City. The Entrance is 0.2km past roundabout on R700 road to New Ross. Relaxed atmosphere maintained old garden with croquet on lawn. Rural bliss with old style charm. Golf and horse riding nearby. Advice given on golf locality.

B & B €23-€30pp, Rooms 2 double, 1 twin, 2 family, most en-suite, No smoking, Children welcome, No dogs, Closed Nov to Mar

Blanchville House Dunbell, Maddoxtown, Co Kilkenny

Monica & Tim Phelan Tel: +353 56 27197 Fax: +353 56 27636
Email: info@blanchville.ie Web: www.blanchville.ie

Blanchville House is an elegant Georgian House, situated five miles from the medieval city of Kilkenny. Offering superior accommodation in the most elegant surroundings. Built in 1800 the house has been sensitively restored by Tim and Monica Phelan and is furnished accordingly, with fine taste. Blanchville is an ideal place from which to explore the south east or simply to relax and get away from it all. There are several golf courses in the area within half an hours drive. Good food and a very warm welcome await you at Blanchville. Self catering coach houses are also available.

B & B €45-€50pp, C-Cards MC VS AE, Rooms 3 double, 3 twin, 1 family, all en-suite,
Restricted smoking, Children over 10, Dogs by arrangement, Closed Nov to Mar

Ashley Park House Nenagh, Co Tipperary

Map Ref: 20
N52

PJ & Margaret Mounsey Tel: +353 67 38223 Fax: +353 67 38013
Email: margaret@ashleypark.com Web: www.ashleypark.com

Ashley Park House is a fine 18th century country house which stands overlooking a private lake which is used for fishing, a boat is available. There are 70 acres of woodland, home to some 300 year old trees, and three fairy forts to ponder, a haven for nature lovers. The house has been decorated with impeccable taste, from the magnificent first floor suites and bedrooms, to the octagonal Chinese reading room off the drawing room. Crystal glasses, silverware and chandeliers decorate the dining room which is warmed by a log fire in winter.

B & B €32-€45pp, Dinner from €30, Rooms 1 single, 1 double, 2 twin, 2 family, all en-suite,
Restricted smoking, Children & dogs welcome, Open all year

Dunbrody Country House & Restaurant Arthurstown, New Ross, Co Wexford

Kevin & Catherine Dundon Tel: +353 51 389600 Fax: +353 51 389601
Email: dunbrody@indigo.ie Web: www.dunbrodyhouse.com

Map Ref: 21
R733

Award winning Dunbrody Country House offers our guests unrivalled hospitality and cuisine. Sumptuous rooms, individually styled and decorated to the highest standard guarantee guests real luxury and comfort. A Georgian house set in 300 acres of gardens and parkland. Dunbrody is renowned for its cuisine, created by owner and Masterchef Kevin Dundon. Meals are served in a large and spacious dining room, there is an attractive bar area and imposing entrance hall. The grounds run down to sea frontage overlooking Waterford Harbour.

B & B €90-€180pp, C-Cards MC VS AE DC, Dinner from €50, Rooms 11 double, 8 twin, 1 family,
all en-suite, Restricted smoking, Children over 12, No dogs, Closed Xmas

Glendine Country House Arthurstown, New Ross, Co Wexford

Map Ref: 21
N29, N25

Tom & Ann Crosbie Tel: +353 51 389258 Fax: +353 51 389677
Mobile: +353 87 6873166 Email: glendinehouse@eircom.net www.glendinehouse.com

Built in 1830, Glendine Country House enjoys sweeping views from an elevated hill top position, of the Barrow Estuary. Steeped in over 60 years of history, and now very much a family home, the emphasis here is on warmth and relaxation, coupled with an appealing olde worlde charm. Glendine is highly recommended, home to the Crosbie family since 1948, guests are assured of a genuine welcome. There are dogs, ponies, sheep and beef cattle. Waterford which is seven miles away, may be reached by car ferry, Rosslare is 30 miles.

B & B €32-€40pp, C-Cards MC VS AE, Rooms 2 double, 2 twin, 1 family, all en-suite,
Restricted smoking, Children welcome, Small charge for dogs, Closed Dec to Feb

se Tagoat, Rosslare, Co Wexford   Map Ref: 22

Tel: +353 53 32555   Fax: +353 53 32577   N25

are@indigo.ie   churchtown-rosslare.com   *see Photo opposite*

Churchtown House was built at the dawn of the 18th century. The families associated with it were amongst the most powerful in a Wexford County of emerging independence. Eight and a half years ago Patricia and Austin Cody reopened and somewhat extended this lovely country house, providing good food and excellent accommodation and all you would expect in a small intimate country house. Perfect for an overnight stay or longer to enjoy history, seafishing, swimming, walking, bird watching and golf amongst other activities. Set in eight acres of mature parkland Churchtown provides a haven of peace and tranquility.

B & B €65-€95pp, C-Cards MC VS AE, Dinner from €35, Rooms 1 single, 5 double, 5 twin, 1 family, all en-suite, No smoking, Children over 10, No dogs, Closed Nov to Mar

---

Ballyduff House   Ballyduff, Thomastown, Co Kilkenny   Map Ref: 23

Breda Thomas   Tel: +353 56 58488   Mobile: +353 8791 50321   N9, R700

Email: ballyd@gofree.indigo.ie

Ballyduff House is an 18th century manor house set in its own grounds, overlooking the River Nore. Very secluded an private. Delightful library, the perfect room to relax. The bedrooms are beautifully decorated, many antiques and crisp white linen. Mount Juliet with its golf course and leisure centre is just ten minutes drive. Riding, hunting and fishing can be arranged. Many beautiful walks. Children welcome.

B & B from €38pp, Rooms 2 double, 1 twin, 1 family, most en-suite, Restricted smoking, Children welcome, No dogs, Closed Nov to Mar

---

Foxmount Country House   Passage East Road, Waterford, Co Waterford   Map Ref: 24

Margaret & David Kent   Tel: +353 51 874308   Fax: +353 51 854906   R683, R684

Email: foxmount@iol.ie   Web: www.iol.ie/tipp/foxmount.htm

Foxmount Farm is an elegant 17th century house on a working dairy farm. There are log fires, antiques and beautifully decorated rooms to enjoy in a relaxed, homely style. The spacious bedrooms overlook the well tended grounds or the beautiful herb garden. The emphasis is on good food cooked by Margaret, the farm supplying home produced beef, lamb, free range eggs and fresh vegetables, there is also local wild salmon to enjoy. There are ten golf courses within easy reach, and safe, sandy beaches locally. Dinner is served at seven, bring your own wine.

B & B from €45pp, Dinner from €30, Rooms 1 twin, 3 double, 1 family, all en-suite, Restricted smoking, Children welcome, No dogs, Closed Nov to mid-Mar

---

Gaultier Lodge   Woodstown, Co Waterford   Map Ref: 25

Sheila Molloy   Tel: +353 51 382549   R684

Email: castleffrench@eircom.net   Web: castleffrench.com/gaultier

Gaultier Lodge is an 18th century Georgian bed and breakfast, situated in Woodstown on the south eastern coast of Co Waterford. The surrounding area is ideal for country walks with excellent views over the Suir Estuary to Dunmore East, where one can enjoy a leisurely lunch over a glass of wine. Woodstown is an ideal base for touring Wexford via the Passage East car ferry to Ballyhack, the quaint picturesque town of New Ross, or the spectacular landscape of the Hook Head are all within easy reach.

B & B from €70pp, C-Cards MC VS, Rooms 4 double, 1 twin, all en-suite, No smoking, Children over 8, Dogs in kennels, Open all year

Churchtown House, Tagoat, near Rosslare, Co Wexford

The Southwest

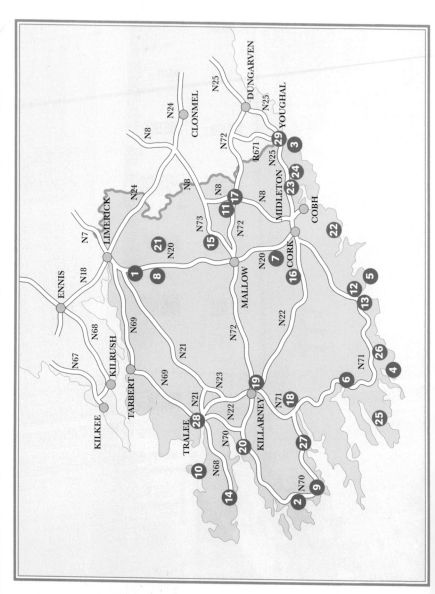

The Blue Map References should be used to locate B & B properties on the pages that follow

The Mustard Seed at Echo Lodge Ballingarry, Co Limerick
Daniel Mullane   Tel: +353 69 68508   Fax: +353 69 68511
Email: mustard@indigo.ie

The Mustard Seed at Echo Lodge stands eight miles from Adare Village, it is a beautiful Victorian country home overlooking the tranquil village of Ballingarry. Built in 1884, the house stands in seven acres of lawns, it has been lovingly restored to combine a gracious elegance, with modern day comforts. Dan Mullane is well travelled, he has interesting collections to bear testimony to his trips which will intrigue visitors here. The bedrooms are individually presented and especially comfortable. Dinner is prepared to order, choosing from the best of Ireland's organic farms.

B & B €42-€64pp, C-Cards MC VS, Dinner from €45, Rooms 6 single, 9 double/twin, 3 double/family, all en-suite, Restricted smoking, No children, Dogs not in house, Open all year

Rascals Old School House Barry's Cross, Ballinskelligs, Co Kerry
Mrs Lillian Morgan   Tel / Fax: +353 66 9479340
Email: oshmb@iol.ie   Web: www.kerry-insight.com/old-school

Map Ref: 2
R567

A truly magical place, your visit will leave you wanting more. The Old School House has a lot to offer the weary traveller, comfort, hospitality, good food and wine, an open turf fire in our lounge, boat trips to Skellig's nature walks and travel tips. Most bedrooms are en-suite, tea and coffee on arrival and a song or two in the evening. Your hosts Dominick and Lillian look forward to meeting you. The kettle is always on.

B & B €23-€33pp, C-Cards MC VS, Dinner from €16, Rooms 4 single, 6 double, 6 twin, 2 family, most en-suite, No smoking, Children welcome, Dogs in outside kennel, Closed Dec to Jan

Spanish Point Ballycotton, Co Cork
John & Mary Tattan   Tel: +353 21 4646177   Fax: +353 21 4646179
Mobile: +353 87 2446535   Email: spanishp@indigo.ie

Map Ref: 3
N25, R633

Spanish Point Seafood Restaurant is perched on a cliff looking over Ballycotton Bay. John has trawlers which supply the fish for the restaurant, Mary trained at the Ballymaloe cookery school, she uses fresh local produce to complement their seafood menus. There are two restaurants, one is in a conservatory overlooking the sea where breakfasts and dinners are served. All the bedrooms are well equipped and comfortably furnished, with views to the sea. Guests are welcome to relax in the cosy sitting room with an open fire. Wonderful for walking, swimming, bird-watching or angling.

B & B from €38.10pp, C-Cards VS DC, Dinner from €35.50, Rooms 2 twin, 3 double, all en-suite, Children & dogs welcome, Closed Dec to Feb

Baltimore Bay Baltimore, Co Cork
Youen Jacob
Tel: +353 28 20600   Fax: +353 28 20495

Map Ref: 4
R595

Baltimore Bay is a restaurant and guesthouse combined, it stands in the corner of a small square on the water front. It seems to be a lively place, there is often a gathering of folk. There are two Youen Jacobs, Youen senior originated from Brittany, there are two restaurants, oysters being a speciality. Accommodation for guests is above a busy cafe. Some rooms have views to the busy harbour, others, overlook a small garden. They all offer en-suite facilities. For seafarers, Baltimore offers boats, sea food and music.

B & B from €25pp, C-Cards MC VS AE DC, Dinner from €25, Rooms 8 double, all en-suite, Children welcome, No dogs, Open all year

Sea Court, Butlerstown, near Bandon, Co Cork

Butlerstown House Butlerstown, Timoleague, Bandon, Co Cork
Elisabeth Jones & Roger Owen   Tel / Fax: +353 23 40137
Email: mail@butlerstownhouse.com   Web: www.butlerstownhouse.com

Lis and Roger welcome you to Butlerstown House, a magnificent small Georgian Irish country residence, set in its own grounds of some ten acres. Elevated at 500 feet above sea level, it offers uninterrupted views of rolling Irish countryside, with the blue haze of the Dunmanway Mountains in the distance. Its position off the beaten tourist routes, and just one mile from the Atlantic coastline, offers peace and tranquillity, jealously guarded by its present owners.

B & B €85-€95pp, C-Cards MC VS, Rooms 2 double, 2 double/twin, 1 twin, No smoking, Children over 12, Dogs by arrangement, Closed Nov to Mar

Sea Court Butlerstown, Bandon, Co Cork
David Elder   Tel: +353 23 40151/40218
Email: seacourt_inn@yahoo.com

Map Ref: 5
R600
see Photo opposite

Sea Court is a Georgian country mansion built in 1760, which has been lovingly restored over the last twenty years by David. The house and grounds have many interesting architectural features, including an impressive fan lighted doorway beneath a pillared porch, an arched belltower, a number of unusual trees and a newly restored orchard. David and Monica, based in Kentucky, visit Sea Court for ten weeks each year, during which time they open for bed and breakfast. For the remainder of the year the property is available for self-catering. Out of season contact the US, tel: +1 513 961 3537 or fax: +1 513 721 5109.

B & B from €35pp, Dinner from €30, Rooms 3 double, 2 twin, 1 family, most en-suite, Restricted smoking, Children welcome, Dogs in outbuilding, Closed Sep to May

Bantry House Bantry, Co Cork
Egerton & Brigitte Shelswell-White   Tel: +353 27 50047   Fax: +353 27 50795
Email: info@bantryhouse.ie   Web: www.bantryhouse.ie

Map Ref: 6
N71

Bantry House overlooks Bantry Bay and is one of the most beautiful properties in Ireland. The views are magnificent over the Bay and Italianate Garden, with its fountains, parterres and 'Stairway to the Sky'. The luxurious furnishings and decor within Bantry House are enhanced by wonderful antiques, priceless furniture and works of art. The house is in three parts, the east and west wing offer en-suite accommodation, whereas the main and imposing frontage houses the reception rooms which are open to the public. Facilities for residents include a sitting room, billiard room and balcony television room.

B & B from €60pp, C-Cards MC VS AE, Rooms 8 double, 1 family, all en-suite, No smoking, Children welcome, No dogs, Closed Nov to Feb

Maranatha Country House Tower, Blarney, Co Cork
Olwen & Douglas Venn   Tel: +353 21 4385102   Fax: +353 21 4382978
Email: info@maranathacountryhouse.com   Web: maranathacountyhouse.com

Map Ref: 7
R617

Built in 1887, this lovely Victorian mansion stands in a secluded position and is surrounded by beautiful, gardens and woodland. The bedrooms are an expression of Olwen's flair for style, each diplays a romantic theme and is richly enhanced with colour. The Regal suite has a four poster bed, a sunken bathroom and a whirlpool. Delicious breakfasts are taken in the flower filled conservatory, they include a choice of juices, cheeses and yogurts, and a traditonal breakfast. Blarney Castle, Blarney woollen mills, two golf courses and angling are nearby.

B & B €21-€35pp, C-Cards MC VS, Rooms 5 double, 1 family, all en-suite, No smoking, Children welcome, Guide dogs only, Closed Dec to mid-March

allyteigue House Rockhill, Bruree, Co Limerick

chard & Margaret Johnson Tel / Fax: +353 63 90575
Email: ballyteigue@eircom.net

Map Ref: 8
N20

Ballyteigue is a Georgian Country House, situated 2km from the N20. Easy to find. Large garden with views of mountains and countryside from all windows. The rooms are large with high ceilings, furnished with antiques. The dining room has separate tables and there is a drawing room for guests use. Ballyteigue is situated near Maigue River and Ballyhoura Mountains. There is an archaeological site and stone circle nearby. Riding can be arranged.

B & B €33-€40pp, C-Cards MC VS, Dinner from €32, Rooms 3 double, 1 twin, all en-suite, 1 single, own bathroom, No smoking, Children welcome, No dogs, Closed Dec to Mar

Iskeroon Bunavalla, Caherdaniel, Co Kerry

Geraldine & David Hare Tel: +353 66 9475119 Fax: +353 66 9475488
Email: info@iskeroon.com Web: www.iskeroon.com

Map Ref: 9
N70

Iskeroon's location overlooking Derrynane harbour makes this house special. It stands in four acres of semi tropical gardens which run down to the sea. The house has been widely praised for its presentation, the rooms being spacious, light and airy. Just two and a half miles off the Ring of Kerry, Iskeroon makes the perfect base for exploring the Iveragh Peninsular. The large drawing room has a turf fire. There's a private pier from which to swim. A self catering apartment is available. Excellent restaurants in Waterville, and pub food nearby.

B & B from €50pp, C-Cards MC VS, Rooms 2 double, 1 twin, all with private bathroom, Restricted smoking, Children over 12, No dogs, Closed Oct to April

The Shores Country House Cappatigue, Connor Pass Road, Castlegregory, Co Kerry

Annette Mahoney Tel / Fax: +353 66 7139196
Email: theshores@eircom.net Web: shores.main-page.com

Map Ref: 10
R560

This highly recommended, award winning, modern, comfortable country house enjoys fine panoramic views to the Dingle peninsula, it is just one mile west of Stradbally. The rooms are luxuriously appointed, they are spacious with Queen size beds, and are presented in a Laura Ashley style, they are privileged with wonderful sea views. Breakfasts are delicious, gourmet dinners using fresh local produce also are an important reason to spend time here, they are served in the attractive dining room. There is a library stocked with an interesting range of guides for guests to browse.

B & B €24-€27pp, C-Cards MC VS, Dinner from €18.50, Rooms 4 double, 1 twin, 1 family, all en-suite, No smoking, Children over 3, No dogs, Closed Dec to Feb

Ballyvolane House Castlelyons, Co Cork

Jeremy & Merrie Green Tel: +353 25 36349 Fax: +353 25 36781
Email: ballyvol@iol.ie Web: www.ballyvolanehouse.ie

Map Ref: 11
N8,R628

A relaxing drink beside an open log fire, followed by an excellent candlelit dinner is a perfect ending to a perfect day at Ballyvolane. The house built in 1728, was remodelled 120 years later in Italianate style. The fine pillared hall features a Bluthner baby grand piano. All our rooms have stunning views overlooking 12 acres of formal gardens, or the parkland with its trout lakes. Ballyvolane has 10km of privately managed salmon fishing on the renowned River Blackwater, with a variety of spring and summer beats.

B & B €70-€75pp, C-Cards MC VS AE, Dinner from €36, Rooms 3 twin, 3 double, all en-suite, Restricted smoking, Well behaved children, No dogs, Closed Xmas & New Year

Ard Na Greine Ballinascarthy, Clonakilty, Co Cork

Norma Walsh Tel: +353 23 39104 Fax: +353 23 39397
Email: normawalsh1@eircom.net Web: www.ardnagreine.com

Map Ref: 12
N71

Ard Na Greine is an imposing house standing near to Ballinascarthy village, it enjoys wonderful views of the surrounding countryside. Warm hospitality is extended to all who come here, Norma's cooking offers the very best in quality of ingredients and care in preparation. Vegetarians and coeliacs are happily catered for, visitors are generous in their praise. Ard Na Greine is well placed for interesting day visits to Kinsale, Bantry, West Cork and Blarney.

B & B €30-€33pp, C-Cards MC VS, Dinner from €19, Children & dogs welcome, Open all year

Dunmore House Muckross, Clonakilty, Co Cork

Mary & Jeremiah O'Donavan Tel: +353 23 33352 Fax: +353 23 34686
Email: ireland@greenbook.ie. Web: www.greenbook.ie

Map Ref: 13
N71

This idyllically situated house overlooks the Atlantic Ocean on the southwest coast of Ireland. Family owned, it is an ideal base for discovering the magic charms of West Cork. Dunmore House is known for its welcoming atmosphere, personal service and uninterrupted breath taking views of the Atlantic coastline. Its excellent restaurant, with the backdrop of the ocean, offers the finest fruits of land and sea. Residents have free use of the adjacent nine hole golf course, the private coastline is ideal for those wishing to pursue water sports.

B & B €55-€65pp, C-Cards MC VS DC, Dinner from €30, Rooms 4 single, 6 twin, 12 double, 2 family, all en-suite, Children welcome, No dogs, Open all year

Greenmount House Upper John Street, Dingle, Co Kerry

Mary & John Curran Tel: +353 66 915 1414 Fax: +353 66 915 1974
Email: mary@greenmounthouse.com Web: www.greenmounthouse.com

Map Ref: 14
N86, R559

Greenmount House is situated on an elevated site overlooking Dingle town and harbour and has been decorated to the highest standard throughout. The house incorporates six top class en-suite rooms and six new developed superior rooms with sea views. All bedrooms have a full bathroom and large sitting area, direct dial telephone, television, and tea/coffee making facilities. Breakfast, served in the conservatory takes advantage of the fabulous view, it is a feast for which the Currans are famous. John and Mary have extensive knowledge of the area and will happily discuss and recommend a local itinerary for you.

B & B €38-€64pp, C-Cards MC VS, Rooms 7 double, 5 twin, all en-suite, No smoking, Children over 8, No dogs, Closed Xmas & New Year

Creagh House Main Street, Doneraile, Co Cork

Michael O'Sullivan & Laura O'Mahony Tel: +353 22 24433 Fax: +353 22 24715
Email: creaghhouse@eircom.net Web: www.creaghhouse.ie

Map Ref: 15
N73, R522

An imposing Regency classical townhouse with stately reception rooms, spacious bedrooms and large bathrooms. Creagh House stands beside the Awbeg River on the edge of Doneraile town, it provides a timeless and gracious atmosphere. Dinner is available with advance notice, there are many restaurants however within a short drive. The historic town of Doneraile is a perfect tour base for visiting scenic, cultural, historic and sporting sites in Munster. Mallow Racecourse and Blarney are nearby. Killarney and Cashel are within an hour's drive, as are Cork and Shannon Airports.

B & B €70-€75pp, C-Cards MC VS AE, Dinner from €30, Rooms 1 double, 2 double/twin, all en-suite, Restricted smoking, Children welcome, No dogs, Closed Nov to Jan

Farran House Farran, Co Cork

Patricia Wiese Tel: +353 21 7331215 Fax: +353 21 7331450 Mobile: +353 86 8111244
Email: info@farranhouse.com Web: www.farranhouse.com

Map Ref: 16

N22

Originally built in the mid 18th century, Farran House was remodelled in 1863 in the elegant Italianate style you see today. It stands in the hills of the Lee valley in 12 acres of beech woodland and rhododendron gardens, overlooking the medieval castle and abbey of Kilcrea. The house has retained its original character and charm. The bedrooms have large bathrooms and beautiful views over the countryside. There are antique furnishings, a grand piano and a billiard room with a full sized table. A wonderful base from which to explore Cork and Kerry.

B & B €62-€70pp, C-Cards MC VS AE, Dinner from €32, Rooms 2 double, 2 family, all en-suite, Restricted smoking, Children welcome, No dogs, Closed Nov to Mar

Glanworth Mill Glanworth, Fermoy, Co Cork

Lynne Glasscoe Tel: +353 25 38555 Fax: +353 25 38560
Email: glanworth@iol.ie Web: www.glanworthmill.com

Map Ref: 17

N8

Glanworth Mill, situated alongside the River Funcheon in the heart of the lush Blackwater valley, offers a resting place for travellers in its unique atmosphere of a water mill. Each en-suite bedroom is individually decorated in the style of the writer it's named after. The Fleece & Loom restaurant offers fine dining, lighter fare is available in the Mill Tea Rooms. The fresh food is served with warmth and care. Tea can be served in the library, or relax in the courtyard garden. There is a wealth of activities nearby including historic trails, walking routes, houses and gardens, horse riding golf and fishing.

B & B €57-€64pp, C-Cards MC VS AE DC, Dinner from €20.50, Rooms 8 double, 2 twin, all en-suite, Restricted smoking, No dogs, Closed Xmas & New Year

Sallyport House Glengarriff Road, Kenmare, Co Kerry

The Arthur Family Tel: +353 64 42066 Fax: +353 64 42067
Email: port@iol.ie Web: www.sallyporthouse.com

Map Ref: 18

N71

Sallyport House is just a few minutes walk from Kenmare town centre in a quiet and secluded place. This elegant Country House is uniquely laid out with lawns and trees overlooking the harbour and with panoramic views of Kenmare Bay and surrounding mountains. The bedrooms are elegantly furnished with antiques, King and Queen size beds, direct dial telephones, colour televisions and large en-suite bathrooms. Sallyport House is personally managed by the Arthur family and has earned itself a place in most major travel guides. Sallyport offers a friendly place to relax and enjoy one of the most beautiful parts of Ireland.

B & B from €63.50pp, Rooms 5 double, all en-suite, No smoking, Children over 12, No dogs, Closed Nov to Apr

Coolclogher House Mill Road, Killarney, Co Kerry

Mary & Maurice Harnett Tel: +353 64 35996 Fax: +353 64 30933
Email: coolclogherhouse@eircom.net Web: www.coolclogherhouse.com

Map Ref: 19

N22, N72

Coolclogher House is a handsome Victorian house, set in a 60 acre walled estate in the suburbs of Killarney. Surrounded by mature gardens and parkland, the house commands fine views to the mountains. Having been sympathetically restored, guests are welcomed to experience high standards in beautifully presented, spacious bedrooms and reception rooms. The Victorian conservatory was specially built around a 170 year old camelia. Coolclogher House is perfectly placed for interesting trips, such as the Ring of Kerry, Dingle, Kenmare and Glen Gariff. Killarney, Waterville and Ballybunion are home to famous golf courses.

B & B €70-€83pp, C-Cards MC VS, Rooms 2 double, 2 twin, all en-suite, Restricted smoking, Children over 8, No dogs, Closed Xmas & New Year

Ash Hill Stud, Ash Hill, near Kilmallock, Co Limerick

Kathleen's Country House Tralee Road, Killarney, Co Kerry
Kathleen O'Regan Sheppard Tel: +353 64 32810 Fax: +353 64 32340
Email: info@kathleens.net Web: www.kathleens.net

Map Ref: 19
N22, N72

Traditional hospitality combined with courteous personal attention has made Kathleens a special place. Irish Tourist Board Four Stars, AA Five Diamond, RAC and Small Hotel Guesthouse of the Year are among its awards. Set on three acres of mature gardens and scenic surroundings. 3km from town centre. Personally supervised. Each bedroom furnished with antique pine, has bathroom, tea/coffee facilities, phone, television, radio and orthopaedic King Coil beds. Guest library. Ideal golfing/touring base.

B & B €45-€62.50pp, C-Cards MC VS, Rooms 2 single, 6 double, 8 twin, 1 family, all en-suite, No smoking, Children over 5, No dogs, Closed Nov to Mar

Carrig House Caragh Lake, Killorglin, Co Kerry
Frank & Mary Slattery Tel: +353 66 9769100 Fax: +353 66 9769166
Email: ireland@greenbook.ie Web: www.greenbook.ie

Map Ref: 20
N70

This charming Victorian property is situated on the shores of the beautiful Caragh Lake on the Ring of Kerry route. It stands amongst gardens and woodlands, with spectacular views across the lake to the Kerry Mountains. The restaurant with views across the lake, is wonderfully situated. The drawing room is full of light and warmth, here one may read, chat in comfort beside a log fire, or enjoy a drink before dinner. The elegant bedrooms, some with lake views, are individually and luxuriously decorated with en-suite bathroom. Four poster suites are available.

B & B €60-€85pp, C-Cards MC VS DC, Dinner from €32, Rooms 2 single, 5 twin, 7 double, 2 family, all en-suite, Children welcome, No dogs, Open all year

Glendalough Caragh Lake, Killorglin, Co Kerry
Josephine Roder Bradshaw Tel / Fax: +353 66 976 9156
Email: kerryweb@eircom.net Web: www.glendalough.mainpage.net

Map Ref: 20
N70

Charming Victorian hunting lodge circa 1840. Just a few steps from beautiful Caragh Lake, with magnificent views of the Lake and McGillycuddy Reeks. Furnished with antiques and old paintings the house has interesting gardens with mature trees and many rare shrubs. Salmon and trout fishing, woodland walks, golf on the many championship courses, tee times arranged. Delicious dinners by candlelight using local organic produce. Succulent moutain lamb, wild salmon. Glendalough is a house for all seasons and an excellent base to tour the Ring of Kerry, The Dingle Peninsula, ancient ruins and historic sites.

B & B from €65 (min 2 nights)pp, C-Cards MC VS AE, Dinner from €35, Rooms 4 double, 3 twin, all en-suite, No smoking, Children over 10, Dogs by arrangement, Closed Dec to Feb

Ash Hill Stud Ash Hill, Kilmallock, Co Limerick
Belinda & Simon Johnson Tel: +353 63 98035 Fax: +353 63 98752
Email: ashhill@iol.ie Web: www.ashhill.com

Map Ref: 21
R512
see Photo on page 411

Ash Hill Stud is a handsome Georgian house of National architectural importance. It stands on a well wooded stud farm way off the road at the end of a long drive. Lots of animals live here. The bedrooms are spacious with large bathrooms, they enjoy views to the 18th century stable yard, or to the surrounding fields. There are fascinating features throughout the house, 18th century ceilings, antique baths, wood panelling and intriguing plasterwork. There is plenty of space for children to play, making this an ideal family place to stay.

B & B €40-€50pp, C-Cards MC VS, Dinner from €30, Rooms 2 double, 1 family, all en-suite, Children & dogs welcome, Open all year ·

The Lighthouse The Rock, Kinsale, Co Cork   Tel: +353 21 4772734
Carmel Kelly-O'Gorman   Fax: +353 21 4773282   Mobile: +353 86 2703179
Email: info@lighthouse-kinsale.com   Web: www.lighthouse-kinsale.com

Map Ref: 22
R600

The lighthouse is a tudor style house, antiques here are a special feature, and there are four poster and canopy beds. The Lighthouse is internationally acclaimed by the Sunday Times, Essentials, Sunday Telegraph, Irish Examiner, Sunday Express and Harpers & Queen. Extensive breakfast menu, including smoked salmon, champagne, freshly roasted coffee, freshly squeezed juices, fresh fruits and a great selection of Irish cheeses. The town has wonderful old pubs, galleries and restaurants.

B & B €38-€58pp, C-Cards MC VS AE, Rooms 4 double, 4 twin, 1 family, all en-suite, Restricted smoking, Children over 10, No dogs, Closed Xmas

Glenview House Midleton, Co Cork
Ken & Beth Sherrard   Tel: +353 21 4631680   Fax: +353 21 4634680
glenviewhouse@esatclear.ie   www.dragnet-systems.ie/dira/glenview

Map Ref: 23
N25
see Photo on page 414

Glenview House built circa 1780, was restored in the 1960s using Georgian features recovered from the demolition of 16 houses in Fitzwilliam Street in Dublin. The house is surrounded by forestry and woodland walks. There is a tennis court and lawns which run into the forest. Without another house in sight, the beautifully presented bedrooms with antique furniture, enjoy undisturbed country views. Guests are spoilt for choice with restaurants in Midleton, though by prior arrangement Beth will cook a country supper. Wonderful walks, history, towns, golf and fishing are all nearby.

B & B €63.50-€70pp, C-Cards MC VS AE, Dinner from €32, Rooms 4 double, 2 double wheelchair accessible, 1 twin, Restricted smoking, Children welcome, Guide dogs only, Open all year

Old Parochial House Castlemartyr, Midleton, Co Cork
Paul & Kathy Sheehy   Tel: +353 21 4667454   Fax: +353 21 4667429
Email: enquiries@oldparochial.com   Web: www.oldparochial.com

Map Ref: 24
N25, R632

Old Parochial House (1784) is a family home where you are invited to relax and enjoy the historic ambience. Log fires, antiques, four poster beds and delicious homemade produce await you. Extra personal touches are guaranteed to make you feel pampered and relaxed. Old Parochial House is the ideal location from which to enjoy wonderful beaches, coarse and sea angling, bird sanctuaries, Fota Wildlife Park, Jameson and Cobh Heritage Centres, sailing, scenic walks, the challenge of wonderful golf courses, an abundance of excellent restaurants and more!

B & B €45-€51pp, C-Cards MC VS, Rooms 2 double, 1 double/twin, 2 family, all en-suite, Restricted smoking, Children welcome, No dogs, Closed Nov to Jan

Rock Cottage Barnatonicane, Schull, Co Cork
Barbara Klotzer   Tel / Fax: +353 28 35538
Email: rockcottage@eircom.net   Web: www.mizen.net/rockcottage

Map Ref: 25
R591

Rock Cottage, a Georgian hunting lodge, dating back to 1826, stands on 17 acres of wooded parkland, fields and heather covered hills. It was built on a slope at the edge of Dunmanus Bay. A short walk leads onto the hills, where stunning views over the bay unfold. The bedrooms are simply decorated, with wooden floors, pine beds and comfortable sitting areas. Dinner is excellent, it should be booked in advance, specials include lobsters and seafood. There are good restaurants locally. Local attractions include water sports, walks, cycle routes and sandy beaches.

B & B €32-€58pp, C-Cards MC VS, Dinner from €32, Rooms 1 double pb, 2 triple en-suite, 1 family cottage, Restricted smoking, Children welcome, No dogs, Open all year

Glenview House, Midleton, Co Cork

Grove House Coolnagurrane, Skibbereen, West Cork, Co Cork

Anna & Peter Warburton   Tel: +353 28 22957   Fax: +353 28 22958
Email: relax@grovehouse.net   Web: www.grovehouse.net

Map Ref: 26
N71

Relax in our authentic Georgian Country house that dates back to the beginning of the 1800's. You can choose between a romantic four poster bedroom or opt for one of our Courtyard Suites which have been converted from the old stables and barns (ask about the one with the en-suite double jacuzzi!) In the evenings, relax in our residents lounge and enjoy a pre-dinner drink from our 'honesty bar' before sampling some first class West Cork cuisine in our dining room. A stay at Grove House is an ideal way to recharge those batteries and as one of our guests put it 'if you can't relax at Grove House, you can't relax anywhere.

B & B from €38pp, C-Cards MC VS, Dinner from €20, Rooms 2 double, 3 family, all en-suite, No smoking, Children welcome, No dogs, Closed Xmas & New Year

Tahilla Cove Country House Tahilla, Sneem, Co Kerry

James & Deirdre Waterhouse   Tel: +353 64 45204   Fax: +353 64 45104
Email: tahillacove@eircom.net   Web: www.tahillacove.com

Map Ref: 27
N70

Travel writers have described this Ring of Kerry sea shore, fully licensed, family-run, guesthouse, established in 1948 by Charles Waterhouse, as 'the most idyllic spot in Ireland or any other country.' Guest bedrooms are in two houses on the 13 acre sea shore estate. All rooms have superb sea or mountain views, most with balcony or terrace overlooking the well tended gardens and extensive lawns which sweep down to the waters edge. The bedrooms are all en-suite with colour television, direct dial telephones and many more home comforts. The drawing room, television room and dining room all have excellent sea views.

B & B from €55pp, C-Cards MC VS AE DC, Dinner from €25, Rooms 6 double/twin, 3 twin, all en-suite, Restricted smoking, Children & dogs welcome, Closed Oct to Easter

Castlemorris House Ballymullen, Tralee, Co Kerry

Mary & Paddy Barry   Tel: +353 66 7180060   Fax: +353 66 7128007
Email: castlemorris@eircom.net

Map Ref: 28
N21, N86

Castlemorris house is a beautiful ivy-clad Georgian home standing in its own grounds, an eight minute walk from the centre of Tralee. Guests enjoy complimentary afternoon tea on arrival, open fires and a friendly atmosphere. The spacious bedrooms have king size beds and they are tastefully decorated. Three have the original fireplaces and two others have sloping ceilings and beams. Meals are delicious, good home baking and irrestible breakfast menus. Dinner needs to be booked by noon. The house is convenient for Kerry, beaches, golf, riding, fishing and walking.

B & B €45-€50pp, C-Cards MC VS AE, Dinner from €26, Rooms 6 twin en-suite, Restricted smoking, Children welcome, No dogs, Open all year

Glenally House Copperalley, Youghal, Co Cork

Herta & Fred Rigney   Tel / Fax: +353 24 91623   Mobile: +353 87 6294609
Email: enquiries@glenally.com   Web: www.glenally.com

Map Ref: 29
N25

A fine Georgian house standing in seven acres of gardens and paddocks with wild areas. Our aim is to provide a relaxed country atmosphere, guests are welcome to enjoy the house and gardens as their own throughout the day. Carefully restored, the period features remain and the house displays a blend of antique and modern furniture coupled with a warm atmosphere which is enhanced with fresh flowers and log fires. The bedrooms are large and light with modern shower rooms. Candlelit dinners by arrangement. Beaches, birdwatching, golf, gardens and excellent pubs nearby.

B & B €40-€50pp, C-Cards MC VS, Dinner from €32, Rooms 3 double en-suite, 1 twin private bathroom, No smoking, Children over 12, No dogs, Closed Dec 22 to end Feb

The West & Northwest

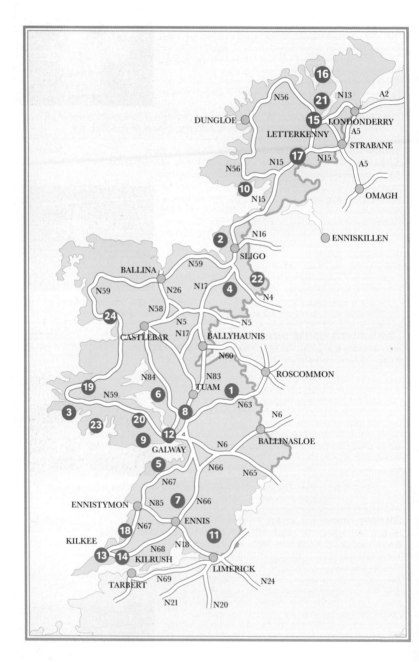

The Blue Map References should be used to locate B & B properties on the pages that follow

Castle ffrench Ballinamore Bridge, Co Galway

Bill & Sheila Bagliani Tel: +353 903 22288 Fax: +353 903 22003
Email: castleffrench@eircom.net Web: www.castleffrench.com

Map Ref: 1
N63
see Photo on page 419

Caste ffrench is a listed Georgian house, built in 1779, set in rolling parkland. With its elaborate plasterwork it has a warm and peaceful atmosphere. Blazing log fires, comfortable rooms, good food and wine, the perfect escape from modern day stresses. Hunting, golf and fishing are available. Nature walks through the peat bogs are organised, with picnic lunches, or relax in the grounds, either painting or bird watching.

B & B from €95pp, C-Cards MC VS, Rooms 4 double, 1 twin, all en-suite, No smoking, No children or dogs, Closed mid-Oct to end Apr

Ardtarmon House Ballinfull, Co Sligo

Charles & Christa Henry Tel / Fax: +353 71 63156
Web: www.ardtarmon.com

Map Ref: 2
N15

Ardtarmon House has been a family home since 1852, it stands among extensive grounds with a 500 metre path through the farm to the beach with safe swimming. The location is beautiful, being on the north coast of Sligo bay. The bedrooms are large and very spacious, they are furnished with period furniture, creating a nineteenth century ambience. There is a games room, a tennis court and various lovely walks. Home grown fruit and vegetables, a house cow and poultry contribute to home cooking. Many opportunities for walking, cycling, boating, fishing and bird watching. Six miles from Drumcliff towards Raghly.

B & B €32-€42pp, C-Cards MC VS, Dinner from €22, Rooms 2 double, 1 twin, 1 family, all en-suite, No smoking, Children welcome, No dogs, Closed Xmas & New Year

Emlaghmore Lodge Ballyconneely, Connemara, Co Galway

Nicholas Tinne Tel: +353 95 23529 Fax: +353 95 23860
Email: info@emlaghmore.com Web: www.emlaghmore.com

Map Ref: 3
R341

Emlaghmore was built as a fishing lodge in 1862, between the beautiful Roundstone Bog and the Atlantic. The river runs through the garden with fly fishing for sea trout, brown trout and the odd salmon. It is approximately eight miles from Clifden, the capital of Connemara, six miles from Roundstone and near to Ballyconneely with its 18 hole links golf course. There are good pubs and restaurants in the area, and local activities include sailing, fishing, riding, walking and wind surfing. Two self catering cottages are available. A very peaceful, quiet situation.

B & B from €60pp, C-Cards MC VS, Dinner from €35, Rooms 1 single pb, 1 double en-suite, 1 twin en-suite, No smoking, No children or dogs, Closed Oct to Easter

Temple House Ballymote, Co Sligo

Deb & Sandy Perceval Tel: +353 71 83329 Fax: +353 71 83808
Email: guest@templehouse.ie Web: www.templehouse.ie

Map Ref: 4
N17

Temple House, a magnificent Georgian Mansion stands in 1000 acres of farm and woodland, which is home to sheep and donkeys. There are six centrally heated bedrooms, with private bathrooms. Meals are thoughtfully prepared, and whenever possible, produce from the walled garden is used; Temple House is highly regarded for its cuisine. There are turf fires to enhance the traditional atmosphere, also some canopied beds. An abundance of wildlife may be found in the pastures, woods, bogs and marshes which surround Temple House Lake. Boats available on Lake. No perfumes please.

B & B from €65pp, C-Cards MC VS AE, Dinner from €30, Rooms 1 single, 3 double, 2 twin, 5 en-suite, 1 private bath, Restricted smoking, Children welcome, No dogs, Closed Dec to Mar

Drumcreehy House   Ballyvaughan, Co Clare   Map Ref: 5

Bernadette & Armin Moloney-Grefkes   Tel: +353 65 7077377   Fax: +353 65 7077379   N67
Email: B&B@drumcreehyhouse.com   Web: www.drumcreehyhouse.com

Delightful country style house overlooking Galway Bay and the surrounding Burren landscape. Open fires, antique furnishings, and a friendly and personal service by conscientious hosts, Armin and Bernadette help to make your stay both enjoyable and memorable. The bedrooms are en-suite, tastefully decorated, and well equipped with television and direct dial telephone. There is an extensive breakfast menu and simple country style cooking in a relaxed atmosphere. Ideally located for touring Clare, Galway and Kerry. One mile from village with craft shops, restaurants and pubs. It is a ten minute walk to the beach.

B & B €28-€38pp, C-Cards MC VS, Dinner from €22, Rooms 5 double, 5 twin, all en-suite, Restricted smoking, Children over 5, Dogs by arrangement, Open all year

Ballywarren House   Cross, Cong, Co Mayo   Map Ref: 6

Diane & David Skelton   Tel / Fax: +353 92 46989   R334, N84
Email: ballywarrenhouse@eircom.net   www.ballywarrenhouse.com   *see Photo on page 420*

Ballywarren is the delightful country home of David and Diane Skelton, which they have lovingly created to reflect the charm and character of the late 18th century, with open fires, oak staircase and four poster and hand carved beds. Each room has many little extras including chocolates, a decanter of sherry, playing cards, glossy magazines and fragrant toileteries by Crabtree & Evelyn. Delicious dinners are cooked by Diane in the Aga and guests may select wine from a short but interesting wine list. For the last 20 years, visitors have been welcomed to this lovely home.

B & B €55-€65pp, C-Cards MC VS AE, Dinner €32, Rooms 3 double, all en-suite, Restricted smoking, Children over 12, Dogs by arrangement, Open all year

Clifden House   Corofin, Co Clare   Map Ref: 7

Jim & Bernadette Robson   Tel / Fax: +353 65 6837692   N18
Email: clifdenhousecountyclare@eircom.net   Web: www.clifdenhouse-countyclare.com

Clifden is an early Georgian manor (circa 1750) standing at the foot of a wooded hill, upon the shore of Lough Inchiquin. The magnificent rock hills of the Burren are viewed from the windows. The River Fergus flows through the gardens. Lough Inchiquin (about 300 acres) is celebrated for its trout fishing. Bernadette is passionate about cooking and her organic fruits, vegetables and meats come from the garden and the nearby family farm. The stable wing, with its cobbled yard and riverside lawn, contains two holiday cottages. Shannon airport is just 20 miles away.

B & B from €60pp, C-Cards MC VS, Dinner from €32, Rooms 3 double, 1 twin, all en-suite, Restricted smoking, Children welcome, No dogs, Closed Nov to mid-Mar

Cregg Castle   Corrandulla, Co Galway   Map Ref: 8

Ann Marie & Pat Broderick   Tel: +353 91 791434   N63
Email: creggcas@indigo.ie   Web: www.creggcastle.com

There is no category in which to place Cregg Castle, we are neither an hotel nor ordinary guest house. The friendly and informal atmosphere means you will live for a while in a 17th century castle and feel completely at home. Sit by the huge open fire and maybe listen to a tune or two. Conversation is the main attraction at Cregg, where many great friendships have been found. Take a walk through Cregg Woods for some well deserved peace and quiet and play with the farmyard animals.

B & B from €60pp, C-Cards MC VS, Dinner from €30, Rooms 2 single, 3 twin, 5 family, all en-suite, Restricted smoking, Children welcome, No dogs, Closed Xmas

Castle ffrench, Ballinamore Bridge, Co Galway

Ballywarren House, Cross, near Cong, Co Mayo

Fermoyle Lodge Costello, Connemara, Co Galway

Nicola Stronach Tel: +353 91 786111   Fax: +353 91 786154

Email: fermoylelodge@eircom.net   Web: www.fermoylelodge.com

Map Ref: 9
N59

A fine Victorian sporting lodge, surrounded by tropical gardens
and tucked away in one of the wildest parts of Connemara.
Fermoyle Lodge is a haven of tranquility with a relaxed
atmosphere. Turf fires, fabulous views and Jean-Pierre's cooking
make staying here an unforgettable experience. Hillwalking, golf,
riding and fishing are popular pastimes. There is excellent wild
salmon and sea trout fishing, and wild brown trout fishing on
nearby Lough Corrib. A ten minute drive enables you to explore
the beautiful Connemara coast, with its sandy beaches, or take a
ferry to the Aran Islands.

*B & B €60-€75pp, C-Cards MC VS, Dinner €35, Rooms 4 double, 2 twin, all en-suite,
Restricted smoking, Children over 10, Dogs not in house, Closed Nov to Mar*

Bruckless House Bruckless, Dunkineely, Co Donegal

Joan & Clive Evans Tel: +353 73 37071   Fax: +353 73 37070

Email: bruc@bruckless.com   Web: www.iol.ie/-bruc/bruckless.html

Map Ref: 10
N56

Bruckless House, the home of Joan and Clive Evans, is an
attractive 18th century Classical house with an award winning
garden with profusions of bluebells and rhododendrons, and a
cobbled courtyard. The beautifully presented, spacious drawing
room and dining room overlook the lawns and the sea. Bruckless
House is run as a Connemara pony stud, in Spring therefore, there
will be mares and foals out at grass. The Atlantic coast is beautiful
and completely unspoilt. There is an abundance of interest locally,
archaeological sites, fishing, golf and riding are all available in the
area.

*B & B €38-€45pp, C-Cards MC VS AE, Rooms 2 single, 1 double en-suite, 1 twin en-suite,
No smoking, Children welcome, No dogs, Closed Oct to Mar*

Ardsollus Farm Quin, Ennis, Co Clare

Pat & Loreto Hannon Tel: +353 65 6825601   Fax: +353 65 6825959

Mobile: +353 87 9210043   Email: ardsollusfarm@ireland.com

Map Ref: 11
N18

A warm welcome is assured at this spacious agri/tourism award-
winning 300 year old farmhouse on a 120 acre working farm
overlooking Dromoland Estate with its 18 hole golf course. The
house is fully modernised, but retains its 'olde worlde' charm. There
are antique furnishings throughout the house which is a fifth
generation family home. There are show jumping horses on the
farm. This is an ideal place to stay as Shannon airport, Bunratty
and Knappogue medieval castles are within a 15 minute drive, the
cliffs of Moher and the Burren are nearby.

*B & B from €32pp, C-Cards MC VS, Dinner from €24, Rooms 2 double, 2 twin, all en-suite,
Restricted smoking, Children welcome, Dogs in kennel, Closed Dec to mid-Feb*

Norman Villa 86 Lower Salthill, Galway, Co Galway

Dee & Mark Keogh Tel / Fax: +353 91 521131

Email: normanvilla@oceanfree.net

Map Ref: 12
N17

Norman Villa is a Victorian townhouse. The house is full of
antiques and a large collection of contemporary Irish art. Each
bedroom sports a lovely antique bed. The most spacious rooms are
very large, and are ideal for family groups. Each bedroom has a
telephone, tea making facilities, snug shower facilities, beautiful art,
books, antiques, original floor boards and shutters. There is a
private enclosed car park and a walled garden. In the evening
there is a great choice of places to walk for dinner. Our highlighted
maps are a must for exploring Burren, Connemara or a day trip to
the Aran Islands.

*B & B €48-€51pp, C-Cards MC VS, Rooms 4 double, 2 family, all en-suite,
Restricted smoking, Children welcome, No dogs, Closed Nov to Feb*

Halpins Hotel　Erin Street, Kilkee, Co Clare

Pat Halpin　Tel: +353 65 9056032　Fax: +353 65 9056317
Email: halpins@iol.ie　Web: www.halpinsprivatehotels.com

Map Ref: 13
N67

This tastefully refurbished Townhouse offers quality, comfort and fine food with a tradition of personal service. The open hearth fire and friendly lounge bar provide a warm welcome for each guest. Halpins also enjoys an excellent reputation for its food in this picturesque Victorian resort village. It is ideally located being close to some of Ireland's premier golf courses. Halpins is close to Shannon Airport and Killimer car ferry, making it an excellent place to stay whilst touring the west and southwest.

B & B €45-€80pp, C-Cards MC VS DC, Dinner from €30, Rooms 1 single, 4 twin, 6 double, 2 family, all en-suite, Children welcome, No dogs, Closed Nov to Mar

Old Parochial House　Cooraclare, Kilrush, Co Clare

Alyson & Sean O'Neill　Tel / Fax: +353 65 9059059
Email: oldparochialhouse@eircom.net　Web: www.oldparochialhouse.com

Map Ref: 14
N68

This stone built former Priest's house standing on four acres of land, built in 1872. The house has been lovingly restored, whilst maintaining all the original features in the very spacious rooms. The sitting room and dining room have marble, turf burning fireplaces, the bedrooms display high corniced ceilings, antique furniture and poster beds. Guests are offered complimentary tea and scones on arrival. It is remote and unspoilt here, with views to Cooraclare Village, the Atlantic Coast with deserted beaches is five miles away. Seafood restaurants locally. Self catering in restored stables is available.

B & B €35-€45pp, C-Cards MC VS, Rooms 2 double, 2 twin, all en-suite, No smoking, Children welcome, No dogs, Closed Oct to Mar

Castle Grove Country House　Letterkenny, Co Donegal

Mary & Raymond Sweeney　Tel: +353 74 51118　Fax: +353 74 51384
Email: ireland@greenbook.ie　Web: www.greenbook.ie

Map Ref: 15
N13, N56

Castle Grove is a Georgian country house set amidst its own estate,it is situated approximately three miles from Letterkenny. The house is approached by a mile long avenue through parkland of mature trees, it commands fine views to Lough Swilly. The restaurant specialises in seafood and the best of Irish fare, it is complemented by an excellent wine cellar. All the bedrooms are en-suite and are individually decorated. The spacious drawing rooms warmed by winter log fires, enjoy wonderful views across one of the most beautiful parts of Ireland.

B & B €50-€85pp, C-Cards MC VS DC, Dinner from €35, Rooms 2 single, 5 twin, 7 double, 2 family, all en-suite, Children welcome, No dogs, Open all year

Croaghross　Portsalon, Letterkenny, Co Donegal

John & Kay Deane　Tel / Fax: +353 74 59548
Email: jkdeane@croaghross.com　Web: www.croaghross.com

Map Ref: 16
R238

A modern elegantly furnished country home. Croaghross enjoys stunning views over Ballymastocker Strand and Portsalon's 18-hole golf course. The bedrooms have colour television and tea making facilities. Two family bedrooms and one double bedroom are at the front, with en-suite bathrooms and french doors to a private terrace. At the side are a small double bedroom and a large twin bedroom specially adapted for wheelchair access, both with en-suite shower rooms. From here, tour the breathtaking Atlantic Drive and visit Glenreagh National Park. A three bedroom self-catering cottage also available.

B & B from €30pp, C-Cards MC VS, Dinner from €22.50, Rooms 2 double, 1 twin, 2 family, all en-suite, Restricted smoking, Children & dogs welcome, Closed Nov to mid-Mar

Ardnamona Lough Eske, Co Donegal

Kieran & Annabel Clarke   Tel: +353 73 22650   Fax: +353 73 22819
Email: info@ardnamona.com   Web: www.ardnamona.com

Ardnamona on Lough Eske under the Blue Stack mountains, is described in the topographical dictionary of Ireland, 1837, as 'one of the most picturesque domains in rural Ireland.' It has glorious gardens planted in the 1880s by Sir Arthur Wallace. Many of the seeds and cuttings came from the Imperial Gardens at Peking and the Palace gardens in Katmandu. It is a designated National Heritage Garden. There are wonderful walks, fishing, boating and swimming. The sea is a 15 minute drive away, and the local town is famous for its handmade tweed.

B & B €58-€64pp, C-Cards MC VS, Dinner from €32, Rooms 3 double, 3 double/twin,
all en-suite, Restricted smoking, Children welcome, Dogs not in house, Closed Xmas & New Year

Berry Lodge Annagh, Spanish Point, Milltown Malbay, Co Clare

Rita Meade   Tel: +353 65 7087022   Fax: +353 65 7087011
Email: info@berrylodge.com   Web: www.berrylodge.com

Charming Victorian family home is now a welcoming guesthouse, restaurant and cookery school operated by Rita Meade. Excellent accommodation in the traditional style with modern comforts of en-suite, television, tea/coffee making in bedrooms is provided. The heart of the house is the kitchen which provides excellent food. Using only fresh local produce and hands-on cookery tuition. Ideally suited for golfing at Lahinch, Doonbeg, Kilkee. The cliffs of Moher Burren area are a great attraction. Special Christmas and New Year breaks. Dinner 7.30 p.m., booking 24 hours, wine licence.

B & B €30-€35pp, C-Cards MC VS, Dinner from €32, Rooms 2 double, 3 twin, all en-suite,
Restricted smoking, Children welcome, No dogs, Closed Jan to mid-Feb

Crocnaraw Moyard, Connemara, Co Galway

Lucy Fretwell   Tel / Fax: +353 95 41068
Email: lucyfretwel@eircom.net   Web: http://homepage.eircom.net/~lucyfretwell

Crocnaraw is an Irish Georgian country house on the shores of Ballinakill Bay, six miles from Clifden, capital of Connemara, on the scenic Clifden to Westport road. Set in 20 acres of gardens, trees and fields, Crocnaraw is the winner of the National Guesthouse gardens competition for four years. Crocnaraw is fully licensed and the excellent cuisine includes milk, cream, eggs, fresh vegetables, salads and fruits from the home farm garden and orchard. Crocnaraw is ideally located for deep sea angling, salmon and trout fishing, championship golf and many other leisure activities.

B & B €32-€50pp, C-Cards VS AE, Dinner from €32, Rooms 1 single, 2 double, 3 twin,
all en-suite, Restricted smoking, Children welcome, Dogs by arrangement, Closed Nov to Mar

Ross Lake Country House Rosscahill, Oughterard, Connemara Co Galway

Henry & Elaine Reid   Tel: +353 91 550109   Fax: +353 91 550184
Email: ireland@greenbook.ie   Web: www.greenbook.ie

Ross Lake House is a graceful Georgian house standing at the end of a winding country road in a panoramic garden setting amidst woods and lawns. The emphasis here is on quality food, served in a warm, comfortable atmosphere. Guests are invited to relax in the elegant drawing room or the intimate bar before retiring to the luxurious bedrooms. Ross Lake House is 22km from Galway city (route N59), it is ideally situated for exploring Connemara, for fishing on Lough Corrib, golfing at the nearby Oughterard 18 hole golf course, or simply enjoying the countryside.

B & B €60-€90pp, C-Cards MC VS DC, Dinner from €32, Rooms 2 single, 3 twin, 8 double,
2 family, all en-suite, Children welcome, No dogs, Closed Nov to Mar

The Anglers Return, Toombeola, Roundstone, Connemara

Frewin Letterkenny Road, Ramelton, Co Donegal
Thomas & Regina Coyle   Tel / Fax: +353 74 51246   Mobile: +353 8797 43347
Email: flaxmill@indigo.ie   Web: www.accommodationdonegal.net

Map Ref: 21
R245

Frewin is a beautifully restored old stone manor house located in mature grounds on the outskirts of historic Ramelton. Formerly a Rectory, it offers its guests an atmosphere of luxury, relaxation and personal attention from its owners, Thomas and Regina. Ramelton is a small historical town and sits on the banks of the river Lennan. It boasts many fine Georgian buildings with popular pubs and restaurants in the area. Within easy reach of golf courses/links, beaches and fishing. Frewin is an ideal base for touring or walking Dongal's wild mountainous countryside and panoramic coastline.

B & B €45-€58pp, C-Cards MC VS, Dinner from €26, Rooms 2 double en-suite, 1 double pb, 1 family en-suite, Restricted smoking, Children over 10, No dogs, Closed Xmas day

Ross House Ross, Riverstown, Co Sligo
Oriel & Nicholas Hill-Wilkinson
Tel / Fax: +353 71 65140   Mobile: +353 8790 56776

Map Ref: 22
N4, R284

The farmhouse is Oriels family home, built in 1890, it has flower bedecked porch with flagstones outside and all around there are cow fields and the consequent sounds, otherwise this is pure peace. Rooms of varying sizes in plain colours with some modern furniture exactly what you would wish for from farmhouse accommodation. Nearby lies the archaeological site of Carrow Keel and its amazing passage tombs which are a sort of tourist secret. Ross House is a short distance away from Lough Arrow, one of Europe's most famous trout lakes, a boat is available. Television and tea/coffee facilities in bedrooms.

B & B from €30pp, C-Cards MC VS, Dinner from €23, Rooms 1 single, 1 double, 1 twin en-suite, 2 family en-suite, Restricted smoking, Children & dogs welcome, Closed Nov to mid-Mar

The Anglers Return Toombeola, Roundstone, Connemara, Co Galway
Lynn Hill   Tel / Fax: +353 95 31091
Email: lynnhill@eircom.net   Web: www.anglersreturn.itgo.com

Map Ref: 23
N59
see Photo opposite

In a lovely corner of Connemara, which is one of the most beautiful landscapes in Europe, nestles this 18th century sporting lodge, now a family run guest house, The Anglers Return. It may be found between the mountains and the sea, at the foot of Derradda Hill. Here there is peace, space, turf fires, books and lovely rambling gardens which create an atmosphere where guests are happy to relax and be cared for, in a timeless elegance. Great walks and fishing (own brown trout lakes) beautiful beaches, sea fishing, golf, excellent restaurants are all nearby. Small groups welcome.

B & B from €35.50pp, Dinner from €19, Rooms 1 twin, 2 double, 1 double en-suite, 1 family, No smoking, Children by arrangement, Dogs in car only, Closed Dec to Mar

Rosturk Woods Rosturk, Mulranny, Westport, Co Mayo
Louisa & Alan Stoney   Tel / Fax: +353 98 36264
Email: stoney@iol.ie   Web: www.rosturk-woods.com

Map Ref: 24
N59

Rosturk Woods is situated on the unspoilt west coast of Ireland, between the historic town of Westport and the landscapes of Achill Island. The house stands in a beautiful setting on the clean, sandy, tidal seashore of Clew Bay and its islands. Very much a family home, we offer both bed and breakfast and self catering accommodation. The bedrooms are charming in that they have stripped pine doors, soft shades of blue, good lighting and views across the bay. Dinner, including fresh, local ingredients, fish and shellfish may be enjoyed by all in the main house.

B & B €32-€45pp, Dinner from €32, Rooms 2 double/twin, 1 family, all-en-suite, Restricted smoking, Children welcome, Dogs by arrangement, Closed Nov to Feb

The Midlands

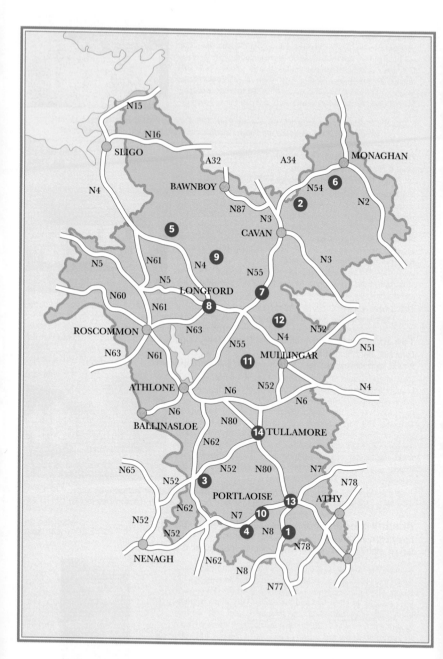

The Blue Map References should be used to locate B & B properties on the pages that follow

Preston House Main Street, Abbeyleix, Co Laois
Alison & Michael Dowling
Tel / Fax: +353 502 31432

Map Ref: 1
N8, R430

Formerly a school established in 1834, Preston House is very much a warm and inviting family home. Guests from afar are invited to enjoy friendly hospitality where reminders of schooldays abound, breakfast is taken in the head teacher's study which is furnished with lovely antiques. The schoolroom now hosts morning coffees and lunches, there is an open fire in there in winter. Bedrooms are large and comfortable, they are furnished with antiques and they overlook the peaceful garden. The famous Heywood Gardens and the Slieve Bloom mountains are nearby.

B & B from €25pp, C-Cards MC VS, Dinner from €34, Rooms 4 double, all en-suite, Restricted smoking, Children over 5, Dogs by arrangement, Closed occasionally

Rockwood House Cloverhill, Belturbet, Co Cavan
James & Susan McCauley Tel: +353 47 55351   Fax: +353 47 55373
Email: jbmac@eircom.net

Map Ref: 2
N3, N54

Rockwood House has been beautifully reconstructed in the style of an old rectory which stood on the grounds since the 1860's. It is in a secluded woodland setting surrounded by lawns and gardens. Cavan is renowned for its Drumlin Hills and is known as 'The Lake Country' of Ireland. Cavan town is about six miles away, Butlersbridge two miles and Belturbet four miles. The house has four guest rooms all with en-suite showers and guests can enjoy breakfast overlooking the gardens and relax by a log fire on colder evenings.

B & B from €28pp, C-Cards MC VS, Rooms 2 double, 2 twin, all en-suite, No smoking in bedrooms, Children welcome, No dogs, Closed Xmas day

Spinners Town House Birr, Co Offaly
A T J Darrah Tel: +353 509 21673   Fax: +353 509 21672   Mobile: +353 8689 63444
Email: spinners@indigo.ie Web: www.spinners-townhouse.com

Map Ref: 3
N6, N7

With an outlook over the majestic walls of Birr Castle, the townhouse offers a modern revival of Georgian architecture and style. An enclosed courtyard garden, a peaceful haven at all times of the day. The bedrooms are spacious, stylish and thoughtfully designed for comfort and relaxation. An hospitable oasis for the weary traveller, young and old. En-suite rooms, direct dial telephones. Enjoy our world renowned Bistro, awarded for its great food and wines and with a setting in a restored seventeenth century woollen mill, a complete hospitality package.

B & B from €32pp, C-Cards MC VS AE DC, Dinner from €16, Rooms 4 double, 5 twin, 4 family, all en-suite, Restricted smoking, Children welcome, Dogs by arrangement, Open all year

Kinnitty Castle Kinnitty, Birr, Co Offaly
Con Ryan Tel: +353 509 37318   Fax: +353 509 37284
Email: ireland@greenbook.ie Web: www.greenbook.ie

Map Ref: 3
N62, N52

This magnificent country residence is an ideal retreat set on a 1,200 acre estate in the foothills of the Slieve Bloom Mountains, yet equi-distant from Dublin, Galway and Limerick. This luxuriously refurbished Gothic revival castle boasts fine bedrooms which are furnished to enhance the original features of this fascinating building. The restaurant is decorated in a classical style, it offers superb gourmet cuisine accompanied by a well chosen wine list. The Dungeon bar which hosts traditional entertainment, provides a pleasant and relaxing way to pass the evening. A wide range of leisure facilities is available.

B & B €115-€160pp, C-Cards MC VS DC, Dinner from €40, Rooms 2 single, 11 twin, 20 double, 4 family, all en-suite, Children welcome, No dogs, Open all year

Viewmount House, Longford, Co Longford

Ballaghmore Castle The Manor House, Borris-in-Ossory, Co Laois
Map Ref: 4
N7

Grace Pym Tel: +353 505 21453 Fax: +353 505 21195 Mobile: +353 8764 84579
Email: gracepym@eircom.net Web: www.castleballaghmore.com

Situated between Roscrea and Borris-in-Ossory Ballaghmore Castle has been lovingly restored by Grainne Ni Cormac, who bought the castle in 1990. Grainne (Grace) will delight you with stories of MacGiollaphadraigs which go back to 500 B.C. The Castle is available to rent weekly or for weekends. The Manor House offers bed and breakfast. Excellent Irish breakfasts are served, also smoked salmon and scrambled eggs, fruit and cheese. Set in 30 acres, both privacy and peace are provided. Ballaghmore Lake is a natural 3 acre lake, cultural tours of the property are happily provided by Grainne. Castle open to rent over Xmas & New Year.

B & B €25-€45pp, C-Cards VS, Rooms 1 single, 2 double en-suite, 1 twin, 1 family suite, Restricted smoking, Children over 5, No dogs, Closed Xmas

Glencarne House Ardcarne, Carrick-on-Shannon, Co Roscommon
Map Ref: 5
N4

Agnes Harrington
Tel / Fax: +353 79 67013   Mobile: +353 8762 10477

Glencarne House is a large country Georgian house. Central heating and log fires create a warm and friendly atmosphere in this newly decorated property. The en-suite bedrooms offer delightful views over open countryside and are very freshly furnished with welcoming brass beds and crisp white linen. The home cooked food is from local farm produce. There is a Golf course half a mile away, boating, fishing and shooting locally.

B & B from €32pp, Dinner from €26, Rooms 1 twin en-suite, 1 double en-suite, 1 family, Restricted smoking, Children welcome, No dogs, Closed mid-Oct to Mar

Riverside House Cootehill, Co Cavan
Map Ref: 6
N54, R187

Una Smith Tel: +353 49 5552150 Fax: +353 49 5559950
Mobile: +353 8763 00262 Email: unasmith@eircom.net

A delightful period property, ideal for exploring Ireland. The five bedrooms all en-suite, have tea/coffee making facilities. Two large lounges complete with video and television. The dining room overlooks the River Annalee, home cooked traditional Irish breakfasts, using local produce whenever possible. Evening meals are availabe upon request. Riverside Guest House locally offers horse riding, boat hire, fishing, walking, cycling, with four golf courses within easy reach. Help on tracing ancestors is a speciality.

B & B from €26pp, C-Cards MC VS, Dinner from €17, Rooms 1 single, 2 double, 2 twin, 1 family, most en-suite, Restricted smoking, Children welcome, Dogs not in house, Closed Xmas & New Year

Toberphelim House Granard, Co Longford
Map Ref: 7
N4, N55

Dan & Mary Smyth Tel / Fax: +353 43 86568 Mobile: +353 87 9963249
Email: tober2@eircom.net Web: www.toberphelimhouse.com

Toberphelim House is a Georgian family home standing in a scenic, elevated position on a 200 acre working sheep and cattle farm, one km from the road. Home to the Smyth family, guests are assured of warm hospitality coupled with good home cooking, breakfasts are served on a large mahogany dining table. Scones and boxty are a speciality, there is water fresh from the spring. There are many historical sites, forest walks and lakes to visit. There is also a cycle trail to enjoy .

B & B €40pp, C-Cards MC VS AE, Rooms 2 double en-suite, 1 twin pb, No smoking, Children welcome, Guide dogs only, Closed Oct to Apr

Viewmount House Dublin Road, Longford, Co Longford
James & Beryl Kearney Tel: +353 43 41919 Fax: +353 43 42906
Email: info@viewmounthouse.com www.viewmounthouse.com

Map Ref: 8
N63, N5
see Photo on page 428

This beautiful former landlords residence adjoins Longford county golf club. Less than a mile from town centre the house is surrounded by four acres of magnificent gardens. En-suite bedrooms are individually styled with period furniture. Breakfast from an extensive menue can be enjoyed in the delightful dining room with its valuted ceilings. While touring Longford you will see some of Irelands best and unspoilt scenery. Its waterways are renowned for fishing and boating. The local attractions include Carriggglas Manor, Ardagh Village, Corlea Centre, Strokestown House and Gardens.

pp, C-Cards MC VS AE, Rooms 4 double, 1 twin, 1 family, all en-suite,
Restricted smoking, Children & dogs welcome, Open all year

Glebe House Ballinamore Road, Mohill, Co Leitrim
Laura Maloney Tel: +353 78 31086 Fax: +353 78 31886
Mobile: +353 87 958 2177 Email: glebe@iol.ie Web: www.glebehouse.com

Map Ref: 9
R202, R201

This lovely Georgian rectory was built in 1823 and stands surrounded by 40 acres of woods and farmland. The house has been completely restored by the Maloney family, who have ensured that every comfort is available to their visitors, many of whom return each year. The bedrooms are ensuite, they have direct dial telephone and television. Breakfasts and dinners are served in the garden dining room. There is much to enjoy in this unspoilt part of the Irish Lakelands. Dublin is two hours, and Belfast two and a half.

B & B €38-€45pp, C-Cards MC VS AE, Dinner from €19, Rooms 2 double, 6 family, all en-suite,
Restricted, Children welcome, Not in public area, Closed Xmas & New Year

Roundwood House Mountrath, Co Laois
Frank & Rosemarie Kennan Tel: +353 502 32120 Fax: +353 502 32711
Email: roundwood@eircom.net Web: www.hidden-ireland.com/roundwood

Map Ref: 10
N7

A wonderful 18th century palladian villa close to the unspoilt Slieve Blooms. 90 minutes from Dublin or Shannon. The house is surrounded by find woods of chestnut, beech and lime. The dining room, drawing room and study contain a large collection of books, paintings and antiques. Rinding and three gold courses available locally. There is abundant wildlife in the neighbouring woods and morrs. For children there are games to play, animals to feed and woods to explore. Birr with its famous gardens is just 20 miles and Kilkenny is 30 miles away.

B & B €65pp, C-Cards MC VS AE DC, Dinner from €40, Rooms 5 double, 3 twin, 2 family,
all en-suite, Restricted smoking, Children welcome, Dogs not in house, Closed 6 Jan to 2 Feb

Meares Court House Rathconrath, Mullingar, Co Westmeath
Brendan and Eithne Pendred
Tel: +353 44 55112

Map Ref: 11
R392

Mearescourt House is a gracious mansion which stands proudly in 350 acres of wonderfully green Midlands countryside. Visitors here may experience a gentle Georgian elegance, combined with present day comforts and facilities. Large bedrooms with brass beds have fine uninterrupted views, whilst downstairs the drawing room and cosy sitting rooms look out to the walled garden. There is always a warm welcome, and good home cooking awaiting guests here, delicious country house dinners should be booked by noon. This is a perfect location for touring, walking, fishing, golf and riding.

B & B from €38pp, C-Cards MC VS, Rooms 1 twin, 2 double en-suite, 1 family en-suite,
Restricted smoking, Children welcome, Dogs outside only, Closed Xmas & New Year

Mornington House, Mornington near Mullingar, Co Westmeath

Mornington House Mornington, Multyfarnham near Mullingar, Co Westmeath Map: 12

Anne & Warwick O'Hara Tel: +353 44 72191 Fax: +353 44 72338 N4, R394

Email: info@mornington.ie Web: www.mornington.ie *see Photo on page 431*

Tranquility and warm hospitality are the essence of Mornington, home to the O'Haras since 1858. Set in an unexplored corner of Westmeath with its charming landscape of rolling hills, forests and lakes, Mornington is truly part of the real hidden Ireland, yet 60 miles from Dublin. Built in 1710, this gracious home has a reputation for delicious meals prepared in the tradition of the Irish country house. Anne is a member of Euro-toques, the international fraternity of serious chefs. Golf, fishing and equestrian activities can be arranged. Neolithic sites, castles and gardens are within easy reach.

B & B €50-€60pp, C-Cards, Dinner from €32.50, Rooms 2 double 1 en-suite, 1 twin, 1 family, both en-suite, Restricted smoking, Children welcome, Dogs by arrangement, Closed Nov to Mar

Ivyleigh Bank Place, Portlaoise, Co Laois Map Ref: 13

Dinah & Jerry Campion Tel: +353 502 22081 Fax: +353 502 63343 M7, N7, N80

Mobile: +353 8623 04789 Email: info@ivyleigh.com Web: www.ivyleigh.com

Georgian family home in the town centre. Restored to a very high standard in accommodation, but equally a depth of character with a profusion of antiques, period furnishings, comfortable bedrooms individually styled with tea/coffee facilities and television, on request. Breakfasts are a treat with selections of freshly baked breads, porridge, Dinah's muesli, followed by full Irish breakfast or scrambled eggs with smoked salmon or Cashel blue cheesecakes. Recreational facilities include golfing, fishing, equestrian, hill walking, theatre, pubs. Award winning restaurants are all close by. A good base for touring around Ireland.

B & B €52.50pp, C-Cards MC VS, Rooms 1 single, 3 double, 2 twin, all en-suite, No smoking, Children over 8, No dogs, Closed Xmas & New Year

Pine Lodge Ross Road, Tullamore, Co Offaly Map Ref: 14

Claudia Krygel N52

Tel / Fax: +353 506 51927

This award winning retreat is located in a peaceful setting just four miles from Tullamore, Offaly's county town in the heart of Ireland. There is much to appeal here. Swimming in the Indoor Pool, cycling, playing golf on the nearby course, even horseriding locally, or just relax in the Sauna or Steam room and finally to dinner in town. The bedrooms are mainly stripped pine furniture. There is much wood everywhere, to give a warm feel to the whole house. The breakfast menu is delicious and has won prizes!

B & B from €38pp, Rooms 2 double, 2 twin, all en suite, Restricted smoking, Children over 12, No dogs, Closed Oct to Mar

Rahan Lodge Rahan, Tullamore, Co Offaly Map Ref: 14

Carole McDermott Tel: +353 506 55796 Fax: +353 506 55606 N52

Mobile: +353 86 2419665 Email: rahan@eircom.net Web: www.rahanlodge.com

Rahan Lodge is a 1740 Country Retreat set in the tranquillity of farming and woodlands in Ireland's midland region. Good food and open fires makes this house a place to relax away from the hustle and bustle of every day life. Located off the N52 for Birr out of Tullamore brings Rahan Lodge close to all amenities. Evening meals are cooked only by arrangement, advance booking essential.

B & B from €45.50pp, C-Cards MC VS AE, Dinner from €30, Rooms 4 double, 1 twin, Children over 12, No dogs

Property Index

Property Index

Property Index

Property Index

Town Index

Town Index

Town Index

Report Form

Please photocopy and use this form to let us know about your stay.
We value your comments, good or bad, and we will take the
appropriate action where necessary.

Property Name: _____

Address: _____

_____ Postcode: _____

Comments:

_____

_____

_____

_____

_____

_____

_____

_____

_____

_____

_____

_____

_____

_____

From:

Name: _____

Address: _____

_____ Postcode: _____

Please send the completed form to:
The Editor (GBB), Tomorrow's Red Books, PO Box 7677,
Hungerford RG17 0FX *or email*: editor@tomorrows.co.uk

Recommendations

Please photocopy and use this form to tell us about any other Homes
that you would recommend for listing in future editions.

Property Name: _____

Address: _____

_____ Postcode: _____

Comments:

_____

_____

_____

_____

_____

_____

_____

_____

_____

_____

_____

_____

_____

_____

From:

Name: _____

Address: _____

_____ Postcode: _____

Please send the completed form to:
The Editor (GBB), Tomorrow's Red Books, PO Box 7677,
Hungerford RG17 0FX *or email*: editor@tomorrows.co.uk

Notes